# THE FORGOTTEN FLEET COMPLETE TRILOGY

---

CRAIG ANDREWS

Created with Vellum

# ALSO BY CRAIG ANDREWS

**Ashes & Empires**

The Heir of Archonia

The Scars of Archonia (Fall 2025)

**The Forgotten Fleet:**

Wings of Honor

Wings of Mourning

Wings of Redemption

**The Machinists:**

Fracture

Splinter

Martyr

Capture

Exposure (Coming 2026)

*For Ender and Callan.*
*This series was supposed to be about*
*aliens and starfighters going pew pew.*
*Instead it became a series about sons and fathers.*
*I hope you know how proud you make me every day*
*And how I'll forever do anything for you.*

# AUTHOR'S NOTE

This book exists for two very specific reasons: because I've been dreaming about X-Wings since the first time I saw Star Wars, and because my oldest son is named after the title character in my favorite book of all time, *Ender's Game*.

So when my youngest son was old enough to realize that his brother had a book of his own and he didn't, I decided that I would write one for him. Dusting off an old idea, I set out to write the awesomest, geekiest book I could write, filling pages with my version of epic X-Wing battles, and writing a character my son could look up to, just as my son Ender can look up to Ender Wiggin.

I hope you enjoyed reading it, and I hope Callan does too (when he's old enough), because I had a blast writing it.

# WINGS OF HONOR

THE FORGOTTEN FLEET BOOK ONE

# 1

*Coliseum, Terran Fleet Academy*
*Sol System, Earth, High Orbit*

Callan "Coda" O'Neil slipped on his virtual-reality helmet, muffling the surrounding voices and sounds of excited anticipation. The VR's imaging display flickered to life, and the real-life image of his squadron donning their own simulation helmets on the floor of the Coliseum was replaced by a simulated first-person view of the inside of his fighter drone. Resistant to radar, lidar, and other forms of detection, the matte-black Z-18 Hornet flew silently through the digital representation of space.

This calm before the battle, the silence before the rest of his squadron plugged into the simulation and the radio chatter began, was usually one of Coda's favorite moments. But the upcoming battle was with Andrei Krylov's Shadow Squadron, and Coda's nerves and overwhelming desire to win spoiled whatever personal heaven the prebattle isolation normally provided.

Andrei Krylov, call sign "Moscow," was one of the finest drone pilots in the Terran Fleet Academy and, in Coda's opinion, its biggest prick. More importantly, Shadow Squadron was tied with Coda's own Viking

Squadron for first place in the academy's standings. In addition to determining the Ace Squadron of their class, the battle would be one of the deciding factors in determining the pilots' post-graduation assignments.

Coda already knew where he would be stationed. The image of the sleek black hull of the SAS *Americas* filled his mind's eye. The battle cruiser was the flagship vessel in the Sol Fleet and home to the *Nonpareil*, the finest drone squadron the Sol Fleet had ever assembled. Coda would soon be one of them, fighting battles that weren't simulated, battles that actually meant something. He couldn't wait to rub Moscow's smug face in it.

*One thing at a time,* Coda told himself, dismissing the daydream. *Don't get ahead of yourself.*

"Heads-up," he said softly, and his heads-up display overlaid his view of space, providing him with important flight data and a small three-dimensional map displaying a full view of the battle. The battle map, which was relegated to the bottom right-hand corner of his vision, would soon be teeming with green and red dots indicating friendly ships and enemy fighters. For the moment, however, a white dot of the friendly capital ship cruised behind the friendly green symbol that marked his fighter.

Above the floor of the Coliseum, where Shadow and Viking Squadrons were plugged in, was a much larger version of the battle map. Nearly four stories tall and almost as deep, the battle map gave the spectators front-row seats to the upcoming incursion. Instead of the green and red dots on Coda's HUD, though, the spectators enjoyed three-dimensional, photo-real images of the fighter crafts.

There, the extensive view would shift to where the battle was thickest, like the vids of a space race moving to where the race was most interesting. A normal battle would draw most of the student body—it was a perfect opportunity to study a fellow squadron's tactics, after all—but there wouldn't be an empty seat in the house tonight. Even the faculty would attend. Not to mention representatives from Fleet Command.

Coda turned, the view in his VR helmet shifting seamlessly with him, and saw the rest of his squadron formed up beside him. Every battle simulation began this way, with the sixteen drones of the squadron stretched out in a simple line that gave each squadron leader a block of clay that they could shape into a formation of their choosing.

"All right, report in." Coda listened as all of his pilots announced they were plugged in and ready for action. When the last radioed that he was ready, Coda ordered the squadron to move into standard formation, and in practiced unison, the drones shifted into a V with Coda at its point.

He didn't intend to remain in the standard formation for long, but it gave the spectators something to see and provided his pilots with an opportunity to put their drones in action. Not that they needed the practice, of course; they'd logged thousands of hours in their drone operation bays, but Coda had long since learned that even the best pilot could hesitate during the early moments of battle. Having them shift formations before it began allowed them to get control of their nerves and avoid any serious mistakes.

"Contact!" Buster boomed suddenly.

"Copy that, Buster," Coda said. "What do we have?"

"Looks like your standard smash-and-go scenario," Buster said.

Coda glanced at his battle map, noting the newly appeared red dots marking the enemy fighters. They were two minutes out and zipping toward Coda's fighters, away from a capital ship of their own.

"Let's get some space between us and our ship." Coda keyed an intercept course and sent it to his squadron. "Seventy percent burn for sixty seconds on my mark... Mark."

Viking Squadron moved as one, angling below their previous flight path, and creating some space between them and their capital ship. The scenario's objective was simple: destroy the opposing side's capital ship and the easiest way to accomplish that was to destroy the opposing squadron then go for the capital ship itself.

The way this particular scenario had been constructed seemed to push them toward that inevitability. There was no cover, no territory to hold, nothing that would make their sensors go haywire. Not even a planet and an associated gravity well to contend with. Just empty space. The academy leadership wanted an old-fashioned duel. But Coda wasn't interested in giving them what they wanted. He was interested in winning. Thoroughly.

He wasn't planning on taking on the second-best pilot in the academy straight on, either.

"Vikings, form up in the Revised Coleman Diamond and wait for my mark."

The Coleman Diamond was a formation named after the famed pilot Commander Chadwick Coleman, a hero from the early days of the Baranyk War before drone warfare had replaced real pilots in real starfighters. Commander Coleman had used the formation in a suicidal attack on the Baranyk Fleet, the battle that had turned the tide of the war —or at least staved off imminent defeat, depending on who was telling the story.

The tactic was simple enough to understand though rarely leveraged. Unlike the starfighters of old, drones could be fielded in much greater numbers, replenished faster, and more importantly, since their pilots were tens of thousands of kilometers away, not limited by the same physical constraints the former star pilots had been.

As a result, the newer formations employed on the front were more fluid, capable of shifting strategies at a moment's notice. They more closely resembled a school of fish, changing directions on a dime, yet still coordinated, moving as one, never colliding. With that in mind, Coda hoped the formation would distract Moscow enough that he wouldn't notice the new wrinkle Coda had put on it.

Coda remained in position while thirteen drones formed a diamond behind him, its top and bottom points equal distances above and below the plane of the impending battle. Coda's wrinkle was to have the remaining two fighters throttle down to fall behind the formation then match speed before going completely dark. Their dark hulls would make them all but invisible to visual identification, and their lack of heat signatures would help hide them from computer detection.

The plan wasn't foolproof since radar or lidar could still detect the drones, and their residual heat signatures might intermittently pop up on enemy HUDs. Of course, anyone paying attention might also notice that the incoming squad was suddenly two fighters short, but that would be easy enough to miss since the fighters would go dark while the formation was coming together.

As soon as Viking Squadron completed its formation, Moscow countered it with one of his own.

"Coda, this is Buster. Are you seeing this?"

"I am," Coda said. Shadow Squadron had slipped into a spear with Moscow at its tip. "He means to punch through our diamond."

"What are we going to do?"

"We're going to let him."

"We're going to do what?"

"Three seconds before collision, break formation and form up into seven battle pairs twelve degrees positive-Z," Coda said. "That will give us a better attack angle as they break though. If they don't engage, burn hard in pursuit. If we do this right, we'll have time to break their formation before they're able to get to our capital ship."

"That's not going to give us a lot of time," Buster said. As Coda's best friend and flight leader, he was the only one who could get away with directly question Coda's orders.

"Then don't miss," Coda said. "Every shot counts. Vikings Fifteen and Sixteen, remain dark and maintain your trajectory. We're going to end this before they know what hit them."

They were committed now. Even if Coda wanted to alter strategies, they didn't have time.

"Contact in fifteen seconds." Coda shifted excitedly in his seat. All his time spent at the prestigious military academy, everything he'd worked for, every test he'd aced, and each battle he'd won culminated in this moment. Anything short of a decisive victory would be a supreme disappointment. "Ten seconds. Prepare to break formation."

At seven seconds, Coda fired a volley of digital projectiles at the incoming drone spear. He hadn't given the order, but the other ships in the formation followed his lead, firing as well. The odds of them hitting one of the incoming vessels was slim, the distances were too great, but like before, the action allowed his fighters to get the first shots out of the way.

"Five seconds," Coda said. Then three. "Break!"

The diamond shattered, breaking into seven shards of two fighters apiece, all darting above the battle plane. There was no up or down in space, but if there were, the new position would have given Coda's fighters the high ground. They blanketed Shadow Squadron's flight trajectory with cannon fire.

Moscow didn't have time to adjust course and lost four fighters as they sped through the barrage. Unfortunately, the losses weren't enough to force them into a different strategy.

Coda keyed in his pursuit and maximized thrust, burning hard. His wingman, Hound, just off his wing in the dash-two position, did the same. Panic flared in Coda's chest as Shadow Squadron showed no signs of breaking course. He keyed in on the nearest enemy fighter, thumbing the switch on his joystick, activating his missiles. A red square appeared around the target, and a second indicator, larger than the first, tracked behind it.

The target took evasive actions, trying to slip missile lock. But this is where Coda shined. He countered the target's moves almost as if he knew what the other pilot was going to do before they did it, and quickly closed the distance. As he did, he toggled the lead fighter and the Viking capital ship. A countdown appeared in the corner of his vision, counting down the time before the tip of the spear was within firing range of Viking Squadron's capital ship.

*This is going to be close.*

The two indicators came into alignment on the enemy target, then glowed more brightly and was accompanied by a steady tone. Coda had missile lock.

"Viking One," Coda announced. "Fox three!"

Coda launched the first of his eight AIM-220s. He didn't have visual on the missile, it was too small to register in the black, but a yellow indicator identified it on his HUD. It zipped from his fighter, streaking toward its target.

"Splash five!" Coda shouted as the enemy drone exploded in a brief flash of light. He shoved the joystick forward, avoiding the debris from the destroyed drone as another flash of light flared, and another red dot disappeared from his battle map.

*Six down. Ten to go.*

Five fighters remained in the haft of the spear, the rest creating a V at its head. Positive-Z, Coda and his wingman had a clear firing angle, but just as they got missile lock again the haft of the spear broke away, streaking toward its pursuers. Half of Coda's squadron was forced to take evasive action and engage the enemy.

Coda and Hound held course. *Not me. Not today, Moscow.*

He eyed the countdown to their firing range, then searched the battle map hoping to see signs of life from Vikings Fifteen and Sixteen. Viking Squadron's best chance of winning was if the two fighters could get to Shadow Squadron's capital ship before Moscow got to theirs. It was a race, and one Coda was beginning to feel less confident about winning.

Two more fighters broke away from Shadow Squadron, flipping nose to tail and plotting an intercept course with Coda and Hound. It was a maneuver only a drone could perform. At a minimum a real pilot would have blacked out under the immense strain. More likely, the inside of the cockpit would have been coated in human soup.

"Evasive maneuvers," Coda ordered, and he and his wingman split, allowing the attacking fighters to slip between them.

"They're coming around on our tails," Hound said.

"Break off," Coda said. "Stall them. Keep them off my six. I'm staying on the leader."

"Roger."

Hound flipped, then spun and shot toward the nearest enemy fighter, opening up his cannons. Coda stayed focused on the tip of the spear, trusting his wingman would keep him safe. Moscow was at the tip of that spear. He knew it.

A glint caught his eye, something closer to a lesser darkness than to light, then was followed by another flash of light just off Moscow's wing. Coda looked back at his battle map, and all became clear. Buster, on a cleaner attack vector, had fallen into firing range. Coda could almost see Moscow calculating his chances. Could he get into missile range before Buster eliminated him and his wingman?

*Not likely.*

Moscow must have come to the same conclusion. He aborted their attack run, diving negative-Z below the battle plane and racing back toward the dogfight. Grinning, Coda flipped his drone, plotting a new intercept course.

In his all-or-nothing gambit Moscow had accepted catastrophic casualties and was now significantly outnumbered. Coda's squadron remained at full strength, while Moscow's was down nearly two-thirds. If Coda had been in Moscow's shoes, he would have doubled down on the attack, but the risk of losing that way, losing without firing a single shot, would have been too much for Moscow to bear. At least this way, he could save a little face in front of the room full of superiors and say he'd taken some of Viking Squadron with him.

*The battle's over, Moscow. The rest is just a formality.*

Moscow entered the dogfight, attacking with desperate ferocity. His pilots were on the run, most with tails, and disappearing by the second.

Moscow provided aid where he could, guiding his pilots into trajectories that brought their pursuers into his firing range. It wasn't enough to turn the tide of the battle, but Moscow had drawn blood. And as each friendly indicator disappeared from his HUD, Coda grew more and more frustrated.

As the battle had played out, he'd had illusions of completing it without a single casualty. That dream had disappeared.

Coda weaved through the fray, staying on Moscow, and little by little gained on him. Then, as Moscow slipped through the edge of the dogfight, he flipped nose to tail and rocketed directly toward Coda's fighter.

*He knows it's me. He knows I'm coming.*

Coda settled into his seat, blinking to ensure his vision was clear. He wanted Moscow. Wanted to destroy him. Grind him into oblivion. He would only get one shot at this. If he made a mistake, Moscow would turn him to dust, and regardless of whether Viking Squadron won or not, Coda would never live it down.

Coda tightened his grip on the joystick. He and Moscow opened fire at the same time, the two ships speeding toward each other at incredible speeds. They juked and janked, tracer fire ripping passed their cockpits, somehow avoiding the incoming slugs and staying on course.

*Three seconds.*

Coda held course, continuing the barrage, finger held firmly on the trigger, rounds erupting from the six-barrel gatling gun to the tune of four thousand per minute. Moscow did the same.

Jerking his joystick to the side, Coda pitched his drone into a wide aileron roll. He came out of it slightly below the battle plane expecting to have a clear shot at Moscow's underbelly. The other pilot had anticipated the maneuver. They were now on a direct collision course. Slugs slammed into each other, giving the pilots a preview of what was to come.

Coda screamed, finger still pressed against the trigger as his ammo ran out. Moscow was still—

The simulation faded to black. The image of Moscow's incoming drone dissolved in Coda's VR display.

"No!" Coda bellowed.

He yanked off his helmet and stood, his eyes immediately going to the large battle map overhead. Moscow had killed him. The thought was nearly enough to make him sick. The only thing worse than losing was losing to Andrei fucking Krylov, asshat extraordinaire. Except when his eyes found the vid screen above, it too was black.

Confused, Coda looked around to find the rest of his squad throwing their helmets aside, screaming and high-fiving those close to them. Before he could register what had happened, Buster was pulling him into a hug, slapping his back hard enough to knock the wind out of him.

"We did it!" Buster yelled into his ear. "Oh my god, we did it."

"Did what?" Coda said. "What happened?"

Buster pushed Coda away and gave him a pointed look. "What happened? We won!"

"We what?"

"I said we won!" Buster grabbed Coda by the back of his head and drew Coda's forehead to his. "Your nearly disastrous strategy actually paid off."

Coda finally allowed himself to smile. Maybe Moscow hadn't killed him after all.

"You really didn't know?" Buster asked. "What did you think happened?"

Coda didn't respond. He'd grown obsessed with Moscow and had lost sight of the larger objective. He'd completely missed it when Viking Fifteen or Sixteen—he didn't even know who had fired the winning shot—had ended the simulation and claimed victory. Then in ripping off his helmet in frustration, he'd missed the victory message that would have been displayed across his HUD.

His superiors wouldn't miss that act of arrogance and attitude unbecoming of a drone pilot. But he refused to worry about that now. He'd just beaten Andrei Krylov and Shadow Squadron, and his Vikings were the Ace Squadron of their graduating class. Everything Coda had dreamt about for the last several years was about to become a reality.

# 2

*Viking Squadron Ready Room, Terran Fleet Academy*
*Sol System, Earth, High Orbit*

CHILLED CHAMPAGNE WAITED FOR THE VICTORS IN THE VIKING SQUADRON ready room. The pilots rushed forward, pushing and shoving their way to the bottles, ready to shake, uncork, and spray their fellow victors as though they had just won the World Series.

"Wait! Wait! Wait!" Coda screamed over the din. "Hold up a second!"

His pilots did as ordered, though they reminded him of a group of puppies, unable to sit still without trembling with excitement. They still wore their slate-gray flight suits fashioned after the ones worn by twenty-first-century fighter pilots.

Coda surveyed the room, milking the moment and testing their patience. "I just want to say a few words," he said. "When I took command of this squadron a year ago, I didn't know what we had. But I do now. We have the best damn pilots in the academy!"

Cheers erupted.

"And so does every other pilot, teacher, civilian, janitor, and commander in this place! You are the best. The best of the best. And it's been a pleasure serving as your squadron leader."

This was met with an even more enthusiastic chorus of cheers, and some of the pilots took things further, shouting their own gratitude.

"The pleasure is ours, Coda!" Buster shouted.

"You're the best!" Hound added. Coda's wingman had somehow found time to unzip his flight suit, exposing a black tank top underneath.

"Moscow ain't got nothing on you!" Hot Rod shouted.

The last one made Coda laugh, even if it was a break from decorum. He should have reprimanded the pilot, but their time was coming to an end, and he didn't want to mar an otherwise joyous moment. Besides, the ready room was a place of confidence for the pilots, a place where everyone was equal and could speak his or her mind.

"No, he doesn't," Coda said. "And Shadow Squadron ain't got nothing on you, either." He turned to Buster, who was holding an unopened bottle of champagne. "Let me see that."

His friend handed him the bottle, and Coda quickly uncorked it. He held it high so all could see. "To Viking Squadron!"

Coda took a long pull from the bottle and handed it back to Buster, who echoed the sentiment with a drink of his own then handed it to the next pilot. Around the room the bottle went, until it found its way to Hot Rod, who finished it off. Another cheer went up, then the true celebration got underway.

Sometime later, Coda found himself sitting with Buster at the back of the ready room, watching as the pilots of Viking Squadron joked and told stories, enjoying their final moments as a group. It was one of the rare moments Coda had seen his fellow pilots completely without inhibition.

They'd gone through their formal victory celebration, where Captain Hughes himself presented their victory pins, before returning to the ready room. With that behind them, they were left completely without supervision. No senior officers. No commanders. They could finally be themselves, and they weren't letting such an opportunity go to waste.

"I can't believe it's over," Buster said.

"Me, neither," Coda said. "You going to miss it?"

Buster shrugged. "Probably."

"I will," Coda said. "We really did do something special, you know?"

"Of course I do. We beat Moscow." Buster shoved Coda playfully. "I'll tell you what I'm *not* going to miss, though. I won't miss having to juggle studies with simulations. Life's about to get a lot simpler."

"You think?"

Buster leaned back in his seat, throwing a foot on the back of the chair in front of him. "Definitely."

Coda wasn't sure he agreed. Their time at the academy was coming to an end, but that only meant they would be joining the real war effort. Flying with real drone squadrons. Fighting in real battles. Stationed on battle cruisers and capital ships, not a floating school orbiting the Earth. But he didn't want to argue with his friend and spoil his mood. *Not today.*

"When do you think we'll get our orders?" Coda asked.

"You're the Squadron Leader. I was hoping you knew."

"They haven't told me anything yet."

"It's got to be soon, though, right? I mean, what else are we going to do? Sit around and jerk off all day?"

Coda laughed. Like all young men, if Buster wasn't playing with his junk, he was talking about it. The familiarity of the male banter put Coda at ease, though. "You're right. It'll probably be soon. So do me a favor."

"Of course."

"Don't think about it. Just enjoy it. Enjoy this." *Because I don't think life is going to be as simple as you think it is.*

# 3

*Viking Squadron Ready Room, Terran Fleet Academy*
*Sol System, Earth, High Orbit*

Once Viking Squadron had emptied the remaining champagne bottles and were feeling more than a little light in the head, they left the ready room for the final time.

Coda lingered behind, soaking up the view, committing it all to memory. At some distant point in the future, he knew he would think back on this moment and remember when and where his journey had *truly* begun. He knew that wherever his orders took him, he would be successful. He didn't have a choice. He was fighting for something greater than himself.

The ready room emptied into a wide corridor, where the floor curved upward in both directions. The Terran Fleet Academy, like all space stations designed before humanity had reverse-engineered Baranyk technology and learned to manipulate gravity, was built around a central axis with a spinning wheel providing artificial gravity. Students and pilots loitered in the corridor, reliving the recent battle. Coda stopped just outside the ready room. Moscow stood with a few members of

Shadow Squadron outside a nearby doorway, their eyes intent on the Viking Squadron ready room.

*They've been waiting for us.*

Adrenaline pulsed through Coda's veins, making his arms and legs feel light. He knew better than to think that Moscow simply wanted to congratulate him. Coda looked down the corridor to where the rest of his squadron was already disappearing from view, too invested in their celebration to notice their squadron leader had fallen behind.

Coda briefly thought about ignoring Moscow and his thugs, acting as if he hadn't seen them, but his supreme dislike for the man won out. Besides, he wasn't one to back down from a fight. It wasn't in his blood. It was the same reason he'd sought out Moscow during the simulation.

*It's also why you have several demerits on your academy record.*

Coda leaned his back against the corridor wall just outside the ready room, directly across the corridor from Moscow and his six thugs. "Come to congratulate us on our victory?" Coda looked down at the Ace Squadron pin at his breast then back up at Moscow with a patronizing grin.

Moscow spat at his feet and crossed the hallway. "You know as well as I do that your *victory* was luck."

"It doesn't look that way in the standings."

Moscow stopped directly in front of Coda, his face inches from Coda's. "I had you, *O'Neil*."

In most instances, calling a pilot by something other than their call sign wasn't necessarily a form of disrespect, but Coda knew better. He saw it in the way Moscow sneered as he said Coda's last name. He was trying to connect Coda to his father, to remind him who Joseph O'Neil had been… and what he had done.

Burying his anger, Coda feigned nonchalance. "You didn't have dick."

"You and me, O'Neil, let's go. One on one."

"What the hell's going on?"

Coda looked up, spotting the rest of Viking Squadron heading back down the corridor. Buster was at their head, his pace quick, eyes on Moscow as if expecting the other squadron leader to do something.

"Moscow didn't get enough of Viking Squadron," Coda said. "He wants a rematch." It wasn't exactly what Moscow had proposed, but

Coda didn't care. He didn't have any intention of honoring the request anyway.

Moscow shot an uneasy look at the approaching mob of Viking pilots. Even with his gang, he was outnumbered. "That's not—"

"Thing is," Coda interrupted, turning back to Moscow, "what's in it for me? Battling you would be like arm wrestling a girl. If I win, who cares? I already beat you. But if I *lose*, well, then I got beat by a girl. It's a lose-lose. You know what I mean?"

Laughter filled the corridor. Coda smiled and made for his squadron, turning his back to Moscow.

"You're just like him, aren't you, O'Neil?" Moscow's voice was cold and sharp, and it cut like a knife driven into Coda's back. "You're just like your father."

Coda froze.

"A *coward*."

Before Coda knew what he was doing, he'd spun, his right fist rocketing through the air in a vicious right hook. It connected cleanly with Moscow's jaw, dropping the larger man. But Coda wasn't done. He was on top of Moscow in an instant, one fist holding his flight suit, the other driving into Moscow's nose. Blood sprayed across Coda's pale knuckles, staining the clean metallic surface of the corridor crimson. He heard shouts and screams as someone tried to pull him away, but Coda shoved them off.

Nobody talked about his father like that. Nobody disrespected his family. Nobody could do that but him. The primal instinct buried deep inside him meant to use Andrei as an example of what happened when someone broke that unspoken rule.

When someone finally wrestled him off Moscow, Coda's eyes stung with tears, and he could barely lift his arms. Lying helpless on the floor, his face barely recognizable, Moscow groaned, moving slowly.

"We need to get out of here," Buster said. "Come on."

Buster pulled Coda away from the scene, dragging him up the corridor through the group of Viking pilots. They watched him in shock, eyes wide, mouths agape. Coda's face burned with shame. He'd lost control of his emotions and let Moscow goad him into doing something stupid.

*Maybe he was right. Maybe you* are *like your father.*

Buster hauled him to his private quarters. "Get inside." Buster shoved him again, and Coda fell into the small room, catching himself on the edge of his bed. His friend followed him into the room, closing the door behind him. "What the hell was that? Christ, man! What was going through that tiny-ass brain of yours?"

"He insulted my family," Coda said.

"I don't care what he did. We're twenty-four hours away from graduation and receiving our orders. Do you have any idea what you just jeopardized?"

Coda didn't know what to say. He couldn't believe the sudden turn of events. An hour ago, he'd been primed to become one of the newest recruits on a ship on the front, and now he was... what? He had no idea what the future held in store now.

"I know your family name doesn't have the best... *reputation*," Buster continued, "and Moscow can be a royal ass. But you can't go around hitting everyone who insults your family's honor."

"You don't understand—"

"No, Coda. I do. Your father disgraced himself and everyone he's ever known. And you've taken it upon yourself to undo that."

Coda opened his mouth to speak, but the words died on his tongue.

"You see," Buster said. "I understand more than you think, and I respect the hell out of you for it. But you're not going to do any good if you're kicked out of the academy."

Coda found the edge of his bed and took a seat. He ran a hand over his closely cropped hair. "You don't think it'll come to that, do you?"

"You beat him pretty bloody." Buster crossed the small room, grabbed the only other seat, and dragged it in front of Coda. "But no, I don't think they'll kick you out. You're too damn good. Besides, what do they think will happen when they put five hundred soldiers together in a metal container floating through space and tell them to battle one another? And it wasn't like Andrei didn't deserve it. He had you up against the wall. Had his boys with him. What you did to him was self-defense."

Buster's version of the story wasn't entirely accurate, but it was close enough to the truth that it gave Coda hope.

"Thank you," Coda said.

"No problem."

"No. I mean it."

Coda had spent so much time planning for his future that he hadn't thought about who would be in it, and for the first time, he realized Buster probably wouldn't be a part of it. Meeting his friend's gaze, he saw that Buster had come to the same conclusion a long time ago.

*No wonder he's so angry. I took away what was supposed to be his final happy moments with his squad mates.*

"Go on back," Coda said. "Find the guys. Celebrate. Tell them I'll join them when I can."

"I'm not leaving you here, Coda."

"I'll be fine. They'll be worried, and I don't want to ruin their night. Please, go."

"You sure?"

But Coda didn't get a chance to answer. There was a knock at his door. Then a moment later, it opened, and two officers stepped inside.

"Ensign O'Neil," the first officer said, "come with us. Captain Hughes demands your presence."

The cold hands of despair strangled Coda's remaining hope. If Captain Hughes, Commander of the Terran Fleet Academy, wanted to see him, he was in more trouble than he'd realized.

# 4

*Captain Hughes's Office, Terran Fleet Academy*
*Sol System, Earth, High Orbit*

"Tell me, Ensign," Captain Gary Hughes said, "do you consider yourself a special kind of stupid?"

If Coda hadn't been standing at attention, his eyes on the wall behind his commanding officer, he might have stirred under the weight of Captain Hughes's gaze. Even sitting behind his desk, he was nearly as tall as Coda.

"No, sir."

"No?" Captain Hughes feigned surprise. "Then tell me how someone can be dumb enough to beat up one of their fellow students on the same day they were supposed to graduate."

"It was a temporary lapse in judgment, sir."

"A temporary lapse in judgment." Captain Hughes chewed on the words. He stood from behind his desk, his broad, two-meter frame towering over Coda. Space stations weren't built for men like Captain Hughes, whose clean-shaven head nearly touched the stainless-steel ceiling. Combine that with his square face, and he looked every bit like the career military man he was. "A temporary lapse in judgment."

The amusement in his voice terrified Coda more than anything else about the situation. Good things rarely followed a superior's laughter.

Captain Hughes rounded the desk and took a seat on its edge, crossing his arms. His cold eyes didn't match the amusement in his voice. "Tell me, Ensign, do you consider yourself an honest man?"

"Yes, sir."

"How about someone who takes responsibility for their mistakes?"

"I... I think so, sir."

"Then I'm confused, Ensign. Because from my perspective, striking Ensign Krylov once, maybe even twice, would have constituted a 'temporary lapse in judgment.' But three times? Four? Having to be dragged away by your fellow wingmen? That doesn't strike me as temporary. So either you're lying to me, *or* you're refusing to accept responsibility for your actions. So which is it? Are you lying or acting like a child?"

"Sir?"

"I asked if you're dishonest or immature."

"It was a mistake, sir. One I was goaded into."

"Ah, so it's the latter."

"Excuse me, sir?"

"I said it's the latter," Captain Hughes repeated. "Actions of a *boy*. An inability to accept responsibility. Not too surprising, given your family situation."

Coda's eyes slipped from the rear wall, finding Captain Hughes's.

"You have a weak spot, Ensign. One your enemies will exploit if you don't take better care of hiding it."

"With all due respect, sir, I don't see how I can hide my family *situation*. Our name is known throughout the galaxy, and it isn't thought of kindly."

"No, it's not, but that doesn't mean you have to wear it as a badge of shame. It drives you, Ensign. I can see that. But it also holds you back. Three times, you've been in this office, and all for the same reason: because you can't keep your anger in check. All because you thought defending your family honor was more important than defending the human race."

"Sir, that's not—"

"Another lapse in judgment?" Captain Hughes asked, raising any eyebrow. "Arguing with your commanding officer?"

"I'm sorry, sir."

"You're a damn fine pilot, son—nobody will debate that. Squadron Leader of the Ace Squadron of your graduating class, you should have your pick of commissions. Unfortunately, I can't recommend you for deployment. Not until you've learned to control your anger."

Coda's head spun. *This can't be happening.* It was his worst nightmare —beyond his worst nightmare.

"Permission to speak freely, sir?"

"Granted."

"You're making a mistake, sir." Coda kept his voice cool, devoid of all emotion. If getting angry had jeopardized everything he'd worked for, he wasn't about to make that mistake again. "I am a very good pilot, one of the best in my class, and from what I understand, there's a shortage of those skills on the front."

"That's where you're mistaken, Ensign. You're one of over one hundred fifty pilots in a single graduating class from a single academy. There are others like it. Pilots, we have, Ensign. Drones, on the other hand... So maybe if you were in a more demanding field like advanced manufacturing or robotic engineering, something where you had to use that tiny brain of yours, I might be more lenient."

"This isn't just any academy, though, sir. This is the Terran Fleet Academy. The best of the best. And I'm in command of its top squadron. Surely that counts for something."

"It does," Captain Hughes said. "Which is why you're being allowed to graduate. You'll be stationed either in the Orbital Defense Force or on one of the smaller vessels deeper in the black. But you won't be on the front."

"All because of a little fistfight, sir?" Coda couldn't believe what he was hearing. The Terran Fleet Academy was a *military* institution. Violence wasn't just encouraged; it was taught.

"Because you clearly don't understand what it takes to be a part of a squadron. When you're in battle, a real battle, your fellow wingmen need to have absolute trust in you. There's no room for grudges. There's no room for ego. And there sure as hell isn't room for pilots who aren't capable of learning from their mistakes."

The jumble of emotions inside Coda was nearly enough to break him. Anger, frustration, devastation, confusion—he could barely tell them apart. They mixed with the fear he'd already felt, causing sweat to drip down his back and his eyes to water. He attempted to blink the emotion away, but it was too much. Captain Hughes was right. Controlling emotions was a requirement for any great pilot. And Coda just didn't have it.

But buried deeper was something that kept Coda standing, kept him from lashing out, from giving up. Determination.

He was Callan *O'Neil*. The cards had been stacked against him his entire life. He'd been through worse, faced stiffer odds, and still been accepted to the most prestigious flight academy in the Sol Fleet. This was only a setback, and one he refused to accept. He would fight. He would succeed. And when he won, he would smile at Andrei, Captain Hughes, and anyone else who had tried to stand in his way. He would make fools out of *all* of them.

"Let me remind you, son," Captain Hughes continued, his voice taking on a more somber tone. "We are at war with an enemy more terrifying than you can imagine. They have the advantage in technology. They have the advantage of numbers. And they've had us on the defensive for longer than you've been alive. We're the only thing that stands between them and the destruction of the human race. They don't give a damn about your family history or personal grudges. Do I make myself clear?"

"Yes, sir," Coda said.

"Good," Captain Hughes said. "Because if you're to stay in the drone fleet, you will begin your career elsewhere."

Coda blinked. "*If*, sir?"

Captain Hughes uncrossed his arms and stood with a sigh. "You're being given a choice, Ensign."

"Between what, sir?" Coda tried to temper the hope blooming in his chest.

Captain Hughes didn't respond, though. Instead, the door opened behind Coda, and another man strode in. He was shorter than the captain by a few centimeters though still thickly built, with ebony skin and closely cropped black hair peppered with white. Lines creased his forehead and the edges of his mouth, drawing Coda's eye to his brown eyes and full lips.

Coda struggled not to stare. The man in front of him was straight out of military legend. He'd killed more Baranyk than any other known pilot and was someone Coda had studied and tried to emulate during his time at the academy. Commander Chadwick Coleman.

"Ensign," Commander Coleman said. "You know who I am?"

"Yes, sir. It's an honor, sir."

"Spare it, Ensign," Commander Coleman said. "There's no time for flattery. I have a number of these to get through, so I'll be brief. I'm putting together a special squadron, and I want you to compete for a spot in it."

"Sir, I—"

"Before you give me your answer, Ensign, there are a few things you need to understand. There are no guarantees. You'll have to earn your place. And by 'special,' I mean top secret. Nobody can know who or what's involved. Understood?"

"Yes, sir."

"And it'll be dangerous. Far more dangerous than anything you've experienced, maybe even more dangerous than being on the front itself. But I'm offering you a chance to fly, Ensign."

"How many other pilots will be in the squadron, sir?"

"A few."

"Any I know, sir?"

"Perhaps."

"And who might I expect, sir?"

"Other pilots like yourself, Ensign. Pilots who have shown a knack for flying but might not have all the qualities Captain Hughes is looking for."

"How long will the deployment last, sir?"

"That depends on how successful we are."

Despite the commander's elusive answers, Coda wanted to say yes on the spot. Very few pilots had the chance to fly under the great Commander Coleman. But he had one last question. One that was essential to his longer-term goals.

"Will I get to kill Baranyk, sir?"

A smile parted Commander Coleman's face, exposing teeth as white as porcelain. "You might, Ensign. You very well might."

For the first time since beating Shadow Squadron, Coda felt like smiling. "Then sign me up, sir."

Commander Coleman pulled a tablet from the inside of his uniform and held it before Coda. "Just need your prints, Ensign."

Coda should have been more nervous than he was, but he placed the palm of his hand against the tablet, allowing it to scan and record his prints. Little green boxes similar to his targeting-guidance system appeared around his fingertips, then when the tablet had taken a proper scan, they flashed, indicating a successful scan.

"Welcome to the training program, Ensign," Commander Coleman said. "Or should I say Lieutenant?"

Coda let himself smile. He wouldn't be promoted a full lieutenant yet, of course, merely a lieutenant junior grade, but it was a start, and it was certainly more than he'd expected only a few minutes before. "Thank you, sir."

"Don't thank me yet, Lieutenant. Grab any personal belongings you have and meet me in Shuttle Bay Three at sixteen hundred, ready to ship out."

"Yes, sir." Coda saluted and spun on his heels, dismissed.

"And, Lieutenant..."

Coda stopped in the doorway.

"You should know I flew with your father. He was a good man and a hell of a pilot. If you're half of what he was, I expect great things out of you."

For the first time in forever, Coda was speechless. He couldn't remember the last time someone had spoken kindly of his father, let alone compared Coda to him and meant it as a compliment. Eyes brimming with tears, and not knowing what else to do, he nodded to Commander Coleman then exited Captain Hughes's office.

"Ah, shit," Buster said as he entered Coda's quarters and saw Coda's personal belongings strewn about his bed. "That bad?"

"No," Coda said. "Not at all. Well, that's not true. Captain Hughes *did* rail into me for fifteen minutes and tell me that I wouldn't be joining any of the ships on the front, but then..." Coda paused, trying to figure out how he could tell his friend what had happened. "Then, well... it's classified, but it's really exciting."

"That's good," Buster said, sounding relieved but sharing none of the excitement Coda felt. "I think. What can you tell me about it?"

"Not much. Mostly that I won't be serving my time on a third-rate ship patrolling the belt or something."

"Glad to hear it." Buster took a seat, watching Coda place the rest of his personal belongings in his bag. There was something off about him.

"You okay?"

"Me? Of course." Buster smiled, but the expression didn't reach his eyes.

"You're full of it. What's up?"

"It's nothing, Coda. Really."

"Damn it, Buster, we've trained together for months. I can tell something's wrong."

"That's just it. We've trained with each other for months. You and me. Us and Viking Squadron. We're the Ace Squadron, and you're shipping out with barely a goodbye."

"It's the nature of the beast, Buster. But trust me, this is better than the alternative."

"I guess."

"It is." He zipped up his bag and set it aside. "Commander... the other officer said he had a few other meetings. I think he's recruiting other pilots. If you haven't been invited yet, I'm sure you will be."

"Why?" Buster asked. "Why me?"

"Because we were the Ace Squadron, and you played an integral part in that."

Buster laughed. It was livelier this time. More real. "I just kept your ass out of trouble."

"Which is a difficult job," Coda said. "Obviously."

"Obviously. What time do you ship out?"

"Sixteen hundred."

Buster looked up at the clock inset in the wall above the door. "Better get a move on it then."

Coda grabbed his bag and slapped Buster on the shoulder. "I'll see you on the ship."

"What if you don't?"

Coda didn't want to think about it. "Then you're going to kill a lot of bugs on the front."

"What do I tell the squad?"

"Tell them I'm doing something exciting and not to worry. They'll hear about it soon."

Buster nodded. "I will." He crossed the distance between them and pulled Coda into a tight hug. "Take care of yourself, Coda."

Coda hugged Buster back, slapping his friend hard on the back. "You too, man."

When the embrace ended, Buster smacked him on the arm. "And stay out of trouble. You're not going to have me looking after you."

Coda laughed. "I'll try. Probably fail, but I'll try."

"All right."

Coda nodded a final time, and not wanting to extend the moment out any longer, he left his quarters and best friend behind, headed toward the true unknown.

# 5

*Docking Umbilical, Terran Fleet Academy*
*Sol System, Earth, High Orbit*

Coda floated through the docking umbilical connecting the academy to Commander Coleman's transport ship. Away from the spinning operational facilities of the rest of the space station, he didn't experience the simulated gravity felt elsewhere, instead relished the seldom-felt, disorienting zero-g experience. He and the rest of the academy pilots operated their drones in three-dimensional space, but those were simulations, and while simulations could train the mind how to think, they couldn't train the body how to react. As a result, his body wanted to panick, unsure whether it was floating, falling, or flying.

The umbilical was mostly transparent, giving Coda a breathtaking view of the Earth below. Two years had passed since he'd left, leaving behind everyone he'd ever known or loved. He and his mother hadn't separated on great terms—Coda had seen to that when he'd applied for the Terran Fleet Academy against her wishes.

"I lost my husband to the war," she had said, tears streaming down her face. "I won't lose my only son too."

But lost him, she had. And her words continued to haunt him. His actions had driven a wedge between them, and she hadn't been there for his graduation from basic. She hadn't responded to his letter informing her that he'd been accepted into the prestigious Terran Fleet Academy. And she wouldn't have been at his academy graduation, either. It was as if he were already dead to her.

Looking down at the beautiful planet below, Coda realized why he'd been so quick to say yes to Commander Coleman. There was nothing left for him on Earth. Nothing in those blue oceans, sandy beaches, green forests, or snow-peaked mountains. Nothing but a mother who didn't want anything to do with him and a past he desperately wanted to rewrite.

The transport ship had a traditional winged design that resembled NASA's original space shuttle and was large enough to seat twenty or thirty passengers and crew. Able to fly in atmospheric conditions and land planetside in an emergency, the ship was truly meant for space travel with metallic walkways, rounded edges and corners, and a seating design that would make a terrestrian nauseous.

The ship's crew greeted him at the air lock, took his bag, and led him to his seat—a formfitting gel seat with a five-point harness meant to keep him in place and protect him during hard burns and excessive G's. He floated into position and latched the lap belt, keeping his eyes focused on the air lock.

Jose "Uno" Hernandez, Raptor Squadron's top pilot, was the first to arrive. He looked surprised when he saw Coda, but he masked it quickly and took his seat across the aisle from Coda.

"Coming with us, huh?" Coda asked. "I was starting to think I was the only one."

"Not today," Uno said. "I'm surprised to see you, though. Thought you'd be going to the front."

Word of Coda's demise apparently hadn't spread throughout the rest of the academy yet. That was one of the benefits of shipping out prior to graduation, he supposed.

"I couldn't pass up the opportunity to fly with a legend," Coda said.

Uno grinned. "Me, neither."

"Any idea where we're headed?"

Uno shook his head. "You?"

"Nope. I'm in the dark too."

"Well, I'm not going to lie, Coda. I feel better knowing you're going too."

Coda nodded. He'd spoken with Uno on only a few occasions, but the Raptor pilot had always struck him as someone he could get along with. He was also damn good at what he did, and if Uno was the caliber of pilot Commander Coleman was after, then he was truly building something special.

More pilots trickled in after Uno, fifteen in all, including David "Squawks" Anderson and Benjamin "Noodle" Campbell. After joining Coda and Uno, the other two pilots chatted amicably, doing their best to hide their anxious anticipation.

Coda kept one eye on the air lock, hoping to see Buster, but as the minutes ticked by and the transport began to fill up, his hopes dimmed. When Commander Coleman arrived, he did have another student in tow, but it wasn't the one Coda was hoping for.

"You've got to be kidding me," Coda mumbled.

Moscow floated behind the commander, sneering as he surveyed the shuttle's occupants. He'd been cleaned up since his fight with Coda but still sported a split lip and swollen eyes that were beginning to purple. A pair of butterfly bandages crossed his right cheek, and another held together a cut above his left eye. If Moscow was embarrassed by his injuries, he didn't show it. Instead, his sneer turned into something more sinister when he spotted Coda.

"What is he doing here?" Uno asked as Moscow found a seat and strapped in.

"Bringing some talent to this sorry-ass group," Moscow said, apparently having heard the remark. "Isn't that right, O'Neil?"

Coda ignored him and took some sadistic pleasure in hearing how Moscow's injuries made his words come out with a slight lisp. Commander Coleman floated down the aisle toward the front of the ship. Once there, he anchored his feet in a pair of handholds and peered over the gathered pilots.

"Welcome aboard," Commander Coleman said. "The Sol Fleet doesn't often show its appreciation for its service members—there are ceremonies and awards for that sort of thing. But as I look over you now, I want you to know that *I* appreciate you taking this risk and joining me. I know you have a lot of questions, and I promise you, answers are coming. But in the spirit of military efficiency, we'll wait until the rest of the squad has arrived."

Commander Coleman gave them a small grin, drawing a few nervous laughs.

"But when you look around this shuttle and see the quality of pilots we've assembled, I hope you agree we're beginning something special. I can't tell you what that is yet, but I can tell you where we'll go to begin our journey."

Coda perked up. Only a few hours had passed since his discussion with Commander Coleman, but already he felt like a man drowning in a sea of questions, grasping for answers.

"We fly to Jumpgate Sol Four, where we'll hyperjump to Proxima Centauri B, and rendezvous with the SAS *Jamestown* and the rest of your squadron. There, you'll get your answers and begin your training. So buckle up and get comfortable. We'll be at the jumpgate in four hours."

---

CODA COULD IMAGINE WORSE THINGS THAN BEING STRAPPED INTO THE GEL seat of a transport vessel for four hours but not many. Unlike the battle cruisers and capital ships that made up the bulk of the Sol Fleet, transport vessels weren't equipped with much in the way of entertainment or facilities. They ate terrible food, shat in something closer to a bag than a toilet, and were forced to entertain themselves. That mostly meant conversation and simple games, and Coda, leery of Moscow, had to force himself to partake in any of it.

He knew it was an important bonding time for the squadron: friendships would be made, alliances solidified, and old rivalries made worse by adding new players. In typical Moscow fashion, he was already making new friends and turning them against Coda. He could feel their eyes, hear their laughter and caught more than one glance in his direction.

Coda tried to ignore it and focus on the group he was engaged with, but it was easier said than done.

"So something I'm trying to figure out," Squawks said, speaking fast and loose in something that resembled a verbal swagger, "is how you all earn your call signs? I mean some make sense, right? Squawks—I talk a lot. Squawk, squawk, squawk. Makes sense. Uno—first, I thought it was cause you only had one nut or something, but then you shot me down with one shot. Boom. Dead. Uno. Makes sense. But then you got Noodle." Squawks gestured toward the thin pilot. "I have a few guesses, but tell us, what's your story. Someone just razzing you or what?"

Noodle's pale faced colored. There were two kinds of call signs: those that were earned and those that were given. The ones that were earned were generally forms of respect like Uno, but the ones that were given were an altogether different story.

Some could be innocuous, little more than simple jokes. Buster had given a new pilot in Viking Squadron the call sign "Crash" due to his early propensity to, well, crash. But others could be downright insulting. A guy in the class ahead of Coda had been called "Sluf," which had been given to him because someone had overheard one of the female pilots calling him a "short little ugly fucker." The call sign Sluf was born, and it had stuck.

If Noodle's embarrassed reaction was any indication, his call sign had been given, not earned. "I just don't like working out," Noodle said quietly.

Squawks looked at him skeptically, then his face split into a broad smile. "Noodle. Cause you've got noodle arms?" He laughed. "That's good. Accurate too. I've seen skeletons with more muscle than you."

Noodle's face burned crimson, something he tried to hide with a fake laugh. If Squawks noticed or cared that he'd made his squad mate uncomfortable he didn't show it.

"What about you?" Squawks said, turning his attention to Coda. "What's Coda even mean?"

Coda bit back a sarcastic comment about looking it up in the dictionary. Like Noodle, he wasn't comfortable talking about his call sign. His hadn't been given *or* earned. He'd come up with it himself and convinced the other pilots to call him by it—not an easy feat since that wasn't how things were supposed to work.

"I don't want to talk about it," Coda said.

"C'mon, man. We're supposed to be getting to know each other."

"Another time."

"You're no fun."

DECELERATION BEGAN THIRTY MINUTES BEFORE THE TRANSPORT SHIP docked with the jumpgate. The ship flipped on its axis so that the thrust of the engines pointed *away* from the direction they were traveling, and as if to remind them why their seats were made from a soft gel material, the pilots were shaken, battered, and bruised for the duration.

Jumpgates were a modern marvel—the first faster-than-light travel conceived by the human race. The how and the why were closely guarded secrets, and while its science well above Coda's pay grade, he did understand it on a crude, fundamental level.

The jumpgate itself was like a giant gun that the transport ship would be loaded into, though instead of being shot across space, the ship was shot *through* it, arriving almost instantaneously at its destination. The jumpgate had limits on how far it could send them, of course, just as the ships equipped with EmDrives had similar, albeit much larger, limitations. However, Alpha Centauri, only 4.367 light-years away, was well within jumpgate capabilities.

As the transport vessel slid down the chamber of the jumpgate, Coda found himself growing increasingly uneasy. He had never given much thought to how he would die—he'd always assumed it would be somewhere on the front as his battle cruiser went down in a hail of gunfire—but he thought about it now. He could almost hear the news reporter on the vids.

"Lieutenant Callan 'Coda' O'Neil and fourteen other Terran Academy graduates, along with the heroic Nighthawk pilot, Commander Chadwick Coleman, are confirmed dead after a jumpgate malfunction."

The reporter would keep her tone somber, her lips slightly downturned in mock sadness before she sent the program to a commercial break. It would be another tragic chapter in the O'Neil family story and one that would bring his father's mistakes back to the forefront of public consciousness.

Coda did his best to hide his growing unease. Jump travel was, after all, a common form of travel these days, especially among the Sol Fleet.

The front was uncomprehendingly far away and only accessible via the jumpgates, so fearing it was useless. But fear, like all emotion, was an irrational beast, and no matter how much Coda attempted to talk himself through it, his back still grew wet with sweat, his hands clammy and trembling, his breath shallow.

The loading procedure took several minutes, but once complete, the power-up process began. Blue bands of energy like a tempest of pure electricity stretched throughout the interior of the jumpgate, shining bright enough to wash out the backdrop of distant stars.

The ship began to vibrate. It wasn't painful or nearly as violent as the acceleration and deceleration burns. Instead, Coda felt as if he and everything around him were brimming with energy, trembling with adrenaline-infused anticipation. Then, without any word from the ship's pilot, the length of the ship appeared to *stretch*, the seat in front of Coda seemingly pulling away from him. When he reached out to touch it, his fingers brushed against the back of the gel cushion, and his arm looked as if it had stretched too.

The sensation was beyond disorienting, and he fought with everything he had not to vomit. Then, just as before and without warning, the world snapped back into perspective, and everything around him returned to normal. Even without being able to confirm it, Coda knew they had arrived in the Alpha Centauri System.

# 6

*Hangar Deck, SAS* Jamestown
*Alpha Centauri System, Proxima B, High Orbit*

LESS THAN A FULL DAY AFTER HAVING HIS FUTURE RIPPED AWAY FROM HIM, Coda found himself and the rest of the select group of pilots from the Terran Fleet Academy on the hangar deck of the SAS *Jamestown.* Commander Coleman stood in front of a squadron of Hornets.

Coda fell into parade rest with the rest of the squadron, watching his commander but wishing more than anything that he could run his hands along the dark exterior of the drones, feel the contours of its smooth body, trace its fuselage with his fingers. Seeing the ships felt like seeing an old girlfriend. Buried emotions swelled to the surface.

"Welcome aboard the SAS *Jamestown,*" Commander Coleman said. "This is Hangar Bay 7B. We'll be spending much of our time here, but right now, follow me." He spun on his heels and strode across the hangar through a set of double doors that hissed open as he approached.

They entered into a light-gray corridor lit with series of artificial lights set into the wall near the floor and ceiling. Having spent a year and a half in the wheel of the academy's space station, it was odd seeing the corridor stretch out straight in front of him. The SAS *Jamestown* was one of the oldest ships in the fleet equipped with artificial gravity, and the lack of curve somehow made everything appear both bigger and farther away.

The *Jamestown* was a warship through and through, the evidence plain for all to see. The corners of the walls were rounded and coated with a compound that was soft to the touch, and spread throughout the corridors were various handholds to grab should the ship shake or spin in the heat of battle.

Coda found himself smiling as a sense of satisfaction welled up inside him. He couldn't help feeling as if he'd made it. He was aboard a warship. The opportunity for glory rested at his feet.

Commander Coleman led them into an area of the ship that was less busy. "These will be your quarters," Commander Coleman said. "These four barracks sleep twenty-five a piece. The rest of the squadron will be arriving shortly. In the meantime, the facilities are that direction." He pointed down the corridor back the way they had come. "So, take a shower, get in a workout, do whatever you need to do to mentally prepare yourself for what comes next."

"The rest of the squadron?" someone asked.

"Yes," Commander Coleman said. "You didn't think you were the only pilots vying for a spot in this squadron, did you?"

The pilot who asked the question, Autumn "Whiskey" Jones, stirred under the commander's patronizing gaze.

"There aren't even enough pilots here to fill out a squadron, let alone build one," Commander Coleman said. "Yes, other pilots will be joining us. A lot more, in fact. I said each of these barracks sleeps twenty-five, and we have four of them, so even the worst student here should be able to figure out that means one hundred pilots. You number only fourteen. So you can expect to see a lot of new faces. Now get ready—your briefing begins in two hours."

Commander Coleman disappeared down the corridor, and the pilots began filing into the various barracks. Coda noted which barracks Moscow entered and avoided it.

"Bunk together?" Uno asked Coda and the two other pilots who had enjoyed the flight with them.

"Sure." Coda pointed toward the nearest barracks, the one farthest from Moscow's. "This work?"

"Doubt any of them are different," Squawks said. "And it's closest to the crapper, so it works for me."

When nobody voiced disapproval, Coda stepped inside. Like the rest of the ship, the barracks was long and narrow, with bunks stacked two high and inset into the wall on either side of the room. At the foot of each bed was a vid screen, and each was provided with a privacy shade that could block out light and muffle unwanted noise. It was a step down from his private quarters at the academy, but as far as sleeping arrangements went, he'd heard of worse.

"Back or front?" Coda asked. "Less privacy up front, but it has its advantages too."

"Like what?" Noodle asked.

"You're the first people the commander sees when he enters, and the last he sees when he leaves," Uno said. "And squadron leaders are traditionally near the door. I vote the front."

"Oh god," Squawks said. "I didn't know you were a kiss ass. We can't be friends." He smiled as he said it, clearly making sure Uno understood it was a joke.

"So... you vote rear?" Coda asked.

"Oh no," Squawks said. "I vote front too. Too hard to sneak my drunken rendezvous through an entire barracks of sexually pent-up twenty-something-year-old men, you know?"

"Do you always talk this much?" Uno asked.

"Call sign's 'Squawks,' remember?"

"Great."

"It's settled then," Coda said. "We bunk at the front."

The group dispersed, each grabbing the bunk nearest them. That left Coda with the bottom bunk two bunks deep into the room. Uno grabbed the bunk above him, with Squawks and Noodle across from him.

Coda quickly surveyed his new space, pushing a hand against the gel mattress. It felt like standard military issue, which meant it was only a few centimeters thick and barely softer than concrete. He opened the two drawers under the mattress and a locker with a handprint security system, finding each of them empty.

*We'll probably get our flight gear when the rest of the squadron arrives.*

Coda slipped away from the barracks alone, took a shower in the communal facility, changed back into his clothes, and returned to his bunk, where he pulled the privacy shade closed. Something Commander Coleman had said had been gnawing at him since they'd arrived. He'd said more pilots would be joining them, a lot more, and that the squadron would soon number one hundred.

Squadrons in the academy were on the small side, numbering only sixteen in all, but on the front, squadrons numbered an even twenty-four. Commander Coleman had said he was building a squadron. Not a wing. And not a group. If one hundred other pilots were vying for a position within its ranks, that meant more than seventy-five would wash out.

*He's going to whittle us down,* Coda thought. *Only take the best of the best.*

Coda's previous feelings of accomplishment vanished, immediately replaced by an anxious pit in his stomach. The odds were stacked against him. Again. And something told him this would be his toughest challenge yet.

He gritted his teeth, his resolve hardening. He would meet the challenges head-on, and he would succeed. He didn't have a choice.

# 7

*Ready Room, SAS* Jamestown
*Alpha Centauri System, Proxima B, High Orbit*

THE READY ROOM OF THE SAS *JAMESTOWN* WAS EASILY TWICE THE SIZE OF those back at the academy, though it lacked the polish of the newer space station. The chairs were worn, their cushions cracked, and the paint on the walls had faded with age. Commander Coleman stood behind a podium at the front of the ready room, prepared to address the pilots, who had already found their places. Behind him, a large digital display board, the only technological upgrade in the aging room, stood out like a new button on a well-worn suit.

The rest of the squadron had trickled in over the last couple hours. Always in groups of ten or twenty, they were as diverse as their dress. Like Coda and the rest from the academy, some seemed have been recruited from other flight schools, but others wore the light blues of stationed officers, insignias proudly displayed on their uniforms.

The uncomfortable pit that had been balling up in Coda's gut blossomed into full-blown anxiety. Competing for a spot against other students was one thing, but how was he to compete with pilots who'd flown in real battles?

The others seemed to feel the same way too. Noodle and Uno wore uneasy expressions, their lips tight, eyes slightly downcast, and Squawks, for once, had nothing to say. Most of the officers ignored Coda and the rest of the academy graduates, but others weren't so kind and regarded them as if they were nothing more than fresh meat for the grinder.

"Good morning," Commander Coleman said, his voice easily carrying to the back of the room. "I stand before you, looking at a sight I never expected to see again. Take a look around, ladies and gentlemen. Take note of your fellow wingmen. You all come from different backgrounds. Some just graduated and are serving in your first deployments. Others have already been deployed and have fought on the front. Still others have made a name for yourselves through years of battle. But listen to me when I say this: in this, you are all students. Your backgrounds and any previous successes mean exactly dick. Here, you are all *nuggets*."

The lights suddenly dimmed, and the digital display behind the commander flickered to life. A chill of excitement snapped down Coda's back, and he found himself sitting forward in his seat, staring at a still image taken from battle. The sleek Hornet drones of the Sol Fleet were engaged in a massive space battle with the insectoid ships of the Baranyk.

"What I'm about to show you is a galactic secret that will not be discussed beyond these walls. Failure to comply with this order will result in *stiff* punishment." Commander Coleman stepped away from the podium, stopping in front of the first row of seats. "This is your last chance, nuggets. If any of you are having second thoughts, now is your chance to leave. You will not get another."

Coda surveyed the room, waiting for someone to take the bait. Nobody did. It appeared everyone else was like him—utterly captivated.

"All right." Commander Coleman toggled something on his tablet, and the still image behind him began to play.

The hornet drones flew in a series of tight formations, wing to wing, nose to tail, with incredible precision. They moved fluidly, attacking like a swarm of their namesakes. And there were dozens, maybe hundreds of squadrons, each assaulting the Baranyk fighters and ships with devastating efficiency.

Coda had seen similar vids in the past, but many of them were classified beyond his clearance level, and without the proper instruction, they were impossible to emulate. That was one of the things that excited him the most about fighting on the front—becoming a fighter pilot and learning the secrets behind such precise tactics.

"This was taken thirteen days ago in the Dakara System," Commander Coleman said. "Our ships had been engaged with the Baranyk Fleet for seventeen minutes when... well, see for yourselves."

The ships on the vid continued their assault. Missile trails and tracer fire filled the vacuum between the larger vessels, carving into the reinforced ship exteriors with little resistance. Smaller points of light flashed briefly then disappeared as drones and Baranyk ships exploded. The human fleet was pressing their advantage and making for the Baranyk capital ship when the drone fleet just... *stopped.*

They didn't stop in the traditional sense—there was no stopping in the vacuum of space—but all navigational movement ceased. As if the pilots had lost all navigational control, the drones continued on their course, never deviating or avoiding fire.

The Baranyk made quick work of the drones, eliminating the human fleet in moments before turning their sights on the human capital ships. As the alien fleet closed on the human vessels, Commander Coleman paused the vid, freezing the enemy fire as it hurled toward the metal constructions with violent intent. He stood silently as if encouraging questions.

"With all due respect, sir," said a pilot in the front row. "But what the hell just happened?"

"According to Fleet Intelligence, the Baranyk have developed a new weapon that knocks out all communication between our drones and the drone pilots aboard our battle cruisers."

"But that would mean..." The pilot's voice trailed off as he came to the silent conclusion.

"That our ships are sitting ducks," Commander Coleman said. "Yes, if Fleet Intelligence is correct, the Baranyk have eliminated our greatest advantage in this war."

Coda ran through the implications in his head. The Baranyk were a fierce enemy with superior firepower and a technological edge. The humans' only advantage, if they even had one, was in numbers. Maybe not human numbers but fighter numbers. And only because drones were easier to replace than pilots.

At some point after the early years of the war, when the fleet had faced catastrophic losses among its fighter wings, Fleet Command had realized it was easier to manufacture new starfighters than it was to train new pilots, and within a year, Fleet Command had shifted away from manned starfighters to drones that could be operated from the relative safety of the heavily armored battle cruisers. The Baranyk, for all their technological advancements, hadn't adopted a similar strategy against their human enemy. *Until now.*

Of the many theories why the Baranyk hadn't altered their original tactics, the prevailing one was that the Baranyk fighters were some kind of lesser creature akin to drones themselves, something easily produced in large numbers. Still, humanity, with its vast network of colonized planets and moons, could manufacture drones faster than the Baranyk, and that had given them the advantage. If that was no longer the case, then the Baranyk had a bigger advantage than they had ever had before.

"Fortunately," Commander Coleman said, "Fleet Intelligence believes the Baranyk were reluctant to use the weapon, which explains why they didn't use it until human victory was clearly at hand, and why we haven't seen it used since."

"Why would they be reluctant to use it again, sir?" another pilot asked. "I understand them wanting to keep it a secret, but use it once, and the secret's out. What advantage do they have by not using it again?"

"Intelligence has a couple of ideas. The first is that it's some sort of new weapon, and with all new weapons come bugs. Maybe they've attempted to use it, but it hasn't worked. Another thought is that since it *is* a new weapon, not all Baranyk ships are equipped with it. In either case, Intelligence is working to counteract the weapon, and that's where you come in."

Coda felt his face contort in confusion. Fleet Intelligence harbored some of the smartest men and women the human race had to offer, and if anyone could solve the latest riddle, it was them. He was no mental slouch, but he wasn't qualified to assist in any intelligence efforts, either.

"Intelligence is working on ways to counter the device so that our ships can retain communication or ways to boost the strength of our signal so that the drones are unaffected when the enemy attempts to use their weapon. But that's not for us to worry about. That's not our mission. We're the backup plan. Hell, we're the backup plan to the backup plan. The redundancy in case everything Intelligence comes up with fails. We're another kind of experiment."

"And what kind of experiment is that, sir?" The words were out of Coda's mouth before he knew it. Squawks and Noodle looked at him, their mouths agape, leaning away as if attempting to distance themselves from him.

"The best kind, Coda. The kind that'll put all of you into the cockpits of real starfighters. The kind that will allow you to become real pilots, just as I was."

Commander Coleman's words cut to Coda's very core. *He wants me to be a pilot. Not a drone pilot—a fighter pilot. Just like my father.* Coda never would have thought it possible. Hell, since the advent of drone warfare, it *hadn't* been possible. Now suddenly placed on the same treacherous path as his father, Coda's doubts resurfaced.

*His blood runs through my veins. What if I'm just as weak? What if I fail? What if I cause death and destruction just as he did?*

It was almost unimaginable. If Coda failed, the O'Neils would never have a place among the military again. They would be disgraced. Discarded. Hated. Coda tried not to think about the riots in his hometown, about the vile threats and vandals terrorizing what little peace his mother still had.

*I can't do it. I won't. I can't risk it.*

Even if he avoided the traps of his father, Fleet Intelligence wanted to put Coda and ninety-nine other rookies into the cockpit of a death machine. Casualties among fighter pilots had been the highest among all Fleet personnel and for good reason. The extreme conditions pilots faced in a starfighter were as dangerous as anything the Baranyk could throw at them. Even with inertial dampeners and other systems meant to lessen the strain, the physical toll alone had accounted for nearly ten percent of all fighter deaths, and many of the pilots who had survived suffered lifelong ailments. Flying a starfighter was akin to looking into the face of death itself.

*But...*

Some of the most renowned military figures had been pilots. It was no coincidence that Coda had recognized Commander Coleman on sight. He could have done the same with a handful of other legendary pilots. Of everyone he looked up to, of all the prestigious drone pilots fighting on the front, he knew their call signs and had maybe even seen a picture or interview with them once or twice, but none of them were as recognized as those original starfighter pilots. If Coda's goal was restoring honor to the family name, what better chance would he have?

*I have too much riding on this.*

It was almost poetic, in a sense. He'd dreamed about righting his father's wrongs, and now he had an opportunity to do it from the same cockpit.

*Can I really turn that down?*

Coda found himself nodding. Nodding in excitement. Nodding in agreement. Ready to get started.

"I see a lot of nervous faces," Commander Coleman said slowly. "And rightfully so. I'm not going to sugarcoat it. This isn't going to be easy. Chances are some of you won't survive. Statistics say that five of you will stroke out before you ever see battle. And even then, the cards are stacked against you. In my day, a pilot spent six weeks at Advanced Preflight Instruction, then six *months* at Primary Flight School, and another eighteen weeks at Advanced Flight Training. We have twenty-six weeks."

Nervous whispers filtered throughout the room.

"The odds are slim," Commander Coleman continued. "I understand that. Fleet Intelligence understands that. Which is why there are one hundred candidates in this room. Out of all of you, only twenty-four will make the squadron. The rest of you will receive new orders. But unlike you, I understood the challenges and expectations when I accepted this post. I understood the odds and the limitations of our timeline. But I also understood what was at stake. There's a very real chance that Fleet Intelligence will fail in their attempt to counteract the Baranyk weapon, and if that happens, we are the *only* thing that stands in the way of our fleet's total destruction."

Commander Coleman paused, letting the words sink in. He knew, just as Coda did, that when it was put like that, when they were faced with the ugly, terrible, terrifying truth that their fleet's destruction meant the eradication of the human race, nobody would quit. They were all here for reason, and they would give it their all or die trying.

"Look around, nuggets. The men and women in this room are the best and brightest fighter minds in the fleet. I personally picked every single one of you, because if there's anyone who can learn to fly a starfighter under these conditions, it's you. We will become the most fearsome squadron in the Sol Fleet. Now grab some food and some sleep, because we begin FAM Phase tomorrow at oh six hundred. Dismissed."

# 8

*Corridor, SAS* Jamestown

*Alpha Centauri System, Proxima B, High Orbit*

Coda was so deep in thought as he left the ready room that he didn't hear Moscow fall into step behind him. Uno and Squawks were at his side, talking animatedly about how they were going to kick Baranyk ass, when Moscow's voice cut through the corridor.

"Gonna be a pilot like your old man, huh, O'Neil?"

Coda's body tightened at Moscow's words, but he continued forward, acting as if he hadn't heard him. He felt his friends' eyes on him, but they took his lead, letting the taunt go unanswered.

"Seeing as your old man went rogue and killed his wingmen," Moscow continued, "I'm not sure I like that very much."

Coda let out a long, slow breath, silently repeating Captain Hughes's words over and over again. *You don't learn from your mistakes. You don't learn from your mistakes. You don't learn from your mistakes.* Letting Moscow goad him into another fight wasn't a mistake he would make again. He wouldn't give Moscow the satisfaction.

"You hear me, O'Neil?" he said even more loudly. "You going to kill us like your old man killed his wingmen?"

Coda's resolve broke. He turned to face his tormenter.

"What do you say—"

"Stow it, Lieutenant!"

Every pilot inside the corridor froze, their eyes falling on Commander Coleman, who had just exited the ready room.

"Do you have an issue with who I assembled for this squadron?" Commander Coleman asked, advancing on Moscow.

The other rookie looked genuinely terrified. His eyes darted to the small gang he had assembled, but each of his new friends gave him a wide berth. He was on his own, and he knew it.

"I asked you a question, Lieutenant!"

"No, sir."

"Then you will cease all talk of Lieutenant O'Neil's family. Do you understand?"

"Understood, sir."

"Are you sure, Lieutenant?" Commander Coleman closed the remaining distance between him and Moscow in a single step, bringing his face inches from the other pilot's. The larger officer made Moscow look like a child by comparison.

"Crystal, sir."

"Good." Commander Coleman surveyed the corridor, looking at Moscow's gang and the others who were milling around. "Anyone else?" When nobody answered, Commander Coleman returned his attention back to Moscow. "Get to your barracks."

"Yes, sir." Moscow turned and started down the corridor. He didn't say anything to Coda as he passed, but his eyes burned with anger and embarrassment. *This isn't over,* they seemed to say. *Not by a long shot.*

As Coda turned toward the barracks, Commander Coleman's gaze settled on him. The Commander's expression was unreadable, and as the moment drew longer, Coda grew increasingly uncomfortable. Turning his back on the commander felt inappropriate, especially since he had just come to Coda's defense. Fortunately, Commander Coleman nodded at him then continued down the corridor in the opposite direction, sparing Coda from further scrutiny.

"Come on," someone said to him, and Coda found himself being pushed toward the barracks.

Back in the privacy of their quarters, Coda's new friends huddled around him.

"What the hell was that all about?" Squawks asked. "I mean, I knew you and Moscow didn't like each other, but damn."

Coda shrugged, not sure how much he wanted to talk about it.

"Seriously," Squawks pressed. "What just happened?"

"Nothing," Coda said quietly.

"Didn't look like nothing."

"It's… complicated," Coda said.

Squawks opened his mouth to say more, but Uno laid a hand on his shoulder. "Lay off him. He obviously doesn't want to talk about it."

"No," Coda said. "It's fine. Me and Andrei have been rivals since our first day at the academy. I don't know why, but we never got along. Actually, I'm pretty sure he hated me since day one. And it only got worse when we got our own squadrons. Anyway, when Commander Coleman recruited me, he told me that he had flown with my father. That he was a good man. I guess hearing Moscow bad-mouth him pissed the commander off as much as it did me."

Coda's friends shared an uneasy look. Joseph O'Neil wasn't someone people usually talked about, and when they did, they certainly didn't praise him. Calling a known war criminal a "good man" just didn't happen—especially from a superior officer.

"The commander flew with your father?" Uno asked tentatively.

Coda nodded.

"Did he say when?" Squawks asked. "I mean, was he there when… you know…"

"When he allowed the Baranyk to wipe out his entire squadron?" Coda asked bitterly. "He didn't say. But I got the impression that they knew each other pretty well. They might have even been friends."

Squawks whistled his surprise.

"Are you going to talk to him about it?" Uno asked. "You know, so you know for sure."

"No."

Another awkward silence, made worse by the other pilots' reluctance to meet his eye, fell over the group. Coda wanted to say something, but he didn't know what. He hated talking about his father, because when he did, things got awkward… and he lost friends.

"Look," Coda said, "I know you've all thought about it, so if we're going to fly together, you deserve to know. Yes, my father is a war criminal. Maybe even a traitor. And his wingmen died because of it. But my father's mistakes were his own. Not mine. And for as long as we fly together, I promise I will do everything in my power to be the best wingman I can be."

"You don't have to say that, Coda," Uno said.

"Yes, I do," Coda said. "It's important to me. And I need all of you to understand that, okay?"

He was met with a series of small nods.

"We're going to kick some serious Baranyk ass, aren't we?" Squawks said, his playful bluster shattering what remained of the awkward moment.

"Hell yeah." Coda was grateful for the new subject and gave Squawks a knowing smile. He reminded him of Buster, who'd had a rare ability to say the right thing at the right time, protecting Coda with words when he resorted to fists.

Uno hooted his own battle cry, and the rest of them followed. Before Coda knew it, they were smiling and laughing again, their nerves and concerns disappearing. Coda took part in all of it, silently noting that for the first time since he could remember, nobody cared who he was or where he came from. In that moment, Coda and his small group of friends were ready for whatever the following day had in store.

# 9

*Hangar Deck, SAS* Jamestown

*Alpha Centauri System, Proxima B, High Orbit*

THE NEXT MORNING, THE PILOTS FORMED UP IN FRONT OF COMMANDER Coleman on Hangar Deck 7B. The Commander stood in front of a squadron of X-23 Nighthawks; the single-manned starfighters were larger than the Z-18 Hornet drones the pilots were more familiar with, sporting a sleek design with angled wings, four rear thrusters, and a narrow cockpit. Matte black and ornamented with a full armament of missiles and a nose-mounted cannon, the Nighthawks looked every bit like the big brother to the Hornets that Coda had imagined them to be.

"Welcome to FAM Phase," Commander Coleman said, "also known as the Familiarization Phase. Over the next two weeks, you will familiarize yourself with every nut, bolt, nook, and cranny of the X-23 so that when we are done, you will be able to rebuild your Nighthawk in space with nothing more than your flight suit and fingernails.

"Make no mistake, ladies and gentlemen, the next two weeks will be one of the most trying times of your lives. It will test your patience and mental endurance more than ever before. FAM Phase is not fun, but it is important, and I expect you to treat it as such. Is that understood?"

"Yes, sir!" the squadron echoed in unison.

"Good," Commander Coleman said. "There are one hundred of you and only twenty-five X-23s, so form into groups of four and find a fighter. Over the next hour, I want you to acquaint yourself with it. Run your hand along her body. Sit in her seat. Look her up and down, inside and out, then we'll begin the real fun."

Coda quickly formed a group with Squawks, Uno, and Noodle and found an X-23 that wasn't already surrounded by overly excited pilots. Squawks bounded up the ladder and climbed into the cockpit before anyone had an opportunity to argue, grinning as he took in the various gauges and screens.

Coda circled the X-23, studying its contours. The Nighthawk wasn't just bigger than the Hornet, there were subtle variations in the curve of the body and a slightly different angle to its wings. Its navigational thrusters were more numerous and spaced out more evenly to increase maneuverability.

Like the Z-18, however, the Nighthawk's matte-black exterior seemed to absorb the light of the hangar, and Coda knew from his studies that it was resistant to radar, lidar, and other forms of detection. Most of the battles on the front were fought at range with missiles, but the larger battles often devolved into close-quarter combat—dogfighting—and the fighter's dark exterior made it difficult to spot amid the black of space.

Uno took Squawks's place in the cockpit, easily outmuscling Noodle for the next position in line. Coda didn't mind. He would get his turn, and besides, he was equally fascinated by how the fighter's hundreds of plates fit together so perfectly that the ship almost looked as though it had been carved from a solid block of metal.

When he finally took a seat in the cockpit, the childlike excitement that had consumed the others overcame him as well. Where the Hornet drones were little more than cold predators, there was something majestic about the Nighthawk. A history. A connection to every pilot who had sat in its cockpit. Beyond the luminous dials, instrument panels, buttons, switches, and triggers was the smell of sweat, blood, and human resolve. Squawks was right—the fighter *was* awesome. Coda couldn't wait to see what it could do.

Unfortunately, the commander had other ideas, and by "real fun," he had actually meant unbelievably tedious. After their session with the

Nighthawks, Commander Coleman brought each of them to a private room no larger than a broom closet and had each sit on a deck-mounted metal chair in front of an embarrassingly old computer terminal.

"What is this, sir?" Coda asked, sitting down on the uncomfortable chair.

"This is your Computer Assisted Instruction," Commander Coleman said. "It will guide you through all of the technical workings of your starfighter."

Coda looked at the ancient screen skeptically. It looked like it would sooner project a grainy black-and-white image than it would anything Coda was accustomed to.

"Is there an issue, Lieutenant?"

"No, sir," Coda said. "It's just that... sir, how old is this?"

"The *Jamestown* is one of the oldest ships in the fleet, and it's not equipped with the *fancy* technology you were pampered with at the academy. If you're looking for state-of-the-art equipment, Coda, you signed up for the wrong squadron."

With that, the commander turned to leave. Coda watched him go, silently cursing himself. As far as early impressions went, he wasn't making a very good one. Turning back to the terminal, he sighed, ready to begin. There was only one problem.

"Sir!" Coda shouted as the door hissed closed. "I don't even know how to turn this thing on."

The Commander didn't return. He didn't even respond.

"Great," Coda mumbled. He looked over the terminal and, seeing no buttons or switches, touched the screen. It immediately came to life, displaying a propaganda-like image of a squadron of X-23s overlaid with a menu of options. There were seventy-five modules to choose from, and with a sigh, Coda toggled the first one, titled Program Overview.

The menu disappeared, replaced by a clean-cut private citizen who no doubt worked for the contractor who had built the X-23. The man gave a standard introduction, highlighting the Nighthawks' capabilities, top speed, and success in battle as if he were reading straight from a brochure—which he no doubt was. Contractors were every bit as concerned about securing their *next* contract as they were about fulfilling their present one, and that meant constantly touting their successes.

Ten minutes into the program overview, Coda's legs began to tingle. The metal chair was cutting off the circulation to his lower half. Worse yet, since it was bolted to the floor, he had no way to move it to a more comfortable position.

*Two weeks,* Coda thought. *I've got two weeks of this.* The thought filled him with dread, but failure wasn't an option. He had to get through it so he could get to the good stuff.

When the overview ended, Coda immediately moved onto the next module, and for the next two hours, he listened and took notes on an introduction to the miniature Shaw Drive equipped on the X-23. It was dry stuff, which the presenter made worse with a slow, monotone voice that catered to the lowest common denominator.

Coda's eyes burned, and at one point, he nearly fell asleep. He would have let himself if the video didn't stop periodically to give him a short quiz, making sure he was paying attention. And the longer the video played, the more difficult the quizzes got. Coda began missing questions, and the module responded by forcing him to rewatch entire sections until he passed the mid-module exam.

He felt triumphant when he finally got to the end of the first module, but the feeling quickly turned to despair when he saw the one-hundred-question test that awaited him. Despair then turned to irritation when he failed the test and was forced to retake the module from the beginning.

After a brief meltdown, he forced himself to take the module more slowly, often replaying certain parts so he could take more detailed notes and ensure he understood the content. When he came to the test again, he passed it without issue, though not with the score he would have liked. Still, passing was passing, and as the old saying went, "Cs get degrees."

That afternoon, Coda and his group of friends met in the mess hall. The room was like every other mess he'd eaten in. Stainless-steel tables and chairs lined the room and were all bolted securely to the floor. Refreshment stations serving recycled water and black coffee framed the food buffet, where cooks lethargically spooned slop onto their plates.

"What is this?" Squawks asked, staring at his tray. "Looks like you puked on my plate and called it a meal."

He wasn't far from the truth. The food, if one could call it that, was a brown paste that resembled something between meatloaf and Jell-O.

"Why can't I have some of that?" Squawks pointed at a tray of hamburgers piled on a warming tray.

"You're with the new squadron, right?" the cook asked.

"Yeah."

"Then this is what you get." The cook spooned a second helping onto Squawks's plate and gave him a sarcastic look.

"This is some horseshit," Squawks said.

"I don't think we're going to get prime rib and scallops," Coda said as the cook scooped a spoonful onto his tray. "Come on. Let's find a place to sit."

They found a table near the refreshment station and sat, poking their food as if it were a strange creature that had washed up on the beach. Noodle was the first to brave a bite. The rest of the group watched as he chewed, swallowed, and made a face Coda couldn't read.

"Well?" Squawks asked.

Noodle just shrugged. "Tastes like someone mixed some proteins, fats, vitamins, and water in a blender and called it good. It's not going to win any cooking awards, but I've had worse."

Hearing it wasn't as bad as it looked, Coda took a bite of his own and was pleasantly surprised by its lack of taste. Like Noodle, he shrugged and helped himself to more.

"If we're saving the fleet, we should at least eat like it," Squawks said, stirring his food with a disgusted expression.

"We *are* eating like it," Uno said.

"What do you mean?" Coda asked.

"Think about it," Uno said. "Flying a starfighter takes a serious toll on the body. Whatever's in here, it's more than just fat and protein."

"What are you saying? You think there's steroids or growth hormones in here or something?" Coda's appetite was disappearing by the second.

"Of course there is," Uno said. "They said there would be."

"Who did?" Squawks asked.

"The commander."

"He didn't say anything like that to me."

"Me, neither," Coda said.

"It was in the paperwork." Uno looked around the table and was met with a series of blank expressions. "I'm the only one who read the release, aren't I?"

The group nodded.

"Wow," Uno said. "You guys signed up for something without reading what would be required?"

"They said it was classified," Noodle said.

"The mission was classified," Uno said. "Not what would be required to fulfill that mission."

"What did it say?" Coda asked.

"You pretty much figured it out already. They have us on a special diet chocked-full of your standard fat and proteins but with an added helping of experimental growth hormones meant to strengthen our bodies for the stresses of space flight."

Coda slid his tray away. The word "experimental" turned his stomach, and he was left with a mental image of himself growing a third arm.

Noodle came to a very different conclusion. "I'm going to get jacked, aren't I?"

"Sorry, Noodle," Squawks said. "He said '*experimental,*' not '*miracle.*'

"Shut it, Squawks."

"It's okay, little guy. One of these days, you'll hit puberty."

"And one of these days, I'm going to kick your ass."

"You're welcome to try," Squawks said. "Just remember, I've got bigger muscles."

"You've got a bigger mouth too," Noodle said.

Laughter erupted around the table. Squawks took the jibe in stride, laughing the loudest of all.

"Well played," Squawks said, giving Noodle a fist bump. "There's hope for you yet."

The banter was familiar to Coda, even welcomed. Viking Squadron had bickered like family too, and Coda believed it was a true sign of camaraderie. When your wingmen made fun of you, that meant they liked you. If they ignored you... well, that was an altogether different story.

"Whether Noodle will ever fill out remains to be seen," Uno said. "But either way, I'm sure the commander will have us in the gym soon. So eat up. It might be the difference between life and death out there."

"If I don't die of boredom first." Squawks pushed his tray away. "Seriously. FAM Phase can suck it. Who knew being a pilot would be so *boring*?"

Noodle began mimicking the instructor's slow monotone voice, and everyone laughed again.

"I don't know," Uno said. "It's not that bad."

"*What?*" the other pilots said in unison.

Uno's face colored, and he kept his eyes on his tray, absently poking at the food paste with his fork. "I kind of like it. It's interesting."

"You're messed up in the head, man," Squawks said.

The conversation eventually drifted in other directions, but Coda's mind was occupied with what Uno had said. Like the pilots in Viking Squadron, those in Commander Coleman's would have their own strengths and weaknesses, and it would be vital that their squadron leader know how to use them accordingly.

Coda made a mental note of Uno's. He didn't know if he would ever be in a leadership position again, but if he was, he promised himself he would be ready.

# 10

*Ready Room, SAS* Jamestown

*Alpha Centauri System, Proxima B, High Orbit*

UNO'S PREDICTION THAT THEY WOULD SPEND PLENTY OF TIME IN THE GYM proved to be true. Apart from their mealtimes and daily briefings, it offered the only reprieve from their computer-aided training.

Coda had never been much for working out, but he took to it immediately, relishing the opportunity to get away from the droll voice of the narrator. The highly technical overview of the inner workings of the X-23's guidance system had been more than enough to turn his brain to mush, and he was growing increasingly frustrated with the process.

He was a pilot. Building a fighter wasn't his job—flying one was. Who cared how the guidance system worked as long as it did? But after making a less-than-ideal first impression, he wasn't about to voice his displeasure. Instead, he took his aggression out in the gym.

The only person who seemed to hate the gym more than the CAI was Noodle. He complained about it as much as Squawks griped about the food.

The goal of their workouts, Commander Coleman had said, wasn't to bulk up. They weren't interested in pure strength; it would only get in the way. Instead, they were after enhanced flexibility and muscular endurance. That meant, in addition to heavy cardio and partner stretching, they focused on exercises that strengthened their cores, utilizing low weight with high reps. After the gym and the mental undertaking of the CAI, Coda went to bed exhausted, both mentally and physically.

Three days into FAM Phase, Commander Coleman posted their first progress report on the display boards of the ready room, and to Coda's great surprise, he was dead last. Every other pilot had completed more CAI modules than he had, and most had better scores. Worse yet, Moscow was in the top ten and made sure Coda knew it. The only thing that kept Coda sane was that Uno had not only finished the most but had also remarkably scored the highest on each of the evaluations.

When Coda asked him how he'd scored so high, Uno had just shrugged and repeated that he found the subject matter interesting. Unfortunately, such advice wasn't helpful, and even after reapplying himself, Coda didn't make up enough ground to dig his way out of the bottom quarter of the class by the end of the week. For the first time in his life, Coda was failing at something, and he had no idea how to fix it.

That night, during their daily briefing, Commander Coleman reviewed their progress, calling out everyone in the bottom half by name. It was public humiliation at its worst. When he got to Coda's name, Moscow snickered and muttered something to one of the nearby pilots. Coda couldn't make out what he'd said, but the outburst had drawn the commander's attention.

"What was that?" Commander Coleman asked, pausing his review.

Moscow stiffened, his smile disappearing immediately.

"I asked you a question, Lieutenant."

"Yes, sir."

"Then answer it."

"Sir," Moscow said, "I just wonder when the first cuts are going to be made. You know, when the first pilots will be sent home."

"Afraid of your competition, Lieutenant Krylov?"

"No, sir," Moscow said, apparently refusing to take the bait. "I'm more afraid of flying with pilots who can't pass a simple test, sir."

Commander Coleman chewed on the words, his face a mask of displeasure. Coda waited for him to scold Moscow, but to his surprise, the commander did the opposite. “I would be too, Moscow. That is why any pilots who haven’t completed their computer-aided instruction by the end of next week will be cut from the program.” He surveyed the ready room. “Hear me now, nuggets. You have seven days. Make them count.”

# 11

*Gym, SAS* Jamestown

*Alpha Centauri System, Proxima B, High Orbit*

Uno was the first pilot to complete his CAI, finishing four full days before the deadline, with an impressive cumulative score of ninety-six percent. The next batch of graduates came a day later, and to Coda's great frustration, Moscow was among them.

"Ninety-three percent," Moscow said when Coda passed him in the gym. "That's what I scored, O'Neil. Did you see it? You won't even make it through ninety-three percent of the material."

Coda seethed but said nothing. He strode past Moscow, making for the free weights on the other side of the gym. When he got to the bench press, he slapped a series of weights on either side of the bar and lay down into position.

"What are you doing?" Noodle asked, appearing above him. "We're not supposed to be using these weights."

Coda ignored the question—it should have been pretty damn obvious what he was doing. "Spot me."

"Coda—"

"Spot me," Coda repeated, then without waiting for a response, he lifted the bar from the bracket and lowered it onto his chest. It felt lighter than he'd expected. Fewer than two weeks into the program, his body was growing stronger and showing signs of increased muscle definition. He finished the first four reps without issue. By the fifth, the bar began to get heavy. By seven, he was noticeably slower, and by the ninth, his arms were shaking.

"One more," Noodle said, placing his hands under the bar in case Coda's arms gave out. "Come on, Coda. One more."

Feeling as though he was lifting the weight of the world itself, Coda pushed with everything he had. When the bar slammed back into place with a satisfying *clang*, he let out a triumphant scream then, breathing heavily, sat up. Noodle was grinning at him.

"Thanks," Coda said.

"You're welcome," Noodle said. "What was that all about, anyway?"

Coda just shook his head. He didn't want to be reminded of the CAI.

"How'd your session with the computer go?" Noodle asked, proving there was no getting away from it.

"Not good."

"It couldn't have been that bad."

"I've got three days left, Noodle, and I'm only seventy-five percent of the way through it. I might as well start packing."

"That's a bit dramatic."

"Yeah? And what should I be doing?"

"Well, for starters, I wouldn't be in here. There's only so much time in the day, Coda, and you can't afford to waste any of it in here."

"I'm not sure the commander would agree."

"The commander isn't here," Noodle said. "Neither is Squawks or Uno or a bunch of other people."

Coda surveyed the room with fresh eyes. Noodle was right. Squawks and Uno were nowhere to be found, and the gym was noticeably emptier than usual.

"Where are they?" Coda asked.

Noodle raised an eyebrow as if the answer was obvious.

"Both of them?"

"Yeah."

"But Uno completed his... wait, Uno's helping him?"

"That's what you do when you need help, isn't it? You ask for it. Just like you did when you asked me to spot you."

"Can he do that?"

"Did anyone say he couldn't? Seriously, Coda, if you're not resourceful enough to figure this out, maybe you don't belong in a cockpit."

Noodle smiled as if to suggest he was joking, but there was too much truth in the statement for Coda to laugh. He hadn't thought to ask for help, partly because he didn't know he could, but also because he didn't like doing it. He'd always wanted to succeed on his own, and if that meant failing on his own too, then so be it. But if he didn't get through a quarter of the program in the next forty-eight hours, that hypothetical situation would become a very real possibility.

"So, uh, you think you could help me out?" Coda asked awkwardly.

"Me?" Noodle said. "Coda, I think you misunderstood. I'm not doing much better than you are. I'll finish, but just barely, and that's with me putting in extra work. No, you're going to have to talk to Uno or something."

"All right," Coda said. "I'll do that."

---

CODA FOUND UNO AND SQUAWKS IN ONE OF THE TRAINING ROOMS, huddled close to the screen. Uno was pointing at something and explaining it in simpler terms. Coda didn't recognize it, so it must have been from a later module. That was a good sign. If Squawks was closer to completing the CAI, that meant Uno would have more time to help him, wouldn't it?

"Making progress?" Coda asked from the doorway.

Uno and Squawks looked up immediately then at each other. Coda couldn't tell for sure, but Squawks appeared to be trying to decide whether to be embarrassed and concerned.

"Relax," Coda said. "Noodle said I could find you here. What module is that?"

"Fifty-seven," Uno said. "The inner workings of Shaw Drive mechanics."

Coda couldn't believe his luck. Just before heading to the gym, he'd completed module fifty-six. Squawks was literally working his way through the very course he was set to begin.

"Do you have room for one more?"

"Are you wanting to help too?" Uno asked.

"Actually, no." Coda's face grew hot. "I'm looking for a tutor if you have space for another student."

"You need help?" Uno asked, a hint of surprise in his voice.

Coda nodded. "A lot of it. I'm actually on module fifty-seven too."

"No way," Squawks asked.

"Yep."

Squawks looked at Uno and shrugged as if saying the decision was up to him.

"I don't mind," Uno said. "But there's no way for you to undock and work in here with us."

"That's fine," Coda said. "What I need is someone who helps me understand this stuff. I can figure the rest out."

"Then grab a chair," Uno said.

"Thank you," Coda said.

In a nearby room, Coda found a chair that wasn't bolted to the floor then squeezed it in next to the two pilots. The room was already tight with two and was completely crammed with three, but even as the room grew hot, nobody complained.

Uno was a born teacher. He often paused the videos, taking time to explain them in greater detail and with less technical language. He answered their questions patiently and without condescension, and even though the video took twice as long to get through, they completed the module in half the time Coda had taken to complete the previous one.

They worked late into the night, not stopping until a full two hours after the three of them were supposed to be in bed. In that time, they had wrapped up two other modules, ending on the sixtieth. With Uno's help, Squawks had completed eighty-percent of the program and had rising evaluation scores.

Armed with a tablet full of notes, his eyes bleary with exhaustion, Coda returned to his training room and fired up the computer. There was no way to fast forward through the video, so he was forced to watch it from the beginning. At first, he tried to tell himself that he would watch it again, but ten minutes into the first video, Coda was struggling to hold his eyes open. Scared he would fall asleep and lose an entire night, he pulled out his personal hand terminal and set an alarm for every ten minutes.

When he got to the exam, he was pleased to find that the questions were the same questions Squawks had answered, only in a different order. Between his familiarization with them and Uno's tutelage, Coda breezed through the evaluation, posting his best score yet.

Suddenly feeling better than he had in days, he began the next module.

# 12

*CAI Room, SAS* Jamestown

*Alpha Centauri System, Proxima B, High Orbit*

For two full days, Coda worked with Uno and Squawks, and for two full nights, he took what he'd learned from their group study and applied it to his own evaluations. By the end of the second night, Coda wasn't worried about completing the remaining modules in time, but he was growing increasingly concerned that his test scores wouldn't be high enough to pass.

Commander Coleman had set the benchmark at a cumulative eighty percent, and while Coda was within spitting distance of that mark, the long days and nights were beginning to take their toll. In the last forty-eight hours, he hadn't managed more than thirty minutes of continuous sleep, and faced with severe sleep deprivation, he found himself making stupid mistakes—misreading questions, making basic arithmetic errors, and simply highlighting the wrong answers.

By the time he was ready to begin the final module his uptick in scores had taken a dive, and he would have to score a ninety-six on his final exam to meet the commander's benchmark.

As with nearly every other test, the questions began simple: *Identify the various components of the X-23's navigational thrusters. The X-23 leverages how many navigational thrusters for its X, Y, and Z-axis maneuvers? Unlike the Shaw Drive propulsion system, which leverages electromagnetic propulsion, the navigational thrusters used what fuel?*

Coda calmly punched in the answers for each, and it wasn't until he was a third of the way through the exam that he even needed to consult his notes.

*Name the optimal compression range for the aft- and port-side nose thrusters. In the event the liquid oxygen compressor is damaged, what other system can provide emergency navigational abilities? What steps are required to bypass the compressor to make this possible?*

He was halfway through the exam when he got his first question wrong. It was a ridiculous question about hydrogen composition mixes where the four possible answers varied by less than a tenth of a percent. By that point, almost an hour into the exam, his adrenaline rush of having nearly completed FAM Phase had worn off, and he made his second mistake, simply miscounting the correct number of zeroes after a decimal point. It was exactly the kind of question that pissed him off.

*Who cares what the optimum hydrogen composition mix is for the navigational thrusters? That's not my job.*

Captain Hughes had criticized him for not trusting others—well, he sure as hell trusted that the Deck Chief knew how to service the X-23 better than he did.

Seething, Coda queued up the next question and immediately erupted into a series of curses. Of course it was a follow-up question. It only made sense that the test was doubling down on something he obviously didn't understand. Something he didn't care about. Worse still, he had twenty-five questions to go, and if he got another question wrong, he would have to answer every other question correctly in order to score marks high enough.

His emotions getting the better of him, Coda punched in the first answer he thought might be correct, and to his welcomed surprise, the terminal flashed green.

Sometimes it was better to be lucky than good. Knowing he'd somehow dodged a self-inflicted bullet, Coda put himself through a relaxing exercise that his anger counselor at the academy had taught him. He closed his eyes and breathed in slowly through his mouth for ten seconds, held it for ten seconds, then out his nose for an equal amount of time. After five long breaths, he opened his eyes. Feeling a renewed sense of clarity, he read the next question.

The monitor flashed green with another correct answer.

Five questions later, five right answers. Then ten. Twenty. Before he knew it, he had five to go and only needed to get four correct.

Three left. Then two.

His body trembled as he read the second-to-last question. It would almost be fitting if he missed the last two questions—to come so close only to fail. That was something his father would have done.

Coda read the question three times, and his answer five more, consulting his notes every time to ensure he wasn't making a stupid mistake. Satisfied he wasn't, he held his breath and punched in the answer with a shaky hand. His eyes welled with tears as the green bracket appeared, and alone in the small room, Coda let them flow freely down his face.

*I did it,* he thought. *I did it.*

The words of the final question were blurry through his tears, but even then, barely able to read them, he still got it right.

---

Walking into the ready room that night, Coda was hit with a strange mix of excitement and dejection. The pilots milling around the auditorium seating wore grim expressions that randomly broke into smiles. Everyone in the room had lost someone they'd known to the commander's exceedingly high benchmark, and while it was tough to say goodbye, it was equally tough not to feel proud of what they had accomplished.

Coda found Uno and Squawks talking to Noodle. Unlike the rest, they wore openly relieved expressions, smiles shining through bloodshot eyes and pale faces. Their excitement only grew when they spotted Coda.

"You did it?" Uno asked.

"Ninety-eight percent!" Coda shouted triumphantly.

"I told you!" Uno slapped him on the chest and gave him a friendly shove. "I knew you could do it."

"By the skin of my teeth," Coda said. "I wouldn't have been able to do it without you. Any of you. Thank you."

Uno beamed, and the others inclined their heads in recognition. Before anyone could say anything more, the door to the ready room opened. Commander Coleman strode in.

"Attention on deck!" someone shouted, and every pilot inside the ready room snapped to attention.

"At ease," Commander Coleman said. "And find your seats."

It wasn't until everyone had sat down that Coda noticed just how empty the room was. He couldn't say who was missing, or even how many, but it was a sizable number.

Moscow, unfortunately, wasn't one of them. He met Coda's gaze and didn't look happy. His group was down a member, and Coda's unexpected success was surely salt in the wound. Shoving the thought to the back of his mind, Coda turned his attention back to Commander Coleman, who waited at the front of the room.

"For the last two weeks, you and every member of this squad have been familiarizing yourself with the inner workings of the X-23 Nighthawk. Look around. The pilots you see here are the pilots who passed."

"How many are left, sir?"

"Eighty-seven."

*Eighty-seven,* Coda repeated in his head. Thirteen percent of their total number had already been removed from the program. The commander had said competition was fierce, but Coda hadn't expected it to be this intense.

"FAM Phase is meant to separate the mentally strong from the weak," Commander Coleman continued. "Every pilot who sits with you tonight has displayed the mental fortitude required to pilot an X-23. Like you, they deserve to be congratulated."

Polite applause filled the room, followed by half-hearted hoots of excitement.

"Congratulations," Commander Coleman said without a hint of pride in his voice, "you have completed FAM Phase. Tomorrow, you'll begin to truly understand what it means to fly an X-23 Nighthawk."

# 13

*Simulator, SAS* Jamestown

*Alpha Centauri System, Proxima B, High Orbit*

The operational flight trainer was one of the most beautifully intimidating pieces of equipment Coda had ever seen. Mounted in the center of a gyroscope was an exact working replica of the cockpit of an X-23 Nighthawk, its insides already alive with multicolored lights, screens displaying simulated flight data, gauges, switches, knobs, dials, and more.

Commander Coleman stood in front of it like a proud parent. "Welcome, nuggets, to the simulator."

A wave of awe swept through the pilots, and Coda heard more than a few hushed whispers. Smiling, Coda looked at his friends standing beside him. Squawks and Noodle were smiling too—the kind of smile that was so wide, it had to hurt. Uno, however, looked as though he was going to lose his stomach. His already-pale face had turned a sickly green color.

"Once upon a time," Commander Coleman said, "pilots trained in primitive versions of what you see in front of you. They were static, didn't move, and focused more on training pilots to understand the cockpit than the sensation of flying. That's not the case here, ladies and gentlemen."

Commander Coleman took hold of one of the outer tubes of the gyroscope and gave it a hard push. The various tubes making up the frame of the simulator began to move, and when they did, the cockpit spun with it.

"The Simulator will spin you. It'll twist you. It'll hum, throb, and shake you. And when you crash, it'll hurt. It's not flying, but it's damn close."

Coda was smiling again—he couldn't help it. The commander saw it too.

"What are you smiling at, Coda?" he barked.

"Just excited to get started, sir."

"Good," Commander Coleman said. "That's good. But the pilot with the honor of giving it its first spin is the pilot who completed their CAI first."

"Oh no," Uno whispered.

"Lieutenant Hernandez."

"No, no, no, no, no," Uno continued to whisper. His eyes took on a wild look, as if he were a spooked animal about to flee.

"Uno!" Commander Coleman snapped. "Get up here."

Uno suddenly pitched forward and lost his stomach on the dull-gray deck. The pilots standing in formation around him shied away, giving him a wide berth as he vomited again. Coda looked on in confusion, unsure of whether to laugh or console the friend who had gotten him through the computer-aided training.

Moscow's shrill laugh cut through the sound of Uno's retching.

"Knock it off!" Coda shouted, pointing a finger at Moscow, then was at Uno's side. "You all right?"

Uno turned away.

The sound of heavy bootsteps caught Coda and Uno's attention, and they looked up to find Commander Coleman making his way toward them. Uno sprang to his feet, snapping once again to attention as Commander Coleman stopped.

"Sir," Uno said. "I..."

"Don't just stand there!" Commander Coleman shouted. "Find a mop and clean it up."

"Yes, sir," Uno said.

"And while you're at it, scrub the entire deck. I can't have my Simulation Room smelling like vomit."

"Yes, sir," Uno said then, his face red and eyes bloodshot, darted out of the room.

Commander Coleman watched him leave, shaking his head. "At least he didn't piss himself."

The jibe stoked Coda's anger, but when nobody else, not even Moscow, said anything more, Coda realized what the commander had done. By speaking up first, he'd taken the opportunity away from everyone else and effectively neutralized their response. Despite his previous criticisms of the commander, Coda was growing to respect the man more and more every day.

"Coda!" Commander Coleman said. "Get up here. It looks like you get your chance after all."

"Yes, sir!" Coda said.

"Lucky bastard," Squawks mumbled as Coda left him behind.

Commander Coleman grabbed one of the still-spinning arms of the gyroscope, bringing it to a halt when the cockpit was positioned right-side up. He locked it in place by yanking a nearby lever then looked expectantly at Coda.

"Well? Climb in."

Coda looked at the cockpit, his excitement beginning to give way to nervousness. The gyroscope was nearly twice his height and, since it was spherical in design, just as deep. That meant the cockpit was well off the ground, more or less at Coda's eye level. Surely, he wasn't supposed to climb the arms of the gyroscope to get in, was he?

Commander Coleman cleared his throat, and Coda looked at him then followed his eyes to a ladder set off to the side of the simulator.

*Right. Of course.*

He fetched the ladder and climbed into the cockpit. It was exactly as he'd expected it to be, a complete working replica of the same X-23 cockpit he'd sat in during their first day of FAM Phase. However, resting on the seat was a VR helmet similar to the one he'd worn back at the academy.

Commander Coleman stepped through the labyrinth of arms of the gyroscope, settling in next to the cockpit. "Know what you're doing?" he asked quietly.

"I think so, sir."

"Good. Take it easy. Uno isn't the only nugget I've seen empty his stomach, though they usually wait until *after* they've flown the simulator."

"Yes, sir."

"Fire it up."

Coda reached for the switch that would ignite the X-23's thrusters then paused. He looked to the commander, suddenly unsure. Was it the right switch? He didn't want to break something or embarrass himself.

"What are you waiting for?" Commander Coleman asked, loudly enough for everyone to hear.

Coda flipped the switch, and immediately, his seat began to rumble. In that moment, the two weeks he had spent in front of the computer were worth it.

"It's something, isn't it?" Command Coleman said, his voice quiet again.

"Hell, yeah, sir."

"Nervous?"

"A little, sir."

"I'll be with you the entire time, guiding you through a series of exercises. Stay calm and take it slow. Nobody is going to be an expert their first time out. That's why we use the simulator, understand?"

"How will you see what I'm doing?" Coda asked. "It's just a VR helmet, right?"

Commander Coleman pulled his tablet from his pocket, and after a few short commands, the lights in the room dimmed and an entire wall of the room lit up. It wasn't nearly as impressive as the Coliseum at the academy, but the image on it was as clear as if Coda were floating through space himself.

"We'll see what you see, Coda. Ready?"

"Let's do it, sir."

"Strap in, then."

Coda pulled the shoulder straps down, snapping them into the buckle at his crotch, then buckled another set, completing the five-point harness.

"Good. Put your helmet on and wait for my command."

With that, the commander stepped from the center of the gyroscope, falling in line with the rest of the pilots. Coda pulled on his VR helmet; the same star-speckled sky he'd seen on the imaging wall immediately replaced his view. Except now, when he turned his head left or right, the image rotated with him. Between the rumble of the cockpit and the gentle swaying motion of the gyroscope, he was beginning to grow disoriented.

"Can you hear me, Coda?" Commander Coleman's voice said through the helmet's speakers.

"Loud and clear, sir." Coda heard his own voice echoing throughout the room. *So they can hear me just like I can hear the commander.*

"Good," Commander Coleman said. "This simulation is designed to give you a feel for the X-23, so we're going to go through a small flight course. Your goal is to navigate the course and fly through a series of checkpoints. For this simulation, and this simulation alone, your speed will be computer regulated, so just focus on navigation, understood?"

"Understood, sir."

"Good. Let's see what you got."

The rumble of the thrusters intensified, and Coda's HUD came alive with various pieces of navigational information indicating his speed, coordinates, and weapon counts. A small yellow arrow at the top of his vision pointed upward, and a series of numbers counted down faster than he could read them. He'd gone through similar training exercises when he'd learned to fly the Hornet, so he knew the arrow was pointing toward his first objective.

Coda pulled back on the joystick, and several things happened at once. The display image shifted, mimicking the movement of a real X-23, and with it, the entire gyroscope rotated. Coda was thrust back into his seat then flipped upside down. When he finally got his bearings, he realized he was flying upside down and *away* from the checkpoint.

"Holy shit," Coda said breathlessly, his stomach in his throat.

"Careful, Coda," Commander Coleman said. "You do that in a real Nighthawk, and the chief will have to pull you out in a body bag."

"Yes, sir," Coda said. "She's just a little more sensitive than I'm used to."

"That she is. Be gentle with her."

"Will do, sir."

The yellow icon that pointed to his next objective was at the bottom of his imaging screen now, the numbers growing larger. Coda pushed upward on the stick, more gently than before, and made a series of small course adjustments, bringing the icon into the center of his vision. It grew steadily in size, and the numbers counted down until he was nearly upon it.

The checkpoint was an octagon, and as soon as Coda's fighter sped through it, his navigational information shifted, the yellow indicator pointing to the right side of his vision. Pitching the fighter perpendicular to the battle plane, Coda pulled back on the stick and brought his fighter around in a tight curve. Within moments, he'd sped through another checkpoint.

He flew through two more without incident then brought up the fifth and final one on his battle map. But there was something odd about it. While the other four had been stationary, the last appeared to be moving. The yellow indicator rotated around the perimeter of his HUD, and every time he got it in his sights, it slipped away as if it were an enemy fighter evading his pursuit.

Accepting the challenge, Coda kept on it, countering its movements. He began to gain on it. A few more seconds, and he was flying through its center. Coda hooted, taking his hands off the stick to celebrate. But as he did, the cockpit shook violently and was accompanied by a loud screech.

"What the hell was that?"

Before anyone could answer, his fighter was thrown off course with a sharp jolt, and blue fire shot past the cockpit.

"What is that?"

"You're under attack, Coda. Evasive maneuvers!"

Deep down Coda knew it was only a simulation, but the combination of the movement, the photo-real images, and Commander Coleman's not-messing-around tone made Coda's adrenaline spike. His drone flight training kicked into gear, and he stopped thinking.

He flipped the nose of the fighter around so that he was flying backward but still facing the enemy spacecraft. He couldn't see it with his naked eye, but the targeting system bracketed the ship as it had with the checkpoints before it.

More blue fire erupted from the enemy ship, covering the distance between them in a blink. A last-second course correction was all that saved Coda from becoming simulated slag. Centering the target in his view again, he pulled the trigger.

Nothing happened.

"You have to activate your weapons," Commander Coleman said.

Coda fumbled with the joystick, his thumb searching for the safety switch that would activate his weapons. Flicking it into place, he pulled the trigger again. The cockpit vibrated with a muffled rumble as simulated projectiles barreled out of the Nighthawk's nose-mounted cannon.

Two seconds went by. Then three. Nothing happened. He'd missed. But the enemy vessel *had* altered course, veering off at a ninety-degree angle.

*It's fleeing.*

Since the computer was regulating his speed, Coda flipped his fighter back around, settling on a course that would bring him directly behind the enemy vessel. One eye on the yellow indicator highlighting the enemy craft, Coda kept the other on the distance between them. It wasn't getting any smaller. He wasn't gaining on it. He nearly squeezed the trigger again but flicked the weapons switch instead, toggling his missiles.

Successfully engaged, the targeting system changed. A circle appeared, trailing the enemy fighter. Keeping the enemy in his sights, Coda allowed the targeting system to lock on. Then, when the circle completely surrounded the enemy fighter, it stopped flashing, going solid with the dull sound of missile lock.

Coda squeezed the trigger, and a missile blasted forward. He quickly lost sight of it, but a new bracket appeared on his HUD, tracking it as it streaked toward the enemy fighter. A heartbeat later, and with a flash of light, the enemy ship was destroyed.

"Splash one!" Coda shouted, keeping his hands on the joystick and his eyes on his surroundings. No other fighters came, and a few brief moments later, the simulation dissolved.

"Good!" Commander Coleman said, bringing the ladder up to the edge of the simulator. "Very good. If that had been a real Baranyk fighter, you would have been shot to shit fifteen different ways to Sunday, but you weren't a complete disaster out there, and for today's purposes, that was good enough."

"Thank you, sir." Coda climbed out of the cockpit onto the ladder.

Commander Coleman laid a firm hand on his shoulder as his feet touched the deck. Having been spun every which way imaginable over the last several minutes, he was thankful for the added stability.

"So how was it?"

"Amazing, sir." Coda grinned. "Absolutely amazing."

# 14

*Mess Hall, SAS* Jamestown
*Alpha Centauri System, Proxima B, High Orbit*

Uno didn't come to lunch that day. Coda noted his absence, assuming it had to do with his throwing up in the Simulation Room earlier that morning. Uno was probably embarrassed, mopping the deck, or both, so Coda decided to give his friend some space. But when he didn't show up for dinner either, Coda knew the issue was more serious.

After shoveling in the last of his protein paste, Coda left Noodle and Squawks behind and sought out his friend. There weren't many places a pilot could be—Commander Coleman hadn't granted them access to the larger ship—so when Coda didn't find Uno in his bunk, the gym, or the bathroom, there was only one other place he knew to look.

The Simulation Room was dark when the doors slid open, and Coda almost left right then, but something drew him inside. It could have been his desire to find his friend or the allure of gazing upon the simulator again; he couldn't be sure.

The lights flickered on as Coda stepped inside, the room's motion sensors detecting his movement. Uno sat at the base of the simulator, his arms hugging the knees. He made no motion to see who had walked into the room, just continued to sit there, staring upward at the machine.

"We missed you at dinner," Coda said, stopping to the side and slightly behind Uno.

"Wasn't hungry." Uno still didn't so much as look in Coda's direction.

"Yeah? Still not feeling good?"

Uno took a deep breath but didn't say anything more. He obviously didn't want to talk about what had happened.

"You know what's crazy?" Coda said, deciding to take a different tack. "I grew up designing my own X-23s. Well, not the X-23. I'd call them the X-24 or X-25 or whatever, but I'd design them and print them out on our 3-D printer. They were just toys, of course, but I'd stage mock battles in my room, even run simulations, pitting them against the X-23 to see which was more powerful. The X-23 always won, of course. There was no way a twelve-year-old would design a better starfighter than the military's top minds. But it was fun."

Coda's words echoed off the walls, dissipating into silence. Uno made a face but didn't appear any closer to talking. Coda walked up to the simulator, took hold of one of the arms as Commander Coleman had, and gave it a push. The mechanism went into motion, the various arms and cockpit spinning with it.

"It's crazy," Coda continued, "because after they were decommissioned, I never thought I'd fly one. Hell, I never thought I'd *see* one again, but here we are." Coda turned back to Uno and took an exaggerated breath. "Here we are... And holy shit, do the things scare the crap out of me."

Uno's eyes found his, surprise plainly visible on his face. "No shit?"

"No shit."

"I thought I was the only one."

"No," Coda laughed. "Definitely not. I bet half the people who failed FAM Phase did it on purpose."

"I wish I'd thought about that," Uno said.

"I'm glad you didn't," Coda said. "Viking Squadron was a pretty tight group, and I didn't know if I'd ever find that again. But then I met you guys, and you're all right. I mean *you're* kind of a know-it-all, and I've never heard anyone complain about working out as much as Noodle. And Squawks... well, Squawks just never stops talking. But you've all been there for me. Without you, I wouldn't still be here at all."

"Not sure I did you any favors," Uno said, his lips curling into the tiniest of smiles.

"I'm not sure you did either," Coda said, matching his smile. "But whatever crap we go through, we go through it together, all right?"

Uno nodded, his gaze taking on a distant quality.

"So, are you going to tell me what happened?" Coda asked.

"There's not much to say. I got nervous, and I threw up."

"We both know there's more to it than that."

"Maybe." Uno shrugged.

"Care to elaborate?"

"I'm not like you and Squawks. I don't want the attention. I like to figure things out on my own. Not in front of a group."

Everything suddenly clicked. Coda had misunderstood. Uno wasn't afraid of the simulator. He was afraid of learning in front of everyone, or more specifically, afraid of *failing* in front of everyone. His call sign suddenly took on a different meaning. Uno might have developed a reputation for shooting down fighters in a single shot, but what if he was a bit of a loner too? It made too much sense to be a coincidence.

"That might have worked back at the academy, Uno, but that's not going to fly here. There's too much attention on our entire group. Too much pressure."

"I know."

"That doesn't mean you can't log extra time, though," Coda said. "Try to figure things out on your own after hours. God knows I'm planning on it."

"You are?"

"Of course," Coda said. "I barely squeaked by FAM Phase, remember? I've got some ground to make up. We can do it together."

"You'd do that?"

"Of course. As far as I'm concerned, I owe you one, and like I said, I was already planning on it anyway."

"You're a good guy, Coda."

"Thank you, but don't tell anyone, all right?"

Uno laughed. It was a tentative thing, but it was a start. "All right."

"Here's what I propose. Morning workout is at oh six hundred, so we meet here every day at oh five hundred and get in an extra hour. If we're feeling up to it, we can log more time after hours too."

"Sounds good."

"Good," Coda said. "Let's get started then."

"Now? What happened to tomorrow?"

"You were the only pilot who didn't log simulator time today. I'd be willing to bet the commander has you go first again tomorrow. Let's get you comfortable with it."

Uno looked as though he might be sick again, and shot a nervous glance at the simulator. "Do you even know how to use that thing?"

"I'm sure we can figure it out." Coda slapped Uno on the back. "Come on, let's get to work."

Uno took a deep breath and climbed to his feet, then together, they made for the simulator. Coda suspected it would be the first of many long nights.

# 15

*Barracks, SAS* Jamestown

*Alpha Centauri System, Proxima B, High Orbit*

"Wake up! Wake up!" Commander Coleman shouted as he entered the barracks. "Rise and shine!"

It took Coda two precious seconds to register what was going on. His first thought was that he had overslept their morning workout, but as quickly as the thought came, he dismissed it. Across the room, Uno and Squawks were just as confused as he was. If he had overslept, then they had too, and that was unlikely.

"Get your asses up!" Commander Coleman strode down the center of the barracks, already dressed in the blue of the Sol Fleet. "You can get your beauty sleep on your own time!"

Coda kicked off his blanket and scrambled out of bed, snapping to attention. The metal decking was cold against the bottoms of his feet, and like most of the other pilots in the room, he was dressed in nothing but his underwear.

"What's going on, sir?" Squawks asked. "Workout's not for another hour."

"That was yesterday's schedule," Commander Coleman said.

"Today's is different. You have two minutes to get dressed and meet me in the gym. Move!"

Without another word, Commander Coleman left the room. Coda hastily pulled a navy-colored tank top and pair of gray sweatpants from the drawers below his bunk and threw them on. As soon as he had on his shoes and socks, he was hustling out the door.

Uno caught up to him before he'd made it more than few steps. "What do you think's going on? You think this is part of the training? Sleep deprivation and all that?"

"I have no idea," Coda said. "But I'm sure we're about to find out."

Commander Coleman was waiting for them in the back of the gym, his arms folded across his chest. Another officer stood at his shoulder. With graying hair and a disapproving scowl creasing his tan face, he was at least as old as Commander Coleman and every bit as intimidating.

Coda snapped to attention in front of them, waiting for the rest of the squadron to arrive. They made it seconds later, every one of them beating the commander's time. As the last stragglers fell into formation, Coda realized that the squadron had been split in half. The pilots in the gym had come from two barracks. Unfortunately, the other barracks was Moscow's. He apparently wasn't getting away from his academy rival any time soon.

"Someone tell me what time it is," Commander Coleman said.

"Oh four thirty, sir," someone said from behind Coda.

"That it is," the commander said. "As you've no doubt figured out, our training resources are limited, but in their great resourcefulness, the fleet has mustered up and installed a second simulator. But we still have more pilots than we do equipment, so this group is being rewarded with the morning shift. For the next two weeks, I want your asses in here by oh four thirty, working up a lather. Is that understood?"

"Yes, sir!"

"Good," the commander said. "Let me also introduce you to Commander Chavez, who will be aiding your instruction moving forward. For those that don't already know, the commander and I have flown many missions together, and I consider him one of the finest pilots to have ever flown in the fleet. More than that, before transferring to my squadron, he was my NFO aboard the *Pittsburgh*, making him one of the foremost experts of the X-23's systems and flight capabilities. I'm honored to have him as part of our squadron."

"The honor is all mine, sir," Commander Chavez said.

Commander Coleman nodded and returned his gaze to the squadron. "We'll see you in the Simulation Room at oh six hundred. Get to it."

They got to it, and for once, Noodle wasn't the person who complained the loudest.

"This is horseshit," Squawks wailed. "It's too early for—"

"Stow it," Coda shouted between sets. "No one wants to hear it."

Squawks grumbled some more but largely kept it to himself. By the time their workout was over, Coda felt more awake than he'd ever expected to, and after he'd showered and thrown on a set of clean clothes, he made for the Simulation Room.

True to Commander Coleman's word, a second simulator had been installed on the other end of the room. Having been there late into the evening the night before, Coda had no idea how they had found the time to install it, but there it was, buttons glowing and waiting.

The commander quickly separated them into two groups based on their barracks then muttered the ten scariest words in the English language. "We're going to do things a little bit different today."

The commander had programmed four different training scenarios that escalated in difficulty, each one in the sequence adding a new variable. The pilots, broken into even smaller groups, took turns running through the simulation while the rest looked on. The largest variation between the day's training and the one previous was that after the subgroup's simulated run, they sat down with Commander Coleman or Commander Chavez to review their hop.

Coda was pleased to learn that while the commander could be a hard ass with the larger squadron, he was calm and patient with their smaller number. He went from being their CO to their instructor, and they listened to him all the more closely for it.

"Your approach vector is too shallow here," Commander Coleman would say, pausing the simulation replay. "Tell me how you could have done it differently."

And they would tell him—then put their words to action in their next run, redoing the scenario until the commander was pleased.

For three hours, they took turns running through the simulations, learning from their fellow squad mates and their combined mistakes. By the end of the first session, the vibe had shifted from exhausted frustration to positive excitement, and that carried over through breakfast and into their late-morning practice.

"Where is the rest of the squadron?" Uno asked during one of their evaluation periods. The Simulation Room was still filled with only forty or so members, all from the same two barracks.

"Class," Commander Coleman said simply.

"Class?" Uno asked skeptically. Minus the CAI—which in Coda's estimation barely counted—they hadn't had any class. "For what?"

"You'll find out soon enough," Commander Coleman said. "Now tell me why you flipped nose to tail here instead of altering course with a more gradual barrel roll."

The commander clearly wasn't going to explain further, and Uno didn't press the issue. He gave his explanation to the commander's question instead.

"It's faster, yes," the commander said, "and might have been a good maneuver if you'd had a Baranyk fighter on your ass, but at those speeds, the g-forces are enough to cause black out. Remember, these simulations are designed to help you learn to fly an X-23 correctly. Follow the flight rules until you know where you can bend them."

"Yes, sir."

"But...?" Commander Coleman said, obviously hearing the unspoken question on Uno's lips.

"But the X-23 is equipped with inertial dampeners, isn't it, sir?"

"It is," the commander said slowly. "Otherwise, you'd be ripped apart by even the most basic maneuver. But there are limits to every gravitic drive, even the most advanced, which I can assure you, do *not* come standard with the X-23."

"Which is why you're juicing us up with steroids and experimental growth hormones, right, sir?"

Coda and Squawks, who were in the evaluation group with Uno, shared a nervous look. That information hadn't made it beyond their circle or been spoken about since their first dinner on the *Jamestown*.

"Now where would you get a crazy idea like that?" Commander Coleman asked, the tone of his voice suggesting he was genuinely dismayed. There was something in his eyes, though, a hardness that hinted at his true feelings. Uno's question had made the commander uneasy.

Uno met Commander Coleman's gaze, not backing down but not exactly challenging him, either. "I don't know, sir," he said, obviously deciding not to push the issue. "You're right, though. It's a crazy thought."

Commander Coleman nodded, returning to Uno's evaluation.

At the tail end of their session, the commander posted their evaluations on the display board. Because most of the exercises had been timed, it showed their time of completion, along with accuracy, precision, and other success metrics. Coda's favorite was a calculated measure the commander called their "death probability," which the commander explained as the likelihood that their flight paths, vectors, and speed would either kill them or get them killed by enemy fire. It all culminated in a final score that was measured out of one hundred. The highest score barely cracked fifty.

Before Coda could find his name on the list, Commander Coleman called their attention to a red line separating a small number of pilots at the top of the list from the bulk at the bottom.

"This," Commander Coleman said, "is your failure line. Your training is about to get very real, ladies and gentlemen. I'm not interested in good pilots. I'm not even interested in great pilots. I need the best. The best of the best. And that means any pilots still south of this line at the end of the month will be excused from the program. Work hard, ladies and gentlemen. I'll see you tomorrow at oh four thirty."

Coda strolled out of the Simulation Room to a mix of hushed voices. The commander had changed the rules, upped the pressure. The real competition was about to get started, and Coda had no intention of giving up. He was having too much fun.

# 16

*Corridor, SAS* Jamestown

*Alpha Centauri System, Proxima B, High Orbit*

After their morning session in the simulator, an officer escorted the pilots to a part of the ship they had never seen. Unlike their private section of the ship, the corridors here were occupied with the usual shipboard activity. Coda caught more than one confused look, though in true military fashion, nobody voiced their questions. Those conversations would happen over drinks or quietly over dinner, between shipmates, not out in the open.

"Take a good look, ladies," Squawks said loudly as he jogged past a group of female officers. "Heroes of the fleet, coming through. Heroes of the—"

"Can it, Squawks!" Uno shouted.

"I just want—"

"I said, 'Can it!'"

"Geez!" Squawks threw him an irritated look. "What crawled up your ass?"

"We have our orders. Follow them."

"It's not like they won't know soon enough, anyway," Squawks said.

"There's a huge difference between 'will know' and 'already knows,' so can it."

"What's the big—"

"Squawks!" several pilots shouted at once.

"Your mouth is talking," Coda said. "See to it."

Squawks snapped his mouth shut and defiantly blew a kiss in the officers' direction but remained quiet until they arrived at their destination. The classroom was like every other classroom Coda had ever been in, though like throughout the rest of the ship, the tables and chairs were bolted to the floor. And like the ready room, instead of the three-dimensional displays, the room was equipped with an aging digital touch board that took up the entire front wall.

"Take your seats," the escorting officer said. "Your instructor will be along shortly."

Coda found a seat with Uno, Noodle, and Squawks four rows from the front. Once they sat down, another group of pilots entered, Moscow at their lead. Seeing Coda, he smiled then nodded to his group. They found seats in front of Coda, but instead of sitting down, Moscow took a seat on the table, tossing a foot on the chair so that he was facing Coda.

"Funny thing, O'Neil," Moscow said in an amused voice. "I didn't see your name above the failure line. I guess you're just as much of a shit pilot as your father was."

The room fell into a hushed silence.

Coda opened his mouth to speak, but Squawks beat him to it.

"And your death probability was twenty-four percent. How about you do us all a favor and raise that up a bit, huh?"

Laughter filled the room.

"He keeps talking, and it will," Uno said. "Even if I have to shoot him myself."

"What was that?" Moscow said, his cool voice at odds with his coloring face. "Oh, hold up." Moscow suddenly clutched his stomach and mock vomited in Uno's face. "The only thing you can hit is your own boots."

Coda was on his feet before he knew it, lunging at Moscow.

Squawks was on him immediately, grabbing ahold of him and pulling him back. "Simmer down, Coda. Simmer down. He's all talk."

If Moscow was all talk, Uno wasn't. He was on top of the table and diving at Moscow in an instant. The other man's eyes widened as the human projectile crashed into him, sending them both toppling off the table. They hit the deck with a loud thud and had just enough time to get in a few wild punches before the other pilots separated them.

Squawks let Coda go, and together, they pushed through the throng, making for Uno, then got between him and Moscow, who continued to shout obscenities at one another.

"Officer on deck!"

Years of military training took over, and Coda snapped to attention. Their instructor waited in the doorway, a tablet in her hands, watching the melee with a single raised eyebrow. She couldn't have been much over thirty and was short with closely cropped black hair that was only slightly darker than her skin.

"Someone tell me what the hell's going on in my classroom," she said in a thickly accented voice.

"Just getting in a quick workout, sir," Squawks said. "We're ready to learn."

"Good. Find your seats then."

Coda navigated Uno back to his spot then took a seat. "You didn't have to do that."

"Wasn't doing it for you," Uno muttered under his breath.

"My name is Lieutenant Commander Naidoo, though you may call me Dr. Naidoo. And I am no more a teacher than you are an astrophysicist, but we will make do. I am here because among all of you, I am the only one who has ever seen a Baranyk in person—a mistake we're about to fix together." Dr. Naidoo turned to the door and nodded. "Bring it in."

A pair of men wearing white lab coats wheeled in a gurney, its contents hidden under a thin sheet. They stopped it in front of Dr. Naidoo then turned and left. She thanked the men then, in a single quick motion, ripped the sheet away.

Half the class was on their feet in an instant. Many backed away, while others sat in frozen silence, hands over mouths. Lying on the gurney was a supine mass, flat black in color, with four legs, two arms, large lifeless black eyes, and a pair of thin antennae rising from a triangular head.

"I am not here to give you a shot or check your prostate. I am not that kind of doctor. I am a xenobiologist, and aboard this ship, that means I am the foremost expert of Baranyk biology. An area, if I'm not mistaken, your training has largely ignored. Now, please, return to your seats so we can begin."

Only half of the pilots returned to their seats, though the other half, primarily those nearest the prone Baranyk, refused to move.

"Oh, please," Dr. Naidoo said sarcastically, slapping the Baranyk on its oval-shaped abdomen. "It's not going to bite."

With the doctor making fun of the frightened pilots, the rest slowly made their way back, though if Coda wasn't mistaken, many of the front seats that had been occupied before were now vacant.

"Good," Dr. Naidoo said. "Now will someone tell me what you know about the Baranyk so we can begin?"

Uno raised his hand.

"Yes," Dr. Naidoo said, calling on him.

"The Baranyk—or the 'Astral Montodea,' as they're known officially —most closely resemble the praying mantis of Earth, though, of course, it's much larger and more deadly than anything back at home. Standing above two meters, it has four hind legs, with two forelegs that are bent and equipped with spikes used to snare prey and pin it in place. Their long neck is flexible enough that it can spin almost three hundred sixty degrees, similar to that of an owl. But unlike their cousins at home, the Baranyks' eyes are larger and can see in much clearer detail, though we're unsure if they see as we do or in some sort of infrared.

"Beyond that, they are thought to be tunnel dwellers since in our first encounter with them, they had primarily lived underground, going undetected for months. Since other Baranyk colonies were found underground, the evidence seems to support that theory. Unfortunately, since the fleet's ability to probe belowground remains greatly limited, the Baranyk remain nearly impossible to detect, and that remains one of our biggest challenges with the war."

"Good," Dr. Naidoo said.

"Show off," Squawks muttered.

"But spoken as if read out of a book," Dr. Naidoo said. "Tell me what you *know*, not what you've read."

"I... um..." Uno shifted in his seat. "I guess I don't understand the question, ma'am."

"Tell me its strengths. Its weaknesses. Tell me what they want or *why* we are at war with them."

Uno chewed on his lip, his face making a pained expression, as if not knowing the answer hurt.

"Anyone?"

Nobody took the bait.

"It's okay," Dr. Naidoo said. "We train you to fight, not to think. It doesn't matter *why* we're at war with them if those we are at war with threaten everything we know and love, does it?"

Several pilots voiced their agreement.

"But back to you," Dr. Naidoo continued. "You were trained to fly a drone, to fight distantly, not hand to hand. If you were a squad of marines, you would have no doubt received something similar to what I'm going to teach you, but you didn't. You didn't need to. But if you are to be pilots, you will have a very real chance of meeting one of these things in person, and I'm going to make sure you're ready."

"Ma'am," Ginger said. He was one of the experienced drone pilots who had joined them from the front. "We're fighter pilots. We'll be blowing the Baranyk out of space. Why would we ever run into one in person?"

"A fair question," Dr. Naidoo said. "Have you been trained on ejection procedures yet?"

"No."

"Well, let's just say if you're successful, you may be moored on an alien moon or planet. And if you are shot down, you can bet it'll be Baranyk-infested territory. If you want to survive until a rescue team can be assembled, you'll need to know how the Baranyk think, how they hunt, and where they're vulnerable."

"Understood, ma'am."

"Make no mistake," she continued. "This is not weapons training. It's far more important than that. So download the course curriculum onto your tablets, and we will begin."

An uncomfortable knot settled into Coda's stomach.

*Learn to fly,* Commander Coleman had said. *Save the world. Reclaim your honor.*

No one had ever said anything about battling the Baranyk in person.

One-on-one. Maybe Uno had been right all those nights ago. Maybe he should have read the fine print.

# 17

*Barracks, SAS* Jamestown

*Alpha Centauri System, Proxima B, High Orbit*

CODA RETURNED TO HIS BUNK, MENTALLY AND PHYSICALLY EXHAUSTED. THE two hours of class with Dr. Naidoo had been followed by four more with a different instructor. That alone would have been enough, but the advanced mathematics and physics lessons had been followed by an evening workout, dinner, and evening debriefing. By the time he staggered into the barracks, he felt as though he'd been run through the wringer, so his heart dropped when his tablet vibrated and he read its message.

*My quarters. 2100.* And it was signed by Commander Coleman.

The commander wanted to see him. Why? Even after performing well in the latest simulator scenarios, Coda was still below the failure line, but then again, so was everyone else in their quartet, and nobody else seemed to have received the message.

*The incident in the classroom then?*

That didn't make sense, either. It had been little more than a shoving match, and between Moscow and Uno more than anyone else. Why would Coda be summoned and not one of them?

Commander Coleman's quarters were near the rest of the barracks in their semiprivate section of the ship. Coda stopped outside the door. He looked for a communicator, something similar to what they'd had at the academy, but didn't find one and resorted to knocking.

The door slid open, exposing a small room with a bunk set into the bulkhead. A writing table, bookshelf, and two chairs spaced around a circular table filled the room. Commander Coleman sat in one of the chairs.

"Sir," Coda said, stepping into the room and snapping to attention.

"Have a seat."

"Thank you, sir." Coda made for the second chair and sat down.

"Dr. Naidoo said she walked into an issue in her classroom today."

*It is about the scuffle then. Strange.*

"It was nothing, sir. A few pilots were jarring, and it got a little out of hand. Nothing to be worried about."

"Nothing to worry about." The commander chewed on the words. "Dr. Naidoo said Lieutenant Krylov was at the center of it."

"I suppose, sir."

"There seems to have been a number of incidents between you two."

"Yes, sir."

Commander Coleman took a deep breath, rose from his seat, then made for the small bookshelf where a bottle of brown liquor waited. He poured two fingers' worth into a snifter, swirled its contents, and returned to his seat. After taking a sip, he exhaled through his teeth.

"You see," Commander Coleman said at last, "I've got a problem. My squadron is divided, and you and Moscow are at the heart of it. That's not going to work. The pilots of this squadron need to have complete and absolute trust in their wingmen. And I'm not talking about belief, Coda—they need to *know* that they can count on those they fly with. Do you think they can do that now?"

"No, sir."

"I agree. Unfortunately, it seems you and Moscow are more than just academy adversaries."

"Sir?"

"Do you know what the SAS *Benjamin Franklin* is, Coda?"

Coda's blood went cold. "The *Benjamin Franklin*, sir? Yes. I... It's..."

"The ship your father was stationed on when he turned on his wingmen." Commander Colemen took a sip, his eyes narrowing as they watched Coda over the rim of the glass. "When people speak of your father, they often talk about how many pilots died by his hand. What they usually leave out is how many people aboard the *Benjamin Franklin* perished as well."

"Sir." It was all Coda could do to get the word out of his throat. "What does this have to do with me and Moscow?"

Commander Coleman placed his glass on the table. "I did a little digging, Coda. And it appears that Lieutenant Kyrlov's mother was aboard the *Benjamin Franklin* during the attack."

"And she..." It was somewhere between a question and a statement.

Commander Coleman nodded. "She did. It's all right there if you want to read it." The commander nodded to his tablet that rested on the table between them.

Coda followed the gesture, seeing a woman with a pale complexion and dark hair, before looking away. Even at a glance, he could tell she was Moscow's mother. He could see the pride burning in her eyes, the same pride that pushed Moscow to his limits and never allowed him to accept defeat. The same pride that Coda had thought was at the heart of their issues.

"I... I had no idea, sir. He never said anything about it. About her." Coda fought back the roiling mix of emotions raging inside him. Everything seemed so complicated all of a sudden. So confusing. "I just thought we were rivals."

Commander Coleman grunted. Like Coda, he seemed to be lacking the words and instead swirled his drink. "Then you see I have a serious issue."

"Yes, sir." Coda swallowed a lump in his throat. "Are you... are you sending me home, sir?"

Commander Coleman took another sip then winced from the bite. "No. But if I'd known the severity of the situation, I never would have taken both of you. Unfortunately, the urgency of our predicament didn't allow me enough time to properly vet the background of every candidate, so I focused on other attributes. But here you are, and I can't send either of you packing without a legitimate excuse. That would only divide the squadron even further. Nor do I *want* to send either of you home, to be honest. Despite your issues, you're both developing into a pair of fine young pilots."

"Thank you, sir," Coda said, breathing a little easier.

"But we need to find a way to fix this."

"Of course, sir."

"So here's what we're going to do. We're going to solve this the old-fashioned way—with a competition."

"Sir?"

"You heard me," Commander Coleman said. "I've heard him grumble about you ever since your squadron beat his back at the academy. So, we're going to give him his wish. You two are going to go toe to toe in the simulator."

"No offense, sir," Coda said skeptically, "but do you really think that'll work? That it'll fix our issues?"

Commander Coleman barked a laugh. "Of course not. But I hope it can be a start. And of course, if things don't get better, your one-on-one performance might give me grounds to get rid of one of you." He added the last bit as if it was an afterthought, but Coda knew better. There was likely more truth to that statement than he was letting on.

"Sir, if I may? Why tell me this?"

"A man deserves to know why someone hates him, Coda. More than that... well, I'll let you figure that out for yourself."

Walking back to his bunk, Coda replayed the conversation in his mind. If the commander's goal was to help him understand the true cause of his issues with Moscow, then he had done that, but Coda felt like he was missing something. The commander wanted him to understand something. Something important. But try as he might, Coda couldn't figure out what it was.

# 18

*Simulator, SAS* Jamestown
*Alpha Centauri System, Proxima B, High Orbit*

CODA EXPECTED HIS COMPETITION WITH MOSCOW TO COME THE NEXT DAY, but when they entered the Simulation Room, Commander Coleman made no mention of it and instead walked them through their normal routine. The showdown didn't come during their late-morning session after breakfast, the following day, or the day after, either, and by the end of the week, Coda had begun to wonder if he'd just imagined his entire conversation with Commander Coleman.

Knowing he was working on the commander's timeline, he allowed himself to fall into his new routine: gym in the morning, simulator, evaluations, breakfast, more simulator and evaluations, class, lunch, more class, afternoon workouts, dinner, debriefing with Commander Coleman and the entire squadron, all followed by his private after-hours practice with Uno.

By the end of the second week in the simulator, their fourth overall in the twenty-six-week program, Coda, Noodle, and Squawks were above the failure line. Despite being below the cutoff, Uno had made marked progress, and Coda believed he would make it above the line in time.

That morning, Commander Coleman addressed the pilots as he always did, but his tone held something new.

"Congratulations on completing your first two weeks with the simulator. Every single one of you has put in a considerable amount of work, and you're all the better for it. If we look at the updated standings"—Commander Coleman punched something into his terminal, and the standings appeared on the Simulation Room's wall display—"you'll see that more than half of the pilots in the squadron are above the failure line. That's outstanding. That also means we're ready to move on to our second phase with the simulator: Combat Phase."

A ripple of excitement washed over the gathered pilots. Combat phase. The reason they were all here: not to study Baranyk biology or learn to rebuild a Shaw Drive with spit and gumption, but to feel the rush of flying on their edge of their seats, blasting down Baranyk fighters. As exciting as basic flight was, nothing got a young pilot hard faster than weapons training.

"Over the next two weeks," Commander Coleman continued, "you will face every other pilot in this squadron in a one-on-one competition. The objective is simple: shoot them down before they do you. Any questions?"

There weren't any.

"Good," Commander Coleman said. "Before we begin, there's one last thing I want to bring to your attention. With this new phase, we also enter a new evaluation period. Please see the board with the *updated* standings."

The red failure line that separated the safe pilots from the rest moved up. With one click of a button, Commander Coleman had just changed the fates of more than a dozen pilots.

"I don't understand, sir," one of the pilots in the front row said. "I thought you said anyone with an overall score of seventy would advance."

"You're absolutely correct, Fireball," Commander Coleman said. "There's been enough progress throughout this group that Command and I felt it was time to raise the bar. As I mentioned before, we don't need good pilots. We need the best of the best. That's why of the eighty-seven remaining pilots, only the top fifty will be moving on. Your battles will mean something, so make them count. Coda, Moscow, you're up first. The rest of you get with Lieutenant Commander Chavez and get your assignments. Let's get started."

Coda separated himself from the throng, making for the simulator. Moscow appeared at his shoulder, smirking.

"You ready to be embarrassed, O'Neil?" he asked quietly.

Coda had to chew on the inside of his cheeks to keep from snapping something back. *He lost his mother because of your father. Keep that in mind.* Always *keep that in mind.* "Good luck," he said instead.

Moscow looked at Coda skeptically and muttered something under his breath before they diverted and climbed up the ladders into their separate simulators.

Settling into the cockpit, Coda strapped in and adjusted the straps so that he was snug against the seat. When he was satisfied he wouldn't be thrown out of the simulator once it started rotating, he pulled on his VR helmet.

The simulation was already running, and Coda found himself looking down the barrel of the launch tube. A track nearly one hundred meters in length ran down its center and was attached to a pulley system that would hurl the starfighters out of the side of the battle cruiser like an arrow shot from a bow.

Coda went through his preflight routine, activating the various guidance, tactical, and weapons systems. When all glowed green, he settled into the gel seat and waited for instruction—except it never came. One moment, he was waiting patiently, visualizing his victory, and the next, he was hurtling down the launch tube, his Simulator attempting to replicate the force generated by accelerating to over three hundred kilometers per hour.

The small black dot at the end of the launch tube quickly grew larger until he was hurled into the black of space. The simulated environment nearly took his breath away. He was surrounded by the aftermath of what looked like a full-scale battle. Derelict ships and debris floated in high orbit around a blue-and-green planet, forming something of a ring around it. Streaks crossed the upper atmosphere where pieces of debris burned up, pulled down by the planet's gravity.

Coda punched his fighter to a more suitable combat speed.

"*Speed is life,*" Commander Coleman had taught them, and the old posters and quotes spread throughout their ready room had only reiterated the motto.

He oriented his battle map so that the planet was down. In this simulation, his orientation was a simple exercise, but in the black of space without reference points like the glowing ball below, it was much more difficult to maintain orientation and thus understand where one was located in the greater context of battle.

To solve that challenge, the early brass had devised a strategy allowing pilots to orient their fleet based on an artificial plane extending from their capital ship to the enemy's capital ship. Everything above the plane on the z-axis, called "positive-Z," became up, and everything below, or "negative Z," was down.

The simple exercise allowed battle commanders to keep the battle organized and execute complex strategies that made sense to every ship and fighter, regardless of their personal orientation. Of course, Coda was a fighter pilot, and his orientation might change twelve times in a three-second time span, so the exercise was necessity rather than preference. In the heat of battle, starfighters didn't have time to worry about minor details like up and down.

He set a course that kept him on the upper outskirts of the wreckage. His navigational thrusters spat out puffs of compressed air, allowing him to weave his fighter through the drifting debris as his targeting computer scanned the battlespace for Moscow's signature. In most instances, the computer was quick, easily distinguishing friend from foe, but having to catalog each piece of battle wreckage was slowing it down.

Keeping his eyes alert, Coda spotted the enemy capital ship cresting the curve of the planet at the same moment his targeting system beeped. A red box appeared around the vessel on his screen, marking it as an incoming enemy. Turning sharply and increasing thrust, Coda quickly left the debris field behind, settling into an approach vector. By the time Coda was halfway there, Moscow appeared, his location distinguished only by a red box bracketing his fighter.

Moscow must have seen him too, because in a heartbeat, the two fighters were racing toward each other on an intercept course. These one-on-one scenarios hadn't changed much since the early days of flight, and they almost always began with both fighters racing toward each other, opening fire. Then if both missed, they streaked past one another to loop back around for another pass. That was when things got interesting and when superior flying skills came into play.

As his and Moscow's fighters entered weapons range, Coda opened fire. His seat rumbled as his cannon hurled digital projectiles. Moscow did the same.

Tracer rounds cut through the black of space like shooting stars as Moscow and Coda used their navigational thrusters to juke and jank, avoiding the incoming fire. Then in less than a blink of an eye, they streaked past each other.

Coda watched on his battle map as Moscow flipped and burned, pulling a dangerous high-g maneuver to get on Coda's six. Coda had several options but decided to boost thrust, increasing the distance between them.

He made for Moscow's capital ship. Its dark exterior was accented with the yellow of the Sol Fleet and quickly grew larger. Identical to Coda's own capital ship, it was heavily armed with hundreds of port and starboard cannons, missile turrets, and secondary batteries but didn't open fire as he approached. This was a dogfight, not a race to destroy each other's capital ships.

Coda sped past the top of the vessel then turned in a downward arc that brought him around its underbelly, speeding toward Moscow's incoming ship. Coda opened fire, but Moscow immediately veered to port, bringing his fighter parallel to the capital ship.

Coda fired his forward thrusters, shedding speed, and spun to follow. But just as Moscow came back into view, he immediately disappeared, darting under the larger ship. Coda tried to follow, but he'd shed too much speed. By the time he made it under the ship, Moscow's fighter was nowhere to be seen. Corkscrewing his fighter back around the top of the capital ship, Coda searched for the missing fighter.

Tracer fire streaked past his cockpit. *Where did that come from?*

Wrenching his neck to see behind him, Coda searched for Moscow, but the multipoint harness restricted his movement, making it difficult to get a visual. More tracer fire flashed, and this time Coda's fighter shook violently as Moscow's shot found home.

"Shit!"

Coda was hosed. He maximized thrust and took evasive maneuvers, speeding toward the battle debris.

His fighter shook again. An alarm claxon blared. He wasn't going to make it.

*I'm not a coward, and I won't run like one.*

With Moscow closing on his six, Coda pulled the stick back, ascending above the battle plane, then flipped nose to tail so that he was flying backward, his guns facing his rival's expected trajectory. Tracer fire lit the black as he pulled the trigger, and the slugs ripped through Moscow's rearmost wing in a shower of sparks.

Coda hooted, expecting Moscow's fighter to explode, but excitement quickly turned to disappointment when he realized the damage was only superficial. Like the larger main wings, the offset rear wings were designed for atmospheric flight and weren't required for spaceflight.

Wounded but not yet destroyed, Moscow juked the remaining incoming fire before bringing his fighter into an attack vector. More alarm claxons sounded. They were different, more urgent.

*He's locking on,* Coda realized. *He's going to fire his missiles.*

A bright-yellow target appeared on Coda's HUD. It streaked toward Coda's fighter, closing the distance between them faster than he would have imagined possible. Coda opened fire, targeting the incoming missile, only to have a second one appear.

*You're hosed. You're hosed. You're hosed.*

There was a brilliant flash, then all went black. By the time Coda blinked his vision back, he found himself spinning, a dozen emergency lights flashing. All of his maneuvering thrusters were offline.

It took him a moment to realize what had happened. He'd shot the missile, but it had been too close. Its shrapnel must have peppered his fighter. But that was the least of his worries. The second missile was almost upon him.

*I lost. I lost to Moscow. Thank god it was only a simulation.*

The second, blinding flash was accompanied by a terrible pain that burned through Coda's entire body. He cried out, his body paralyzed. He couldn't move. Couldn't breathe. Could barely think.

By the time the pain dissipated, Coda found himself in complete darkness, his body cold with sweat. With a shaky hand, he pulled his off his VR helmet and found himself back in the simulator.

Moscow was already standing, pumping his fist into the air and screaming his victory. Coda's friends looked on in disappointment, though Coda barely saw them. Deep down, he knew he was in shock, his body struggling to quantify the pain he'd experienced. Wearily removing his restraints, Coda climbed onto the nearby ladder and climbed down to the deck.

"Tremendous flying," Commander Coleman said, stepping forward. "Congratulations on your victory, Lieutenant Krylov."

"Thank you, sir."

"Sir," Coda said. "There at the end, when the simulation ended, there was... I... It *hurt*."

Moscow sneered, obviously not understanding what had happened in the opposite cockpit. Commander Coleman's reaction surprised Coda the most, though. He laughed.

"Of course it hurt," Commander Coleman said. "You were shot down."

"But, sir... It's only a simulation."

"It's a training exercise, Lieutenant. What you felt is a mild deterrent—one meant to prevent my pilots from getting comfortable with being shot down."

"I don't know about 'mild,'" Coda said sarcastically. He hadn't meant to say it aloud, but there was nothing he could do about that now, except mutter a quick "sir" and brace against the commander's wrath.

"The little jolt you felt is nothing compared to the pain of being shot down," Commander Coleman said. "That, I can guarantee you."

"Yes, sir. Of course."

"Good flying, both of you," the commander said. "Now take a seat at the debriefing monitor and wait for me to return."

"Yes, sir," they said in unison and started for the private alcove at the back of the room.

"I told you," Moscow said quietly. "You're nothing. You never were. And now everyone knows it."

Coda took a deep breath, trying like hell to ignore the insult. Commander Coleman had said the squadron was divided. That it needed to be unified. And that the battle was the first step in accomplishing that goal. As much as he wanted to punch Moscow's teeth in or challenge him to a rematch, Coda knew it would only counter whatever the commander was working on. So instead, he forced his best smile and said, "It was a good battle, Moscow. Congratulations."

Moscow sniffed, no doubt expecting the compliment to be followed up with a jab, but when it didn't come, his sneer faltered. He looked genuinely perplexed.

"I mean it, Andrei. Good flying."

Moscow grunted something Coda couldn't decipher and put some distance between them. Coda sighed. Playing nice with Moscow wasn't going to be easy—especially if the other pilot had no intention of meeting him in the middle. Still, considering that their last encounter had ended in a shoving match, he couldn't help but feel like this was an improvement. *At this pace, we'll be friends in no time.*

But even as he thought it, he knew it would never happen. They would never be friends, but maybe they could tolerate being in the same room, fly in the same squadron. That was something Coda wanted. Wasn't it?

# 19

*Simulator, SAS* Jamestown

*Alpha Centauri System, Proxima B, High Orbit*

Battles. It was battles all day, every day as the pilots worked through the remaining roster, taking each other one-on-one in custom simulations built by the commander himself. Battle became life, an all-encompassing game that they lived, breathed, and dreamed. There was no class or studies. Only the gym and the game. Only winning and losing. And losing meant going home, so when they weren't in the simulator, they were watching the battle unfold on the display board.

Coda spent his time studying the other pilots, taking detailed notes about their strengths and weaknesses. He'd then eavesdrop on the commander's evaluation to see how his own reviews stacked up. Oftentimes, he picked up on things that Commander Coleman highlighted, but the commander always had more to add, and Coda, even when he wasn't flying, continued to learn.

By the third day, a hierarchy was already beginning to take shape, and Coda was surprised to find that experience didn't necessarily translate into success within the simulator. He and Moscow continued to be outliers in that regard, both placing within the top fifteen pilots, well above the failure line.

Their friends weren't quite so fortunate. Noodle and Squawks rode the line, above it some days and below it others, while Uno was consistently below it. Moscow's friends were doing even worse.

That night at dinner, after a particularly embarrassing rout, Uno was even more agitated than usual. "I'm sick of it," he said. "It's too complicated. There's too much to keep track of."

He wasn't the first pilot to voice the complaint or the first to be overwhelmed by the sheer number of commands the pilots were responsible for. Unlike transports and bombers, the Nighthawk was a single-pilot starfighter. They didn't have the luxury of a navigator. It was just the pilot and the computer, and regardless of how much slack the computer picked up, there was still far more the pilots had to pay attention to than their previous drone training had prepared them for.

"The stick has over sixty combinations alone," Uno said, resorting to raw numbers and statistics as he always did when he was trying to make a point. "Did you know that? *Sixty!* Just tonight, I was trying to designate a target and turned off the cockpit lights. No joke. Yesterday, I thumbed the wrong weapon and dropped a bomb instead of firing my guns."

They all laughed. Noodle, caught in the unenviable position of having taken a drink of milk a moment before, spit it out all over his food.

"Probably make it taste better," Squawks said, and Noodle almost lost it again.

"I'm serious," Uno said. "I don't know if I can do this."

"You just need to calm down," Coda said.

"I can't," Uno said. "The commander calls it 'finger fire.' Says it's been around for hundreds of years. And he says it's only going to get worse when we start flying for real and there's radio chatter. 'Helmet fire,' he called it. I don't think I'm cut out for this."

"You just need more time in the simulator," Coda said.

Uno barked a laugh. "And when am I going to get that? The commander has it running all day, and we're already putting in extra time as it is."

"Wait," Noodle said. "You've been flying without us?"

"What do you think we've been doing every night?"

"It's the only personal time we get," Squawks said. "For all I know, you've been dating a pretty little lady."

"The only date we've had has been with the simulator," Uno said. "Little good it's done me."

"We'll be there again tonight," Coda said, ignoring Uno's bitter tone. "Come if you want. It might help your scores."

---

Commander Coleman stepped out of the Simulator Room just as Coda and the rest were approaching. Noodle and Squawks had taken Coda up on his offer to join them for after-hours practice, and they all froze as the commander spotted them.

"Good evening, Commander," Coda said.

"Coda," he said. "Gentlemen. You're not looking to sabotage my simulators, are you?"

"Just logging in some extra time, sir," Coda said.

"Personal time was built into your schedules to keep you sharp."

"We understand, sir. Thing is"—Coda nodded toward the door—"that's all we think about. All we dream about. And the way we see it, the better we fly, the better we'll sleep, and the sharper we'll be."

Commander Coleman nodded appreciably. "I completely understand, Lieutenant. Be easy on my equipment."

"Will do, sir."

The commander turned down the corridor as Coda and the rest entered the Simulation Room. Having been the pilots' home for the last few weeks, it smelled strongly of sweat and agitation.

"Squawks, Uno, get ready to go. I'll get you queued up."

"Who put him in charge?" Squawks asked sarcastically as he and Noodle made for their cockpits.

"You did by joining my extra sessions," Coda said then cycled through the various preprogrammed simulations in the control panel on the wall. After selecting one to his liking, he turned to join his squad mates. As he did, the door opened again, and Moscow strode in. He was joined by three of his friends, and all four of them froze, each eyeing the other. Apparently, Coda and his friends weren't the only ones planning to log extra time in the simulator.

Moscow appraised the scene and grimaced. "Come on," he said to the others, turning to go. "We'll come back later."

"No," Coda said as Moscow's friends turned to join him. "Wait."

Moscow stopped in the doorway.

"You're going to fly some extra simulations, right? So are we. Nothing says we can't do it together."

Moscow's eyes slid past Coda, finding the other three pilots behind him. "You want us to fly with you?"

Coda shrugged. "Why not?"

Moscow's friends looked at each other warily. *Why not?* They had a thousand reasons why not. But their common need outweighed them all.

Finally, Moscow shrugged. "Why not?" he repeated then strode into the room.

"Squawks," Coda said. "Take this one off." Then a little more quietly, he said to Moscow, "Uno's flying this one. Let's try to keep things even, yeah?"

"Sure," Moscow said. "Bear, you're up."

Bear, a female pilot with jet-black hair, had earned her call sign because she had a reputation for going "Momma Bear" when defending her friends. Though she and Uno were both below the failure line, Bear was in the bottom third overall, much lower than Uno.

Coda made for Uno's simulator, while Moscow and his group went for the other.

Squawks fell into step at Coda's shoulder. "What are you doing?" His voice was quiet, but there was an edge to it.

Coda felt Moscow's eyes on him. "We don't own the simulator, Squawks." Then just loud enough for Squawks, he added, "Besides, who would you rather shoot down? Uno or one of them?"

Squawks grinned. "Good point."

Coda slapped him on the shoulder. "Just play nice, okay?"

"Only down here," Squawks said. "I'm gonna kick some ass in the simulator."

"There you go." Coda climbed up the ladder. "How you feeling?"

Uno clicked the last latch of the harness into place then set the VR helmet on his lap. "Good."

Coda could hear the nervousness in Uno's voice but didn't mention it.

It would only make him more self-conscious, and the last thing Uno needed was to think about himself instead of his opponent.

"All right," Coda said. "Listen, Bear is slow, and she's overly reliant on missiles. If you get in close and take her with your guns, she won't have a chance."

"Okay."

Coda wasn't sure how it was possible, but Uno somehow sounded even *more* nervous than before. "Hey." He let the word hang there until Uno met his eyes. "It's just us. No statistics. No board. No full squadron, okay?"

"Okay."

"Good," Coda said. "Have fun."

Coda stepped down the ladder then moved it out of the way. When both pilots gave him the thumbs-up, he toggled the start initiative on the wall panel, and the simulation began.

It was a relatively brief encounter, with both pilots flying tentatively, like a pair of amateur boxers unwilling to commit to the fight. Despite Coda's advice, Uno kept his distance, making sweeping movements at full thrust. The strategy played directly into Bear's strength, and Uno met his end when he failed to deploy his chaff in time, allowing Bear's long-range missile to take him clean in the fuselage.

"Sorry," Uno said to Coda as he and Squawks swapped positions.

"No need to apologize."

"I didn't listen to you."

"Maybe you'll fix that next time, huh?" Coda smiled to let Uno know he was joking, but he would've been lying if he'd said there wasn't an element of truth in his words. "Listen, Uno. You're flying stiff because you're thinking too much. Just let it go, and before you know it, the stick will be an extension of your body."

"Is that how it is for you?"

"Me?" Coda asked. "God, no. I'm flying by the seat of my pants too. It's just something my dad used to say…" Coda winced, wishing he could take back the words. "Anyway, just relax. Stop thinking. Let your training kick in."

Squawks's battle was smoother. Unlike Uno, Squawks had all the traits of a talented fighter pilot. Unfortunately, he flew like he talked: fast, confident, and reckless. He took unnecessary risks that worked as often as they got him into trouble. Commander Coleman would have to train that out of him before he ever saw action, though Coda struggled to see how that could be done. Telling Squawks to fly slower and not take as many risks would be akin to telling him to be quiet. It was an assault on who he was.

*Maybe not train it* out *of him then. Maybe the commander can teach him to channel it.*

By the time their hour of personal time was nearing an end, everyone had flown except for Moscow and Coda.

"Rematch?" Moscow asked, smiling wryly.

Coda couldn't tell if Moscow was trying to be an ass, or if his own feelings were still raw from the defeat. He decided Moscow was trying to have fun with it, nothing personal. "Not tonight."

"Still sore?"

*Okay, maybe he is trying to be an ass.* "Something like that."

"You guys here every night?"

"Yeah," Coda said. "I take it you're planning on making it a regular thing?"

"That was the plan," Moscow said. "The group needs the practice."

"So does mine," Coda said. "No reason they can't do it together, right?"

"I guess not."

Just like that, he found himself in a shaky truce with Moscow. Every night during their hour of personal time, Coda and his three friends logged extra time in the simulator, and every night, Moscow's group joined them. They didn't always battle opposing teams. Sometimes, Uno took on Squawks or Noodle flew against Coda, but as the nights wore on, they began to offer each other advice.

"When he's on your ass like that," Moscow said to Noodle one night after Bear had gotten in close and killed him with guns, "you can deploy your chaff. At those speeds, it'll tear her apart. Don't be afraid to think outside the box."

By the end of the week, the extra practice was already beginning to pay off. Moscow had cracked into the top five, with Coda right behind him. Noodle had worked his way into the top twenty, and every member of their alliance had broken into the top sixty. After that, it didn't take long for people to realize they were spending more time in the simulator than the others. Some of the pilots asked to join their after-hours practice sessions, while others complained to the commander.

Commander Coleman simply said that personal time was personal time and that he wasn't going to discipline pilots for working harder than everyone else. After that, the simulator became a buzz of activity, and it became next to impossible to log an extra session.

So Coda spent the time studying the other pilots in excruciating detail, augmenting the notes he'd already begun taking. Subconsciously, Coda knew that when it came to fighting the Baranyk, it wouldn't matter how well he could fly if he couldn't understand and outthink his opponent.

For the remainder of the week, he put the strategy into action, leveraging what he knew about the other pilots' deficiencies to destroy them in battle. When it was all said and done, he, like the rest of his group, had made his mark on the commander's standings. Unfortunately, it wasn't the commander's opinion that he should have been worried about.

# 20

*Commander Chadwick Coleman's Quarters, SAS* Jamestown
*Alpha Centauri System, Proxima B, High Orbit*

COMMANDER CHADWICK COLEMAN SIGHED AS LIEUTENANT HERNANDEZ left his quarters. The meeting hadn't been altogether unexpected. Pilots, after all, left programs for personal reasons all the time, but what *had* surprised him was who the meeting had been with. Lieutenant Hernandez wasn't a bad pilot, and his scores were good enough to graduate to the next phase of his training, but if he didn't think he had what it took, then Coleman wasn't going to argue with him.

Unbuttoning his uniform, Coleman crossed the small room to his bookshelf, where he poured himself a drink. After a small sip that warmed his body from the inside, he returned to the chair and pulled up the flight roster on his tablet. He found Lieutenant Hernandez's name in the top fifty and, with a second frustrated sigh, crossed it out.

The pilots had done well, all things considered, in large part because their drone training had translated better than he had expected. Even then, it still wasn't an equal replacement for basic flight. In his day, any X-23 pilot would have first flown other spacecraft before being selected for the Nighthawk strike fighter program—Commander Coleman himself had built his early reputation on flying long-range reconnaissance vessels, so he'd possessed at least some experience with fast-moving, highly maneuverable spacecraft.

Still, transitioning from the larger, slower ships of the fleet to the X-23 was akin to jumping from a bicycle to a motorcycle. They were similar only in concept. But that concept created a foundation upon which everything else was built. The pilots of Coleman's squadron didn't have that foundation, or if they did, it was incomplete, the concrete not yet solidified into something that could be built atop of. That was why they'd logged so many hours in the simulator. During his day, a pilot only had to complete eight hours of simulated flight before moving to the real thing. Most of his pilots had already logged over fifty.

*They're ready... or at least as ready as they'll ever be.*

The only question left was with Lieutenant Hernandez's sudden departure, would he slide the person from the fifty-first position into the top fifty?

*No,* Coleman decided. *That would be an insult to those who've earned it.*

It was done then. What had been one hundred was now forty-nine. Only half of the original recruits had made it to the midpoint in their training. He took another sip and set his tablet aside, then sinking deeper into his seat, he rested his head back and closed his eyes.

The tablet buzzed. Coleman was alert in a heartbeat, noticing the red border that now filled the edges of his terminal, noting the priority message.

With the development of the Shaw Drive, humanity had unlocked the keys to faster-than-light travel, but faster-than-light communication was still little more than a science fiction concept. That meant the ships of the fleet were often both battle vessels and mail carriers, carrying important information to other ships in the area like a bucket brigade. For high-priority messages, though, command leveraged courier drones whose sole mission was to jump to a single location via a jumpgate and deliver its message. Even with the receiving vessels reusing the courier drones for subsequent communications, the system was beyond expensive and only available to those with a captain's rank or higher. Whoever had sent him the message had gone to a lot of trouble for him to get it as quickly as possible.

Commander Coleman played the message. The man on the screen

was in his early sixties, his skin smooth and showing little sign of his age. His hair, however, was pure white, matching his admiral's uniform, and styled meticulously. But Admiral Orlovsky's lively blue eyes were bloodshot and rimmed by dark circles, as if he hadn't slept in days.

"Commander," the recording of Admiral Orlovsky said, "enclosed, you'll find footage of a recent Baranyk encounter. The target was the mining colony of Numina 3, and as you'll see, the enemy once again employed the use of their Disrupter. Despite recent fleet R&D upgrades, our forces were still rendered inoperable. The colony was lost, as were the *Boston* and *Charleston*."

The admiral paused, taking a deep breath. The hardness of his eyes melted away, and the façade of command disappeared as the admiral turned into the man Coleman had known for his entire military career.

"They're going for our supply lines, Chadwick. Destroying not only our drones, but our ability to manufacture more. The courier carrying this message is equipped with a new Shaw Drive prototype. I need your report, including roster updates, capabilities, and battle readiness. And, Chadwick, I hope your work is going better than it is out here, because we're going to need your pilots. We're going to need you. I look forward to your report. Good luck, Commander."

The image of the admiral disappeared as the screen faded to black. Coleman sat there for several moments before toggling the vid attached to the message. By the time it ended, Coleman was ready for a second drink. It was bad form for a commander to get sloppy drunk, so he did the next best thing: he slid the fifty-first pilot into the fiftieth position.

The rest of the squadron might not know it yet, but they were going to need every pilot they could get.

# 21

*Ready Room, SAS* Jamestown
*Alpha Centauri System, Proxima B, High Orbit*

"WHERE'S UNO?" CODA ASKED, SURVEYING THE HALF-EMPTY READY ROOM.

The remaining pilots of Commander Coleman's squadron mingled, sharing smiles, attempting to ignore the vacancies left behind by their departed friends. That was the fighter pilot way: to move on and act as if the cut, the loss, or the death had never happened. Dwelling on it meant confronting failure. Confronting death. One's own mortality. To a pilot, that meant losing their edge. And the moment a pilot lost their edge, they became slag.

"Have you seen Uno?" Coda asked, turning to Squawks, who, like Noodle, sat next to him.

"He's probably taking a dump," Squawks said.

Noodle snorted, but Coda didn't feel like laughing. "I haven't seen him all morning."

"Maybe it's a stubborn one."

"A what? No, never mind, I don't want to know." Coda shook his head, trying to get the mental image to disappear. "He should be here."

"Settle down," Squawks said. "He will be."

"Yeah..." But for some reason, Squawks's words didn't make Coda feel better. Objectively, Coda knew he shouldn't be worried. Like every other member of their group, Uno had finished above the failure line and would advance to flight status, but Coda still couldn't shake the uneasy feeling in his gut. Something wasn't right.

"Attention on deck!"

The pilots snapped to attention as Commander Coleman stepped into the ready room.

"Take your seats," he said, taking his usual position behind the podium.

Once the pilots had found their seats, the room fell deathly quiet—something that was even more pronounced by the number of empty seats. When the pilots had first arrived, they'd been excited, nearly bursting at the seams, but that energy had suddenly dissipated, leaving a gloom as if the squadron had lost a major battle and taken fifty-percent casualties.

"Congratulations," Commander Coleman said, giving his obligatory speech. "The men and women in this room have advanced to basic flight. The chief is still readying your fighters, so despite my better judgment, I'm giving you the day off. Enjoy it, because it'll be the last one you get before the end of your training."

The room erupted into cheers, pilots clapping and laughing, slapping each other on the back.

A day off. Coda couldn't remember what that was like. Twenty-four hours to himself. He didn't know what he would do. *Sleep.* Yes, that sounded nice. *Sleep.* His eyes felt heavy just thinking about it.

"Flight schedules have been downloaded to your tablets," Commander Coleman said once the ruckus had died down. "Check then double and triple check your flight times and craft number. Failure to arrive on time and at the correct spacecraft will result in an automatic SOD."

A SOD—or a "sign of difficulty"—was the pilots' version of a strike, and as in the great American pastime of baseball, after three strikes, the pilot was out of the program.

"This is the real thing, ladies and gentlemen. I expect you to be ready. I'll see you tomorrow."

Coda turned to his friends as the commander strode out of the room. "Come on."

"Where?" Squawks asked.

"Just follow me."

Coda pushed his way through the pilots, making for the ready room door, then chased the commander down the corridor. "Sir!" Coda shouted. "Sir!"

Commander Coleman stopped and turned to face him. "What is it, Coda?"

"It's Uno, sir," Coda said. "We haven't seen him and were wondering if you knew where he was."

"Lieutenant Hernandez?"

"Yes, sir."

"Coda," Commander Coleman said, "Lieutenant Hernandez is set to depart with the rest of the washouts at oh nine hundred."

"Washouts?" Coda said. "Sir, there must be a mistake. Uno was above the line."

"Yes, he was," Commander Coleman said. "Which is why it was so unexpected when he came to my quarters last night and withdrew from the program."

"He quit?" Coda couldn't believe what he was hearing. "I thought you said we couldn't quit."

Commander Coleman's face grew hard. He apparently didn't like having his words thrown in his face any more than anyone else did. "I won't have a pilot in my squadron who endangers everyone else he flies with. The lieutenant didn't believe he had what it takes, and I didn't disagree with him. Anything more than that, and you'll have to ask him."

"He's still here?"

"As I already said, Coda, he departs at oh nine hundred. You can find him in the hangar bay."

---

THEY FOUND UNO SITTING AGAINST THE WALL, HIS ARMS DRAPED OVER HIS knees, watching as specialists worked under the watchful eye of the chief, frantically trying to get the remaining Nighthawks ready for flight.

When he saw Coda and the rest approaching, his mouth fell open, and his face grew several shades redder than it had been before.

"Hey," Coda said, crossing his arms and stopping in front of him.

"What are you guys doing here?" Uno asked.

"What are we... Uno, what are *you* doing here? The commander said you quit."

Uno turned away.

"Uno—"

Snapping his head around, Uno jumped to his feet. "What do you want me to say? I told you I couldn't do this, but you wouldn't listen. 'You just need more time,'" Uno said, giving Coda an exaggerated impersonation of himself.

Coda felt his blood rise and forced himself to take a deep breath. "Uno, you were above the line. You want to say you couldn't do it? You're full of it. You did it. You passed."

"Anyone can pass a test, Coda."

"What's that supposed to mean?" Coda asked defensively. Was that a shot at Coda nearly failing FAM Phase?

"It just means I can pass whatever test the commander puts in front of me, but that doesn't change anything. I *know* I can't do this. I *know* I don't have what it takes."

"We don't believe that," Noodle said.

"It doesn't matter what you believe," Uno said. "Do you know what I've been doing in my bunk the last few nights?"

"I'm not sure I want to know..." Squawks said.

"I've been watching the flight vids," Uno said, ignoring Squawks's failed attempt at a joke. "Mine. Yours. All of them. And you know what I saw? I saw someone who was slow. Someone who was mechanical. Someone who *thought* too much. Not like you guys. Not like everyone else."

"Uno—"

"No, Coda. I already made my decision."

Coda clamped his mouth shut. There was no arguing that. Uno had quit on his own, and even if Coda somehow convinced him it had been the wrong thing to do, there was little chance the commander would take him back. A fighter pilot with self-confidence issues wasn't exactly a prized commodity.

"You should have said something," Coda said. "We're supposed to be friends."

"I know." Uno blew out a long breath. The anger and frustration in his voice disappeared, and for the first time since they'd confronted him, he seemed truly disappointed. "But you guys know me. I like to fail on my own."

"Deep down, you're just as selfish as I am," Squawks said with a smile.

"I guess so," Uno said, smiling back.

Coda didn't know how Squawks did it. He'd basically just insulted the man, but instead of getting mad, Uno had thought it was funny. If Coda had done something like that, Uno probably would have decked him.

"Where are they sending you?" Coda asked.

"The *Philadelphia*."

"They're sending you to the *front*?" Noodle asked.

"Yeah," Uno said. "I was surprised too. They have me flying a drone again."

The front. The one place Coda had dreamt about since joining the academy. At any other point in time, he would have been jealous, annoyed that a washout was being stationed in the one place he wanted to be while he was left behind. But strangely, he didn't feel any of those things, and if someone had given him the opportunity to swap places, he wasn't sure he would have taken it.

"Anyway, it looks like I've got to go." Uno pointed to where a group of former pilots were boarding a transport ship. "Seriously, though, guys. I'm sorry. Thanks for coming. Thanks for everything."

Coda clapped hands with Uno and pulled him into a quick hug. "Good luck."

"You too, Coda."

Noodle was next, repeating the embrace. "Take care, man."

"Save some Baranyk for us," Squawks said, punching him in the arm.

"No promises," Uno said, then with a final, half-hearted smile, he nodded and turned to go.

Watching Uno walk away, Coda couldn't help feeling as if the squadron had just had its first real casualty. He also knew it wouldn't be the last.

# 22

*Ready Room, SAS* Jamestown

*Alpha Centauri System, Proxima B, High Orbit*

Coda entered the ready room two hours before his scheduled flight. Commander Coleman was already there, sitting in a chair in the front row of the auditorium seating. His eyes were alive in a way Coda hadn't seen since joining the squadron. When the commander stood and strode toward Coda, his step was light, almost giddy.

"Good morning, sir."

"Good morning, Coda. You ready?"

"Can't wait, sir."

"Good." Commander Coleman stepped past Coda and, grabbing a black stylus from the tray, stopped in front of the large digital display board that took up the entire front wall. "You reviewed your flight packet?"

"Yes, sir."

Commander Coleman handed the stylus to Coda. "Write it out for me then."

"Sir?"

"I said write it out for me. Who's flying? What are their call signs?

What are our takeoff and landing times? What ship numbers? Communications frequencies? Diversion information? I want all of it, and I'm going to want to know all of it before every flight."

"Yes, sir."

Coda started writing. *Who's flying? Lieutenant O'Neil and Commander Coleman. Call signs? Coda and Spitfire. Taking off at 0700 from hangar bay 7B in Nighthawks One and Two. Landing at 0800 at the same location.* He listed communications frequencies, both primary and emergency, as well as alternative flight paths in the event of engine trouble, carrier malfunction, and invasion. The whole process took nearly twenty minutes. When he was done, he handed the stylus back to Commander Coleman and stepped back to let him review it.

"Well done."

"Thank you, sir."

"Can you tell me why I had you do this?"

"Because you wanted to be sure I knew it, sir."

"Because it helps avoid accidents. This is your first flight, so your ship is unarmed, but I've flown in training exercises where the pilot accidentally climbed into the wrong fighter and fired real rounds instead of the simulated rounds we'll be working with today. His mistake nearly cost his CAG his life. Don't forget that, Coda. Mistakes cost lives."

"Understood, sir."

"Good, because you'll do this before every flight. I'll take two minutes to review it, but other than that, you'll be on your own to fill it out properly. Get anything wrong, and you're grounded for the day."

"Yes, sir."

"Follow me."

The commander led Coda through the ready room into the adjoining locker room, where they stopped in front of a locker with Coda's call sign. Hanging inside was one of the best presents he'd ever received.

"Do you know how to put that on?"

"I think so, sir."

"Do it."

Coda began shedding clothing until he was dressed in nothing more than his underwear. The black flight suit, known as a G-suit, fit snugly around every part of his body. During flight, it would squeeze his legs and abdomen, preventing the flow of blood from his brain to help avoid grayout, the loss of vision or awareness, or even blackout, the loss of consciousness altogether. Because it was so snug, the commander had to zip it up in the back for him. Coda repaid the favor.

Once dressed, they moved down the short corridor into the hangar. They passed a number of ship personnel, garnering confused looks and double takes. While their presence was becoming known throughout the ship, there was a difference between knowing and seeing, and seeing two pilots striding purposefully down the corridors of their ship, especially the legendary Commander Coleman himself, was akin to seeing a living legend.

Commander Coleman led Coda through the hangar, avoiding technicians and machinery with an efficiency gained through years of practice. Their fighters were set apart from the rest of the hangar, hitched to a pair of forklifts that would assist loading them into the launch tubes. A middle-aged man with thinning dark hair and a round face covered in grease was overseeing the last of their preparations.

"Chief," Commander Coleman said.

The chief looked up. "Sir," he said, giving the commander a quick salute. "We're just wrapping up now, sir."

"Very good. We'll take it from here."

"Of course, sir." The chief stepped away from the fighters and ordered his specialists to do the same. Rather than disappearing entirely, though, they only gave the commander some space.

"What are you doing, sir?" Coda asked, watching as Commander Coleman ran a hand down his fighter's fuselage.

"Visual inspection."

"Isn't that what the chief was doing?"

"Mm-hmm."

"Then why are you doing it again, sir?"

"Because it's *my* ass in the cockpit."

That was good enough for Coda. He circled his own fighter, trying to mimic his commander's steady gaze. The only problem was, he didn't know what to look for. The commander seemed to sense his confusion, and without taking his attention away from his own fighter, he told Coda what to look for.

"Loose parts, dents, cracks, anything that can cause friction or come apart in a high-g maneuver."

Coda started his review again, taking in the finer details of the fighter, running a careful hand down its fuselage, offset wings, and rear thrusters. It was the first time he'd seen one of the fighters since the first day of FAM Phase, and after flying countless simulations since that day, he found it even more impressive.

"Looks good, Chief," Commander Coleman said. "Good work."

"Thank you, sir."

"Coda?"

"Looks good to me, sir."

"All right. We've got four minutes 'til launch. Load up."

One of the specialists rolled over a ladder, which Coda used to climb into his cockpit. Settling down inside, he immediately secured his harness then slid on his helmet. The specialist helped him lock it into place, and a moment later, cold oxygen blew into the flight suit, giving the entire thing a miniature pressurized environment. The cockpit would be pressurized too, of course, but in the event of an emergency, the suit would give him roughly another thirty minutes to get to safety.

Manned spaceflight was built around contingency after contingency after contingency, and while many called it redundant, Coda, who was seconds away from shooting into the cold, lifeless void of space, was beginning to understand that redundancy might save his life.

With everything in place, he closed the cockpit, maneuvered the emergency lever to lock it into place, and powered on his guidance, engine, and communication systems.

"Hawk Two, this is Hawk One. Do you copy?" Commander Coleman's voice sounded slightly tinny through the speakers of Coda's helmet.

"Copy, Hawk One. Loud and clear."

"Copy that, Coda. Begin final systems check and prepare for launch."

"Yes, sir."

Coda ran through the final check, verifying that each of his systems was online and functioning properly. Once confirmed, he radioed back to the commander. "Final systems check complete, sir. I'm good to go."

"Same here, Coda. Strap in and have fun."

"Yes, sir."

The forklift moved him into the launch tube, locking the bottom of his fighter to a pulley that was attached to a track at the bottom of the deck. When it was time to launch, the pulley would rocket forward, dragging his fighter along with it, and hurl it into space.

"*Jamestown* Tower, Hawks One and Two are green and ready for takeoff."

"Roger, Hawk One," Lieutenant Commander Chavez said over the radio. "Hawks One and Two are cleared for launch from launch tubes three and five, firing at one-second intervals in ten seconds."

The prelaunch sensation reminded Coda of being a kid and riding a roller coaster. His legs felt light, and he thought he had to pee. And this time, he didn't have the reassuring smile from his father to let him know everything was going to be all right. Worst of all, just as it had been when he was a child, once he was strapped in and the ride started moving, there was no shutting it down. He was truly at the mercy of whatever came next.

"Five seconds."

*I really do have to take a piss.*

"Three."

There was a muffled banging noise followed by hissing air. Was something wrong?

"Two."

*Two? Why's he still counting down? Where's the emergency abort?*

"One."

Another bang. Another hiss. Both louder than before. Then like a bolt fired from the world's largest ballista, Coda rocketed forward. Thrown back in his seat, he watched as the distant black dot at the end of the tunnel grew alarmingly fast. He had just enough time to blink before he was spit out into the night.

*I'm flying,* Coda thought as the *Jamestown* grew smaller behind him. *I'm actually doing this!*

And then the panic hit him.

# 23

*Cockpit, Nighthawk*
*Alpha Centauri System, Proxima B*

Coda's heart was in his throat. Adrenaline coursed through his veins, making his hands tremble, his movements sharp. The *Jamestown* was little more than a shadow against the orange glow of Proxima B, but its subtle shifting out his starboard window, coupled with the null gravity, was more than enough to send his body into a panic.

Up became down and down became sideways as he fought to find some semblance of gravity. In that terrible moment, he realized that regardless of how realistic the simulator was, nothing could ever truly replicate the experience of spaceflight.

"Breathe," said a calming voice on his radio. Who? Who was talking to him? "Breathe, Coda." Commander Coleman's X-23 appeared at Coda's wing, close enough that Coda could see the other man seated inside the cockpit. "Just follow the blues of my thrusters. Acknowledge?"

"Acknowledged," Coda said, forcing the words through the lump in his throat.

Commander Coleman's fighter moved ahead of Coda's effortlessly. Coda took a deep breath then pushed the throttle forward with his left hand, increasing speed, and formed up behind Commander Coleman's left wing in the dash-two position, using the blue of his Shaw Drive thrusters as much as the navigational path that had popped up on his HUD. They followed the path for several minutes, leaving the various orbits of fleet ships and satellites behind.

"All right, Coda. Just like we practiced in the simulator. Stay with me."

Commander Coleman's fighter rocketed forward, quickly leaving Coda behind. With the aid of his computer, Coda initiated his main thrusters and matched speed. One second, he was moving at a comfortable five kilometers per second; the next, he was moving at more than twice that. Thrown back in his seat, with what felt like the weight of the world on his chest, he finally understood what five G's truly felt like, and along with the sensation came something else: true, unbridled joy.

Letting out a long yell, Coda fell in behind Commander Coleman, but because the commander had launched forward before him, the blue of his thrusters appeared as little more than a pair of blue stars shining in the distance. Coda brought up his targeting computer, identified Commander Coleman's ship, and locked on. No sooner had he done so than the commander strafed right, turning forty-five degrees.

Coda followed, and the G's increased. If he hadn't been harnessed in so tightly, he would have been thrown against the left side of his cockpit. As it was, his body cried out against the restraints, and he could *feel* the blood inside his body forced from his extremities. The flight suit tightened, compensating for the movement, keeping the blood where it belonged and preventing him from blacking out.

Before he'd fully adjusted to the sensation, the commander turned again, bringing his fighter around ninety degrees to the left. Coda followed again, and again, the harness and flight suit adjusted for the increased g-forces. Coda still felt his vision grow fuzzy.

*This is going to take a lot of getting used to.*

Zigging and zagging, they flew, Coda always matching Commander Coleman's maneuvers. For an hour, Coda followed him, doing barrel rolls, corkscrews, aileron rolls, and split-S maneuvers—everything he'd already mastered in the simulator—and by the end of the hour, the overwhelming panic he'd felt when he'd shot out of the *Jamestown* had been replaced by a growing confidence.

"All right, Coda. That's enough for one day. Lead us home."

"Copy that, sir."

With the *Jamestown* behind them, and Coda once again in the dash-two position behind Commander Coleman's starboard wing, the correct maneuver would have been to make a wide one-hundred-eighty-degree turn, but his confidence was growing by the second, and Coda wasn't interested in correct. He wanted some fun.

Coda fired his nose thrusters, flipping the front of his ship backward. It was a maneuver he'd done in the simulator a thousand times, but in the short time since the beginning of the exercise, he had forgotten how little the two had in common. He was thrown up, down, and backward, then all three all over again. By the time he stabilized the fighter, he was still facing the wrong direction.

Breathing heavily, Coda reoriented himself, finding the two other ships, and braced himself against the commander's impending rebuke. However, what he heard was even more unnerving.

Commander Coleman was *laughing*. He appeared in front of Coda, their fighters nose to nose, Commander Coleman flying *backward* so that he was looking directly into Coda's cockpit.

"That didn't look comfortable," Commander Coleman said.

"I feel like my brain was put on spin cycle."

"I bet. Are you hurt?"

"Only my ego, sir."

"What did you learn?"

"That I'm an idiot?"

"I won't argue with you there," Commander Coleman said. "That wasn't very good headwork. But tell me *why* you're an idiot."

"Because I can't do things out here the same way I did them in the simulator."

"Very good, Coda. I won't argue with your stupidity, but part of this was my fault. In my day, a pilot would fly eight simulations before flying their first real flight. You've flown more than eighty. We never had the opportunity to get comfortable in the simulator. You did. And you're going to have to unlearn a lot of it."

"Understood, sir."

"It's going to be a process, and we're going to spend some time getting comfortable. After that, the real work will begin."

"Sounds good, sir."

"All right. Let's try that again, shall we? Home's that way." Commander Coleman pointed behind Coda, laughed again, then used his forward-facing thrusters to create some distance between them, giving Coda space to turn around and plot a course back to the *Jamestown*.

As they drew closer, Coda radioed in. "*Jamestown* Tower, this is Hawk Two requesting clearance to land."

"Roger that, Coda. You are cleared for landing in hangar bay 7C."

"Copy, *Jamestown* Tower. Thank you."

Coda set a course that would bring them into the fighter recovery bay then toggled up the landing procedure on his HUD. Selecting the automated sequence, he let go of his stick. Instead of following the designated path, though, the fighter drifted off course.

Cycling through his systems again, Coda made sure his autopilot was activated. After confirming it was, he reattempted to connect with the *Jamestown*'s auto-docking procedure. It failed a second time.

"Is there an issue, Lieutenant?" Commander Coleman asked.

"My auto-docking isn't engaging."

"That's because we're not using the auto-docking procedure."

"Sir?"

"The enemy has a way to disrupt our connection with our drones. Who's to say they couldn't do the same with an automated landing? We'll be hands-on the whole way in."

*Hands-on.* The words filled Coda with dread. He'd practiced landing in the simulator, of course, but he'd already learned that the simulator wasn't the same. Now he was supposed to land on a ship that was traveling at eight thousand meters per second while coming in on an adjacent flight path.

"Is that going to be a problem, Coda?" Commander Coleman asked.

Coda had no idea what to say. *Yes, sir, I'm petrified?* He would never live that down, especially since he knew his radio communications were being broadcast in the ready room for anyone who wanted to listen. He didn't expect a big draw; he wasn't the first pilot who'd flown, but he had been the first out of his friends. That meant Noodle and Squawks were likely listening in.

"No, sir. Not a problem at all. Plotting my landing now."

Coda readjusted his flight path, aligning it with Hangar Bay 7C, then swung around so that he was flying parallel to it. Once his fighter and the *Jamestown* were traveling at matching speeds, the only thing he had to do was ease the fighter in, like an old car switching lanes on the highway—at eight thousand meters per second.

"Clear one, Coda," the tower officer said. "Call the ball."

"I've got the ball," Coda said.

"Just like the simulator," Commander Coleman said. "Trust your training, and you'll be fine."

It went against every instinct in Coda's body, but trust his training, he did. The digital display on his HUD traced a line moving from left to right. His job was to keep a small circle inside a second, larger one. The farther out he was, the more leniency he had, but as he drew closer to the *Jamestown*, even the smallest movement had amplified effects.

Using the line on the HUD as his guide, Coda used his portside thrusters to ease his fighter starboard closer to the *Jamestown*. It was close enough now that he could make out the individual cannons lining its surface out of his peripheral vision. Coda kept his eyes locked on the ball, sweating as it veered up and down, side to side, fighting him as if the fighter itself were an energetic puppy that didn't want to go back into its kennel.

His gaze never veering from his HUD, Coda felt the lights of the *Jamestown* more than he saw them. Having been in the black for an hour, he found them bright and oppressive. But he was inside the ship now, and squinting against the bright lights of the hangar, Coda brought the fighter gently onto the deck.

After several deep breaths, Coda looked to see if the commander had landed yet. He spotted him only a few meters away, already pulling off his flight helmet. He saw Coda looking and gave him a thumbs-up.

*I did it,* Coda thought, returning the gesture. *I don't know how, but I did it.*

By the time they'd been towed back into the main hangar, Coda had removed his flight helmet and popped the cockpit hatch.

Commander Coleman met him at the bottom of the ladder. "Well done."

"Thank you, sir."

"How are you feeling?"

"A little wet in the breeches, but other than that..."

Commander Coleman laughed. "The first landing is enough to make any pilot's butthole pucker. We'll continue to work on them, and before you know it, you'll be able to land without leaving a mess inside your flight suit." He turned to survey the hangar. "Chief!"

"Yes, sir," the chief said, appearing behind Commander Coleman. "Here you are, sir." He handed something to the commander, who in turn held it out to Coda.

"This is yours," the commander said.

Coda took the small flight badge and studied it. Roughly six centimeters by four, it depicted a stylized pair of Nighthawks flying against the backdrop of the sun. Under the image were the words The Forgotten.

"We'll have it sewn onto your flight suit," the commander said. "You earned it."

"Thank you, sir," Coda said, never looking up. "What are the Forgotten?"

"We are, Coda. The war moved on without fighter pilots. The world left us behind. But where they have forgotten us, so has our enemy, and that will be their downfall. We are the Forgotten Squadron."

Coda rubbed a reverent finger across the flight badge. Usually, only full pilots were given badges.

The Commander seemed to read his mind. "It doesn't mean you've made the squadron yet, Lieutenant. But there aren't a thousand people left in the world who have flown a Nighthawk, so as far as I'm concerned, you're one of us."

It was too much. During the days of manned starfighters, each squadron had its own badge, and Coda could remember early memories of donning his father's flight jacket, looking at himself in the mirror, and dreaming of one day growing up to be just like him. That had been before the incident, but his father's downfall had only increased his desire to earn a badge of his own.

"It's... It's amazing, sir," Coda said, meeting the commander's eye. "Thank you. I'll wear it proudly."

# 24

*Mess Hall, SAS* Jamestown
*Alpha Centauri System, Proxima B, High Orbit*

CODA SET DOWN HIS TRAY. AS HE SLID INTO THE METAL CHAIR, NOODLE sucked in a sharp breath and held it. His eyes twinkled with amusement, darting in Coda's direction. When Noodle didn't release the breath, Coda finally took the bait.

"What's he doing?"

"Breathe, Noodle!" Squawks said in an exaggerated impersonation of Commander Coleman. "Come on, Noodle! Just breathe! Breathe, goddamn it!"

Noodle burst into laughter, and Squawks joined him. A couple people sitting nearby looked at them, obviously wondering what the hell was so funny.

"You guys are assholes," Coda said, which only made them laugh even harder. "Why am I even friends with you?"

"Oh, please," Squawks said, wiping tears from his eyes. "This is *exactly* why. Someone has to keep you from believing your own bullshit."

"You, maybe," Coda said. "But not him. Noodle is more of the cool, quiet type."

"It's true." Noodle nodded.

"Yeah, you're a real rock star," Squawks said sarcastically.

"I take it you guys were listening?" Coda asked.

It hadn't been more than ninety minutes since his flight—just enough time to shower, change, and go through a short preliminary debriefing with Commander Coleman. The full evaluation would come later that night, once more of the pilots had flown.

"Every glorious second of it," Squawks said. "Breathe, Coda! Breathe!"

Squawks and Noodle erupted into laughter again.

"I'm glad I didn't say what I really was feeling then," Coda said, unsure if either of the two assholes even heard him.

"Don't let them razz you too bad, Coda."

Coda looked up to see an older pilot wearing the standard gray flight suit of Commander Coleman's squadron. With thinning salt-and-pepper hair and a face sporting lines of age, he was easily one of the oldest in the squadron. Coda didn't know him well; he bunked in one of the other barracks and was on a different schedule than Coda's.

"There ain't many pilots who wouldn't cry for momma while making a landing in high orbit."

Noodle and Squawks looked at the newcomer and exchanged a look that said, "Who the hell is this guy?" But between the newcomer coming to Coda's defense and his thick southern drawl, Coda immediately liked him.

"It's Tex, right?" Coda asked.

"Yeah."

"I take it you had your first flight?"

"Naw, not yet," Tex said. "Not in the Nighthawk, anyway."

"What do you mean?"

"I've flown other ships. Made some hands-on landings. They ain't fun."

"No, they're not," Coda agreed.

"You mind if I sit?"

"Sure."

"Thanks." Tex slid into the seat Uno normally occupied, a detail that didn't go unnoticed by Noodle and Squawks. Tex must have felt their uneasiness, because he offered them a kind nod.

"So," Coda said, interrupting the growing silence, "you've flown spacecraft before?"

Tex stabbed his food paste and shoveled in a bite. "I'm a puddle jumper," he said, talking around the mouthful.

"A what?" Squawks asked.

Tex swallowed. "A puddle jumper. A bus driver."

Squawks's confused face made it clear he had no idea what the man was talking about, but he shrugged, apparently not interested enough to figure it out.

"You flew transports?" Noodle asked.

Tex pointed at him with his fork, nodding. "Marines, mostly."

"On the front?"

"Where else?"

A quiet appreciation filled the table.

"Then why'd you leave?" Suddenly interested again, Squawks asked the question that was on all of their minds. They all dreamed of getting to the front and making their mark on the war, even if each had his own reason. To leave that behind was like walking away from a winning lottery ticket.

"Same reason I joined the fleet the first time," Tex said. "Wanted to fly a Nighthawk. My folks thought I was crazy. Told 'em I didn't want to wake up at sixty-three and regret not following my dream. 'You won't have to worry about waking up at sixty-three,' they told me. 'You won't make it to thirty-six flying one of them things.' Well, the way I see it, I've already made it to thirty-six, so I don't have to worry about that no more."

Coda grinned. "My mom said something similar when I joined up."

"Mine too," Noodle said. "They wanted me to go to school. Get one of those advanced robotic manufacturing jobs Captain Hughes was always talking about. I couldn't do it, though. The drones were just too damn cool."

"They never did it for me," Tex said. "I was actually in the strike fighter program before they shut it down. Had a chance to be one of the first drone pilots. But like you said, I just couldn't do it. I wanted to *fly*. So when the opportunity came again, I couldn't pass it up."

"But the front..." Squawks said.

"Ain't as glorious as they make it out to be," Tex said. "'Specially for a marine transport pilot. I'd be on the same shit planet, eating the same shit food, sleeping in the same shit housing, staring at the stars, wondering where my life had gone wrong. You don't know how good you got it here."

"I think you've been roughing it for too long," Squawks said, stirring his meat paste with a disgusted look.

Coda laughed with the rest of them. Still, he couldn't help but feel that Tex was right. The food wasn't *that* bad—and whatever Commander Coleman was packing into it was working. They were only about halfway through their training, and he was already working out with twice as much weight and had more than tripled the distance he ran on the treadmill while dropping his per-kilometer time by a third. He'd thought he was in great shape before, but any remaining baby fat had disappeared. Even Noodle, the skinniest person in their squadron, had noticeably filled out.

But it was more than that. Coda had no way to confirm it, but he felt as though his reaction and processing times had improved too. Not to mention his recovery periods. Every day, he was growing faster, stronger, and smarter. To top it all off, they were being trained by the great Commander Coleman himself.

*Yeah, Tex is definitely right. The members of the Forgotten don't have it bad at all.*

That night after their evening debriefing, Commander Coleman told them that because the squadron had shrunk by half, they no longer needed four barracks, and ordered them to reassemble in Barracks One and Two.

Coda groaned. Even though it had only been a day and a half since the other pilots had left, he'd started growing accustomed to the extra space and relative privacy.

*At least I'm in Barracks Two and don't have to move.*

Tex was one of the first pilots to make his way into their barracks. He pointed to the open bunk once occupied by Uno. "You mind?"

Something told Coda that the older man hadn't connected with any of the other pilots in the squadron, likely because of his age and unique background, but he was still reluctant to give up Uno's place in their quartet so easily. To Coda's surprise, though, Squawks answered first.

"It's all yours," he said. "But only if you promise to tell us some stories from the front."

Tex gave him a small laugh and nodded. "Deal. But I ain't gonna promise they'll be interesting."

# 25

*Ready Room, SAS* Jamestown
*Alpha Centauri System, Proxima B, High Orbit*

TEX WAS THE FIRST OF THEIR NEWLY FORMED QUARTET TO FLY AFTER CODA, and the older pilot was what Squawks called "a real hoot to listen to." Every increase in speed and high-g maneuver was accompanied by a hoot, yee-haw, or woo-hoo, and it got so bad that the commander had to tell him to cut the chatter. But that night during their group evaluation, Commander Coleman hadn't been able to keep from smiling with the rest of them.

"Tex was obviously meant to be in the cockpit," Commander Coleman said. "And his excitement is infectious. But if you're going to hoot and holler, Tex, do so off the radio, and make sure you don't miss a critical order."

"Yes, sir," Tex said.

"But I'm glad you're having fun."

Noodle went up after him, and the slender pilot earned high praise from the commander, even if Noodle secretly believed he didn't deserve it.

"I couldn't decide if I wanted to throw up or wet myself," he had said after the flight.

"When?" Squawks asked.

"During all of it," Noodle said. "You don't know what it's like. It's nothing like the simulator; that's for sure."

Squawks just laughed and called him a wuss, but Coda could see that under the bravado, their friend was growing increasingly uneasy. When it was Squawks's turn to go up, Noodle and Coda gathered together in the ready room to listen in. They weren't the only ones, either. Moscow and his gang were hanging out in the back of the auditorium, keeping to themselves.

Since the uneasy truce had been made in the simulator, Coda hadn't had much interaction with Moscow or his gang, and it was a welcomed change since it provided him with fewer distractions.

"All right, Squawks," Commander Coleman's voice said over the ready room speakers, "well done today. Let's bring it in."

"Roger that, sir," Squawks said, his pride barely masked behind military decorum. By all indications, his flight had gone well. Like Coda and Noodle, he'd been able to perform the basic flight maneuvers they'd mastered in the simulator, but as Coda had already found out, when it came to performing a hands-on landing aboard a moving vessel in high orbit, there was a canyon of difference between the simulator and the real thing.

The seconds ticking by, Coda listened to the commander's instruction, piecing together the landing sequence in his mind's eye. Squawks would be parallel to the *Jamestown* by now, ready to begin his landing procedure.

"Squawks, you're a kilometer out. Call the ball."

"Roger that. I have the ball."

Coda slid to the edge of his seat, growing increasingly nervous. This was the most difficult part of the landing sequence, and Squawks was already muttering curses under his breath.

"You're too shallow, Squawks," Commander Coleman said. "Just like in the simulator. Keep the two together, and you'll be fine."

"Copy that, sir," Squawks said, though Coda thought he could hear panic in his voice.

"You're still too shallow, Squawks," Commander Coleman said a few seconds later. "Abort and prepare to circle back for another pass."

"Negative, sir," Squawks said. "I've got this."

"Lieutenant—"

"Almost there, sir."

"Pull up, Lieutenant. Pull up. Squawks, pull up. Pull up! Pull up! Pull up!" Commander Coleman's shouts were followed by an eerie silence.

Silent seconds ticked by, the quiet punctuated only by Commander Coleman's heavy breathing. Coda didn't move, didn't think, fearing the worst.

Had Squawks successfully landed or had he crashed into the side of the *Jamestown*? Would they have felt the impact? Heard the explosion? Or would it be the equivalent of hitting a bug on the freeway, a nuisance that would have to be washed off when it was convenient?

Then he heard it. The faint voice of his friend.

"Oh my god, oh my god, oh my god."

"Oh my god is right." Noodle ran a hand across his closely shaven scalp. "What just happened?"

"Your friend is rubbing off on him," Moscow said, striding down the auditorium stairs. "It's the O'Neil curse."

His emotions already flying high, Coda seethed. His feud with Moscow might have taken on a different tenor lately, but that didn't undo the months of comments, digs, and verbal jabs. Before Coda could reply, Moscow and his gang continued down the stairs, leaving the ready room behind.

"I'm seriously going to kick that guy's ass someday," Noodle said.

"Don't worry about it," Coda said, his words at odds with his emotions. He wanted nothing more than to let Noodle kick Moscow's teeth in—hell, he wanted to do it himself—but he was tired of his temper turning him into a failure.

"You're just going to let him get away with it?"

"We're supposed to be part of the same squadron, Noodle. Fighting him won't do any good. It'll just make it worse."

Noodle stared at him as if he had just turned into a Baranyk. "What happened to you?"

"Nothing."

"He and his gang get to you? Push you into an empty room and have their way with you?"

Coda's anger was quickly moving from Moscow to Noodle. If he wasn't careful, he'd take it out on his friend. "Drop it."

"The commander talk to you? Tell you to bury the hatchet?"

Coda let out a sharp breath, less because Noodle was right, and more because he was being such a persistent little asshole.

"He did, didn't he?" Noodle said. "What did he say?"

"It doesn't matter."

"The hell it doesn't. Look, Coda, you tell me to sic him, and I'll bite his leg like a Jack Russell terrier. If you tell me to stand down, I'll do that too. Just tell me why."

Coda imagined Noodle with his teeth around Moscow's calf and had to hold back a smile. "Then as my friend, listen to me when I say don't worry about him. Moscow's an ass, but..."

"But what? Coda, I don't know what the hell happened, but you spent every day fighting with that guy for months, and now you're defending him? What changed? What do you know that I don't?"

Coda drew in a deep breath. "Let's just say I understand where he's coming from."

"Coda—"

"It's not my story to tell. Okay? Just drop it."

Noodle snapped his mouth shut and looked away, irritated. That was fine as far as Coda was concerned. Noodle could be mad. He could even think that Coda was defending Moscow. Anything was better than having the squadron know that Coda's father was responsible for Moscow's mother's death. That would drive a wedge between him and everyone else in the squadron so deep that there would be no recovering from it. And at that point, the commander wouldn't have to choose between Moscow and Coda. The squadron would choose for him.

---

THE NEARLY BOTCHED LANDING EARNED SQUAWKS THE FIRST SOD IN THE squadron. If he got two more, he would be expelled entirely. For nearly a day and a half, he steamed, running landing simulation after landing simulation, obsessing over the mistake. Tex had tried to help him through it by sharing stories about his own experiences and offering small tips and tricks that he'd learned over the years, but Squawks made it abundantly clear that he wanted none of it.

His mood only improved when other pilots had similar issues. Fortunately for him, the mistakes weren't uncommon. Of the fifty remaining pilots, nearly one third had to abort their approach and try again, and of them, nearly half failed to accomplish a clean landing on the second attempt. Squawks hadn't flown the cleanest, but he wasn't the worst, either, and for the time being, that seemed to be enough for him.

As the weeks wore on, Coda settled into his new routine. Because the squadron had only two instructors, he was lucky to go up every other day, so when he wasn't in class or at the gym, he spent most of his time in the simulator. But after he'd tasted the real thing, simulated flying couldn't scratch the itch. Flying had become a drug and he needed his fix.

When he had gone up the second time, the commander spent the first part of the training session putting him through the same basic flight maneuvers and critiquing him on the finer details, but they spent the majority of their time doing touch-and-go landings aboard the *Jamestown*. Coda flew approach after approach, getting ten for the price of one. It was terrifying work, but by the end of the fourth week Coda could approach without pissing himself.

Once each of the pilots had gone up twice, they began group instruction, flying courses and beginning formations. Then, when the commander was confident they wouldn't accidentally crash into each other, began dogfighting.

Their only reprieve was that their flights were no longer scored and tiered. They had progressed to a review phase, and as Commander Coleman and Lieutenant Commander Chavez had done during one-on-one post-Simulation debriefings, they instructed the pilots instead of graded them. But like all breaks, Coda knew it wouldn't last.

# 26

*Commander Coleman's Quarters, SAS* Jamestown
*Alpha Centauri System, Proxima B, High Orbit*

CODA TOOK A DEEP BREATH, STRAIGHTENED HIS UNIFORM, AND KNOCKED ON Commander Coleman's door.

"Come in," Commander Coleman said as the door slid open. Coda stepped in and snapped to attention. "At ease. And have a seat." The commander gestured at the unoccupied armchair opposite the one the commander had obviously been sitting in.

Coda sat. Commander Coleman had turned his back to Coda and fumbled with something on his bookcase. His eyes drifting from the commander to the small room, Coda made a mental note that it was the second time he had been summoned to the commander's personal quarters, and for the first time, he realized the older man didn't have a personal office.

The realization surprised him. Commander Coleman was a true, real-life war hero on a secret mission to construct a squadron that might very well save humanity, and he couldn't even get a personal office? Secrecy, it appeared, didn't afford luxuries.

When the commander turned around, he was holding two glasses, one filled with a brown liquid, the other with water. He handed the one filled with water to Coda and sat down in the chair across from him.

"Thank you, sir," Coda said, oddly thankful he wasn't holding the glass with the alcohol. It wasn't that he wasn't of age—he was, even if the United States federal government hadn't long since lowered the drinking age for all enlisted personnel to eighteen years old. Drinking hadn't been accepted at the academy, and despite stories of fighter jocks being heavy-drinking womanizers, Coda's experience in the Forgotten had been very different—though he supposed that was likely due to their equally different training circumstances.

"You're doing well," Commander Coleman said, leveling his gaze on him. "You completed FAM Phase by the skin of your teeth, but you were near the top of your class in the simulator, and you've made the transition to real flight look surprisingly easy."

Coda let the smile wash over his face but played it modest. "I don't know about easy, sir."

"Oh?" Commander Coleman took a sip. "Then tell me how you're feeling."

"I feel good, sir. Confident."

"That's good. A timid pilot is a danger to themselves and everyone they fly with."

Coda felt a stab of guilt as his mind wandered to Uno. A lack of confidence had been his friend's undoing. It had rendered him slow and tentative—"mechanical," as Uno had put it. Perhaps the commander was right.

"You don't have to worry about that with me, sir. I feel... at home out there."

Commander Coleman took another sip, his eyes never leaving Coda. "Is that why you're here?"

Coda cocked his head to the side, caught off guard by the question. What was the Commander really asking? "I'm here to become the best fighter pilot in the squadron and protect the fleet, sir."

"No." Commander Coleman shook his head. "Not *here*. I mean here, fighting in this war."

Coda stalled, taking a sip of his water. He hadn't openly expressed his feelings on too many occasions, though they probably wouldn't come as any great surprise, either. After all, Buster had guessed his true motivations, and he hadn't exactly the fastest ship in the hangar. Would it help his cause if the commander knew the truth?

Commander Coleman had flown with his father and had spoken highly of him. Maybe in this instance, separating himself from his father would be counterproductive.

"You obviously know my father's story," Coda said, deciding to take the chance.

Commander Coleman nodded. "It couldn't have been easy growing up under that shadow."

"It wasn't," Coda agreed. "Though it wasn't as bad at home as it was at the academy. Either way, when I'm done, the O'Neil name won't be something to be cursed. It'll be celebrated. Revered."

"You want to be a hero."

"No." Coda shook his head. "I don't *want* to be a hero. I want to restore honor to my family name. Being a hero is just the quickest way to do it."

"That's a very noble goal."

Coda shrugged. Something about the way Commander Coleman had spoken the words made Coda uncertain if the other man truly meant them or if the commander was somehow poking fun at him.

"You know I flew with him."

"That's what you said, sir."

"The man I knew and the man the world *thinks* it knows are very different."

Coda shifted uneasily. Having someone suggest that the person he'd despised his entire life was actually a good person was discomforting. More than discomforting. It went against every mental image he'd crafted of his father and threatened to destroy the entire world he'd built atop it.

"Unfortunately," Coda said, "the man I knew was closer to what everyone else sees."

That wasn't entirely true. Coda had many fond memories of his father: playing catch in the backyard, going to the zoo, sitting in the cockpit of his father's Nighthawk. But the pain caused by his father's betrayal greatly outweighed whatever positive feelings he felt for the man.

Commander Coleman leaned back in his seat, pursing his lips. Coda was growing increasingly confused by how well the commander had known his father and just how close they had been. Coda wasn't interested in getting to the bottom of it at the moment. He wasn't there to talk about this father. He decided to change the subject before the commander had a chance to muster up his response.

"Why are *you* here, sir? What's a decorated war hero doing on an ancient ship flying patrol over a worthless mining colony?"

"I'm here to assemble the best fighter squadron known to man and protect the fleet."

It was obviously a play on Coda's politically correct response, and hearing it from the commander helped him realize just how ridiculous it really sounded. Because the commander had said it without even the hint of a smile, Coda took his true meaning. Commander Coleman wasn't going to tell him a damn thing.

"The truth is, Lieutenant," Commander Coleman continued, "even though this squadron has surpassed even my wildest expectations, it's still woefully behind the schedule the fleet needs us on. As much as I would like to continue with basic flight maneuvers and formations for another month, we simply don't have the time. We need to move forward."

Commander Coleman set down his drink then slid his tablet across the table and gestured for Coda to take a look at it.

"What's this, sir?"

"Your flight."

A "flight" was a smaller subset of fighters from the same squadron, numbering anywhere from four to six. What a squadron was to a wing, a flight was to a squadron.

"This is where the training gets fun, Lieutenant. For the next three months, we're playing war games, and for this mission, I want you to lead other pilots. Assuming you want to, of course."

Coda looked up from the names on the tablet. "Yes, sir. Of course." His eyes went back to the terminal. "But this list... Surely you don't mean..."

"Don't mean what?"

Coda's eyes fell back to the tablet. At the top of the list was Moscow's name. Commander Coleman not only expected them to work together in the same flight, but he expected Moscow to follow Coda's orders. It was almost laughable. But how could he say so?

"Is there a problem, Lieutenant?"

"No," Coda said. "It's just that... well... I think we'd be more successful if I had Noodle and Squawks under my command."

"Which is exactly why I didn't put them there. The squadron needs to fight as a single unit, and that means you must be comfortable flying with *everyone* inside it. More than that, you need to know, in intimate detail, the strengths and weaknesses of everyone around you. That's not possible if you only surround yourself with your friends."

Coda bit his tongue. The Commander was right, of course. Why else had Coda been taking notes on every pilot in the squadron?

"You'll get a chance to fly with your friends," Commander Coleman continued. "There are no set rosters here, not yet. Not until the squadron gets closer to its final number. For now, the pilots that make up each flight will change with every mission. And the person giving orders will change with every mission as well. For now, at least."

"What kind of missions, sir?"

"They'll be simple at first," Commander Coleman said. "Flight versus flight. Basic combat. But after a while, they'll get increasingly complex. Multiple objectives. Stacked odds. Scenarios you can expect on the front."

"When will they start?"

Commander Coleman grinned. "Your pilots are already waiting for you, Lieutenant. Launch is at nineteen hundred."

# 27

*Simulator, SAS* Jamestown

*Alpha Centauri System, Proxima B, High Orbit*

The five pilots that made up Coda's flight were already waiting for him in the Simulation Room when he arrived. If they were surprised to see him, they didn't show it, so Coda assumed they'd received their orders separately and had known to expect him as their leader.

Moscow was there, of course, watching Coda with an expression that he couldn't place. Joining him were Tex and Bear, Reno and NoNo. The only thing he knew of the latter two was that they had performed well in the simulator, finishing in the top thirty overall, and had both been reassigned from drone squadrons on the front.

*At least Commander Coleman isn't giving me a completely green flight.*

"Good morning," Coda said. "Our hop is in two hours. The details are unclear, but our objective is simple: destroy all enemy fighters. Your flight information has already been downloaded to your personal tablets. Read it. Memorize it. Preflight is in one hour. Any questions?"

There weren't any.

"All right. Let's get warmed up."

Coda loaded Reno and NoNo into the simulator first, keying in a scenario that had them flying as a fighter pair against an enemy force outnumbering them three to one. Coupled with the notes he'd taken from their previous simulations, he intended to study their flight patterns and better understand who he was flying with.

Both pilots were deft—even if NoNo had a bit of a habit of shouting, "No! No! No!" when things got hairy—and made short order of the enemy fighters, falling effortlessly into working as a pair. That had likely become second nature to them while on the front, where the drone squadrons flew in complex, highly coordinated formations. To them, staying on the wing of their wingmen was as natural as breathing.

Coda ran Moscow and Bear through the simulator next, with the former flying lead. They weren't nearly so smooth, lacking the training and experience that Reno and NoNo had benefited from, but they weren't completely clueless, either. Having spent dozens of extra hours in the simulator flying with each other, they knew each other's styles well, even if their instincts were often at odds with one another.

He didn't have time to run through the simulation with Tex, so rather than have the other man fly his wing, Coda opted for another strategy. If the others were his scalpels, cutting into the enemy with precise, synchronized attacks, then Tex would be his bat, ready to crush any unfortunate fighters flying into his strike zone.

An hour before flight, they began their preflight routine. Commander Coleman sat in the ready room but made no effort to instruct, direct, or review their preflight information. Coda stepped into the role, ensuring that each of his pilots had memorized their flight information and that there wouldn't be any accidents. After they'd confirmed their information, they stepped into the locker room and suited up. By 1850, they were climbing into their cockpits, ready to be loaded into the launch tubes. Once loaded, Coda radioed his pilots and had them perform systems checks.

"All right, *Jamestown* Tower," Coda said after everyone had confirmed they were green across the board. "We are go for launch.

"Copy that, Coda," the tower said. "You are go for launch at quarter-second intervals. Prepare for launch in five, four, three..."

Coda didn't listen to the rest. He settled into his seat, waiting for the sudden but welcomed g-forces to slam into his body like a stack of bricks. Maybe it was because of his time in the gym. Maybe it was the growth hormones that strengthened his body from the inside out. Or maybe it was just his state of mind. But no matter the reason, when the forces came, they wrapped him like a warm blanket, comforting him.

He'd been anxious before. Now he was calm. At peace. The commander was right. Flying was in his blood. He was born for this.

# 28

*Cockpit, Nighthawk*
*Alpha Centauri System, Proxima B*

Six X-23 Nighthawks shot out of the bow of the *Jamestown*, entering space at quarter-second intervals. It took one-point-five seconds from the time the first fighter entered space to the last.

"All right," Coda said, plotting a course that moved them away from the *Jamestown* toward the coordinates outlined in the mission briefing. "Form up, and keep your eyes peeled. They're out here somewhere."

Silence stretched out before them, interrupted only by the slight rumble of their Shaw Drive thrusters and the soft sounds of breathing through Coda's helmet speakers. The sea of stars and image of the ever-shrinking orange globe behind them might have been relaxing if they hadn't been flying into battle.

"Contact!" NoNo bellowed as a group of red dots appeared on Coda's HUD. "I've got six bogeys, negative-Z twelve degrees. Thirty thousand kilometers and closing."

Coda adjusted the battle map in his HUD, switching the battle plane from the original plane to the new one between his fighters and the enemy bogeys. Once completed, he sent it to the rest of his flight, using his power as flight leader to automatically switch theirs, ensuring they all continued to operate under the same information.

"Copy, NoNo. Let's go get 'em." Coda brought his fighter into an intercept course with the incoming enemy, the rest of his flight falling into formation behind him. "Fighter pairs. Just like we practiced. Tex, you and I will play centerfield."

Several affirmatives came through the coms at once, and Coda dug himself deeper into the gel seat. He had three seconds before the enemy vessels were in firing range, but since they were on a direct heading, their combined speed prevented missile lock. It was all guns.

"Let's see if we can break them up," Coda said. "Fox-four!"

Coda thumbed the firing switch to guns and pulled the trigger. The cockpit came alive, rumbling as the nose-mounted M-66 cannon hurled thirty-millimeter rounds at the incoming enemy to the tune of four thousand rounds per minute. They were simulated rounds, of course, all tracked and cataloged by their onboard computers, but the effect felt very, very real.

The X-23 held only three hundred rounds, so he kept his trigger finger light, shooting in controlled bursts that lasted only a fraction of a second. The firing bursts had their desired effect, and two seconds from contact, the enemy formation broke apart. Two fighter pairs broke off in opposite directions, veering to the three- and nine-o'clock positions relative to Coda's incoming squadron. The last pair held course, splitting Coda's formation down the center.

"Break!" Coda bellowed, and as one, his formation broke apart.

Reno and NoNo who had taken the dash-3 and -4 positions directly behind Coda's portside wing, brougt their fighters around and went after the bogey that had veered off to their left. Moscow and Bear mirrored their movement, going after the fighter to their right, while Coda and Tex dove above and below the battle plane, taking opposite routes but both making for the third pair that had split their formation.

The g-forces were incredible, slamming Coda into his gel seat hard enough that black spots crept into his vision. Coda's G-suit tightened in response, constricting around his extremities, preventing his blood from rushing out of his brain. Without the suit, he would have lost consciousness; instead, he felt as though he were being squeezed in an old trash compactor. It was uncomfortable, but he was alert.

Completing the turn, Coda found that the enemy fighter pair had broken apart, making for opposite ends of the battle. Coda keyed on the nearest one. The pilot brought the fighter around level with the battle plane. The angle left Coda's flank open, and if he had been any slower, the enemy fighter would have managed missile lock. Instead, Coda brought his fighter around, setting himself up on another head-on course.

As he and the other fighter sped toward each other, Coda opened fire, forcing the enemy fighter to dive below the battle plane to avoid the incoming slugs. Coda threw the stick forward then barrel-rolled, bringing his fighter directly behind the other. The steady, single note of missile lock sounded in Coda's ears.

"Hawk One, Fox Two," Coda said, squeezing the trigger. A yellow blip appeared on his HUD, shooting toward the enemy fighter. Half a second later, the fighter's cockpit lights went dark, and the fighter disappeared from the battle map. "Splash one!"

The enemy fighter vanquished, Coda reassessed the battle map just as another enemy fighter disappeared from the battle map.

"Splash two!" Moscow shouted.

He and Bear harried the lone fighter left of their original battle pair while Reno and NoNo were involved in a series of complex flight maneuvers with the second pair struggling to gain the advantage.

"Keep it tight!" Reno yelled. "Don't get acute!"

Acute meant Reno's wingman was too wide to be in firing position. A quick glance at his HUD showed that Reno was manipulating the enemy's flight course in a tactic as old as aerial combat. Time-tested and time-approved, it was still the foundational tactic of space combat.

"You're too acute, NoNo! You're too acute! Goddamn it! Break off and come back around."

"We've got a tail, Bear!" Moscow shouted. "You see it?"

"Uh..." Coda could almost hear Bear processing the information on her battle map. Precious moments ticked by as she searched for the enemy vessel. "Oh, no! It's coming around on our tail. Moscow, it's on our asses."

"Break formation," Moscow said. "See if you can draw it off. I'll stay on this one. Tex, I think it's time you brought your bat."

"Copy that, Moscow," Tex said. "I've got your back."

Coda grinned. His loose strategy had so far proved effective. Now it was up to the individual pilots themselves to ensure their victory.

Bear's fighter altered course, attempting to draw the incoming enemy vessel away, but to everyone's surprise, he stayed on Moscow.

"Tex!" Moscow shouted. "Tex, I need—"

"On it," Tex said. "Three seconds."

"I don't have three seconds." Moscow darted left and right in a series of evasive maneuvers, delaying the inevitable, all while trying to keep the other enemy fighter in his sights. "He's almost got missile lock! Tex, where the hell are you?"

Before Tex could respond, the red marker on Coda's HUD suddenly disappeared.

"Splash three!" Tex shouted. "You're clear, Moscow. I repeat, you're clear."

"Nice shooting, Tex," Moscow said, relief palpable in his voice. "Bear, you still out there?"

"Still here, Moscow."

"Good. I'm sending updated vector information now. We can't let Coda and Tex have all the fun. There's only three left."

"Copy that."

Coda let the words wash over him, keeping his eyes on the larger battle, never listening to any one thing. There was too much going on, too much to keep track of. He had to trust that his brain was able to keep it organized and prioritize what needed to be prioritized. That was easier said than done, though.

Coda screamed as two fighters cut upward through the battle plane, only meters from the nose of his Nighthawk. The thrusters of the other craft cooked the glass of his cockpit, skyrocketing the temperature inside to a near boil. Coda glanced back at the battle map to make sure he wasn't about to become an improbable casualty of a space collision—and saw how truly messy the battle was.

The battle was like a knot that had been tied over itself again and again, the fighters pulling the ends of the string tighter and tighter. In the infiniteness of space, the battle became a single point of violence less than twenty kilometers in the diameter—something impossibly small at their speeds.

Still recovering from the near collision, Coda didn't notice the enemy fighter opening fire. By nothing more than an impossible stroke of luck, the digital projectiles missed, and the enemy fighter zipped past him, but not before Coda caught a single important detail.

Where the wings of both flights were accented with the gold of the Sol Fleet, this one was accented with red. Unlike the rest of the pilots in the squadron, this pilot had earned his colors—he'd shot down enemy fighters. He'd fought real battles. Had drawn real blood. The enemy fighter was piloted by none other than Commander Coleman himself.

# 29

*Cockpit, Nighthawk*
*Alpha Centauri System, Proxima B*

Coda watched as Commander Coleman brought his fighter around, angling for another pass. Such were the ways of fighter combat, both pilots attempting to outmaneuver the other, often making several runs until one of them made a mistake. Unfortunately, Coda knew that if either of them was going to make a mistake, it would be him. If he stood any shot at defeating the commander, he needed help.

"Tex," Coda said, "where are you at?"

"Occupied."

"I'm going to need a hand over here."

"Bite off more than you could chew?"

"You could say that."

"Fifteen seconds."

"Negative," Coda said. "This one's too important. Break off and meet me..." Coda keyed in on a point on his HUD and sent the coordinates to Tex. "There."

Tex sighed. "Breaking off. Rendezvous in six seconds."

Coda cursed silently. Even six seconds was too long. He and

Commander Coleman would be coming around for another pass by then, and already, the commander's more precise flight paths were giving him the advantage. He would have Coda dead in his sights before Tex could come to his aid. Worse, if Coda broke off his attack and tried to run the commander would have a clear path to his six.

*This is why you don't fly solo.* Then again, the commander was flying solo too, and that gave him a chance. *In theory.*

Coda and Commander Coleman's fighters raced toward each other. Coda squeezed the trigger again, loosing another triple burst. But unlike the nugget pilot, Commander Coleman didn't flinch. The commander mirrored Coda's strategy, letting off a burst of his own. Both pilots missed, their fighters zipping past each other faster than their eyes could register.

Coda started his turn almost immediately. Eyeing his HUD, he saw the commander doing the same.

"Tex?"

"Coming. Hang on."

"Trying..." Coda's voice was strained by the excessive G's of the turn. "He's closing... Tex... the commander..."

"Say again, Coda," Tex said. "The commander? You want me to fire at the commander?"

"Yes!"

"This is going to be fun."

Coda leveled off and turned, adjusting course to come around into another pass, but the commander had already completed his maneuver and was coming in on Coda's flank. He would have missile lock any moment.

Coda's Hornet training took over. He threw the joystick to the side, rolling his fighter in a series of tight corkscrews, then with his wings perpendicular to the battle plane, he pulled back, performing a tight high-g turn.

The yellow indicator of a missile appeared on Coda's HUD.

Shoved hard against the gel seat, he prepared to drop his chaff. At worst, the debris would cloud Commander Coleman's missile sensors, hindering its ability to target Coda. At best, the missile would explode against one of the sand particles.

But he never had a chance. Even his G-suit couldn't keep him from blacking out during the high-g maneuver. The last thing he saw was the yellow indicator racing toward him.

He had no idea how long he was out. It could have been a second, an hour, or anything in between. When he returned to consciousness, his head pounded as blood returned to the places it should have been. But with every throbbing pulse, Coda's awareness grew.

He still had controls. By some miracle, his fighter was still operable.

And someone was screaming. No... they were yelling. Moscow. It was Moscow. Why would Moscow be yelling?

Coda blinked, trying to focus. The yellow blip of the missile was gone, as was Tex's fighter, but so was the red marker of the commander. Trying to shake away the remaining cobwebs, Coda worked to make sense of the situation. Something was wrong. Coda had been dead in Commander Coleman's sights.

*Unless...*

Moscow's shouts suddenly made more sense. Lieutenant Andrei "Moscow" Krylov, Coda's former rival at the Terran Fleet Academy, had just eliminated Commander Coleman and saved Coda's ass in the process.

Coda wanted to be sick.

# 30

*Hangar Deck, SAS* Jamestown

*Alpha Centauri System, Proxima B, High Orbit*

A crowd of people was waiting in the hangar as Coda and the rest of the flight arrived. They clapped and cheered as the victorious pilots cracked their cockpits and removed their helmets. The pilots pumped their fists and yelled excitedly in return, celebrating their first win as a unit.

When Moscow took off his helmet, the crowd erupted, and the few people who weren't already around his fighter flocked to it. There was no doubt who the crowd thought the hero of the battle was, and Moscow basked in it. He stood on top of his seat, hollering back at his screaming admirers like a rock star trying to make his audience earn an encore.

Coda removed his own helmet and gloves without fanfare. Except for the specialist who rolled over a ladder so that he could climb out of his starfighter, nobody even seemed to realize he was there. He struggled to swallow the bitter lump in his throat. The recognition Moscow was receiving was the same recognition he'd dreamed about since joining the academy.

Tex was the first to come to him, finding him as Coda began his post-flight visual inspection. "I'm sorry, Coda."

"For what?" Coda asked.

"You needed me, and I wasn't there."

Coda sighed and brushed off his hands. "To be honest, I don't even know what happened. I blacked out from the turn. The last thing I saw was the commander's missile headed my way."

"I took care of that then got the commander's attention before he could turn you into slag. That was a mistake, let me tell you. He's good, Coda, real good. Took care of me in no time. But that's when Moscow snuck up on him and took *him* out."

"Moscow left his wingman?"

"Reckon so."

Coda shot another look in Moscow's direction. He was stepping down the ladder, grinning and high-fiving his admirers. Leaving your wingman was a cardinal sin. Space was too large, too empty, the battles too chaotic for one person. The first pilots had long since learned that when facing that alone, they often ended up like... well, like Coda. An afterthought in battle—or worse. That he'd broken the first rule of flight cheapened Moscow's victory even more.

"You took out the commander's missile?" Coda asked.

Tex grinned, puffing out his chest. "Sure did."

"I'll have to check out the vid," Coda said. "That must have been a hell of a shot."

"Like shooting a can in the backyard."

Coda and Tex found Noodle and Squawks as they headed for the locker room. Even they were commiserating, regarding Coda and Tex as if Coda had lost, as if he'd failed. Coda wanted to scream. He might not have shot down the commander, but damn it, his flight had won! Beginning his breathing exercise, Coda slowly wrestled his emotions back under control. Then Moscow's voice cut through the din.

"You're welcome, O'Neil!"

Coda froze. Hearing Moscow call him out, hearing him address him by his last name took him straight back to their fight at the academy.

Turning, Coda locked eyes with Moscow. He couldn't be sure from the distance, but Moscow's sneer seemed to falter.

"For what?" Coda shouted back.

Moscow looked at the crowd gathered around him as if deciding whether pushing Coda was worth it. He must have decided it was, because when his gaze returned to Coda, so did his smirk. "For saving your ass."

Coda barked a sarcastic laugh then wiped the bottom of his nose with his thumb, starting toward him.

"Don't," Squawks said, attempting to grab him.

Coda ripped his arm from Squawks's grip.

Moscow started toward Coda, ready for his rematch, his admirers falling into step behind him. Moscow had at least twenty to Coda's four, but Coda didn't care. He had to wipe that patronizing sneer off Moscow's face.

Before he got his chance, the commander appeared between them. Still dressed in his flight suit, he stood like a rock ready to withstand the force of two incoming tidal waves. Coda and Moscow froze at the same time, their attention shifting from each other to the commander, who stood unfazed between them.

"Congratulations," Commander Coleman said, though his tone was anything but congratulatory. "It's not often a pilot takes down their instructor in their first battle. Let alone when that instructor is me. Well done, Moscow."

The jubilant atmosphere that had filled the hangar before returned, and Moscow was once again at the center of it. The crowd behind him shouted their praise, slapping him on the shoulders and back in congratulations. Moscow took it in, smiling, though his eyes never left Coda.

Commander Coleman turned his gaze from Moscow to Coda. "You flew well. Whether by skill or sheer dumb luck, you flew *together*. And that's how you're supposed to do it. Together. For each other." He appraised Moscow and Coda again, then apparently content with his ability to de-escalate the situation, he nodded. "Get out of those flight suits and shower up. Your debriefing starts in ten."

With that, the commander strode past Coda without a word, exiting the hangar. Moscow and Coda watched each other for several long seconds before Moscow inclined his head and turned back to his fighter, putting an end to the situation.

Coda started back toward the locker room.

"Well, that was close," Squawks said behind him.

Coda showered up, dressed, and grabbed a seat in the front row of the ready room. The rest of the flight's pilots joined him, and to his surprise, so did the rest of the squadron. The commander's evaluations were going to be a public as public could get.

Any remaining excitement from the flight quickly dissipated when the commander began his evaluation. He was ruthless, cutting into their strategy from every angle. Coda's initial plan had been sound, except Coda and Tex never should have been flying alone.

"Had you been paired up like the other fighters, you would have had me long before the second pass," Commander Coleman said, addressing Coda directly. "You have wingmen—use them. It's no mistake Reno and NoNo killed three fighters to your one. They flew together, and the other pilots didn't stand a chance."

Then he graded their speed, approach vectors, accuracy, flight maneuvers, and reaction times—and declared them all subpar. He grounded every pilot in their flight until they completed the updated exercises and scenarios he'd plugged into the simulator.

"And you will stay grounded," Commander Coleman continued, "until you've completed them to my satisfaction. Before the rest of you get too excited, I recommend you look at them too, because I expect you to learn from your fellow pilots. They were graded harshly today, but I assure you, the pilots who fly next will be graded even harder. And then harder after that. It's a moving goalpost, ladies and gentlemen, but I still expect you to get there."

That night at dinner, Coda watched as Moscow was surrounded by yet another group of admiring pilots. He was retelling the flight from his perspective, using his hands in place of fighters.

"You're going to drive yourself nuts comparing yourself to him," Noodle said.

"I'm not comparing myself to him," Coda said.

"Of course you're not," Squawks said. "I mean, why else would you stare at him your entire dinner?"

"I haven't been..." Coda's face grew hot. How long *had* he been watching him? "Whatever. I'm just trying to figure out why everyone is so infatuated with him all of a sudden. It's not like he shot down the most fighters."

"No," Noodle said. "He only shot down the best one."

"But it was still my strategy that made it happen."

"So?"

"So why is everyone all over him?"

"You mean why isn't everyone all over *you*?" Tex said. "What do you want, Coda? To win? Or to win glory?"

Coda stewed on the question long after dinner and lights out. He lay on his bunk, his curtain closed, wide-awake. The question had been more insightful than Coda would have expected from Tex, whose slow speech and deep-Southern drawl did little to suggest he offered much in the way of intelligence. But after knowing Coda for little more than a few days, Tex had understood the feeling that plagued Coda every day.

When the commander had asked him why he'd joined the Forgotten, the answer had been so clear. But for some reason, life didn't seem as simple as it had before. Things weren't as cut and dry. Even his feud with Moscow was confusing. Were things getting better or staying the same? He couldn't tell. And more than that, did he *want* them to get better?

*Questions, questions, questions. So many questions. What do I want? To win or to win glory?* And most perplexing of all, if he couldn't have both, which would he choose?

# 31

*Mess Hall, SAS* Jamestown
*Alpha Centauri System, Proxima B, High Orbit*

"YOU'RE DOING IT AGAIN," NOODLE SAID. THEN TO EVERYONE ELSE AT THE table, "He's doing it again."

"Yes, he is," Squawks said, his voice somewhere between amused and annoyed. "Hey! Dumbass!"

Something wet and slimy hit the side of Coda's face. He glanced down, saw a glob of food paste on the stainless-steel table, then looked up at Squawks, who was still holding his food-stained spoon, smiling wryly.

"What?" Coda snapped, grabbing his napkin and wiping the meat paste off his face.

"You're staring at him again." Squawks nodded toward Moscow, who sat on the other side of the mess hall. "It's getting creepy."

"I wasn't staring."

"You were staring," Noodle said.

"You looked like you were about to ask him to dance," Tex said.

"Got the hots for Moscow now?" Squawks joked. "Didn't think he was your type, but I guess he is kind of a celebrity now."

"Shut up," Coda said.

"Seriously, Coda," Squawks said. "You're obsessed. You need a hobby."

Coda snorted. "A hobby?"

"I'm not kidding, man. You may be a badass in the cockpit, but you're kind of a stick in the mud outside it."

"A stick in the mud?"

"Are you just going to repeat everything I say?" Squawks asked. "Yes, a stick in the mud. Boring. Dull. Someone who needs a life. And staring at Moscow like you're going to ask him to prom isn't helping."

Coda could feel his face growing red. He stirred his food absently. Squawks wasn't wrong, but Coda liked to think of himself as determined, not boring. He had a goal, and he wasn't going to stop striving for it until he achieved it. He didn't have time for anything else. It was as simple as that.

"And when am I going to find time for a hobby?" Coda asked defensively. "It's not like you guys have anything going on outside of our training, either."

"Are you serious?" Squawks asked, suddenly irritated. He turned to Noodle and Tex, who wore equally vexed expressions. "Is he being serious right now? God, Coda, you can damn near recognize someone by their flight patterns, but when it comes to everything else, you really are clueless, aren't you?"

"What are you talking about?"

"What do you think we do during our free time?"

"I don't know..." Now that Coda thought about it, since Uno's departure, their extra practices in the simulator had all but ended, and most nights during their free time, his friends *did* disappear. He'd never thought to ask where. He'd barely even noticed they were gone.

"Unreal, man. Tex has his own garden in hydroponics, growing carrots and potatoes and crap. And Noodle, you telling me you haven't seen him scribbling in his notebook? He's writing a book, man. By hand. Swords and dragons and all that nerdy stuff. *I'm* working on something more *communal*. Everyone has their own thing. Everyone but you. And it kind of sucks that you didn't know that."

Coda looked at the three of them as if seeing them for the first time. Squawks was right. He barely knew anything about them. He might call them friends, but they were anything but. They were his wingmen, his squad mates, and that was it. He'd known he'd built a wall around himself—he'd done that years ago—but he hadn't realized he hadn't entered anyone else's, either.

"I'm sorry," Coda said. "You're right. I am... Are you really writing a book, Noodle?"

His slender friend nodded, his face turning crimson.

"Mind if I read it sometime? I apparently need a hobby."

"No," Noodle said softly.

"No?" Coda raised an eyebrow. He hadn't expected to be rejected.

"Not until it's finished."

"All right. How long will that be?"

Noodle shrugged as if to say he had no idea. Since he clearly had no desire to talk about it, Coda turned to Tex. "And you, growing food. I thought you said this stuff wasn't so bad."

"It's not," Tex said. "But there's nothing better than fresh veggies."

Squawks snorted. "*Everything* is better than fresh veggies. Well, almost everything," he added, sticking his spoon back into the meat paste.

"I had no idea," Coda said. "I haven't been a good friend, and I'm—"

"Stop," Squawks said. "You don't need to baby us. Just get out of your own head sometime."

"All right."

For the remainder of lunch, Coda tried to play a larger role in the banter, but try as he might, his eyes kept drifting back to Moscow. He'd decided the night before to suck it up and bury the hatchet. And he meant to tell Moscow as much. So when Coda's friends finished and stood to return their trays into the washing dispenser, Coda made for Moscow.

Squawks groaned behind him. "He really is going to ask him to dance."

Ignoring the comment, Coda continued toward Moscow. He was sitting at another table with his friends, and they were laughing, in the middle of a story about how poorly the morning flight had gone. If the commander had heightened expectations following his pep talk the day before, then he must have been very disappointed with the morning's session.

Their laughter died away as they spotted Coda approaching. Bear nodded to him, her previous disdain having been damped down in their hours spent training together in the simulator. Moscow, however, smiled when he noticed Coda, and it wasn't an inviting thing.

"Can I talk to you?" Coda asked.

"Come to congratulate me on our victory yesterday?" Moscow asked. "Or maybe thank me for saving your bacon?"

Coda ground his teeth. *Why can't he make this easy?* "Something like that."

Moscow shrugged and rose from the table. Coda quickly led him out of the mess hall into an adjoining corridor.

"Look," Moscow said before Coda could start. "I'm just busting your balls, okay? Nothing personal. If you didn't take offense to everything, people might tone it down."

"That's good," Coda said, "because that's exactly what I wanted to talk to you about. This thing, this rivalry—it needs to stop. Because like it or not, we're two of the best pilots in this squadron, but even that won't guarantee our spot in the squadron. *If* we make it, then we have to trust each other, and we can't do that if we're constantly looking over our shoulders."

"Why wouldn't we both make it?"

"Huh?"

"If we're two of the best pilots, why wouldn't we both make it? Why would one of us get reassigned?"

"That's not the point," Coda said, trying to steer the conversation back to center. "I'm just saying—"

"It's not the point, but it's important. Why wouldn't we both make it?"

"Because there's a chasm in the middle of our squadron a mile wide, Moscow. We were about to go at it in the hangar and it wouldn't have just been us. It would have been your group and mine. It would have been a brawl."

"You sound like the commander."

"Well, he's right." Coda regretted the words the moment they left his mouth. Moscow was already suspicious, and the way Coda had phrased his reply left little doubt that he'd had help coming to the conclusions.

"You talked to him?" Moscow voice went quiet. "What did you talk about?"

"Nothing," Coda said. "He just told me to fix this."

Moscow eyed him as if deciding whether or not to believe him. Was he always this on guard? This suspicious?

Moscow shook his head. "And here I thought you were doing something honorable. Instead, you're just following orders."

"I was!" Coda said, exasperated. "I am. Damn it, Moscow, what's wrong with you? I'm trying to make life easier for both of us."

"Just stay away from me, O'Neil, and we'll be fine." Moscow started back toward the mess.

Coda grabbed his arm, stopping him. "It doesn't work that way, and you know it. Yes, I talked to the commander, and if we can't get this stuff worked out, one of us is going home."

"Then you better step up your game, Coda, because it ain't going to be me."

Moscow tried to pull away again, but Coda wasn't letting go. "Look, man, I know why you hate me, and I get it—"

"You don't know anything."

Coda had stepped on a land mine, and he knew it. He let out a long breath. "No, Moscow, I don't know everything, but I know enough. And for what it's worth, I'd hate me too. Hell, I already do."

Moscow's eyes blazed in anger. "Who told you?"

"Nobody," Coda lied. "And nobody else knows. Just me."

"You're lying."

"I'm serious. I was doing research on my father when I came across her name on a file. I'm s—"

"Don't!" Moscow shoved a finger in Coda's face. "Don't."

"Andrei..."

Moscow's hand became a fist, and for a second, Coda thought Moscow was going to hit him. Moscow regained control at the last moment, though, his fist falling to his side. "Stay away from me, O'Neil. If anyone finds out about this, I swear on my mother's grave, I *will* kill you."

"Fine," Coda said.

"I mean it, Coda."

Coda shrugged. "So do I."

They stared at each other for several moments. When Moscow

finally turned to go, Coda let out a long breath. *Maybe he's right. Maybe I just need to leave him alone.*

But even as he thought the words, Coda knew keeping his distance wouldn't be enough. He would never feel comfortable flying in a squadron where he knew someone hated him. Where someone wanted him dead. No, the commander was right. There was only enough room in the squadron for one of them. The only thing Coda could do was make sure that person was him.

# 32

*SAS* Jamestown

*Alpha Centauri System, Proxima B, High Orbit*

Avoiding Moscow proved to be simpler than Coda anticipated. With flights occurring every day, the squadron's previous schedule was thrown out the air lock. Workouts and classes on Baranyk physiology and biology were still required, and they still logged dozens of hours a week in the simulator, but all of those things came in at a distant second to logging time in their starfighters.

When they did occupy the same space, mostly during dining hours and squadron briefings, Coda didn't so much as even acknowledge Moscow's presence. And Moscow did the same. If the commander noticed the sudden change in how they stepped around each other, he didn't say anything.

As the days turned into weeks, Coda spent more and more time in the cockpit, flying hop after hop, sometimes as flight leader, sometimes not, sometimes as the flight with offensive objectives, sometimes as the defending force. And he dedicated himself to his training like never before. When he wasn't in the cockpit, he was in the simulator, and when he wasn't in the simulator, he was studying the recent flight vids, analyzing and learning from his fellow pilots. Squawks had said he needed a hobby, but that was a luxury Coda couldn't afford. Not yet.

He won, he lost, and he was shot down, but every hour of every day, he grew more confident. As his notebook filled up, he began to understand his wingmen like never before. He leveraged the knowledge when he was flying with them and exploited it when he was flying against them. Their flight strategies became as recognizable to him as their voice, their laugh, or even their walk.

After their fourth week of Nighthawk battles, the commander unveiled his new leaderboard. Coda wasn't surprised to find his name near the top but had to grind his teeth when he saw he was still trailing Moscow.

The commander never said as much, but Coda assumed it was because the quality of kills were weighted in the ranking. Shooting down a pilot who was in the bottom quarter didn't count as much as shooting down someone in the top or, for that matter, shooting down the commander himself. Moscow's kill of Commander Coleman continued to pay dividends, but Coda was gaining on him, and he knew that before long, he would knock his rival out of the top spot.

But seeing Moscow's name atop the leaderboard proved to Coda one thing above all else—try as he might, there was no way he could avoid Moscow forever. Sooner or later, their paths would cross again. What he didn't know was just how soon that would be.

Or that it would coincide with the first catastrophic training accident.

# 33

*Cockpit, Nighthawk*
*Alpha Centauri System, Proxima B*

Coda didn't know what he enjoyed more: the silence or the stars. The brief moments between sliding on his VR helmet and the following radio chatter had always been one of his favorite moments back at the academy. It offered freedom, as if he were floating on a pristine lake nestled somewhere deep in the heart of Earth. There was no responsibility, no rivalry, no fight to regain honor. There was... nothing. And because Coda knew the silence would never last, it was something to be cherished.

But those moments, like the simulator he'd experienced them through, had been artificial. Here, though, the silence was real, and it was unique. The absence of radio chatter was new, different, and unnerving. Not like the stars. They burned like distant embers, flashing and flickering blue, white, and gold. They called to him, inviting him to join them like beautiful sirens beckoning an old seafaring captain.

But both moments had one thing in common: they were always interrupted.

"Something feels different about this one," Squawks said. His voice was slightly muffled, cracking through the speakers of Coda's helmet.

"Forget your lucky underwear?" Noodle asked. It was the first time Coda had flown with the two of them together.

"No," Squawks said. "It isn't that. I've got them on, and I didn't wash them either."

"That's disgusting," Noodle said.

"Gotta keep the streak alive, you know?" Squawks added.

"What kind of streak are you talking about?" Tex asked.

"Okay, too far, too far," Noodle said. But he was laughing. Laughing was good. Laughing kept them loose. Because Squawks was right—something *did* feel different.

"Stay sharp," Coda said. "This one feels different because it's bigger."

He didn't necessarily believe his own words, but they seemed to sate the growing concern among his wingmen. Like all good lies, there was just enough truth sprinkled in to make it sound credible. Of course, it really was a bigger hop, the largest they'd flown yet, and unless Coda was mistaken, it was about to turn into a real mess.

He glanced at his HUD. Twelve fighters made up two flights of six. He was flight leader of Alpha Flight, Tex the flight leader of Bravo. Their recent hops had put them up against increasingly numerous enemies, often outnumbering them by fifty percent. If that trend continued, how many enemies could they expect today? Sixteen? Twenty? The latter would mean more than thirty Nighthawks in the entire engagement. Not a small number by any stretch.

At the moment, though, the HUD was empty, showing only the green indicators of the two flights and the Proxima B's moon to their left. Like Earth's moon, its surface was rough and littered with craters, though instead of the light gray that Coda was accustomed to, Theseus was a mix of reds and oranges, almost like the surface of Mars.

Coda eyed it closely. According to their mission detail, an enemy mining colony existed on the back side of the moon, but intelligence was spotty, and they didn't know the size of its defensive force. The primary mission was to scout the moon and relay the information to Command, but if the mining station was vulnerable, they were to take it out. In Coda's mind, that left only one option.

"Bravo One, Alpha One," Coda said. "Tex, you copy?"

"Loud and clear, Coda."

"You ready to see what they got cooking?"

"Is a frog's ass watertight?"

"Say again, Tex?"

"Does Howdy Doody have wooden balls?"

"Uh..."

"Yes, you dumb Yankee!"

"All right," Coda said, still more than a little confused. "Then take your flight around the moon, full burn, and we'll meet you on the other side."

"Sounds good, boss."

The green indicators marking Tex's flight on Coda's HUD veered away, darting toward the moon.

"All right, Alpha Flight," Coda said, "new coordinates coming your way. Keep the formation tight and stay on me."

A series of affirmatives came in through the radio, and Coda punched it, settling in on a course that would have him rendezvous with Tex's flight on the back side of the moon. The flight path brought them close enough to the moon that he could make out individual rock formations. Their red peaks glinted in the sunlight, hinting at the valuable metals beneath the surface. Like Proxima B, Theseus was critical to the Centauri system's mining operation, and being the closest star system to Sol, the operation was one of the most important in the fleet.

"Entering communications blackout," Tex said. "See you on the other side, Coda."

Since they didn't have access to the satellite system orbiting the moon, the moon's natural body would restrict their window of communication, creating dead zones proportionate to where the two forces were in relation to each other. For the next two minutes, each flight would be entirely alone.

"Acknowledged," Coda said. "Good luck."

The next two minutes felt like an eternity. Coda didn't know what to expect, and his imagination ran amok. He imagined the entire squadron waiting for them, thirty-eight fighters ready to take on Coda's twelve, and helmed by the commander himself. It would never happen, at least not this early in their training. Besides, Coda knew that his imagination was always worse than whatever reality held in store.

Except when it wasn't.

"Coda!" Tex's voice erupted on Coda's radio. "Coda! Goddamn it, can you hear me? Requesting immediate assistance! I repeat, immediate assistance!"

"Coda copies." He struggled to keep his voice even. "Approaching from the east, two degrees positive-Z in... fifteen seconds. I repeat, Alpha Flight, rendezvous in fifteen seconds."

"Hurry, Coda," Tex's voice came again. "They're on us like a pent-up bull."

Coda toggled his flight's private frequency. "Be alert and prepare for contact. We're coming in hot."

The curve of the moon blocked their view of the battle, but after a few moments, it came into focus. From the distance, it looked like little more than a swarm of mosquitos flying above a pool of water, but as they sped closer, Coda was able to take in the full situation. His HUD showed almost thirty contacts, and it was changing every second as green dots disappeared and more reds materialized. It was a true rat's nest, and even with Coda's flight, their total forces would still be outnumbered nearly two to one. Fortunately, despite the previous panic in Tex's voice, his flight appeared to be holding up better than expected.

The enemy had obviously known they were coming, but in space, there was only so much they could do to prepare. The enemy could come from any position, from any angle, at any time, and that meant defending forces were limited in the defensive measures they could prepare. Space combat had become a mano a mano fistfight built around three foundational pillars: track, deploy, and attack.

Coda had scratched off the first two. It was time to move to the third.

# 34

*Cockpit, Nighthawk*

*Alpha Centauri System, Theseus*

"FIGHTER PAIRS," CODA SAID. "TARGET THE PURSUING FIGHTERS FIRST. Let's get them off our friends' backs. Prepare to break in... three, two, one, break."

Coda's formation broke into three pairs. Squawks, who was in the dash-two position, was his wingman, and together, they zipped into the fray. Toggling his weapons switch, Coda ensured it was set to missiles and let his computer select a nearby enemy fighter harassing one of Bravo Flight's pilots. Then matching course, Coda performed a tight maneuver to get on its six.

"Bravo Four," Coda said. "Bravo Four, this is Alpha One. I've got your enemy in my sights. Prepare to break to positive-Z, six degrees in three. Acknowledge."

"Acknowledged, Coda," came the voice on the radio. "It sure is good to see you."

With the enemy fighter nearly in his sights, Coda didn't have time to chat. "Break!"

Bravo Four suddenly veered course, and as Coda expected, the enemy pilot took the bait. Moving to intercept, Coda waited for his targeting computer to get a lock. The X-23's anti-radar did its job, slipping missile lock like a banana peel in an old cartoon, but that would delay the inevitable for only so long.

After two more breaths, Coda had lock and fired his first missile. The yellow icon streaked toward the red indicator on this HUD, and a moment later, the enemy vessel disappeared from the battle map. In real life, the fighter went completely dark, save for its emergency markers as the ship's onboard computer steered it safely from the battle.

"Splash one!" Coda boomed into the radio.

"Thank you, Coda."

"No problem, Bravo Four. Let's get back in there."

Coda brought his fighter around in a wide arc, targeting the next fighter that had unwittingly opened up its flank to Coda's incoming vector. As quickly as Coda registered the opportunity, he got tone. Less than a second later, another missile was on its way.

"Splash two!"

Coda completed the arc and made for another pass through the knot of fighters. It was the equivalent of running through a swarm of yellow jackets. At breakneck speeds, fighters zipped in every direction. He and Squawks took out two more fighters before they erupted through the far edge.

Coda brought his fighter back around, preparing for another pass, then spotted an enemy fighter in pursuit. "Evasive maneuvers," Coda said.

Squawks split from Coda, pulling above the battle plane. The enemy stayed with Coda, moving into firing position.

"He's coming around on my six," Coda said. "Where are you, Squawks?"

"I've got you, Coda. Continue course."

Coda strafed left and right, weaving in and out of the edges of the dogfight, using its natural chaos to his advantage. Fighters were everywhere, blazing so fast that he barely had time to see them, let alone take evasive maneuvers to avoid a collision. He was nearly clipped more than once, and the encounters left him in a cold sweat. The commander had armed them with digital rounds and missiles, and he'd even put restrictions on speed and elevation as it pertained to the moon—there would be no canyon runs on this flight—but there was nothing the commander could do to prevent fighters from colliding with each other.

Despite his attempts to shake him, the enemy drew closer. "I can't hold him much longer, Squawks!"

"Two seconds."

An alarm claxon blared. Coda didn't have two seconds.

"Alpha Two!" Squawks shouted. "Fox Three. Bingo!"

The enemy indicator disappeared from Coda's HUD. "Good shooting, Squawks. I owe you one."

"Like shooting fish in a barrel, right, Tex?"

Tex's laughter echoed through the comm. "Easy as fallin' off a log."

"Whatever that means," Squawks said, reappearing on Coda's wing.

Coda focused his HUD, studying the mass of ships. "Squawks, break formation. It's not going to do us any good in there."

"The commander's going to have your ass," Squawks said, reminding Coda of the commander's disdain for fighters going at it alone.

"Break formation but follow my lead. Make it appear as if I'm a lone wolf and see who takes the bait."

"Copy that."

Squawks's fighter veered off perpendicular to Coda's, darting into the mass of fighters with complete disregard for his own safety. Coda followed a moment later, entering from a different angle.

Fighters zigged and zagged in every direction, moving faster than Coda could track, but though he'd been overwhelmed in his first two passes, the world seemed to slow now. His actions were measured, never rushed. His heartbeat remained within its resting boundaries. Again, he allowed the computer to analyze the various flight trajectories. This time, he let it select his targets for him.

Targeting brackets appeared around another enemy fighter. It moved more slowly than the rest, its movements timid, as if the pilot was afraid of making a mistake.

*Uno was right. He never would have made it out here.* Coda followed his target through the mass of fighters, recognizing the other pilot by her flight style. *Bear, how many times has the commander told you that speed is life?*

Getting into firing range took less than three seconds, and even then, seeing no reason to waste his missiles, Coda switched to guns. As the fighter moved into his crosshairs, Coda let off a quick double burst.

Bear's cockpit went black as she vanished from Coda's HUD. Coda didn't take any time to celebrate before moving on to the next target. He thumbed the switch back to missiles, then took out two more fighters before spotting an incoming third.

Pulling back on the stick, Coda darted above the battle plane, then rolled into a steep-pitch turn, and let the enemy craft fly beneath him. Then he pulled out of the turn directly behind the other fighter. The pilot never saw him coming.

"Splash twelve!" Coda boomed as its cockpit went dark. "Keep it going, boys. We've got them on the ropes now."

But Coda's celebration was interrupted as Squawks's voice cut through the rest of the radio chatter. "Coda, you've got company. Incoming bogeys. Ten o'clock, six degrees positive-Z."

Coda found the fighter pair on his HUD. "I see them."

"Move to intercept and hold course," Squawks said. "I'll provide cover."

"Acknowledged."

Coda pulled his fighter into a head-on course, daring the incoming fighters to engage. Tiny sparks shot from the front of the crafts as their cannons came alive. Coda fired his own bursts, but like the enemy fighters', his weren't effective. Squawks's cannons, however, were. He cut in from negative-z, taking out the enemy wingman from below.

"Sorry, Coda," he said as he zipped past the lead fighter. "Thought I could get both of them."

Coda had no time to respond. The incoming fighter was coming in too hot. Coda offset left, avoiding a collision as he and the other fighter passed each other in the black, then he pulled above the battle plane in a tight loop. Crossing over, Coda rolled out behind the other fighter, who was angling for another pass.

The other fighter saw his own mistake and increased speed to get away from Coda's pursuit. Only one pilot had the ability to recognize his own mistake so quickly: Moscow.

Grinning, Coda punched the throttle, going after the other fighter. He toggled his long-range targeting system, preparing to switch to the accompanying long-range missiles, but Moscow was too elusive. He ducked and dodged, flying dangerously close to other spacecraft, providing himself with cover, just as Coda had done before.

Coda kept pursuit, giving chase as if he were playing a childhood game of tag. And like those early games, it was only a matter of time before the pursuer gained the advantage. Little by little, Coda drew closer.

Moscow must have seen it too, because he suddenly veered off course, diving steeply below the battle plane in what looked like a reverse high yo-yo maneuver. At their increased speeds, Coda barely had time to replicate the maneuver...

And spot his mistake.

Moscow wasn't performing a high yo-yo—he was performing a high yo-yo *defense*. Where the first maneuver was designed to maintain speed, the high yo-yo defense was deceptive, allowing the defender to shed velocity and cause the pursuer to overshoot. Moscow was trying to force Coda in front of him, where he could turn the pursuer into the pursued. But it worked too well. Coda was coming in hot—way too hot.

Throwing the stick hard to the right, Coda tried to avoid colliding with Moscow's fighter. His nose missed, but a terrible shriek crossed the underbelly of his fighter. After a brief flash of light, Coda was spinning.

Up became down then down became forward as his fighter tumbled out of the fray. He had just enough time between spins to see Moscow's fighter spiraling out of the battle too, its starboard wing completely ripped away. A second flash illuminated the dark, this time brighter and tinged with orange.

An explosion.

*Oh god!* A third fighter had collided with the wreckage from Moscow's fighter.

"Mayday! Mayday!" the voice on the radio screamed. Coda couldn't tell who it was. "Multiple collisions. I repeat: multiple collisions. Send immediate recovery!"

Coda shut away the panicked voice. Multiple claxons in his cockpit told him he had more immediate problems of his own.

Quickly assessing the situation, he found the underbelly of his fighter had been breached, and the collision had knocked out several of his portside navigational thrusters. The cockpit was leaking oxygen and losing pressure, but his flight suit was designed to protect him in situations like that. Correcting the spin without full navigational thrusters would be much more difficult, though.

Worst of all, his HUD showed that he was well below the battle plane and streaking toward the moon. With no friction to slow him down, he was flying toward the moon at nearly the same speed that he had been flying in pursuit of Moscow. If he didn't correct it and fast, he would provide the moon with a brand-new crater. Fortunately, his onboard computer was still active, and the fighter's spin was correctable—even with his fighter's damaged thrusters.

Coda had the computer measure his spin and leveraged the autopilot to counter its rotation with several well-timed bursts. Almost immediately, he felt the spin subside, then quickly thereafter, it stopped altogether.

And that was when he saw it.

Like Coda, Moscow was streaking toward the moon's surface, but his fighter appeared to be entirely inoperable. Its cockpit and marker lights were completely dark, and there was no sign of its navigational thrusters. The X-23 was little more than battle debris caught up in the moon's gravitational pull.

"*Jamestown* Tower," Coda said. "Alpha One. What's the ETA on the recovery vessels?"

"Alpha One, *Jamestown* Tower. ETA in four minutes."

"Four minutes." Coda chewed on the words. Moscow didn't have four minutes. He didn't have anything even close to that. Unless Coda did something, it wouldn't be him that would be leaving a fresh crater on Theseus.

It would be Moscow.

# 35

*Cockpit, Nighthawk*
*Alpha Centauri System, Theseus*

Coda's first thought was to let Moscow fall, let his fighter crash into the surface of Proxima B's only moon. That would certainly solve many of his problems. No more rivalry. No more looking over his shoulder. No more trying to play nice with a man who wanted nothing of it. And Commander Coleman wouldn't have to choose between two of his best pilots—chance would do it for him.

But even as the thought came to him, Coda knew he couldn't let it happen. He wasn't wired that way. He hadn't grown up drowning in his father's misdeeds only to let something similar happen on his watch—regardless of how much he hated Moscow. Shoving the throttle forward, Coda directed his damaged fighter toward Moscow's.

Halfway there, he realized he had no idea what he would do once he got there. He didn't have any tow cables or anything to latch to Moscow's fighter that he could use to pull him to safety. What was he going to do?

*I'll crash into him again if I have to. Throw him off course. Wait...* That gave him an idea.

Coda adjusted his course. Rather than intercepting Moscow's spacecraft, he would arrive at a point *below* it. Only, no, that wouldn't be enough. He had to arrive well below Moscow's fighter in order to provide himself with enough time.

*That means I'll only get one shot at this.*

Well, if he was only going to get one shot at it, he had to give himself as much room for error as possible. Plotting a revised course, he settled into his seat, preparing himself for what would amount to little more than a suicide run.

*What are you doing, Coda? Why are you risking your life for the only person you hate more than your... The only person more than your father?*

That was it, wasn't it? He was willing to risk his life to save Moscow's because he had dedicated his entire military existence to undoing the damage his father had done. He couldn't undo the deaths, and he couldn't bring back Moscow's mother, but he could do everything he could to save her son.

"Charlie One, Charlie One, this is Alpha One. Do you copy?" Coda waited for a response, then when none came, tried again. "Moscow, it's Coda. Do you copy?"

Still nothing.

Following the flight path indicated on his HUD, Coda moved into position, bringing his Nighthawk into a low orbit around Theseus and directly into the middle of Moscow's incoming trajectory.

"Andrei, it's Coda. Are you there?"

Moscow never responded. His comms were likely dead. After all, Coda hadn't heard his mayday on the radio.

*Unless he's injured... or worse.*

Was Coda trying to save someone who couldn't be saved? Risking his life for someone who was already dead? There was no way to be sure, and he didn't have time to radio the tower and have them check the vitals measured by his flight suit. Moscow's fighter was coming in too hot.

Coda brought up Moscow's Nighthawk on his HUD, measuring its incoming velocity and rate of spin. Like an outfielder tracking down a pop fly, Coda calculated the multiple points where he could catch Moscow's vessel. Then, firing his forward thrusters, he propelled his fighter *backward*, deeper into the moon's gravitational pull. The maneuver meant that Moscow's fighter was still gaining on his but at a slower rate than before.

As Moscow's fighter came closer, Coda feathered his thrusters, gaining more reverse speed, thereby slowing the rate of Moscow's pursuit until they had nearly matched speed. Moscow's fighter was in visual range now. Its portside wing was missing, and the glass of his cockpit was cracked.

Still plummeting toward the moon, Moscow's fighter closed the remaining distance. With one eye on the catch point, Coda gave his rear thrusters a single short burst, slowing his rate of descent. Half a second later the two fighters collided in a second crash of metal and...

...Coda *caught* Moscow's damaged fighter.

"I've got you!"

The two fighters were lodged against each other, their wings and fuselages intertwined like two hooks looped together. The positioning brought their two cockpits side by side, and Coda could finally see Moscow. The other pilot was slumped against his seat, not moving. He was either dead or unconscious, but there was nothing Coda could do about that at the moment. Increasing power to his rear thrusters, Coda gently slowed their descent. His Nighthawk groaned under the combined strain. The fighters were designed to deal with intense g-forces. They wouldn't break apart, would they?

Coda couldn't do anything about that, either. He continued to increase his thruster power, and within seconds, they had settled into a dangerously shallow orbit, neither falling nor climbing.

"Come on," Coda said, encouraging the fighter. "You've got this. You can do it. Come on."

Little by little, he increased thruster power, never more than half a percent at a time. His fighter was intact, with only moderate damage, but Moscow's was barely hanging together.

The seconds ticked by, becoming minutes, and despite the occasional metal groan, they eventually escaped the moon's gravity well. Breathing a sigh of relief, Coda surveyed the battle space. The other fighters had disappeared, and a quick glance at his HUD showed that they had all returned to the *Jamestown*.

"*Jamestown* Tower, this is Alpha One. What's the ETA on that recovery ship?"

"There was a malfunction with the hangar bay doors, Alpha One. The recovery ship is still several minutes out."

Coda cursed. After literally catching him in space, Coda couldn't afford to sit around and wait.

"Copy that, *Jamestown* Tower. Alpha One requesting clearance for emergency landing."

"Coda," Commander Coleman's voice said over the radio. "What's your status?"

"I've got Moscow, sir. His ship is... *attached* to mine."

"Alpha One, repeat," Commander Coleman said.

"I said he's attached to me, sir. Our wings are crisscrossed, wedged together. It's not pretty, but I've got him."

"What's his condition?"

"Unknown, sir," Coda said. "His ship is intact, but..." Coda heard other voices in the background and realized the commander hadn't been talking to him.

"Increased heart rate... blood pressure dropping..." He could barely make out the words, but what he heard didn't sound encouraging.

"Coda," Commander Coleman said. "This is what you're going to do..."

Coda's mouth went dry as the commander gave him his emergency landing orders.

"Do you copy?"

"Copy, sir."

"All right. We'll see you aboard soon."

"Alpha One, *Jamestown* Tower. Proceed to Landing Bay 7C and prepare for emergency landing."

"Acknowledged. Proceeding to Landing Bay 7C. Coda, out."

Coda's ship was already moving—slowing down would likely mean their two fighters would separate again—so he angled the nose of his ship around to point toward the *Jamestown*. Or at least where the *Jamestown* would be. They'd practiced emergency landings in the simulator but never anything like what Coda was about to attempt.

His course plotted and speed set, Coda's only job was to make the small adjustments needed to keep his fighter on the designated path indicated on his HUD. This far out, that task was simple, but as he grew closer, it would become increasingly difficult. What he hadn't counted on, and what his computer struggled to compensate for, was the added mass of Moscow's fighter and the reduced navigability due to his damaged thrusters.

For the first time since the first week practicing landings, Coda almost succumbed to his fear. But what he had now that he hadn't had before was hours of training. Experience.

Banishing the emotions from his mind, he focused only on the task at hand. He adjusted, readjusted, and felt the ship moving under him, always anticipating what he would need to do next. When the *Jamestown* finally came into view, he was still green, his ship well within the range of error. But then he realized just how fast he was truly going.

Unable to slow down, Coda and Moscow were approaching the *Jamestown* at more than ten times the speed of a normal landing. Terror seized him as the *Jamestown* grew at an alarming rate.

*This is going to hurt,* Coda thought, squeezing his eyes shut.

The last thing he saw before shooting into the landing bay was the giant net that had been erected in its center. Then there was groaning, crashing, sparks, and above all, incredible, excruciating pain, followed by deep, impenetrable darkness.

# 36

*Sick Bay, SAS* Jamestown
*Alpha Centauri System, Proxima B, High Orbit*

Coda's eyelids felt as if they were weighed down with lead weights. It took nearly everything he had to open them, and when he finally succeeded, keeping them open was twice as difficult. The blinding white light wasn't doing him any favors, either.

He found himself in sick bay, surrounded by empty gurneys and a distracted medical staff. Unlike the rest of the *Jamestown*, the sick bay was pristine. No industrial walls accented with the signs of old battles. No dated equipment or furniture. The place was immaculate. Everything was white or chrome, and it all seemed to be alive, glistening from the lights of the various monitors and equipment spread throughout the room.

A nurse appeared at his side. She laid a hand on his forehead and shushed him, telling him to take it easy, then brought a small cup of water up to his dry lips. The water was cool and soothing and felt like heaven as it tamed his scratchy throat.

"Thanks," Coda said once he'd drunk his fill. "How long have I been out?"

"Shhh," she said again. "Save your questions."

"For what?"

The telltale sound of a door hissing open caught her attention, and she looked up. "For him."

Coda followed her eyes, spotting a thickly built man with closely cropped black and white hair and ebony skin. Commander Coleman. Coda swallowed reflexively, but the commander's customary hard expression softened when he saw Coda was alert.

"Sir," Coda said, trying to sit up to give him a proper salute.

"No," Commander Coleman said, stopping beside Coda's bed. "No need for that."

Coda was thankful for the commander's sudden lack of military decorum. The movement had *hurt*.

"How are you feeling?" Commander Coleman asked as the nurse left to go back to whatever she'd been doing before Coda had woken up.

Coda laughed softly, and even that stirred more pain. "Funny. I was just thinking my body felt like a giant bruise."

"Something that's not far from the truth, I'm afraid. There's a reason we don't practice emergency landings. They're... *painful*."

Coda couldn't argue with him there. "How bad is it?"

The commander shrugged. "You had some significant bruising, a couple broken ribs, multiple lacerations, separated shoulder, whiplash, and a minor concussion. Nothing too serious."

*Nothing too serious.* Any one of the ailments the commander had mentioned would have been enough to send anyone to the doctor. With all of them combined, there was no telling how long he was going to be grounded. Still, even as pained as he was, he didn't feel as bad as the commander's words suggested.

"How long have I been out?"

"Two days. You're healing quite nicely."

*Two days.* That wasn't enough time to heal but only the most minor of cuts. *What exactly are they pumping me full of?* The thought brought another to the front of his mind. "How's Moscow?"

"Moscow's fine. Better than you. He was discharged this morning."

Coda closed his eyes, nodding. The pain was worth it then.

"That was a brave thing you did," Commander Coleman said. "And for someone you dislike."

"He's part of my squadron," Coda said.

"*Your* squadron?"

Was that a smile at the edges of the commander's lips? "Don't make me laugh, sir."

"My apologies." There was something else in the commander's expression, something he left unsaid.

"He would have done the same thing for me, sir."

"Would he?" Commander Coleman raised an eyebrow. "Perhaps. I pray we never have to find out. In either case, you have my thanks. You prevented a terrible accident from claiming even more lives."

"Even more lives, sir?"

Commander Coleman's gentle demeanor vanished, replaced by the hard expression Coda was more accustomed to. "Sooner or later, death comes to all pilots, Coda."

"Who was it?"

"Don't worry about that right now," Commander Coleman said. "Right now, you need to—"

"Who was it, sir?"

Commander Coleman exhaled. He had to know that if Coda didn't get the information out of him now, he would get it from his next visitor. At least this way, he could control the message. "Whiskey."

"Whiskey..." Coda repeated, ashamed of the sudden wave of relief flooding through him. It hadn't been Squawks or Noodle. Hadn't been Tex. Coda closed his eyes, trying to reconcile the guilt.

Commander Coleman must have misunderstood the gesture, because he rested a hand on Coda's shoulder. "Do this long enough, Coda, and you will know more. Whether we're dealing it out or falling victim to it, death will always surround us. Get some rest." The commander patted him on the shoulder before making back toward the door.

"Sir?"

Commander Coleman stopped and turned.

"When will I fly again?"

"I don't know, Coda. All flights have been grounded until the investigation has been completed."

Coda felt his blood go cold. "Investigation, sir?"

"Yes. A review board is being assembled to investigate the death of

Lieutenant Jones. It's standard procedure following a mishap of this nature."

"Who's being investigated, sir?" Coda asked, already knowing the answer.

"Coda—"

"No, sir, I need to know what to expect."

Commander Coleman sighed. "You and Lieutenant Krylov are under investigation for exhibiting a trend of unsafe behavior that culminated in the death of one of your squad mates. After a review of the facts by the officer board, you, Lieutenant Krylov, or both may be expelled from the squadron and never allowed in the cockpit of a Nighthawk again."

Coda watched as Commander Coleman turned to go. *This can't be happening! It's a nightmare... an absolute nightmare. No matter how hard I try, I'm no better than my father.*

Struggling to cope with the array of conflicting emotions, Coda replayed the training scenario again and again in his mind. When he could do that no more, he requested his personal tablet back then watched the training scenario itself, deconstructing the flight from every angle.

The simple fact of the matter was Coda had a blind spot the size of the Milky Way where Moscow was concerned. He'd abandoned the battle at large, focusing all of his effort and energy on shooting down the one fighter that would bring him the most personal gain. And it had cost him. Again.

"When you're in battle," Captain Hughes had said after Coda had beaten Moscow to a bloody pulp in the Terran Fleet Academy corridors, "your fellow wingmen need to have absolute trust in you. There's no room for grudges. There's no room for ego. And there sure as hell isn't room for pilots who aren't capable of learning from their mistakes."

Captain Hughes had been right. Not only was there no room for personal animosity, but Coda also couldn't learn from his mistakes.

The realization was like a blow to the gut. Coda thought he'd been doing well. God knew there'd been times when he'd wanted to slam Moscow's head into the deck, but he'd held back. He'd even *stopped* a fight between Moscow and Uno in Dr. Naidoo's classroom. But it was all fool's gold. When push came to shove, Coda could always be counted on to follow Moscow into a foxhole. This time, neither he nor Moscow had died. Whiskey had.

There was no question who the review board would conclude was at fault. Bile crept into the back of Coda's throat. He could taste its sour burn. He was responsible.

"The hero is awake," Noodle said as he strode into sick bay with Squawks and Tex.

Coda looked at his friends. The words cut deep. "Don't feel like a hero."

"Please," Squawks said. "Everyone's talking about it. Even Moscow doesn't have anything bad to say for once."

"Yeah?" Coda asked. "And what are they saying about Whiskey?"

His friends' smiles and easygoing nature vanished, and it quickly became obvious that they had talked prior to coming in. Make sure Coda was in good spirits. Don't pull him into the muck with everyone else.

"Nobody's saying much," Squawks said. "You know how it is. Everyone acts like nothing happened."

"Well, it happened," Coda said, then he told them about the pending investigation.

"I was wondering why everyone was grounded," Noodle said.

"It's standard procedure," Tex said. "Maybe not grounding the entire squadron, but that's how these things go. The top brass needs to find something to cover their ass."

"You mean someone to blame," Coda said.

"It's really not a big deal," Tex said.

"Not a big deal?" Coda repeated. "Tex, Whiskey is *dead*."

"I wasn't talking about that," Tex said. "I was talking about the review itself. I've been through one too."

"You have?" Squawks said. "For what?"

"Failure to complete a training syllabus," Tex said as if reciting the description from an official memo. "But they can be called for almost any reason. Too many SODs, a failure to meet goals, actions discrediting space aviation, mishaps—whatever blows their hair back."

"Exhibiting a trend of unsafe behavior that culminated in the death of one of your squad mates?" Coda said. "That's what me and Moscow are under investigation for."

Tex whistled. "That's not good, Coda. That means they'll be elbows deep in your cookie jar. They'll dig into your whole life. Not just what's happened on the *Jamestown*, but everything. The academy. Your school. Your..."

"My what?"

"Your family, Coda," Noodle said.

"You think they'll rope his dad into this?" Squawks asked.

All eyes went back to Tex, but the older man looked like he was trying to find a place to hide. Unlike Squawks and Noodle, who had spoken with Coda about his father on a few occasions, the subject was still taboo to the older pilot.

"I..." Tex stammered. "I wouldn't be surprised."

"That's ridiculous," Noodle said. "He had nothing to do with it."

"It doesn't matter," Coda said softly. "It's never mattered. Whatever weakness flowed through him flows through me. That's how everyone's always acted. How everyone has ever looked at me."

"That's not true," Noodle said.

"Isn't it?"

"No," Squawks said. "Noodle is right. Forty-eight pilots and Commander Coleman himself just watched you risk your life to save Moscow's. Whatever they say, your squad mates know you're nothing like your father."

"We'll see," Coda said. It was the only thing he could think of. He didn't want to talk about it anymore, but he didn't have anything else to talk about. Except for the vids on his terminal and the random conversation with the medical staff, nothing else had happened. There was nothing to share with his friends.

"Keep your head up," Tex said. "You'll get a chance to speak your piece. Just know what you want to say before you go in there, and you should be all right."

"You don't think they're coming *here*, do you?" Noodle asked.

"Well," Tex said, "that's how mine were done."

"Yeah, but you were at a training facility with training staff. We're light-years away from the top brass."

"That's true," Tex said. "Huh. I don't know what they're going to do then."

The sudden uncertainty did little to improve Coda's mood. At least in a face-to-face conversation, he would have had a chance to make his argument. The board could see his remorse, and he could explain what had been going through his mind. He would have been able to attack the questions about his father head-on and quell any similarities that could be drawn between the two.

"I bet they do it through written questions," Noodle said. "They'll get their information, and it'll be cheaper than shuttling them out here."

"That makes sense," Tex said. He turned his attention back to Coda. "Know what you want to say, and say it. That's the best advice I can give. And be honest. They can smell bullshit like it's stuck to the bottom of your boot."

# 37

*Private Room, SAS* Jamestown
*Alpha Centauri System, Proxima B, High Orbit*

Noodle's prediction that the review board would use written questions and statements was only partially true. When the official questions came in, they did arrive in a written format but only to supplement the video messages they accompanied. The commander brought Coda, who was still recovering from his injuries, into a private room and moderated the interview, recording Coda's responses to the video's questions.

Tex's prediction was spot on, though. For two hours, Coda was grilled about his time at the academy, including every minor and major success and failure. Fortunately, his time there had been marked more with awards of excellence than demerits. They reviewed his scores and recommendations, even shared statements his former squad mates had made about him, always asking him to respond.

Admiral Orlovsky, whom Coda couldn't believe was overseeing the review, asked specific questions about Coda's first interactions with Moscow: when and where they'd met, how, and in Coda's estimation, why their feud had escalated.

Coda attempted to keep his answers short and succinct, relaying the facts as he remembered them. When it came to the why, he purposely left out all knowledge of Moscow's mother's death. The information had helped Coda understand the true depths of Moscow's hatred and even helped him understand Moscow himself, but it wouldn't do anything to help his case with the board.

The questions about his time in Commander Coleman's squadron were even more tedious. They questioned the speed of the training and the mental and physical strain it put on all the pilots. They compared brain scans, heart rates, and other information taken during his physicals on the *Jamestown* with his previous records from the academy to show his deteriorating psychological state.

The longer the questions about the squadron's training wore on, the more Coda began to get the impression that he and Moscow weren't the only people under review. Commander Coleman didn't flinch or show any outward sign of emotion, but Coda could feel the anxiety emanating from him like heat from a fire. But why would the commander be under review? Accidents happened, and death was no stranger to the pilots. So why the extra scrutiny now?

*Because not everyone in the fleet wants the commander to succeed,* Coda realized. The idea was tantamount to treason. Commander Coleman's squadron was the ultimate fallback, a redundancy of a redundancy of a redundancy, only to be used if all other methods to counteract the Baranyk disrupter failed. Rooting for the squadron's failure was the equivalent of rooting for the destruction of the human race.

But it was never that simple. The military was the ultimate bureaucracy full of competing desires, agendas, and methodologies that all battled for the same limited budget. On some line of some memo in some stack of papers on some admiral's desk there was a cost breakdown of Commander Coleman's efforts. From the direct costs of transporting, housing, and feeding the pilots to the indirect costs of pulling them from other service, everything had a dollar sign. And even those paled in comparison to the money required to supply, retrofit, and repair a full squadron of aging X-23 Nighthawks.

Surely someone somewhere thought that money could be better spent elsewhere. More scientists researching the Baranyk weapon. More engineers trying to counteract its effects. More manufacturing equipment to rebuild the drones that had been destroyed during battle. It was no wonder the entire squadron had been grounded.

The realization that he wasn't just fighting for his own future but the future of everything they had been working toward woke something inside him. The anger strengthened his resolve, banishing the self-pity that had been plaguing him since he'd woken up in the infirmary. He knew what he was fighting for now, and he wasn't going to go down without giving it everything he had.

His first answers had been short and succinct, offering little additional insight. However, Coda let himself embellish his answers about the squadron. He talked about the growing camaraderie, their unprecedented skill and confidence, and how they would be ready when the fleet called on their aid. Keeping his flattery to a minimum, he praised the commander's instruction, using specific examples of how his one-on-one evaluations had improved their piloting skills and how his reputation meant his students listened to him all the more.

He fell into a groove, his words coming out smoothly and exactly as he intended them. When the conversation shifted abruptly to his father, Coda went blank. He stared at the camera recording the interview as if he had just been bludgeoned in the back of the head and forgotten his name.

"Coda?" Commander Coleman said from behind the device.

"I'm sorry," Coda said. "Could you repeat the question?"

"The captain asked what you know of your father."

"Right," Coda said. "Thank you, sir. My father..." He'd known the question was coming and had followed Tex's advice. He'd even written out his responses beforehand, but in that moment, his mind was as empty as space itself. "I know what most anyone knows, I suppose. The official information is classified, but the general understanding is that he turned on his wingmen, resulting in the loss of his squadron and the subsequent deaths of hundreds more aboard the *Benjamin Franklin*. He was executed for treason and wasn't given a proper military burial. But I doubt that's what you were asking.

"Unlike the rest of the other sixteen billion people that populate the Sol System, I also knew Lieutenant O'Neil as my father. He taught me how to play catch, how to ride a bike, a hoverboard. He..." Coda's vision went blurry. "He wasn't the man I saw on the vids or the man I read about on the web. To me, as much as they're the same person, they're different.

"Lieutenant O'Neil betrayed those he had sworn to protect, but Joseph O'Neil tucked me in at night and read me stories of great heroes. He taught me what it meant to be selfless, how to put others ahead of myself. That man, the man I knew, loved the fleet. He loved flying. I don't know why he did what he did, but I know in my heart that he would have had a damn fine explanation."

Coda blinked. The words had slipped out of his mouth as little more than a stream of consciousness. For those brief moments, he was alone with his memories, pen to paper, writing out a path to his deepest secrets —secrets that even he hadn't acknowledged in a long time.

Commander Coleman watched him for several silent seconds, for some reason, his face growing harder.

*Did I do something wrong? Was I too honest?*

Coda replayed his words in his head, trying to figure out how they had sounded to his audience. He cursed himself. There was no doubt about it, he had gone too far. The review board wouldn't care about his father teaching him how to throw a baseball, and they wouldn't like hearing Coda defend him.

Part of him wanted to backtrack and attempt to clarify what he had said. But what would he say? And how could he say it without sounding like he wasn't trying to backpedal? The commander moved on to the next question before Coda figured it out.

When the strange interview finally ended, Commander Coleman dismissed Coda, remaining behind to provide his own statements. As Coda left the small room and returned to his barracks, he couldn't tell if he'd helped his case or doomed the military careers of himself and everyone else in the squadron for good.

# 38

*Hangar Deck, SAS* Jamestown

*Alpha Centauri System, Proxima B, High Orbit*

A day later, Coda assembled with the rest of the Forgotten in the hangar bay for Whiskey's funeral. A squadron of Nighthawks surrounded their group, providing them with an element of privacy from the rest of the ship's personnel.

The ceremony itself was conducted in crisp military fashion. Because Whiskey was from the United States, her casket was draped with the stars and stripes of the American flag. An old bugle recording played over the speakers as her casket was loaded into one of the X-23 launch bays. Something about the scene, combined with the aftermath of uncovering his deep-seated emotions during his interview, made it difficult not to compare the proceedings to his father's burial—or lack thereof.

For Lieutenant Joseph O'Neil, there had been no lamenting music. No tears. No gathered friends to say their final farewells. Not even a casket. He'd just been spaced out an air lock, where the frigid black and lack of pressure ravaged his traitorous body and did the fleet's dirty work for them. The whole thing made him angry. Lieutenant O'Neil might have deserved that, but Coda and his mother hadn't. They had deserved a chance to say goodbye. A chance to find closure.

Commander Coleman said a few words—more talk about how death was too often a pilot's unwelcomed friend—then they gave Lieutenant Autumn "Whiskey" Jones her final salute and watched as her casket was launched from the tube into her final resting place.

Noodle blew out a breath as the proceedings concluded. "What now?"

It was a good question. The squadron was still grounded, and save for the gym and the simulator, there was little else to do.

"I've got just the thing," Squawks said, giving Tex a knowing look. "Follow me."

---

Squawks's idea, it turned out, was to get well and truly drunk. How, exactly, Coda didn't know at first, but Squawks led them to a secluded corner in a seldom-used parts locker where he and Tex, with the aid of a couple handy crewmen, had built a metal contraption that looked like little more than two buckets connected by a copper tube.

"What is that?" Coda asked, thoroughly confused.

"A still."

"A what?"

"I thought your old man was in the military?" Squawks said. "It's a still, Coda. You know, to make alcohol?"

"Oh," Coda said, finally understanding what he was looking at. "What kind?"

"The kind that'll get us messed up."

"And hopefully not make us go blind," Tex added.

"Blind?" Noodle asked, suddenly looking nervous.

"Yeah," Tex said. "Bad alcohol can make you go blind."

"Seriously?"

Tex erupted into laughter, his deep voice booming off the walls.

"Quiet, you dumb hick," Squawks said. "If we get caught with this, going blind will be the last thing we have to worry about." He grabbed the container that the metal hose emptied into and held it out to Coda, who reluctantly took it.

The container was nearly three-quarters full with a brown liquid. Coda sniffed the bottle's contents and instantly regretted it. Pulling his head away in disgust, he held the container as far away as possible. "It smells like engine solvent."

"That's how you know it's the good stuff," Squawks said, taking the cup back. He took a sniff of it himself and smiled. "Oh yeah, definitely the good stuff." He handed the cup to Tex. "You did most of the work. You do the honors."

Tex held the cup to his nose and took in a long, slow breath before taking a sip. He immediately started coughing. It was a deep, raspy sound, as if his lungs were full of smoke, but even before he was finished, he was smiling. "Not bad," he said between coughs then handed the cup to Noodle.

The slender pilot looked at the cup's contents as if it were poison. "If this makes me go blind, I'm going to kick your ass."

"You'll have to find it first," Squawks said.

Noodle shrugged at Coda then took a sip. Like Tex, he immediately began coughing, his face turning red. But also like Tex, he smiled, his eyes glassy. "This is terrible." But that didn't stop him from taking another, bigger sip before passing the cup to Coda.

"I'm going to regret this, aren't I?" Coda asked.

"You know what the commander says," Squawks said. "If you aren't making mistakes, you aren't trying new things. Well, try that."

Coda sighed and brought the cup to his lips. The alcohol, whatever it was, may have smelled like engine solvent, but it tasted like pure rubbing alcohol, and it burned like liquid fire. In an instant, his entire midsection was warm, and his face felt flushed.

"There you go," Squawks said like a proud parent. He took the cup from Coda then gave each of the four pilots a smaller cup and filled them with the alcohol. "All right. Let's do this."

They settled into a small circle, sitting on various boxes and pieces of equipment as if sitting around a campfire.

Tex held his cup high. "To Whiskey."

"To Whiskey," they repeated then took a sip in salute.

Coda winced as the fluid burned its way down his throat. "It's weird," he said. "I've been so focused on making the squadron, I barely knew her."

"None of us one did," Noodle said.

"That's what I'm talking about," Coda said. "You guys were right when you said I was clueless. Outside of you three and Moscow, I barely know anyone. Hell, I barely know anything about you guys." He turned to Tex. "Like, I know you were in the Nighthawk program before it was discontinued, but that's it. I don't even know where you're from."

"His call sign is 'Tex,' dumbass," Squawks said sarcastically. "Where do you think he's from?"

"I'm from Georgia," Tex said, throwing an amused look in Squawks's direction. "But you dumb Yankees can't tell one southerner from another."

Everyone laughed.

"Other than that, there's not much to know."

"There's always more to know," Coda said. "You lived there your whole life?"

"Yeah," Tex said. "Family's owned a cotton farm for eight generations. My brother's running it now."

"Didn't want to go into the family business?" Noodle asked.

"No." Tex shook his head. "When you ain't ever been more than a hundred miles away from home your whole life, sometimes all you want to do is get as far away as possible. And you can't get no farther away than space, you know?"

Coda found himself nodding. He knew all too well what it meant to get away, but the one thing he wanted to run away from was the one thing he could never escape. "You been back since you left?"

"Naw," Tex said. "They wouldn't want me back, anyway. I didn't leave on the best terms."

"Me, neither," Noodle said. He stared into his cup as if it held the secrets of life. "Parents both went to Stanford. Dad's in Advanced Robotics. Oversees the plant that builds the processors for the Hornets. Mom's in Communications. They both expected me to follow in their footsteps, go to the family school and all that. But I grew up around the drones, saw the early models, and watched as they became what they are today. When it came down to it, I didn't want to build them. I wanted to *fly* one. So I joined the academy."

"How'd they take it?" Coda asked, knowing how his own mother had taken his decision to enlist.

"Dad blew a gasket, and Mom..." Noodle winced. "Well, I've never seen anyone cry so much." He took a deep pull. Coda couldn't tell if Noodle's glassy eyes were from the drink, the memory, or both. "I get it," Noodle continued. "I'm their only kid. Their whole life. And I just up and abandoned them."

"A man needs to find his own way," Tex said.

Noodle's eyes found Tex, and he nodded. The two couldn't have come from more different backgrounds, and yet in that moment, they were the same.

"So why join the Forgotten?" Coda asked. "If flying Hornets was your dream, then why are you here?"

Noodle grinned. "Because as cool as the Hornets were, the Nighthawks are even cooler. Besides, as Squawks likes to say, chicks dig pilots."

"Damn right," Squawks said.

Everyone laughed. Coda found that his smile lingered. He couldn't remember the last time he'd sat around with friends, with nothing to do except enjoy each other's company. It had probably been his last day at the academy, before his fight with Moscow, before his entire world had been upended. He'd forgotten how *good* it felt.

Coda's story was well known to everyone, his friends most of all, so it didn't come as any surprise when their eyes passed over him, falling on Squawks. What did surprise him was how much it stung. His friends might know about his father and how driven Coda was to fix his mistakes, but they knew little about the person he was. Before he'd been Coda, he'd been Callan O'Neil, with his own hopes and dreams, his own hobbies and loves. And some day after his service, he would become that man again. It hurt that his friends didn't want to know who that person was.

Squawks, it seemed, wasn't enthused, either. He stared back at Noodle and Tex as if irritated that he was expected to share next. "Are we here to talk or to drink?"

"Both," Noodle said. "Come on."

"It's not a happy story," Squawks said.

"Has anyone's been?" Noodle pressed.

"Well..." Squawks paused, winced, and shifted uncomfortably. "While all of you were disappointing your families, I was trying to find out who I was. I grew up in the system. Don't know who my mom or dad are. They could be drug dealers or Stanford grads—I don't know. Maybe I'll never know, but I can guess. You guys wanted to fly? You wanted to wipe the shit off your family name? That's great. I was just looking for some clothes, three squares, and a place I didn't need to move out of every six months."

A heavy silence fell over the group. Coda looked from Squawks to Noodle then to Tex. Nobody said anything.

"I don't know what to say, Squawks," Coda said, breaking the silence. "None of us knew."

"It's not something I usually talk about." Squawks looked toward Tex. "Every man needs to find his own way, right? Well, every man has his own secrets too."

"I wish I was entitled to my own secrets," Coda said. "I can't take a dump without it being compared to my father."

He'd meant it as a joke, but he didn't get more than a slight chuckle.

"This is going to sound sappy, or maybe this stuff's stronger than I thought it was," Noodle said, twirling the remaining alcohol in his cup. "But I think you found more than some clothes, three squares, and a roof, Squawks."

"Yeah?"

"Yeah. You found us, man."

"Lucky me," Squawks grinned. "A hick, a nerd, and a traitor's son. The three worst friends anyone could ask for."

"Says a guy who talks more in his sleep than most do awake," Noodle said. "We didn't do much better."

"Ha! No, you didn't." Squawks said. Then again, more introspect. "No, you didn't."

A gentle quiet permeated the group. In the wake of their squad mate's death, they had found a way to grow closer, to become better friends. Three of them had shared something deeply personal about themselves. Coda couldn't believe it, but he had the strong urge to participate. His mind drifted back to the first time they came together as a group, the first time they had shared something else about themselves.

Coda turned to Squawks. "You once asked me where my callsign came from." He kept his voice soft, not wanting to violate the peace. "The truth is, it's something I came up with."

"What's it mean?" Squawks asked.

"A coda is something that comes at the end of a play or a dance," Coda said. "Like the final moment when the actors come back on stage to be recognized for their performance. To me it's the end of the whole story with my family... to my father. And when I'm done it'll reshape the way the world looks at us."

Coda took a sip, too afraid to make eye contact with any of his friends. Said out loud, it sounded ridiculous. Somewhere between arrogant and self-righteous.

"The call sign's a constant reminder of why I'm here, what I'm fighting for," Coda continued. "That's the idea anyway."

"You fly with the weight of the world on your shoulders," Squawks said.

"Yeah." It really felt like it sometimes.

"No wonder you're so slow," Squawks deadpanned. "You're overloading your thrusters every time you go out."

"I was going to say 'no wonder he's so short,'" Noodle added, "but he's taller than I am so that wouldn't have made sense."

"Or so frumpy all the time," Tex added.

The three of them roared with laughter. Coda couldn't believe it. He had shared something about himself that he hadn't shared with anyone, not even Buster, and they were *laughing* at him. Anger growing, he shot a look at Squawks... and saw something in his expression that calmed his frayed emotions.

"You're such an asshole," Coda said.

"That's what you like about me," Squawks said.

Coda shook his head, eyeing the three of them. "You really are the three worst friends anyone could ask for."

"Hell yeah." Noodle raised his cup, laughing. "To the three worst friends anyone could ask for."

Tex followed his lead. "To the three worst friends anyone could ask for."

Coda and Squawks shared a look, then did the same. "To the three worst friends anyone could ask for."

Taking a swig, Coda's eyes fell on the group, and he was struck with an overwhelming sense of camaraderie. It was even stronger than what he'd felt at the academy. He wanted to graduate with these men. Fly with them. Fight with them. More than anything in his entire life, he wanted to remain part of the Forgotten. But he also knew that the decision wasn't up to him. In that, he was completely and utterly powerless.

"Guys?"

"Yeah, Squawks?" Noodle said.

"Do I really talk that much in my sleep?"

Laughing, Coda banished thoughts of the squadron from his mind. For tonight at least, he was with friends.

# 39

*Hangar Deck, SAS* Jamestown
*Alpha Centauri System, Proxima B, High Orbit*

COMMANDER CHADWICK COLEMAN TRACED A FINGER ALONG THE WRECKED fuselage of Coda's Nighthawk. Unlike Moscow's fighter, which had lost a wing, Coda's was mostly intact. The main damage was to the navigational thrusters along its nose and the puncture in the fuselage's belly. Had the X-23 still relied on combustible fuel instead of the electromagnetic propulsion created by the Shaw Drive, the accident would certainly have claimed another life. Unfortunately, one death had been enough to ground the entire squadron for over a week.

Coleman sighed, rounding the back of the fighter and starting back toward its nose. Their training was falling farther and farther behind schedule, something he couldn't afford. The timelines had already been tight. Beyond tight. They'd been downright impossible. And in all reality, it was remarkable how far his pilots had come. Still, for the first time since accepting the post, he felt that the squadron had no chance of success.

*If I just had another eight weeks, we could have built something special. Something to be honored. Something to be feared.*

But no, that wasn't the whole story. He'd been challenged with more than just compressed timelines. Coda and Moscow had been able to set aside their differences or if he hadn't uncovered the root cause of their rivalry before inviting both to join the squadron. He'd made so many mistakes. So many *unnecessary* mistakes.

*What's done is done. There's nothing you can do about that now.*

The real question keeping him up at night was whether or not he would get a chance to correct those mistakes. Whether his squadron would ever get a chance to fly. To fight. To prove to the world that their time—and Whiskey's sacrifice—had been worth it.

Coleman's tablet vibrated, and for a moment, he wondered if some sardonic god had heard him and granted his wish.

Pulling the device from his pocket, Coleman froze. The edges of the normally transparent tablet were outlined in red, marking the message as urgent. Even more concerning, the message was from Captain Baez, commander of the *Jamestown*, not someone at Sol Command. The emergency was local, maybe even aboard the ship. Had one of his pilots gotten into trouble?

Coleman opened the message to find a simple note requesting his immediate presence in Captain Baez's quarters. Coleman sent his reply, saying he was on his way, and started across the hangar. He was barely halfway across when his tablet vibrated again. Thinking it was the Captain's reply, Coleman pulled the tablet back out of his pocket.

His step faltered.

The message was from Admiral Orlovsky and was coded *Priority One*. Like the first, the second message was text-based, allowing Coleman to read it where he stood without fear of a security breach, and what he read sent shivers down his spine. Commander Coleman broke into a run. His wish had been heard and granted.

# 40

*Barracks, SAS* Jamestown

*Alpha Centauri System, Proxima B, High Orbit*

Claxons blared.

Coda's eyes snapped open. Flashing red lights bathed the barracks in a bloody light, intensifying the alarm as fifty pilots woke to the same scene. He was out of his bunk in a flash. His bare feet touched the cold floor, the sensation bringing with it a level of alertness that banished any lingering fatigue.

Tex rolled out of the upper bunk, colliding with Coda. The larger man was denser than Coda had expected, the collision rattling his teeth.

"Sorry," Tex muttered, his drawl more pronounced in his sleepiness.

"You're fine." Dressed in only his underwear, Coda pulled out a pair of standard issue flight pants and began pulling them on. "What do you think is going on?"

Before Tex could answer, the door to the barracks opened, and Commander Coleman, already dressed in a full flight suit, stopped in the doorway. "I need you in the ready room in two minutes. This is not a drill."

Commander Coleman disappeared, no doubt going to the second

barracks. Coda's eyes moved from the doorway to Tex. The other pilot's wide-eyed expression mirrored Coda's. Without another word, Coda pulled a tank top over his head, threw on his socks and boots, and was out the barracks door in less than a minute.

Commander Coleman was already in the ready room by the time Coda arrived. He watched with a grim expression as the pilots filed in and took their seats. Coda grabbed a seat in the second row. Noodle, Tex, and Squawks found seats beside him. Two minutes after the claxons had sounded, Commander Coleman stepped up to the podium.

"At oh one hundred this morning," he began, "the SAS *Jamestown* received an emergency alert from Sol Command. The forward mining operation of Toavis is under heavy Baranyk bombardment. Our fleet, which arrived minutes after the attack began, has been rendered useless by the Baranyk Disrupter, and we have been called in to issue aid."

Excited whispers filled the room as Coda exchanged wide-eyed looks with his friends.

"We picked the wrong night to drink ourselves into a stupor," Squawks said quietly.

Coda chuckled then realized he didn't feel as bad as he'd expected to. Either the alcohol from Squawks's still was some magical concoction that left its drinkers without a hangover, or the additives in their food helped his body metabolize the alcohol quicker than normal.

"This is the real thing," Commander Coleman continued. "This is what we've been training for. Toavis is critical to the fleet's ability to maintain its forward operating bases, and we have over one hundred thousand people on the ground. I don't need to tell you how important it is. I only need to tell you to trust your training. Trust your fellow pilots. Do that, and I have no doubt you'll be victorious."

Commander Coleman hit a button on his tablet, dimming the lights and calling up the display at the front of the room. A moment later, the display showed an updated flight roster of thirty-six pilots.

"We're being called in before your training could be completed, so the final cuts to the squadron never occurred," Commander Coleman said. "For this mission, we will be going with the following flight roster. The first twenty-three pilots here will make up Alpha Squadron." He clicked another button, and a thin red line separated the pilots of Alpha Squadron from the rest. "The next twelve will be standby, loaded up and ready to launch in our extra Nighthawks. The rest of you, stay alert and be ready for additional orders. Any questions?"

Coda had a thousand questions but one in particular. His name wasn't included in either list... neither was Moscow's. He found the other pilot seated in the row in front of him, the same silent question on his lips. Like Coda, though, he seemed to have decided to hold his tongue. This sort of thing was better to talk to the commander about directly.

"Twenty-three pilots, sir?" someone behind Coda asked. "A squadron has twenty-four."

"I'll be leading Alpha Squadron," Commander Coleman said.

"Hell yeah, sir."

"All right," Commander Coleman said. "Your orders have been sent to your tablets. I'll meet you in the hangar once we've arrived. Good luck, godspeed, and let's kill some Baranyk."

Fifty pilots rose as one. Alpha Squadron and the standby pilots made for the adjoining locker room, while the rest waited behind for what would become of them. Though they were part of the first wave, Coda's friends lingered, watching Coda awkwardly and offering sympathetic looks.

"You're the best of us," Noodle said. "You should be out there too."

Coda shrugged, attempting to ignore the terrible feeling of disappointment eating him alive. "Don't worry about me. Just take care of each other and kill some Baranyk for me."

"Oh, we're definitely going to do that," Squawks said, but even his boast fell flat.

With a tight smile, Noodle nodded then turned and strode down the stairs, making for the locker room. Tex and Squawks followed after offering their own disappointed expressions. Coda watched them go, wondering if he should have said something more. They were going to battle, going to war, and there were no guarantees they would come back.

He didn't call out, but he also made sure to watch until they disappeared from view. *Stay safe, guys.*

As soon as they had entered the locker room, Coda dashed down the stairs. He had his own business to attend to. If the commander wasn't following his pilots into the locker room, there was only one place he was going: the *Jamestown* CIC.

Sprinting through the corridors, Coda caught up to the commander before he made it to the bowels of the ship where the commander center was located.

"Sir!" Coda closed the distance between them. "Sir, please."

Commander Coleman stopped and turned to face Coda. "What is it, Coda?"

"It's just that my name wasn't included on the active roster, sir."

"You and Lieutenant Krylov are part of an active investigation, Coda. Why would you expect otherwise?"

"I just thought..."

"No, Coda. We don't have time for this. You and Lieutenant Krylov were left off the flight roster intentionally, and unless some act of God convinces me to change my mind and break all military regulation, it will stay that way. Now if you'll excuse me, I've got a battle to plan."

Commander Coleman strode away, rounding another corner and leaving Coda behind. Coda waited there, lost and, for the first time in a long time, unsure of what to do. He'd had his chance, and he had ruined it. He was a failure. A disgrace. He was just like his father.

# 41

*CIC, SAS* Jamestown

*Alpha Centauri System, Proxima B, High Orbit*

THE CIC BUZZED WITH ACTIVITY AS COMMANDER COLEMAN STRODE IN. Laid out in a rough circular shape, the CIC was made up of two levels: an outer ring and the pit, which was taken up almost entirely by a three-dimensional hologram that displayed a frozen image of battle. Coleman didn't immediately recognize the image, but he assumed it had been taken from Toavis.

Captain Baez stood in the pit, studying the image. His XO, Commander Zhang, was at his side, receiving a steady flow of information that would help them prepare the ship for the upcoming battle.

"Docking into Jumpgate Centauri-3, sir," a voice said as Commander Coleman made for the pit. "Jump sequence initiating. Jump in two minutes."

"Understood," Captain Baez said, glancing from the image to one of the officers on the upper ring. The gesture brought his eyes to Coleman. He nodded. "Commander."

"Sir," Coleman said. "The squadron has their orders. They're ready when you are."

"Good," Captain Baez said. "We're going to need them." His attention returned to the battle image. "Another drone jumped in while you briefed them. The battle isn't going well."

Coleman grimaced then studied the image closer. Toavis was a green planet, so rich in color that it almost looked like a gas giant, but underneath a thick atmosphere was a rocky surface rich in nickel, lithium, and other precious metals vital to the Terran manufacturing operations. Stretched out in front of it, however, were six Baranyk carriers.

Like all Baranyk ships, they had an organic appearance, as if they had been born instead of built. The Sol Fleet had recovered more than one ship during the war and had found that the appearance wasn't too far from reality. While not alive as some of the conspiracy theorists on Earth and Mars believed, the ships weren't manufactured in the same way the human ships were either. There were no separate panels fastened together, no rivets, bolts, or rebar. But the results were just as lethal.

The orange, red, and yellowed claw-shaped Baranyk ships were actively engaged with the human vessels, and even outnumbering the Baranyk fleet by two ships, the humans were clearly overmatched. Humanity, it seemed, had come to rely too heavily on the drone attack and had truly forgotten about how deadly the early days of the Baranyk War had been.

"How old is this?" Coleman asked.

"We received the message less than ten minutes ago," Captain Baez said. "But the image itself is over an hour old."

Coleman cursed. An hour old? There was no telling how much damage had been done since the image was taken.

"Recent intel suggests," Captain Baez said, as if reading his mind, "that one of the Baranyk ships has broken away from the larger force and has begun assaulting the planet. The *Virginia* has been called in as well, which should sway the odds back into our favor."

The *Virginia*. Admiral Orlovsky's personal ship was one of the most advanced ships in the entire fleet. If it had been called in, the situation was even direr than Coleman had first thought.

"Docking procedure complete, sir," the same voice from before said. "Initiating jump sequence on your command."

Captain Baez cast Commanders Coleman and Zhang a weary look. "Let's see what we've got." Then to the officer above, he said, "Jump."

"Yes, sir. Initiating jump sequence in five, four, three..."

Coleman studied the map, wondering what they were about to step into, as the odd feeling that always accompanied a jump overcame him. The world seemed to stretch in front of him, his own sense of self and consciousness stretching with it. Gripping the padded rail around the pit, Commander Coleman steadied his breathing, waiting for the sensation to end. When it did, the CIC came alive with fresh activity.

"Arrived at Toavis, sir. Data streaming in now."

The holographic image at the center of the pit had gone dark but was slowly updating as the information, moving at the speed of light from the battle, streamed in. It wasn't a smooth process, however. The images of the ships that had been clear and easily recognizable before had become grainy, as if they had been taken with a low-resolution camera then blown up to a larger size. It was more than enough, though, to see that even the arrival of the famed *Virginia* hadn't been enough to turn the tide of the battle.

All six of the Baranyk carriers still remained, but of the original human ships, only six still offered resistance. The other two were ruined wrecks, slowly descending into Toavis's gravity well. Joining them were hundreds of the inoperable human drones. They were still, lifeless, almost like a school of dead fish floating listlessly on the surface of the ocean. As Captain Baez had indicated, one of the Baranyk ships had begun assaulting the planet's surface without opposition.

"Get to your fighter," Captain Baez said, "and have your pilots provide support to the remaining battle cruisers. Without their combined firepower, we don't stand a chance."

# 42

*Cockpit, Nighthawk*
*Arradin System, Toavis*

COMMANDER COLEMAN CLOSED THE HATCH AND SETTLED INTO THE cockpit of his Nighthawk. Going through his preflight routine, he buckled and unbuckled his harness three times then yanked on the straps another three times after it had clicked into place. Satisfied he was strapped in properly, he flipped on the switch to the Shaw Drive thrusters.

To some outside the pilot brotherhood, the preflight routine might look a little obsessive-compulsive, and maybe it was, but Coleman was convinced it kept him alive and one couldn't argue with results.

The final step to his preflight routine was pulling the creased and faded picture from the inside of his G-suit. He hadn't flown in battle since losing his wife and daughter, since his wife had given him the ultimatum: his Nighthawk or them. And Coleman, not knowing that the X-23 program was about to be discontinued, had picked his fighter.

Well, that was only half true. He hadn't necessarily picked his fighter; he just hadn't picked her. Any person who forced another to pick between two things they loved wasn't a person he wanted to spend his life with. It was Aniyah, though, who had suffered the true tragedy. Growing up without her father couldn't have been easy, and had he known his ex-wife would win sole custody of their child then refuse to let him see her, he might have chosen differently.

Stroking the side of his daughter's young face with his thumb, Coleman apologized, uttered a quiet prayer, then set the picture on the instrument panel where it would be on the edges of his vision, just as his family would forever be on the edges of his mind. One day, he would see them again. One day, he would hug his daughter tightly enough to make up for the countless hugs they'd missed over the years. But first, Commander Coleman needed to win the battle.

Being the last to arrive, Coleman was the last pilot loaded into the launch tube. His pilots were antsy, chattering over the comm.

"All right, quiet down," Commander Coleman said. "Launching in one minute. Sound off. Hawk One is a go."

"Hawk Two is a go."

"Hawk Three is a go."

One by one, they sounded off, confirming there were no malfunctions and that they were green to go. When the final confirmation came in, they had twenty seconds to launch.

"Remember," Commander Coleman said, "keep it tight. Fly together. And trust your training."

"We'll do you proud, sir," Squawks said.

"Good to hear it, Squawks. It's my pleasure to fly with each and every one of you. Now settle in. Here we go."

Coleman was thrown back in his seat as his fighter raced through the launch tube. The pulley screamed, the seat of the Nighthawk vibrated, then... Commander Coleman was hurled into the silent black. The other twenty-three Nighthawks were shot out of the bow in less than four seconds.

"Form up," Commander Coleman ordered. "Delta formations."

Behind him, the rest of the squadron fell into four separate V-shaped formations made up of six fighters apiece. He plotted a course for the nearest human vessel, the SAS *Washington*, which was little more than a black dot against the green of the planet behind it.

"Looks like we've been spotted, sir. I've got five Baranyk fighters closing."

Commander Coleman glanced at his HUD, seeing the red indicators marking the incoming Baranyk fighters. Only five? Against a number five times that?

*They think we're drones.*

"*Jamestown* actual, this is Commander Coleman. Are you reading the signal of the Baranyk Disrupter?"

"Affirmative, Commander," Captain Baez said. "It appears as if the Baranyk are attempting to use it against you."

"Well, it's good to know it doesn't work on us." Truth be told, Coleman had harbored a nagging concern before their training had ever begun that the Baranyk weapon would fry the Nighthawk computers just as it did the Hornets. "Can you tell where it's coming from?"

"There's a lot of distortion," Captain Baez said. "We're working on it."

"Acknowledged. We have other fish to fry, but if you locate the source of that signal, you let me know."

"Of course, Commander."

"Thank you, sir." Coleman closed the channel then reopened the one with his pilots. "Do not engage the incoming fighters. I repeat, do not engage. Stay on me. Three-quarter thrust."

Punching the throttle, he swerved, plotting a new course that would keep them wide of the incoming fighters. The rest of his squadron followed.

"They're swinging around!" came a panicked voice on the radio. "They're moving onto our six."

*They're scared,* Commander Coleman realized. *Nervous and not thinking straight.* "They're not in firing range," he said calmly. "Shooting them down might have alerted the enemy that their weapon doesn't work on us. We need to provide support to our ships *before* that happens. Understood?"

"Understood, sir."

"Good, because it looks like we've piqued more interest."

More of the enemy fighters attacking the *Washington* broke off their assault, moving into an attack vector to meet the Forgotten head on. They moved as a single unit, like a flock of birds or school of fish. Early on, Sol Intelligence had thought the Baranyk were a hive mind, not unlike aliens in the popular science fiction novels of the twentieth century, but that wasn't the case at all. Like their human counterparts, the Baranyk were capable of individual thought.

"Prepare to break formation and fire on my mark." Commander Coleman watched as the enemy fighters closed the distance. "Break!"

The human fighters broke formation, twelve pairs shooting off in twelve different directions. Commander Coleman's Nighthawk came alive, vibrating as he opened fire. Two incoming Baranyk fighters broke apart as he zipped through the threshold and into the thick of the battle. It was pure chaos, with ships everywhere, flying at speeds human evolution hadn't yet caught up with.

Alternating between manual guns and computer-aided targeting, Coleman shot down four Baranyk fighters in as many seconds then brought his Nighthawk parallel with the *Washington*, though at a safe distance from its point-defense cannons. Not that there was a true "safe distance," of course, but there were perhaps a hundred Baranyk fighters between him and the *Washington*, and that, at least, gave him the illusion of cover.

The maneuver kept him in prime firing position. He opened fire again. There were more flashes of light as Baranyk mass became space dust. Missiles streaked in from other vectors as more of his pilots came to the *Washington*'s aid.

With the exception of a few enemy fighters, the Baranyk focused all of their effort on the larger capital ship. Seeing the larger vessel up close, Commander Coleman understood why. Gaping holes littered its hull, spewing fire along its length, and fewer than half of its point-defense cannons still appeared operable. The ship was a wounded bird, and the enemy knew it.

"All fighters," Commander Coleman said, "focus on the main contingent. The *Washington* doesn't have long."

Coleman squeezed off several more shots, eliminating three more fighters as the rest of his squadron arrived. Two flights, one beginning at the *Washington*'s bow, the other at the stern, sliced through the enemy like a propeller through water. They mowed down more than half of the enemy's force in a single pass.

The remaining Baranyk fighters broke into two flights of their own as if finally taking the human force seriously. But it was already too late.

The next wave of human pilots arrived, flanking them from the *Washington* port side and using it as a backstop. The Forgotten had the remaining Baranyk fighters in a vise, and within moments, they were no more.

Bringing his fighter around, Coleman surveyed the battle. The *Washington* was still engaged with the Baranyk carrier, each ship throwing volley after volley of torpedoes and medium-range artillery at their enemy. In the distance and partially hidden by the curvature of Toavis, the *Virginia*, *Oregon*, and other three human battle cruisers were involved in a similar slugfest with all but one of the remaining Baranyk carriers. The last one was somewhere below the planet's thick atmosphere.

*Come on, Baez. Get the* Jamestown *into the battle. We won't have numbers for long.*

The human squadron had provided much-needed support and had bought the *Washington* some extra time, but the battle was far from over. And now the enemy knew the human fleet had an advantage of its own. But as severely outnumbered as the human pilots were, would the advantage be enough?

"All fighters form up and prepare for an attack run."

They hadn't gotten to the point in their training that would have focused on bombing runs. As a result, Coleman hadn't ordered the Nighthawks equipped with the heavier artillery used to assault the Baranyk carriers. They'd have to do the job with missiles... and a little bit of luck.

"Two missiles apiece. The *Washington* has done a number on her. We don't need to exhaust our reserves."

Coleman triple-checked that his weapons switch was selected to missiles, then with his pilots forming up behind him, he angled his Nighthawk on a flight path that would have them streak past the center of the enemy carrier in a high-speed pass. The Baranyk carrier, perhaps sensing the danger, shifted focus from the *Washington* to the Forgotten. Point-defense cannons lit up their flight path.

"Evasive maneuvers!" Coleman shouted, throwing his fighter starboard to avoid a stream of incoming projectiles. "And fire!"

Trails of white vapor streaked from the quick-moving fighters toward the massive ship, then a moment later, more than twenty explosions ravaged its hull. Not three seconds after the last explosion lit the void, white-hot fire ballooned out of the center of the Baranyk vessel, splitting it in two and throwing the two ends of the ship in opposite directions. Cheers sounded over the comm as the pilots celebrated their victory.

"Well done," Coleman said. "Prepare for delta formations. We're not done yet. There's still five more of these bastards to go."

# 43

*Ready Room, SAS* Jamestown
*Arradin System, Toavis*

Coda sat alone in the ready room, bathing in the battle's radio chatter. He hadn't found a way to tap into the holographic display that they had in the CIC, but he had found a way to pipe into the radio frequencies and play it across the ready room's speakers. It wasn't the same as being in the battle. It wasn't even the same as watching it, but it was the best he had been able to come up with.

He listened with bated breath, often having to remind himself to breathe at all. There had been some panicked chatter at the beginning of the battle then mostly silence as the pilots focused on the task at hand. Now, though, it was beginning again.

"*Jamestown* actual, this is Commander Coleman. Were you able to identify the source of the Baranyk signal?"

"We have, Commander," Captain Baez said. "Sending you the information now. What do you have in mind?"

"With their fighters, they've still got us outnumbered out here," Commander Coleman said. "If we can eliminate the weapon, we eliminate the signal. Then we get full use of our drones and the odds swing back into our favor."

"As long as one of their other ships isn't equipped with the weapon," Captain Baez said.

"Yes," Commander Coleman said. "As long as none of the others are equipped with the weapon."

Coda could almost hear the two men thinking. How much would it cost them to assault one of the Baranyk carriers? Was it worth the risk?

"Make it happen, Commander. The *Washington* and *Jamestown* will provide cover."

"Copy that, sir," Commander Coleman said. "Form up. Our job is to distract the enemy and provide aid for the *Oregon* until the *Jamestown* and *Washington* can arrive. Our target is *this* Baranyk carrier." He must have identified the carrier in question and sent it directly to their onboard computers. "According to the *Jamestown*, this is the ship with the weapon that renders our drones inoperable. We destroy it, and we turn this battle in our favor. Any questions?"

There weren't any.

"All right. Let's do this."

Coda leaned forward in his seat. Something told him that the next battle wouldn't go as smoothly as the last. From the sound of things, the Baranyk hadn't thought the new human fighters were much of a threat, but they wouldn't make that mistake a second time.

*Come on, guys. You can do this.*

So focused on the sounds of the battle, Coda almost didn't hear the door to the ready room slide open. Moscow stepped inside then, spotting Coda, froze. He clearly hadn't expected company.

"Here they come," Commander Coleman said over the speakers. "Forty contacts, positive-Z six degrees, one hundred thousand meters and closing. Break in three, two, one. Break!"

Moscow's eyes slid from Coda's to the walls of the ready room, no doubt looking for the speakers, then still refusing to look in Coda's direction, he made his way across the ready room and took a seat on a far chair.

Screams and panicked voices filled the room.

"They're everywhere!"

"There's too many of them!"

"I lost sight of Hawk Twelve!"

"He's on my six! Bear, you see them?"

"Where's my wingman? Where's Hawk Four?"

"Hard left! Hard left! Bring it around. I've got them."

"I can't shake them!"

"Break right and two degrees negative-Z. Now!"

"Mayday! Mayday! Hawk Six is down. I repeat, Hawk Six is down."

Coda tried to remember who Hawk Six was. Dot? Burn? Baldy? And who were Hawks Twelve and Four? He hadn't studied the flight roster closely enough to remember. He listened, half hoping to hear one of his friends over the radio. That would mean they were in trouble, but it would also mean they were alive.

"Damn it!"

"Keep it level. That's it. Two sec—"

"Ahhh!"

"Hawk Fourteen is down."

Coda flinched with every confirmation of another human death. They were getting cut to shreds out there.

"I'm hit! I'm hit!"

"*Jamestown* actual," Commander Coleman bellowed, "where the hell are you?"

"Sixty seconds, Commander."

"You're going to have to do better than that." Commander Coleman's voice was more concerned than Coda had ever heard it. "We don't have sixty seconds."

"Negative, Commander. If we increase thrust any more, we won't be able to slow down in time."

"Then jump!"

Silence.

"What are they waiting for?" Moscow asked, speaking for the first time. He was looking in Coda's direction, his eyes wide.

"Probably seeing if it's doable," Coda said.

"Of course it's doable," Moscow said. "The Shaw Drive can't make galactic jumps, but intersolar jumps are... bah, you already know all that."

"The *Jamestown* is a defensive ship around a quiet mining colony," Coda said. "Captain Baez probably hasn't ever seen real action, let alone made a quantum jump mid battle. And you and I know how difficult those are to plot. One tiny mistake, and they'll jump into the planet's core."

"Doesn't matter," Moscow said. "Captain Baez needs to do something. We're getting destroyed out there."

Coda couldn't argue with that. If the battle was even half as bad as it sounded, the squadron couldn't hold out much longer.

"Commander, *Jamestown* actual. Jump coordinates sent to your computer. Avoid the area at all costs."

"Copy that," Commander Coleman said. "All pilots fall back. The *Jamestown* is jumping in. Let's see if we can draw a few of these fighters away from the rest in the meantime."

"He's dividing their forces," Moscow said.

Coda nodded.

"We should be out there," Moscow added. "Not locked in here."

They weren't technically locked in the ready room, but Coda knew what Moscow was getting at. "Yeah, well, we sure did a damn good job of messing that up."

"Yeah..." Moscow's voice was tinged with regret. "You think we'll ever fly again?"

Coda blew out a long breath. "No idea." He toyed with the idea of telling Moscow of his exchange with Commander Coleman in the corridor but decided it wouldn't make either of them feel any better. "Thanks for putting in a good word, by the way. You know, during the review."

The last step in the investigation had been for Coda to review all statements and offer a counter or clarification statement of his own. In doing so, he'd been privy to all statements made about him and had been surprised to see that Moscow had come to his defense, going so far as to say that he believed the squadron was better off, and its pilots safer, with Coda in it.

Moscow shrugged. "It's true."

"Well, I still apprecia—"

The world stretched in front of Coda. The *Jamestown* initiated its jump. Coda held his breath, wondering if it would be his last, then let it out as the world snapped back to normal, the jump completed.

"All pilots," Commander Coleman's voice boomed over the radio, "reverse course and engage. Use the *Jamestown* to your advantage. Smash them like a bug under your foot."

Coda tried to picture the battle outside, only dimly aware that he and Moscow were now a part of it. The *Jamestown* would have likely arrived parallel to the Baranyk carrier, with the *Oregon* flanking it from the other side. The distant rumble of cannon fire vibrated through the floor of the ready room as the *Jamestown* opened its main batteries. With it, the radio chatter changed pitch again, becoming more encouraging.

"Here we go!"

"Nice shot!"

"Take it! Take it!"

"Bingo!"

The chatter brought a smile to his face. Even tucked away in the relative safety of the *Jamestown*, Coda felt as though he were playing a role in their success. Those were his wingmen out there. His friends. He rubbed his hands together as if washing them, his eyes drifting back to Moscow.

"For what it's worth, I feel the same way. You're a damn good pilot, Moscow. And if I'm allowed back into the squadron, I want you there with me."

"Thanks, Coda." It was the first time Coda could remember Moscow calling him by his call sign instead of his last name. "I never said that, you know, after the accident. I never said thank you."

It was Coda's turn to shrug, though in truth, he didn't want the conversation to end. For the first time he thought he and Moscow were really getting somewhere. "You didn't have to. I didn't save you for any other reason than because I'd want someone to do it for me. Golden rule and all that crap, you know?"

Moscow grinned. It was a small thing but further proof that the ice was thawing between them. "Either way, I was an ass. You tried to talk to me, tried to be the better man, and well, I didn't help things."

"I just wanted to keep flying," Coda said with a knowing grin.

Ha! Well, I should have followed your example. Instead, I let my emotions get the best of me. If I had, we'd be out there right now. You're not a bad guy, Coda. You're not your... You're not your father. Whatever happens, I want you to know that."

Coda fought back a strange swell of emotion, biting the inside of his cheeks to distract him from the lump in his chest. "I appreciate that," he said softly. "You have no idea how much I appreciate that."

Moscow made a satisfied face and nodded.

"You know," Coda said, "when this is all over, we need to grab a drink. Clear the air. Completely. With us on the same side, nothing stands a chance."

"Hell yeah," Moscow said. "There's only one problem: there's no alcohol on board."

"That's where you're wrong."

"Yeah?"

"Yeah."

"Screw it, then," Moscow said. "It's a deal."

# 44

*Cockpit, Nighthawk*
*Arradin System, Toavis*

"GIVE IT EVERYTHING YOU'VE GOT," COLEMAN SAID OVER THE COMM. "Press the advantage."

He didn't receive a reply, though he wasn't expecting one, either. His pilots had other things to worry about—things like the hundred or so Baranyk fighters that they had drawn away from the carrier before the *Jamestown* had jumped in. The vessel was now in a pitched battle, flanking the Baranyk capital ship and laying into it with heavy close-range fire. The rest of the pilots were still focused on the single-manned Baranyk fighters, though the point-defense cannons on the *Jamestown*'s starboard side aided them.

Like the rest of his pilots, Coleman had taken longer than he would have liked to settle into the rhythm of the battle. They had never experienced it, and he hadn't in years. But things were different now. Things felt good. Things felt *right*.

He pulled a high-g turn, caught an enemy fighter with cannon fire as it streaked past in pursuit of one of his squad mates, spun out of its expanding debris field, then pushed the stick forward, diving below the

Z-axis of the battle plane. Another short burst later, another Baranyk fighter was gone. Spinning again, he pulled back up then leveled out, cutting a path along the top of the *Jamestown* and laying waste to the fighters attacking it.

But despite how well the squadron was faring, they were still facing a significant numbers disadvantage. The worst of the battle was still ahead.

Strafing across the stern of the *Jamestown*, Commander Coleman flipped, preparing for another pass. Rather than flying toward the bow, he veered starboard, turning back into the thick of the battle. He targeted the nearest friendly fighters and provided aid to those with enemy tails. He could continue to pick off unsuspecting fighters almost at will, but unless some of his pilots were left to assist, it would all be in vain.

He juked, janked, shifted, dove, and climbed, moving with the never-ending music of battle. It was a silent battle, of course. The sounds of gunfire, missile launches, and ship explosions had no way of traveling across the vacuum of space, but the music was in his head. All he had to do was write it down.

Coleman was about to request a status of the Baranyk vessel when a terrible, white-hot explosion erupted from the *Oregon*.

"What the hell was that?" someone shouted over the comm.

"No!"

Coleman watched in horror as additional explosions ravaged what was left of the *Oregon*. In seconds, what had been the pinnacle of human ingenuity and invention was nothing more than an expanding debris cloud.

"Someone get me the goddamned status of that enemy vessel," Coleman bellowed into the comm.

"We're showing significant damage along its port and starboard sides," a female voice replied. "If we'd had another twenty seconds, it would have been slag. Without the *Oregon*..."

Coleman hated the tone of her voice. She sounded defeated. *Goddamn it, the battle isn't over. Not yet.*

"Launch all remaining fighters," Coleman said. "I repeat, launch all remaining fighters. We *have* to destroy that ship." He didn't get a reply, but a few moments later, twelve more fighters shot out of the *Jamestown* in rapid succession. "All right, *Jamestown*. Keep up the attack. We'll provide the extra firepower."

"What are you doing, Commander?" It was Captain Baez again.

"What we were trained to do, sir," Coleman said. "We're going to unload everything we have on that ship. When we're done, it'll be nothing but slag."

"And so will you."

"No faith, sir." Coleman tried to keep his voice lighthearted. "Either way, with that ship gone, the Baranyks' advantage is gone too. Our drone reinforcements can do their job."

There was a slight pause, followed by "Get it done."

"With pleasure, sir." Coleman switched back to his squadron's frequency. "Take heart, pilots. The men and women of the *Oregon* honored your sacrifice. Now it's time to honor theirs. Prepare for an attack run. It's time we reminded everyone why we're here."

Bringing his fighter around in what would become its attack vector, Coleman watched as the rest of his squadron broke off their attacks and fell into a loose formation behind him. The remaining Baranyk fighters saw the sudden change and moved to press the advantage. Their pursuit didn't go unnoticed by the other pilots of the Forgotten, and Coleman could hear his pilots' concern. It was evident in the way their breathing increased, the way they cursed under their breath, forgetting that everyone else in the squadron could hear them.

Coleman ignored all of it, keeping one eye on the path in front of him, the other on the pursuing fighters behind. The attack vector would bring them around the stern of the *Jamestown* and slightly above the Baranyk vessel in what would allow them to devastate the entire length of the enemy ship. But they weren't there yet, and the enemy fighters were nearing missile range.

*Close enough.*

"Release your chaff," Coleman ordered.

Flying in formation, the pilots had little concern of hitting their friendly fighters behind them, and almost as one, the pilots dropped their chaff. Moments later, the canisters detonated, creating clouds of expanding sand particles. At the high velocity, individual grains would be more than enough to wreak havoc on the pursuing fighters, but as close as they were, the fighters entered a thick cloud of it. The pursuing force was decimated, only a handful of the remaining Baranyk fighters able to successfully navigate the debris cloud.

"Good headwork, sir," Noodle said over the radio.

"We're not done yet," Coleman said. "Switch to missiles, and lock onto the enemy craft. Fire everything you have. We *have* to take out that ship."

Coleman crested the bow of the *Jamestown* then brought his fighter around for his attack run. *We can do this.*

Coleman unloaded his entire arsenal. And so did his pilots. In one glorious moment, nearly one hundred missiles streaked toward the enemy vessel. With its point-defense cannons focusing on the *Jamestown*, the missiles wreaked havoc across its hull. Explosions—more than he could count—riddled the enemy ship, and as he streaked past the bow of the ship, he brought his fighter around, watching, waiting for some sign that the attack had been enough.

It started with what looked like a normal explosion. And then there was a second gout of flame. Then a third. Before he knew it, the entire ship was coming apart.

Coleman screamed into the radio, his voice mixing with the voices of the remaining fighters. They had done it. It had cost them the *Oregon* and nearly a quarter of their squadron, but they had destroyed the enemy vessel armed with the Baranyk weapon. Toavis had a chance.

"*Jamestown,*" Coleman said triumphantly, keying the entire squadron into the communication. "Prepare to launch drone fighters, and instruct the rest of the fleet to do the same."

No answer came.

"*Jamestown*, acknowledge."

Still no answer.

"Did the explosion knock out their communications?" one of his pilots offered.

*Maybe.* But the uneasy feeling seeping into his gut suggested otherwise.

"*Jamestown* actual, this is Commander Coleman. Release all drone fighters. Acknowledge."

"Negative, Commander," Captain Baez said. His voice was low, breathless. Defeated.

"Why not, sir?" Coleman said. "We just watched the Baranyk ship turn to slag. It's time to press the advantage."

"Because, Commander. That ship wasn't the only one equipped with the weapon."

"Say again, sir?" There had to be a mistake. They had unloaded everything they had on the ship. They didn't have anything left.

"I said that ship wasn't the only one equipped with the weapon. We're still registering the Baranyk signal from at least one other source. Our drones are useless. It's just us."

*It's just us. But that won't be enough.*

Coleman's reply died on his lips.

# 45

*Ready Room, SAS* Jamestown
*Arradin System, Toavis*

"We're still registering the Baranyk signal from at least one other source," Captain Baez said. "Our drones are useless. It's just us."

Coda saw Moscow looking at him out of the corner of his eye. He ignored him, trying to focus on what Captain Baez had just said. Another signal? Commander Coleman had just bet everything on the fact that the Baranyk ship they just destroyed was the only one equipped with the Disrupter. How could they repel the Baranyk forces now?

"Don't do it," Moscow said. "Don't do it."

"Don't do what?" Coda asked.

"The commander's going to order an assault on the other Baranyk carrier."

Coda thought for a moment, trying to come up with another option. There wasn't one. "He doesn't have a choice."

"Sure he does," Moscow said. "Order the remaining fighters back to base for rearmament. It took every missile we had to destroy that carrier, and that was after it was already heavily damaged."

"There's not enough time. Even ten years ago, it took twenty minutes to rearm a single Nighthawk and re-launch. And that was when the crews were well versed in the process. How long would it take now? Thirty minutes? Forty? The battle will be over by then."

"Then do it in waves," Moscow said. "Ten fighters at a time."

Coda thought for a moment. That made more sense, but he still didn't think it would work. And the commander didn't, either.

"*All fighters,*" Commander Coleman said. "Prepare to assault the second Baranyk carrier."

"I knew it!" Moscow shouted. "Damn it, this isn't a battle we can win."

"He has to try," Coda said. "That's his job. That's *our* job."

"Fine," Moscow said, casting him a frustrated look. "But he can't win this way. He has to think outside the box, the same way he did when he used chaff against the incoming fighters."

"What, though?"

"I don't know." Moscow pinched his forehead as if attempting to massage an idea into being. "I don't know. But sometimes it's not about sheer force. It's about getting creative. Have you ever heard of a Molotov cocktail?"

"Of course," Coda said. "They were used during World War II to help fight tanks."

"Not exactly," Moscow said. "They were actually created before then and gained notoriety when the Soviet Union invaded Finland. Molotov, who was the Foreign Minister of the Soviet Union and involved in the invasion, said that he was just providing aid to the starving Finns. The Finns knew it was a lie, of course, and attacked the invading tanks with what they called 'Molotov bread baskets.' The weapons worked so well, the Finns began mass-producing them, and the Molotov Bread Baskets became Molotov Cocktails. Point is, even the underequipped and outnumbered Finns were able to repel Soviet tanks with little more than glass jars filled with gasoline. That's what we need."

"Flaming jars of gas?"

"Something that turns a weakness into a strength," Moscow said. "Or a strength into a weakness. The Molotov cocktail didn't work because it was powerful. It worked because it exploited the tanks' weaknesses."

"The Baranyk carriers don't have a weakness," Coda said. "That's the problem."

"No," Moscow said. "Everything has a weakness. But that's not what I was thinking. What's *our* biggest weakness?"

"Numbers," Coda said slowly. "Numbers because our drones are inoperable."

"Exactly."

"Holy shit!" Coda said, finally understanding Moscow's train of thought. "Moscow, that's genius!" He jumped to his feet, rushing to the terminal on the wall of the ready room. Unlike his personal tablet, it was linked to the *Jamestown*'s shipboard communication.

"What are you doing?" Moscow asked.

Coda ignored him, punching in the correct frequency. When he had it correctly inputted, he opened the channel. "Commander Coleman? Commander Coleman, do you copy?"

"Who is this?" Commander Coleman asked.

Coda shot a look toward Moscow, whose eyes were wide with disbelief. "It's Coda, sir. We have—"

"Coda, this is a private—"

"Sir, please—"

"—channel. You are to confine yourself—"

"Moscow and I know how to defeat the Baranyk."

There was a slight pause.

"Out with it then, Lieutenant."

"The drones, sir," Coda said.

Commander Coleman cursed. "The drones are inoperable. Now remove your—"

"No," Coda said. "The drones are not inoperable. We just can't navigate them once they're outside our hull. But this is space, sir. Nothing can stop them once they're *moving*."

"You're not making any sense, Lieutenant. You have three seconds."

"We launch the drones *at* the ship, sir. They're kamikazes. Space-age Molotov cocktails. And they'll inflict just as much damage as our missiles. Maybe more, depending how much kinetic energy we can create."

Coda held his breath. One second. Two. Four. He looked at Moscow helplessly. It was their best idea. Their *only* idea. If Commander Coleman didn't use it, if he didn't appreciate Coda's butting in, then

Coda was sure he had just doomed any chance he would have at ever piloting a Nighthawk again.

"Captain Baez," Commander Coleman said. "Are you listening to this?"

"I am, Commander."

"How many drones do we have on board?"

"Two squadrons of pilots," Captain Baez said. "With twice as many drones."

Two squadrons. Forty-eight pilots. Ninety-six drones. And that was just aboard the *Jamestown*. Coda's heart lurched in his chest. They had more than enough drones. They had hope. They could win.

"Make it happen, Lieutenant," Commander Coleman said.

Coda beamed. "Yes, sir."

"We're counting on you, Lieutenant. You understand?"

"I understand, sir."

"Good. Get down to the Drone Operation Center, and radio me when you're set."

"Yes, sir." Coda ended the transmission then turned to face Moscow, who was wearing a grin of his own. "We did it."

"Not yet," Moscow said. "But we gave ourselves a chance."

# 46

*Drone Operation Center, SAS* Jamestown
*Arradin System, Toavis*

THE DRONE OPERATION CENTER REMINDED CODA OF THE COLISEUM BACK at the Terran Fleet Academy. Rows of steep stadium seating circled a three-dimensional imaging display. Only here, there were no spectators. Coda and Moscow had arrived only moments before, finding the display already showing the battle and the drone pilots plugged in.

The *Jamestown* continued to defend itself against the enemy fighters that remained from the destroyed Baranyk carrier, but it was otherwise on the outskirts of the battle. Nearer to the planet, the remains of the human fleet were engaged with three Baranyk carriers in orbit, and even with numbers squarely on their side, they were showing signs of losing the battle. The human ships took heavy fire, burning in multiple locations, their once-pristine hulls pocked and damaged, smoke spewing from them like steam from a kettle.

Coda and Moscow remained on a platform at the base of the image, the seating spiraling up around them. Unlike the Nighthawks, which had to be manually loaded into the launch tubes, the drones were already preloaded, their activation handled by their pilots remotely.

As the last of the pilots settled into their seats, Coda began his briefing. "We don't have a lot of time, and our mission, as simple as it may be, is critical to the success of this battle. As we speak, the *Jamestown* is navigating toward the Baranyk ship equipped with the Disrupter. Once in position, we will launch our drones, piloting them at full thrust into a collision course with the Baranyk carrier itself."

"Won't the weapon render all controls useless?" one of the drone pilots asked.

Unable to tell which pilot had asked the question, Coda looked in the general direction of the voice. "Yes, but the Baranyk signal isn't omnidirectional. It needs to be pointed at its target. That will give us the precious time needed to plot our course of attack. Any other questions?"

"How long are we talking?"

"From the moment our drones are spotted? Two to three seconds. Maybe. We can't count on more than five from the moment our drones leave the launch tubes."

Hushed voices filled the large space as the pilots muttered their disbelief.

"Fortunately," Coda said above the din, "our target is huge and vulnerable. We're not fighter pilots here. We're shooting a gun. Just point it at its target, and let it fly."

There were no further questions after that, and Coda sat down at his own station beside Moscow. "You ready to do this?"

"Just like our days back at the academy."

"Only now, we're on the same side," Coda said.

"I can hear the Baranyk crying for mercy already."

The world as Coda saw it disappeared as he slid on his VR helmet. Gone was the Drone Operation Center, replaced by the first-person view of the inside of a drone cockpit. After spending so much time in the Nighthawk, Coda needed several moments to refamiliarize himself with the view. He brought his drone online then activated his radio, patching in the rest of the drone pilots into Commander Coleman's squadron's line.

"Coda to Commander Coleman. We're ready, sir."

"Excellent," Commander Coleman said. "Prepare to launch on my mark."

Coda shifted in his seat, listening to the accompanying radio chatter.

Commander Coleman and Captain Baez were working through the intricacies of the plan, moving the *Jamestown* into position.

For the first time since radioing the commander, nerves fluttered in his stomach. His arms and legs felt weak, and he felt like he needed to throw up, piss, or both. Steadying his breathing, he put himself through a quick relaxing exercise.

The thought of sitting in that office back at the academy brought a smile to his lips. So much had changed since those days, not the least of which was his relationship with Moscow. Things had been bad then had become worse, and now they sat side by side, having come up with a battle plan that would save the other members of their squadron.

"Still with me, Coda?" Commander Coleman asked.

"Still here, sir. Waiting for your order."

"Show them what you've got," Commander Coleman said. "Mark!"

Someone other than Coda handled the launch, but at the commander's order, the launch tube became a blur, and at one-sixteenth-of-a-second intervals, he and the rest of the forty-nine pilots were hurled into the black.

There was no time for formations, no time to form up. As soon as Coda's drone was beyond the *Jamestown*, he directed it at the Baranyk carrier. At the distance, it was nearly invisible, so he relied on the *Jamestown*'s computer to target it and plot a collision course. Once it was within his sights, Coda punched it, accelerating the drone to full throttle. Aside from the ever-increasing speedometer and the subtle shift of space, there was no way to tell if the drone had responded to his command or not. No accompanying g-forces. No sudden weight on his chest. Nothing.

"Hornet One is a go and on course," Coda said.

"Hornet Two is a go," Moscow echoed then gave an enthusiastic hoot.

More pilots announced their successful course.

Coda tried to determine how much time had passed since his launch. Three seconds? Four? He would lose operational control at any moment. Spinning around, he saw nearly two full squadrons of drones racing through the black. It was a beautiful sight. One he had dreamed about during his early days at the academy.

... and then it disappeared.

The Baranyk had hit them with their weapon.

# 47

*Cockpit, Nighthawk*
*Arradin System, Toavis*

"Hawk One, this is Hornet One," Coda said over the radio. "We have lost control. I repeat, the Baranyk have targeted our drones and we have lost navigation."

Coleman let the words wash over him. The drone pilots had launched only seconds ago. Had they had enough time?

"Captain Baez," Coleman asked, "how many drones were able to successfully plot a collision course?"

"Looks like forty-three, Commander."

"Copy that," Coleman said.

Forty-three out of an even fifty. That number was remarkable, considering the small window they'd been given to work with. Commander Coleman had often discounted the drone piloting program. In his opinion, flying what amounted to a glorified paper airplane wasn't flying. But there was little doubt that their pilots were good at what they did.

*I'll have to go easier on them in the future.*

As expected, a number of Baranyk fighters broke away from the battle, moving to intercept the incoming drones. They would make short order of the human attack force if it had no backup.

"All right, ladies and gentlemen," Coleman said. "The drones are away. Time to make sure they find their target. Let's go. Time to plow the road!"

He punched the throttle, rocketing toward the battle and Baranyk vessels. Positioned as they were, the Nighthawks were a full two seconds ahead of the drones and approaching the incoming enemy from their flank. The Baranyk flew in a tight formation, which was a mistake, given that Coleman and the rest of his fighters were out of missiles.

As the first fighter came into range, Coleman opened fire, squeezing the trigger in short, controlled bursts. He shot down two fighters before the rest of his squadron opened fire. Within moments, a dozen more became space dust. With the smaller human force the larger immediate threat, the Baranyk fighters altered course, moving to engage the Forgotten. Coleman hooted as the drone ships zipped past unmolested, their path to the capital ship clear.

Then the dogfight began. He swerved, avoiding an incoming Baranyk fighter, opened fire, and shot down a second. Then he veered, peppering a third while bringing the capital ship back into view. Its point-defense cannons shot down many of the incoming drones, but dozens of explosions erupted against its hull. Terrible gouts of flame inflicted more damage than anything his missiles had been able to accomplish.

Coda had been right.

But would it be enough? Coleman longed to have more kamikaze drones, but they had purposely left the second squadron aboard the *Jamestown*. The Baranyk weapon would be pointing in the *Jamestown*'s direction already, further shortening the drones' operational window. More importantly, if their attack succeeded in destroying the Disrupter, the remaining drones would become fully operational and able to enter the battle. For that same reason, they had reserved the drones on the other ships as well. They would need them. Because god be damned, they were going to succeed.

Coleman went positive-Z. The Baranyk ship disappeared from view just as more explosions riddled its hull. The sudden change of course was the only thing that saved Coleman's eyes. A triumphant explosion lit up the black as the second Baranyk carrier erupted into flames.

Jubilant shouts filled the radio.

"Captain Baez," Coleman said as he shot down another Baranyk fighter. "Tell me that did it. Tell me we've eliminated the Baranyk signal."

The radio remained silent as the *Jamestown* was no doubt running the diagnostics. Coleman spun then pulled a tight, high-g turn, catching another fighter in his sights. But he wasn't done. He shot down two more before Captain Baez's voice came on the radio.

"All ships, this is Captain Baez. The Baranyk signal has been eliminated. Launch all drones. I repeat, launch all drones."

More triumphant cheers echoed across the line.

Coleman opened a private channel. "Sir, what if there's a third signal? We just committed every drone in our fleet."

"This battle is over, either way, Commander," Captain Baez said. "Either the signal is destroyed and our drones can engage, or it's not, and we're forced to retreat."

"Forced to retreat?" Coleman repeated. "The strategy worked. If there's another ship with the weapon, we can—"

"The Baranyk will just shoot down the next wave of drones. The strategy could only work once. And my intel shows me that nearly all of your fighters are down to their last ten percent of ammunition. You are ordered to return to base."

Coleman wanted to argue. He wasn't done. He'd waited years to get back into the cockpit, to get back into battle, and he wasn't ready to give that up. But he'd been given a direct order, and besides that, Captain Baez was right. They were all dangerously low on ammunition.

"Acknowledged." Coleman switched to his pilots' channel. "All fighters, this is the commander. Good work. We've done our jobs and given the fleet a chance. RTB for rearmament and await further instruction."

Coleman shot down another Baranyk fighter before flipping around and blazing a trail back to the *Jamestown*. He passed the *Jamestown* drones headed to battle, and something told him that Coda and Moscow, who had led the previous assault, wouldn't have given up their place in the squadron. Despite everything that had happened, they would get their chance to fight after all.

*Do your squad mates proud, gentlemen. You've already earned my admiration.*

# 48

*Drone Operation Center, SAS* Jamestown
*Arradin System, Toavis*

IT WAS JOY. PURE, UNBRIDLED, GLORIOUS, NEVER-FELT-BEFORE JOY.

Tucked away in the safety of the drone fighter pod in the Drone Operation Center, Coda grinned as his drone belched fire and death, tearing through Baranyk fighters with reckless abandon. He zigged and zagged, through and around, above and below hordes of Baranyk fighters still taking part in the battle. Even after the destruction of the second Baranyk carrier, they showed no signs of giving up. Their carriers and the remaining vessels from the Sol Fleet duked it out about Toavis like heavyweight boxers trading haymakers. Hornet drones poured from the human carriers, assaulting the Baranyk carriers like swarms of angry bees.

Moscow was on his wing the entire time, mirroring Coda's flight when Coda wasn't mirroring his. Coda had spent so much time studying his former rival that Moscow's flight strategy was as familiar as his own, and together, they created a true fighter pair. They cut through the Baranyk droves like a knife through water. Coda had already lost count of how many fighters he had shot down, but he was sure it was over twenty.

*This is what the commander meant,* Coda realized. *This is what he meant when he said that a pilot needed to know everything about his wingmen. If the entire squadron was this comfortable with each other, nothing could stop us.*

"Coda, you've got one on your tail. Drop negative-Z, twenty degrees, and loop right in three, two, one, break!"

Trusting Moscow completely, Coda dove below the battle plane and pulled his drone around in what would have been an excessive high-g maneuver capable of causing blackout. Separated from the stresses of spaceflight, Coda took out another pair of fighters while Moscow cleared his tail.

"Thank you," Coda said, meaning every word. Though he was safely tucked away in the bowels of the *Jamestown*, they had expended their extra drones in the process of destroying the Baranyk carrier. If his drone was shot down, he would be out of the battle.

"Does that make us even?" Moscow said.

"Even?" Coda barked a laugh. "For that? Yeah, right! I saved your ass from becoming a new crater on Theseus. You've got a long way to go."

"You never know 'til you ask."

Coda laughed then squeezed off another burst, taking down two more fighters. Moscow's drone appeared beside Coda's, and together, they performed a gentle turn, bringing the heart of the battle into view. The remaining Baranyk carriers were flanked on both sides by their human counterparts, taking heavy fire. The various drone squadrons attacked in coordinated wave after coordinated wave.

"All *Jamestown* drone pilots, this is Captain Baez. You are to join ranks with the drone squadrons from the *Virginia*, *Oregon*, and *Edmonton* and focus all your efforts on the carrier assaulting the Toavis installation."

A sudden, blinding explosion punctuated the captain's words as another of the Baranyk carriers exploded.

*Three down. How much longer will they hold out?*

"Let's go," Coda said. "They're on the run now."

"Right behind you," Moscow said.

Coda darted below the battle plane, plotting a course through the Toavis atmosphere toward the Baranyk carrier. He and Moscow flew with hundreds of Hornets, each on its own slightly different course. Having never flown in a proper Hornet squadron before, Coda and Moscow had fallen back to their Nighthawk training, flying as a fighter pair and leaving the formations to their counterparts.

Atmospheric flight was entirely different from space flight. It was slower, with more drag, and under the constant effect of gravity. In space, the drones could flip and reverse course in less time than it took to say the words, but atmospheric attacks were closer to bombing exercises—something they hadn't been trained in.

*We'll have to make do.*

Dropping his speed, Coda brought his drone behind the *Jamestown*'s Coyote Squadron and prepared for his attack run. The battle had been so thick with Baranyk fighters that he hadn't needed to use his missiles and had instead relied heavily on his cannons. He flipped the switch on his stick to missiles then targeted multiple points along the Baranyk carrier's length. Zooming into position, he squeezed, and two missiles launched away in rapid fire.

Coda spun, watching the missiles streak toward their mark. Accompanying them were hundreds of additional bands of white vapor cutting across the Toavis atmosphere, ending in explosions that tore into the organic Baranyk hull.

As a single unit, the Hornet drones looped around, preparing for their next run. Baranyk point-defense weapons cut through their ranks but not before more missiles found their target. More explosions tore through the hull. Some, Coda noticed, came from *inside* the ship. The Baranyk ship suddenly careened, smoke billowing from thousands of impact holes, and began to lose altitude.

"One more," Coda said, digging himself deeper into his seat. "One more."

And as if they could hear him, the drone squadron leaders brought their fighters around for a final pass. Coda, who only had two missiles remaining, targeted two more points on the Baranyk vessel and squeezed the trigger. His missiles joined ranks with another volley, and a moment later, a terrible explosion lit up the Toavis sky.

*Boom.* Coda watched as the Baranyk ship disintegrated, falling to the planet's surface. It was a beautiful sight.

"*Jamestown* pilots, this is Captain Baez. It's time to come home. The remaining Baranyk carriers are bugging out."

Cheers echoed across the line and through the Drone Operation Center. Coda added his to the mix.

# 49

*Drone Operation Center, SAS* Jamestown
*Arradin System, Toavis*

Coda removed his helmet and placed it on the hook inside the drone operation pod. The Drone Operation Center vibrated with the sounds of pilots cheering. There were screams and hoots, trash talk, and hugging. Victory had never sounded so sweet.

Someone grabbed him under his arms, yanking him to his feet. It was Moscow. He yelled victoriously, hugged Coda tightly, then gave him a vicious shove.

"We did it!" he shouted. "We sent them back to their hole!"

Coda grinned, excited and proud. But something was off. He wasn't as excited as he had expected to be.

Moscow saw it, his own smile faltering. "Are you all right?"

"Yeah." Coda didn't know how else to respond. He didn't know what was wrong. Didn't know how he felt.

"Bullshit," Moscow said. "I know you well enough to know to know something's up."

"I don't know how to describe it," Coda said. "I just feel... *relieved*. It's stupid, I know."

"Your idea just saved a lot of lives, Coda."

"It was your idea, not mine."

"No." Moscow shook his head. "I only knew *something* needed to be done. Not *what*. That was you."

Coda wasn't buying it. Moscow was just trying to cheer him up. "And I wouldn't have thought of it without you."

"Fine," Moscow said. "We came up with it together."

The door to the Drone Operation Center slid open, interrupting their argument. The remains of the Forgotten streamed in, their cheers adding to the rest, making the celebration damn near deafening. Squawks and Noodle saw Coda and broke into a sprint that covered the distance between them in a blink.

Squawks crashed into Coda, nearly sending them both to the deck. "You crazy son of a bitch! You've got some balls on you, you know that? Barging into the commander's communications like that. What the hell got into you?"

Coda laughed and pushed Squawks off him. "I channeled my inner Squawks, that's all."

"What does that mean?"

"It means that I had something to say, and I wanted everyone to hear it."

Squawks thought about the words for a moment. "So if I'm hearing you right," he said slowly, "you're saying that without me, you never would have told the commander your plan."

"I guess so," Coda said.

"Then I'm a hero." Squawks turned to Noodle, giving him a playful shove. "You hear that, twig? I'm a hero. I'm a goddamned hero!"

"Someone stop him," Noodle said, failing to hold back a smile. "Please."

But Coda was too busy laughing. It felt too good to have all of his friends back together again.

*Except...*

"Where's Tex?" Coda asked.

Noodle's smile disappeared, and he looked to Squawks, whose own jubilant attitude faltered.

"What?" Coda already knew the answer but needed confirmation. "What happened?"

"It was hell out there for a while," Squawks said, his voice haunted. "He... He didn't make it."

Coda shook his head, refusing to believe it, refusing to let himself be consumed by his emotions again. Tex was gone. Coda would never laugh at one of his ridiculous sayings again... or be put at ease by his genuine concern. It was almost unthinkable. And Tex wasn't the only one. The squadron had suffered major losses. How many other pilots would never return home? Would never see their loved ones again? The celebration in the room suddenly felt very wrong.

"He died doing what he loved," Noodle said. "He wanted to fly a Nighthawk so bad, he joined the program twice. And you know what? His family told him he wouldn't live to see thirty-six, and he proved them wrong, didn't he?"

"That, he did." Coda swallowed the lump in his throat. "That, he did."

The intense feelings of reflection returned. It was in that moment that he finally understood the true meaning of the name Commander Coleman had chosen for his squadron. Thinking of his friends and follow wingmen, everyone who had joined the program with them, Coda made them a promise.

*You won't be forgotten.*

# 50

*Commander Coleman's Quarters, SAS* Jamestown
*Arradin System, Toavis*

Commander Coleman had his back to Coda as he stepped into the commander's personal quarters. Even after a decisive victory, it seemed the commander still couldn't get an office worthy of his station.

"Have a seat, Lieutenant," Commander Coleman said.

Coda did as instructed, watching as the commander turned to him, holding a pair of glasses. This time they were both filled with a brown liquid. He handed one to Coda then sat down opposite him.

"Thank you, sir," Coda said.

"Falcon Rare," Commander Coleman said, nodding at the glass.

That obviously meant something to Commander Coleman, something Coda didn't understand. He sniffed the alcohol then took a sip. It tasted the same as any other whiskey he'd ever drank, but the commander obviously thought highly of it, so he wasn't going to argue.

"So how does it feel to be a hero, Coda?"

Coda shifted in his seat. Squawks had taken no issue with calling himself a hero and shouting it for the entire world to hear, but the idea that Coda was one made him uncomfortable. "I'm not sure I'm a hero, sir."

"That's how it always works, Coda. You never *feel* like a hero, just like a villain never feels like a bad guy. But make no mistake, you and Lieutenant Krylov are to be commended." Commander Coleman took a sip, watching Coda over the rim of his glass. "Your father would be proud."

Coda stirred again. If being called a hero was enough to make him uncomfortable, then being called a hero in the same sentence as his father was damn near unsettling. But Coda had learned something in the three days since the battle.

"Permission to speak freely, sir?"

"Granted."

"You once said that my father cast a huge shadow over my life. And you were right. When I was a kid, my father was a decorated war veteran, one of the best fighter pilots in the fleet. Then as I got older, his mistakes overshadowed me. For the longest time, all I've thought about was making my own way, earning my own glory, and using that to restore honor to my family name. But you know what I realized? I've been lying to myself, sir, and I don't even know for how long.

"I realized after the accident that I haven't wanted to bring honor back to my family name for *me*. I want to do it for *him*. It's clear to me now. I loved my father, and it's terrible to say, but I was angrier at him for leaving me than I was for what he did. And as much as I try to act like I don't, I miss him. Restoring honor to his family name is the single greatest gift I could ever give to him. It's the only way I can truly undo what he did. It's the only way he can ever truly rest. So that's what this has been all about. I didn't do it for me. I did it for him."

Coda took a deep, shuddering breath then a sip from the glass, letting the alcohol burn away the emotion in his throat. The words were finally out. He'd been wrestling with them for a lifetime, trying to comprehend them, accept them, and put them into action.

"Your father was a good man," Commander Coleman finally said. "I know I've said that, but it's true. And it's a shame things turned out as they did."

"You were there, weren't you, sir? Everything about that mission is classified, but... I know it. I can see it in your eyes. You were there. You know what happened."

Commander Coleman's eyes fell from Coda to his glass. He stared into its contents and licked his lips. "I was there."

"What happened, sir?" Coda knew that he was breaking a thousand military regulations and putting the commander in an uncomfortable spot on top of it, but he couldn't hold back. He had to know the truth.

Commander Coleman looked up from his glass with a sad expression. Whether it was from the memory or what he was about to say, Coda couldn't tell. "One of these days, Coda, I'll tell you. But now is not the time."

Coda let out a disappointed breath. He hadn't expected the commander to answer, but he hadn't been able to keep himself from hoping, either. Fighting every urge to ask again, to press the commander into action, Coda nodded. He could live with getting answers someday in the future, as long as he knew he would get them.

Commander Coleman took another sip. "I also thought you'd like to know that the results of your review have come back."

"The review?" The last three days had been such a whirlwind that he'd completely forgotten about the review. Apparently, their victory at Toavis hadn't settled that. Coda couldn't help but feel as though he'd been thrown from one inferno to the next.

"Cleared of all transgressions."

Coda blinked. "Just like that?"

"Just like that."

"I'm not going to lie, sir," Coda said, letting himself smile. "That's the best news I've heard in a while."

Commander Coleman smiled back. "I'm sure it is, Coda. It also means there's a place within my squadron if you want it. We could use you, Coda. Command is creating an entire fighter group. Ten squadrons. Your former school is being retrofitted to train future Nighthawk pilots until the Baranyk Disrupter can be countered. Even then, I'm not convinced they'll discontinue the program altogether. The Nighthawks and Hornets made a hell of a one-two punch."

Coda studied the commander. There was something in his eyes. Something that told him that, just like when he'd agreed to compete for a spot among the Forgotten, this might be one of the most important decisions of his life. And just as he'd felt back at the academy, he had no way of turning the opportunity down.

"What about Moscow, sir?"

"Lieutenant Krylov? What about him?"

"Will he be a part of your squadron?"

"Your newfound friendship continues, I take it?" Commander Coleman gave him a sarcastic smirk. "That's good to know. Lieutenant Krylov accepted his position twenty minutes ago. He will be a member of the Forgotten."

Coda smiled again. For the first time since Joseph O'Neil's treasonous actions, Coda felt as though he belonged. That his life was finally *his*. The world might not know it yet, but the O'Neil family name once again had honor.

"Then I accept, sir. It would be an honor to fly with you."

# WINGS OF MOURNING

THE FORGOTTEN FLEET BOOK TWO

# 1

*Office, Chrylis Mining Facility*
*Chrylis*

ALICIA MENENDEZ WORE HER BEST SMILE. DAVID WOULD KNOW IT WAS fake, of course—he'd learned that much in their six years of marriage. The important thing was that none of their coworkers would be able to tell the difference. To them, she was the supportive wife who had left behind everything and everyone she had ever loved and cared about to fly halfway across the galaxy in support of her husband. The worst part about the lie was that everyone else's smiles, David's included, were genuine.

The mood was light, festive, and relieved—a stark contrast to the usual day-to-day. They had done it. Work rotations on Chrylis lasted two long, miserable years, but due to the extended hours, inhospitable conditions, and proximity to the warfront, the job was very lucrative. After two years on Chrylis, she and David would be able to afford the life they'd always dreamt about. That was how he'd sold the idea to her, anyway.

And now the two years were up. To say they'd passed by like a blink would have been an even bigger lie than the smile she wore, but after the first three months, things had gotten easier. Her heart still ached at the thought of the children they'd left behind, but deep down, she knew things were better this way. Chrylis wasn't a place for children.

To combat the longing, she'd embraced their new routine: David in the mines, Alicia working in Operations. They sent video letters to their kids every day, of course, and had gotten them back with nearly the same frequency. They had eventually grown shorter than the long, rambling messages from the early days. Her kids were strangers now. Jenny was seven, Mark had just turned five, and Caleb, who had lived more of his life without his parents than he had with them, was three.

*So why aren't I smiling? We're done. I'm going home to my babies!*

She just couldn't shake the sense that everything felt premature. The new work crews wouldn't arrive until tomorrow, and the celebration should have waited until then.

*No,* she reminded herself. *That wouldn't have been possible.*

The company ran a tight ship—she and her crewmates were allotted only half a day off every two weeks. The moment the new crews landed, they headed straight into the mines, and the exiting crew would board the returning shuttle. If they didn't celebrate *before* the new crew arrived, they would never get the opportunity.

David put a thick arm around her and pulled her close. The planet had made him hard. His arms and chest were corded in thick muscle and stained black from the dust. She wondered if they would ever be able to wash it off, ever be fully free from Chrylis's grasp.

"What's wrong?" he whispered into her ear.

"Nothing." She gave him an exaggerated smile that said, *See? Everything's okay here.* She hoped he understood the subtext of the gesture. Unfortunately, like most men, David had as much of a nose for subtlety as a rock and was nearly as dense.

"C'mon," he said. "I can tell something's wrong."

"This isn't the place to talk about it."

He pulled her away from the group and found a quiet corner in the office. The work colony didn't have much in the way of comfort, and they had been forced to arrange the party in the same modular office where she'd spent the last two years working. To make room for everyone, they had pulled the desks and chairs from the center of the room, arranging them against the walls. David sat on one and patted the space beside him, motioning for her to sit.

"I know it's been hard," he said. "But it's over, Ali. It's over."

Did he think she was suddenly nostalgic for this godforsaken planet? "It's not that. I'm just tired. That's all."

"You sure?"

"Promise."

That brought a smile back to his face. The sight was nearly enough to break her. She couldn't remember the last time she'd seen him so happy.

*I'm not the only one who has made sacrifices. He might not talk about it, but this hasn't been easy on him, either.*

She smiled back, a real one this time, and was surprised to feel tears welling in her eyes. David saw them and pulled her into a tight hug. She fell into him, her head resting against his chest.

"We're going home," he said softly.

"I know." It was all she could say. Two years of pent-up emotion was suddenly ready to explode.

David's arms loosened. She compensated by hugging him tighter, but even as she did, his arms fell away from her completely.

"What's wrong?" she asked, looking up.

David's attention wasn't on her anymore. It was focused on the window and the rocky landscape outside. The horizon was the same pink and violet she'd grown used to. The sun was a white-hot glow that, due to the axis of the planet, was constantly low on the horizon, creating long shadows and a constant feeling of twilight. Wind buffeted the modular building, kicking loose rocks and gravel against its side, but his attention was on the streaks of light entering from the upper atmosphere.

"What is that?" Alicia asked. "Meteor shower?"

David leaned across the table, drawing closer to the window. It was tough to see, but something was definitely out there. More than two dozen in all, the streaks burned across the sky like shooting stars. They were accompanied by a roaring sound reminiscent of an approaching shuttle. Growing louder, the noise drowned out the sounds of the celebration.

The first projectile disappeared on the horizon, then a terrible crash shook the building. The lights flickered as pictures and other mementos from nearby desks clattered to the floor. Someone screamed, but the sound was cut short as the remaining objects crashed to the planet's surface, each impact more intense than the last.

Like the deep lumbering steps of a terrible monster, the objects drew closer. As the last one struck, a shock wave of dirt and rock slammed into the side of the building, knocking out the lights and bathing David and Ali in darkness.

There were more screams, and suddenly everyone was rushing toward the exit.

"Stop!" Charles Dilawar waved a pair of flashlights at the rattled group. As Site D's mine manager, he was used to yelling, but they had all learned to listen to him. "It seems our festivities are—"

"Turn those off," David said. He seemed to be the only one in the room not looking at Charles. His eyes were still focused on the horizon.

"What?" Charles asked, irritated.

"I said turn off the damn flashlights!"

"Listen, David—"

"There's something out there."

That got Charles's attention. He turned off the flashlight then shuffled toward David. "What is it?"

The dim light from the window was barely enough to illuminate the two men's faces. David squinted, his eyes attempting to pierce the dust that still hung in the air. Alicia could see it too. Shadows moved through the dust, drawing closer. Was somebody out there? Had the new crew arrived early?

"Get everyone inside," David said. "Now."

"We *are* inside," Charles said, confused.

"The mines," David said. "Get everyone inside the mines. Go."

"But—"

A terrible, high-pitched shriek cut off Charles.

"Baranyk!"

David took Alicia's hand and dashed through the room, making for the door. Unfortunately, everyone else had the same idea. They bottlenecked, pushing, shoving, fighting for the same exit. Something crashed against the top of the building.

"They're on the roof," David said.

"What do we d—"

The building shuddered as the door was ripped off its hinges. Someone screamed, and suddenly, the mass of people pushing for the door rushed *away* from it. David and Alicia were ripped away from each other, and she was thrown to the ground, where she was kicked and trampled as people rushed to get away.

"Ali!" David shouted. "Ali!" Then he was there, pulling her to her feet.

She froze. Standing in the doorway with a human body at its feet was a two-meter monstrosity. With a triangular head and spear-like forelimbs, the Baranyk warrior was the pinnacle of its evolutionary line. It regarded them with cold, black eyes then cocked its head to the side and shrieked.

Even though she covered her ears, the sound seemed to pierce Alicia's brain. It was followed by two more clunks atop the building.

*It called for reinforcements.*

Alicia snapped into action, yanking David away as the Baranyk and two of its counterparts entered the building. "The emergency exit. Come on!"

She pulled him past a mass of cowering miners, through another door, and into the back offices. The entire structure was built like a giant L, with the back offices reserved mostly for the management team. The emergency exit was set into the wall and opened by turning a large wheel counterclockwise and pulling the door inward.

David took the wheel in both hands, but before he could pull, the door to the front of the offices crashed open. Several terror-stricken miners raced inside. What Alicia saw through the door was something straight out of a nightmare.

The Baranyk tore through her friends and coworkers with terrifying efficiency, pinning them with razor-sharp forelimbs then dragging them into the open air of Chrylis like a predator taking its prey back to its lair. The nearest warrior had a miner pinned facedown against the ground and ripped his head from his shoulders with a single sharp jerk. Blood cascaded into the air, coating the black exoskeleton as it threw the body aside and started toward the back section of the office.

"David!" Alicia screamed. "It's coming!"

Eyes and tendons bulging, David heaved the wheel. Metal screeched but didn't budge. One of the other men grabbed the wheel, too, and together, they pulled. The wheel spun more freely this time, and then it was loose. David ripped the door from the wall. Wind whipped into the office, buffeting the interior with detritus.

There was a scream somewhere. Distant. Were the Baranyk taking her friends alive?

The Baranyk that had seen them through the door advanced, squeezing itself through the small opening, then lunged with its forelimbs. David hurled the door at it, the corner striking it in its triangular head. It shrieked, retreating a step, shaking its head in pain.

"Go! Go! Go!"

David shoved her out the open hatch. She crashed against the hard ground, rocks slicing her hands and arms. David was there a second later, pulling her to her feet. They were on the back side of the building, facing the direction the invaders had come from. More were on their way. Close. They couldn't outrun the monsters. The enemy was too fast.

"To the mines!" David shouted. "Come on! We can make it!"

David ducked under the modular building. The prefabricated design was built with the floor of the building a meter above ground, leaving a small gap between it and the planet's surface. Alicia rolled under the building, trailed by the remaining survivors.

Just as they did, the hind limbs of the Baranyk crunched onto the ground. The warrior made a strange guttural sound, its body twisting left and right, no doubt searching for its human prey.

David held his fingers to his lips.

The Baranyk's feet scraped against the ground, moving away. Only then did Alicia let herself breathe. David nodded, and together, they began crawling. With the four other survivors in tow, they made their way across rocky surface to the front of the building, the side overlooking the mining operation.

Set deep within the mountainous regions of the planet, the office was only one hundred meters from the mine's entrance. From their position, Ali could see its open mouth and the dark illusion of safety beyond.

"When I say 'go,' you run," David said as if talking only to her. "Don't look back. Don't stop. You understand me? Don't. Stop. No matter what happens. You get to that mine, and you close those doors."

He was talking like he didn't expect to make it.

"You too," she said. "You stay with me." Tears streamed down her face.

He cupped her face with his hand, wiping away the tears with his thumb. "It's going to be okay. I promise."

She nodded, afraid her emotion would betray her voice.

"Okay." David turned back to the expanse in front of them. It was nothing but open space from the office to the mine's opening. No cover. Nowhere to hide. When they moved, there was no going back. They would make it, or they wouldn't.

Above them, the sounds of the attack had subsided. Alicia didn't want to think about what that meant. Didn't want to accept the idea that almost everyone she had known for the last two years was gone. Dead. Captured. Or worse. And for what? A nightmare of a planet rich in precious metals?

*Why did I agree to come to this place? How could I leave my children behind?*

Their dream of a better life suddenly paled in comparison to her longing to hold her children one last time. To hug them. To kiss them. To tell them how much she loved them.

*Please, God, give me another chance.*

"Go!" David lunged forward, using his arms to pull the lower half of his body out from under the building, then instead of running, he turned and took hold of her, pulling her into the open. "Run!"

He was already reaching for the next person.

"Not without you!" She reached for him.

He swatted her hand away. "Run, Alicia! I'll catch up."

"David—"

"Go!"

Tears streaming down her face, she obeyed. The first step was the hardest. The second was easier, then the third. By the fourth, she had momentum.

Another ear-splitting Baranyk shriek sliced the air. She didn't dare look or even turn around. David had made her promise. But he had also promised he would be by her side. Her steps faltered as she turned. David ran toward her, but he was at least ten meters behind, bringing up the rear.

"David!" she screamed as the other survivors darted past her.

"Go!" he shouted.

But she wasn't looking at him. Her eyes were on the Baranyk that stood atop the single-level building, watching them flee. With another shriek, the warrior lunged off the top of the building, covering five meters through the air as if it was nothing, then landed with a crunch and raced toward them.

"Run!" Alicia shouted, but she knew it was too late. The Baranyk warrior was covering too much ground, its powerful legs propelling it too quickly. Alicia bent to the ground, grabbing a fist-sized rock.

"No!" David shouted. "Run!"

She ignored him. She was committed now. With a form that would have made her father proud, she hurled the jagged rock as hard as she could at the Baranyk. It sailed over David and struck the monster squarely in the head. It shrieked and skidded to the ground.

David was on her now, taking her hand and pulling her toward the mine's entrance with him. Running hand in hand with him, Alicia promised herself she would never let him go. Her children would not grow up without a father. The thought was interrupted by another angry screech.

Still running, David glanced over his shoulder. "It's getting up! Faster!"

Alicia willed her legs to move faster. They were almost there. The others had made it—they were inside the mine. One person was already at the terminal, ready to close the blast doors once she and David made it inside.

"Wait!" David shouted. "We're almost there!"

That's when Alicia saw it. The man wasn't ready to punch commands into the terminal—he *already* had.

"Wait!" Alicia's voice joined David's.

The man ignored them, hitting a final button. The ground shuddered as the thirty-meter-tall, reinforced-steel doors began to close.

"No!" David screamed. "Wait!"

"Please!" Alicia added.

The man disappeared into the bowels of the mine, the doors closing behind him with booming finality. Alicia and David arrived two seconds later.

"No!" David bellowed. He slapped the doors in futility. Then quieter, defeated, he added, "We were so close."

Alicia turned. The injured Baranyk was advancing, though with a noticeable limp. Flanking it were four more warriors, and behind them were even more, perhaps twenty in all. They took their time, as if savoring the fear in their prey's eyes.

"I'm sorry," David said. "I never should have brought us here."

"Don't," she said. "Whatever choices we made, we made together."

"I just wish..."

"I know," she said.

"I love you."

"I love you too."

He pulled her close, bringing her head to his chest, shielding her from the incoming nightmare. She closed her eyes, waiting for the terrible inevitability to pass.

*I love you, Jenny. I love you too, Mark. And I love you, Caleb. Please forgive me, my babies.*

A new sound entered the fray. Behind the scrapes of exoskeletons scratching against the rocky surface was something else. Aerial. Familiar. She opened her eyes, looking past the advancing Baranyk.

*There!*

In the distance, two streaks of light cut through the clouds. Instead of falling, though, they were *flying*. And unlike the organic structure of the Baranyk vessels, these were made of true, human-machined metal.

The fleet had arrived.

The massing Baranyk horde broke apart, scurrying for cover, but there was none to be had. Alicia dropped to the surface, cradling her head, David's weight on her as he shielded her with his body.

Cannons opened fire. The terribly beautiful sound reverberated off the mine's blast doors. She felt slugs punch into the ground, listened as pained shrieks filled the air, and smiled as the thunderous fighters drew closer.

And then they were gone, their pass complete.

Alicia looked up, surveying the scene. Of the Baranyk warriors who had pursued them, only one remained. It writhed in pain, its exoskeleton blasted to pieces and leaking yellow blood. Alicia grabbed another rock and started toward the wounded alien.

"Ali," David said. "What are you doing?"

She ignored him. The words seemed to have caught the Baranyk's attention, though, and it watched as Alicia approached.

"Fuck you." Alicia drove the rock down into the alien's head. "Fuck you and your whole fucking species."

Again and again, she drove the point of the rock into its skull. A blow for each of her kids, for every friend and coworker they had attacked. She didn't stop until her arms were covered in its yellow blood. Until it was long past dead.

# 2

*Cockpit, Nighthawk*
*Chrylis*

Coda looped around, angling for another pass. Flying in atmo, the maneuver was slower and more gradual than he was accustomed to. The atmosphere created drag, reducing speed, but it also caused less strain on his body. After flying almost every day for six months, his body definitely felt the strain.

"What are you seeing down there, Moscow?" Coda asked over the comm. "Any survivors?"

Moscow, his former adversary, was now a close friend and wingman. He flew in the dash-two position of their two-man formation, only meters off Coda's port-side wing.

"Looks like we shredded them pretty good," Moscow said. "Wait. We've got movement. There are survivors down there, Coda. *Human* survivors!"

"You sure?" Coda asked.

"Positive."

Coda pulled harder on the joystick, tightening the turn, the straps of his harness digging into his tender body. Without a word, Moscow matched Coda's course—flying together nearly every day for six months had its advantages. Leveling out his Nighthawk, Coda made for the survivors.

"*Berlin* actual, this is Coda. You read?"

"Loud and clear, Coda. What's your status?"

"We have human survivors down here. Requesting immediate evac."

"Copy that, Coda. How many do you have?"

"I have visual on two," Coda said. "The rest may have blockaded themselves behind the blast doors of one of the mines. Can't be more than a handful."

"Copy that. Releasing the Stork now. ETA in four minutes. Keep those survivors alive down there, Coda."

"Roger."

Streaking in for another pass, Coda surveyed the ground. It appeared they'd eliminated the Baranyk around the survivors. His attention shifted elsewhere. Baranyk dropships continued to streak through the atmosphere. Shaped like fleshy purple eggs, the alien dropships fell from the sky with little resistance, bouncing on impact until finally coming to rest. It was then that the Baranyk warriors inside would tear through the membrane, emerging like newly hatched insects.

"They're still coming," Moscow said. "What the hell do they want down here?"

Coda had no clue. He couldn't even remember what planet they were on or what the colony had been mining. He'd seen too many to tell one from another anymore. All he knew was the Baranyk wanted it—and Baranyk success meant human casualties. As the last line of defense, the Forgotten were tasked with preventing that from happening.

He and Moscow circled the survivors, patrolling the area and picking off alien troops. Without the aid of air support, it was a slaughter, not all that different from crushing bugs under one's foot.

That was the biggest flaw of the Baranyk drop strategy. While they could launch hundreds or even thousands of the drop eggs, they couldn't use the same carriers for retreat. They were completely at the mercy of their capital ships in orbit to retrieve them. Coda had often wondered how the Baranyk leadership convinced their warriors to fight what amounted to little more than a suicide run in battle after battle.

Fleet Intelligence was adamant that each of the Baranyk warriors was capable of independent thought, but nobody could explain why they were so eager to throw away their own lives.

The Stork emerged from a thick blanket of clouds. Coda and Moscow escorted it to the blast doors. A squad of marines dashed out of the rear hatch, secured the area, and ushered the two human survivors inside. A moment later, the blast doors opened, and the other survivors made for the dropship. The woman who had been outside the blast doors charged down the ramp into the human mass, swinging her fists wildly.

"Looks like they're going to have a long flight up," Moscow said.

Coda smiled. He couldn't blame the woman. From the looks of it, she and her companion had been locked outside the mine. If all the other survivors got was a fist to the face, then they would get off easily.

With the area clear, Coda found his eyes flicking to the sky. He itched to get into orbit, where the rest of his squadron was engaged with the main Baranyk force.

Once the Stork's ramp closed, it began its ascent. Coda and Moscow flew in the dash-two and dash-three positions, escorting it back into orbit to the *Berlin*.

As they flew through the final layer of atmosphere, the gentle haze washed away, giving way to the pure black of vacuum. In the distance, Coda could just make out the main battle. The *Berlin* was exchanging long-range fire with a single Baranyk carrier. The rest of the Forgotten had engaged and were greatly outnumbered by the Baranyk's single-man fighters.

Since the Baranyk had rendered the Sol Fleet's Hornet Drones inoperable, the Baranyk had pressed their advantage, reclaiming worlds and mining operations long held by the Sol Fleet. With their main defenses inoperable, humanity hadn't sat idle, either. In the months since Coda had graduated from Commander Coleman's training program, the Sol Fleet had assembled two other squadrons, both manned by aging pilots long past their prime. Though not as effective as the Forgotten, they were all that stood in the way of even more destruction.

Perhaps sensing humanity's strain, the Baranyk had shifted strategies. Instead of conducting near-all-out assaults as they had at Toavis, the Baranyk now conducted raiding attacks at multiple locations, placing the human fleet under constant bombardment. Humanity was on the ropes, absorbing blow after blow, trying to remain standing. They just had to hold out until the bell, the moment the fleet's reinforcements would arrive.

"Thank you for the escort, Lieutenant," the Stork captain said over the radio.

"Anytime," Coda said, then patched into the main *Berlin* frequency. "*Berlin*, the Stork is safely en route. Permission to reengage."

"Copy that, Coda," the tower said. "Permission granted."

Coda took a deep breath, reorienting his battle map so that it matched the rest of the Forgotten, then plotted an attack vector. "All right, Moscow. Let's go to work."

# 3

*Cockpit, Nighthawk*
*Chrylis*

CODA AND MOSCOW ERASED THE DISTANCE BETWEEN THE *BERLIN* AND THE Baranyk carrier in less than three minutes. The two enormous vessels were in matched orbits, separated only by forty thousand meters, hurling volley after volley of missiles and anticarrier slugs at each other. Coda plotted a course for the center of the fray, where the larger battle would be won.

What remained of the Forgotten was engaged with a force almost four times its number. The sleek black Nighthawks flew as fighter pairs, using nose-mounted cannons and guided missiles to lay waste to the smaller and more agile Baranyk fighters. But where the human fighters fought as a pair, the Baranyk moved as multiple swarms.

Like a school of fish, they changed direction at seemingly random intervals, diverging as they enveloped target after target then reconverging into formation when their enemies had been vanquished. The tactic made them difficult to predict, but the formations provided the human fighters with an advantage.

With the Baranyk clustered, the Forgotten could be less precise with their attacks, spraying antifighter slugs across a wide swath of space, and know that they would connect with multiple fighters. Missile explosions aimed at the center of the formation also did heavy damage, usually taking out several fighters with a single missile, debris and shrapnel taking out even more.

"All right, Moscow," Coda said. "Here we go. You ready?"

"Does a polar bear shit ice cubes?"

"Uh..."

Another voice piped through the chatter. "That was weirder than the shit Tex used to say." The other voice belonged to Squawks, the fastest-talking pilot in the Forgotten and one of Coda's closest friends.

"Does Howdy Doody have wooden balls?" Noodle added, mimicking their fallen friend's Southern drawl. Noodle was Squawks's wingman and a Terran Fleet Academy graduate, like Coda, Squawks, and Moscow.

The banter brought a smile to Coda's lips. Talking of fallen pilots was supposed to be taboo, but Coda had made a promise to Tex and the rest of their former comrades that they wouldn't be forgotten. One way they honored Tex was by coming up with the most random jokes they could think of, something they thought he would have said. Coda prepared a joke of his own but was brought short by greater authority.

"Cut the chatter." Commander Coleman's voice was light, but his pilots took his meaning. Radio banter was accepted, even encouraged, but not at the expense of losing focus.

The chatter eased as Coda and Moscow passed through the invisible bubble that his onboard computer designated as the battle area. He let his targeting computer autoselect the nearest targets for him, then designated them Targets A, B, and C, and moved to engage.

They took enemy fire almost immediately and were forced to dart starboard. At their speed, the inertial dampeners could only compensate for so much, and Coda felt the equivalent of four Gs. It felt like someone had jumped onto his chest without warning. He felt a rib on the back side of his ribcage twisting out of position under his flight harness, ripping his breath from his lungs.

Coda's G-suit tightened, preventing too much blood from flowing from his brain to his extremities. The odd sensation was painful since it was combined with the flight harness that cut into him, but it kept him from blacking out.

As he brought his fighter back around, the weight lessened, allowing him to breathe again. The workouts, low weight with high reps designed to strengthen muscles but not add bulk, had continued even after flight training, as had the stretching. The terrible food pumped full of experimental growth hormones that helped his body remain strong and heal faster than normal had continued as well, but the body could only take so much. Flying was as physically taxing as it was mentally.

*I'll need another trip to the doc after this.*

A small group of Baranyk fighters came into range. They didn't often fly in such small groups, so Coda took advantage. Flying perpendicular to their attack vector, Coda and Moscow sprayed the Baranyk flight path with cannon fire, using short, controlled bursts to avoid burning through their ammunition.

In a single fluid motion, the Baranyk ships altered course, moving to intercept. Moscow, however, had expected the maneuver and had a missile burning away a quarter second later. It exploded center mass, taking out all four Baranyk fighters in a single blast.

"Bingo!" Moscow shouted.

"Nice shot," Coda said.

"Easy as killing grass," Moscow said.

"That actually wasn't half bad," Squawks said. "Now you just got to teach that wingman of yours something decent, because his jokes are downright terrible."

Coda smiled. Ten seconds was all it took for them to disregard Commander Coleman's orders. If the man was angered by it, he kept it to himself. Like Coda, their commander probably knew that Squawks was at his best when his mouth was moving as fast as he was. And that helped keep all of them alive.

With their first targets vanquished, Coda's computer automatically prioritized the next based on proximity. Target B was a slightly larger mass of Baranyk fighters, eight in all, and as Coda and Squawks moved to intercept, the fighters split into two equal forces, darting in opposite directions.

"They're moving to flank us," Moscow said.

"I see that," Coda said. "Maintain course. Lateral spin, ninety degrees. Take them out."

Coda didn't wait for an affirmative. Using his navigational thrusters, he spun the nose of his ship counterclockwise so that his cannons were facing toward the incoming enemy. Then, using his port-side thrusters, he stabilized his fighter. His course remained unchanged as his fighter flew *sideways* in the direction of his starboard wing, allowing him to keep the enemy in his sights.

Coda opened fire. Two of the yellow-, orange-, and red-streaked fighters broke apart, spraying mucus and other fluids into space. Unlike the human ships, the Baranyk fighters were made of an organic compound. While not alive in the traditional, sentient sense, they were believed to be alive much like a tree or coral reef. Undamaged, the other two fighters split again, and again, they attempted to flank Coda.

"No, you don't." Coda launched a missile after the first, then he rotated to track the second and took it out with his guns. "Boom! That's four for Coda. How are you doing over there, Moscow?"

Coda spun his fighter around, completing the maneuver just in time to see the last enemy ship explode. Its red indicator on his HUD disappeared.

"As easy as killing kittens," Moscow said.

Coda winced. "Too morbid."

"Damn," Moscow said. "Sorry."

A break in the battle brought the enemy carrier into view. Streams of needle-shaped projectiles blasted from dozens of turrets along its starboard side, targeting incoming volleys of torpedoes from the *Berlin*.

"Commander, we've got a clear angle on the Baranyk carrier."

"Copy that, Coda," Commander Coleman said. "Execute attack run Alpha-2."

"Roger."

Coda charted a course that would bring them closer to the carrier but not directly at it. He didn't want to draw its attention. Not yet. They were just two more birds in the sky.

Unlike attack procedure Alpha One, which had been developed after their victory at Toavis and relied on using drones as blunt-force instruments, Alpha-2 was a coordinated effort with the *Berlin*.

The human capital ship launched a wave of torpedoes, followed by two more in carefully calculated bursts. Suddenly inundated with incoming projectiles, the Baranyk ship focused on blasting them out of the sky, opening its flank to the human fighters.

Nighthawks were already zipping in, breaking away from the dogfight to unload Haymakers into its hull. The standard-issue Nighthawk missiles were like the starfighters themselves—fast and maneuverable, designed for fighter-to-fighter attacks. The Haymakers, though, had one purpose and one purpose only—to pack a hell of a punch.

With the carrier in range, Coda altered course, moving into an attack vector, and increased thrust. Offset by fifteen degrees instead of ninety, he and Squawks would have plenty of time to launch both of their Haymakers into the belly of the beast.

"Hawk Three," Coda said, announcing his intent to fire. "Fox Four."

Coda's fighter lurched as the two missiles unlatched from his fighter and streaked toward the enemy capital ship. They hit center mass, and terrible gouts of flame and organic material exploded into the void. Moscow's capital killers struck a millisecond later, having a similar effect.

"Bingo!" Moscow shouted. "Four direct hits."

"Good work," Commander Coleman said. "Hawks One and Two moving into an attack vector now. ETA in—"

"We've picked up a tail, sir." Ginger sounded worried. He'd been selected as Commander Coleman's wingman for the mission.

Coda glanced at his HUD, spotting the enemy trio cutting through the larger battle to get onto their six.

"Cancel formation and prepare to—"

"Negative, Commander," Coda said. "Continue course and let those birds fly. Moscow and I are coming around now. We'll get your tail."

"Copy that, Coda," Commander Coleman said. "You let them shoot me down and there's going to be hell to pay."

"Never happen, sir."

"Maintaining course," Commander Coleman said, back to business. "Prepare to fire Haymakers in three..."

Coda settled himself deeper into the gel of his seat, his eyes focused on the red brackets indicating the enemy fighters on his HUD. His finger massaged the trigger, preparing to fire. Flying as fast as they were, he would only get one shot at this, and if he missed, he would never live it down.

Commander Coleman and Ginger ripped past him. Opting for his cannons, Coda opened fire. He laid on the trigger, spraying slugs indiscriminately across the enemy's trajectory. Moscow did the same.

The incoming fighters had no chance. They hit the projectiles at more than twenty thousand kilometers per hour, becoming space dust before they even realized they were dead.

Coda let out a victorious shout. "Splash three more for Coda."

"The hell you did," Moscow said. "I took out at least two of those."

"I fired first," Coda said. "Early bird gets the worm, Moscow."

"Mornings suck, and worms are gross," Moscow said. "We should split it."

"You got one and *a half* kills?" Ginger mocked over the comm. "How does someone get half a kill?"

"Because their wingman is a greedy bastard."

Coda laughed. Six months ago, he might have taken offense at the *bastard* jab, but things had changed since Coda and Moscow had secured the Forgotten's victory at Toavis. The O'Neil name wasn't as tarnished, and as a result, Coda wasn't as bitter. He'd also realized that many of the feelings he'd been harboring were misplaced. That wasn't to say he didn't still struggle with the fact that his father had been convicted of treason and promptly thrown out an airlock when Coda was an adolescent, but the wound wasn't as raw as it had once been. He'd started to heal.

"Commander?" Moscow asked. "What do you think? Care to give a ruling?"

"Two for Coda," Commander Coleman said. "One for Moscow."

"Why does he get two?"

"Because it was his ide—"

Coda's fighter gave a violent shudder. There was a brilliant-orange flash then terrible, searing pain. The next thing Coda knew, he was spinning, the world a blur. He reached for the stick but couldn't find it. He reached again. Still nothing. And that was when he realized the horrifying reality. The stick wasn't there. He was in space, still strapped to his seat in what remained of his cockpit, his fighter a ball of wreckage behind him.

He had been shot down, but by some miracle, he was still alive—and flying away from the battle at the same speed his fighter had been traveling.

Into the empty void of space.

How long did his suit have? Were his emergency beacons functioning? Would the rescue bird be able to get to him in time? Would it even be sent out?

*Yes,* Coda thought. *I'm alive. For now...*

# 4

*Shattered Cockpit, Nighthawk*
*Chrylis*

Coda didn't know how long he'd been spinning. For the first several minutes, he'd attempted to find a way to counteract the spin, but separated from the guts of his fighter, he had no control. He accepted the new reality, talking himself through the growing nausea, assuming that like his first encounters with zero-g environments, his body would grow used to the sensation. Instead, it was like being stuck on a merry-go-round with no ability to get off.

*At least I only threw up inside my helmet twice.*

And the second time hadn't exactly been his fault. The spinning motion had gotten to him first, causing him to lose his stomach. The smell was the culprit the second time. The yellow fluid, thick with the day's half-digested breakfast, had congealed into circular balls that floated around the inside of his helmet. The worst of it was that he had no way of wiping it away.

By the time the floodlights found him, he was green, shivering, and wishing for death. Since the interior of his helmet visor was caked in vomit, he hadn't seen the mechanical arm of the recovery vessel reach out and take hold of the cockpit remains, halting the spin in a single, jarring *bang*. Nor had he seen his savior exit the recovery craft, wearing nothing but a spacesuit and tether. But he felt the gloved hands and heard his voice when he held his helmet to Coda's.

"It's going to be all right, Coda," the man had said, his voice muffled. The sound waves didn't transmit through the glass of his flight helmet very well. "I'm going to take you home."

*Home. Where is that?*

He hadn't had a home since he'd left Earth, and even that wasn't a home anymore—his mother had seen to that. The closest thing to home he'd come to know was the Terran Fleet Academy, and that was only because he'd spent almost two years of his life there. He'd also been successful there, and success brought security, if not comfort. But since those days, he'd been on ship after ship, never on the same one for more than a few weeks at a time.

When the ship they were stationed on took on too much damage, the Forgotten were moved to another and shipped back out. Such was the life of those who stood alone between the enemy and humanity's annihilation. But their casualties were adding up. Fighters were getting sloppier, either due to overconfidence, lack of sleep, or the shear odds finally catching up to them. If something didn't change soon, everyone in his squadron would pay the ultimate price.

Coda's savior clipped himself to Coda then returned to the recovery vessel. They entered through a large hatch that opened like the mouth of a dropship. Once the environment inside had pressurized, the man took off Coda's helmet. Coda took in a long, deep breath. For the first time in what might have been hours, he inhaled air that smelled like something other than his own vomit.

"Here." The man handed him a towel. He had taken his helmet off, too, and looked to be about Coda's age, with blue eyes and a friendly face.

"Thank you," Coda said.

"Of course. We couldn't let the Hero of Toavis float away, now could we?"

*The Hero of Toavis?*

That was a new one. People had congratulated him, of course. Some had even bought him a few drinks. A few *very* grateful, if overly intoxicated, women had wanted to express just how grateful they were. Still, he had never been called a hero to his face. Not since Commander Coleman had asked him what it felt like to be one. Just like that day, Coda didn't feel like a hero, and covered in his own vomit, he couldn't imagine he looked like one, either.

---

BY THE TIME THE RECOVERY SHUTTLE RETURNED TO THE *BERLIN*, MOST OF his squadron had already showered and left the locker room for parts unknown. Noodle and Squawks were waiting for him, though.

"You look like shit," Squawks said as Coda entered.

"I feel like it." Coda set his helmet on the bench that extended down the center of the room then sat down and began pulling off his flight suit. "You guys didn't have to wait for me."

"We were worried," Noodle said.

"*He* was anyway," Squawks said. "I knew you were fine. Took one up the ol' cornhole, though, huh? How'd that feel?"

"Not good," Coda said. "I'm not even sure what happened. I had no visual, no radio. I didn't even know we won the battle until the recovery ship came and got me."

"The Baranyk carrier jumped away right after you were shot down," Noodle said.

"Bad timing on my part, then." Coda removed the top part of his flight suit and tossed it into the cleaner then shed the tank top and trousers he wore underneath. Like the rest of him, they smelled of vomit.

"We're supposed to tell you that the commander is waiting for you after you get cleaned up," Noodle said.

"Great," Coda said. "He want to grill me for getting too cocky?"

"Who knows?" Squawks said.

"You really do look like shit," Noodle said. "You all right?"

"Yeah." It was an automatic response, but once it had escaped his lips, he wasn't sure. He was still in shock and hadn't had an opportunity to analyze his mental condition.

"All right," Noodle said skeptically. "We'll leave you be. But we really *are* glad you're okay."

"Thanks," Coda said.

Squawks patted him on the arm as he and Noodle left the locker room.

Letting out a deep sigh, Coda shed the rest of his clothing then stepped into the shower. If the commander asked what had taken him so long, he would just tell him that he didn't want his office to smell like vomit. The truth was, though, he needed a moment to himself.

*I almost died today.*

The sudden realization made his hands tremble. One moment, he'd been in complete control. The next, well… it had all happened so quickly. And that was the worst part. He didn't even know what had gone wrong. How was he supposed to correct his mistakes if he didn't know what his mistakes were?

He rested his head against the shower bulkhead, letting the recycled water stream down his head and back. He stayed there until the timer went off and the water stopped flowing then toweled off and put on a fresh pair of sweatpants and a clean top. Finally presentable, he went to see Commander Coleman.

As the *Berlin's* CAG, Commander Coleman had his own private office near the flight deck. It wasn't a permanent position—nothing about their squadron was permanent. They'd bounced from ship to ship like a troubled foster child, but while he had it, Commander Coleman made good use of the private space.

The office was small, furnished with a desk, two chairs, and a digital display on the wall opposite the window that overlooked the pilots' wing. Commander Coleman sat behind his desk, reviewing something on his tablet, when Coda walked in.

"Sir," Coda said, snapping to attention.

"At ease." Commander Coleman pointed to a vacant chair on Coda's side of the desk. "Sit."

"Thank you, sir," Coda said, taking a seat.

Commander Coleman placed his tablet on the desk and leaned back, steepling his fingers in front of his mouth in an appraising gaze. "That was a close call out there. How are you holding up?"

"I'll be fine, sir."

Commander Coleman's expression didn't change. "These things can have lasting effects. Pilots can lose confidence. Become tentative. Cautious. I don't need to tell you what happens after that."

"A slow pilot is a dead pilot," Coda said, repeating the mantra Commander Coleman had instilled in them since the beginning of their training.

"Speed is life," Commander Coleman said. "Tentative pilots become a danger to themselves and those they fly with. So I'll ask you again, Coda. How are you holding up?"

"Honestly, sir, I haven't had much time to think about it. And with as many battles as we've faced, I doubt I'll have the time to dwell on it, either."

"You're tired."

"I'm exhausted. We all are. We've been in a constant state of alert for six months, and that's after nearly another six months of intense training." Coda let out a long breath. "I'm not complaining, sir. We all know what's at stake, but it's a lot."

Commander Coleman's mask of authority cracked, and for a brief moment, he wasn't the CAG but just another pilot. Coda had known the commander was just as exhausted as they were. He'd seen it in the dark circles around the man's eyes, the way his skin had lost its luster, and the extra gray in his hair. The commander had also been quicker to anger, his patience having worn thin months ago. But for those briefest of moments, Coda could see the true exhaustion plaguing the commander. He could see what it truly meant to be a hero.

Commander Coleman leaned forward in his seat, placing his hands on the desk. He looked at them absently, picking at a callus on the inside of his index finger. "It *has* been a lot. Fortunately, reinforcements are coming."

"Sir?"

"The first graduates of the new Nighthawk training program are joining the fleet."

"That's... great, sir." Using the same curriculum and schedule Commander Coleman had devised to train the Forgotten, the Terran Fleet Academy and other, less prestigious drone-flight programs had been overhauled to train pilots to fly the Nighthawk instead of the Z-18 Hornet drones the cadets had signed up for. Coda and the rest of the pilots in the squadron had been counting down the weeks until the new graduates arrived.

"We're falling back to the forward operational facility on Meitas, where we'll get our reinforcements and receive our next orders."

"We're switching ships again, sir?"

"Yes," Commander Coleman said. "The *Berlin* sustained heavy damage and will need to spend a few months in dry dock. But you don't need to be concerned with that. I want you to integrate the new pilots into the squadron. See what they're made of. Show them what we're about."

"Me, sir?"

"Yes."

"Don't take this the wrong way, sir, but isn't that the CAG's responsibility?" Under normal circumstances, the question might have earned him a firm rebuke, but he and the commander had been through the shit together, and that provided some extra latitude.

"Yes, Coda. It is. But something tells me Command has other plans for me."

A chill went down Coda's spine. "What kind of plans, sir?"

"Oh," Commander Coleman said. "We'll see. We should be at Meitas in just over seventy-two hours. In the meantime, I want you back into the cockpit as quickly as possible. Get some rest. You're flying CAP as soon as we start for the JumpGate."

# 5

*Admiral Orlovsky's Office, SAS Abraham Lincoln*
*Meitas Station, High Orbit*

MEITAS HAD BEEN NAMED BY SOMEONE WHO'D ATTEMPTED TO CONNECT THE story of King Midas and the might of the Sol Fleet. It was a dry and desolate planet located on the outskirts of the inhabitable zone, and it was prone to electrical storms, wind gusts, and tornados that would kick up the golden-colored soil that had inspired the planet's name. The advanced military base was in high, geosynchronous orbit.

Commander Coleman had briefed his pilots before they left. They were officially orderless, which provided them an element of freedom they hadn't had in months. But he warned them against taking that freedom too far. Drinking was expected. Getting blackout drunk and assaulting an officer was not. He wanted his pilots to behave, but he knew better than to expect it. Coleman was sure he would get more than one call about their behavior. That was just in a fighter jock's nature.

*Lord knows I've caused my share of trouble.*

There was no temporary leave for Coleman. He was still very much on duty, with an appointment he couldn't afford to be late to.

Admiral Orlovsky's office was aboard his personal ship, the *Abraham*

*Lincoln*, which was also currently docked at Meitas Station. After Commander Coleman deboarded the *Berlin*, a pair of junior officers escorted him to the admiral's ship then to his private quarters buried deep within its belly.

The *Abraham Lincoln* couldn't have been more different from the old, industrial ships the Forgotten had served on. While the other ships had been dark, with recessed lighting buried into the tops and bottoms of corridors, the *Abraham Lincoln* was bright. The white bulkhead radiated light itself, and the ship had the shine of technological promise. It felt like a private yacht rather than a warship, and Admiral Orlovsky's personal office felt no different.

Admiral Orlovsky himself appeared as bright and clean-cut as always. With stark-white hair and a square face, the man had the look that officers in the Sol Fleet were supposed to have—regal, strong, and fair. Like the *Abraham Lincoln* itself, he showed no signs of the stress and exhaustion that Commander Coleman and the rest of his squadron felt. The admiral hadn't endured what they had endured or suffered through the same front-row seat to death. Where they were broken, he was whole.

He smiled, rising from a leather-backed chair, revealing teeth as white as his hair. "Chadwick," he said. "It's been too long."

Coleman smiled back. He and the admiral had been friends for a long time, long before he had risen to one of the top stations in the fleet.

"Yes, it has, sir," Coleman said.

"Please." Orlovsky waved a hand in front of his face as if warding off a bad smell. "No sir. It's just us. Two old friends."

Coleman knew better, of course. He hadn't been summoned to a private meeting with one of the most powerful men in the fleet because they were old drinking buddies. They'd stopped being *that* kind of friends years ago. They were closer to friendly acquaintances who shared a fond past.

"Of course," Coleman said.

"Sit." Orlovsky pointed to one of the chairs on Coleman's side of the desk.

Coleman sat and crossed his legs. "How's the family?"

"Getting too old too fast," Orlovsky said. "I'm married to an old woman now."

Coleman laughed. "And she's married to an old man."

"That, she is. When did that happen, Chadwick?"

"Sometime in the last twenty years would be my guess," Coleman said. "What about Victor? He must be about finished with his officer's training. Will I see him on a ship soon?"

"He already is," Orlovsky said. "He's aboard the *Munich*."

Commander Coleman raised his eyebrows. "That's a nice ship."

"Being an admiral's son has its advantages," Orlovsky said with a wry smile. "He's older now than we were when we enlisted. Did you realize that?"

"Now you're making *me* feel old."

"Good. I couldn't be the only one." Orlovsky rose and strode over to a small bar tucked away into the corner of the office. "Want a drink?"

"Of course."

Orlovsky filled two small glasses with brown liquor, handed one to Coleman, then sat in the chair beside him.

"Thank you." Coleman sniffed the glass's contents then took a small sip. The bourbon went down smooth, with a smoky aftertaste that lingered on his tongue. Coleman held the glass to the light appraisingly. "Impressive."

"Another perk." Orlovsky enjoyed a sip of his own then took a deep breath before exhaling through his teeth over several long seconds. "I bet you're wondering why you're here."

"You mean I'm not here to get plastered with an old friend and go streaking through the station?"

Orlovsky let out a booming laugh. "No, but those were the days, weren't they?"

"Some of the best," Coleman agreed. "Before life grew... complicated."

"And it's about to grow even more complicated, old friend." Orlovsky grabbed his tablet and typed in a command before spinning it around so that Coleman could see. "Fleet Intelligence suggests that after their most recent attack, Baranyk forces have begun pulling back from some of their forward operating territories."

Coleman watched a compilation of time-lapse videos showing Baranyk ships in orbit of several Baranyk-controlled territories. One moment they were there, then after a flash of light, the Baranyk ships were gone.

"What happened?" Coleman asked, taking the bait. While the recently vacated worlds had been under human control prior to the Baranyk's development of the disruptor weapon, humanity wasn't in a position to launch an offensive. Not yet. Reinforcements *were* coming, but for the time being, humanity was still very much fighting a defensive war.

"We don't know," Orlovsky said. "But look at the time signatures."

Coleman studied the videos, noting the timestamp on each. At precisely the same millisecond, all four Baranyk capital ships disappeared from the four Baranyk-controlled worlds.

It defied all logic. Commander Coleman had been part of many such retreats, and never in his experience had every ship and shuttle jumped at exactly the same time. Retreats, even planned fallbacks, were more of a haphazard affair and usually deliberately staggered to provide some semblance of order.

"Where are they going?" he asked.

"That's what we want you to find out," Orlovsky said.

"Me?"

"Command is putting together a crew to investigate the disappearance of the Baranyk forces and determine what they're planning next. And we want you to lead it."

Coleman drew his lips into a disapproving frown. It was the same one he used when his pilots made a mistake that they should have known better than to make. "Admiral, we've been through this..."

"I know we have, Chadwick, and let me just stop you right there, because it's not going to work this time. Command was all too happy to let you work on your pet projects, but you were little more than a glorified mechanic. Something well below your rank's credentials. Command was okay with it, because it kept you out of their hair, and they recognized the war had moved past your specific set of abilities. But that's no longer the case. This war, this mission, plays directly into your strengths, Chadwick. There is no more qualified person to lead this mission than you."

"Are those Command's words or yours?" Coleman asked.

"Both."

"I belong in the cockpit. You know that."

"No." Orlovsky regarded his drink. "You *belonged* in the cockpit, but you don't anymore. I've seen your scans. You keep yourself in optimum shape—there's no question—and you're pumping yourself full of steroids and hormones usually reserved for advanced-combat personnel, but you're still forty-six years old. Father Time has finally caught up with you, and unlike this bourbon here, age hasn't made you better. Your body is breaking down. It can't take much more of it."

Coleman regarded the other man for a second then took a sip, giving himself another couple moments to respond. Orlovsky's words were an assault on his ego. He, the soft-bellied, silver-haired desk jockey, was calling *him* old. His first instinct was to show Orlovsky just how *old* he was, but as Orlovsky had said before, the rank of admiral came with a certain set of perks. One of them, Coleman supposed, was that Orlovsky didn't have to worry about angry lower-level officers trying to beat his ass.

Worse, the admiral wasn't wrong. While Coleman liked to tell himself that age was just a number, it came with its own set of realities. No matter how much time he spent in the gym, his body *was* breaking down. He injured easier and took longer to recover, and those were just the physical ailments. The heart and brain scans were more troubling. But damn it, he was a fighter pilot, and he belonged in the cockpit.

"That was a low blow," Coleman said.

Orlovsky shrugged and offered Coleman a small grin. "The perks of—"

"Of rank, I know."

"Of being your friend," Orlovsky finished. "I can tell you the hard truths, and you'll believe me."

*Well, didn't I just shove my foot into my mouth?*

Orlovsky knew he had Coleman in an awkward spot. His grin grew wider. "The truth is, Chadwick, you're afraid of the responsibilities that come with a captainship. You want to be in the cockpit because it's just you in there. If you make a mistake, you're dead, but it's only you. You aren't responsible for the other thousand souls onboard."

"I'm not afraid—"

"Reluctant. Hesitant. Whatever. The point is the same. You don't want the responsibility. But here's where your logic falls apart. In this new war, you're already responsible for every soul onboard, in the fleet and otherwise. If your squadron fails, we're dead. It's as simple as that."

"It's *not* that simple," Coleman said. "I have other pilots to back me up if I fail."

"You're splitting hairs," Orlovsky said, waving his hand. "You assembled the roster, trained them, outlined objectives, and devised the strategy. You do that wrong, and the fleet is gone. You can try and hide from responsibility, Chadwick, but it's already been placed on your shoulders. And you know that, so don't try and argue with me."

Coleman took a deep breath. "You're not going to give me a choice, are you?"

"I told you arguing about it wasn't going to work this time."

"Tell me about the crew," Coleman said.

Orlovsky beamed, obviously sensing victory.

"I'm *not* agreeing to anything yet," Coleman added.

"Of course, of course," Orlovsky said, but it was clear he didn't believe him. "You'll lead it from the state-of-the-art, first-off-the-assembly-line, though recently retrofitted, *Redemption*."

Coleman frowned. "Why would a state-of-the-art ship need to be retrofitted?"

"To accommodate the two squadrons of Nighthawks that will be stationed onboard."

"Two?" No other ship in the fleet had more than the standard one. There was no need. If they got into a battle large enough to necessitate more fighters, then they either retreated or called in additional firepower.

Orlovsky only nodded. "With another two drone squadrons and full platoon of marines. I wasn't lying when I said you were uniquely qualified to lead this mission, Chadwick."

Coleman tapped a finger on the arm of his chair, his eyes boring into Orlovsky's. The admiral was an old friend, but he was still the admiral—and he was looking out for his own neck. Still, he'd brought up some good points, and Coleman would be lying if he said he'd never thought about a captainship. To lead his own ship, to be in charge... he'd served under too many incompetent captains to know that even with the heightened responsibility, the position had advantages too.

Moving in for the kill, Orlovsky stood and rounded his desk. He reached into a drawer and pulled out a small box, removing its top. He slid it across the table. Two gold captain's bars glistened under the artificial light.

"They're yours, Chadwick. All you have to do is say yes."

Coleman took the box, regarding the contents inside. They gleamed at him invitingly. "Under one condition."

"Name it."

"I get to pick my executive crew."

"Done."

"And I want my squadron."

Orlovsky winced. "That, I can't allow. They're the best pilots in the fleet. We need them to lead the other squadrons."

"You have the Old-Timers. Surely, they can—"

Orlovsky waved the suggestion away. "No. They'll be leveraged as well, you can be sure, but your pilots are the true vets of this new war, and we need to leverage their experience."

Coleman understood the challenge. The fleet couldn't integrate several hundred new pilots, all with zero battle experience, and expect the best. "A compromise then. Give me twelve pilots. That'll give me four flight leaders, four seconds, and four more to fill my ranks."

"That's half of your remaining force," Orlovsky said.

"Those are my conditions."

Orlovsky seemed to stew it over for a moment. "That's still too many, Chadwick. I'll never get it approved. Eight. That'll still give you four flight leaders and four seconds. That's the best I can do."

It was more than Coleman had expected to be able to retain. "Fine." He nodded as if to say the negotiation was over.

Orlovsky's stoic face split into a smile. "Congratulations, Commander. Or should I say, *Captain*."

The word rang like an ominous bell. "Thank you, sir."

"Let's get you to your ship."

# 6

*Station Bar*
*Meitas Station, High Orbit*

The bar aboard Meitas Station was the best kind of bar: dirty, cramped, and full of an equal number of men and women. Coda wanted to find a table in the back, somewhere they could be alone to observe the festivities, but Squawks and Noodle overruled him, selecting a high-top table at the center of the room, within shouting distance of the bar and near the makeshift dance floor.

Half a beer deep and having only drunk sparingly over the last six months, Coda was already more than a little foggy headed. The slight buzz was a welcomed feeling, providing him with the escape and liquid looseness he'd been craving for some time.

Since their time aboard the *Jamestown*, Coda had only partaken in the traditional fighter pilot festivities on two occasions: once after Whiskey's funeral and after their first victory as a squadron. On both occasions, he had been called to battle within hours of falling asleep, and regardless of whether or not his body was better equipped to metabolize the alcohol, he hadn't wanted to repeat the mistake. He'd even been reluctant to partake tonight, but again, Squawks and Noodle had won out.

"We're on leave, Coda," Squawks had said. "It's not only allowed; it's *expected*. Didn't you hear the commander?"

"Yeah," Coda said. "He warned us against getting into too much trouble."

"Key word," Squawks said. "*Too much*."

"That's two words," Noodle chimed in.

"Can it, Noodle," Squawks said. "We're expected to blow off steam. And what better way to do that then get annihilated drunk and make bad decisions?"

"Sounds fun," Coda said.

"Damn right, it does," Squawks said, seemingly oblivious to Coda's sarcastic tone.

Coda hadn't fought anymore after that—not because Squawks had won but because it *did* sound fun. After months of being on high alert, the ability to drown his senses was a welcome opportunity. Still, as enticing as it had sounded, he couldn't help but feel they were making a mistake. Maybe it was the months spent in battle or the fact that even now, little stood in the way of a Baranyk attack, but Coda couldn't get comfortable.

The bartender showed up with another tray full of drinks and began placing them onto the table in front of the three men.

"Uh," Coda said, stepping back as if the drink were a viper about to attack. "We didn't order those."

"Compliments of the girls at the bar," the bartender said. "Said to say thank you for all your efforts."

Coda followed his gaze, finding a pair of women sitting at the bar. Their physiques indicated they were servicewomen, which, Coda assumed, wasn't a dangerous assumption as they were on a military station. But unlike the three men, they were dressed in their finest.

"You don't say." Squawks eyed the women, who were now giggling and smiling. "Let's go say you're welcome." Squawks rose from his seat, and Noodle joined him. "Not you."

"What?" Noodle asked.

"Not you," Squawks repeated. "I need a real wingman. I've seen you talk to women. It's embarrassing. Come on, Coda."

Coda didn't move, eyes darting from the women to the drinks. One of the girls smiled coyly, tucking a strand of dark hair behind her ear, giving him a clear view of her slender neck.

*What's wrong with you? Get off your ass and go talk to them!*

But as if frozen in place, Coda still didn't move.

"What the hell's wrong with you?" Squawks asked. "Let's go."

*You're being ridiculous. You have no fear going into battle, but you can't talk to a couple of girls who bought you a drink?*

Coda's tablet vibrated, giving him an excuse to look away and spare him from further embarrassment. It was a message from Commander Coleman.

*This is why I don't drink.*

"What's that?" Squawks asked.

"The commander wants to see me," Coda said.

"What does he want?" Noodle asked.

"I don't know, but it looks like you're up." Coda nodded at the two women.

"Great," Squawks said. "I knew the commander was a dick, but I didn't know he was a cockblock too."

"Good luck." Coda took a final swig then headed toward the door. The last thing he heard before he was out of earshot was Squawks telling Noodle to let him do the talking.

Leaving the bar behind, Coda followed the directions Commander Coleman had sent to his tablet. They led him to a dock on the other side of the station. Commander Coleman waited outside an airlock, still dressed in full uniform. Like the rest of the pilots, Coda had changed into something less formal, sporting a T-shirt and some standard-issue trousers.

"Thank you for coming," Commander Coleman said as Coda approached.

"Of course, sir. What's going on?"

"Walk with me."

Commander Coleman toggled something on the wall pad, opening the airlock, then strode into the umbilical. Unlike the docking umbilicals at the Terran Fleet Academy, this one was hard and within the station's artificial gravity field, allowing the two men to walk down its length.

When they got to the end, Commander Coleman opened the second airlock, entering the ship proper.

Coda found himself in a large corridor leading into the belly of the ship. The ship was new. Its bulkhead was a pristine white, showed no signs of battle, and seemed to glow. As a result, the corridors were well lit, feeling more like a passenger liner than an old twentieth-century submarine.

The commander continued his stroll through the adjoining corridors, en route to his destination. The farther they ventured into the ship, the more it became clear that the commander knew exactly where he was going.

"What is this, sir?" Coda asked. "Our new ship?"

Rather than answer, Commander Coleman stepped through another door, entering an enormous hangar bay. At least twice the size of anything Coda had served on previously, it stretched out in front of him far enough that he couldn't throw a wrench and hit the far wall. He wasn't even sure he could hit the ceiling. And lined up as far as he could see were squadrons of Nighthawks and Hornets.

"Welcome aboard the *Redemption*," Commander Coleman said. He slipped between the Nighthawks, absently running a hand along their matte-black fuselages. Coda followed, trying to take in the grand sight and failing. "Fresh off the assembly line and already retrofitted to accommodate two squadrons of Nighthawks and another two Hornet squadrons, she's about to embark on her maiden voyage."

"She's incredible, sir."

"That she is, Coda." Commander Coleman stopped and turned to face him. "And she's mine."

"Sir?"

"I've accepted command of the *Redemption*."

"Oh." Coda couldn't help but feel a shred of disappointment. Commander Coleman had been the only commander the Forgotten had ever had. He'd assembled them, trained them, flown with them, and mourned with them. If he'd accepted a captainship, then who was in charge of their squadron?

As if sensing Coda's frustration, Commander Coleman continued. "I never wanted this, Coda. I'm a pilot. I've always *been* a pilot. My place has always been out there." He nodded toward the massive bay doors at the far end of the room that emptied into space. "But times change, and sometimes we need to move forward."

"I don't disagree, sir. And I'm happy for you. But if I may, what does this mean for the Forgotten?"

Commander Coleman nodded for Coda to follow, then exited through a door that led into the pilots' section of the ship. Just inside the door, adjacent to the locker room and barracks, was a small office furnished with a desk, two chairs, and a digital display board. The CAG's office. Commander Coleman stood in the doorway, looking into the office.

"I accepted the position on one condition, Coda. That I would get to choose my executive crew and handpick the pilots serving under me. You're one of the finest pilots in the squadron, Coda. I want you out there with me."

The shred of disappointment bloomed into something else. The commander wasn't abandoning him after all. "Of course, sir. It would be an honor. I would have requested it anyway."

"And I want you to be my CAG."

"Sir?"

"I said I want you to lead the squadrons of the *Redemption*."

"Me?" Coda couldn't believe what he was hearing. He'd thought the commander was leaving. Now he was being asked to accompany him, to lead with him. "Sir, I've been flying for less than a year and in battle less than that. I want to fly for you, but surely there's someone more qualified."

"How many battles have you seen, Coda?"

Coda let out a long breath, thinking. "Dozens."

"Which makes you one of the foremost veterans the fleet has to offer. You have also served as flight leader under me for the last three months and led Viking Squadron back at the academy. Except for Moscow, no other pilot in this squadron has as much leadership experience as you do."

"What about your old wingmen? Surely one of them would be available."

"No," Commander Coleman said. "Unlike me, they moved on when the war passed them by. They're either commanding ships of their own or out of the service altogether. Even the Old-Timers are being disbanded and used to train the new graduates. But even if they weren't, they're like me—old and slow, losing their battle with age. I need someone like you, Coda. Young. Experienced. Driven."

Coda looked away from the commander—or was he a captain now? —taking in the office. Captain Coleman was offering it to him. All he had to do was say yes. Could he do it? Did he *want* to do it?

The questions brought with them something else that had been plaguing him of late. For his entire military career, he'd had a single goal: restore honor to his family name. He'd done that. He was a hero of the fleet. When he went to bars, people recognized him and bought him drinks. By all indications, he had succeeded, but if that were the case, why did he still feel like his job was unfinished? Why didn't he feel like the man everyone saw him as? What drove him now? All questions he'd been unable to answer.

Coda stepped into the office. "What's the mission?"

"Baranyk ships are retreating from newly conquered territory. We're to find out why and what they're planning."

"A recon mission."

"Something like that."

"And yet, if the number of fighters in the hangar were any indication, they're expecting heavy resistance."

Captain Coleman shrugged. "We're at war, Coda. We expect it every day." He stepped into the room and slid a finger across the display that took up the entire wall. The screen came to life, displaying forty-eight fighters divided into four flights of twelve.

"Two squadrons," Captain Coleman said. "Each with their own squadron leader and flight leaders made up of the Forgotten. The rest will be made up of reinforcements."

*Reinforcements*. Meaning green pilots yet to see battle.

"Would I get to pick my squadron and flight leaders?" Coda asked.

"Of course," Captain Coleman said. "Off of the flight roster that I've assembled, anyway. I think you'll be comfortable with my choices, though."

Captain Coleman swiped the images to the left side of the display and brought up a list of pilots on the right. Seeing his friends' names on the roster, Coda smiled. He placed an index finger on one of the names, slid it over, and dropped it on top of the gold fighter that indicated the squadron leader of Silver Squadron. He repeated the process, completing the flight roster with its flight leaders, and stepped back, allowing the captain to see.

The captain smiled and nodded his approval. "Should I take this as a yes?"

Coda cast a final look at the board and took a deep breath. Like Captain Coleman, Coda wouldn't be in this alone. He would have his friends and flight leaders, along with four more seconds, all made up of people he had flown with and trusted.

"Yes, sir. It's an honor to be your CAG."

"Good," Captain Coleman said. There's one last thing."

"Sir?"

"It's there on your desk." Captain Coleman pointed toward a small black box sitting on the desktop.

Coda grabbed the box and, casting a questioning eye toward the captain, opened it. Inside was a gold-leaf collar device. "Sir, I... thank you, sir."

"Welcome aboard the *Redemption*, Lieutenant Commander."

# 7

*Meeting Room, SAS Redemption*
*Meitas Station, High Orbit*

A week later, Captain Coleman stood at the head of the table in the *Redemption*'s officers' meeting room, feeling more than a little uncomfortable with the room's eyes trained solely on him. Just off the ship's bridge, the room felt very different from the ship's command center. The meeting room was devoid of the electronics that fueled the navigational, communication, and tactical displays.

The table, made of solid old-fashioned wood instead of the composite materials used throughout the rest of the ship, could have belonged to a navy vessel four hundred years in the past. The steel anchors that bolted it to the floor, keeping it from becoming a five-hundred-kilogram projectile should the ship's artificial gravity fail, were all that suggested the desk was aboard a starship and not an old sealiner.

Like the table, Coleman couldn't help but feel like a relic, something that would have been out of place if not for tradition. As he returned the gazes of his officers, Coleman's new reality hit home for the first time. A week ago, he had been the commander of one of three Nighthawk squadrons left in the fleet. Now he was the captain of a starship with orders to venture into Baranyk space and answer one of the biggest questions plaguing Fleet Command. With the new position had come new responsibilities, and the first had been to handpick the very people seated in front of him—most of whom hadn't met each other yet, which was the first point of his meeting agenda.

"Thank you for coming," he began. "I know it's early for some of you, late for others. It's going to take a little time to get acclimated to the ship's schedule. First order of business is some quick introductions." He pointed to Coda, who sat immediately to his left. He was the youngest person in the room by a wide margin and seemed to realize it, shifting uneasily in his chair.

"Lieutenant Commander O'Neil is our CAG, the person in charge of integrating the newly graduated Nighthawk pilots into the fighter squadrons we have aboard the *Redemption* and leading them in battle. I have personally flown with Commander O'Neil, and he was the one who devised the strategy that ensured our victory above Toavis."

Coda sat a little straighter and nodded to the officers seated around the table. *So, I'm not the only one who feels like a fish out of water.* Something about that made Coleman more comfortable.

"Seated beside him is Chief Engineer Brahm Payton."

Tall and slender, Payton had thin black hair that he kept dangerously close to exceeding regulations and wore the kind of smirk that said he was smarter than everyone else in the room and wanted everyone else to know it too.

"The chief will keep all of us warm and cozy inside our little ship as we venture into the cold, dark unknown." This got a few chuckles from around the table, though none from the chief.

Payton pursed his lips together, his eyes narrowing at those who laughed. *Why are the best engineers born without a sense of humor?*

"On the other side of the table, we have Chief Science Officer Indira Naidoo. One of the foremost experts in Baranyk biology and theoretical communication, Dr. Naidoo will be joining us until we have provided Fleet Command with a viable answer to their most pressing questions."

Dr. Naidoo had her black hair pulled into a tight bun. Where Payton wore his disdain openly, Naidoo was reserved, her face showing no hint of emotion. Coleman had met her aboard the *Jamestown*, and in the few conversations he'd had with the woman, he'd found her highly intelligent and more than capable.

"Lastly, my longtime friend and XO, Commander Jaime Garcia."

A former fighter pilot in his own right, Garcia hadn't aged well. His once-chiseled frame had gone soft with age. His belly pushed against the buttons of his jacket, and the skin of his neck was loose and drooping. But his calling card had always been his hair, and that was as thick as ever, even if it was peppered with gray.

"Happy to be aboard," Garcia said. His voice was deep and warm, but Coleman knew it could cut and growl with the best of them. "I never thought I'd see the day where the great Commander Coleman took a captainship. Had to see it for myself."

"And it never would have come to pass if I hadn't been allowed to handpick each and every one of you," Coleman said. "Our mission is of extreme importance and likely extremely dangerous."

"A mission I'm still a little fuzzy on, if I'm being honest," Garcia said.

"Which brings us to agenda point number two." Coleman toggled a couple buttons on his tablet, dimming the lights, and called up the display at the back of the room. "As I have shared with all of you individually, our recon drones have observed enemy carriers jumping out of Baranyk-controlled territories, leaving them unprotected and open to human counterattack. What I haven't shared with you is this."

Coleman pulled up four separate images from four different systems with a global clock at the bottom of the screen. As the admiral had shown him, he showed his officers.

"They jumped at the same time?" Payton asked.

Coleman nodded. "At *exactly* the same time."

"Is that even possible?" Coda asked.

"It's possible," Payton said. "If their ships are equipped with jump drives similar to ours, it's just a matter of entering in the time of the jump and allowing the AI to coordinate it over the network. Pretty simple really. Now whether or not it's probable is another story. We've never been able to detect a Baranyk network."

"You're attempting to project a human thought process onto an alien species," Dr. Naidoo said. "What may be improbable or strange to us may be the way they naturally operate."

"I'm less concerned with the how," Coleman said, "and more

concerned with the why. Where did they go? What are they planning? Why leave hard-fought territory open for retaking? And why do it in system after system?"

"There's only one strategic reason to leave territory unguarded," Garcia said. "Because you're massing forces somewhere else."

"Which explains Command's concern," Coleman said.

A heavy silence fell over the room as each of its occupants watched the display repeat the Baranyk disappearances in a steady loop.

"Were they left unoccupied?" Coda asked, interrupting the quiet. "I mean, have all Baranyk forces left those systems?"

"No," Coleman said. "Each system has what amounts to a small rear guard. A single ship, medium size, no doubt to monitor our movements."

"And on the ground?" Coda asked.

"We don't know," Coleman said. "Our recon drones haven't been able to provide anything definitive. Early signs point to no ground activity, though."

"Then we could be walking into a trap," Garcia said. "They could be massing a large fleet somewhere and then jump in the moment our ship is detected."

"Then you understand the stakes," Coleman said. "We need to be prepared for anything. Commander O'Neil, how are the new pilots falling in?"

"They're still arriving, sir," Coda said. "From what I can tell, they're well trained, but I won't know what I have until I put them in the simulator. And even then, we won't truly know what they're made of until we've seen them in action."

"Keep on them," Coleman said. "They have to be ready. Our success depends on it." He took a deep breath, shifting his attention to the larger audience. "We're flying into the unknown, ladies and gentlemen, and something tells me our collective mettle will be tested. Stay focused, and prepare your people. We jump in forty-eight hours."

# 8

*Nighthawk Ready Room, SAS Redemption*
*Meitas Station, High Orbit*

THE MOMENT THE LAST PILOT REPORTED ABOARD THE *REDEMPTION*, CODA ordered his squadrons to the Nighthawk ready room. He gave them two minutes to assemble and find seats in the room's stadium seating before stepping through the door and making for the podium at the front of the room, his three other flight leaders in tow.

"Officers on deck!" someone shouted, and as one, forty-eight pilots rose to their feet and snapped to attention.

"At ease," Coda said, falling into position behind the podium. "And take your seats." His flight leaders stopped a step behind him, flanking him on either side, not unlike their standard finger-four flight formation.

Captain Coleman hadn't been surprised when Coda had selected Moscow, Squawks, and Noodle as his flight leaders, though he had raised an eyebrow when Coda told him that Moscow was his second-in-command and leader of Silver Squadron. It seemed that while Coda and Moscow had largely put their past issues behind them and had even supported each other as wingmen, Captain Coleman didn't fully trust them. Coda couldn't blame him. To say he and Moscow had been rivals was like saying the sun was hot.

Once his pilots had retaken their seats and silence again filled the ready room, Coda began. "Welcome to the Forgotten. I am Lieutenant Commander Callan O'Neil, your CAG, but in the cockpit and in nonformal situations, you may call me by my call sign, Coda. Behind me are your flight leaders, and like me, they have been in this squadron since the beginning. They have flown in battle, and they have been victorious. I trust them with my life."

Coda paused, letting the words sink in.

"The unfortunate reality is that while I trust them, I do not trust you. You're no doubt great pilots, the best the Sol Fleet has produced. But trust is earned, ladies and gentlemen. Through hours in the cockpit. Through blood, sweat, and tears. From you being there when I need you and me being there when you need me. And until that day comes, what will they be, Squawks?"

"FNGs, sir," Squawks said.

"FNGs," Coda repeated.

"Fucking new guys," Squawks said.

A small wave of laughter filtered through the room, and Coda allowed himself a smirk. "Fucking new guys," he repeated. "I don't tell you this to make you angry. I don't tell you this to make you feel inadequate. It's simple common sense. Until we've flown with you, we don't know if you're more likely to kill us or the enemy. And until each of you proves that you're more likely to kill the enemy than one of your wingmen, you will remain FNGs. Any questions?"

"When will we get an opportunity to prove that we belong, sir?" The question came from a pilot in the front row. She leaned back in her seat so that her long legs stretched out in front of her. Her no-nonsense expression reminded Coda of Captain Coleman.

"The rest of the crew is still boarding the *Redemption*," Coda said. "We'll remain at Meitas Station for another sixteen hours. After that, the decision is up to the Baranyk. In the meantime, each of you has been assigned to a flight leader, and that information has already been sent to your tablets. Line up according to flight, and prepare to move."

The pilots checked their tablets, rose, and slowly milled about to determine who was in each flight. Coda turned to Moscow, raising an eyebrow.

"Move!" Moscow bellowed. "This isn't Sunday school. Go! Go! Go!"

Chaos ensued. The pilots frantically formed into four lines based on flight. Coda smiled, taking his place at the head of his flight. His other flight leaders did the same, then he led them out of the ready room. They jogged down the corridor, entering a nearby room that had been equipped with four simulators. His pilots formed four neat rows, eyes on Coda and the simulators.

"Until I say otherwise," Coda began, "you will spend every waking moment in these simulators. Make no mistake, FNGs—you're still very much in training, and until my flight leaders know what to do with you, you will keep working. Is that understood?"

"Yes, sir!" the pilots shouted in unison.

"Good," Coda said. "Let's begin."

Coda selected the first member in line from each of the four flights and told them to strap into the simulators. One of the pilots was the woman who had asked when she would have a chance to prove herself.

Over the course of several hours, Coda and his flight leaders ran the new pilots through the preprogrammed scenarios Coda had built within the simulator. Flying in small flights of four, they had a simple objective: hold off a growing swarm of Baranyk fighters for as long as possible. There was no "winning" the scenario; it simply grew more and more difficult until the pilots were finally overwhelmed. Still, it allowed him to see how far their previous training had taken them.

It didn't come as any surprise that the woman—he'd learned her call sign was Nails—was good. *Really* good. Her flight lasted longer than any of the others', and she had more kills than any other pilot. Through it all, Coda felt a growing sense of familiarity. From the cool confidence in how she held herself to her precise flying that had a flair of swagger, Coda couldn't escape the feeling that he'd met her before.

When every pilot had taken their turn in the simulator, Coda cued up another scenario and had them begin again. He was met with a few frustrated murmurs, but nobody questioned him outright. Not even Nails. He understood their frustration, of course. It was getting late, and he'd told them they would be shipping out in a matter of hours. That meant that some of them would be in the cockpit again with little to no sleep, and since they were entering Baranyk space, there was no telling when they would catch up.

*There's no other way. I have to know what I have.*

Another four hours and more than twenty flights later, practice came to an end. All in all, Coda was surprised by how well they'd flown. They were technically competent, confident, and aggressive. Still, he was only cautiously optimistic. Simulated battle was far from the real thing. When the real bullets started flying and mistakes meant death, he didn't know how many of his pilots would lose their edge or snap under the pressure.

"Good work today," he said in their debriefing. "You've had some good training. In time, you'll be worthy of your position among the Forgotten. Over the next few days, my flight leaders and I will assign you to your wingmen and fill out the flight rosters. That's when the real work will begin, because while you show promise, you're still what?"

"FNGs," they repeated in amused exhaustion.

Coda let himself smile. He couldn't be a hard-ass *all* the time. Fighter pilots and their leaders shared a different kind of bond than other military units—it was good for his pilots to see him as something more than just their superior.

"FNGs," Coda repeated. "Exactly. Now get some rest. We'll reconvene at zero six hundred. Dismissed."

The pilots filed out of the room in an exhausted shuffle. As the door slid closed behind the final one, he let out a long breath and turned to his flight leaders. "We have our work cut out for us."

"Yes, we do," Noodle agreed. "I wouldn't trust a single one of them to understand a complex set of orders, let alone be able to carry them out."

"They're green," Moscow said. "Greener than green."

"Fucking FNGs," Squawks said.

"What are we going to do?" Noodle asked.

"Exactly what I said we were going to do. We'll assign them to their wingmen as soon as possible and get them flying CAP and logging time in the simulator. Then we need to fill out the flight rosters. We need to pair them up by skill set and flying styles. They need to be better together than they would be individually."

"And you think you have enough information from only two training scenarios?" Moscow asked skeptically.

"No," Coda said. "It'll be a fluid process, and things will change, but we don't have time to wait."

"When do we get started?" Noodle asked.

"Right now," Coda said. "Come on."

They exited the Simulation Room and found Nails waiting in the corridor. She took one look at Coda and started to speak then noticed the others behind him and closed her mouth as if she'd thought better of whatever she was going to say.

"Can I help you with something?" Coda asked.

She hesitated, her attention darting between Coda and the rest. "No, sir. Good night." She gave him a crisp salute and disappeared down the corridor.

"That was weird," Squawks said, watching her go.

"Yeah, it was," Noodle said.

"What do you think she wanted?" Moscow asked.

"I'm not sure," Coda admitted. Then, as if the thought had just come to him, he added, "Does she remind you of anyone?"

"No..." Noodle said. "Should she?"

"I don't know. I just feel like—"

"Captain Coleman," Squawks said, cutting him off. "It's that whole take-no-shit, tough-as-nails attitude that the captain has, which is where she no doubt got her call sign. Hell, she even looks like him."

Coda looked back down the corridor. She'd long since turned down an adjoining corridor, but in his mind's eye, Coda could still see her. Now that Squawks mentioned it, she *did* look like the captain. Coda couldn't imagine him having a daughter. Captain Coleman was many things, but fatherly wasn't one of them. If anything, he was married to his service, and the Nighthawks were his children.

"Yeah, that must be it," Coda said. "Come on. It's already late."

Even as he led the flight leaders into his office to begin their work assembling the fighter pairs, the questioned needled at him. He struggled to focus as they watched clips of the flight scenarios on the left side of the digital display and moved names around on the right, putting together tentative pairs, then rewatched clips of both pilots side by side. Two hours into the process, with his flight leaders having taken over, Coda pulled up Nails's file.

Lieutenant Aniyah Robinson had graduated from the recently refurbished Terran Fleet Academy, with marks good enough to place her within the top five percent of her class. Her instructors raved about her all-business attitude and ruminated on how she felt as though she had grown up in the cockpit. It was the latter comments that made Coda dig deeper. While Nails's family name was different from Captain Coleman's, he couldn't shake the feeling that the two were related. It only took a few minutes of digging before Coda found his confirmation.

He found it in the form of a divorce filing. Lisa Robinson had filed for divorce from Chadwick Coleman, citing irreconcilable differences, and had promptly been awarded sole custody of their only child, Aniyah Robinson. The processing dates were eerily close to when the Sol Fleet had shut down the Nighthawk program. Was that why the captain had never returned to Earth, even after the war had left him behind? Because he had nothing to go back to?

Coda doubted he would ever fully get answers to the questions. It didn't matter anyway, because new questions quickly replaced the first. Did the captain know his daughter was onboard, having joined the ranks of the most dangerous squadron in the fleet? If he did, why hadn't he said anything to Coda about it? Or even more puzzling, if he didn't know, was it simply coincidence that she'd found her way to her father's ship, or had someone higher up within Fleet Command placed her there? And if the latter was true, what other surprises could the Forgotten expect?

Sitting behind his desk inside his new office, watching as his flight leaders argued about fighter pairs, Coda was left with an unsettling feeling.

*Nothing about this mission is what it seems.*

# 9

*Bridge, SAS Redemption*
*JumpGate Meitas-2, High Orbit*

THE BRIDGE OF THE *REDEMPTION* WAS MUCH LIKE THE BRIDGES OF THE other ships Captain Coleman had served on. It was made up of three descending levels, with the more critical crew members closer to the center and bottom circle, where the captain and XO were stationed. The biggest difference was the size. It wasn't necessarily bigger to accommodate more crew but to give them more space to operate in.

Commander Garcia stood at the center of the bottommost layer, his eyes firmly on the three-dimensional display that ascended to the ceiling. Coleman had known Garcia since his days as a pilot, when both had served aboard the *George Washington.* When the Nighthawk program was shut down, Coleman had refused advancement, staying as close to the fighters as possible, while Garcia had moved on with the times.

Like many of the other former pilots Coleman had known, Garcia hadn't aged well. The wrinkles that stretched out from his eyes and mouth were the worst. Not only were they wrinkles of age but stress as well. Fleet Command hadn't been kind to him—that was one of the reasons Garcia had taken Coleman up on his offer to join him.

The display showed three-dimensional wireframe images of the space surrounding the *Redemption.* Like the other sensors aboard the ship, the images were updated automatically as new data came in. Having undocked from Meitas Station hours ago, the only wireframe was of the *Redemption*, its fighters flying CAP, and JumpGate Meitas-2.

The JumpGate was shaped like a pistol, the *Redemption* hovering above what would be the barrel, moving slowly downward as if being loaded from above—which, for all intents and purposes, it was.

"How are we looking, Commander?" Coleman asked as he descended the final step into the bottom layer of the bridge.

"Approaching the JumpGate now, sir," Garcia said. "Docking procedure to commence in five minutes."

"Good," Coleman said.

Whether it was Garcia's words or having the bridge crew looking down upon him, Coleman couldn't help but feel like the eyes of everyone in Fleet Command were on him. It was a far cry from the days when he'd made decisions from the privacy of his own cockpit. There had been no eyes there, and when he didn't want to hear other people, he'd just needed to order radio silence. This was going to take some getting used to—as was the earpiece he and the rest of his command had been fitted with.

Coleman toggled the piece, opening a channel between him and his CAG. "Coda, we're approaching the JumpGate now. Bring in the CAP."

"Yes, sir," Coda said.

Watching the battle map, Coleman saw that Coda relayed his command immediately. The green wireframes of the four Nighthawks on patrol altered course, moving to dock with the *Redemption*.

"How are things looking down there?" Coleman asked.

"Good, sir. We've finalized our flight rosters and fighter pairs, and each of the flight leaders have run their pilots through various scenarios in the simulator. They're green, sir, but they're well trained."

"Good," Coleman said. "Get your best two flights in the tubes and ready to launch. Let me know when they're ready."

"On it, sir."

"Keep up the good work."

"Will do, sir."

Colman closed the line and opened a new one with his chief engineer. "I'm reading all green down here, Chief. How are my engines looking on your end?"

"Green down here too, sir," Payton said. "The ship's sensors should alert you if there's any trouble. No need to get my approval before every jump."

"Old habits die hard, Chief," Coleman said. "I'll be a fighter pilot until the day I die, and that means I'll double-, triple-, and sometimes quadruple-check our processes. I've known too many good men who died because they trusted the word 'should.'"

"Understood, sir." Payton's tone was sharp, as if he were annoyed. He likely took questioning the integrity of the sensors as questioning Payton himself. Well, his chief engineer would just have to get used to his captain being overly cautious.

"We'll be entering enemy space within minutes," Coleman continued. "I'll expect regular status updates."

"And you'll have them, sir."

Coleman closed the channel. On the digital battle map, Coleman watched as the wireframe image of the *Redemption* slid into the barrel of the JumpGate.

"We're loaded, sir," Ensign Richey, his communications officer, said. Her dark hair was pulled back into a bun, framing a young face. "The gate crew is awaiting your order to begin the jump-initiation sequence."

"Begin," Coleman said.

"Yes, sir."

Coleman took a deep breath then toggled his earpiece to channel communication with the entire ship. It was his responsibility to inform the crew what they could expect, to prepare them, and to keep them together when shit hit the fan. But damn it if it wasn't unnerving. He wasn't one to make speeches.

"This is the captain," he began, his voice reverberating through the bridge's speakers. "We're about to jump into Baranyk territory. Command has all but assured us that the enemy forces have mostly fled, but I don't hold to that, and neither should you. As a fighter pilot, I learned to always expect the worst. By doing so, I had a plan in place to fix whatever situation I fell into, long before it ever happened. That's how I lived where others died. That's why I am here and they are not. So

I challenge each and every one of you: think, expect, and prepare. For *every* possible scenario. Coleman out."

Coleman toggled the earpiece off.

"Riveting, sir," Garcia said under his breath. "I got chills."

"I wouldn't be surprised if that was the most nerve-wracking thing I have to do all day." Coleman sighed.

"You're a natural, sir."

"And you're still a smartass, Commander. I was up half the night putting that together." He turned back to Richey. "Where are we with the jump initiation?"

"Just finished, sir."

"Good," Coleman said. "Tell the gate crew to initiate jump on my mark."

"Yes, sir."

Coleman opened a new channel. "Coda, what's the status of my Nighthawks?"

"The deck crew just loaded the last one, sir. We're good to go."

"Understood. Stay alert." Then to Garcia, "You ready?"

"Let's see what our old friends have cooking."

Coleman spotted Richey on the ring above him. Her eyes were already locked on him, awaiting his order.

"Jump."

# 10

*Bridge, SAS Redemption*
*Cerian-7*

Captain Coleman had been aboard more than a dozen ships and jumped more times than he could count, but he still never got used to the sensation. Most people described it as having the world stretch out in front of them, as if their sense of reality were somehow elongated.

For Coleman, however, it felt like being ripped out of his body altogether. It wasn't painful, just disorienting. The world *did* stretch out in front of him, but as it did, so did he. He watched himself, seeing the back of his head as if he were dreaming in the third person. He felt and saw every movement during the jump sequence, which only made him even more disoriented. So he had long since instituted a practice that kept him stock-still until the jump was completed.

For several long moments, the sensation continued. Then in the span of an eyeblink, the world snapped back into focus. Coleman's sweaty palms gripped the railing nearby to keep him from staggering.

"Report," Coleman said, his eyes moving back to the three-dimensional battle map in the center of the bridge.

"Sensor data coming in now," Tactical Officer Lieutenant Poiu said, not looking up from his terminal. Like many aboard the *Redemption*, he was young but had come with strong recommendations and high marks from the academy. "We've arrived at Cerian-7, sir."

The image of the planet suddenly appeared on the display. Like Earth, it was a mix of blues, greens, oranges, and yellows. Cerian-7, though, was actually a moon that orbited the gas giant Cerian, which gave the system its name. The moon's close proximity to the gas giant created tidal forces and volcanic activity that kept the moon, which was well out of the sun's Goldilocks zone, warm enough for human habitation.

The real treasure of the system was Cerian itself. Rich in hydrogen and helium-3, the planet provided many of the raw materials used in the fleet's fusion reactors. Like Toavis and many other planets before it, Cerian-7 was a requirement for advancing the human fleet. Supply lines had always been a challenge during planetary war, but they were an impossibility in intergalactic warfare. The challenge had finally been solved by the advanced mining operations of the Sol Fleet. Now, though, Coleman saw none of the standard ships, scoopers, or other mining vessels that would normally be harvesting the raw gases from the planet's atmosphere.

He had chosen to begin his mission at Cerian-7 for two reasons: If they were able to reclaim the moon, mining operations could restart, providing vital materials to the fleet. It was also the farthest the Baranyk had ventured into human space. The end of their line had become the beginning of his.

"Readings?" Coleman asked.

"Nothing, sir," Poiu said. "No activity coming from the planet or the moon."

"Plot a cour—"

"Wait," Poiu said, "I'm picking something up."

The data slowly visualized on the display. Something was coming around the moon. Coleman recognized the carrier before Lieutenant Poiu confirmed it.

"It's the Baranyk, sir! One carrier. And... it's breaking orbit. We've been spotted."

"Set Condition One throughout the ship," Coleman said. "Launch fighters and plot an intercept course."

"They left someone behind, after all," Garcia said.

"Yes, they did," Coleman said.

"They want to know if we came knocking?"

"Or left as bait to draw us into a trap."

Coleman watched the display as twenty-four Nighthawks blasted out of the side of the *Redemption*. Immediately clear of the larger ship's hull, they split into two flights of twelve. Forming up on the nose of the *Redemption*, they looked every bit like the tip of the spear that they truly were.

"Time to intercept?" Coleman asked.

"At this speed," Lieutenant Poiu said, running the calculations on his terminal. "Four minutes."

Coleman stared at the image of the incoming vessel, running through his options. The old starfighter's adage rang through his head. *Speed is life.*

"Increase thrust twelve percent, Lieutenant Poiu," Coleman said.

"Course, sir?"

"Same course, Lieutenant."

Although Lieutenant Poiu didn't question the order, he watched Coleman for half a second too long. All chatter on the bridge seemed to die, and Coleman thought he felt the eyes of the entire bridge staff. The order to increase speed ran contrary to typical engagement tactics. With their ten-meter-thick, reinforced-steel hulls, the human battle cruisers were built for strength, not speed, but as Coleman was beginning to learn, old habits died hard.

"You heard the captain!" Garcia bellowed. "Increase thrust twelve percent. Same course."

"Increasing thrust twelve percent." Lieutenant Poiu's fingers moved like lightning across his terminal.

"Bring us within ten kilometers on the starboard side," Coleman said. "I want every cannon firing the moment that ship enters range, and don't stop until it's out. We're going to hit it with everything we have while we pass."

"Course is set," Lieutenant Poiu said.

"Good," Coleman said. "Once we're past the enemy vessel, slingshot around the moon and prepare for another pass."

"At that speed, that won't give us a lot of time on the second pass," Garcia said quietly.

"We do our jobs right on the first and we won't need it." Coleman brought up the frequency to his fighter squadrons. "Coda, do you read me?"

"Loud and clear, sir."

"Good. Lieutenant Poiu is transferring flight data to you now. You're my spear. We're going to strafe past the enemy vessel, and I want you to poke as many holes in it as possible."

"What about their fighters, sir?"

Smaller red dots were streaming out of the carrier now, moving to intercept the human force.

"Open fire, but do not pursue."

"Sir?"

"Your primary objective is the carrier," Coleman said. "Once the *Redemption* has passed, engage the fighters and draw them away. We'll continue around the moon and assault the unprotected carrier."

"Copy that."

"That'll leave you in communications blackout until we make it around the moon."

"We'll be fine, sir."

"Happy hunting, Commander." Coleman closed the channel.

"Weapons range in one minute," Lieutenant Poiu said.

The two massive vessels drifted toward each other. The vastness of space made the dance look slow, but Coleman knew they were moving at incredible speeds, and the window of time for bombardment would be very short. Still, strafing runs were less dangerous, and with only one Baranyk carrier present, there was no reason to take any undue risk.

"Ten seconds," Lieutenant Poiu said. "Five, four, three..."

*Here we go.*

The Nighthawks opened fire first, cutting into the enemy fighters with a volley of missiles. Red wireframes disappeared from the display as enemy fighters were blown out of space. True to Coleman's command, the Nighthawks continued course, heading straight for the unguarded enemy carrier. A moment later, a volley of Haymakers were on their way. Red circles appeared around the carrier's image, marking multiple hits. Then in a blink, the Nighthawks were past, and it was Coleman's turn.

Unlike being in the cockpit, his role in the battle was relatively limited. He had to give the order and trust his crew to carry it out. The distant rumble of batteries echoed through the ship, reverberating through the bulkhead, vibrating the deck. The display lit up as rounds streaked from the *Redemption* toward the enemy vessel. Over six meters in length and two meters in diameter, the capital-ship killers nicknamed the Rods from God weighed more than ten thousand kilograms and packed a significant punch. Better yet, since they relied exclusively on kinetic energy, there was no disarming them. The Baranyk's only hope was avoiding them altogether.

"I'm showing multiple hits," Lieutenant Poiu said. "Between the fighters and our—"

The ship shook violently as the first Baranyk slugs tore into the *Redemption.* The enemy didn't let up, and due to their ships' close proximity, there were no evasive maneuvers Coleman could take. He and the rest of his crew were at the mercy of the strength of the *Redemption*'s hull.

"Damage report!" Coleman bellowed.

"Multiple hits along our starboard side, decks five through seventeen," Lieutenant Poiu said. "No breaches. They're hitting us, but they're little more than glancing blows. Looks like our speed is making it difficult for them to get off a clean shot."

"Good," Coleman said, perhaps a little too triumphantly—which he was reminded of when the ship shuddered again, the already dim lights of the bridge flickering.

"That one got through," Lieutenant Poiu said. "Decompression in decks twelve through sixteen."

"Get our people down there," Coleman said.

"Already done, sir."

The deck continued to vibrate as the men and women of his gunnery department kept their systems online and batteries firing. More red circles on the Baranyk ship's wireframe showed additional hits. The ship was taking a hell of a beating, but would it be enough? The *Redemption* shook again with another direct hit. The enemy had adjusted their ordinance. Lieutenant Poiu shouted as decks suffered breaches and decompression.

Sweat trickled down Coleman's back. He wasn't used to taking direct hits. If something like that happened in a fighter, the pilot was done for.

The ship continued to vibrate as it belched fire and death on its enemy, the two ships passing in the black. And then it stopped. An eerie silence fell over the bridge, interrupted only by the heavy breathing of its personnel and the soft beeping from the shipboard computers.

"We're out of range, sir," Lieutenant Poiu said.

"Status of the enemy vessel?"

"Showing signs of major damage. Dozens of breaches and signs of power failure. We did quite a number on her, sir."

"Good." Coleman allowed himself a sigh of relief, watching the display as his fighters still at the tip of the *Redemption* broke off at opposite angles. The fighters swung around wide, reversing course, and prepared to engage the Baranyk fighters pursuing the human force.

"Lieutenant Poiu," Coleman said, "plot a course around the moon. We're going to slingshot around and finish the job."

"Yes, sir."

*Good luck, Coda. You're on your own for now.*

# 11

*Cockpit, Nighthawk*
*Cerian-7*

CODA FIRED HIS FORWARD THRUSTERS, SHEDDING SPEED. HIS FLIGHT harness dug into his chest, shoulders, and crotch, sending spikes of pain through his body. Gritting his teeth, he assessed the situation on his HUD.

The Baranyk carrier had launched its fighters before the *Redemption* opened fire, likely expecting a standard engagement. Captain Coleman's unique strategy had thrown them off, though, rendering their fighters ineffective, except for a couple lucky shots from distance. The larger ships were slower and more sluggish, but the smaller, more nimble crafts had altered course to begin harrowing the human capital ship from behind.

Coda's computer counted four squadrons of Baranyk fighters, leaving his squadron badly outnumbered. They were also without the cover fire of the *Redemption*'s point-defense cannons and the safety net the ship provided if they were forced to retreat. Fortunately, the enemy had been preoccupied with the human capital ship and had massed their fighters in offsetting square-shaped formations that allowed maximum offensive fire. It also gave the first wave of Coda's fighters a clear shot as they came into firing range.

Targeting the nearest Baranyk fighters, Coda and Nails, his wingman on the hop, released a pair of missiles in less than a heartbeat. Four small points of light, barely brighter than the sky's brightest star, flashed for a brief moment then winked out. Red dots on Coda's battle map disappeared a moment later, confirming the enemy crafts' destruction.

"Splash two!" Coda shouted.

"Splash four," Nails echoed.

There were more flashes of light as the rest of the squadrons' missiles cut into the meaty part of the formation. The radio rang with more triumphant shouts as the Baranyk squadrons were cut down by almost half.

*That'll make this a fair fight.*

"Like shooting pigs in a barrel," Squawks said over the comm.

"I don't think that's how it goes," Coda said.

"That's the joke, dumbass. Did you lose all sense of humor when you became CAG?"

Coda laughed, wondering what the new pilots thought of the strange banter. Then the Baranyk formations shattered, breaking into quads of fighters darting in every direction. Coda's Nighthawk shuddered and came alive as he switched to cannons and opened fire. Tracer fire disappeared into the black, narrowly missing a quad of Baranyk. It seemed to get their attention, though, because they altered course, darting in pursuit.

Coda flipped his Nighthawk nose to tail, expecting Nails to do the same. She didn't, leaving Coda alone against the incoming enemy fighters. Worse yet, she'd picked up a tail of her own. Busy taking evasive maneuvers, she wouldn't be able to come to his aid.

Fortunately, his maneuver left him flying backward, his nose-mounted cannon pointed directly at the pursuing enemy fighters. Firing in controlled bursts, Coda took out the lead fighter. Its organic hull exploded like a squashed bug on concrete.

He opened fire on the next fighter and instructed his computer to get missile lock on the third and fourth. A well-placed shot in the middle of the formation would likely destroy all three remaining vessels, but before Coda could launch the missile, the Baranyk formation broke apart. Two fighters moved to his starboard side, the other to his port. It was the same strategy the enemy had taken in the battle of Chrylis when they'd tried to take down Coda and Moscow. It hadn't worked then, but he didn't have Moscow now—the other pilot was in charge of Silver Squadron, which wasn't in this battle—and his new wingman had her own issues.

Coda ran through his options. He could spin horizontally, follow the pair of Baranyk fighters, and allow the third to get onto his six. If he could eliminate the pair of fighters fast enough and turn his attention to the third...

*No. There's no time.*

He did the only other thing he could think of. He fired his main thrusters. Since they were pointed in the direction his craft was flying, the maneuver slowed his speed—*dramatically*. Coda slammed into his gel seat, feeling something twist in his chest. All-too-familiar pain erupted.

*Another broken rib.*

That would be his fourth, and if he wasn't mistaken, they were breaking with more regularity now. Bones were supposed to heal stronger, but that was only the case if they were given enough time to heal to begin with.

Still, pain meant he was alive, and the three fighters had overshot, giving him a few precious seconds to escape. He weaved in and out of the melee, using the battle's natural chaos to put some distance between him and his pursuers. At some point, the Baranyk fighters gave up, having found an easier target, and disappeared from his six altogether.

Coda found himself on the outskirts of the battle. His HUD showed a snarled mess. He'd heard dogfights described as a tangled knot that was tied back over itself tighter and tighter as the battle progressed, but he liked to think of it more as a swarm of angry bees. The swarm was roughly circular in shape, and so was the battlespace. And instead of empty space between the buzzing insects, the dogfight was filled with antifighter slugs and missiles. But the chaos, the impossibility of keeping an eye on a single object within the larger mass—that was the same.

Fortunately, where he couldn't track every fighter, his computer could, and it told him his green pilots were holding their own. While not flying with the same precision he'd come to expect from the Forgotten, they weren't exactly fresh meat for the grinder, either.

Since decimating half the enemy force in the initial wave, his pilots had shot down another third of their remaining forces while only taking a handful of casualties themselves. And they only needed to hold out for another couple minutes. Then the *Redemption* would return.

Thinking of the *Redemption*, Coda found the Baranyk carrier and was surprised to see it hadn't altered course. It seemed to have slowed but had carried on its original trajectory. Had the *Redemption* inflicted that much damage?

Coda blinked as a pair of Nighthawks buzzed his wing. He cursed. He'd been flying on the same trajectory at the same speed for several seconds.

*Too long.*

He was as close to a sitting duck as there was in space combat. Settling back into the gel of his seat, he reentered the fray. Guns blazing, he shot down two enemy fighters while allowing his computer to autoselect missile targets. Getting a lock, he fired then dove negative-Z, trusting the computer-guided missiles to find their targets. When the other two red indicators disappeared from his battle map, he knew they had.

Spinning in a tight corkscrew, he went back positive-Z, cutting into the battle from its underside. If it had been a battle on the open seas of Earth, he would have had all the advantage in the world, but this was space. There was no up or down—only the battle plane, an artificial line that the fighters used as a directional reference. Although the fighters were roughly aligned to the same battle plane, they pointed and moved in every direction, so he wasn't surprised when he found himself on a head-on course with three enemy fighters instead of below the bellies of Baranyk ships.

Moving on instinct alone, Coda went hard to starboard, performing a high-G turn. His ribs screamed at him, ripping the air from his lungs. Darkness crept in from the edges of his vision.

*No, no, no*, Coda thought, widening his eyes as if to keep the darkness at bay. He couldn't black out. Not now. Not with three enemy fighters on his tail.

A strange thought came to him. Were they the same three fighters he had engaged with before? Distinguishing between Baranyk fighters was impossible, but he swore he saw scorch marks on the side of one—scorch marks from the explosion of one of his missiles. Could they have been tracking him? He didn't want to find out.

"All fighters, this is Coda. I've got a few clingers. Who wants to be on my good side today and wipe them for me?"

"I'm coming, Coda," Nails said. "ETA in… four seconds."

Coda cursed. Four seconds was an eternity in combat. "Copy. Just do what you can."

He swung his fighter back and forth in a series of basic maneuvers to keep the enemy at bay. His battle map lit up as the enemy fighters opened fire. Smaller dots streaked through the digital space, racing toward him. He held his breath, corkscrewing, waiting for the inevitable. When none of the slugs struck, he veered positive-Z then performed a tight, high yo-yo defense maneuver.

In atmosphere, the maneuver would have shed speed, causing the enemy to overshoot, but since there was no drag in space, it was no different than a standard high yo-yo. To compensate, he fired his forward thrusters, creating his own drag, slowing his fighter. Again, his body screamed. Something inside him broke. Another rib. Maybe two. And this time, his collarbone sent agonizing waves of pain up his neck.

But the sudden maneuver worked. The three Baranyk vessels zipped in front of him then attempted to veer off. Coda shoved the throttle forward, racing after them. These three had put him through hell, and he wasn't about to let them get away with it. He took out the first with guns, while his computer got a lock on the other two. When he got tone, he fired.

As if sensing their impending doom, the two ships veered in opposite directions. But it was too late. The two missiles pursued, and unable to shake them, the pair of enemy fighters exploded in a burst of organic material.

Coda bellowed, pumping his fist, and immediately regretted it. Goddamn, his body *hurt*. He prepared to reenter the battle when something caught his eye. His pursuit of the enemy fighters had left him facing the gas giant, and racing around it, just coming into view, was the *Redemption*.

"All fighters," Ensign Richey said over the comm, "you're to disengage and provide cover fire for the *Redemption*."

"Copy that." Coda winced. Even talking hurt. *How long am I going to spend in the medical bay?* "Gold and Silver Flights, form up. Full throttle. It's time to catch the bus."

Coda darted out of the swarm of fighters, making for the coordinates that Ensign Richey had provided, and maximized thrust. The G-forces pushed him into his seat, pressing against his ravaged body like an enemy crushing him in a vise.

"You know," Squawks said as he and the fighters of both flights moved into position behind Coda, "we're going to have to rethink this whole Gold and Silver Flight thing. It makes me feel inferior."

"You are inferior, Squawks," Coda said. "Especially in the head. That's how they keep convincing you to climb into these deathtraps."

"Touché," Squawks said.

"For what it's worth, Squawks," someone else said, "you'll always be gold in my book."

"Thanks, Stubbs."

"Gold-plated, at least."

"I hate you guys."

Laughter filled the comm then died away as the enemy fighters regrouped, moving into an attack formation of their own. The battle wasn't over yet.

# 12

*Bridge, SAS Redemption*
*Cerian-7*

"All Nighthawks are en route, Captain," Lieutenant Poiu said.

"Good." Coleman kept his eyes firmly on the large battle map. His Nighthawks had plotted an intercept course that would have them rendezvous with the *Redemption* only moments before it intercepted the damaged Baranyk carrier. "What's the status of the enemy vessel?"

"Showing significant damage along its port side, Captain. Sensors are also picking up massive power fluctuations."

"Radioactive material?" Coleman asked.

"Not that the sensors are picking up."

Power fluctuations without the detection of radioactive mass... he supposed it was too much to hope that they had damaged the main reactor.

"Thank you, Lieutenant," he said. "Maintain current course and speed."

Once again, Coleman felt every eye on the bridge on him. And once again, it was his XO who voiced the unspoken questions.

"That slingshot significantly increased our velocity, sir," he said quietly. "We'll have an even smaller window to fire than before."

Coleman's eyes snapped to Commander Garcia. The man was his friend—he had taken the position *because* he was his friend—but the questioning had gone on long enough. Coleman didn't intend to reprimand the man, he believed his actions and their subsequent success should do the talking, but he needed to instill confidence, let his crew know that he had a plan and that he wasn't another flyboy flying by the seat of his pants.

"We won't need as much time this time around." Coleman let his gaze linger, driving his point home.

Garcia met his eye, seeming to understand Coleman's intensity. He nodded. "Maintain current course and speed."

"Nighthawks reporting that the Baranyk fighters are in pursuit, Captain," Ensign Richey said. "In pursuit and attempting to get through their guard. They're trying to get to the *Redemption*, sir."

"They know their ship is nearly lost," Garcia said.

"Time to weapons range?" Coleman asked.

"Fifteen seconds, sir."

"They don't have enough time," Coleman said. "Tell the squadron to keep up the good work. The battle is nearly over."

The seconds ticked by with impossible slowness. Coleman watched as the green and red indicators danced behind the *Redemption*. For every one that winked out, a pilot had died with it. Their forces were already down four fighters.

*And this was just one battle. One battle with one ship.*

But like the original one hundred candidates for the Forgotten, Coleman knew that this was just war's way of whittling down the best. Those four pilots would have been chiseled away regardless. It was a morbid thought, but the cream rose to the top, and for pilots, that meant the best stayed alive to fight another day. Even if they lost twenty fighters, the remaining force would be just as deadly, maybe even more so, given their newfound experience and battle-hardened readiness.

"Five seconds, sir," Lieutenant Poiu said, continuing the countdown to firing range.

"You know what to do, Lieutenant. Take them out."

"With pleasure, sir."

Barely more than a second after the words were out of his mouth, the *Redemption* rumbled with the sounds of their batteries opening up. On the battle map, small circles expanded from the enemy carrier like ripples in water, each one representing a direct hit. The enemy vessel was taking terrible damage.

"Two seconds," Garcia said, counting down the time left in firing range.

The *Redemption* continued to rumble. Coleman leaned closer to the battle map, his eyes nearly level with the wireframe of the enemy vessel.

*Come on. Come on!*

The ship was traveling too fast. If he was forced to angle for a third pass, it would take precious time his fighters didn't have. He was already down another Nighthawk since his last count.

*We need to end this now.*

The rumbling stopped, the firing ceasing.

"Status!" Coleman bellowed. The enemy ship hadn't disappeared from the battle map. Had he failed?

"Reading high levels of radioactive material, Captain," Lieutenant Poiu said. "Looks like the reactor is going critical."

Relief flooded through Coleman's body. He hadn't realized it, but at some point during the conflict, he had taken hold of the railing again. His palms were sweaty, leaving the surface smudged as he let go.

"Reverse course," Coleman said. "Ninety-second burn. Let's shed some of this speed and settle into orbit."

"Yes, sir."

There were no unspoken questions this time.

"Nighthawks are requesting orders, sir," Ensign Richey said.

"Tell them to RTB. Battle landings," Coleman said, trusting the *Redemption*'s point-defense cannons to eliminate any remaining enemy pursuit.

As the Nighthawks made for the *Redemption*, beginning their landing procedures, the enemy carrier disappeared from the battle map.

"The reactor has gone critical, sir," Lieutenant Poiu said. "The enemy vessel is gone."

Cheers erupted inside the bridge as the dozen bridge crew began clapping and hooting.

"Quiet!" Coleman bellowed. The din ended immediately. "All scanners, scan all frequencies."

"You still thinking this was a trap?" In the quiet of the bridge, even Garcia's soft voice was audible in the corners of the room.

"Always plan for the worst, Commander," Coleman said.

A heavy silence fell over the bridge, extending for several long seconds as everyone watched their terminal, waiting for an enemy fleet to jump in. The only sound was of the ship's rumbling and creaking as its thrusters shed velocity. Ten seconds went by. Then twenty. Thirty. A minute. Coleman let himself exhale.

"Looks like we're in the clear, sir." Garcia extended a hand. "Well done. A little unconventional, but well done."

Coleman took his XO's hand, shaking it with satisfaction. "Thank you, Commander. You as well." Then louder, so that the entire bridge could hear him. "All of you. Well done. Now let's get to the moon, and see why—"

"Captain!" Ensign Richey said. "I'm picking up a signal from the moon. It's a distress signal, sir. One of ours."

Coleman darted up the stairs to Richey's communications terminal. "How old is it? Could it have been from the original Baranyk invasion?"

"Doubtful, sir," Richey said. "We've been scanning human frequencies since we arrived. It wasn't there before."

"The Baranyk have been here for months," Garcia said. "That's a long time for a human resistance to hold out. And those weren't soldiers down there."

"No," Coleman said. "But if there are survivors, we can't let them languish any longer. I want a squad of marines on the surface the moment we've settled into orbit. It's time to see what the hell is going on down there."

# 13

*Flight Deck, SAS Redemption*
*Cerian-7, High Orbit*

Coda winced as he removed his flight helmet. With the battle officially behind him, his body had stopped pumping itself full of adrenaline, and now all of his bumps, bruises, and cracked and broken bones were flexing their terrifyingly painful muscles. His personal injuries aside, the battle had been a costly one, with five of his pilots having flown their last flight.

*Five out of twenty-four birds. We can't continue with those kinds of losses.*

On the deck, one of the specialists rolled a ladder over. Coda cracked open his hatch then stood, grabbing the ladder's railing with his good hand, and slowly descended its steps.

"Thank you," Coda said, stepping from the final rung.

The deck was alive with activity. The deck chief was shouting orders to over a dozen specialists as forklifts moved the now-empty Nighthawks into their stalls for inspection, repairs, and rearmament. As Captain Coleman had taught him, Coda inspected his own fighter.

He ran a hand along the cold exterior of the fuselage, his eyes scanning for anything amiss. Its matte-black exterior was coated with

Baranyk material and dented and scratched from having been peppered by the remnants of their fighters' organic hulls, but nothing appeared overly alarming.

"She's all yours," Coda said to the specialist who was now rolling the ladder away. "Take care of her."

"Will do, Commander."

Coda strolled across the hangar, making for the pilots' quarters through a nearby door. Most of his pilots had already returned to the ship and removed their flight gear, but some lingered behind, telling animated stories of the battle. They saw their CO, saluted, then got as far away as possible, leaving him alone in the locker room.

With one hand, Coda removed his flight suit—which was more difficult and painful than he ever imagined possible—and redressed in a pair of sweats and a tank top before making for the ready room for his debriefing.

The ready room was so loud with excitement and celebration, nobody heard the door slide open or saw their CO standing in the doorway. Coda watched them for a moment, not yet wanting to spoil their mood.

For as long as pilots had taken to the skies in defense of their family and country, the pilots' ready room had been an open space to voice opinions. Step into any ready room across the fleet, and one was likely to hear complaints about the ineptitude of government, the shortsightedness of command, clueless voters, and a slew of other things humanity had bitched about for centuries.

The strike fighter ready rooms, however, were a different beast altogether. Where most ready rooms across the fleet were moderately informal, the strike fighter ready room had an added layer of respect. FNGs were expected to be deferential, to shut up unless spoken to. They occupied the space somewhere between invisible and insignificant. But that was only until they had flown their first mission.

"Officer on deck!" someone shouted as Coda moved into the room. Smiles faltered and laughter faded as Coda strode from the edge of the room to the front, where he stopped behind the podium.

"Take your seats," Coda said.

The pilots found their seats and watched Coda with unenthused expressions.

"Before I get started, I just wanted to say... not too bad out there." He smiled, letting everyone else in the room know that it was okay for them to smile too. What he got in return was a half-hearted response. "I mean it. Good work."

The cheers intensified, some of the excitement from before returning.

"The bridge just sent me the preliminary numbers," Coda continued, "and it looks like we had over thirty-seven confirmed kills. Not bad for a squadron that was still flying with training wheels only two weeks ago."

More laughter.

Holding his bad arm against his chest, he toggled a few commands into his tablet with his other, dimming the lights and calling up a scoreboard at the front of the room. "Of those thirty-seven kills, your individual kill totals are as follows."

Coda turned to look at the display. Unsurprisingly, his veteran pilots were grouped toward the top, but ahead of every other FNG was the daughter of Captain Coleman himself.

"Nails," Coda said. "Stand up."

She climbed from her seat, face beaming with an "I told you so" expression.

"Nails single-handedly accounted for eight kills," Coda said. "Well done."

"Thank you, sir," she said, a defiant edge to her voice.

His eyes lingered on her even after she took her seat again. If the attitude continued, he would have to talk to her about it. Disrespect was one thing—hell, complaining about superiors was as old as military itself—but insubordination was unacceptable.

"Unfortunately," Coda said, "it wasn't all sunshine and buttercups out there. Remove Nails, Squawks, and myself from the equation, and the numbers for many of you are downright dreadful. Factor in the five pilots who are no longer with us, and our performance leaves a lot to be desired. These kinds of numbers cannot continue. Remember, ladies and gentlemen, you're not just fighting for yourselves out there—you're fighting for your fellow wingmen. And every mistake you make, every shot you miss, puts them at risk."

Coda took a deep breath, surveying his pilots. Any semblance of joy had vanished. They looked on with hard expressions, many refusing to meet his eye. He was losing them; he could feel it. But it didn't stop him from criticizing them.

"Even you, Nails," Coda continued. "You were to fly my wing this mission, and the moment we encountered resistance, I lost you. It nearly cost me my fighter. It nearly cost you your CAG."

"Sir, I—"

"Can it, Nails," Coda snapped. "If your first thought is to defend yourself, you're missing the point."

Nails shifted in her seat. "What *is* the point, sir?"

"You have to do better. *We* have to do better. Not for ourselves but for the people sitting beside you. We lost five pilots today. Five pilots in a single battle against a single Baranyk carrier in a system they abandoned. Five. We have to do better for *them*. Flight leaders, with me."

Coda strode to the door as his flight leaders rose and moved to join him.

"Damn, Coda," Squawks said once they were into the corridor. "I've heard of a wet blanket before, but holy shit. They weren't *that* bad."

"I'm their commander, Squawks, not their friend. It's my job to give them the hard truths. It's yours to be the hero who spares them extra duty. We're not there yet, though. Once they've had a chance to decompress, get them back in the simulators. Maybe they weren't as bad as I made them sound. I need to review the flight data first. But we still have work to do and not a lot of time to do it."

"Of course, but..."

"What is it, Squawks?"

Squawks took a deep breath and shot a look toward Moscow and Noodle as if silently pleading with them to come to his defense.

"They're not just FNGs anymore," Noodle said. "We can't continue with the us-and-them stuff."

"You agree?" Coda asked, turning to Moscow.

"I do," Moscow said. "They've earned the right to become part of the squadron."

"What do you have in mind?" Coda asked.

"They need to be properly initiated," Squawks said with a grin.

Coda rubbed his forehead. Squawks was proposing a celebration. The idea grated on him. They shouldn't be celebrating. They should be reflecting. Getting better. Working harder. But even as he thought it, something in Coda understood the value. To fly as one, they needed to become one. And in order to do that, they first needed to become closer.

"All right," Coda said. "But I need them in condition to fly. Can you do that?"

"I've got a few ideas."

"Make it happen, then" Coda said. "I'll be in sick bay if anyone needs me."

# 14

*Gas Mining Complex, Cerian-7*
*Surface*

JOIN THE MARINES AND SEE THE GALAXY. THAT'S HOW SERGEANT HANIGER had been sold on enlisting. See the galaxy, visit alien planets, make a difference. All of the brochures and recruitment material had shown vibrant, alluring planets that looked like tropical paradises. Marines in full combat gear stormed beaches and ran over windswept plains, the might of the Sol forces behind them and looking every bit the heroes the recruiters portrayed them as.

Sergeant Haniger hadn't joined for that reason alone; it was more of the icing on top. And after boot, he'd promptly shipped out to planet after planet, fulfilling the recruiters' promise.

*Join the marines and see the galaxy.*

Unfortunately, the galaxy was a dumpster fire, and most planets were shitholes.

Cerian-7 was different. The dropship had dropped them at the heart of a mining operation in the northern hemisphere. The ground was rocky, largely devoid of flora or fauna, not unlike Earth's moon or even Mars. *But that view... my god, what a view.*

Beyond the metal structures, pipes, and conveyer tubes was Cerian itself. It dominated the skyline the same way Haniger expected Jupiter would from Europa, and like the gas giant of the Sol system, it was a vibrant mix of reds, oranges, and whites. It left the moon with a strange feeling of being in a perpetual state of sunset.

Haniger had seen it for the briefest of moments when he'd raced down the dropship ramp, taking position, rifle raised as the rest of his squad fanned out. In that briefest of moments, he'd snapped a mental image and stored it away for future reflection. He and his marines now raced across the metal walkways, moving with precision, eyes scanning their surroundings, advancing toward the distress beacon.

They'd been told to expect Baranyk activity, but thus far, he hadn't seen a single alien monster. No signs of life at all, in fact. The mining facility was quiet and dark, having lost power at some point. The only light came from the planet and the soldiers' barrel-mounted flashlights.

"Sir!" Corporal Abernathy said. His rifle was angled down at the metal grating of the walkway. The dark metal was stained red.

"Blood?" Haniger asked, stepping closer to see for himself.

"Looks that way, sir." Abernathy lit more of the area. "Lots of it."

"We're getting close," Haniger said. He scanned their surroundings. The distress beacon was coming from the center of the installation, where a single structure doubled as living and office quarters. "Let's go."

They passed more remnants of battle as they moved toward the structure, blood and human remains, even the distinct yellow blood of the enemy.

*So, there was some resistance. Good work, people. I hope you gave them hell and took a few of the bastards with you.*

The living quarters and office building formed a square, two-story structure with windows that gave views of the operation. Like the rest of the installation, the windows were dark, showing no signs of life. They advanced toward the entrance, finding the door damaged and hanging sideways off its track, partially blocking their path inside. Corporal Abernathy and his fire team set up on the left side of the door, Corporal Hosaka and his team took the right. On Haniger's order, they streamed inside, Haniger close behind.

Death waited for them inside. Blood coated the floor and walls.

Human limbs were scattered about like refuse, bodies torn in two, heads ripped free, dead eyes staring lifelessly at the world they'd left behind.

See the galaxy. Visit alien worlds. That was the dream. This was the reality.

The fire teams continued their search, securing nearby rooms and corridors. Every now and then, they would pass a Baranyk corpse, though the death toll was significantly in the enemy's favor. The miners had tried to mount a resistance but had learned firsthand just how deadly the enemy was.

Coming to a central staircase, Haniger ordered his fire teams to split up—one clearing the rest of the first level and another the top floor while he took two marines to search the lower levels. It was growing increasingly obvious that the Baranyk had fled, but that signal was coming from somewhere, and most of these installations were equipped with a security bunker. Within two-meter-thick steel walls in a bunker fully stocked with supplies, a group of survivors could hold out for days, maybe weeks. The question was, how long had these miners been hiding?

The basement level was darker than the main floor, devoid of all windows and natural light. The darkness was suffocating, almost cave-like, and even the sixty-watt barrel-mounted flashlight struggled to penetrate it, casting long shadows. Dust hung in the air, giving it a slightly hazy feel, reflecting the light and making it hard to see through.

They fanned out wide and moved slowly, advancing through the large room. Where the top level of the building was comprised of personal quarters and the main level for business functions, the basement was largely for the building's infrastructure. Water heaters, purification systems, and heating-and-cooling systems occupied the room. Pipes and vents were exposed in the ceiling. There were no corridors or rooms, just a single space that took up the entire floor. Although the main level had shown signs of a resistance, this area was devoid of blood and bodies.

*They made their resistance above while others sought shelter here.*

Haniger checked the signal. He was right on top of it. He surveyed the room, slowly training his flashlight on the walls, expecting to see a door or hatch. While all of these structures had a safe room, there was some variability to where it was actually located. *If not in the walls, then—*

He spotted it on the floor and closed the distance in a second. Kneeling beside it, he traced the telltale grooves with a gloved hand. "I've got it."

His marines were on him in an instant. Private Lopez dropped to his knees while Private Kennedy kept his eyes on the room. Haniger and Lopez slid their fingers into the crack and lifted, but the hatch wouldn't budge.

"It's locked from the inside," Haniger said. *That's a good sign, isn't it?* "Hey!" he yelled, slamming an open hand on the hatch. "Hey! It's okay. You're safe to come out."

Haniger waited for a response, for the lock to click or the hatch to open. But it remained as still and lifeless as the room. He pounded on it again, more urgently this time, voice louder. Still no response.

"Blow it," Haniger said.

Private Lopez pulled a cartridge from his tactical vest then filled the crack with blast foam. After he'd gently inserted the primer, the three of them retreated, ducking behind a water tank.

"Clear!" Private Lopez shouted, and half a second later, the blast foam detonated.

Haniger darted out from around the tank, rifle raised, his scope illuminating the smoke from the blasts. Private Kennedy advanced from the other side, his scope lighting the chamber below. There was movement. Shadows. Dark shapes inside the space. Haniger's finger squeezed the trigger, riding the millimeter between holding and firing.

One of the shadows emerged, and Haniger's breath caught in his throat.

*Holy shit.*

# 15

*Sick Bay, SAS Redemption*
*Cerian-7, High Orbit*

Dr. Rydell wasn't happy to see Coda as he walked into sick bay. Frowning, she gave him a slight shake of the head then pointed to an open examination table. Coda climbed atop it and waited as she finished with her current patient. Dr. Rydell was a middle-aged woman with short brown-and-gray hair and a friendly, motherly face.

"You're making this too much of a habit," she said, coming over.

"I figured if I didn't pop in every week, you might get worried," Coda said.

She gave him a small laugh. Using her tablet, she ran a series of scans across his ribs, spine, and collarbone, and to nobody's surprise, Coda's self-diagnosis had proven largely accurate. He had two cracked ribs, a bruised shoulder and collarbone, and swelling around the spine.

"Keep this up and you're liable to kill yourself," she had said before getting started on a sling for his injured collarbone. "Displaced ribs alone can cause hemopneumothorax, pneumothorax, pneumonia, and internal bleeding from the laceration of internal organs including your lungs. And don't get me started on the swelling. I have half a mind to remove you from flight status altogether."

"Doc," Coda said, giving her his best smile, "you can't do that. I'm CAG now."

"Don't test me." Dr. Rydell pointed at him, driving the point home. "The only person on a ship with more power than its captain is its doctor. If I tell you you're unfit for duty, then you're unfit for duty. Nobody can say otherwise."

Coda held his hands in front of him as if to keep her at bay, though he knew that behind her stern words, she wasn't being hard on him out of spite. Like all good doctors, she cared about her patients and genuinely didn't want to see any harm come to them.

"I know, I know," Coda said patiently. "I'm not saying you *can't*. I'm only saying that you shouldn't." He winced. "That came out wrong. It's just that—"

"I get it," she said. "You're a big dog with big responsibilities. Well, *I'm* just saying that unless you start taking it easier out there, there's going to be a new big dog with big responsibilities."

He smiled, the cocky kind that he knew would aggravate her. "Speed is life, Doc. You know that."

"Speed is also death. I know that too."

Dr. Rydell turned and strolled toward a closed locker. She unlocked it and pulled out a small white tube. "You know what this is?" she asked, making her way back to the examination table.

"Growth hormone," Coda said.

"Somatotropin. A peptide hormone that promotes growth, cell reproduction, and regeneration. Engineered, of course, to expedite recovery, but the fact that you recognize it even though this tube doesn't have any labels is terrifying. This alone can cause joint swelling, joint pain, and increase your likelihood for certain cancers."

"Come on, Doc," Coda said. "We both know they've been spoon-feeding this stuff to us since we signed up."

"And we *also* both know that like this *experimental* concoction, your squadron was supposed to be a short-term solution to a very specific problem. Just be careful. That's all I'm saying." She handed him the tube.

"Thanks, Doc. I will."

"Mm-hmm," she said skeptically. "You know how to apply that, I'm assuming?"

"Rub it on twice a day," Coda said, as if reading the instructions from a bottle. "Twelve hours apart."

"And?"

"And use a glove to limit skin exposure. You don't want me growing a third arm."

"Exactly."

Coda gave her a thoughtful expression. "Say, Doc? Can this make... um, certain body parts grow bigger too? I'm asking for a friend."

"Oh, get out!" Rydell hit him on his bad shoulder with an open hand.

"Ouch, okay, ow! Bad joke. I get it. Squawks is rubbing off on me. He's a bad influence, you know." He slid off the examination table and headed toward the door.

"Be careful out there, Coda. I mean it. And I promise you, if I find out that stuff went anywhere near your... *extremities*, I'll amputate it. Understood?"

Coda didn't turn around. "I'll see you again soon, Doc."

---

BEING CAG CAME WITH ITS OWN SET OF ADVANTAGES, INCLUDING PRIVATE quarters. In his room, Coda stripped his top half naked and prepared the cream. He may have given Dr. Rydell a hard time, but he took careful note to follow her instructions.

With a gloved hand, he squeezed a line of the cream from his shoulder down his chest and began rubbing it across his injured areas. The stuff smelled like a mix of vomit and spoiled food, but it left a numbing sensation in its wake, banishing the pain. After applying a generous amount over his ribs and collarbone, he screwed the cap back on, removed the glove, and lay down on his bunk.

It was then that he was reminded of one of the *disadvantages* of being CAG: leadership was lonely. His pilots would be in their barracks, celebrating, telling stories, reenacting key moments of the battle, smiling, laughing, and honoring the fallen pilots. They would be growing close. Becoming one. Learning why it was so important to fight for each other and not just themselves. His flight leaders might even be taking part in the celebration. He knew Squawks would. Squawks wasn't the kind of person who would let a good time go by without taking part.

*What about Moscow and Noodle?* Coda laughed at himself. *Even if they weren't participating in the festivities, what would you do? Call them up and ask them to come sit with you because you're lonely?*

Not knowing what else to do, he grabbed his tablet and propped it up with his knees. Operating it with his good hand, he went into his mail, half thinking of writing his old squad mate Uno or Buster, who had been his best friend at the Terran Fleet Academy. Both were serving aboard capital ships, members of the drone squadrons, though Coda had heard Buster was part of the *Nonpareil* now—the finest drone squadron in the fleet.

He was curious how things were going, wondered if they were seeing action or if they'd heard any rumors about Fleet Intelligence finally finding a way to counter the Baranyk jammer and make the Hornets operable again.

But as he opened up his mail, he found that someone had already written him, and it had come from the unlikeliest of people—his mother.

The message was short and, if not sweet, at least to the point.

*Hello Callan,*

*I have received your Air Medal for your participation in the battle above Toavis, though why you thought to send it to me, I don't understand. We've been through this, and you know my feelings, so sending it to me feels like you're rubbing my nose in what you consider to be your accomplishments. In any case, since you seem destined to repeat your father's mistakes, I have stored it with all of his awards and accommodations. If you return, you'll know where to find it.*

*Good luck out there,*
*Mom*

If it had been a paper letter, he would have crumpled it up and thrown it away. Because it was digital, the best he could do was throw it in the electronic trash bin, which wasn't nearly as satisfying. They hadn't ended on good terms—hell, they'd ended on about the worst terms imaginable—but she was still his mother. He was still her only son. More than two years had gone by. Was she still that mad? Had he hurt her that deeply? Something about that made him feel even worse.

He flung his tablet across the room and tossed his good arm over his eyes as if shielding himself from the world. Bitter thoughts plagued him as he drifted off to a restless sleep: why couldn't she see he was doing this for their family? For her. For his father. For every other past, present, and future O'Neil. If she loved him, why couldn't she support him?

He woke to the sound of a voice in his quarters, and it took him several moments to realize that it was coming through the walls.

"Coda, do you read?" It was Captain Coleman. "Coda, are you there?"

"I'm here, sir," Coda said, his throat dry, voice scratchy. He wasn't sure how long he had been asleep.

"Get down here right away. We've uncovered something on the moon."

# 16

*Sick Bay, SAS Redemption*
*Cerian-7, High Orbit*

For the second time that day, Coda returned to sick bay. This time, instead of being greeted by a grumpy but well-meaning doctor and a handful of under-the-weather officers, he found the medical facility crammed with dirty strangers wearing little more than rags. Captain Coleman stood beside Dr. Rydell, speaking to a bald man who wore filth like a second pair of clothes.

"Sir," Coda said, stopping beside Captain Coleman and Dr. Rydell. "What's going on? Who are these people?"

"Survivors," Captain Coleman said.

Coda looked at the newcomers with fresh eyes. Grease and solvent covered their skin, matting their hair. But there was more to it than that. Their faces were gaunt, eyes haunted, arms and legs dangerously thin. These weren't survivors; they were the dried husks of the living. The difference between them and the dead was a matter of choice, and seeing the haunted looks in their eyes, Coda knew they were on the edge of a dangerous precipice.

"How is that possible?" Coda asked. "The system has been under Baranyk control for weeks."

"That," Captain Coleman said, "is just what we were getting ready to discuss."

Captain Coleman kept his eyes on the man on the examination table until Dr. Rydell finished her scan.

"He's malnourished, dehydrated, and suffering from a dozen other minor ailments, but he'll live. My staff and I will administer IVs to help with the dehydration, and I'll have the kitchen staff bring up some simple MREs. Beyond that, these people need rest. So be easy on them."

"Thank you, Doctor."

Rydell strode across the room and stopped beside another doctor to give him her orders. Maybe she truly did have more power on the ship than even Captain Coleman—at least when it came to her domain.

"What's your name?" Captain Coleman asked.

"Gary." The man's voice was low and scratchy, as if he'd walked across the desert.

"Welcome aboard the *Redemption,* Gary. I'm Captain Coleman, and this is my CAG, Commander O'Neil. Can you tell us what you did on the moon?"

"I was a mechanic. Worked on the scoopers."

The scoopers were the custom-built shuttles the miners used to collect raw gasses from Cerian. The process was simple and surprisingly low tech. Unlike the mines of old that relied on railcars and belts to transport mined materials, the gas miners of Cerian-7 flew from its moon to the gas giant. They manually operated booms that scooped its compressed gasses and stored it in airtight containers that were brought back to Cerian-7 for processing, storage, and transportation.

"Good-paying jobs are hard to find in Sol," Gary continued. "So I came out here. Thought I could make enough money to start a new life. I was wrong. Very, very wrong."

"What happened?" Captain Coleman asked.

Gary met the captain's eye. There was a sudden life to him, fueled by an intense anger. "You left us to die."

Captain Coleman blinked and cocked his head to the side, eyes narrow, confused. "We weren't—"

"The Baranyk appeared in our skies," Gary said, cutting him off. "But

I knew you'd show up. I knew you wouldn't leave your own behind. Even after our orbital defenses were destroyed, I knew you'd come. When they began bombarding our moon, I knew it was only a matter of time. I didn't lose hope until I saw the Baranyk in person. Saw them..."

"Saw them what, Gary?" Captain Coleman asked.

"Where were you?" Gary growled.

"I assure you—"

"Where *were* you?"

The room went deathly quiet, every pair of eyes focused on the three of them. Judging by the looks from the other survivors, Gary wasn't the only one seeking answers.

Coda turned to the captain, wondering how he would respond. To his surprise, Captain Coleman's usually stoic face softened, and he crouched down so that he and Gary were at eye level.

"I'm sorry for everything that happened here," Captain Coleman said. "But unfortunately, this isn't the only system that's fallen. The enemy has developed a new weapon, and we were on the defensive..."

"Were?"

"Were." He shot a glance up at Coda. "Not anymore."

Gary followed his gaze, as if seeing Coda for the first time. The anger in his eyes cooled, though it didn't burn away entirely.

"How did you hold out for so long?" Coda asked.

"The operation was equipped with blast bunkers in case of a reactor meltdown. We stayed there, only leaving to find food and water when we ran out. Even found a weapons locker and thought about offering up some kind of resistance, but the Baranyk found one of our raiding parties and... they... they..."

Gary didn't have to finish for Coda to know what had happened. The Baranyk were ruthless. They killed on sight and never took prisoners. If the raiding party had been spotted and hadn't returned, that meant only one thing.

"They took them," Gary continued.

Coda blinked. "They what?" The words were out of his mouth before he realized it.

"They took them." Gary's eyes grew haunted, his face losing all hint of emotion, everything making him human disappearing. He'd suddenly become nothing more than a husk of a person. "We heard their screams for hours."

"What did the enemy want with them?" Captain Coleman asked.

"I don't know." Gary finally looked up, eyes wide and glistening with tears. "I don't want to know."

"Okay, Gary," Captain Coleman said. "Thank you. You're in a safe place now. If there's anything you need, just let me know, okay?"

"I just want to forget, Captain," Gary said. "Help me forget."

Captain Coleman returned to his full height and looked to Dr. Rydell, who was administering aid to another of the survivors across the room. "We'll see what we can do. In the meantime, get some rest."

He strode away, and Coda followed.

"What the hell was that, sir?" Coda asked as soon as they were out of sick bay. "The Baranyk never take prisoners."

"I don't know," Captain Coleman said. "But something tells me we haven't found everything we're going to find on this moon. Double the CAP and get me visual on the other moons around Cerian. I don't want any surprises."

"Yes, sir."

It was clearly a dismissal, but Coda lingered. As much as he would rather avoid the subject, he had other things he needed to talk to the captain about.

"Is there something else, Commander?" Captain Coleman asked.

"It's one of my pilots, sir," Coda said.

"Command comes with its own set of challenges, Coda. Difficult pilots are one of them. Use your best judgment. If things don't improve, let me know."

"It's not that, sir. This is different. It's..."

"I've got a million other things to see to, Coda. Stop dancing around the subject and come out with it."

This wasn't going as planned. Coda wished he could just leave the subject alone and tell the captain another day, but he knew he'd gone too far. Captain Coleman wouldn't let him get away without saying anything more.

"I believe one of the pilots in my squadron is your daughter, sir."

Captain Coleman staggered back a step. "What did you... why..." He licked his lips, his eyes darting up and down the corridor to ensure that they were away from prying ears. Outside sick bay as they were, it apparently wasn't as quiet as the captain would have liked.

He stepped closer, dropping his voice. "Aniyah is here?"

"Yes, sir. The squadron leaders and I were reviewing the new pilots, and she came up. Has a chip on her shoulder the size of Texas, and, well, she reminded us of you, so I started doing some digging. She adopted her mother's maiden name, but she's your daughter all right."

Captain Coleman rubbed his forehead. He was more troubled than Coda had ever seen him. He'd known that the captain and his wife had split and that she had been granted full custody, but there had to be more to it than that. How deep had their falling out been? How long had it been since he'd seen his daughter? Coda's mind went back to the letter from his own mother.

*And how would I feel if she showed up here unannounced?*

"Who else knows?" Captain Coleman asked.

"Nobody," Coda said. "I don't think anyone even suspects it."

That seemed to mollify the captain. He took a deep breath, regaining some of his normal stature. His face returned to the same stoic expression Coda had come to know. "Good. Let's keep this between you and me for now. At least until I've had an opportunity to address it."

"Yes, sir," Coda said. "To be honest, sir, I'm a little surprised you didn't know. I figured you would've played a more active role in who served aboard your ship."

"It doesn't work that way, Commander. I was lucky to pick my executive crew and name you as CAG. The rest of the roster—well, that was picked by the department leaders and Command."

"You think they did it on purpose, sir?"

"No," Coleman said. "As bureaucratic as Command is, there's nothing to be gained by a move like that. Aniyah's mother and I haven't had any communication in years, and I haven't seen her in longer. I'm sure it's just a coincidence. I appreciate you coming to me about this, though. I'll take it from here."

"With all due respect, sir, that's not going to be good enough. She's under my command. If this is going to cause an issue..."

"There won't be any issues, Commander. I assure you. Now get my CAP doubled and get eyes on the other moons. Remember, no surprises."

“Of course, sir. I’ll see it done.”

Not wanting to ignore a second dismissal, Coda left the captain behind, making for the pilots’ section of the ship. He would do as ordered, but he couldn’t help but feel like the captain was using the pretense of additional Baranyk forces as a means to end the discussion. Regardless of the captain’s assurances, he was sure the situation with Nails was anything but resolved.

# 17

*Corridor, SAS Redemption*
*Cerian-7, High Orbit*

Coleman's hands tightened into fists as he watched Coda disappear around the corridor. Aniyah was here? Aboard his ship? It felt like a slap to the face. A chaotic swell of emotion warred inside his chest. His thoughts were a jumbled mess. His face grew hot, blazing like the sun, as he started down the corridor toward his quarters.

Once inside, he unbuttoned his jacket then made for the bookshelf at the back of the space, passing the small armchairs, couch, and table in the center of the room. Coleman poured himself a drink and took a mouthful. Trying to quell the anger, he ran through a squared breathing exercise: inhale for four seconds, hold for an equal amount of time, then exhale for four seconds; repeat four times or as many times as needed. Coleman did ten, imagining the heat dissipating with every long breath, breathing out his anger and frustration.

Finally, he settled onto the couch, the last remnants of the heightened emotion making him feel weak. His personal quarters were plush by fleet standards, easily nicer than anything he had enjoyed in the last year—hell, the last *ten* years. He'd had a similar configuration aboard the *Berlin,* but here, he had *space*, which was at a premium aboard a starship. And the furnishings were new. The chair cushions were plush. The couch wasn't sunken in, and the mattress wasn't torn and hastily repaired with tough sewing thread that irritated his skin when he slept.

And he *hated* it. Now more than ever. The space was a waste. The furnishings would only make him soft. They were *already* making him soft.

The bathroom was nice—he wouldn't argue with that, it was great not to have to share a toilet with one thousand other people—but it all felt so unnecessary. He was on duty for sixteen hours a day and on call twenty-four; he didn't *need* all of this.

With a sigh, Coleman took another sip of his drink, letting its warmth battle the last vestiges of his unease. What the hell was Aniyah doing aboard his ship? And a Nighthawk pilot? He couldn't imagine his ex-wife allowing her to follow in his footsteps, but Aniyah was of age now, and there was nothing her mother could legally do to stop her. Still, what were the odds? His first command, and his estranged daughter was aboard. God was playing a cruel joke on him.

From his jacket pocket, he pulled out the picture of her. It was over ten years old, creased and faded, its edges frayed and worn. It had been with him since the day the picture was taken, and save for the official pictures from her school he'd called up on his tablet, it was the only one of her he had.

*Oh, how long I have dreamed of talking to you. Of hugging you and telling you I'm sorry, that I made a mistake.*

Now that she was here, he realized something else: he was well and truly terrified. If someone had asked him a week ago what he would do if he saw her again, he would have said he would run to her, pick her up, and twirl her about as if she were still the little girl he remembered, the little girl he carried with him in his pocket. Now that the day was here, he understood that it was much more complicated than that.

*Would I call her here or meet her somewhere else? Show up announced in the pilots' barracks? What would I even say? How would she react? What would* she *say?*

He was frozen with fear. He had no idea what to do, so he did nothing. How funny it was that the great Commander Coleman, no, the great *Captain* Coleman, decorated war hero and Baranyk killer, was afraid of his own daughter.

*You're a coward, Chadwick.*

It was more than that, though. He wasn't just afraid of her or uncomfortable with the situation. He was... *powerless*. In all of his dreams, he'd been the one to go to her. It'd been his decision, something he would do when he was ready, when the time was right. But that control had been ripped from him, and he wasn't used to someone else calling the shots.

Coda had asked if Command was somehow behind the situation, and Coleman had meant it when he said no. Command probably didn't even know who she was. She had done this. Aniyah. Nails. His daughter.

She'd commandeered his plan of arriving unexpectedly and starting their relationship anew. He hadn't spoken or written to her in years. She was a stranger through and through, but even separated by years, they were the same. Try as she might, Coleman's ex-wife hadn't been able to keep Aniyah from becoming just like her father. He couldn't have been prouder.

Returning the picture to his pocket, he took another sip. The Aniyah situation—he refused to think of it as a problem anymore—was of a personal nature, and as confusing and potentially crushing as it was, he had other responsibilities.

His conversation with the survivor of Cerian-7 troubled him. Something he wasn't seeing was at play. He was trying to put together a puzzle without having all the pieces. His marines had completed their sweep of the area and found nothing. No other survivors or clues to what the Baranyk were using the prisoners for. Whatever the enemy had done with them, it'd happened off world.

The fleet could do nothing for the prisoners now, but Coleman had a whole sick bay full of people he could help. He grabbed his tablet from the inside of his jacket pocket and began typing his report. With the system clear, it was time the fleet returned. He could transfer the survivors to a medical ship that would take them back to the core planets, and new personnel could restart mining operations.

As for the *Redemption*, they needed to venture farther into Baranyk territory. Their investigation needed to continue. Once his report was finished, he brought up his map and list of worlds they'd lost to the Baranyk. By the time reinforcements arrived, he would have plotted their next course of action.

This, he could control.

# 18

*Corridor, SAS Redemption*
*Cerian-7, High Orbit*

Coda heard his pilots long before he made it back to the barracks. Their cheers, laughter, and—was that singing?—echoed through the corridors. More than one of the ship's passing personnel gave him a knowing smile.

Fighter pilots had a reputation for heavy drinking, womanizing, and living life as if they were in the fast lane, and the Forgotten were only living up to it. They'd earned it. And in some way, the other members of the crew got to enjoy the spoils—even if it was through osmosis. As Coda drew closer to the barracks, though, the lyrics became clearer, and he was suddenly less forgiving.

Coda cursed. Of all the songs they could have been singing, they had to be singing one of the most offensive songs from the twentieth century. It had been updated, of course, to fall more in line with the times, but certain things had been left alone. Tradition, they'd been called. Timeless. But it was interesting how those "timeless" lyrics always tended to be the raunchiest.

The door slid open as he neared, and as before, nobody seemed to notice when he entered. The entire squadron was gathered in the barracks, crammed in as tight as a college bar during dollar-beer night. At the front of the room were the green members of the Forgotten who had flown in the battle. Stripped down to nothing but their underwear, they were drinking out of a flight helmet as Squawks egged them on.

*I told him to go easy on the alcohol!* Whatever Squawks was making them do, Coda was going to make him do, too, then do extra duty on top of it.

Pushing through the shoulder-to-shoulder pilots, Coda made his way to the front of the room. By the time he had shoved himself through, the song was nearly finished. Squawks was even singing now, flanked by the other flight leaders.

Those who hadn't seen Coda erupted into cheers. Even those who had seen him celebrated, though with less vigor. The people at the front of the room, however, were completely oblivious to his presence. They screamed as if shouting at the fighter gods to let them into the mile-high club. As the helmet of booze made the rounds, they took long pulls.

Nails, the last pilot to take a drink, polished off what was left, then the entire room erupted into celebration. Coda clapped and kept clapping until he was the only one left cheering. Those who hadn't seen him come in saw him now, and drunken smiles turned into nervous expressions. The pilots looked from him to each other, then to the flight leaders, who had obviously orchestrated the entire thing.

Still, Coda clapped. The sound, the only one in the room, echoed off the bulkhead. When he stopped, the uneasy silence was thick, and even Squawks, who was obviously drunk, struggled to meet Coda's eye.

*It's not their fault. Don't take it out on them. And don't dress down their leaders who brought them into the group. Not if you want them to stay true to you.*

Still not happy with the situation, Coda forced himself to smile. Those who knew him well enough would likely see the insincerity behind it, but he hoped the rest were fooled.

"Welcome to the squadron!" Coda bellowed.

The room erupted into applause that was even louder than before, and he was surprised that with it came a genuine smile this time. These were his squadrons, his pilots, and Squawks had made good on his promise. They were growing closer, and Coda had no doubt that they would fly better because of it. He just couldn't let it get too far out of hand.

"You're not FNGs anymore!"

More cheering.

"But that doesn't mean you don't have other responsibilities. Flight leaders, with me." Coda turned to leave the room, trusting his fellow leadership staff to follow. Before he could get more than a couple steps, a voice stopped him in his tracks.

"What's wrong, sir? Afraid to drink with your squadron?"

Coda turned to his instigator. Still standing at the front of the room, Nails had separated herself from the rest of the newly initiated. Her dark face wore a defiant expression, and her lips curled into a sneer.

"Lieutenant!" Squawks bellowed, his voice suddenly sounding very sober. "Stand do—"

Coda held up a hand, silencing his flight leader, then strode up to Nails. Stopping only when he was inches from her face, Coda met her defiant gaze, attempting to give her his best take-no-shit expression.

*I should have practiced this in the mirror. I feel ridiculous.*

To her credit, she didn't shrink or shy away. Either she truly wasn't intimidated by him or she was a damn fine actor. Neither would have surprised him. Without saying a word, Coda snatched the helmet from her hand then held it out to the side.

"Fill it up," Coda said.

Hushed whispers echoed through the room, growing louder as Squawks filled the helmet with drink.

Taking the helmet back, Coda turned to the side so all could see, held up the helmet for effect, then began to drink. The alcohol was lighter than the alcohol Squawks and Tex had brewed on the *Jamestown*, beer instead of whiskey, but it still wasn't something you'd find at a respected establishment. Coda forced down gulp after gulp, and with every swallow, the murmurs grew. By the end, the noise was deafening.

Coda tossed the empty helmet into the crowd then belched long and loud—not exactly in Nails's face, but close enough. Cheers turned to laughter, and Coda took advantage of the sudden noise.

"I know your secret, Lieutenant," he said quietly, so only she could hear. "I know who you are."

She staggered backward a step, her reaction nearly identical to her father's. Coda took another step forward. He wasn't going to let her get away that easily.

"I don't know what you're talking about," she said.

"Whatever you say, Aniyah *Robinson*." He put heavy emphasis on her last name.

"Who else knows?"

"Only me," Coda said. "And the captain."

Her eyes blazed with anger for a moment, but she quickly wrangled it under control. Her lightning-fast ability to control herself impressed him. He'd thought her outbursts were driven by anger, but if this were any indication, they weren't. She might not be cold, but she was definitely calculating.

*I could learn a lot from her.*

"It was only a matter of time before he found out anyway." Her eyes darted over his shoulder. The din in the room was beginning to fade.

"I take it nobody else knows?" Coda asked.

She shook her head. Well, at least there was that. Coda wouldn't have to worry about her pedigree being a distraction.

"And you know who *I* am, right?" Coda asked. "Who my family is."

She nodded.

"Well, as one person who's struggled to crawl out from under a long shadow of his own, if you ever need to talk, my door is open."

Coda took a step back, and his eyes found hers. They were narrowed, distrusting. *God, what has this woman gone through?* He gave her a small nod, which he hoped came across as reaffirming, then turned and started for the door again.

"Flight leaders..." He looked over the crowd. Maybe it was the atmosphere, maybe it was the alcohol that was already warming him from the inside, or maybe he just wasn't as much of a hard-ass as he thought he was, but Coda couldn't bring himself to break it up. "Belay my last order. Have fun."

Coda left the room to a cacophony of cheers.

# 19

*Bridge, SAS Redemption*
*Cerian-7, High Orbit*

Reinforcements arrived two days after Captain Coleman sent his report. The newly refurbished *SAS Oregon*, having been in dry dock since the battle of Toavis, was sent to oversee operations and provide support should the Baranyk return. In addition, the admiral had sent the light cruiser *Mercy Heart* for the survivors. They would get immediate medical attention and return to the core worlds for further evaluation.

The crew of the *Redemption* had other responsibilities. The moment the survivors were transferred to the *Mercy Heart* and Captain Coleman have given Captain Suarez of the *Oregon* his briefing, Captain Coleman ordered a meeting in the briefing room with his executive crew to align on the next steps of their mission.

They sat around the table, occupying the same seats they had during their initial introduction, with Captain Coleman at their head. "With the aid of Fleet Intelligence," he said, "we were able to reconstruct the path the Baranyk took in claiming our systems."

The display wall behind him showed a two-dimensional representation of space, complete with labels for human- and Baranyk-occupied systems. With a click of a button, the image began to play, showing the Baranyk's slow march. As human systems fell, the labels changed and turned from blue to red, indicating their fall to enemy forces.

"As you can see, it wasn't a linear progression. The Baranyk hit hard, knowing we were stretched thin, and if they hit in enough locations, we wouldn't be able to stop them."

The image ran through its cycle, showing the Baranyk advance, then froze to show how the situation stood currently. It started over, and Coleman paused at the beginning, stopping a series of red lines branching from a Baranyk-controlled world.

"But," Coleman continued, "if we trace this back far enough, we find that they initiated the assault from the Koburn System. It's there that our mission will continue."

"Sir," Coda said. "If I may?"

"Please."

"We found survivors here. Couldn't there be survivors in the other fallen systems as well?"

"There could be. But rescuing potential survivors isn't our objective."

"It doesn't feel right." Coda shook his head. "You heard the survivors. We abandoned their people to this fate. Now we have the power to do something about it, and we won't?"

"It's not our mission."

"There could be other clues in those systems," Coda said. "And—"

Coleman held up a hand, silencing his CAG. "I understand what you're saying, Coda. And it feels as wrong to me as it does to you, but we have our orders. Beyond that, the clock is ticking. Down to what, we don't know. We have to stop whatever is coming before it gets here and *prevent* other people from the fate already experienced by these people. Koburn gives us the best chance at that."

"Koburn was a forward base on the front before the Baranyk advance," Commander Garcia said. "Won't it be more heavily guarded than the human worlds?"

"I wondered that as well." Coleman zoomed in on an image of Koburn showing a stylized representation of the system. There were five planets altogether, each with at least two moons. Only one was capable of supporting life: Koburn-2 was a superplanet roughly six times the size of Earth. "Sensor data indicates Baranyk forces have retreated from here as well."

"Retreated from their own system?" Garcia asked.

"Leaving a single carrier as rear guard, just like Cerian, but yes."

"It doesn't make any sense," Garcia pressed. "Why advance, only to retreat even farther?"

"That's what we're going to find out." He surveyed the table. "We've got a full platoon of marines aboard this ship, and I have every expectation to put them to use. Dr. Naidoo, you've been asking to study a Baranyk world, observe their natural habitat. It's time you get that chance."

"Thank you, sir."

"Any questions?"

There were none.

"Then prepare your teams. We're jumping at zero six hundred."

---

"JUMP COORDINATES SET, SIR," ENSIGN RICHEY SAID FROM HER TERMINAL. "The JumpGate awaits your order."

"Good," Coleman said. He stood in the pit, studying the image of Koburn-2. It was a beautiful planet. Inviting. The image didn't show the immensity of the planet, though with its blues, greens, and whites, it looked like a distant cousin of Earth. He'd called it a Baranyk natural habitat in his briefing, though it was anything but, and Dr. Naidoo had had the grace not to correct him. That didn't mean danger wasn't lurking on its surface. Coleman didn't know why, but he couldn't shake the feeling that something menacing waited in its depths. Beneath its beautiful façade was surely a terrible monster.

"The moment we arrive, set Condition One throughout the ship," Coleman said. "The Forgotten are on standby, loaded and ready for deployment. At the first sign of enemy contact, I want them launched and setting up a defensive formation."

"Yes, sir."

"You feel it too?" Garcia asked, his voice quiet enough that only Coleman could hear.

Coleman nodded. He'd ordered Lieutenant Poiu to plot jump coordinates back to Cerian-7. It wouldn't be a single jump, of course—the distance was far too great for that. But if they ran into a sticky situation, it would get them to safety, where they could regroup. He'd also kept the order between himself, Commander Garcia, and Lieutenant Poiu. It was one thing to go in prepared. It was something else to broadcast the thought of retreat before they'd even arrived. That type of mindset could create a self-fulfilling prophecy.

Confirming his own unease to Garcia already bordered on that. Either way, something pulled him to Koburn. It had been pulling him there for a while. Despite the uneasy feeling, it was time to see what mysteries the planet held.

Coleman took hold of the railing surrounding the battle map. "Jump."

Ensign Richey hit her terminal, and a moment later, the world stretched. Coleman closed his eyes, taking in a slow, deep breath and exhaling for an equal set of time. By the time he was done, the sensation had disappeared.

"Arrived, sir," Lieutenant Poiu said. "Scanning."

The lights dimmed as Condition One was set throughout the ship. The battle map reset, going dark, then updated with new sensor data. They'd arrived more than two hundred thousand kilometers from Koburn-2, as Coleman had erred on the side of caution. If the enemy was still present, then he would have plenty of time to initiate the first jump back toward Cerian-7.

A red dot appeared on the battle map, and half a second later, Lieutenant Poiu confirmed it. "Contact. Baranyk carrier in orbit. It doesn't appear to be moving to engage."

"Hold course," Coleman said.

"Launching fighters," Lieutenant Poiu announced.

Sensor data continued to come in, updating the battle map in real time. The deck thumped as Nighthawks launched from the ship, showing up as green indicators on the battle map, forming up into defensive formations. Five seconds went by then ten. No other contacts registered. The Baranyk carrier didn't alter course.

"What's the status of that ship?" Coleman asked.

"Reading steady power and life support systems," Lieutenant Poiu said. "It appears fully functional."

"Why aren't they doing anything?" Commander Garcia asked.

"I don't know," Coleman said. "Ensign Richey, are there any signals coming from the planet?"

"Nothing yet, sir."

"Are they baiting us?" Commander Garcia asked.

"Maybe," Coleman said. "Or maybe it's a standoff. Lieutenant Poiu, plot an intercept course. Five percent thrust. Let's let them know we're coming."

"Yes, sir. Moving to intercept. Five percent thrust."

They were moving too slowly for the battle map to noticeably change, though that didn't stop Coleman from refusing to look away. With his eyes glued to the image, Coleman saw the moment the red indicator of the Baranyk ship disappeared.

"Sir," Lieutenant Poiu said, his voice confused. "The Baranyk carrier is gone, sir. It... I'm reading a jump signature."

"It jumped?" Commander Garcia asked.

"It appears that way, sir."

Coleman exchanged a look with Garcia. "Maintain course. Increase thrust to ten percent and deploy reconnaissance drones. I want visual on that planet."

"Yes, sir."

"Ensign Richey, still nothing from the planet?"

"Nothing, sir."

"Maybe they heard about what we did to their friends on Cerian," Garcia said.

"Maybe," Coleman said. "They were interested in the planet enough to leave a carrier behind. I don't know why it didn't engage, but they wanted eyes on the planet. The question is why. What do they expect us to find? And why was it so important for them to know when we found it?"

"I don't know," Garcia said. "But something tells me we're about to find out."

# 20

*Cockpit, Nighthawk*
*Koburn-2*

CODA'S EYES BURNED. HIDDEN SECURELY INSIDE HIS FLIGHT HELMET, HE had no way of rubbing them. No way of easing the discomfort. It was the little things like this that nobody ever talked about. Anytime pilots got together, it was rip-roaring tales of speed, high stakes, and near death. Nobody ever talked about the mundane, the small annoyances that only a pilot would understand. The way dripping sweat couldn't be wiped away. The way an itch could never be scratched. The fact that if you sneezed, you sprayed the inside of your flight helmet and had to deal with that for the rest of the hop.

He flew in atmo, his Nighthawk bucking under him because of the planet's high winds. From orbit, Koburn-2 bore a close resemblance to Earth, but in reality, the planet was a cheap knockoff of humanity's home world.

The vegetation was short and squat, more bramble than forest, with sharp branch systems and no leaves. The trees, if they could be called that, more closely resembled cacti than oak or pine. Instead of rolling hills of grass, the ground was rocky, covered in what appeared to be a thick carpet of moss. Even its water, a beautiful mix of blues, greens, and pinks, was super-heated by an active volcanic system and teeming with microorganisms that fed on the acidic ecosystem. For mad spacers looking for a quick dip, the boiling water would melt the skin from their bones, leaving little indication that they'd ever submerged themselves into their inviting depths to begin with.

He'd been in the cockpit since they'd arrived in the system. For six hours, he'd been prisoner to his own sweat, urine, and discomfort, but as far as he and his squadron could tell, there was no sign of Baranyk activity. It appeared that despite all odds, the enemy had indeed left the planet behind. The marines had landed two hours ago. Coda himself had escorted their dropships to the drop zone, a mountainous region in the northern hemisphere, where thermal imaging had uncovered a complex network of tunnels.

Like many insects of Earth, the Baranyk were tunnel dwellers. Coda had never seen a native Baranyk planet, but where steel was the mark of human habitation, tunnels were the mark of the Baranyk. It was one of the things that made them so difficult to track. Different geology absorbed the different detection mechanisms in different ways. On one planet, acoustic processing might work, whereas another required electromagnetic or RF energy. Aside from putting boots on the ground, there was no universal way to determine whether a planet was infested with Baranyk or not.

"Coda," a voice said over his comm. "It's Captain Coleman. How are you holding up out there?"

"Well, sir," Coda said. "The best way I can put it is this. I'm cold but sweaty. I have to pee, but I'm thirsty. Tired but alert."

Captain Coleman laughed. "It isn't the glamorous job you signed up for, is it?"

"Not at the moment, sir."

"Well, I'm going to need you to stay out there for a little longer. Sergeant Haniger's squad found something down there."

"Found something, sir?"

"Yes. I don't know what yet. Dr. Naidoo was on the second shuttle you escorted to the planet, and all she'll tell me is that it's best to be seen."

Coda frowned. It was unorthodox for the captain himself to go planetside, though nothing about this mission was orthodox. Coda was reminded of Dr. Rydell ordering the captain about in her sick bay. Doctors, Coda supposed, liked to do things their own way, and Coleman, trusting their judgment, granted her that freedom.

"Interesting, sir."

"That's one way to put it," Captain Coleman said. "I'm headed planetside now. Maintain the CAP and have a flight patrol the area. If something is amiss, I want you there."

"Understood, sir. Good luck."

"Thank you, Coda. I hope I won't need it."

---

Coleman's transport ship landed at the base of the mountain range. The hatch opened, and a sharp wind assaulted the interior of the shuttle. The high concentration of sulfur on the planet gave it the smell of a spent match. Coleman felt his face scrunch up in a disgusted expression. One of his marine escorts must have seen it, because he handed Coleman a breathing mask.

"Here, sir. This'll help."

"Thank you, Corporal Abernathy." Coleman slid the mask into place then took a tentative breath. The soldier was right—the smell didn't go away entirely but was greatly muted.

The corporal led Coleman down the ramp of the dropship. The rest of his squad fanned out, assault rifles in hand, eyes scanning the perimeter. They believed the area was secure, but seeing the stiffness of the soldiers' bodies, the alertness of their eyes, Coleman realized how little those scans meant to the marines. They didn't trust anything but their own eyes. Their own gut.

They eventually came to the mouth of a cave, but before entering, they had to give way to a medical evac team. The medics pushed a glass-enclosed gurney that floated a few feet off the ground. Inside was a woman who looked to be in her thirties or forties, her pallid face covered in dirt and grime. Monitors on the side of the medical bed showed her vital signs.

"There's survivors?" Coleman hadn't expected to find any human life on the planet. None of their scans had turned up anything, and there hadn't been any recent distress calls that indicated there might be.

"*Survivor*, sir," Corporal Abernathy said, emphasizing the singular nature of the word. "So far."

Coleman nodded. "Lead on." He wondered what the hell the marines had found inside.

Corporal Abernathy led Coleman into the mouth of the tunnel. Marker lights had been placed on the ground, lighting a narrow passage. The walls were tight, just centimeters from his shoulders, but the high ceiling gave the system an oddly oppressive feeling.

Following the path downward, they eventually came to a wide chamber. Circular in shape, it was ringed like the bridge of the *Redemption* with a lower section and two higher rings that looked down upon it. Spotlights had been set up around the perimeter, lighting the central space, which was occupied by Sergeant Haniger's marine squad and a team of scientists.

He picked out his chief science officer almost immediately. His movement must have caught her eye, because she spotted him as well and climbed up the earthen rings to greet him.

"Captain," Dr. Naidoo said. "Thanks for coming."

"Of course, Doctor. What have we got?"

"I've never seen anything like it, sir. Follow me. I'll warn you, though, it's... not pretty."

He followed her down into the lower tier as his marine escort fanned out through the room, positioning themselves so that they were looking outward. It was then that he realized that the chamber had multiple entrances and exit points, most leading deeper into the mountains, but it was what was at the center of the chamber that took his breath away.

Stretched out along four smooth rocky slabs were an equal number of human bodies. They had been stripped naked and bound to the slabs with a thick organic material not unlike a spiderweb. Their pallid skin had gone a milky white color but showed no other sign of injury or torture, except...

Coleman was suddenly thankful for the breathing mask. It must have muted the smell, but it also hid the look of horror that covered his face. The skullcaps of the four human bodies had been removed, exposing their brains.

"What the hell is this, Doctor?" Coleman asked.

"I don't know, sir," Dr. Naidoo said. "We've found evidence of the

Baranyk studying human remains before, but nothing like this. These people had no other injuries. No signs that suggest the Baranyk were interested in anything but their brains. There's more too, sir."

She lifted the hand of the nearest body, a middle-aged man with a thick chest and a thicker midsection, and held it for Coleman to see. His fingertips were encrusted with dry blood, the fingernails ripped away. The rocky slab under his fingers was scratched and bloodied as if he had tried to claw his way free. Horror accompanied the realization, stabbing at his gut like a Baranyk forelimb.

"They were alive," Coleman said, looking up at Dr. Naidoo. "They were alive when the Baranyk did this to them."

"That's what my team and I believe too," Dr. Naidoo said.

"Why?"

"Best guess? They were experimenting on them. See here?" She pointed to a spot on the side of the man's brain. "This one shows damage to the temporal lobe. In fact, they *all* show damage to the same spot, only... *different*."

"Excuse my ignorance, Doctor, but the..."

"Temporal lobe. It's the area of the brain that interprets language and influences behavior, memory, and hearing."

"I thought the frontal lobe was responsible for speech," Coleman said.

"I said *communication*, sir. Speech is the result of the need to communicate, but it's not communication in itself."

"What are you saying?" Coleman said. "The Baranyk are trying to find a way to communicate?"

"No," Dr. Naidoo said. "I'm saying that the Baranyk are experimenting with the parts of the human brain that deal with communication. All we have here is the what, not the why."

"But—"

"I'm a scientist, Captain. I make observations. I'll make a hypothesis, too, when there's evidence to support it. I can also conduct experiments to prove or disprove that hypothesis. What I won't do is speculate. I'll leave that to you."

Coleman frowned. Scientists could be infuriating sometimes. Why was it so difficult to provide even a simple guess? To verbalize a gut feeling? "Thank you, Doctor."

"There's something else." Dr. Naidoo stepped away from the slabs and human bodies, moving toward a dark corner of the chamber. From the distance, and away from the spotlights, Coleman had thought the mound was a rock formation, but as he drew closer, he realized how wrong he had been.

In the corner was a stack of human bodies, piled atop each other and discarded like a pile of broken ship parts. Like the others at the center of the chamber, their skullcaps had been removed.

"How many are there?" Coleman's voice was tight.

"Unknown, sir. There are other corpses deeper in the tunnel system. Older. Their skin displaying greater signs of decomposition. These were just the most recent."

"And they all had the same experiments? To the same area of the brain?"

"Actually, no, sir. Many of them show signs of different experiments. All still on the brain, but different areas."

"But *why*?"

"Like I said, Captain, I'll leave the speculation up to you."

Coleman took a deep, shuddering breath. The human cost of the war was staggering, so vast that the number of dead had lost all meaning. It was just a number until one saw the death and destruction firsthand. Saw the human toll with their own eyes. Saw the blood, the injuries, the missing skullcaps.

"There's a survivor, though," Coleman said. "I saw her on my way in. Maybe she can tell us what happened here."

Dr. Naidoo winced. "We'll see, sir. There were actually three survivors when we found them. The first two died before we could provide medical aid. And the woman is showing significant signs of dehydration, malnourishment, and other, more serious ailments. To say she's touch and go would be an understatement. Dr. Rydell will do what she can, but I wouldn't get your hopes up."

"Understood, Doc," Coleman said. Dr. Rydell was a miracle worker, and he would need her to be one again. "Carry—"

A sound from one of the tunnels silenced him. At first, Coleman thought it was a rock falling, but as his mind caught up, reprocessing the sound, he realized it wasn't something falling at all but something *scraping*. Like rock against rock. *Or carapace against rock.*

"Away from the wall!" Sergeant Haniger bellowed as he and the rest of his squad moved into position. They formed up on either side of the wall, four marines deep on each side. The front two dropped to their knees, all with guns trained on the cave's opening. Coleman backed away, his step carrying him all the way back to the stone slabs.

Gunfire erupted as the first Baranyk warrior burst from the cave's opening.

# 21

*Cave, Koburn-2*
*Surface*

THE FIRST BARANYK WARRIOR WENT DOWN IN A WAVE OF BULLETS BUT WAS immediately replaced by a second. The two-meter-tall alien pierced one of the kneeling marines with its jagged forelimbs, lifting him into the air, then slammed him headfirst into the rocky wall with a sickening crunch. Two more Baranyk warriors emerged behind it, then two more after that, and before Captain Coleman realized it, another marine was down.

"Get the captain back to the shuttle!" Sergeant Haniger bellowed.

The two rearmost marines fell back, moving down toward Captain Coleman, Dr. Naidoo, and the rest of the science staff in the center of the chamber.

"Let's go, sir," Corporal Abernathy said. He grabbed Coleman by the arm and hauled him toward the original entrance. They were too late. More Baranyk streamed into the room from one of the other entrances closer to their destination.

"Shit!" a marine shouted. "We're surrounded."

"Fall back," Sergeant Haniger bellowed. "Defensive formations. Protect the captain!"

Coleman and the scientists were herded to the center of the chamber like cattle for the slaughter. There were only seven marines left, and they formed a defensive perimeter while the science team fell to their knees, terrified. Coleman remained standing, surveying the situation as it took a terrifying, unexpected turn.

For every Baranyk the marines took down, two more seemed to take its place. Unprepared to fight a prolonged battle, the marines began shooting in more controlled bursts, only firing when one of the enemy warriors lunged forward.

"Abernathy," Sergeant Haniger screamed. "On the horn."

"On it, sir." Corporal Abernathy pulled away from the defensive formation, yanking something from his pack, and kneeled to the ground. He held the device to his ear then cursed.

"It's no use, sir. I'm not getting a signal. We're too deep."

"Damn it, Abernathy, you're surrounded by half a dozen scientists. Figure out a way to boost the signal."

*They're trying to radio for reinforcements. But none are coming. We're on our own.*

Coleman tried his own earpiece, but buried in the mountains, he didn't have a signal, either. It was worth a try. With no other options, he sprang into action. "Corporal! Give me your sidearm."

"Can't do that, sir," Corporal Abernathy shouted back, firing another burst into the massing enemy. The Baranyk had them completely surrounded now, outnumbering them at least three to one and occupying the high ground.

"I'm not going to ask again, soldier. Your sidearm."

Abernathy cursed. Keeping his rifle stock against his shoulder, he pulled his sidearm free with his other hand and held it out to Coleman. The captain took it, immediately flipping the safety off. He chambered a round, and training it on one of the enemy warriors, he unloaded two bullets into a triangular head.

"Hand them all over," Coleman shouted over the gunfire. "All of you!"

"Sir—"

"Do it!" Haniger yelled.

Dr. Naidoo was the first to take one of the weapons, though her team expressed far more reluctance. They seemed more content to hide.

"Fight, damn it!" Coleman shouted. "Fight, or we're all dead."

Three more of the scientists stood, taking weapons. Only one seemed to remember their weapons training, though, switching off the safety and chambering a round. She helped those beside her do the same, then more of the scientists took weapons. In a moment, their defensive force had doubled.

*It won't be enough. Even if they were all expert marksmen, we're still outnumbered. And the contained environment takes away our guns' biggest advantage.*

Another of the Baranyk lunged forward and was met with a barrage of gunfire. It shuddered, taking half a dozen rounds in the midsection before retreating. Yellow blood oozed from the wounds, but the creature showed no other signs that it was injured.

*Damn, these things are tough bastards. Ugly fuckers too.*

More gunfire rang out as a pair of Baranyk darted forward.

"What are they doing?" someone asked.

"Testing our perimeter," Haniger shouted. "Stand firm!"

That was easier said than done. The bulk of their number were scientists who had only ever seen the enemy as a corpse or in a highly controlled environment. They were terrified, shaky, and just as likely to shoot one of their own as they were the enemy.

Sergeant Haniger must have seen it too. "We need to move, sir."

"Where to, Sergeant?" Coleman asked.

"Any of the other cave entrances," Haniger said. "We can use the narrow passages to our advantage. Their numbers won't mean jack there."

Coleman surveyed the scene with fresh eyes. The creatures' height made it difficult to see past them, and from the bottom ring of the perimeter, Coleman had trouble spotting one of the entrances.

*There!*

"Seven o'clock," Coleman said. "Their numbers are thinner. We can push through."

"That'll lead us deeper into the mountain," Corporal Abernathy said.

"We don't have a choice," Haniger said. "Prepare to move." He unclipped a grenade from his tactical vest and removed the electronic pin. "We're pushing for the entrance." He hurled the grenade into the mass of Baranyk that stood between them and their destination. It detonated a moment later, rocking the chamber, drowning out all other noise, and leaving a terrible ringing in its wake.

Coleman couldn't hear anything beyond that ringing, couldn't hear the marines shouting to move forward, but he felt their insistence. The human force sprayed gunfire, carving a hole toward their destination. Someone behind him was cut down. He couldn't tell if it was scientist or marine, the warm blood indistinguishable.

The human push slowed, meeting resistance as the Baranyk regrouped. Coleman drove his shoulder into the person in front of him, pushed, seeing up close the horror of Baranyk forelimbs tearing through human flesh.

There was another explosion, and suddenly, the bottleneck loosened. Coleman stumbled forward, tripping over fallen human and Baranyk alike. He crashed into the tunnel then spun, facing the marine rear guard as they streamed into the tunnel. Baranyk forelimbs ripped through them from behind with terrifying brutality. Blood washed over Coleman's face, then he was moving again.

It was darkness. The only light in the tunnel came from the lights in the main chamber. He felt more than heard the enemy pursuit. He ran, firing wildly behind himself. He knew it was useless—his bullets were more likely hitting the walls of the tunnel—but didn't care. It had been years since he'd shot a firearm, and that had never been under this kind of duress. He wasn't a marine. He was a pilot, used to a different kind of fight.

Light appeared ahead of him. Multiple lights.

*Flashlights.*

They were moving away.

*Wait!*

He tried calling ahead but couldn't hear his own voice. Had the grenades ruptured his eardrums? Was he deaf?

*Doesn't matter. Keep pushing.*

Then blessedly, there was light behind him too. Someone pushed him. There were marines behind him too.

*Of course there are. They're trained soldiers. They aren't going to leave their captain behind. And I was shooting toward them.*

There was another explosion behind him, and Coleman stumbled as rock and detritus fell from the roof of the tunnel, narrowing the passage.

The enemy could still get through but would be slowed. Someone pushed him forward, keeping their position as rear guard. The rest of the barrel lamps were still ahead. They'd come to a complete stop, though.

*Dead end?*

As Coleman neared, he realized that it wasn't that they didn't have any options—it was that they had too many. The small chamber opened up into several adjoining hallways. Some led up, others down, none giving any hint of whether they would lead out of the cave system at all.

"This way!" Haniger said. "Go! Go! Go!"

Two marines, followed by the mass of scientists, rushed into the dark opening, Coleman right on their heels. The rest of the marines formed their rear guard.

Down, up, left, right they went, having to duck under rocky protrusions hanging from the ceiling, climbing over boulders on the ground. The scraping sounds of the advancing Baranyk echoed behind them.

And then there was light ahead. Not the swaying lights of the barrel-mounted flashlights but real, true light from the outside. The group rushed toward it as if they were thirsty travelers in the sand-blown dunes of the Sahara. The little resolve that remained in the scientists cracked, their panic finally winning over. They surged toward the light, taking little heed of those around them, pushing their captain and protective marines out of the way, trampling the sorry souls who had fallen.

Bursting into the light, Coleman was temporarily blinded. He blinked hurriedly then squinted, trying to get his bearings.

They'd come out of another tunnel, not even a full kilometer from the original entrance, and parked in the same position was the dropship that had brought Coleman to the surface. Blessedly, there were no Baranyk in sight.

"To the dropship!" Haniger shouted, waving the scientists forward, though he hadn't needed to. The scientists sprinted forward, while Coleman lagged behind with the marine rear guard.

"Fire in the hole!" Abernathy hurled a grenade into the cave's opening. It exploded just as the first Baranyk came into sight, sending limbs and carapace flying with bits of rock and stone. The entrance collapsed, blocking the enemy's exit.

"That should hold them for a while," Abernathy said.

Along with the remaining marines, Coleman broke into a jog toward the dropship. They made it onto its ramp just as the first Baranyk exited the other entrance. The enemy surged forward, showing no signs of giving up the chase.

"Get us in the air," Coleman said to the pilot. He backed into the belly of the dropship, where the rest of the group was strapping in. The Baranyk streamed from the caves as the ship rose. There were hundreds of them, and more still poured out.

Above the whine of the dropship's engines was a familiar sound. A moment later, a flight of Nighthawks in delta formation ripped past the dropship. They opened fire, carving through the massed Baranyk below. The door to the dropship closed as the Nighthawks turned, preparing for another pass.

Coleman finally took his seat. Safe and secure but still feeling the heightened effects of the adrenaline pulsing through his body, he took a deep breath. It was over. He had made it.

Five marines and a handful of the science staff remained. There had been at least twice as many. Like Coleman, now that they were safe in the dropship, their emotions caught up to them. Those who weren't crying wore haunted expressions. The physical part of the battle was over, but their emotional and psychological war was just beginning.

The shuttle bucked as it gained altitude. Coleman closed his eyes, resting the back of his head against the bulkhead, letting the swaying ship calm his nerves.

The Baranyk had never left, he realized. *Was it a trap then? Did they want us to find those bodies?*

So many questions. Everywhere they went, the questions grew, and they were no closer to finding answers.

# 22

*Cockpit, Nighthawk*
*Koburn-2*

EVERYTHING ABOUT KOBURN FELT OFF. FROM ORBIT, THE PLANET'S COLORS were strikingly similar to Earth's, but the landmasses were in the wrong places, the shade of the water slightly off. It was the equivalent of a person painting what they thought Earth *should* be, not what it was. The result was just similar enough to feel familiar but different enough to make Coda uncomfortable.

The cockpit of his Nighthawk *was* familiar, comfortable, and a welcomed retreat. At some point during the months of training and the following months of battle, it had become home. They'd moved from ship to ship, the only constants being his cockpit and his wingmen. It was like moving from his childhood home to another. The yard and the address were different, but the things that were *his*—his bed, his belongings, and his friends—remained the same.

Coda melted into the gel of his seat, completely relaxed by the slight vibration of his thrusters. He had no doubt he could fall asleep if he closed his eyes. Instead, he and Nails flew CAP, their fighter pair augmented by four other pairs on staggered two-hour blocks.

He'd had little contact with Nails since their encounter during Squawks's initiation ritual, but he hadn't been able to escape the feeling that he'd been forced to end their short conversation prematurely. Between that and his overwhelming desire to get back into the cockpit, Coda had made last-minute changes to the CAP schedule, ensuring that he and Nails would fly it together.

For nearly two hours, they'd flown with the *Redemption*, one eye on the planet, the other eye on the battle map. Just like everyone else, Coda knew the inactivity on their sensors was a false negative. The planet was teeming with the enemy. As always, the challenge was that the Baranyk were tunnel dwellers who built complex underground networks of tunnels and open chambers. They'd always been nearly impossible to spot. Since the attack on the captain, the Forgotten had been on high alert, prepared for an inevitable attack, one that had, thus far, never come.

Nails let out a deep sigh, her boredom as loud as a jackhammer at Mass.

"Almost done," Coda said. "Squawks and Tinman will be taking over soon. One more pass should do it."

Coda had staggered the CAP so that it would receive a new pair of fresh fighters every hour, with each pair in the air for twice that. Coda and Nails's rotation was nearly up.

"Who would have thought flying a Nighthawk in enemy territory would be so *boring*?" Nails said.

Coda couldn't help but smile. Like nearly every fighter pilot he'd ever known, Nails had an overly confident attitude that bordered on cockiness. Not even a week removed from her first battle, she was already complaining about a lack of action.

"Recent history aside," Coda said, "that's the nature of war. Long moments of inaction followed by brief, chaotic flashes that flip your world upside down."

"That's not how my father always described it."

"Yeah, well, he flew in a different time, during a different kind of war. Over the last few years, the war has slowed to a grind, becoming less about large-scale battles and more about the development of new technologies. Despite all the work we're putting in, Nails, this war will be won by some egghead who comes up with a new technology or weapon that will give us the critical edge we need."

"Or lose it because they didn't think of it soon enough."

"That's a possibility too," Coda said. "It nearly happened a year ago when they discovered a way to render our Hornets inoperable. If it hadn't been for your father—"

"Please don't."

"Don't what?"

"Don't talk about him as if he's some kind of hero."

"Sorry to break it to you, Lieutenant," Coda said, "but he is. And he's earned the title many times over. There's a reason he was named captain of the *Redemption* without ever serving as an XO or position of true command."

"Just because everyone believes it doesn't make it true," Nails said. "Or do you believe your father is a traitor because everyone else thinks he is?"

Coda bristled at the question. Had she asked him a year ago, he would have said yes without a moment's hesitation, but the act of flying in the same Nighthawk cockpits and undergoing many of the same experiences as his father had opened his eyes. Without ever speaking to the man, Coda had grown closer to him, coming to understand the man better than he ever had. The truth was complicated, and he wasn't sure how he felt anymore.

"My father's sins aside, *I* believe your father's a hero too. Without him, we wouldn't have repelled the Baranyk at Toavis, and there's no telling what would have happened after that."

Nails went quiet. Coda could tell he had struck a nerve. Thing was, he was finally getting somewhere. She had opened up more than she had before. And while he wasn't her counselor or psychiatrist, he needed to understand her well enough to determine whether or not her feelings would interfere with her ability to do her job. He had to keep prying but not pry hard enough to make her close up.

"He *can* be a bit cold, though," Coda added, almost as if it were an afterthought. "The effects of war, I suppose."

"Your father was the same way?" Nails asked.

"Mine?" Coda said. "No. He spent so much time away that when he was around, things were... well, things were good. My father was a completely different man outside of the uniform."

"Mine wasn't," Nails said. "He was always the military man. Always thinking about flying. His mind always in the cockpit."

"It *is* addicting," Coda said, thinking of his injured ribs and how he was flying against the doc's recommendation.

"I'm still waiting to see the allure," Nails said bitterly.

Her words rattled something loose in his brain, and the pieces finally fell into place. Coda had thought Nails had joined the Sol Fleet for reasons similar to his own—to get out of her father's shadow and create a legacy of her own—but that hadn't been the case at all. She'd applied for the recently reopened Nighthawk program to *understand* the father who had left her behind. To understand why flying had led the great Captain Coleman to choose the cockpit over his family.

*That's why she's so angry.* It wasn't because of half-buried feelings but because the thing he'd chosen over her had failed to live up to her lofty expectations. Nails was like a child meeting her father's new wife for the first time. No matter how beautiful, smart, or kind she was, the new woman would never live up to her own mother.

"They cast a wide shadow, don't they?" Coda said. "Our fathers."

"Yes, they do," Nails said. "But at least you're only contending with your father's memory. Not the person himself."

"Sometimes the past can be more difficult to overcome than the present, but I get your point."

Coda's gaze drifted toward the *Redemption.* They flew close to it by space standards, still within visual range. It maintained an orbit around Koburn, turrets and batteries ready to open fire should the enemy return. Who would have thought such an intimidating warship would house so many personal conflicts?

"He hasn't even come to see me," Nails said, interrupting the brief silence. "Did you know that?"

"I didn't." He'd had his suspicions but hadn't been willing to ask the captain about it. It wasn't his business, and while he and the captain were close by commander–subordinate standards, they were not friends.

"I'd hoped... I don't know what I'd hoped, but it wasn't this. If he doesn't say something soon, I will. I'll show up outside his quarters and force him to talk to me."

"Nails..."

"I'm serious."

"Lieutenant," Coda said, addressing her by her title to assume control over the conversation. "Don't. I can't speak for your father, and I can only imagine what you're going through, but forcing the issue never makes it better. Your father is a stubborn man who works in his own way and on his own schedule. I'm not saying it's right, but you have to give him the space to process things. You've been planning this for years. He's only had a couple weeks. Be patient."

For once, Nails didn't reply. Coda understood—he wasn't even convinced of his own explanation. The captain needed to resolve his issues with his daughter. Couldn't he see that he was only making the situation worse? Potentially putting the entire ship in danger? Coda couldn't risk Nails showing up at his door, but if the captain remained aloof for too much longer, Coda would force his hand.

"Thank you."

Coda blinked, the words surprising him. "For what?"

"For listening. There's not a lot of people I can talk to about him."

He wasn't sure how to respond. His motives hadn't been putting her at ease. They were to determine her mental state and assess the risk she posed, but he couldn't tell her that. "You're welcome, Nails. Moscow and Cougar will be launching any moment. What do you say we bring it in?"

"Sounds good, Coda."

"You've got point. Take us home."

"Yes, sir."

Coda cast a final uneasy look back toward the strangely earthlike planet below before bringing the *Redemption* back into his sights. He followed the blues of Nails's thrusters back into the Nighthawk hangar bay.

# 23

*Sick Bay, SAS Redemption*
*Koburn-2, High Orbit*

Something about sick bay could wilt even the strongest man. Coleman watched as the normally calm, confident, and stern Commander Garcia stepped into the medical ward and seemed to deflate. His face grew somber, his shoulders dipped, eyes drifting downward as if his very gaze would disrupt the sick.

Captain Coleman spotted him from the back of the ward, where he and Dr. Naidoo were in deep conversation, and waved him over. As the man neared, Coleman could see the dark circles under his eyes and wondered how long he had been on duty.

"Don't take this the wrong way," Garcia said, his voice quiet, "but you look like shit."

Coleman gave him a half-hearted laugh. "I was just thinking the same thing about you."

"Tried to give the enemy a snack, did you?"

Coleman looked toward Dr. Naidoo uncomfortably. Gallows humor was fine—it was how some people processed their experiences—but this close to the attack and after witnessing the Baranyk's violence up close,

Coleman wasn't one of those people. People had died down there, their heads and limbs torn from their bodies, blood sprayed across the tunnel walls like paint from an expressionist painter. And that didn't even account for the dozens of humans who'd had their skullcaps removed and brains experimented on. No, it wasn't a laughing matter at all.

"I appreciate you coming," Coleman said, taking control of the conversation.

"Of course, sir." Garcia glanced at Dr. Naidoo. "What's going on?"

"It's easier shown than explained," Coleman said. "Follow me."

Coleman stepped away from the group, making for the partition drawn across the back of the ward, blocking the back section from view. Dr. Naidoo and Garcia followed. Coleman opened the partition, nodding for Garcia to enter, then stepped in once everyone was inside.

Inside was a single occupant, a middle-aged woman with stringy hair and a weather-worn face. She was dressed in the gray uniform of the Koburn miners. Her face and hands had been washed clean, but they were so pale the skin bordered on translucent. She eyed Garcia as he stopped at the foot of her bed, then in a single sudden movement, she lunged at him.

Garcia jumped back, crashing into a tray holding various medical instruments, sending them to the floor in a noisy clatter. He shot a look at Coleman then back to the woman. She was still lunging, fighting with the restraints that bound her wrists and ankles to the railing of the bed.

"You said this would be easier seen than explained," Garcia said. "Well, I still don't understand what the hell is going on. What am I supposed to see, Chadwick?"

The woman calmed and cocked her head to the side, her eyes narrowing as if she heard him but didn't understand. Garcia's expression grew contemplative. There was something off about the woman, and Coleman's XO was beginning to see it.

"Does she not... do you not speak English?"

The idea was unthinkable. Walk in any city across human-occupied space, and one would hear dozens of languages, but for all fleetwide communications, English was the standard. The woman continued to look at Garcia as if she had just discovered the second sentient alien species in the galaxy.

"Who is she?" Garcia asked, finally taking the bait.

"We found her in the caves," Coleman said.

"I wasn't aware there were survivors," Garcia said.

"I haven't finished my report yet," Coleman said. "You'll get it. In the meantime, she was the only one. Things were dicey with her too. Dr. Rydell has done wonders to stabilize her condition. Physically, she's doing better, but mentally…"

"It's like she doesn't understand what we're saying," Garcia said. "But that shouldn't be possible, so what are we talking about? Amnesia? A head injury?"

"None of the above," Dr. Naidoo said. "What the captain left out is that we only found one survivor in those tunnels, but there were dozens of dead, all showing signs that the Baranyk had been experimenting on their brains."

"They cut them open, Jaime. Opened their skulls, exposed their brains. Poked, prodded, cut parts away."

Garcia ran a hand through his dark hair. "Jesus…"

"It gets worse," Coleman said. "They did it while the poor souls were alive."

Garcia gave him a pointed look, opening his mouth to speak, but nothing came out. He looked back at the woman, his face growing sympathetic. "Why?"

"Your guess is as good as mine, but Dr. Rydell and Dr. Naidoo say they experimented with the… the…" He waved his hands in front of himself, trying to remember the medical term.

"With the temporal lobe," Dr. Naidoo said. "It's the area of the brain that allows for communication."

"Wait," Garcia said. "Are you saying they're trying to communicate with us?"

"We don't know yet," Coleman said.

"Maybe they're looking to negotiate a truce," Garcia said. "Thirty years of war is a hell of a commitment for any species. Hundreds of millions dead. Infrastructure destroyed. The war showing no signs of ending."

"Then why attack? If their goal was to communicate, why kill our scientists?"

"I don't know, Chadwick. But this is—"

"Baseless speculation," Dr. Naidoo interrupted. "And not supported by the facts."

Garcia clamped his mouth shut then nodded. "Understood. Tell me what I'm missing."

"We originally thought this woman didn't show any signs of experimentation," Dr. Naidoo said. "As you can see, her skullcap is still very much intact."

Save for bumps, bruises, and raw skin from pulling on her restraints, the woman showed no signs of injury.

"Originally thought?"

"Follow me, Commander." Dr. Naidoo stepped out of the partitioned area.

Garcia gave the survivor a final look before following the doctor. Coleman could have been wrong, but he thought the man was relieved to escape the woman's gaze. Coleman closed the partition behind them and followed.

Dr. Naidoo stopped beside a nearby terminal and brought up a three-dimensional image of the survivor's brain. One of the areas in the lower middle of the brain was highlighted red.

"The temporal lobe," Dr. Naidoo said. "Part of the cerebral cortex, has both left and right hemispheres and is responsible for processing sensory input, including pain and auditory stimuli."

"English, Doc," Garcia said. "I'm a dumb fighter jock, remember?"

"It helps us understand language," Coleman said.

"It's more than that," Dr. Naidoo said. "Without the temporal lobe, we'd be unable to form long-term memories or interpret visual stimuli. We know right now that we're looking at an image of a brain, but for vision to be useful, we have to *understand* what we're looking at. The ventral part of the lobe provides meaning to what we see. The auditory cortex is key to hearing and understanding human speech, but the lobe gives it meaning. Wernicke's area in particular—"

"Okay," Garcia said, holding up a hand. "That's more than enough." He turned to Coleman. "So, she doesn't show any sign of experimentation, but her temporal lobe is... damaged?"

"It appears that way," Coleman said.

"Then what happened?" Garcia pointed at the damaged area on the brain scan. "What caused this?"

Dr. Naidoo let out a deep sigh.

"What?" Garcia asked.

"The doctor doesn't like speculation," Coleman said. "Our *hypothesis* is the enemy found what they were looking for. Enough to advance to a different experiment anyway."

"So instead of cutting into her brain, they did what? Targeted that area of her brain with an alien communication of some kind?"

"Maybe," Coleman said. "Or maybe they did something to see how that part of the brain would react. It's impossible to say, which is why the doctor loathes this kind of discussion. In either case, it appears the enemy has developed some kind of technology that effects the human brain. For what purpose, we don't know. But I don't have to stress how important this information is."

Garcia rubbed his forehead. "That's horrifying."

Coleman only nodded. The worst part was he had seen something like this before, years ago. That information was classified, and he didn't have enough to go on yet, but if his hunch was correct, the situation was even more dire than any of them knew.

He opened his mouth to speak—

The lights of the medical bay dimmed, emergency lights kicking on. Condition One had been set throughout the ship. Coleman and Commander Garcia shared a look then raced out of the room toward the bridge.

"Captain," Lieutenant Poiu said in his earpiece, "a Baranyk carrier just jumped into system."

# 24

*Bridge, SAS Redemption*
*Koburn-2, High Orbit*

"REPORT!" CAPTAIN COLEMAN BELLOWED AS HE AND COMMANDER GARCIA stepped onto the bridge. The room was alive with activity, his crew manning their stations alert and crisp. His eyes immediately went to the battle map, where a red wireframe of a Baranyk cruiser floated through space.

"Baranyk cruiser inbound," Lieutenant Poiu said. "Maintaining an intercept. ETA in eight minutes."

"Where did it come from?" Commander Garcia asked, descending the steps to the inner ring with Coleman.

"Unknown, sir," Lieutenant Poiu said. "It jumped in two minutes ago at a distant orbit of several hundred thousand kilometers. Within moments, it plotted an intercept course toward us."

"What about fighters?" Coleman asked. There wasn't any indication of them on the display.

"Nothing yet, sir," Lieutenant Poiu said.

*Odd*, Coleman thought, rubbing his jaw. If the ship was planning to engage, it should have already deployed its fighters. It was in the space *between* capital ships that the battle was normally won. Only on rare occasions did the capital ships engage directly.

"What about ours?" Coleman asked.

"Locked and loaded, sir," Lieutenant Poiu said.

"Good," Coleman said. "Hold them unless the enemy launches theirs or closes within a hundred thousand kilometers."

"Copy that."

Eyes glued on the display, Coleman and his crew watched as the enemy vessel closed the distance between them. The ship didn't veer or alter course, maintaining a steady pace toward the inevitable.

"One hundred twenty-five thousand kilometers and closing."

Coleman grabbed the railing that circled the battle map, the padded metal cool in his hand. He worked to keep his breathing steady, his heart rate slow, but his mind raced with images from the tunnels. The Baranyk mere inches from him, their spear-like forelimbs cutting through armored marines and helpless scientists alike. Blood cascaded through the air, speckling the walls. Then the images shifted. The Baranyk were in the ship, their black carapaces a menacing juxtaposition with the gleaming white bulkhead of the *Redemption*.

"One hundred five thousand kilometers," Lieutenant Poiu said.

"It's not slowing down," Commander Garcia said.

"Launch fighters," Coleman said.

"Launching fighters," Poiu repeated.

The deck thumped with the subtle beat of Nighthawks shot into space. The feeling was accompanied by additional images appearing on the battle map. Twenty-four in all, a full squadron. Names indicated each fighter, noting the pilot. Coda was out there. So was Nails. With the Nighthawks entering the battle space, Coleman expected the Baranyk to launch its own fighters, but after several moments, the battlespace remained empty.

*What are they waiting for?*

The relative speed between the two ships was growing increasingly disproportionate. Old instincts kicked in. "Move to intercept," Coleman said. "Full burn."

*Speed is life.*

"Yes, sir. Moving to intercept. Full burn."

The railing rumbled under his hand as the whole ship vibrated from the immense power of the *Redemption*'s thrusters.

"Sir!" Ensign Richey shouted. "I'm reading some kind of electromagnetic signature."

Coleman bounded the steps two at a time, stopping beside Richey's station. The young officer wore a single earpiece tuned in to the ship's communication. Her terminal displayed the signature in visual form.

"What is it?" Coleman asked. "Some kind of communication?"

"No, sir. The frequency is too high to be a radio wave. It... I've never seen anything like it, sir."

"Is it just emitting it, or is the signal localized?"

"It's definitely targeted toward our ship, sir."

The pit in Coleman's stomach grew worse. Something was off. When the enemy shifted tactics, he took special notice. "Scan all critical systems," Coleman bellowed. "Life support, weapons systems, communications. If *anything* looks off, I need to know now."

There was a furious rush of activity as each of the members of the bridge scanned and reviewed their critical systems. The confirmations came in a rush.

"All green, sir."

"Weapons systems online."

"Navigation online."

Nothing was amiss.

Coleman's thoughts drifted back to the woman in sick bay, to her brain scans, and to the only other person he'd seen with something similar. He toggled his earpiece, opening a channel with his CAG. "Coda, we're reading some kind of strange signal down here. Are you..." How could he ask this question without raising suspicion? "Are you seeing or experiencing anything odd out there?"

"Experiencing anything odd?" Coda asked. "No, sir."

Coleman exhaled a relieved breath. Maybe there was no connection at all. Maybe it was, as Dr. Naidoo liked to say, baseless speculation.

"Captain!" Ensign Richey said. "It's gone."

The image on her display had gone flat, no readings. Silence. "Keep scanning. If it reappears, I want to know."

"Yes, sir."

The ship recorded all inbound and outbound communication and would have a log of the signal for analysis, but Coleman had more immediate concerns.

"Lieutenant Poiu, order our fighters to engage."

"Copy that, sir."

Coleman stepped away from Ensign Richey's station, moving back toward the inner ring.

The Baranyk ship disappeared.

"It's gone, sir," Lieutenant Poiu said. "It jumped."

Coleman froze halfway down the staircase. Silence stretched throughout the room. What the hell was going on? The enemy had jumped in, hit them with an unknown signal, then jumped away.

"Scan systems again," Coleman said. "They hit us with that signal for some reason, and I want to know why."

"Captain."

It took him a moment to realize the voice was coming from his earpiece and not from someone on the bridge.

"Captain, it's Dr. Rydell."

"What is it, Doc?"

"It's the survivor, sir. She's dead."

Coleman's breath caught in his throat. "Say again, Doc?"

"The survivor is dead, sir."

Coleman's eyes found Commander Garcia's. The other man wouldn't be hearing the same thing he was, but it was clear he knew Coleman was getting a private message.

"What is it?" Commander Garcia asked.

"The survivor in sick bay is dead," Coleman said.

"Dead?" Garcia asked. "How?"

"I don't know, but I'm going to find out." Coleman started for the exit. "You've got the bridge."

"Yes, sir."

Coleman raced through the ship's corridors. In sick bay, he found Rydell and Naidoo at the back of the medical ward. The woman lay on the gurney, her half-crazed eyes now vacant and staring at the ceiling. Blood ran down her neck, soaking into the white sheets and pooling on the floor.

"Captain," Dr. Rydell said, finally seeing him.

"What happened?"

"We don't know, sir. Her vitals spiked, and when we came rushing, we found her like this."

"Found her?" Coleman repeated. "You mean she did this to herself?"

Dr. Rydell nodded.

"How is that possible? She was restrained."

Coleman strode closer to the woman then crouched to look at the hand that hung limply off the side of the gurney. It was no longer bound. The thumb had been pushed inward, broken or out of the socket, and under the drying blood, the skin was a tattered mess, as if it had been ripped away.

"Degloved," Dr. Rydell said. "She broke her thumb and slipped her hand free, then broke a piece of metal free from the gurney and—"

"Stabbed herself with it," Coleman finished.

"Yes."

"And you didn't hear it?"

"There was no sound. Not until she broke the railing off the gurney. By the time we realized something was happening, we were too late."

Coleman pinched his forehead. "You're telling me she broke her thumb and ripped the skin of her hand off without so much as a cry of pain?"

"Yes," Dr. Rydell said. "That's exactly what I'm saying."

Coleman shook his head. None of this should have been possible. He looked at the woman again. Wireless electrodes still stuck to her head, marring an otherwise-serene face. "You were monitoring her?"

"Yes, sir."

"Good. I need you to look at her scans from the last five minutes. We were hit by an unknown Baranyk signal and unable to determine its effects. This"—he pointed at the woman—"can't be a coincidence."

"Will do, sir."

"And, Doc, if you find something, get with Ensign Richey and Dr. Naidoo to compare timestamps. Determine if the new brain activity began and ended with the signal's beginning and end."

"Of course, sir."

Coleman nodded and turned to leave the sick bay. He didn't need to wait for Dr. Rydell's confirmation. Deep in his gut, he already knew the truth. The Baranyk ship had jumped in, targeted the survivor with its signal, and somehow forced her to kill herself before jumping away.

They were covering their tracks, hiding the results of their experiments, but what Coleman had seen confirmed his greatest fears. The Baranyk had discovered a way to manipulate human action.

He had to get word to Command, but first, he had to wait for Dr. Rydell's confirmation. Without it, the idea was too absurd. Command would call him an alarmist. He would need to get Dr. Naidoo's opinion as well. Combined, they might be able to convince someone of the danger.

But even then, he knew they would require more information. How strong was the signal? What was its range? How widespread was it? Could it affect more than one person at a time? In order to counteract it and give humanity a fighting chance, they needed more information. But where to look?

In his favorite books and vids growing up, clever detectives were always led from one clue to the next. A card, a matchbook, a phone number—something always led them to a person or location where they would find their next clue. If they followed it far enough, they would find their answers, and the mystery would be solved. His problem was that he didn't have that next place, and nothing that he had collected thus far pointed him toward somewhere in particular.

He could pick a system at random, but that didn't feel right. What had those investigators and detectives done when they ran into a roadblock?

Coleman froze in the center of the corridor, an idea coming to him. *Yes...* as much as he'd tried to discount the idea, the similarities were uncanny. The brain scans, the changes in behavior, people acting against their will.

What did the detectives do when they were looking for that last clue? They went back to the beginning. To the place where the original crime happened.

It was time to go to Kryos.

# 25

*CAG's Office, SAS Redemption*
*Koburn-2, High Orbit*

THE DAY AFTER THE MYSTERIOUS BARANYK APPEARANCE, CODA FOUND himself in his CAG's office with his squadron leaders, struggling to concentrate on the task in front of him. He'd summoned them first thing that morning under the pretense of optimizing the flight roster, but he was really just looking for company. Needed to hear the friendly banter between friends. Laugh at the shit-talking between rivals.

He'd known leadership would come with added responsibility, that his actions would decide the fate of his pilots, and that there would be a certain animosity among the ranks toward him. But he'd expected to have his flight leaders with him every step of the way. What he found was that there were actually two walls—one between him and his pilots and another between him and his former friends.

It wasn't that they didn't joke, banter, or shit-talk—they just didn't include him the same way they had before. The situation had changed. Their responsibilities had changed. Even their rank. His most of all. The worst part was, he didn't necessarily think it was wrong. There *should* be a line between him and those under his command. Get too close, and he might not be able to order them into risky situations. He just couldn't help but feel like he'd lost something.

During his most difficult times at the Terran Fleet Academy, Coda hadn't handled tough situations as well as he could have. He hadn't crumpled under the pressure, but he hadn't always risen to the challenge either. There were outbursts—usually punctuated by fights with Moscow and followed by trips to Captain Hughes's office. He'd skipped more than one practice, but that had been while they were fighting simulated battles, when the responsibility was a responsibility of training for the future, not the responsibility of keeping his pilots safe today.

Losing a battle there meant he might drop in the standings. Losing a battle here meant his friends died. Walls and lines, that was what life had become. Walls and lines. So Coda buried himself in his work.

"We're good with this?" Coda asked from behind his desk.

The rest of his flight leaders sat on the other side of the office, their attention focused on the digital display board that listed the names of their pilots. For the last two hours, they had been reshuffling the flight roster, compensating for lost pilots and equalizing numbers. Despite the work they'd put in assembling fighter pairs, some of their initial pairings hadn't worked out. They needed to adjust the roster to compensate for losses, but it was also an opportunity to increase the remaining pilots' effectiveness.

"I still don't think it's perfect," Moscow said. "But it's an improvement."

"How many times do we need to go through this?" Noodle asked, agitated. "We won't know how well it'll work until we get them in the simulator and see how they look."

"Agreed," Coda said.

Noodle and Moscow glared at each other. They'd been through this before—tensions were high, and the two pilots had never gotten along. A lot of that was a byproduct of Coda's former rivalry with Moscow, but unlike Coda, Noodle hadn't put those old feelings behind him. They'd been at each other's throats all morning.

"I want the simulators running twenty-four hours a day," Coda said. "When the new pilots aren't in them, I want them flying CAP, and when they're not doing that, I want them in the cockpit flying training exercises. I don't know how long we have until our next battle, but I know however long it is, it won't be long enough."

"Good god, man," Squawks said. "You sound just like the captain. I swear, if I just closed my eyes..."

"It's the chair," Noodle said. "There's something about that chair that makes all commanders sound the same."

Coda bristled, his blood rising. *You're damn right it's the chair. And the responsibility that comes with it.* But as soon as the thoughts crossed his mind, he realized the wall between him and his friends had come down—even if only for a brief moment. Squawks had an innate ability to read a situation and know what to say. It was one of the qualities that made him a great flight leader and a great friend.

Coda grinned, trying to think of a retort, but he was too slow, and the moment passed.

"They really didn't do too bad," Moscow said, steering the conversation back on track. "All things considered. We've only lost five fighters, none since the initial engagement. And even with our retooling, more than sixty percent of our original fighter pairs remain intact."

"I know, Moscow," Coda said. "But we both know how many kills the squadron had once you removed the Forgotten veterans from the equation. They may have had good training, but they're still green. Unless we can improve their effectiveness, I'm afraid our streak of victories will come to an end."

"Everyone but Nails," Squawks said. "That girl is something else, let me tell you."

"If she can learn to stay with her wingman, she'll be even better," Coda said.

"You really are the most pessimistic person I've ever met." Squawks added a grin to let Coda know he was joking, but there was too much truth to the statement. "I wouldn't mind flying with her, Coda, if you're up for making another tweak to the roster."

"No," Coda said. "She stays with me."

"She's one of the best," Noodle added.

"Which is exactly why she's staying with the CAG," Squawks said, apparently not willing to let Coda off the hook. "Coda's watching out for his own ass."

"You're damn right I am," Coda said with a wry grin. "Unless you want me to get shot down so you can take over…"

"And sit in that chair?" Squawks said. "No thank you. I can't start talking like the captain too. It'll ruin my best trait."

Coda laughed. It wasn't a hearty thing or even terribly deep, but it was a start. And it felt good. *Thank you, Squawks. I needed this.* "All right. You know what needs to be done, so make it happen. I want daily progress reports and honest assessments with a critical eye. If the new pairs don't take to each other immediately, we'll try something new. We don't have—"

"Time," Squawks finished for him. "We know."

Coda didn't know how other squadrons operated, but he was pretty sure other flight leaders didn't interrupt their CAGs. But this was the Forgotten—their whole existence was an abnormality.

Before Coda could respond, a knock at his door drew their attention, and Captain Coleman stepped into the room.

"Sir," Coda said, jumping from his seat and snapping to attention. The rest of his flight leaders followed suit.

"At ease," Captain Coleman said. "Gentlemen, I need a word with my CAG."

"Of course, sir," Squawks said. "We were just finishing up anyway."

The three squadron leaders gave the captain a final salute then exited the office, closing the door behind them.

Captain Coleman's eyes fell on the display board. "Tweaking the roster?"

"Just making some small adjustments, sir. Balancing the squadrons, tweaking fighter pairs, trying to increase their battle effectiveness."

"It was a successful first battle," the captain said.

"There's always room for improvement, sir."

Captain Coleman smiled a knowing smile. "That, there is, Coda. That, there is. And every loss hurts."

"Yes, it does."

"It gets easier."

"To be honest, sir, I'm not sure I want it to."

"Oh?" Captain Coleman raised an eyebrow. "You like the guilt that comes with losing pilots?"

"No, sir. But I don't want to get to a place where their losses don't affect me, either." His thoughts went back to the original members of the Forgotten who'd died during training or above Toavis and the promise he'd made to ensure their memory was never lost.

"There's a balance, Coda. You have to accept the fact that those under your command will die. That sometimes you will have to *order* them to die. And you can't collapse under that responsibility. You can't let those actions define you or, worse, break you."

"I understand, sir. What is it you wanted to talk to me about?"

Captain Coleman made no effort to sit, and his face took on an expression Coda couldn't place. Whatever the captain had to say, it must have been difficult.

"I've decided where we're headed next." Captain Coleman's eyes went hard. "Kryos."

"Kryos? I've never heard of it."

"No," Captain Coleman said, his voice suddenly somber. "I suppose you haven't. Coda... Kryos is the Baranyk planet we were assaulting when your father... the battle of Kryos is where *it* happened."

The words slapped him, sending him spinning. He fell into his chair. "Why?" was all he managed to get out.

"I'm looking into something," Captain Coleman said. "Something that might be related. That might give us answers. Anything more than that, I can't say. But I wanted you to know."

"I... don't know what to say, sir."

"Just tell me you'll be ready."

Coda thought he saw concern in Captain Coleman's expression. Maybe guilt.

"And if you see or feel anything... abnormal," Captain Coleman added.

"Abnormal, sir?"

"Yes."

It was clear the captain wasn't going to elaborate further. "Of course, sir."

"I know I'm being vague. But you'll know what I'm talking about if it happens."

"I'm sure I will, sir," Coda said, having no idea what the hell the captain was talking about.

"Good." Captain Coleman nodded and seemed to stand up

straighter, as if a terrible burden had been removed from his shoulders. "Kryos is deep in Baranyk-occupied space, and Fleet Intelligence hasn't been able to get us an update. Even if they had, Koburn reminded us that that kind of intelligence isn't worth the paper you wipe your ass with."

"Understood, sir," Coda said. "We'll be ready."

"We aren't near any JumpGates, so Tactical is plotting a series of jumps now. We expect to begin in twelve hours. You've got that time to work out any remaining kinks." He nodded toward the display board.

"We're on it, sir."

"Thank you, Commander."

Coda saluted Captain Coleman again then watched as he walked out of the office. *What the hell was that all about?* He wasn't sure what the captain was hoping to find on Kryos—or what it had to do with his father. *What is he not telling me?*

His mind preoccupied, Coda barely noticed the captain stop dead in his tracks. Someone was approaching him.

Nails. And she didn't look happy.

*Apparently, I'm not the only one confronting demons today.*

# 26

*Corridor, SAS Redemption*
*Koburn-2, High Orbit*

Captain Chadwick Coleman had been a member of the Sol Fleet for nearly thirty years. He'd flown starfighters at speeds beyond human comprehension, fought in battles that had claimed the lives of tens of thousands of people, been hunted, pursued, and nearly blown to atoms. He'd stared into the cold, lifeless eyes of death itself, yet nothing he'd ever faced unnerved him as much as his daughter's chocolate-colored eyes.

Aniyah was both younger and older than he had expected. On some fundamental level, he had known she was twenty years old—or was she twenty-one now?—and she looked every bit the part. A full-grown woman, she was taller than her mother and broad-shouldered like him. Her skin was smooth, missing the stress wrinkles that scarred his own face. But those eyes—they blazed with a simmering hatred in a way that only a child's eyes could. And yet there was more. Pain. Loss. Distance.

*Oh, child. Life isn't fair, is it?*

"Uh," he said as the moment stretched into an uncomfortable length. "Hello, Lieutenant."

"Sir." She said the word without even a hint of emotion. A perfect military greeting, replying to decorum with decorum. A subordinate to her commanding officer, not a daughter greeting a missing father. And why should it be any other way? He hadn't been her father for years.

"Welcome aboard *Redemption*." He stuck with the role of her CO, the one he was more comfortable and familiar with. "Congratulations on your recent success in the cockpit. You've been the talk of your squadron leaders."

"Thank you, sir. I've been fortunate to train under the best fighters in the fleet. My success is a testament to their leadership."

*The best fighters in the fleet. Was that a slight?* The hint of a grin on her lips certainly indicated it was.

"Commander O'Neil is a good man and a better pilot," Coleman said, deciding to play dumb and not take the bait. "And one of my own students. You'd do well to listen to him. He can teach you much." *Okay, maybe not completely dumb.*

"Of course, sir."

He meant it as a dismissal, but she didn't seem to be taking it as such. Did she want to talk? Did he?

*Maybe*. But he didn't know the first thing to say, and she wasn't helping things. As first meetings went, things could have gone far worse, though.

"Carry on, Lieutenant."

"Yes, sir."

Coleman stepped past Aniyah, moving down the corridor. He felt her eyes on him all the way to the door. He glanced her way as it slid open. Sure enough, her eyes followed him, her face expressionless. When his eyes met hers, though, she turned away, returning to her original path.

"And, Lieutenant," he called out.

She turned back to him.

"It's good to have you aboard."

She didn't respond, didn't so much as nod. That was fine with him. Their first awkward encounter was behind them. The ice was broken. Their first steps had been taken. They would talk again, and when they did, it would be a *real* conversation. The one they had both been dreaming about for years. That scared him more than whatever waited for them on Kryos.

# 27

*Corridor, SAS Redemption*
*Koburn-2, High Orbit*

Coda left his office in a haze, only conscious enough to want to give the captain and his daughter a modicum of privacy. His mind was a jumbled mix of half-formed thoughts, his emotions a tangled web of anger, confusion, surprise, and hope. Captain Coleman was taking them back to Kryos. Back to the planet where his father had turned on his wingmen.

*I flew with your father. He was a good man.*

The words echoed in Coda's memory. Captain Coleman had said them the first time he and Coda met. Coda had known then that Coleman knew something he wasn't telling Coda. And now he was taking him back to the beginning.

Coda strolled through the corridors, unsure where he was going. He had to move. Couldn't sit still. To remain still was to confront uncomfortable feelings. Eventually, he found himself in the Simulation Room, which, despite his order, was empty.

For once, he didn't care. In this moment, he wasn't a commander. He was just another man looking for a distraction, and the amazing machines in front of him offered the best kind. He toggled through the various scenarios preprogrammed into the simulator then settled on the one that would require the least thought: a simple sole-survivor scenario that pitted him against wave after wave of enemy fighters. There were no objectives except to stay alive as long as possible.

Once inside the cockpit, Coda pulled on the VR helmet and waited for the simulation to begin. In the simulated Nighthawk cockpit, an empty abyss of stars stretched to infinity around him. There had been times when the moments in the empty vista and accompanying silence were his most cherished moments, but after the bombshell the captain had dropped on him, it was oppressive and restricting, giving him too much time to think.

His HUD beeped as the first wave of enemy contacts appeared. Half a dozen in all, they flew in a wall formation, three fighters wide, two tall. Coda initiated his thrusters, darting toward them. They saw him then shifted formation, moving from the wall into a line that stretched away from him, each of the fighters hidden behind the one at its head.

Coda locked on to the first target and launched his first missile. As soon as it was away, he opened his guns and fired four bursts. The first enemy fighter exploded, taken out by the missile, and then his bursts took the next one in line. Debris eliminated a third.

*That's why you don't play follow-the-leader.*

The remaining three fighters broke formation, veering off in three separate directions.

*And now the real game begins.*

Coda selected another fighter that had darted positive-Z. He moved after it, easily falling in on its six and achieving missile lock. Each wave of the simulation would replenish his weapons, so he didn't worry about wasting a missile on easy prey. He squeezed the trigger, launching his second missile.

*Four down, two to go. For the first wave at least.*

He took the next fighter out as easily as the previous one then moved on to the last. It came at him from his right flank. Coda dove negative-Z, narrowly avoiding an incoming barrage of fire, then swung his fighter around ninety degrees and punched the throttle. In a real battle, the maneuver would have been dangerous, and even the idea of it caused Coda's ribs to ache, but within the confines of the simulator, the pain was nothing more than a memory—and he used that to his advantage.

Coda closed in on the last fighter, countering its evasive maneuvers with his own, keeping it in his sights until his computer got missile lock. He fired another missile and watched it as it disappeared into the black. The yellow indicator on his HUD streaked toward the enemy fighter. There was a distant flash, and the fighter disappeared, destroyed.

Silence and stillness returned as the simulator began its next phase.

*You were there, weren't you, sir?*

In the silence, more memories invaded his consciousness. This time, he replayed the conversation he had with Commander Coleman after the Battle of Toavis. Like it had during so many of their previous conversations, the specter of Joseph O'Neil had hung large, and it was the closest Commander Coleman had ever come to opening up about what he'd seen.

*I was there.*

The captain hadn't said anything more. He'd given Coda a vague promise to tell him when the time was right. *That was six months ago, and things have changed. The time is right now. Tell me.*

But like the real Captain Coleman, the imagined version wasn't talking. He remained silent. And unlike the real thing, this one didn't have answers.

Coda's HUD beeped as the next wave of fighters appeared. There were twelve in all, and from Coda's experience, each would fly with more skill than any had during the initial wave.

He settled into the seat of his cockpit and fought wave after wave, falling into the rhythm of the battle. He lost track sometime after the seventh. By the time he was done, he was sticky with sweat and mentally spent. He had no idea how long he'd been in the simulator, but by the time he removed his VR helmet, his eyes burned with fatigue.

Getting out of the simulator was a difficult task. With the cockpit located in the center of a gyroscope, a ladder had to be moved into position to let the pilot into the cockpit and then moved out of the way once he was in. Coda had been able to get into the cockpit then shove the rolling ladder away. Getting out was an altogether different task.

Someone was rolling the ladder to him, though. Coda realized he wasn't alone.

"Not bad, sir," Nails said as she moved the ladder into position.

"Thank you," Coda slid out of the cockpit and took a series of uneasy steps down the ladder. Her presence annoyed him. He'd come here seeking solace, not to confront a pilot who had given him a hard time from the moment she'd joined the squadron. "Is there something I can help you with, Lieutenant?"

He regretted the words the moment they left his lips. So deep in his own issues, he had completely forgotten that she and the captain had run into each other outside his office. He could see the hurt in her eyes now. Her normally razor-sharp posture was compromised. Her shoulders slumped, chin downcast.

"No, sir." Nails nodded toward the simulator. "We had the same idea. You just beat me to it." Even her voice was somber.

"It can be a hell of a stress reliever," Coda said. "Do you want to take a run?"

Nails shook her head. "I'm good. Thanks. You flew well."

"Not in that last run. I was overconfident, and it did me in."

"I guess," Nails said. "Though in a real battle, you'd never be out there alone."

"As long as my wingman doesn't leave me behind." Coda meant it as a half-hearted jibe, but his delivery was off. "Sorry. That came out wrong."

"No," Nails said. "It's okay. You're right. I've been studying you. Watching old battle vids. Watched you today. When we go into battle next, I'll be ready."

"Yeah?"

"Yeah. I grew up playing sports, and the best watch game film to prepare for their opponent. Battles are like that to me. They're complex, and every one is different, but if you break it down to its individual parts, your targets become more predictable."

"Most people only have three or four moves," Coda said.

"And they usually only use one or two," Nails said. "It never becomes a problem, because the enemy is always different. We never face the same targets twice. They never have time to learn our individual tics. But I did."

Coda found himself smiling.

"I'm serious," Nails said, obviously taking the expression the wrong way.

"No," Coda said. "I get it. I was just realizing how similar we actually are."

"What do you mean?"

"I studied pilots too. Only then, we were all competing for a position in the squadron, and I did it to beat them."

"It worked."

"Yeah, it did," Coda said. "You've got me curious, though. We can't wait until the next battle. Grab a helmet, and let's see what you've learned."

"All right."

Coda toggled the next battle simulation as Nails found a VR helmet. When the simulation began, Nails proved to be a woman of her word. She *was* better. She wasn't perfect, of course—there was a difference between knowing what your wingman was going to do and reacting to it and flying together as one. But with time, Coda had zero doubt they would make a hell of a fighter pair.

With every passing moment, every blast of cannon fire, and every missile launch, he and Nails understood each other a little more. Not only on the superficial level but down to the core. He could almost feel her anger toward Captain Coleman. After years of abandonment, their first conversation had been a brief encounter filled with military decorum. Coda thought she could feel his continued desire to prove himself. He was always fighting with the specter of his father in front of him, shadowing his every deed—almost the same way Nails's father outshined her own achievements. Their backgrounds were different, but there was enough overlap to be hauntingly familiar.

Coda didn't know what to expect at Kryos, but he was learning what to expect on his wing. And for the first time since accepting the role of CAG, he was ready for what the next day would bring.

# 28

*Bridge, SAS Redemption*
*Deep Space*

CODA NODDED TO THE PASSING OFFICERS AS HE MADE HIS WAY TO THE bridge. Already dressed in his flight suit, he was ready for whatever awaited them on the other side of their next jump. Tensions were high, especially in this part of the ship. They had jumped more than two dozen times, drawing closer to Kryos with every leap. Now, all that stood between them and the alien planet was a final jump, which would happen within the hour.

Moscow's squadron was already loaded into the *Redemption*'s fighter bays, ready to be launched the moment the ship arrived at its destination.

*Kryos.*

There was more waiting for them on the alien planet than any of them were privy to. Its skies were a mystery, but the planet represented the very foundation Coda's adult life had been built atop. He might have been going to the planet for the first time, but in many ways, he felt like he was returning—and he didn't know what kind of welcome he would receive.

The bridge was alive with activity as Coda entered. Officers relayed orders to and from the executive deck, counting down the moments to the jump. Captain Coleman and Commander Garcia stood at its center, observing the three-dimensional display. Coda had never seen it in person but was impressed by the quality of the images. It might not have been as grand as the one at the academy, but it was damn close.

"Condition One has been set throughout the ship, Captain," Commander Garcia said. "Battery-loading operations complete, and the engineering and emergency crews are on standby."

"What about my fighters?" Captain Coleman asked.

Coda didn't think the captain had seen him enter, but he spoke up anyway. "Squadrons are locked and loaded, sir. Just waiting for your order."

For the first time since Coda had stepped onto the bridge, the captain tore his eyes off the display. He looked at Coda with a surprised expression. "Very good, Commander. But shouldn't you be with your pilots?"

"Loading and preflight operations are complete, sir. Moscow's squadron will launch first. The rest are on standby and already manning their ships. The flight crew will begin loading operations as soon as Moscow's are launched. There was nothing left to do but await further orders, and I thought I could do that here, sir."

Captain Coleman grunted his response, something Coda took as approval, or at least not disapproval.

"EmDrive charged and stable, sir," Lieutenant Poiu said. "Awaiting your order."

Coleman nodded. His hands tightened around the waist-high rail surrounding the imaging display. Coda steadied his breathing, taking long, slow breaths in and out of his nose in an effort to quell the adrenaline coursing through his veins.

The exercise brought with it an added level of clarity. His senses were heightened; the world seemed to slow. He could make out details he hadn't been able to make out before. The small sweat marks that Captain Coleman's hands left behind on the rail. The subtle creaking noise they made against its metal surface. The space between the cacophony of beeps, clicks, and hums emanating from the various electronics on the bridge. The hushed voices of the crew. Their heightened breathing. For a split second, Coda thought he could hear the hearts of the crew beating as one as they waited for Captain Coleman to give the order.

"Jump."

Barely more than a second later, the jump sensation interrupted what was left of the moment. Coda's perception of reality shifted, stretching out before him as if he were suddenly having an out-of-body experience. He *saw* himself more than he felt himself, and what he saw was elongated by the infiniteness of time and space.

Then it was over. The world snapped back, and Coda felt for a moment as if he were going to fall over. He didn't, blessedly, but others did, and he thought he saw more than one holding on to their terminals for support.

"Jump complete, sir," Lieutenant Poiu said.

The battle display was already updating, the first readouts becoming available. At first, it was a yellowish blob, pixelated and roughly spherical in shape. As the scans continued to come in, the image grew clearer, and Coda found himself looking at what looked like an arid planet, its yellow surface accented with browns and oranges, marking canyons, valleys, and deserts. Blue-green water dotted the landscape, looking like little more than puddles against the vast rocky surface. Kryos looked like an entire planet that personified the worst that Earth could throw at them. A hellish planet if Coda had ever seen one.

"Launch fighters," Commander Garcia said.

Lieutenant Poiu relayed the order, and half a second later, Coda felt the telltale signs of the ship's launch mechanisms reverberating through the deck. He'd never known they could be felt here, deep within the belly of the ship. There was something comforting about that, even if his stomach did twist into a knot at the thought of his pilots being hurled toward that terrible, desolate planet.

"Sir!" The urgency in Ensign Richey's voice cut through the din of the bridge like a line through water. "I'm picking up..."

"What is it, Ensign?" Captain Coleman moved so that his back was to the display and he was looking up directly at the young communications officer.

"I don't know, sir. The scans are still coming in, but—"

"The planet is under attack, sir," Lieutenant Poiu interrupted.

"Under attack?" Captain Coleman turned back to the display, which continued its update. "Where?"

"Isolating." The display shifted, moving toward the ice-capped northern hemisphere. Two black dots, little more than dark shadows against the warm colors of the planet's surface, became visible.

"What the hell is that?" Commander Garcia asked.

Captain Coleman didn't answer. He turned to Lieutenant Poiu. "Have the loading procedures begun for the standby squadrons?"

"Yes, sir."

"I want them launched as soon as possible. But keep them tight. Defensive positions only. Don't go after the targets until my order." Captain Coleman turned back to the screen as the black dots resolved into the telltale images of two Baranyk carriers.

"They're attacking their own installations," Commander Garcia said. "Why would they do that?"

Captain Coleman gave Coda a knowing look. "Because they don't want us to find whatever's there. Get to your ship, Commander. I want you in the next wave of fighters."

"Yes, sir." Coda turned to leave.

"And, Coda."

Coda stopped, turning back to the captain.

"Be quick about it. We can't let them succeed. We *have* to know what's on that planet."

# 29

*Cockpit, Nighthawk*
*Kryos*

CODA WAS THRUST INTO HIS GEL SEAT AS HIS FIGHTER RACED DOWN THE launch tube. For a brief moment, it felt as if the weight of the universe stood on his chest. It subsided the moment he shot into the black and his inertial dampeners kicked in, offsetting some of the Gs.

Calling up the battle map on his HUD, he immediately reassessed the situation. His squadrons formed a defensive perimeter around the *Redemption*. One of the Baranyk carriers maintained its assault on the planet's surface, but the other had broken away. They were still several minutes out, and this far away from the enemy vessels, there wasn't any danger. Still, Coda knew the Baranyk would be analyzing them every bit as much as they were analyzing the enemy.

Coda radioed Captain Coleman directly. "Captain, it's Coda. I'm out."

"Good," the captain said. "One of the Baranyk carriers is moving to intercept. They'll deploy fighters any minute. Prepare to engage."

"Yes, sir." Coda returned to the all-squadrons frequency. "All right, everyone. Bad Dogs, Yellow Jackets, and Dragonflies, on me. Scarecrows, stay close to home in case any of these buggers get through."

A series of affirmatives echoed through his speakers.

"Finger-four formations and prepare to break on my mark."

The three flights broke in half, moving into six smaller formations, their flight lead and seconds flying point. Coda moved to intercept, having his onboard computer calculate the incoming Baranyk carrier's distance and time to intercept.

*Six minutes.*

Except he knew the enemy would never get that close. And as soon as the thought solidified in his mind, the enemy's confirmation came.

"It's launching fighters," Moscow said as the swarm of Baranyk fighter crafts barreled toward them at much higher speeds than the larger carrier.

"Prepare to engage in… one minute," Coda said.

"Just a single carrier's worth?" Squawks asked.

It took a moment for Coda to realize what Squawks was talking about. The second carrier could have easily launched its fighters as well but hadn't. Something didn't make sense about that, but Coda forced it to the back of his mind. Squawks's bravado aside, the incoming enemy fighters posed a very real threat.

"They're trying to stall us," Coda said.

"Yeah, well, they better send in the cavalry, because my Bad Dogs are going to be on them like a geriatric who popped his first happy pill."

There were a series of groans across the comm.

Each of his flight leaders had named their flights. Squawks had originally chosen Horn Dogs, but Coda wouldn't let that fly, and they'd settled on Bad Dogs instead.

"Stay focused," Coda said, biting back a smile. If there was one thing he could always count on during their prebattle banter, it was Squawks doing his best to make everyone laugh, keeping everyone loose. "I don't want anything flashy—understood? Quick and efficient."

"He means boring and by the book," Squawks added.

*And sometimes he can take things too far.* Coda watched as the alien fighters neared. They were almost into firing range.

"Let's do this," Coda said. "Break!"

On Coda's command, the various finger-four formations broke in half, breaking into fighter pairs. Nails matched Coda's course effortlessly, veering from their original vector to come around at the incoming force at an angle.

*She's good. Learns fast.*

Aside from the time they'd spent in the simulator and their battle at Cerian-7, this was the only conflict they had flown together. Something had changed since that first flight, and it felt like they'd been on each other's wings for years. They cut through the first line of fighters with gratifying efficiency, leaving nothing but broken organic parts and viscera in their wake.

Once the two waves of fighters had passed each other, they brought their fighters around, and the real battle began. Coda let his targeting computer identify potential targets. Each was given a numerical representation: B1 through B15, representing the bogey and its original position within their formation.

He selected one that was close in proximity and matched a similar vector—or as his old friend Tex would have said, "Easy pickings." He sent the targeting information to Nails and altered course, moving into an attack vector.

The enemy never saw them coming. The moment the fighter winked from his HUD, another took its place, glowing more brightly to indicate that it was the computer's recommended target. There was no need to disagree, and so again, Coda and Nails knifed through space, hot on the enemy's tail.

The enemy fighter saw their approach and began evasive maneuvers, increasing speed and darting back and forth in an illogical pattern that made it difficult to lock on to. Coda was forced to counter every maneuver and was tossed around the inside of his cockpit like a pinball. For the thousandth time, he was thankful for the gel seat, five-point harness, and healthy dose of growth hormones that the fleet had been feeding him since he'd first begun his training.

Through it all, Coda's missile lock drew closer, the square bracket nearly encasing the enemy fighter on his HUD. But Nails got off the shot before he did.

Nails let out a whoop. "Splash Three!" she bellowed. "Come on, Coda, don't let me have all the fun."

"Sounds like you should be *her* wingman," Squawks added.

Coda ignored the banter, already focused on the next fighter, which had inadvertently flown into their current trajectory. Squawks and Nails weren't even done laughing by the time he had taken it out.

"Stay focused," Coda said in his best take-no-shit voice. "That could have just as easily been one of you."

Altering course to the edge of the battle, Coda zoomed out on his battle map, getting a God's-eye view of the entanglement. Of the first wave of Baranyk fighters, only about half remained, and with every moment, another seemed to blink out of existence. It was a rout, and the enemy saw it too.

In a single, unified maneuver, the remaining enemy crafts disengaged, retreating to their carrier. Under normal circumstances, Coda would have ordered a pursuit, harrowing their six until they entered a more vulnerable place in Baranyk space. But that had been before the squadron's numbers had been reinforced. Before they'd been tested. Before Captain Coleman had brought him to Kryos to face his personal demons.

"Moscow, Squawks, pursue the enemy fighters. Dragonflies, stay with me."

Squawks and Moscow voiced their affirmative, and a moment later, they were zipping toward the enemy fighters. It would be a race to see how many they could take out before the Baranyk fighters got back to their carrier, and that number would be determined by how good the enemy was at slipping missile lock.

"All right, Dragonflies—"

A terrible, high-pitched squeal sliced through Coda's eardrums. It felt as if someone stabbed directly in the soft tissue of his brain and twisted the knife. His mouth gaped, though no words or sounds came out. Eyes bulging, he couldn't breathe. Couldn't think. Couldn't move. It was complete and utter torment.

Then, as quickly as it started, it stopped. Coda gasped, sucking a lungful of air into his oxygen-depleted lungs. He couldn't tell how long the noise had lasted.

"Coda?" Nails sounded worried. "Coda, can you hear me?"

"What the hell was that?" Coda asked between gasps.

"What was what?"

"That noise," Coda said. "I've never heard anything like it."

"Noise?" Nails sounded genuinely perplexed. "I didn't hear anything."

*Didn't hear anything? My brain felt like it was going to explode!* Coda blinked, trying to refocus. "Never mind. Must have been feedback of some kind."

"Feedback?"

Coda ignored the question, flipping his comm to the all-squadrons channel—except he was already on it. Everybody had heard his conversation with Nails.

*Shit!*

"Coda," Captain Coleman said, and this time, it *was* a private frequency, "what's going on out there?"

"It's nothing, sir." Coda blinked, squeezing the flight stick between his legs, trying to refocus and return to the battle zone he'd been in before. The focus eluded him, slipping away like a talented enemy pilot. The subtle ringing in his head didn't help.

"It's nothing," Coda repeated, not sure if it was for him or the captain. "Plotting an intercept course now." He didn't wait for the captain to respond. "Dragonflies, hammer formation. Let's end this. Biscuit, lead us out."

"Yes, sir," Biscuit, Coda's second in the Dragonflies, said. "Dragonflies, on me."

Coda and Nails took up a position at the rear of the formation, and within moments, they were off, ready to be the hammer that crushed the first carrier.

*I just hope we're not too la—*

The shriek returned, twofold this time, blinding him with pain. His head shook, and his body spasmed as if he were having a seizure. Then he went rigid. The pain continued, but Coda's response to it died away. It was like he entered a state of shock. Even his mind felt alien.

Coda reached for his helmet, except... his hand didn't move. Panicking, he tried again. Nothing happened. Same with the other hand. His entire body was unresponsive. He wasn't paralyzed—he could still *feel* his hands and feet. He just couldn't move them. Couldn't move *anything.*

*What the hell is happening?*

He tried speaking, but his mouth wouldn't work. Tried blinking commands to his HUD, but his eyes wouldn't respond. He was trapped in his own mind. A prisoner in his own body.

And then his body moved on its own. He felt his hands tighten around the joystick, thumb switching to missiles. He watched helplessly as he overrode his targeting system to target the pilots of Dragonfly Flight. He screamed in his head as his index finger pressed the firing mechanism. His fighter rocked as the missile launched toward his friends and fellow wingmen.

To everyone watching, it would appear as if Callan "Coda" O'Neil had betrayed his wingmen, just as his father had done above the same skies of Kryos.

# 30

*Cockpit, Nighthawk*
*Kryos*

Chaos. For an undefined amount of time, Coda's reality devolved to madness. Prisoner in his own body, he could do nothing but watch, listen, and dread what happened next. It started with the radio, a dozen voices speaking at once.

"What the—"

"Contact!"

"Coda!"

"—hell was that?!"

"Grizzly, do you copy?"

Pause.

"Coda, do you copy?"

The voices were coming in so quickly that he had trouble deciphering who was speaking. Half a dozen more spoke over each other, making their words incomprehensible.

"Coda, what are your orders?"

There was another break in the communication, and it was then that his body, as if it were a drone being controlled from some distant location, made its next move.

He launched his second volley of missiles. This time, though, his pilots saw them appear on their HUDs and took immediate action.

"Evasive maneuvers!"

The formation broke apart; even the fighter pairs shattered. It was every pilot for themselves, and four of them had missiles on their tails. As tight as the formation had been, they had no time to escape. They erupted into four separate flashes of light—four more deaths caused by Coda's hand.

It was a nightmare. Worse than a nightmare. It was as if his every fear had been realized, and he was powerless to stop it. He had no control over his actions. No control over his body. He couldn't help. He couldn't even voice a warning.

"Coda!" Squawks said, terror and betrayal in his voice. "What the hell is going on?"

Another barrage of missiles streaked away. The only saving grace was that with this volley, he was out of missiles. His ability to dole out death was severely hampered. Then his thumb switched the firing mechanism from missiles to cannons. Whoever—whatever—was behind this wasn't done yet.

"Coda!"

His fighter thrummed as his cannons opened up with short bursts that he felt more than he heard. His fighter turned hard, throwing him against the side of his cockpit. His G-suit tightened around his extremities and midsection, preventing his blood from ending up in his feet and staving off blackout.

Another flash of light. Another death. Coda's hand was bringing his ship around, seeking its next target. He tried to talk, to warn them, to shout to get the hell away, but like the rest of his body, his mouth didn't work. All he had were his thoughts.

"Goddamn it—"

The line went dead in mid-sentence.

*They've shifted frequencies. I am now an enemy target.* Coda could see it in the way the squadrons were regrouping, fighter pairs reassembling, the way he was being flanked in five different directions at once. *This is how I die. As an enemy to my own people. Shot down by my own pilots. By my friends.*

Whatever was controlling him had no intention of going down without a fight. His hand shoved the throttle forward, increasing thrust, then altered course so that he was on a direct heading toward an incoming fighter pair. His missiles expended, he launched a burst from his cannons across their incoming trajectory.

Cannon fire took one of the Nighthawks across the tail of the ship, ripping off its rear starboard wing. The fighter veered, emitting puffs of gas from its navigational thrusters as its pilot worked to regain control. And then it was past, safe from further fire.

Coda turned toward another pair of fighters. These had already opened fire on him, missiles streaking in his direction. He tracked them on his HUD. His stomach lurched as the fighter dove negative-Z then performed a tight, high-G maneuver, spinning toward the reassembling Bad Dog Flight.

*Please no. Not Squawks. Don't make me kill Squawks.*

His finger tightened around the firing stud. One burst. Then two. Three. He sprayed cannon fire across multiple trajectories. It was like throwing nails into the middle of the highway. Sooner or later, one of the fighters would get hit. The bursts also provided cover fire as his Nighthawk blasted into the incoming formations.

Fighter pairs from Bad Dog Flight veered from the incoming fire, giving Coda a clear path through. The moment he was past the first fighter, he yanked hard on the stick, bringing his fighter around perpendicular to the other fighters, jumping straight into their flight path. It was a highly dangerous maneuver that would likely result in a mid-space collision.

Coda tried to scream. Still, nothing came out. He couldn't even close his eyes. To his great surprise, his fighter somehow avoided a collision. The two missiles hot on his tail didn't have the same luck, however, striking two helpless Nighthawks.

The blasts shook his fighter, throwing him off course and sending him spinning. Coda's hands fumbled with the controls, struggling to reorient his ship. It took longer than expected, and by the time his fighter was back under control, the remaining squadrons had fully regrouped.

Four more missiles were heading his way, and eight other fighters nearly had a firing angle.

Looking at what amounted to his imminent death, Coda couldn't help but feel a moment of pride. A hawk had attacked the chicken coop, bombarding the pilots when they were most vulnerable. And yet they'd fought well, wasting little time before doing what needed to be done: marking him as an enemy and neutralizing the threat he posed. He didn't know how many pilots had lost their lives due to his actions, but that number had been smaller than it could have been.

And yet, whoever was behind his movements still wasn't finished. His hand reached for the throttle, throwing it forward to max thrust. More missiles closed in. A Nighthawk's maximum thrust wasn't enough to outrun the Terran weapons.

He emptied his chaff. A pair of explosions erupted behind him, but it wasn't enough. Two more were hot on his tail. He had three seconds, maybe four, before they caught up to his fighter.

His hand remained steady on the stick, not veering course. Despite his attempt to run, whoever was behind his actions wasn't interested in fighting anymore. They were content to let him die.

*Finally.* He wouldn't have to watch his friends and comrades die by his hand anymore. That, at least, was a blessing.

Something zipped by his fighter. Then another. And another. They were flying in the opposite direction.

*Baranyk fighters.*

The second Baranyk carrier, done bombarding the planet, had entered the fight. There were a series of blasts behind him as Baranyk fighters threw themselves at the incoming missiles, sacrificing themselves to save Coda. He couldn't believe it. Refused to believe it. The Baranyk were killing themselves to save him.

*What the hell is going on?*

Despite their best efforts, they were unable to destroy every missile. One slipped through the cracks of the incoming enemy, taking Coda's fighter directly in the bow. There was a flash, searing pain, then darkness.

Coda's last thought was of his father and how he would never know what had happened to him above the same alien world. How he would never know what had happened to himself.

# 31

*Unknown*
*Kryos*

CONSCIOUSNESS CAME IN FRAGMENTS, SMALL GLIMPSES OF LIFE, AS IF HE was looking at the universe through a tiny hole. Coda was floating, spinning slowly toward a yellow planet.

*Kryos*, he remembered distantly. *No. That's somewhere else. This is...* He didn't have a name for it, just a feeling. A series of images that in themselves made no sense.

*No. It is Kryos.* Or at least that's what he had called it. Did it have two names? Two meanings? And why did it feel familiar?

Darkness was followed by a bright light. It appeared and disappeared. Pressure. He stopped spinning and was pulled toward the light. Pain.

Coda kicked, punched, flailed, bit, elbowed, kneed, lunged, and headbutted. He was savage, like a cornered animal with no other recourse. Out for blood to... to... what? Why was he fighting?

He didn't stop. If anything, he fought with even more urgency. He swung wildly, his gloved hand connecting with something solid. A distant part of him thought that was odd, but he didn't have time to think on it. The next moment, something hard slammed into the back of his head, and again, all he saw was blackness.

More lights. Flashing this time. No, not flashing—streaking. He was moving, being pushed down a long corridor. Heavy steps echoed around him as if he were being marched toward an inevitable doom. He tried to sit, roll, slide off the gurney, make a run for it, save himself, but his body didn't respond. Again, he realized he was wrong. His body wasn't the issue. It was the restraints.

Panic coursed through his veins, his heart rate spiking. He had to get out. Had to get to freedom. Safety. The blackness returned.

When the images returned, they came faster but were less vivid. With them came additional coherence. He was dreaming but was somehow more aware. It was an unnerving sensation. Kryos's yellow hue called to him like a siren from deep space. She was inviting and comforting, familiar in all the right ways. But there was something else beneath the surface, something that a part of him rebelled against.

The feeling made him nauseous, but it also scared him more than the armored guards, restraints, or anything else. He didn't trust it, knew its calling was false. The feeling became more insistent, as if it were forcing its will on him. What did it want?

The feeling was demanding. It refused to accept disobedience, and that was when Coda became aware of its true nature. It was madness, violence, and slavery. An overlord with incredible power. And yet he didn't withdraw. Among the madness, violence, and suppression was something else. It wasn't coming from the overlord, not directly, but it was *part* of it. And it felt familiar.

Coda moved toward it, knowing on a fundamental level that it was only his consciousness that moved. Somewhere else, his body was strapped to a gurney, his imprisoners doing God knew what to him. The Coda that remained didn't care. He was here, a part of a network of sorts, and despite the overwhelming will of the overlord, he went deeper, toward the only beacon of light visible to him.

The closer he drew, the stronger the will of the overlord grew. It was scared, Coda realized. Scared of what he would find. That fear strengthened Coda's resolve, and he pushed harder. Moving faster, he streaked through the network of consciousness as if he were a speeder through water. Bubbles of other consciousness drifted by, and despite any interactions, Coda knew that those bubbles were like him. They were other people. Other beings. All with their own will and sense of self. All part of the same network.

The light grew brighter. He was almost there. If he hadn't had the overlord's full attention before, he did now. Almost immediately, Coda's progress was halted. The light was just beyond his reach. He imagined himself extending a hand toward it, reaching, grasping, and pleading with everything he had. That light felt familiar. Warm. Of home and family.

But he was pushed back. Pulled away. The light grew more distant, and with it, the sense of warmth and home diminished.

*No!* Coda couldn't speak in the network, but his defiance radiated through it. And the light seemed to notice. Coda couldn't move toward it, but *it* moved toward him. As fast as the overlord pushed him away, the light flew toward Coda.

Coda reached for it again, and this time, he was met with the image of it reaching for him too. An arm, familiar hands, though older. More calloused and wrinkled. He'd seen them before. Held them. Been comforted by them. Pushed them away.

*No more.*

Coda dug in his heels, fighting back, resisting the overlord with every fiber of his being. Distantly, he felt his body tense and heard his own screams. He was giving everything he had to this fight—mind, body, and spirit. Nothing would stand in his way. He'd waited too long for this.

He didn't know how, but he felt his momentum change. He was still being pulled away from the light, but it was somehow slower. The light grew brighter, closing the gap between them. His resistance was working, and his success fueled his determination. He'd thought he'd given everything to the fight before, but he'd been wrong.

*Now.* He committed himself fully. *Now.* He fought with the determination of a being who knew his own survival and that of everything they'd ever loved and cherished was at stake.

The overlord met his enhanced determination with its own. He thought he heard it growl, and in his mind's eye, he saw terrible fangs. Thick saliva dripped from their jagged tips, coating its exoskeleton, giving its dark coloring a slick look. For the first time since the battle of wills had begun, Coda saw his enemy. It was terrible, huge, and... only a Baranyk.

*No... this one's different.*

It was bigger, not just in height but in girth. Its legs were wider, more powerful, and its coloring was off. Instead of the matte-black exoskeleton, this one had charcoal-colored stripes cutting across its armor. And its eyes burned with sharp intelligence.

Coda had never seen a live Baranyk up close. He had either shot them down from a safe distance or seen them dead on a gurney, but he knew they didn't look like this. The monstrosity in front of him was different. More dangerous. A leader of the soldiers he'd destroyed. And even that word—*soldiers*—felt off.

Behind the terrible beast, the light grew brighter. The overlord's triangular head turned toward it then back to Coda. It roared at him, and Coda could almost feel its warm, humid breath on his face and smell its stench of death and decay. The Baranyk leader lunged toward Coda a final time, snapping its jaws at him, but in an instant, the overlord disappeared, and Coda was one with the light.

Images flashed before him, faster than before. He saw himself in the third person, reliving moments from his childhood. He was a kid on Earth then an adult in space. He was swinging then flying. Hugging then pushing. Throwing. Jumping. Running. Always running. The images kept coming, more furious now, so fast that they were more feelings than images. Love. Loss. Despair. Rebellion.

It was more than Coda could take. He tried to pull away. But he was in the light's grasp now, and as insistent as it had been before, it was even more so now. It wasn't going to let him go without a fight, probably not even then.

More feelings. Regret. Sorrow. Longing.

And through it all was a voice, different yet familiar, distant but close. It was both the greatest sound in the world and one that brought him to his knees.

*Callan?*

# 32

*Sick Bay, SAS Redemption*
*Deep Space*

Coda had no idea how long he was out. Waking was a slow process, and as he made his way through the corridors of his consciousness, he was beset with a tangle of memories, thoughts, and emotions. They mixed together like the ingredients of a soup, becoming something greater than their individual parts, all boiling and threatening to blow the lid off the whole pot.

It was the voices that had brought him back and shown him the way. Not the same voice as before but equally familiar.

"I still want you to proceed with—"

"Extreme caution. I know, Doctor."

The voices belonged to Dr. Naidoo and Captain Coleman.

"You've made that abundantly clear," Captain Coleman continued. "Am I clear to see my pilot now?"

Coda opened his eyes slowly. He was in the medical bay, flat on his back, and it appeared they had cordoned off the back area, leaving him alone and away from view.

"One last thing, sir," Dr. Naidoo said. The voices came from the other side of the partition that blocked off Coda's section of the room. "Until we know the signal's limits, or if there are any traces of it left embedded in his consciousness, he remains a risk. He should remain bound and under guard at all times."

"Understood, Doctor."

"And by no means is he to be allowed back into the cockpit."

It wasn't until the last bit that he realized they were talking about him. He tried to sit up, but his body refused to cooperate. Panic flared through his veins. *Not again.*

But no, it had *tried* to move. Something held him in place. Bound him.

Captain Coleman appeared from around the curtain, his step faltering when he saw that Coda was awake.

"Sir," Coda said, tilting his eyes so that they met the captain's.

"Coda," Captain Coleman said then called for Dr. Naidoo.

She appeared a moment later and stopped beside the captain, keeping her distance. "How are you feeling, Commander?"

"I can't move."

Captain Coleman's eyes traced Coda from his head to his toes and back again, a sad expression on his face. "We had to bind you, Coda. For our protection."

The comment actually relieved him. His body was his own again. He was just restrained. They also confirmed his nightmare—and the horrible things he had done. He took a sharp breath and looked away, trying to hide, but there was no escape. Tears welled in his eyes and fell unrestrained to the gurney's sheets.

"Coda." Captain Coleman stepped closer, moving from the foot of the gurney toward its head. "I need you to tell me what happened."

"I don't know..."

"Coda." The captain's voice took on a softer tone, consoling and compassionate, that of a loved one talking to someone they cared about. "I can't fix it if I don't know what's wrong."

Coda looked back to the captain and saw the sympathy in his eyes. "I wish I knew. We were..." Coda grimaced, trying to replay the sequence of events. "We were preparing for our attack run and then... there was a terrible noise. It hurt. Bad. It felt like it was splitting my head open. Nobody else heard it, though."

"Nobody else heard it?"

"I thought it was feedback."

Captain Coleman shared a look with Dr. Naidoo. "What happened after that?"

"It happened twice. It was worse the second time. And then..."

"Then what, Coda?"

"I lost control."

"Lost control, *how?* What do you mean?"

"My hands... they moved, but I wasn't the one moving them. I couldn't control them. Couldn't stop them. It's like I was a..." He struggled to come up with an apt comparison. "A puppet. Like one of our drones. I knew what I was doing, but I was powerless to stop it. I was a prisoner in my own mind."

Captain Coleman's face went hard. Coda recognized it as the mask of authority; he had even tried to emulate it a time or two. But in the moment, it was terrifying.

"Sir," Coda said, growing frantic. "You have to believe me. I can't explain it, but that wasn't me out there. I wouldn't do that. I would never... you know that!"

Something in the captain collapsed. His mask broke, his eyes falling to the deck, refusing or unable to meet Coda's.

"You know me..." Coda's voice fell, losing all of its frantic intensity. "I know how it sounds. I wouldn't believe myself either." His vision went blurry, and it was his time to look away.

"I believe you." The words were soft, quiet, a secret held for years finally spoken.

"You do?"

Captain Coleman nodded. "Dr. Naidoo, undo this man's restraints."

"Sir," Dr. Naidoo said, "I don't think that's a good idea."

"We're four jumps from Kryos, well out of range from the enemy. And as you can see, he's no longer under any form of Baranyk control."

"We have no evidence to support that."

"Doctor." Captain Coleman was more forceful this time, fixing Dr. Naidoo with his best glare. "I trust this man. Undo his restraints."

Dr. Naidoo let out a curse but did as instructed. She started with his legs, then moved up to his wrists and arms before undoing separate straps on his chest and forehead. It was no wonder he hadn't been able to move.

Coda sat up gingerly.

"Easy, Coda," Captain Coleman said. He watched Coda, but with a focus that suggested he was more worried about him hurting himself than anyone else around him. Dr. Naidoo, on the other hand, watched Coda with an intense glare as if he were a loosed predator. When it became apparent Coda wasn't going to attack either one of them, she exhaled, though she didn't fully relax.

"What happens now?" Coda asked.

"Now," Captain Coleman said, "we have an honest conversation about what we think happened out there. Make no mistake, though, Coda. What I'm about to tell you is both highly classified and includes a significant degree of speculation. This is a working theory at best, understood?"

"Understood, sir."

"What happened to you..." Captain Coleman paused. "What *appears* to have happened to you has happened before. Do you remember Koburn?"

"Of course, sir," Coda said. "You found people in those caves. The Baranyk had rounded them up and slaughtered them."

"Yes," Captain Coleman said. "And no. It appeared they had taken prisoners with the purpose of experimenting on them. We found dozens of them, Coda, each with their skullcaps removed. The enemy was experimenting on their brains. More specifically, the area of the brain that enables communication. And we found a survivor. She was in a terrible state, and Dr. Rydell was able to get her stabilized, but she was... *off*. Then when the Baranyk returned, and... well, come with me."

Captain Coleman nodded to the side and stepped out of the partitioned area of the medical bay, walking to a display mounted against the bulkhead. Dr. Naidoo and Coda followed. Captain Coleman punched in a series of commands, bringing up a pair of images. One appeared to have been taken from the exterior of the *Redemption*; the other showed a frail woman strapped to a gurney. She looked to be in the same partitioned area of the medical bay that Coda had been in.

"I remember this," Coda said. "The Baranyk carrier jumped in, plotted an intercept course, then jumped away."

"Exactly." Captain Coleman played the video. The Baranyk ship grew larger, but Coda wasn't watching the enemy. He was watching the survivor.

She fought against her binds, letting them dig into her skin, then pulled. Her hand came free and her skin with it. Blood soaked the gurney. Her hand was a mangled mess, but she didn't appear to be in any pain. She broke a small metal support off the gurney, then to Coda's horror, she viciously stabbed herself in the neck with it. Falling back to the gurney, her body spasmed as blood pooled on the floor.

The medical staff rushed in and tried to provide aid, but it was too late. The woman went still. At that same moment, the Baranyk ship disappeared. An uncomfortable knot formed in Coda's stomach. The way that woman had moved was inhuman. Still, it wasn't outside the realm of possibility for a survivor of unspeakable violence to end their life. Stress and trauma could do terrible things to the human mind.

Captain Coleman brought up two more images and began the vid. One appeared to be a brain scan. The other was some kind of waveform. The same moment the waveform spiked, the color on the brain scan changed. It was also the same moment the woman began to fight her binds to break free. The signal continued until the woman lay dead on the gurney. Moments after the signal stopped, the Baranyk ship jumped away.

"Okay..." Coda ran a hand through his closely cropped hair, thinking. "The ship jumped in, hit us with some sort of signal, her brain activity goes crazy, the survivor kills herself, and then it jumps away? You're saying that ship brought her under Baranyk control?"

"Watch it again." Captain Coleman began the vid again. This time, he stopped it the moment the signal spiked then backtracked to the millisecond before it began. When he advanced it one hundredth of a second forward, the signal spiked, and the brain registered abnormal activity. "I've watched this image a thousand times. The time signatures match exactly. There's no doubt that whatever signal the Baranyk hit us with was intended for that woman. And it caused her to take her own life."

The parallel was uncanny. The horrible image on the screen darkened his mood, but Coda couldn't help feeling vindicated in some way. He *hadn't* been in control. He'd known it, but here was his proof.

"We've also gone through your scans, Coda," Captain Coleman said. "Your flight helmet gives us a steady stream of data. We were hit with the same signal at Kryos. We'll have to run an analysis, but my guess is it was right before you started complaining about feedback. Then again when you..."

Coda met his gaze. Captain Coleman's face was as soft as he'd ever seen it. "We don't know how it's possible, but if we're correct, Coda, we have proof you were under control of the enemy."

Coda wanted to shout, to scream, to laugh, to cry. It wasn't his fault. He hadn't turned on his wingmen, hadn't had some sort of mental break like his father had. He wasn't a traitor. But even as he thought it, he knew that regardless of who or what was responsible, his pilots were still dead.

"You said it yourself," Captain Coleman continued. "It was like you were a puppet. A drone. You *were*, Coda. Once they hit you with that signal, you weren't in control."

"I... I don't know what to say, sir," Coda said, attempting to put his feelings into words. "It's a relief in a way, but... why me? And how? If they could do this to two of us, why not to everyone else?"

"We're working on that," Captain Coleman said. "And we have some ideas. Fortunately, we have additional evidence."

The captain let the words hang in the air, obviously thinking they would have some sort of profound impact. Coda was missing something. He scanned the images of the woman, the signal, the Baranyk carrier, and the brain scan. What other evidence could they have? The only thing that wasn't on the screen were the images of his own brain. Captain Coleman had said they'd retrieved those from his flight helmet.

*What am I missing? Something about the flight helmet...*

The answer hit Coda like six Gs, ripping the air from his lungs. The flight helmet design hadn't changed since the early days of the Baranyk war, when Captain Coleman and the rest of the Sol Fleet had relied on human flight—when his father had flown.

"My father..." Coda whispered.

"Yes," Captain Coleman said. "What if he, just like that woman, just like you, was under control of the enemy?"

It was too much. Coda couldn't think. He staggered, found a medical bed, and sat down. He held his head in his hands, his eyes staring blankly at the dull gray of the deck.

"You knew..." Coda said softly.

"No, Coda," Captain Coleman said. "I never even suspected. But this tells a different story. When we take this information back to Fleet Command, your father will be vindicated."

"You were there," Coda said. He'd known the captain had flown with his father when he'd turned on his squadron. Coda had even pressed the captain to tell him what had happened, but the captain had refused. He'd said the conversation was for another time. That time had come. He looked up, feeling his face grow hard as he met the captain's eye. "I need to know what happened, sir."

Captain Coleman's lips parted, but whatever he had been about to say died on them.

"It's time, sir."

Captain Coleman looked to Dr. Naidoo, either for support or for another opinion, but the doctor remained expressionless. This wasn't her decision to make. Finally, the captain nodded. "Fine, but not here."

He led Coda to his private quarters, told him to sit, then toggled something on his tablet. "The truth about your father is classified high enough that I would be court-martialed and thrown in a military prison just for telling you. So it goes without saying that this conversation doesn't leave this room."

"I understand," Coda said. "You can trust me, sir."

"The official story about your father was that he went AWOL, disobeying a direct order that resulted in the death of his wingmen and many more aboard the *Benjamin Franklin*. That's what's been leaked to personnel to quell questions, a story to tell over drinks at the base bar. The truth, however, is much different."

Coda leaned forward in his chair, resting his elbows on his knees. He had to force himself to breathe.

"I could tell you what happened," Captain Coleman said, "give you my firsthand account, because, as you have already guessed, I was there. But it would be easier if I showed you."

Captain Coleman held the tablet out to Coda. The image on it was dark and looked to be a first-person view taken from the pilot's helmet cam, the only lights being those from the cockpit's buttons and switches.

Coda grabbed the tablet and held it reverently before him. His hands were shaking. An odd mix of conflicting emotions roiled inside him.

He'd been looking forward to this moment for years. The story of what had happened to his father had always felt incomplete. It wasn't until recently that Coda had gotten over his feelings of anger and abandonment to realize that the man he knew and the man his father had been made out to be didn't match. His anger had twisted then, some being directed at himself for harboring undeserved resentment, while the rest was directed at those driving the false narrative.

It had become apparent to him that his father had been turned into a scapegoat. A distraction from something much worse. But what happened if the man Coda had come to remember wasn't accurate either? What if he *was* the villain? What would that do to him?

"Hit Play, Coda," Captain Coleman said.

Looking up from the tablet, Coda found Captain Coleman as he'd never seen him. His face was soft, his eyes understanding. The only two men who still cared about Joseph O'Neil were his son and his former friend, and both were in this room.

"Hit Play."

Coda thumbed the triangular shape on the center of the tablet, and the vid began to play.

# 33

*Captain Coleman's Quarters, SAS Redemption*
*Deep Space*

THE WORLD DISAPPEARED AROUND CODA. THE MOMENT THE VIDEO BEGAN to play, he was transported directly into the cockpit with the pilot—a pilot he quickly realized was Captain Coleman himself.

*Lieutenant Coleman*, Coda reminded himself. *This is the captain before a series of promotions, when he was just a fighter jock like me.*

The visuals were hauntingly familiar. The cockpit of the X-23 Nighthawk was identical to his own, the radio chatter was familiar, and most of all, the arid landscape of Kryos was the same.

"All right, everyone," Lieutenant Coleman said, "form up. Arrow formations. Delta Flight, offset forty-five degrees at five thousand meters."

"Roger that," a familiar voice said. "Delta Flight, you heard the man. On my wing."

The point of view shifted as Lieutenant Coleman's eyes flicked toward the battle map on his HUD, following the green indicators that moved into formation behind his own flight. There were twenty-four fighters in all, a full squadron, with Lieutenant Coleman the squadron leader in command of Alpha Flight. The other flight leader was Coda's father. Behind them was a larger ship, a legacy-class carrier much like the *Jamestown*. The only other objects on the HUD were a blue line that arced from one edge of the HUD to the other, symbolizing the curvature of the planet, and a series of medium-sized red dots.

Coda watched the red dots intently, but unlike the human fighters, the red dots didn't move. What were they? An enemy fleet in waiting? Orbital platforms? The latter seemed unlikely—Coda had never heard of the Baranyk leveraging anything of the sort, but the war had taken on many different iterations, so it wasn't outside the realm of possibility.

"Remember, Warriors," Lieutenant Coleman said, addressing his squadron, "this is a hit-and-run only. We're poking them with a stick to see how many little bees come out of the hive. Contact in three minutes."

The fighters raced toward the red indicators. Their pilots spent the time bantering. It was the same prebattle bravado Coda had grown accustomed to. He'd known on a fundamental level that all fighter jocks were cut from a similar cloth. In every flight, squadron, and wing, there was a Squawks who talked faster than he flew, a Noodle who often became the butt of their jokes, a Moscow who flew for honor, a Nails who was out to prove herself, and a leader who kept them all together.

To Coda's surprise, his father was none of these. He was quiet, staying out of the banter, not even laughing. Was that normal or a precursor to what was to come? He'd somehow almost forgotten that he was watching a video of death and betrayal. That many of these pilots were flying to their doom.

"Contact in sixty seconds," Lieutenant Coleman said. "Commence radio silence. Good luck, Warriors."

As the fighters drew closer, the objects that the red dots represented began to come into view. They were diamond shaped and enormous, almost as big as a ship, and there was activity around them.

*It's a Baranyk mining operation.*

Kryos was originally an unoccupied planet, something humanity and the Baranyk had fought over due to the wealth of its mineral deposits. To those who succeeded in capturing it, the planet was a great forward base, limiting the dangers of long supply lines and bringing those much-needed supplies to the front.

Without further orders, the human fighters closed in on the larger vessels, appearing like specters in the night, opening fire. Missiles rained down on the vessels, explosions riddling their surfaces like ripples in water. In moments, the vessels were destroyed, cracking open like giant eggs, spewing slime and organic material into space.

The human fleet split, moving with a grace that Coda had never thought possible. Alpha Flight, helmed by Lieutenant Coleman, altered their vector, moving toward another of the orbiting supply ships. Bravo Flight, led by Joseph O'Neil, moved toward the other. The action took them on diverging paths, blasting away from each other at incredible speeds.

Although tens of thousands of kilometers apart, the orbiting supply ships were close to each other by space standards. Lieutenant Coleman left his battle map alone as the green indicators of Bravo Flight disappeared from its edges. He focused on the next vessel, changing the flight's formation so that they would attack the installation in two waves. There still wasn't any resistance, and Alpha Flight easily took out the installation. By then, the enemy was inbound.

"Contact!" a voice bellowed. "Enemy fighters inbound. Two hundred thousand kilometers and closing, nine-o'clock, positive-Z twenty-six degrees."

"I see them." Lieutenant Coleman's eyes were on the battle map. A full squadron of Baranyk fighters was closing the distance between them. "It's only the vanguard. No capital ship, though it's no doubt en route. Break off your attack and prepare to engage."

"Roger that," the first voice said and was followed by other affirmatives.

"Here we go," an eager voice said. The giddiness reminded him of Squawks, though the slight Southern twang kicked up memories of Tex.

*I miss you, you big silly bastard.*

"Fighter pairs!" Lieutenant Coleman bellowed. "Break!"

The twelve fighters within the flight broke as one, splitting into six battle pairs with an efficiency that continued to impress Coda.

*This is what Captain Coleman needs us to be.* Coda made a mental note to request access to more battle footage from the early days of the war. His fighters were a blade, but he hadn't realized how sharp they could be until watching a true squadron in action.

*Together, we'll sharpen them. Me and my wingmen... if I get the chance.*

Lieutenant Coleman and his wingman, Tank, sliced through the incoming Baranyk formation, getting missile lock on one enemy vessel before changing course and going after another. A quick glance at the HUD by Lieutenant Coleman told Coda that he was tracking the missile via the battle map, though he was obviously confident it would find its target.

*If it doesn't run out of maneuvering fuel first.*

The Nighthawks themselves hadn't had any sort of upgrades since they'd been decommissioned, meaning the fighter Lieutenant Coleman had flown was the exact same fighter Coda's squadron flew. But the armament, primarily its missiles and the new torpedoes used by the newly formed bombing squadrons, *had* been upgraded. More fuel provided longer range and more navigability, while enhanced AI helped use it more effectively.

Lieutenant Coleman was right not to worry about this one. The Baranyk fighter either didn't realize that the missile had lock, or it didn't care. The craft altered course to make a pass at a human fighter pair. Before the fighter could engage, Lieutenant Coleman's missile struck, blasting it to atoms.

With his missiles running low, Lieutenant Coleman flew aggressively, moving into short range and opening his cannons. Coda imagined his trigger finger riding the edge of the firing stud, the slightest of movements the difference between firing and not, between a double burst and a triple.

Within moments, Lieutenant Coleman and Tank had eliminated another enemy fighter. Coleman had baited it by spraying ahead of its vector, forcing it to alter course. Tank was waiting for it and opened fire a split second after Coleman, anticipating the enemy's new flight path. He guessed correctly, peppering the enemy craft with his cannons. Organic material leaked into space as the fighter flipped end over end.

It was a fantastically performed maneuver, which Coda had done with his wingmen before. The biggest difference was that Lieutenant Coleman and his wingman had done it without a word, working as two arms of the same body, each knowing exactly where the other one was and what it was doing. The maneuver wasn't just more efficient; it was many magnitudes more deadly.

Lieutenant Coleman eyed his HUD, using the small break to assess the battle. His other pilots were just as deadly. Already, the enemy squadron was down more than half its number, with the remaining fighters broken and alone. The human fleet pounced on them like a lion, claws and teeth ready to sink into flesh in the glory of the kill.

Lieutenant Coleman's radio lit up with screaming, shouts, and curses. The sudden shift in tenor jarred Coda almost as much as it had Lieutenant Coleman. His eyes lingered on the battle map, and for a second, Coda didn't know why. Then it dawned on him.

*He's trying to understand. To see what he's missing.*

The human forces had already shot down another pair of Baranyk fighters. The screaming wasn't coming from Lieutenant Coleman's flight, which meant...

Coda took a shaky breath. He looked up from the tablet for the first time since hitting Play. Captain Coleman was seated across from him, his eyes on the floor.

*As painful as this is for me, it's twice as much for him. He didn't just lose a friend that day; he lost several. All under his command.*

"Merlin! Merlin, come in!"

"Where the *fuck* did that come from?"

"Another missile! Break! Break! Brea—"

Lieutenant Coleman disengaged, his wingmen only a split second behind. "Bravo Flight, this is Alpha. What the hell is going on over there?"

He waited for two breaths. The only reply he got was more confused radio chatter.

"I can't shake it!"

"Eject! Eject! Eject!"

"Ghost, get out of there!"

"Razor, what the fuck is going on over there?"

Still no answer, except...

"It's one of ours!"

"Ghost!

"Nooo!"

Coda tried to swallow the lump in his throat but found that his mouth had gone dry. The radio distress was too familiar. He'd heard the same when he was under Baranyk control. It was almost too much to bear. He almost turned the video off right there, but he'd asked for this. Demanded it, even. And as painful as it was, he had to see it through.

Lieutenant Coleman's hands jetted across the navigational controls to plot a course back toward Bravo Flight. "Alpha Flight, on me. We're going to see what the hell is going on over there."

Lieutenant Coleman broke away from the battle, his fighters in a loose formation, hot on his tail. They blasted toward the other flight, accelerating at speeds that were high even for space combat.

"Razor, I don't know what the hell's going on, but we're on our way. Acknowledge."

No response.

"Razor, this is Spitfire. Acknowledge."

Still nothing. The radio chatter continued—screams, shouts for help, cries for fallen comrades. As fast as Lieutenant Coleman was traveling, it seemed like he was still going to be too late. His fighters would be dead before he arrived.

"Malice, Malice, it's Spitfire. We're on our way."

Malice didn't reply.

"Goddamn it, someone fucking acknowledge!"

"It's Cherokee, sir," one of the pilots said, but what he said after was unintelligible.

"Come again, Cherokee?"

"I said it's the flight leader, sir. It's Razor."

"*What* is Razor, Lieutenant?"

Coda knew what was coming, which somehow made everything worse.

"The attack, sir," Cherokee said. "I don't know what happened, but Lieutenant O'Neil opened fire. We can't keep him and the enemy off our backs, sir. We need to retreat."

"You're not making any sense, Cherokee. Alpha Flight is en route and will be there in..." Lieutenant Coleman glance at his HUD. "Twelve seconds. Stay engaged."

"He's coming around on my tail!" Cherokee suddenly bellowed. "Troll! Troll! I need immediate assistance."

From the inside of Lieutenant Coleman's cockpit, Coda watched as the green indicators on the HUD grew ever closer. One in particular, with the ID Razor, was indeed moving behind Cherokee. Under normal circumstances, it would have been impossible to tell if Razor was moving to engage or to assist. Coda, though, already knew the outcome.

"He's moving into firing range," Cherokee continued to scream. "Troll, where the fuck are you? I need immediate—"

"Lieutenant O'Neil!" Lieutenant Coleman broke in. "Break off immediately and move to heading zero-six-five. I repeat, break off and move to heading—"

"He's firing!"

"Goddamn it!" Lieutenant Coleman screamed. "Razor, disengage! Shut off guidance on that missile and disengage. That's an order!"

His missile away, Lieutenant O'Neil altered course, ignoring a swarm of Baranyk fighters, making for another human vessel.

"Razor!" Coleman bellowed one last time, but like every other attempt, this one went unanswered. Two more shuddering breaths later, Lieutenant Coleman gave the order. "All fighters, this is the CAG. Eliminate Lieutenant O'Neil. I repeat, eliminate Lieutenant O'Neil."

Coda's eyes went blurry. Not only because he'd just heard the order for his father's death but because of the profound pain he heard in Lieutenant Coleman's voice. This was a man sentencing one of his best friends to death. The weight of leadership was heavy, but rarely was it *that* heavy.

Lieutenant Coleman's fingers typed in a series of commands, combining the remnants of Alpha and Bravo Flights into designation Charlie and marking Razor's fighter as an unknown enemy vessel. His final step before entering the battle himself was to shift the radio frequency so that it excluded Coda's father.

With Lieutenant Coleman's fighters entering the fray, the battle took on a fevered pitch. The radio went silent as the pilots focused on two things and two things only: staying alive and dealing out death to all enemies, including the traitor in their midst.

Lieutenant Coleman had eyes for only one ship, though. His former friend and flight leader.

"Why?" Lieutenant Coleman said, his tone mournful. "Just tell me that, Joseph. Why are you doing this?"

The radio remained silent as Lieutenant Coleman cut through an enemy formation, Tank still on his wing. He preserved his missiles, opening fire with his cannons. Two ships broke apart before Coleman was through the formation, angling around to move into an attack run. If Lieutenant O'Neil saw him, he didn't indicate as such and instead terrorized the human lines, targeting fighters at will.

"Please don't make me do this."

Coda wasn't sure if the CAG had opened up a private line with Lieutenant O'Neil or if he was just talking to him from the inside of his cockpit. It didn't matter. Razor wouldn't have replied anyway—even if he'd wanted to. Coda knew that much for certain.

Lieutenant Coleman's fighter drew closer, almost into firing range, but not before another human ship exploded into a ball of light. Coda flinched with every human loss. They were like body blows that struck at his very core. He wanted to yell at his father, to scream, to tell him to break off, plead with him, but he knew it would never do any good. He was watching a specter of the past. A memory that Captain Coleman had lived with for more than a decade. A nightmare that he himself had imagined for just as long.

"I'm sorry," Lieutenant Coleman whispered the moment he got tone. His finger squeezed the firing stud. His fighter rocked as the missile sped away.

Coda couldn't watch. He let the tablet fall between his legs and covered his eyes with his other hand.

"Coda..."

"No." Coda shook his head. "I can't do this."

"Coda, finish the video. You have to see how it ends."

"I know how it ends," Coda said. "He dies. You killed him. His friend."

"Finish the video, Coda."

"I can't."

"You can, and you need to."

There was something in Captain Coleman's voice that Coda couldn't describe but that compelled him to finish the video. Coda pulled the tablet back up and tapped the screen—it had paused when he'd let it fall.

The missile blasted out of sight, disappearing into the inky void of space. Lieutenant Coleman tracked it on his HUD. The yellow indicator streaked on a course that would intercept Razor's fighter. Before it reached it, though, a mass of Baranyk fighters flew in front of it. There was a brief flash, then the yellow indicator disappeared from Lieutenant Coleman's HUD.

"They sacrificed themselves," Coda said, eyes fixed on the video.

"Why?" Captain Coleman asked.

Another missile, Coleman's last, rocketed from his wing. It erased the distance between the two fighters in a matter of seconds, but like the first, it didn't find its intended target. Just as before, a wave of enemy vessels swarmed in, smothering the missile's flight path until it struck a Baranyk fighter.

"They did it again," Coda said.

"Why?" Captain Coleman repeated.

"They're protecting him."

Captain Coleman nodded. "Why would they do that?"

"He's under their control."

On the screen, Captain Coleman and a host of other fighters expended their remaining missiles in what the lieutenant had explained would overwhelm the protecting forces. They only needed one to get through. But the Baranyk fighters were too numerous, the missiles too few. When the last of them had been intercepted, the human fighters were left with too few options.

Lieutenant Coleman cursed, his eyes focused solely on the indicator of Lieutenant O'Neil's fighter. After a few moments of indecision, he gave the order. "Full retreat. All fighters back to..."

The Baranyk fighters altered their vectors. No longer concerned with the human fighters, they were swarming toward the *Benjamin Franklin*, and because the human fighters were out of long-range weapons, there was little they could do to stop them.

"All fighters, full burn! Back to the *Franklin*!" Lieutenant Coleman's hands flew across the controls, plotting an intercept course to the heart of the Baranyk swarm. They didn't have enough time. The enemy would get a full wave of attacks in, maybe two, before the human crafts would cut into their flank.

"*Benjamin Franklin, Benjamin Franklin*," Lieutenant Coleman bellowed. "This is the CAG. Enemy fighters inbound. I repeat, enemy fighters inbound."

"We see them, Lieutenant," said a voice on the radio. "Launching emergency fighters and preparing antifighter bombardment."

"Roger that," Coleman said. "We are hot on their tails, but we won't make it before they get a couple shots at you."

"Negative, Lieutenant." It was a new voice on the radio this time. Older. More authoritative. Coda had little doubt that it was the captain of the *Benjamin Franklin*. "At that range, our antifighter batteries won't be able to distinguish between you and the enemy. Move to heading two-four-five, forty degrees positive-Z, and prepare to engage."

There was a slight pause, followed by, "Yes, sir."

Lieutenant Coleman set a course that would take them beyond the *Benjamin Franklin*, out of danger from friendly fire and ready to engage once the enemy completed their attack run. It also left the human capital ship completely exposed.

The enemy fighters cut across the bow of the ship a moment later, and terrible gouts of flame and precious fluids and gasses billowed out of its reinforced hulls. But even without the Nighthawks, the ship wasn't defenseless. Antifighter gun turrets fired without discrimination, firing into the center mass of the swarm. Baranyk ships burst apart, spraying thick, mucus-like material against the side of the *Franklin* and coating its dark hull yellow.

As the enemy altered course, preparing for another attack run, Lieutenant Coleman's fighters cut into them. Without long-range weapons, they had to fly dangerously close, shifting from snipers to bare-knuckled brawlers, and Lieutenant Coleman was the best. He sliced through the enemy formations with a controlled aggressiveness Coda had never seen. His captain had always been precise, not necessarily by the book, but clean. This was entirely different.

His finger squeezed in a steady rhythm, his guns shooting in bursts that almost had a musical quality to them. If it was a song, it was a song of death and destruction. He shot down three fighters, then four, staying hard on the enemy tail. The Baranyk fighters shifted this way and that, trying to shake him, but Lieutenant Coleman and his wingman had their teeth in them and weren't letting go.

By the time the enemy swarm broke apart and left the coordinated formations behind to shift to an every-man-for-himself battle, more than half their number had been cut down. Still, the Nighthawks didn't let up, and the *Franklin*'s batteries caught any enemy spacecraft that ventured too close.

Three-quarters of the enemy was destroyed, but their work wasn't without success. Another ten percent of the human force was gone, and the rest were dangerously low on ammunition. Then, as quickly as the battle had begun, it ended, the remaining Baranyk vessels bugging out.

"They're retreating," one of the pilots said, her voice an equal mix of surprise and exhaustion.

And that was when Coda heard it. Crying. Lieutenant Coleman heard it, too, because he sat forward in his seat, his hands going to the side of his helmet as if trying to hear better.

"I'm sorry," the crying voice said. Coda's father. "I'm so sorry."

"Razor?" Lieutenant Coleman found him on his HUD. He had been part of the Baranyk swarm, but now that it had disengaged, he was left to drift aimlessly.

"I don't know what happened," Lieutenant O'Neil said. "It wasn't me. I swear. That wasn't me."

Nobody said anything. Silence filled the radio, broken only by Lieutenant O'Neil's quiet pleas. "You have to believe me. I would never..."

Before Lieutenant Coleman or any of the other wingmen had a chance to respond, two new indicators appeared on the battle map. They'd been fired from the *Benjamin Franklin* itself and were streaking toward Razor's ship.

"No!" Lieutenant Coleman bellowed. "*Benjamin Franklin*, this is Lieutenant Coleman. Cease fire! That is a human vessel. I repeat, that is one of ours!"

He desperately punched a series of commands into his computer, changing the designation of Lieutenant O'Neil's fighter from enemy to friendly, then sent it out to his fighters. But while he had the ability to override the fighters' computers, he didn't with the command ship. The two missiles streaked toward the human fighter.

Lieutenant O'Neil's pleas intensified. "I had no control. They were my men. I would never—"

"Razor!" Lieutenant Coleman interrupted. "You have two missiles inbound. Evasive maneuvers!"

Lieutenant O'Neil's ship didn't alter course.

"Evasive maneuvers, goddamn it!"

Nothing.

"Eject! Eject! Eject!"

There was a flash of light, then Lieutenant O'Neil's fighter disappeared.

Coda blinked, pulling the tablet closer. Lieutenant Coleman had a similar reaction inside the cockpit, making the battle map larger. The two yellow indicators of the *Benjamin Franklin*'s missiles were still there, now shooting into the depths of space, but Lieutenant O'Neil's fighter was nowhere to be seen.

"*Franklin* actual, this is the CAG. What the hell just happened?"

"We're reading a jump signature, Lieutenant," the voice said.

"Jump signature? To where?"

"We don't know. Gather your remaining fighters and return to base."

"Damn it, Lieutenant Gwynne," Lieutenant Coleman said, his voice tight. "What the fuck happened to Razor's ship?"

"It's gone."

The words hung in the air long enough that it took Coda several moments to realize that the video had ended. Confused, he looked up at Captain Coleman then back down to the tablet as if the frozen video held more answers.

"I don't understand, sir. My father died. But this..."

"No, Coda. The official *story* is that your father was executed for treason, but as you can see from that video, your father was alive at the end of the battle."

"Alive?" Coda nearly choked on the word.

"Yes, Coda. And he was under enemy control. He wasn't the villain he's been made out to be."

Coda wasn't listening. His mind was in another place on another voice.

*Callan?* The voice had been so clear. So familiar. Tinged with genuine human surprise. It couldn't have been a figment of his imagination. Couldn't have been a dream. Couldn't have been a symptom of being under Baranyk control. No, something had been there, a presence every bit as real as the overlord. He was as certain as he'd ever been about anything in his life. But how was it all connected?

"What happened after he jumped?"

"Well, the jump range on the Nighthawks is very limited. We drew a perimeter then cross-referenced it with known habitable planets and moons and began a search. But we never found any trace of him."

"He's still alive." It was less a comment than it was a realization. Coda jumped to his feet and began pacing.

"No, Coda. I don't want you to get your hopes up. He likely jumped and ran out of oxygen before he found refuge."

"No." Coda was grinning now. "No. Something happened after I was shot down, something I haven't told you. Before I regained consciousness, I was... somewhere else. I don't know how to explain it. But I was *connected* to some kind of network. And there was this force. It drew me in, tried to command me. To control me."

Coda paused, closed his eyes, thinking back to the moment. The experience had felt like a dream, but now he was sure it had been something more. "I fled. It was like I was racing through space, and I passed other things. Other beings, all connected to the same network. Then there was something else. A newer presence. A light. It was familiar and comforting, and I raced toward it. That's when I heard it."

Coda opened his eyes, meeting Captain Coleman's. "I heard him. I heard my father."

Silence stretched out between them, as vast as space itself. Spoken out loud, the whole thing sounded ridiculous.

"It was him," Coda repeated, as much to fill the empty silence as to reaffirm his belief. "I know it sounds crazy, but he said my name, and he sounded as surprised to see me as I was him. He's alive, sir. I *know* it. I can feel it with every fiber of my being."

Captain Coleman rose from his seat and walked past Coda to his bookshelf, where he poured himself a glass of water. "It doesn't sound crazy, Commander. Not after everything we've seen. Collect your thoughts. I need a full report, everything you can remember. In the meantime, I need to think. We still have a mission to complete, and we have information Fleet Command needs, but there are other things at play here. Things we can't ignore."

"I can do that, sir. It'll be good to get it written down. It might help me remember something I'm missing."

"Good," Captain Coleman said. "And thank you, Coda. I know none of this is easy. But we'll unravel this mystery."

# 34

*Brig, SAS Redemption*
*Deep Space*

HUMAN PROGRESS HAS OFTEN BEEN MEASURED BY TECHNOLOGICAL advancement, from the development of electricity to the first automobile, commercial aviation, or even the EmDrive that helped humanity claim the stars. The *Redemption* itself was progress for the Sol Fleet, the pinnacle of human engineering. With an upgraded EmDrive, improved weaponry, powerful scanners, and quantum computing, it was everything the best and brightest minds of humanity could assemble. Although the ship was a great example of human ingenuity and the culmination of hundreds of years of pushing the limits, its brig was a timeless construction.

Coda's cell was the most basic of human structures: three solid walls and a fourth of round steel bars. Eight small cells filled the brig, each equipped with a cot, sink, and toilet. Coda sat on the cot, his back resting against the bulkhead. He hadn't been surprised when Captain Coleman had ordered him here or even when he had escorted Coda himself. Whether it was Coda's fault or not, his hand had killed five human pilots, and his being under Baranyk influence was not common knowledge. To everyone beyond Coda, the captain, and Doctors Naidoo and Rydell, he was a traitor—not only to his own men but to his entire race.

In the loneliness of the brig, Coda couldn't help but think about the things that were likely being said about him. He had a pretty good idea —he'd heard them said about his father. His pilots would be commiserating over drinks, some quiet, others telling anyone who would listen that they had seen this coming.

"Of course Coda was a traitor," they would say. "He had traitor blood flowing through his traitor veins. They should just kill him and his whole family to keep the disease from spreading. Cull the herd."

The worst part wasn't even what the others thought of him—it was what he thought of himself. He knew he wasn't responsible, that the enemy had played him like a puppet, but that didn't stop him from remembering the joystick in his hand or the feeling of his finger pressed against the firing stud. That knowledge didn't erase the images of missiles streaking from his fighter or the flashes in the dark as ships were destroyed. It didn't drown out the voices of his squad mates dying.

He tried to sleep but couldn't escape the feeling that he was somehow at fault. It didn't help that the bed was harder than concrete and the pillow thinner than paper. He hadn't expected comfortable accommodations, but whoever had designed the brig had outdone themselves.

Captain Coleman had left a tablet with him so he could complete his report, and seeking a distraction, Coda had jumped into it full force. He included everything, from the moment he'd heard that terrible noise to the odd feeling of being a spectator in his own body. He explained the odd sensations that had come after he was shot down, of being in another place, something outside his body, pursued by an evil force, and finding refuge in a familiar light.

In doing so, he realized that during his conversations with the captain, he had never mentioned the strange Baranyk he'd come to think of as the Overlord. He didn't know who or what it was aside from the fact that it was evil. Was it some kind of leader? A king? An emperor? He didn't have any answers, but something about the strange being felt important.

Unfortunately, even with thinking through the encounter and explaining it in painstaking detail, Coda completed the report in a couple hours. And after giving the tablet to the marine on guard, who had it sent to the captain, Coda was reacquainted with the silent loneliness that allowed his mind too much time to wander.

Coda had often heard that imagination was generally worse than reality. The imaginary monster was scarier than the real thing. That theory was tested when the door to the brig opened and three sets of heavy boots thudded to a stop outside his cell.

Coda found himself looking at his three flight leaders. They had been drinking, their faces flushed, eyes glassy, and they watched him as if he were an alien creature on exhibit. Coda opened his mouth to speak but thought better of it. What could he say? He was bound by secrecy, tied by pride, and overcome by shame. Coda lowered his head in resignation, eyes falling to the deck.

Squawks spoke first. He stepped forward, taking the bars in his hands, resting his head between them. "How could you?" he asked, his voice quiet. "You promised us, Coda."

Coda didn't respond. Didn't even look up. He couldn't meet his friend's eyes. The words were well timed and well placed, striking the most vulnerable parts of his soul.

"You promised us!"

The worst part was Coda knew exactly what his friend was talking about. He remembered the day like it was yesterday. They'd been standing in their barracks aboard the *Jamestown* during the early days of their training. Coda, so sure of himself, had told them that he wasn't like his father, that he would never hurt them. He had looked each of them in the eye and offered his heartfelt promise.

When it became obvious Coda wasn't going to respond, Squawks muttered a curse and stepped away.

Noodle took a different tactic. "What happened out there, Coda? What are we missing?" His voice was soft but somehow tinged with hope. Even after the death of five of their companions, he believed in Coda. He trusted that everything would make sense after a simple explanation.

Coda wanted to hug the man, to tell him how much that meant to him, but he couldn't even look up from the deck.

"It's really like this, huh?" Moscow said. "After everything, you really are just like your father?"

It was too much. Couldn't they see he was quiet because he couldn't say anything? That he was bound by orders? He couldn't tell them because doing so would only put him and the captain at risk. It would put them at risk too.

"Unbelievable," Moscow spat.

The anger and shame broke Coda. "You don't know anything," he said.

"Then tell us, Coda," Noodle said. There was that hopeful tone again. "Tell us what happened."

"I can't." Coda turned his back on his friends. "Go away."

"Coda..."

But Coda wasn't listening anymore. He found a room in his mind and locked the door. Nobody could hurt him there. Not the Baranyk who tried to control him. Not his friends who wanted more than he could give. Not even himself and his dark thoughts.

"Come on, Noodle," Squawks said, a disappointed tone in his voice.

Moscow left him one last parting gift. "I thought you were better than this."

The door to the brig opened, and his friends left. Coda curled into a ball, eyes on the bulkhead, back to the world. He'd thought he was lonely before, but what he found now was a profound emptiness. Everyone he had ever known, everyone he had ever grown close to, had abandoned him. And he was powerless to bring them back. To help them understand. There, in the dim light of the brig, Coda finally understood what it felt like to be his father.

*I'm sorry, Dad. I'm so sorry.*

Something stirred in the back of his mind, like a sun-starved flower rising on the first warm spring morning. Coda felt himself compelled, drawn toward a conclusion he hadn't seen until this moment. The idea snapped together as if it had been a forgone conclusion.

*Thank you, Moscow. You don't realize it, but you just saved me.*

# 35

*Captain Coleman's Quarters, SAS Redemption*
*Deep Space*

Captain Coleman read his report from the top. It was vital he was as clear and concise as possible without overblowing or oversimplifying the threat. He was trying to deliver terrifying news without implicating Coda as a person—and that was easier said than done, especially with his family's background.

He'd included all of the key details they'd uncovered so far, including their data on the Baranyk signal as well as Dr. Naidoo's assessment including the data points they had shared with Coda, but Coleman didn't feel like it was enough.

They were no closer to discovering where the Baranyk had retreated to or if they were massing at an unknown location. They had no idea how strong the Baranyk signal was, if it was mechanized or a natural ability inherent to their physiology, how widespread it was, or most importantly, how many humans were susceptible.

Doctors Rydell and Naidoo continued to pore over data, and Coleman had been clear in his report that these questions were still unanswered. He couldn't wait anymore. They had proof that the Baranyk had developed capabilities to control humanity and further proof that they had used that ability before. One of the biggest unknown questions was how long had the enemy been doing it? How many sleeper agents did they have within the fleet?

Satisfied with the report, Coleman deployed an emergency communication drone and sent it in. With that behind him, he left his quarters. He knew he should sleep while he had the chance, but he also knew that wasn't in the cards right now. Even if he were to lie down, he wouldn't be able to fall asleep. He had too much on his mind. So he did what he always did when he needed to think—he moved.

The corridors were active. The ship ran on a twenty-four-hour schedule with staggered shifts. His crew saluted him as he passed, and deep in thought, he offered small nods in return.

He couldn't help but feel like he was being pulled in opposite directions, torn between duty and personal ambition. His duty was to his ship, his crew, the entire fleet. He had information that put them all in serious danger, and he owed it to them to get to the bottom of it. But it was also his duty to answer the other questions plaguing Fleet Command.

The problem was his thoughts kept returning to what Coda had said about his father. Coleman couldn't remember the last time he'd watched the vid of Joseph turning on his wingmen. He hadn't needed to—he'd experienced it and watched it enough times to have it memorized. He'd dissected it, broken it down frame by frame, searching for answers but never finding them. Finally, he'd succumbed to the reality that it was a mystery he would never solve.

Except he had—or at least he was getting close. If Coda was right, then the answers were before him, and all he had to do was seek them out. And based on everything they had found so far, the new Baranyk signal signified a greater threat than a massing fleet.

For that reason, Coleman had convinced himself to continue the search for his old friend. Joseph was connected to all of this—that much was clear—and Coda was certain he was alive.

*Could it be true? How is that possible?* Coleman had been part of the search party. He'd scanned those systems, looking for signs of his fighter, put visual on the ground with his own eyes. In every instance, he'd come up empty. The universe was bigger than humanity could fathom, but due to that size and habitation requirements, there weren't a lot of places for an unprepared human to hide.

But Coda was so damn adamant. If his story that his father had found him inside the Baranyk network and saved him from the Overlord was true, then Coleman's old friend could not only access the Baranyk network but could manipulate it. With that kind of access, he might have vital information about the enemy, how they communicated, their command structure, and who knew what else.

*That's a worthwhile diversion, isn't it?*

As far as he knew, Joseph O'Neil was the only other human who had succumbed to the Baranyk signal. He might even offer further insight into the signal. Coleman roamed the halls, mulling over his thoughts, reviewing the situation from every angle, trying to ensure that his decisions weren't swayed too far toward the personal direction.

"Captain?" Dr. Naidoo said in his ear.

Coleman pushed the top of his ear to his head, activating the earpiece. "Yes, Doctor. What's going on?"

"I've found something you should see."

Coleman surveyed his surroundings for the first time in a while. It took him a moment to determine where he was—deep in the heart of the ship toward its bow, where the main engineering facility was. It was about as far from the medical bay as he could be. "What is it?"

"I've found a commonality between Commander O'Neil, his father, and the woman from Koburn."

Coleman stopped in the middle of the corridor. "Say again, Doc?"

"I said I've found a common trait among the three people we know have been vulnerable to the Baranyk signal. It might help answer why they were targeted and give us insight into how widespread our vulnerability is."

*This is it. This is what you've been waiting for.* "I'll be right there."

He was halfway to the medical ward when his tablet vibrated. He slowed, pulling it from his pocket. The message was from Coda, and he'd deemed it a high priority. With luck already on his side, Coleman opened it and scanned its contents.

Coda had a plan—an audacious plan—and depending on what the

doc had to say, it might offer them the quickest path to answers. He slid the tablet back into his pocket, moving with more speed now. First things first, he had to see what the doctor had uncovered. He hoped everything would fall into place after that.

# 36

*Brig, SAS Redemption*
*Deep Space*

Coda's flight leaders didn't return, and no other pilots came to visit. The captain came twice to clarify different points of Coda's report and ask a series of follow-up questions, but he didn't elaborate on his own thoughts. Coda didn't press. Either the captain didn't trust him or he would tell Coda in his own time. In either case, there was nothing Coda could do to pull information from the man. So he waited.

Having told the captain everything, Coda was able to keep the worst of the despair at bay. That wasn't to say he was always successful. In his worst moments, he was almost comatose in his grief, but fortunately, those moments were becoming fewer and farther between. He had a plan, and with that plan came a purpose. All he had to do was wait.

That moment came three days after he'd been sent to the brig. The marine guards didn't say much, just unlocked his cell door and ordered him out.

"Where are we going?"

"Hands," one said while the other waited nearby, gripping a stun gun.

Coda held his hands in front of him. The marine cuffed him and pushed him toward the door. They escorted him toward the captain's quarters. It was a humiliating walk, flanked by armed guards, hands in cuffs, seeing personnel he knew, feeling the weight of their gazes. Many wore their hostile emotions on their sleeves. Others muttered curses. One even acted as if he would spit on Coda. Blessedly, they were far from the pilots' section of the ship, and he didn't see any of his pilots.

Another pair of marine guards stood outside the door to the captain's meeting room, and seeing Coda near, one banged on the door. A second later, the captain appeared and ordered Coda in.

Stepping through the portal, Coda froze. The *Redemption*'s entire senior command sat around the table at the center of the room: Commander Garcia, Dr. Naidoo, Chief Engineer Brahm Payton, and to Coda's biggest surprise, his three flight leaders. He'd expected he was on his way to talk to the captain, maybe work out the finer points of their plan. He hadn't expected this.

Noodle shot a look toward Squawks, but for once, the mouthy pilot seemed speechless. Moscow did little to hide his disapproval, wearing an angry expression that was all narrowed eyes and sharp eyebrows.

*They didn't know I was coming either.*

The door closed behind him, and the captain returned to his seat at the head of the table. "Sit down, Commander," he said, motioning toward an empty seat near him.

Coda sat, placing his bound hands on the table.

"Now that we're all here, we can begin," Captain Coleman said. "The truth is, we've uncovered a real shitstorm. We've discovered what we believe is a new Baranyk weapon—one that strikes at the very heart of the Sol Fleet. At the men and women who fill its ranks." He turned to Dr. Naidoo. "Doctor?"

He and his chief science officer must have prepped ahead of time, because she picked up where he left off. "The Baranyk are targeting us with an ultra-high-frequency signal that penetrates the temporal lobe of the human brain in a way we've never seen before. In doing so, it replicates the signals our brain sends to our body, taking complete control. The subjects we've uncovered who have been hit with this signal convey losing all mobile faculties, and our data appears to confirm their statements."

"We first uncovered evidence on Koburn," Captain Coleman said. "But we were unsure until Kryos." He glanced at Coda. "We have clear evidence that suggests Commander O'Neil was hit with a Baranyk signal that intercepted his bodily control and essentially turned him, against his will, into an enemy combatant."

Feeling the eyes of everyone in the room on him, Coda kept his eyes on his hands, picking absently at his calloused fingers. He'd expected the truth to give way to relief, but he was just as hollow as before. He couldn't shake the feeling that something was wrong with him. That he was weak. That everyone else in the room could see it.

"Fortunately," Captain Coleman said, "the signal appears to be highly limited. We'll get into more of that later, but it appears to have a limited effective range and needs to be hyperfocused. It's not something they can broadcast widely to turn dozens of our people against us. We believe they can only target a single individual at a time. Still, I need to stress the implications of this. If the enemy can turn individuals on a whim, then the entire integrity of our fleet is in jeopardy.

"I've already sent an emergency communication to Admiral Orlovsky detailing our discovery and outlining our evidence. I have made that report available to you as well, but for our purposes here, it's important to understand that the weapon has also given us vital information about the enemy. Following the attack, Coda was connected to some kind of Baranyk network—their hive mind, if you will—and saw a special kind of Baranyk no one has ever seen before. It appears to be some kind of leader. We don't know any more than that, but we're calling him the Overlord. Unfortunately, Coda couldn't uncover more. Our thinking is that if we can lure the Baranyk into using the weapon again, it'll allow Coda to reconnect to the Baranyk network and learn more."

"How do we do that, sir?" Squawks asked.

"We return to Kryos," Captain Coleman said, "and feign an attack. We expect them to hit Coda with the signal again, and when they do, he'll connect to the hive mind and uncover why the Baranyk have fled occupied systems and discover where they're massing. It will also give Doctors Naidoo and Rydell another opportunity to study the signal."

"What's to stop them from targeting someone else?" Commander Garcia asked. "What's to stop them from hitting me with that signal? Or you?"

"The three brains we've analyzed that have been vulnerable to the Baranyk signal have been structurally different from other brains," Dr. Naidoo said. "They have a thinner temporal cortex. The nucleus accumbens and amygdala appear smaller as well, but with only three samples to study, we can't say for certain."

"It's a risk," Captain Coleman said. "There's no getting around that, Jaime. But it appears only a subsection of the population is susceptible to the new weapon, which might explain why it hasn't been used more broadly."

"Or why we haven't discovered it until now," Moscow added. "Who knows how long they've had it."

Captain Coleman nodded. "That's a good observation, Moscow. And the truth is... we have evidence they've had it for some time." The captain's voice was slow and deliberate. It was clear he wasn't going to say more, but it was also clear he didn't think he had to.

Moscow's mother had died aboard the *Benjamin Franklin* when Coda's father had been hit with the same signal at Kryos. Moscow could draw the obvious conclusion, and in a moment, it seemed he had. He flinched as the realization struck, his eyes going wide, mouth opening as unspoken words died on his lips.

Coda looked away when Moscow's attention turned to him. He picked absently at his hands.

"Like I said," Captain Coleman added, "the signal, while devastating, appears to be highly limited. The good doctors have also analyzed the rest of the squadron, plus everyone in this room, and are working through the rest of the crew. So far, no one else appears to have the abnormality."

"Sir," Squawks said. "Are you saying Coda isn't right in the head? Because we all knew that already."

Noodle groaned but couldn't help but laugh. Even Moscow smirked, but if the rest of the executive staff saw the humor, they didn't show it.

"He's not, Lieutenant," Captain Coleman deadpanned. "None of you are. It takes a special kind of crazy to climb into the cockpit."

"Amen, sir."

"But to your point—Coda's brain structure is rare. And that's why we believe if anyone is hit with the weapon, it'll be him."

Coda looked up from his hands. Squawks was already looking at him and gave him the smallest of smiles.

*He's trying to move on. Trying to apologize.*

Only Squawks would apologize with an insult. Coda nodded back, letting him know he appreciated it, a silent promise that they would talk later.

"That's a lot of ifs and shoulds," Commander Garcia said. "And isn't there something we're missing? What happens when the enemy hits Coda with that signal? It was devastating enough last time. He killed five of our pilots."

"He didn't," Captain Coleman said. "*They* did. Coda was powerless to stop it. And we'll take precautions. We can have the chief remove his missiles and cannons. He'll still be able to fly, but we'll neuter his ability to attack our own."

"Won't that tip the enemy off to the ruse?" Noodle asked.

"From all the data we've been able to gather," Dr. Naidoo said, "it appears the Baranyk can take control of bodily function, but they don't have access to thoughts. For lack of a better example, it really is like how we control our drone fighters."

"But you also mentioned Coda connecting to the Baranyk network," Noodle pressed. "If Coda can get information from them, isn't it also possible for them to get information from him?"

Captain Coleman tapped the top of the table with his finger. "That's a good point, Lieutenant." He looked around the table. "Any ideas?"

"We could minimize the fuel in the missiles," Chief Engineer Payton asked. "Give them just enough to fire but run out before they cause damage. We could disarm them too."

"Disarmed or not," Commander Garcia said, "there'd still be a missile in the battle space. One more thing to avoid."

"We'll manage," Squawks said.

"I'm sure you will, Lieutenant," Commander Garcia said. "My other concern is what stops Coda from a suicide run? If it becomes apparent that his weapons are malfunctioning, we obviously run the risk of showing our hand, but they might also try to run him into the ship itself, kamikaze style."

"During basic flight instruction, our instructors had an override," Captain Coleman said. "A button they could push that would shut the fighters down in the event a pilot blacked out or was out of control. I'll see if the chief has something he can rig up."

This seemed to quell the commander's concern.

"Any other concerns?" Captain Coleman asked. "What else are we missing?"

"The only thing I can think of, sir," Squawks said, "is what do we tell the other pilots? I'm sure this isn't something you want getting out, but they'll ask questions if Coda's out there."

Captain Coleman thought for a moment. "Tell them you're incorporating a new pilot into the squadron but because they're green to give them a wide berth."

Squawks made a face. He clearly didn't think that would be enough.

"One of the benefits of command, Lieutenant," Coleman said, "is that you don't have to get their permission or offer an explanation. Tell them to focus on themselves and their wingmen, and that'll buy us enough time. We can worry about other questions later."

"Yes, sir," Squawks said.

"Okay." Captain Coleman looked around the table, giving each member of the crew an opportunity to raise additional objections. When he got to Coda, he gave the smallest of shrugs. It was a question.

"I'm ready, sir," Coda said.

The captain nodded. "We have our plan, then. Arm Coda's fighter with missile duds and fake cannon fire and assemble a disarm device. When that's ready, we'll jump back to Kryos, feign an attack, and allow Coda to tap into the hive mind to learn what he can. We'll use the disarm device to disable his ship, recover him and his fighter, then jump back to safety to debrief and regroup. Any questions?"

"No questions, sir," Squawks said. "But that has to be the craziest plan ever concocted."

"It's a good thing I've got pilots crazy enough to pull it off then, isn't it?"

"Touché, sir. Coda isn't the only one messed up in the brain."

"We already knew that," Noodle said.

"All right," Captain Coleman said, back to business. "You have your orders. Let's get started."

# 37

*Meeting Room, SAS Redemption*
*Deep Space*

"CODA," CAPTAIN COLEMAN SAID, "HOLD UP A MOMENT."

Coda, who had just risen from the table, nodded and remained close, letting the rest of the room's occupants filter through the door behind him. When it was just him and Captain Coleman, the captain gestured at the cuffs binding his wrists.

"I'm sorry I had to do that," Captain Coleman said. "I feared the response we would've got if you showed up unbound."

"I understand, sir."

"How are you holding up?"

"Fine, sir."

Captain Coleman gave him an appraising look, the kind that said he didn't believe Coda and expected an honest answer out of him.

Coda's façade collapsed under that gaze. "It's been hard, sir. But I'm working through it."

"We have a way of beating ourselves up even when we're the victim. It's one of the curses of humanity. Some can avoid all feelings of responsibility, casting blame on anything and anyone around them, but people like us accept it even if it's not ours to bear. We accept it and do something about it. We act. It's one of the qualities of a leader."

Coda studied the captain for a moment. Captain Coleman was hinting at something that had never crossed his mind. *He knew about the signal. He knew about your father. He blames himself.*

The realization brought a wave of... not anger. It was nothing as clear as that, but for a brief moment, Coda had a path out of the darkness. The captain was responsible. It was his fault. He alone had known the dangers and hadn't taken proper precautions or even warned his crew of the *possibility* of danger.

But even as he thought it, Coda knew he couldn't follow that road. As the captain said, people too often avoided responsibility, letting someone else take the blame. He wasn't that kind of person and never had been.

Captain Coleman must have misread his silence, because he reinforced the point. "I'm serious, Coda."

"I know, sir. And I agree. It's not easy, but it's a burden I'm willing to bear as long as it helps keep the rest of our crew alive."

"You're a good man, Coda. Be careful. We don't know how the Baranyk network works or what we're exposing ourselves to. As Noodle alluded to, there's a very real possibility that the enemy can extract information from you just as easily as you can from them. Probably easier. So get in, get what you need, and get out. Understood?"

*In other words, focus on the mission and don't get distracted by your father's presence.* "Understood, sir."

"Good. The guards outside will take you back to your cell. I'll send for you when we're ready."

"Sir," Coda said. Unable to salute, he inclined his head then strode out of the room.

The guards fell into step behind him, prepared to escort him back to his cell, but Coda stopped a few steps into the corridor. Squawks, Noodle, and Moscow stood at the junction. They saw him and waited, obviously torn between waiting for Coda to come to them or closing the distance and joining him. They chose the latter.

"One moment," Coda said to the guards behind him. "Please."

Surprisingly, the guards gave him some space. Coda wondered what orders Captain Coleman had given them.

"Hey," Coda said as his friends stopped in front of him.

"Hey," they said.

An awkward silence stretched between them. Squawks opened his mouth to speak then closed it again, obviously at a loss for words. Moscow wore a hard expression that Coda couldn't make out, and Noodle was... *smiling.*

"I *knew* there was something you weren't telling us," Noodle said.

His friend's joy nearly brought a smile to Coda's own face. "Yeah... I wish I could've said something. Not being able to tell you guys nearly destroyed me."

"But you're good now, right?" Noodle said, then he seemed to notice Coda's wrists were still cuffed.

"Not yet. But I will be. We'll talk more once this is all over." Coda glanced at the two marines behind him. They were starting to get antsy. "I'm not sure if I'll see you guys again before the mission, but if I don't, stay safe out there. I have a feeling it's not going to be as straightforward as we all hope."

"You too," Moscow said. His voice was forceful, ripe with other meaning.

Smiling, Coda nodded and started down the corridor.

"Coda." Squawks's voice drew him up short again.

He turned, barely able to see his friend and his troubled look through the gap between the two guards.

"We really *are* sorry."

"I know, Squawks," Coda said. "I am too."

With that, Coda and his guards strode back to the brig, back to his private cell of seclusion. But for the first time since that terrible battle, he didn't feel alone.

# 38

*Cockpit, Nighthawk*
*Deep Space*

CODA RAN HIS FINGERS GENTLY ACROSS THE INSTRUMENT PANEL OF HIS Nighthawk. It felt *good* to be back in the cockpit. For once, he didn't mind the confined nature of the G-suit or the warm recycled air that blew through it. He wasn't nervous or anxious, settling into the gel seat with a calm determination. After everything he'd been through, including several days in the brig, he was *home*.

Radio chatter filled the line as Coda went through his preflight sequence. He was muted, of course. His presence in this flight was meant to be a secret. They'd even given him a fake call sign, one aptly named Trickster. But if he spoke, the secret was out. Nobody would mistake the voice of their CAG.

Moscow was filling in that role, and the captain hadn't made any mention of whether that was a temporary promotion or permanent. It didn't matter. Coda was back in the cockpit, where he belonged. Everything else would fall into place around that.

"Trickster is go for launch," Coda said over a private line.

"Copy that, Trickster," Moscow said. Then softer, in the voice of a friend, not the CAG, he asked, "You good?"

"Couldn't be better," Coda said.

"Glad to hear it. Time for some payback, huh?"

"Definitely."

Coda's Nighthawk jerked as one of the forklifts on the flight deck hitched to it and dragged it into the launch bay. There were more thumps and clicks as the craft was locked into the skid. It was attached to a pulley system that would throw his fighter out the bow of the ship like a bullet from a gun.

After several minutes, the launch bays were loaded with the full squadron of Nighthawks, and the chatter that had been so prevalent before died away. This was always a quiet time, a moment for self-reflection and coming to peace with the fact that many of them might never return.

Coda wasn't a religious man. He'd always used this time to focus, to shed away distraction and review the mission plan. Today, there wasn't much to review. He wasn't to engage, had no weapons, and wouldn't partake in any formations or maneuvers. He was out there to draw the attention of the enemy and coerce them into striking with their new weapon.

Once that happened, he had no idea how things would play out. Before, he hadn't connected to the Baranyk network until after the battle, when he'd been in a state of semiconsciousness. Would it be the same again, or since he had connected once, would he connect faster this time? And what happened once he did? The experience before had been like floating through a dream. What if he didn't know how to find the information they needed? What if he failed?

They were all normal feelings and concerns, the type that Coda would normally have been able to banish with preparation and visualization. But he was venturing into the true unknown. As far as he knew, he was only one of three people to have ever connected with the Baranyk network. He couldn't know what to expect, and the two people who had weren't available to give advice.

Feeling his heart rate increase, Coda forced himself to go through a squared breathing exercise. Coda took a slow breath, five seconds in length, as Moscow did his final roll call. He held it for an equal amount of time as the squadron checked in, then exhaled as he privately sent his green status.

"All right, Captain," Moscow said over the main frequency. "Loading and preflight checks are complete. Nighthawks are go for flight."

"Copy that, Moscow," Captain Coleman said. "Prepare to jump in two minutes."

That time went by quickly and in silence. One moment, Coda was waiting patiently in his cockpit. The next, the world stretched before him. When it snapped back into place, Coda knew they had arrived at Kryos.

A presence wormed its way into the back of his head. It had already been there, Coda realized, and had been since they'd abandoned Kryos days ago. But it had been muted, somehow lesser. The presence stirred, washing over his consciousness like oil coating the bottom of a pan. It didn't hurt or pry. If anything, it felt curious.

Coda's breath grew short, coming in quick bursts. He knew that presence, recognizing the way it made him itch, as if it were a spider crawling across his brain. It took everything Coda had not to try to swipe it away. Doing so would only alert the Overlord that Coda knew of his presence.

But something was wrong. He hadn't anticipated the presence being so quick. He had expected it after the engagement had begun. He needed to do something, to warn the captain. He opened his mouth to speak and—

Nothing happened.

*Oh no.*

Coda panicked, trying to fight, trying to move, but he was little more than a prisoner beating against the bars of his cell, unable to escape. His hand moved against his will toward the joystick, slow and methodical. His hand cupped it, fingers tightening around the firing stud, thumb moving toward the safety switch.

His missiles were disarmed, but if fired, they would still launch from his fighter. It might not cause the catastrophic damage the enemy wanted, but it would damage the launch bay and potentially more.

Coda's thumb switched the firing mechanism to missiles. His fingers squeezed, and... he lurched forward. The launch bay raced past him, the black dot of space advancing like an incoming target. Then he was free.

The *Redemption* fell away from him as he was blasted from its hull.

Around him, the other Nighthawks formed up by subflight, creating six delta formations. Coda didn't have a visual, but his HUD showed an enemy carrier in the distance, and it was launching fighters.

His fighter raced forward on the same launch trajectory. The sudden launch seemed to have thrown off the Overlord's plans. He could still feel it, and he didn't have control of his body, but the presence was somehow lessened, distracted. When it returned, it returned in full force. Gone were the slow, methodical movements. Instead, it was sharp and decisive.

Coda's Nighthawk banked hard, angling toward a subflight. He toggled one of his own ships, the Nighthawk getting missile lock, then launched the first missile. In an instant, the flight broke into three fighter pairs. With the enemy in their midst, the other flights did the same. And then the fight was on.

Coda watched in alarm as his fighter raced after fighters, firing indiscriminately. If the Overlord realized the missiles were disarmed or that its cannons had been replaced by digital projectiles, there were no signs of it.

For the moment, his friends were relatively safe—at least until the enemy fighters arrived, which appeared to be imminent. But those, they could handle.

He had a different task. Unable to control his body, Coda imagined himself taking a deep breath and closing his eyes. He focused on the presence, fixated on its weight, and let it envelop him. Then there was *more.*

Not just the Overlord but hundreds of other presences. Thousands. Millions. More than he could ever dream to count. It was as if he had entered another galaxy. He was connected to the Baranyk network.

# 39

*Cockpit, Nighthawk*
*Kryos*

CODA COULD MOVE. IT WASN'T A PHYSICAL THING, AS HE HAD NO BODY IN this strange place, but he was able to *compel* his presence forward. The world seemed to shift around him. Bubbles of consciousness streamed by like bubbles of air rising toward the surface of water.

They didn't appear to be congregated or massed in any sort of order, no resemblance to the squadrons of human and Baranyk around him in the real world. Coda couldn't be sure, but it appeared that real-world location and proximity had little to do with the associated location of the consciousness in the network.

He moved toward a single bubble, somehow knowing the presence represented someone like him, a life-form connected to the Baranyk network. Little more than a speck of light in the darkness, an image of a black Baranyk warrior formed in his mind's eye as he drew closer. It didn't seem to notice him, focused on its own task. Coda withdrew, and the image dissipated.

He kept moving, passing other bubbles of consciousness, close enough to form images in his head. More Baranyk warriors. Thousands more. Millions.

He moved faster, the bubbles floating by like a river. Most were Baranyk, but other things passed as well. Planets, moons, and other life-forms. Some were like the Baranyk, resembling insects from Earth. Others were land dwellers, while more lived in vast seas or the skies of gas giants. Many were truly monstrous in their alienness.

Humanity had questioned its place in the universe, asking for centuries if it was alone in the cosmos and had learned in horror it wasn't. But in the decades since the first Baranyk was discovered, on all the planets and habitable moons humanity had colonized, it had never encountered another intelligent life-form.

Some had come to question again just how populated their neighborhood of the galaxy was, even questioning if the Baranyk themselves were some sort of punishment sent to put humanity in its place. But here, Coda could see that the universe was more expansive than they'd ever realized. There were millions of habitable planets and moons, hundreds of millions, their ecosystems diverse and complex. He reveled in it, amazed and overwhelmed.

He moved through the network. There was no sense of time, but he knew he'd grown distracted. He continued to search the consciousness, letting impressions wash over him, but he struggled to assemble them. It was as if he were on a beach, trying to paint a picture of the landscape by studying a single grain of sand at a time.

The network was *vast*, as broad and expansive as the universe itself. How could he ever hope to search it? How could he ever hope to find what he was looking for?

He paused, letting his presence drift. And that was when he felt it. A shadow fell over him. The presence blanketed him, compelling, controlling, demanding. But Coda resisted. He'd felt the Overlord's presence before, the way he had tried to subjugate him through violence and bonds of slavery.

Coda kept his distance. Somehow, he knew that if he ventured too close, the Overlord's power and influence would overwhelm him. Already, he was trying to bend Coda to his will. He fled, racing through the network as if it were a highway. The Overlord pursued. Coda was in his realm. There was nowhere to hide, and Coda wasn't fast enough. The

Overlord was gaining on him, his strength growing with every moment. Coda screamed, growing frantic.

He zigged, zagged, and turned as if piloting a Nighthawk, but it was to no avail. The Overlord couldn't be shaken. He was on Coda's tail and wasn't giving up.

Then as before, there was suddenly another presence. Where the Overlord was darkness, hatred, and subjugation, this was warmer, familiar, and caring. It raced toward Coda with purpose, extending itself as if extending a hand, and Coda went to it, reached for it, letting their two consciousnesses collide.

The network vanished.

Coda stood on a grassy plain. Straws of golden grass rose to his waist, their tips tickling the palms of his hands. It almost reminded Coda of wheat, but it was different in a way he couldn't place. The air was warm. A gentle breeze carried the scent of seawater. Waves crashed against a rocky shore in the distance. It could have been Earth, except for the purple sky. The entire image had a dreamlike quality to it, as if Coda were looking at it through a foggy glass.

"Callan?"

Coda started. He knew that voice, had heard it before, had grown up with it. He turned slowly, nervously.

A man stood in front of him. He was Coda's height but broader in the shoulders and thicker in the chest and midsection, and there was more gray in his dark hair than Coda remembered. But there was no mistaking him. No mistaking those brown eyes, nearly black, that square jaw, or the compassionate expression.

"It's okay. You're safe now."

"Dad?" Coda's voice came out soft.

The man smiled. Coda covered the ground between them in an instant. Collapsing into the man, Coda squeezed him, holding him as if he could disappear at any moment. His father squeezed him in return, slapping Coda's back with enough force to knock the wind out of him. But Coda didn't care. The pain made everything feel more real.

"How?" Coda said. "How is this possible? Where are we?"

"Shhh," his father said. He held Coda for several more moments, his tears wetting the side of Coda's face, before stepping back to appraise him. "You've grown."

Coda laughed, wiping tears from his own eyes. "I'm not the same kid you left behind."

"No, you're not. You've grown into a man. A fighter pilot, too, I see."

Coda looked down. He hadn't realized it before, but he was still dressed in his flight suit.

"You'll have to tell me how you convinced your mom to let you join. She hated me flying and the Nighthawks even more. She always said she wouldn't let you near one."

Coda felt a tinge of regret. His mother hadn't approved of him joining the Sol Fleet, and that had been when Coda was joining to become a drone pilot, not joining the experimental Nighthawk program. Things had only gotten worse since then. Best to leave that topic alone for now.

"I thought you were dead," Coda said. "That's what they said. For years, I thought you were gone."

"No, not dead. Gone might be a different story, though." He strode over to a large rock, took a seat, then patted a spot next to him. "Sit with your old man for a minute."

Coda obliged, sitting next to his father. The vantage had them overlooking the cliff, watching bioluminescent waves of blue, green, and purple crash against the white shore below. It was breathtaking, more beautiful than anything Coda had ever seen in his life.

"I still can't believe you're here," his father said.

"Where are we?" Coda said. "What is this place?"

For the second time in as many minutes, his father avoided the question. "I'm sorry, Callan. I haven't been there for you. I've missed so much. But my love for you has never stopped. You were my world. My everything. Still are. I need you to know that."

Coda nodded—it was all he could do. Talking would mean losing control. He had to keep his mouth shut to lock the emotion away. Not only because of the words and the strength behind them but because Coda hadn't always been so loyal. How many years had he been bitter? How long had he thought of his father as a villain instead of a victim?

Exhaling slowly, Coda turned to the man. He had an easy quality about him. Calm and confident with a natural swagger. A fighter jock, even to this day. He wasn't in a flight suit like Coda, though. Instead, he wore a simple shirt and pants.

"Tell me how to find you," Coda said. "I'm under Chadwick Coleman's command. He's always spoken highly of you. If you tell me where you are, we'll come for you. You don't have to hide anymore. We've discovered—"

"No. Not here. It's not safe."

Coda closed his mouth, surveying their surroundings with fresh eyes. They were alone, not a soul or other life-form in sight, but the space had the same dreamlike quality as before. Warm. Idyllic.

"This isn't real," Coda said. He'd somehow already known that. Of course it wasn't—it was too good to be true. His father couldn't be alive, let alone sitting beside him, telling him how much he loved him.

"It's real," his father said. "Just not in the way you mean it. We're in *his* domain."

"The Overlord."

"Is that what they're calling him?" his father asked.

"It's what I call him," Coda said.

"I guess that's as good as any description I've come up with."

"What is he?" Coda asked.

"Evil. A slave master. One over an entire race and more. He'll bring us under his power if we let him." His father let out a long breath. "But it's not safe to talk about that here, and we don't have much time."

"Why not?" Coda asked. Then before his father could answer, he added, "I need your help. I..." How could he say this without sharing too much? "I'm here because I was looking for something. But this place—this network or whatever it is—is too big. I don't know how to find what I'm looking for. But you obviously know more about this. Maybe you can find it. Maybe you could help us."

"Callan—"

But Coda wasn't listening. The plan was solidifying in his head. "We can prove what happened to you, but if you help us, there wouldn't be any doubt. Help us, Dad. Help *me*."

"Callan, *stop*."

Coda's pleas died on his tongue. He looked at his father in shocked resignation. Had he just refused to help him?

"I need you to listen and not say anything, okay? Just listen."

Coda nodded.

"When you were little, I took you to a baseball game. Just me and you, remember? And somehow, we got separated and I couldn't find you, remember?"

"Yeah, but, Dad—"

"No." His father shook his head. "No talking. I couldn't find you, and even to this day, that was the scariest moment of my life. An usher found you alone and crying. You were scared and hiding behind a garbage can."

Coda wanted to say something. He remembered the moment vividly. That sense of true terror, being surrounded by thousands in a gigantic world but feeling alone and not knowing what to do. What did that have to do with anything? Coda needed information, and his father was the only one who could help him find it.

"We've been separated again, Callan. But this time it's me who's missing. It's me who's hiding. Understand? It's me who's at the baseball stadium, hiding behind the garbage can." His father gave him a knowing look.

"I don't understand," Coda said.

"You will," his father said. "I'm hiding at the stadium."

"Dad—"

"Think on it, son." His father stood and gave him a warm smile. "Please."

Coda blinked, not understanding. He was growing frustrated. Why couldn't his father just say what he meant?

"Please, Callan."

"I will."

His father seemed to relax, his shoulders loosening. "Good. Now come here and give me a hug before you go."

"Go?"

"He's coming, Callan."

Panic spiked in Coda's chest again. With his father's warning, he could feel it now, that sense of foreboding. The Overlord's presence was growing stronger. He pushed it down, not letting the feeling spoil the precious moments he had left.

Coda stood and hugged his father tighter than before. For all he knew, this was the last time he would ever see him. The last time he would ever talk to him. His first, last, and only chance to say goodbye.

"I love you, Dad."

"I love you too, son. It was good to see you."

"It was good to see you too."

Then he whispered in Coda's ear, "Remember. I'm at the baseball stadium."

Coda tried to say he would. He tried to nod, but couldn't. The grip of emotion was too strong.

"*Remember.*"

# 40

*Sick Bay, SAS Redemption*
*Kryos*

Captain Coleman paced the medical ward. He'd been there with Dr. Naidoo and Dr. Rydell since the second battle of Kryos had ended. Their part had gone as well as he could have hoped. Much of the Baranyk force had already withdrawn from the planet, leaving a single carrier in reserve as they had at previous abandoned systems. His squadrons had engaged, and they'd detected the signal. Coda had once again fallen under the influence of the enemy.

Though unlike before, the threat had been neutralized. Without missiles or cannons, Coda was toothless. Not harmless exactly, but a lion without claws. Shortly after they'd engaged and before the *Redemption* and the Forgotten could inflict too much damage, the enemy had bugged out. With it, Coda's fighter had gone lifeless, making no maneuvers whatsoever.

They'd found him unconscious, and though he showed no signs of being under Baranyk influence, he displayed heightened brain activity reminiscent of before. Something was happening, and his doctors couldn't explain it.

*Come on, Coda. Pull through. Whatever's going on, fight like hell. We need the information in your head.*

"Captain!" Dr. Rydell said.

Coleman's back was to her, his steps having taken him close to the door. He spun. Coda was strapped to the gurney—they were still taking precautions—and sensors of all kinds were stuck to his temples, forehead, and exposed chest. The monitors surrounding him gave readouts of his heart rate, oxygen levels, blood pressure, and brain activity. The scan showing his brain, which had been a wild array of colors before, had gone still. Not devoid of activity, which would obviously be a bad sign, but it had changed.

Coleman strode toward Coda, stopping at Dr. Rydell's shoulder, watching from beside the bed. Coda's fingers moved first, then his legs. His head rocked back and forth sluggishly. Then his lips parted, and he took a long, deep breath.

"Easy, Commander," Dr. Rydell said. "Take it slow."

Coda showed no signs that he'd heard the doctor. His eyes opened slowly. They were clouded, pupils constricting against the light slowly as if he were drugged.

"Can you hear me? It's Dr. Rydell. I'm right here, Coda. Can you hear me?"

Coda gave her the slightest of nods.

"Good," she said. "You're doing good. Just take it slow."

Coleman waited impatiently. Coda hadn't taken this long to come out of the trance before.

Coda was blinking now, growing more alert by the second. He tried to move, pushing against the straps, then groaned as they held him in place.

"Coda, it's Captain Coleman. Can you hear me?"

Coda groaned again, but it was different this time. Coleman took it as an affirmative.

"Good. You're tied down, Coda. For our protection. Nod if you understand."

Coda nodded. "It's okay," he said, his voice barely a whisper. "It's me." Then again, stronger, "It's me."

"Undo his binds," Coleman said.

Dr. Rydell didn't protest; they'd been through this before. And maybe it was his lethargic state or lack of Baranyk-induced brain activity, but Coda didn't appear to be a threat. Dr. Rydell undid the binds then helped Coda sit up.

"Welcome back," Coleman said.

"Thank you, sir." Coda grimaced, shifting on the bed. "How long was I out?"

"Nearly sixteen hours. You're safe now." Coleman wanted to say more, to question his pilot and pull everything he could from him, but he knew that would only overwhelm him. They needed to take it slow. "You look like hell, Commander."

Coda gave him a half-hearted chuckle, but the expression faded quickly.

"What is it, Coda? What's wrong?"

"I failed, sir," Coda said, his eyes falling from Coleman's. "I connected to the Baranyk network, but... I failed. I couldn't find what we were looking for."

Coleman drew his lips into a line, refusing to believe it. "Listen to the doc, Coda. Take it slow. I'm sure you'll remember more as you come around."

"No," Coda said. His voice was forceful, erasing any doubt. "It was too big. Too many connections. I can't explain it, sir, but I couldn't do it."

Coleman remained expressionless. He was already running through the series of other options he'd come up with, trying to decide on their next move.

"I couldn't do it," Coda repeated. "But I know who can."

Coleman's attention snapped back to his pilot. "What did you say, Commander?"

"I said I know who can." Coda smiled. "I saw him, sir. He's alive. He helped me. The Overlord was pursuing me, and I don't know what would have happened if he caught me, but my father was there. He... I don't know what he did. He took me somewhere safe. Somewhere we could talk."

Coleman hesitated. If it had been any other pilot at any other time, he would have dismissed the idea, chalked it up to battle fatigue or some such. But Coda was dependable. Trustworthy. His CAG. This was a thread, and the conviction in Coda's expression told him they needed to pull on it.

"Tell me what happened," Coleman said. "Start at the beginning."

Coda paused, seemingly collecting his thoughts, then began his report. Coleman listened, never interrupting, letting his pilot explain the unexplainable in the only way he knew how. Coleman didn't understand half of it and struggled to believe the other, but Coda was so *sure*.

"He wouldn't tell me where he was," Coda said. "He said we were in *his* domain, and I think he was worried about being overheard, like he was worried about being found."

"By the Overlord?" Coleman clarified.

"Yes," Coda said. "He said he was evil, a Baranyk that had enslaved an entire species and more. That he would bring us under his power if we let him." He looked up, eyes going wide. "Sir, he was right. Before my encounter with my father, I came across other presences. They weren't human or Baranyk, something different, other alien life-forms."

"What else did he say?" Coleman asked, trying to steer the conversation back. Fleet Intelligence had long assumed there was other intelligent life in the galaxy, and while the information was potentially groundbreaking, it wasn't entirely pertinent to their mission.

"He's building an empire," Coda said. "Expanding his influence across the galaxy. How do we defeat that, sir? How do we defeat not one alien race but several?"

"That's a problem for another day, Commander. Tell me why you think your father can help us."

Coda looked at Coleman, suddenly aware he'd gone off on a tangent. "He knows how to navigate the network. He found me and created somewhere we could talk. Somewhere safe from the Overlord, at least temporarily. I'm sure he can find other things. Maybe I'm wrong, but he's our best chance. And..."

Coda didn't need to finish the thought. Coleman could see the want clearly on his face. For as long as Coleman had known Joseph O'Neil's son, the young man had been driven by a desire to restore honor to his family. He'd done that above Toavis, but this was an opportunity to vindicate the man entirely.

*No, it's more than that. This is about reuniting father and son and rebuilding a family.*

Coleman's thoughts drifted to his own broken family, of the daughter he hadn't spoken fifty words to since she'd been assigned to his ship, and felt a sudden longing. He'd let fear control him, let shame hold him back, and used the excuse of duty to justify it.

"It's a good idea, Coda. But there's a problem. We don't know how to find him. As I told you before, your father disappeared. We searched but never found him. Not even a trace. What makes you think it'll be any different this time?"

"This time, he wants to be found," Coda said. "Just before I left, he told me a story about when I was a kid. He took me to a baseball game, and we got separated. I got scared and hid. He told me he's the one hiding now. He told me he was at the stadium."

"At the stadium?"

"Yeah."

"He's on Earth?" Coleman didn't believe it, and Coda clearly didn't either.

"No. It doesn't make any sense, but it was important to him that I remember."

"What was the name of the stadium?" Coleman asked.

"I don't know," Coda said. "I was too young. I don't even remember the name of the team. The Plymouth… something. They were a—"

"What did you say?" A chill went down Coleman's spine. "Did you say *Plymouth*?"

"Yeah, why?"

"Coda, one of the planets within jump range of your father's Nighthawk was New Plymouth."

Coda's eyes went wide.

"He didn't want to tell you because he couldn't risk the Overlord coming for him, but he gave you a clue that only you could use to find him."

"Oh my god." Coda ran a hand across his head. "What do we do now, sir?"

"We're going to New Plymouth, Coda. If you're right, your father will be expecting us. And if we're lucky, he can get us the information we need before it's too late."

# 41

*Brig, SAS Redemption*
*Kryos*

Despite the captain's excitement and mutual desire to find Coda's father, there was still planning to be done. So Coda was sent back to his cell. It was an odd contradiction: having the captain's complete trust, sharing a secret only the two of them were in on, and being viewed as a villain by the rest of the crew.

Fortunately, appearances only had to go so far. This time, the captain had sent Coda his tablet. The captain needed his report, but after completing it, he was free to do as he wished.

Coda spent the time researching New Plymouth. From the satellite images, it was a beautiful planet. If Kryos represented the worst of Earth, then New Plymouth was the best of their biological home.

As green as polished emerald, New Plymouth had four major continents, all located within ten degrees of the equator and covered in mountainous ranges, deep valleys, and expansive plains. Deep-blue seas surrounded them, with small ice caps at the poles. With a thick atmosphere, New Plymouth was warmer than Earth, closer in climate to Central America and just as fertile. Its biggest downside was that it was located on the edge of human-controlled space and lacked the rich metal deposits of other planets to make it a strategic resource.

Instead, its rich soil and multiple water sources made it an ideal farming planet, where the homesteaders grew genetically modified wheat and other staples. It was home to people craving a simpler life that harkened back to an earlier time. The promise of their piece of land in the galaxy beckoned to them as the modern version of forty acres and a mule. It was, on the surface, a perfect spot for a deserter to hide.

Eventually, Coda shut off the tablet and tried to sleep. It was a fitful rest full of incomplete dream fragments as his unconscious mind stored and categorized recent memories. When he woke, he felt worse than before and was about to attempt to return to sleep when he noticed the dimmed lights and yellow lighting. The amber alert meant a jump was imminent.

How many had Captain Coleman said it would take to get to New Plymouth? Coda didn't know how many of those he'd slept through already, but the result was the same. With every thirty-minute interval, the time it took to spool the EmDrive back up and plot their next jump, Coda was getting closer to his father.

---

CAPTAIN COLEMAN LET GO OF THE RAILING AS THE WORLD SNAPPED BACK into focus. He stood on the bridge, letting the sound of his tactical and communications chatter wash over him.

"Jump twenty-eight complete, sir." Lieutenant Poiu said. "Beginning the final jump sequence now."

"Good," Captain Coleman said.

Twenty-eight jumps. That was more than he'd taken in his last year, and had it been any other ship in the fleet, they would have been forced to take an eight-hour break after ten, but with the *Redemption*'s upgraded EmDrive, they'd been able to push through. Even with the improved spooling time, it had taken them just over fourteen hours to make it this far—a relatively short distance by galactic standards.

"You've got the bridge, Commander," Coleman said to his XO. "I'm headed to the flight deck."

"Yes, sir. Good luck."

His bridge crew saluted him as he walked out. Instead of heading to the flight deck, however, he made for the brig. It was located in the bowels of the ship, and Coleman arrived less than five minutes later. He found Coda sitting on the edge of his bed, scanning through something on his tablet. He looked up as Coleman strode in, jumping to his feet and offering a quick salute.

"At ease." Captain Coleman palmed the cell door, overriding its lock command. It popped open, and Coleman held it wide. "It's time to go."

Coleman led Coda out of the brig and down several decks to the Forgotten's Ready Room. From there, they entered the adjoining locker room, where they put on their flight suits. All told, from the time he'd left the bridge to the time he and Coda set foot on the flight deck, no more than twenty minutes had passed.

Sergeant Haniger waited with his squad of marines, standing in a crisp line in front of the dropship. Coleman may not have been expecting a fight, but that didn't mean he wasn't going in prepared for one. They snapped to attention as he neared.

"At ease," Coleman said. "Your men ready to go?"

"Yes, sir," Sergeant Haniger said. "Ready to rock and roll."

"Good," Coleman said. "Strap in. We jump in five."

"You heard the captain!" Haniger bellowed. "Load up!"

The dropship, nicknamed the Stork by those it carried, was more elegant than Coda had originally imagined. With long wings, a broad fuselage meant to carry up to twenty-five passengers, and a large tail, it couldn't have been farther away from the bird it was named after, but the fleet's nicknames had never made much sense.

Captain Coleman and Coda made their way past the marines through the belly of the ship to the cockpit, where they strapped in. Coleman took the pilot's chair. He powered up the ship, closed the rear hatch, went through a quick flight check, and began pressurizing the ship. With all systems go, he radioed Commander Garcia.

"I'm strapped in and green for flight," Coleman said.

"Yes, sir," Garcia said. "Have I told you that I don't agree with you going down there? Not after what happened on Koburn."

"Only about a dozen times," Coleman said.

"Let's make it a baker's dozen then," Garcia said.

Coleman laughed, shooting Coda a glance. He'd intentionally

communicated through the radio instead of the implant in his ear, choosing to keep Coda in the conversation.

"It'll be fine," Coleman said.

"You still haven't told me what to expect down there," Garcia said.

"I will."

"You know, sir, I expected the XO would be included in making more decisions."

"Noted, Commander," Coleman said. "Chalk it up to growing pains on my end. I'll do better at including you in the future." The conversation was taking a turn, and Coleman was suddenly regretting the decision to use the ship's radio. Fortunately, Coda didn't seem to be paying any attention.

"Thank you, sir," Garcia said. "Setting amber alert throughout the ship. Jump in thirty seconds. Good luck down there, sir."

"You too, Commander."

The lights of the flight deck suddenly dimmed, turning amber. At the same time, the interior compression doors began to close, isolating the Stork on a deck that would shortly be an unpressurized chamber. Unlike the Nighthawks, the Stork wouldn't be hurled into space. It took off directly from the unpressurized area of the flight deck.

Ten seconds after the compression doors closed, the ship jumped. Shortly after the world returned to focus, the exterior blast doors opened, and Coleman piloted the Stork from the *Redemption*.

They'd jumped directly into orbit of New Plymouth. The beautiful emerald planet shone brightly below. Sensor data sent directly to the *Redemption* was immediately patched through to the Stork's onboard computer. There were several settlements on New Plymouth, each with a few thousand residents. Unlike the mining and manufacturing operations on other planets, farming, it seemed, didn't require as many people.

"There," Coda said, pointing to an installation near the coast of the western continent.

"Why there?" Coleman asked, already plotting his course. They had nothing more to go on other than a vague hint from an impossible vision, but it was as good a place as any to start. If anything, it would give them a logical starting point, allowing them to work north to south, west to east from there.

"It was always my father's dream to live on the beach," Coda said. "And that's where we were during our conversation."

The Stork bucked as they entered atmo, its outer hull glowing orange from the heat and friction. The ship may not have looked like its namesake, but it was a tough bird and got them through without incident. White clouds gave way to a green-and-blue expanse. The mountains were several hundred kilometers to the north and east. Coleman flew low, gliding across the land.

The installation was located several miles inland, but there was a single structure on the coastline. Coleman didn't need Coda to tell him where to go—he made directly for that residence. It was a small dome-like structure, one of the prefabricated units supplied to the planet's inhabitants. It would be short on amenities but wired and plumbed, ready to hook up to the local infrastructure. There were worse ways to begin a new life.

Coleman circled the establishment, looking for signs of life. There were none, but his sensors were picking up multiple signals and heat signatures. Something was down there. He brought the Stork down in a flat area a couple hundred meters from the structure, deployed the rear ramp, and shut down the engines.

Sergeant Haniger's marines were out a moment later, securing the landing site. Coda took an exaggerated breath as he unbuckled and removed his helmet. His eyes were wide and alert; he was nervous with anticipation. Coleman motioned for Coda to go ahead of him, then followed the younger pilot through the ship and down the ramp.

The wind gusted as they set foot on the soft ground, smelling of brine and seaweed, though with a sweeter scent than Earth. The thin, waist-high grass swayed in the wind, making a swishing sound like soft static. Coda seemed to notice none of it, however. His eyes were focused solely on the structure ahead and the man who stood outside it.

He was bigger than Coleman remembered. His once-chiseled frame had gone soft since it no longer had to deal with the rigors of spaceflight. His hair was longer and tinged with gray, and his face, lined with age like Coleman's, was covered in a shaggy beard. But that smile, the way it rose higher on one side of his face like a cocky grin, was the same. He was staring at his old friend.

*Coda was right.*

"Stand down," Coleman said to Sergeant Haniger. "There's no danger here."

Sergeant Haniger ordered his marines back, leaving him, Coda, and Joseph O'Neil alone on the cliffside. Coda moved first, something between a walk and a bound, and his father moved to join him. Coleman kept his distance, giving father and son their moment.

Joseph and Coda came together in a crash, a gesture punctuated by the sound of cresting waves below. It was a long, fierce hug. Joseph squeezed his son's flight suit as if afraid to let go, then slapped him on the back, hard enough Coleman could hear from ten meters away. Their laughter mixed with cries, their joy overcoming years of pain. They reveled in seeing and holding each other again, regretting the years they hadn't. Their happiness was the kind only possible after years of tremendous pain.

This was what Coleman had wanted to share with Aniyah, but he had screwed that up. Instead of a warm embrace and making up for lost time and lost hugs, instead of holding on like he would never let go again, instead of even calling her by her name, he'd hidden behind decorum. Frustrated with himself, he was still happy for Coda and Joseph. After everything they'd been through, they deserved this moment.

When their embrace ended, Joseph laughed, wiping tears from his eyes, and Coleman moved to join them.

"You look different," Coda said.

"Fatter, you mean," Joseph said, his smile bigger than Coleman had ever seen.

"And this wasn't there before." Coda rubbed his own chin, stroking an imaginary beard.

"Yeah," Joseph said, "well, when you don't have to keep it short for regs or have to worry about it itching under your flight helmet, you have a little more freedom."

"I mean it wasn't in the vision, or whatever that was."

"Ah, I see. No, it wasn't. I'll explain later." Joseph's eyes fell on Chadwick, his smile faltering a little.

The lack of reciprocated happiness surprised Coleman. He hadn't expected the same kind of reunion as Coda, but he hadn't expected hostility, either.

"Hey, Joe," Coleman said.

"Chadwick." Joseph looked over Coleman's shoulder at the Stork behind him and the marines standing guard.

*He's wondering if I'm here to arrest him.*

"Don't worry about them," Coleman said, nodding toward the dropship. "They're here for my protection. Last time I went planetside, I nearly became lunch for some angry Baranyk. It's good to see you, old friend." He offered his hand.

Joseph eyed it, then his smile returned. He took Coleman's hand in his, giving it a firm shake. "It's good to see you too. Come on. Let's go inside."

He pulled Coleman in his direction and slapped him on the shoulder as he passed. With Coleman leading the way, Joseph wrapped an arm around his son as they walked toward the small home.

"We have a lot to talk about."

# 42

*House, New Plymouth*
*Surface*

His father's house was small and utilitarian. Like many things throughout humanity's colonies, the single-room residence was a templated design, likely printed through additive manufacturing and assembled onsite. The dull-gray walls were unadorned, and aside from the bed, it housed a kitchenette, space for two chairs, and a private bathroom. Coda's quarters at the Terran Fleet Academy had almost been more accommodating.

Coda and Captain Coleman took a seat in the chairs, while his father sat on the edge of the bed.

"I still can't believe you're here," his father said. "I couldn't tell if you'd understood the hint."

"I almost didn't," Coda said. "Why couldn't you just tell me where you were?"

His father started to reply but stopped short when Captain Coleman cleared his throat. "We'll get to that," he said instead. "Right now, I think we have other ground to cover first. What's on your mind, Chadwick?"

"We don't have a lot of time," Captain Coleman said. "If we start in the middle, we'll miss something. Start at the beginning. We have our theories about what happened on that first mission at Kryos, but I need to hear it from you. What happened? Why'd you run? And how the hell have you stayed hidden this long?"

His father's happy playfulness disappeared, replaced by a haunted expression as he recounted his story. It had been years, but he still remembered it like yesterday, and all told, it wasn't that different from Coda's own story. The ships and people were different, and so was the mission, but the way he'd lost all control and become a bystander in his own body was all too familiar.

Though where Coda had explained it as being a drone, his father compared the experience to being a marionette. His actions were controlled by someone else, directing him with invisible strings. The worst part was that it was only a physical experience.

"I knew nobody would ever believe me," his father continued. "That was made clear when the *Franklin* launched its missiles. I panicked. By then, I had regained control, and I had two choices. I could die there, forever known as a traitor, or flee. I didn't know what the second choice held, and had I known, I might have chosen death. But in that moment, I wasn't ready to go. So I ran."

The story twisted Coda's insides. He understood the guilt all too well. He may not have been in control, but it had still been his hand that had killed his friends and wingmen. He could *feel* it, and try as he might, he could never forget that.

He wanted to tell his father that he understood, to give his father the comfort he so desperately wanted himself, but Captain Coleman was his commanding officer and in control of the conversation.

"So you ran," Captain Coleman repeated. "Here."

"Yes," his father said. "Sort of. I didn't have a plan and had no idea where I was going. I just knew I had to get away. But after a couple jumps, I slowed down and started to think it through, and I went as far away as I could manage. I barely made it here before my oxygen ran out, but when I did, I ditched my fighter and laid low."

"We searched for you here, you know," Captain Coleman said. "Swept the whole planet with every sort of sweep you could imagine, including visual. There was no trace of you."

"I destroyed the transponder and other sensors," his father said with a shrug. "They taught us how to do a lot more than that during FAM Phase."

Coda found himself smiling. His own experience in FAM Phase hadn't been so helpful, but the idea of his father using it to best the fleet was amusing.

"What about the locals?" Captain Coleman pressed. "The population here isn't big enough to assimilate unseen, and everyone would be part of the manifest."

"The people here are different, Chadwick. There's a strong live-and-let-live streak. If you show up, work hard, and keep your mouth shut, they don't ask many questions. And they sure as hell weren't going to give me up."

"And you've been here the whole time?" Coda asked, finally rejoining the conversation.

"Yes. Life here is hard, nothing but early mornings, long days, and no vacations, but there are worse ways to live. No, my days aren't what haunt me. It's what I missed while I've been here."

He gave Coda a pained expression. "That's my story. Now I need some answers of my own. Why'd you come for me after all of these years, and why was my son a part of the Baranyk network?"

"For that," Captain Coleman said, "we need to back up too."

Captain Coleman proceeded to explain how the Baranyk war had changed, the fleet turning to drone fighters instead of human-piloted Nighthawks and how that had left them vulnerable when the enemy developed a new weapon that jammed the signal. Desperate, the fleet had recruited a number of pilots to assemble an experimental squadron and had Captain Coleman instruct them.

He explained how the enemy had pulled back and that they'd been ordered to investigate where they had pulled back to and why. He left nothing out, telling Coda's father about the survivor on Koburn, Coda's own experience, and the discovery of the signal. Captain Coleman stressed the latter part—how it was evidence that what had happened to him was nothing more than another enemy attack. But his father wasn't listening. His eyes were back on Coda. And they looked angry.

"They did it to you too?" his father asked.

"Yeah," Coda said.

"That bastard." His father ground his teeth, his hands squeezing into fists. "I'm going to kill that son of a bitch! He's taken everything from me, and now he's taking it from you too."

His father's anger scared Coda. It was hot and unbridled, the raw kind of emotion that was real and burdened with personal experience. He'd never seen this side of his father before, but he'd seen it in himself. He'd felt that anger too often and had lost control of it a great number of times.

"It's okay," Coda found himself saying.

"It's not okay, Callan. You don't know what he is. What he's capable of."

"That's why we're here," Captain Coleman said. "We need your help. Our mission was to determine where the Baranyk are retreating to and why. Recent events have uncovered a greater threat. If the enemy can control us as they did you and Coda, how many more have been used? How many other *accidents* have there been? How many are still under enemy influence?"

Coda's father was shaking his head now. "It doesn't work that way. The Baranyk are all part of a collective network, some kind of hive consciousness. From what I can tell, it's how they communicate. But one in particular, the one you call the Overlord, can control other creatures within the network. They're like hands and arms to him. Billions of hands and arms, billions of fingers. But we're different. I don't know what it is. Maybe its humanity's strong sense of individualism or something. But he can only control us one at a time. When he's done, we regain control, but part of us remains connected to the hive."

"That still doesn't answer the question of how many other people have been used," Captain Coleman pressed. "Our research suggests only a small percentage of humans are vulnerable to the Baranyk signal, but even a small percentage across billions can add up to a catastrophic liability."

"What makes us vulnerable?" his father asked.

"Some sort of brain abnormality," Captain Coleman said. "Dr. Naidoo can explain it better than I can when we get back to the ship."

Captain Coleman spoke as if his father's return to the fleet was a foregone conclusion, but Coda could see in his father's body language that it was anything but. Even with his anger subsided a bit, Coda could see his discomfort. His antsy gestures, the way he never stopped moving, his leg bouncing up and down, the way he was wringing his hands.

This was a man who'd been hiding for a decade. He'd been used, chewed up, and spit out, and now his son and old friend were at his doorstep, asking him to return to the grinder. Whatever man he'd been before, the sense of duty he'd harbored had disappeared when the enemy turned him into a puppet, had died when his own fired on him.

"Hey," Coda said, keeping his voice firm and reassuring. "You never told me why you couldn't just tell me where you were." He hoped the subject was something his father would know better and be less threatening.

"Because he's looking for me, Callan. We were in his domain, and he was already in pursuit. If I'd told you, I might have led him directly to me."

"Why is he looking for you, though? You're just one man on a distant planet."

"One man on a distant planet who can access the Baranyk consciousness. Who can... control it in a way." He nodded toward Captain Coleman. "You're worried about Baranyk spies. Well, so is he."

"So you're hiding," Coda said. "Not just from the fleet but from the enemy as well."

"Yes."

"This is your opportunity to change that."

Coda's father looked at him. Coda saw fear, not just of repercussions but of leaving a life he'd lived for the past decade. Whether it was the life he would have chosen to live was irrelevant; it was the life he knew. Leaving meant change. It meant facing his past. Maybe even accepting punishment. Regardless of what Coda and Captain Coleman thought, it wasn't a simple request.

"Mom hates that I joined up," Coda said. "She told me that following in your footsteps was the biggest betrayal she could ever imagine and that the day I left would be the day she mourned my death. And she's pretty much kept her word. She didn't send me off or attend my graduation, and the only letter I've got from her only reinforced her stance. As far as she knows, she's lost two men to the war."

"Callan..."

"But what she's never been able to understand is that I didn't sign up for myself. I did it for her. I did it for *you*. I didn't know the truth, so I've been trying to undo the damage you did to our name. I've even succeeded a little. But the only person who can truly do that is you. I know you feel responsible for what happened. I know you can still feel your finger on that trigger. Still hear your wingmen screaming at you, their last moments believing they were betrayed by one they trusted. Still see the explosions, each one another sign of a life you've taken. I know you experience all of that, because I do too. But this is our chance to tell the world the truth. This is our chance to clear *our* name. So I'm asking you to come with us. Help us. Help *me*."

There were tears in his father's eyes, and Coda knew that he'd gotten through to him.

"What do you need me to do?"

"Captain?" Coda asked.

"Coda accessed the network himself, looking for information about the Baranyk fleet, but couldn't find anything. He wasn't proficient enough in navigating it. But you are."

"You said it yourself," Coda said. "The Overlord is afraid of you. Afraid of what you're capable of. Well, prove him right. Show him that he *should* be afraid of you."

"Help us find the Baranyk fleet," Captain Coleman added.

"I don't have to fly again?"

It took Coda a moment to process the words. His father wasn't just afraid of leaving his life behind or of returning to the fleet. He was terrified of being back in the cockpit.

"No," Captain Coleman said. "Just access the Baranyk network and help us find answers."

"Okay."

"Okay?"

"I can do that," his father said.

"Good." Captain Coleman rose to his feet. "Take a moment and grab your belongings. We're up against the clock with this one."

"I don't have anything to take," his father said. "The only belonging I care about is right here."

He pulled a faded picture from his pocket. The edges were rough, and one corner had been ripped away, but Coda recognized it instantly. He'd seen it on his father's cockpit display dozens of times and knew that he'd kept it there every time he went out. It was a picture of the three of them together, taken by a stranger while they'd been on a hike. The last picture taken of their family before his father's disappearance.

"It's the only thing I have from before."

"Let's fix tha—" Captain Coleman froze, his words dying on his lips. He raised a hand to his ear, obviously getting a communication in his earpiece. "Repeat!"

Coda watched the captain intently.

"We're on our way." Captain Coleman dropped his hand from his ear, eyes hard. The captain was back. "Three Baranyk carriers just jumped into the system and are inbound. I don't know how, but I think we just led the enemy directly to your doorstep."

# 43

*New Plymouth*
*Surface*

THEY DOUBLED-TIMED IT BACK TO THE SHUTTLE, COLEMAN IN THE LEAD, Coda and his father close behind. The marines inside the shuttle saw them coming and fanned out, guns raised, expecting an ambush.

"Stand down," Coleman said as he neared. "The enemy's out there, but inbound. Strap in and prepare for takeoff."

Coleman strode through the belly of the ship and into the cockpit and settled behind the controls. His hand raced across them, initiating the prelaunch sequence, closing the hatch, pressurizing the cabin, and starting the engines. The shipboard computer synced with the *Redemption*'s, giving him his first view of the incoming enemy.

As Lieutenant Poiu had said, three Baranyk carriers were inbound. They'd already launched fighters, and judging by the number of enemy icons on the display, they'd launched *every* available one.

Coda fell into the copilot's chair beside Captain Coleman and began putting on his flight helmet. Coleman hesitated, watching him. The other pilot was still susceptible to the enemy weapon, and he couldn't risk Coda losing control again. Not here.

"Sorry, Coda," Coleman said. "I'll take this one."

Coda seemed to understand and returned to the cabin, where he strapped in to one of the harnesses that lined the sides of the fuselage. Coleman knew that wouldn't be enough. He grabbed two pairs of restraints from a central compartment and found Coda and his father in the cabin. Coda looked at the restraints then at Coleman.

"It's for everyone's protection," Coleman said.

"I understand," Coda said, resigned, then held out his hands.

Coleman quickly bound them and turned to Joseph, who sat on the other side of the cabin. He didn't look as comfortable as Coda.

"I'm sorry, Joseph, but we can't take the risk."

Joseph wavered. He was a wanted man; the fleet would likely execute him on the spot if they got the chance. Allowing himself to be bound was akin to turning himself in, which wasn't something he was prepared to do.

"It's only temporary," Coleman added.

Joseph finally relented, holding out his hands. With both potential risks mitigated, Coleman returned to the cockpit, strapped in, and prepared for takeoff.

"Lieutenant Poiu," he said, channeling the *Redemption*'s command frequency. "We're on our way. Rendezvous in thirteen minutes."

"Copy that," Lieutenant Poiu said. "The enemy's launched fighters. Our squadrons are preparing to engage, and I've sent an escort your way. Good luck, sir."

"Thank you, Lieutenant."

Coleman increased thrust and brought the belly of the ship off the ground, angling the engines to increase altitude. As the dropship climbed, Coleman took another look at the battle map. His escort was en route, only forty seconds out, while the rest of the force—marked by an overwhelming number of red indicators—was still inbound. Damn, there were a lot of birds out there.

The ship rocked against the coastal wind, gaining altitude. Moments later, two Nighthawks broke through the clouds above, shot past the dropship, then circled around and formed up on each of the Stork's wings.

"Good to see you, Captain," Lieutenant Little said. He was one of the newer members of the Forgotten, having joined the squadron after his recent graduation. "Let's see if we can get you back to the ship in one piece, shall we?"

"Sounds good, Tiny," Coleman said.

The other pilot remained quiet, and together, the three ships entered the clouds. Losing visual, Coleman's eyes drifted back to the display. His fighters engaged the incoming enemy, who... didn't engage back. The enemy slipped past the human squadrons, maintaining course, heading straight for the planet.

A cold sense of dread formed in Coleman's gut. The tactic was little more than a suicide run. The enemy left their flank open, something the Forgotten were already making them pay for, but greatly outnumbering the human force as they did, it wouldn't matter.

"Lieutenant," Coleman said, channeling Tiny's fighter. "Are you seeing what I'm seeing?"

"Yes, sir. The enemy is slipping through our defenses."

"And if I'm not mistaken, headed straight toward our ship."

There was silence on the other end, followed by a soft curse.

"What do we do, sir?"

Coleman studied the display. Their trajectory had them flying toward the *Redemption*, but it also had them closing the distance with the enemy. Meanwhile, the inbound fighters, exposed as they were, took on heavy losses.

"What's our ETA with the *Redemption* compared to the ETA of the enemy fighters?"

"Looks like... shit. ETA with the *Redemption* is four minutes *after* the enemy fighters enter firing range."

"Okay," Coleman said. "Here's what we're going to do. The *Redemption* is in geosynchronous orbit roughly above our position. I'll have her plot a new rendezvous point to this region here." He sent the coordinates to Tiny's fighter. "That should buy us some time and give our fighters a chance to inflict more damage. With any luck, it'll force the enemy to engage."

"I like it, sir."

"Okay, plot a new course and break on my mark." Coleman channeled his radio to the *Redemption*'s frequency. "Commander Garcia, we need more time. I'm sending you coordinates now. Bring the *Redemption* around to a new rendezvous point."

"Yes, sir," Commander Garcia said. "Coordinates received. Plotting a course now."

Coleman channeled back to Tiny. "All right, Tiny. Here we go. Follow my lead."

Coleman pulled the joystick back and angled it toward his inner left thigh, bringing the dropship around to port. It bounced and swayed under the strain, sending his stomach into his throat. God, he hated flying in atmo. It was a completely different sensation than flying in the black.

On Coleman's display, the *Redemption* started to move. The Stork's tactical display wasn't as sophisticated as the Nighthawk's, but Coleman could imagine the two trajectories moving to a single intercept point—solid lines showing where they'd traveled, dotted lines showing the space to cover.

"Tiny," Coleman said, "what's the updated ETA?"

"Calculating, sir." It took a moment for Tiny to come back. "It's going to be close, but I think that did it."

"Good," Coleman said, the cold sense of dread melting slightly. Every moment, more and more of the enemy fighters were shot down. At some point, the Nighthawks would inflict too much damage, and the Baranyk would have to engage. This was going to work. It had to work.

"Sir!"

Coleman saw it the moment the urgent voice came over the radio. The incoming fighters had altered tactics. The bulk of them flipped to engage the Nighthawks, while the remaining force, little more than a dozen fighters, continued pursuit, somehow increasing thrust.

*That shouldn't be possible!*

"I'm reading increased heat and radiation signatures," Tiny said. "They're overloading their engines, sir."

Coleman didn't need to have Tiny recalculate the rendezvous. If it had been tight before, then they weren't going to make it now. The only question was how long could the overworked Baranyk propulsion systems withstand the added stress?

"New plan," Coleman said. "Drop back fifty meters and stay on me."

"Roger."

Coleman dove. The ship shook as it cut through the clouds, angling back toward the surface. The Stork wasn't designed for high-G maneuvers like this, and it groaned under the stress. It could withstand them if necessary, but it was going to let him know it didn't like it.

He kept the ship on a course that took them away from the incoming fighters. His only hope was that their overloaded engines would give out first or at least that their numbers would be decimated enough that his escort could engage and be victorious.

They fell toward the planet's surface in a steep dive that was damn near free fall, thousands of feet per second. Supplies rattled in the cabin behind him, and he thought he heard someone throw up. At ten thousand meters, he pulled back on the stick gently, beginning to level out. The ship shook violently, screaming and grinding. An alert sounded, ringing loudly, accompanied by flashing red lights. Like the incoming enemy, he was pushing the limits of his ship.

"Come on!" Coleman said, urging his ship on, still pulling back on the stick. "Come on!"

The ship leveled out, and the shaking subsided as it skimmed the surface at a thousand meters. Ten fighters were still inbound and—

They fired.

Blue plasma fire reminiscent of arcs of lightning streaked past his ship. At the enemy's range, it was a lucky shot to even be so close, but it was too close for comfort. The escort didn't wait for a command. They broke formation, turning to engage the enemy. Four fighters broke with them, engaging and leaving the rest in pursuit.

Coleman cursed. They weren't going to make it. He scanned the countryside, looking for something, anything, that could buy them time. They were nearing one of the large farming installations, but a few hundred kilometers beyond it was a canyon. His hand tightened on the stick as he envisioned a canyon run. He just needed time. Only time.

Unfortunately, time was the one thing he didn't have. A second blast arced past the cockpit, this one dangerously close. He tried to take evasive maneuvers, but the Stork was too bulky. And the enemy outnumbered him.

The next blast took the starboard wing. The explosion rocked the ship, shrapnel shattering the cockpit window. The ship lurched and spun, diving toward the surface. Coleman screamed as wind buffeted him and the ground raced up to meet them.

For the first time in his life, he'd been shot down outside the simulator. In the deepest parts of his brain, he'd always known it would happen. Death came for all fighter pilots who flew long enough.

# 44

*New Plymouth*
*Surface*

THE BLISTERING HEAT BROUGHT CODA AROUND. HIS EYES OPENED sluggishly, his thoughts coming even more slowly, taking precious moments to realize the fire nearby was burning him. Searing pain lanced down his face and neck as he fumbled with his straps. Several agonizing seconds went by before he realized his problem—he was still bound.

Coda groaned, taking in his surroundings, looking for someone who could help. The dropship was destroyed. Terrible rents in the bulkhead offered a glimpse of the surrounding landscape. Guns, ammunition, and other supplies littered the cabin and were strewn outside like a trail of history, showing the direction they had come from.

Many of the other occupants were still strapped in. Others littered the ground like the cast-about supplies, while more, still held by their harnesses, bore multiple shrapnel wounds. The marine nearest him had been sliced clean through, his upper half ending abruptly at his waist, dripping blood onto the deck. His legs were nowhere to be seen. The smell of burnt plastic, blood, and viscera hung thick in the air.

The sights barely registered with Coda, though. The pain was too great, demanding all of his attention.

"Help," he croaked. Then he managed, more loudly, "Help!"

Nobody moved.

"Help!" Coda tried again. "I can't move!" He was growing more alert with every passing second, the agony increasing with it. He could *feel* his skin bubbling and blistering. "Please! I'm stuck!"

This time, he thought he heard something from the front of the ship. The cockpit was in ruins, the front windshield was shattered, and the navigational display was shooting sparks. Remarkably, a figured appeared. Blood dripped from his head, the crimson a stark contrast against his dark skin, and he held a hand to his side, where another wound was bleeding through.

"Sir!" Coda shouted. He tried to move, tried to give himself an extra inch or two from the fire. Coda shook, pulled, and fought, growing frantic now that he had hope, but the straps held firm. "I need help!"

Coda succumbed to the pain, letting out a terrible scream, his pain and terror creating an awful chorus. The captain staggered his way, dazed, as if barely aware of his surroundings. Something else moved from the other side of the cabin. Not something—someone. Sergeant Haniger knelt in front of Coda, shielding himself from the flames, and cut Coda free. He fell, and the sergeant caught him.

"Can you walk?"

Coda nodded, though the response must have been habit, because the moment Sergeant Haniger let go, he dropped to the deck. His hands slipped in something wet, sending him sprawling. He rolled to his feet, more carefully this time, using a nearby bench for support. He took great lengths not to look at the fallen marines still strapped in as he stumbled out the back of the ship.

Four other marines waited outside, eyes glassy and faces burnt but alert. They held rifles in hand, keeping their attention on the sky. His father was with them, bloodied like the rest of them, but alive. He looked at Coda, relief on his pain-stricken face. They'd crashed in the middle of a field of crops. Shoulder-height golden-colored genetically modified wheat stretched out for hundreds of meters in all directions.

In the distance, their Nighthawk escorts were engaged in a dogfight with the enemy, but the enemy fighters that had shot them down were already angling for another pass, ready to mop up their remains. The farming installation was close. Sunlight glistened off the tops of its metal silos and girders like a beacon.

"Move!" someone shouted. "Make for the facility and take cover!"

Needing no other prompting, Coda ran. His bound hands made the effort awkward, but he moved, driving his legs as fast as they would carry him. Around him, the marines formed a defensive circle with Coda, his father, and Captain Coleman at the center. The soft terrain squished under his feet. The wheat was long and thin, but fortunately, there were no rocks hiding among it.

With a roar, the incoming Baranyk fighters closed the distance. Coda knew that sound and compelled his legs to move faster, but he knew he could never outrun it. The sound grew closer, and as it did, it changed tenor.

"Down!"

Coda dove then rolled sideways, putting distance between himself and where he'd been. Four Baranyk fighters streaked past, and blue plasma fire rained from the sky, leaving small craters in its wake. Wet soil splattered around him. Coda jumped to his feet and was running again. The complex was getting closer with every step, but the enemy was already angling for another pass.

Coda repeated his move, diving, rolling, and hiding. He had no idea what had happened to the rest of their group, but he assumed they'd scattered. Bunched together, they offered an easy target, but spread out and taking cover, they had a chance.

Two more times, the Baranyk fighters came, and two more times, Coda was able to avoid their fire. This time when he ran, he made it to the complex. It was little more than a few dozen buildings. Most were massive one-story structures, big enough to have stored large spacecraft. Instead, they held industrial farming equipment and massive bales of wheat and other crops. A solar farm made up another section of the installation, while huge grain siloes occupied its center.

As Coda raced from the surrounding fields into the complex, he was joined by the survivors of their group. It appeared most of their number had avoided the Baranyk fire. They ran toward Coda, who ducked inside one of the large structures. Once inside, they kept moving until they were at its center then hid under one of the massive tractors. The fighters screamed above but blessedly didn't fire on the installation.

"Thoughts?" Captain Coleman asked.

"It's too big," Sergeant Haniger said, "with too many entrances. We need something we can protect with minimal forces. Preferably something with multiple fallback positions. If not that, something with multiple levels."

"I'm not sure we're going to find something like that." Coleman scanned the upper levels of the building, where a raised walkway ran its length. At the back of the building, it ended at a man door. "What about up there?"

"We'll make it work, sir."

"Good," Captain Coleman said. "Move."

As Sergeant Haniger ordered his marines into position, Coleman held a hand to his earpiece. "*Redemption* actual, this is Captain Coleman. We've been shot down and are taking shelter in a farming complex. Sending our coordinates now. Requesting immediate evac."

Coda and his father left the captain behind, following the marines to a set of metal stairs that led to the second-story walkway. They stopped on the landing.

"You all right?" his father asked as he inspected the side of Coda's head, where the skin still burned.

"It hurts like hell," Coda said. "But I'll manage. You?"

"I'm one of the lucky ones. We all are, I suppose."

They scanned their surroundings. Sergeant Haniger had positioned his marines toward either end of the building, ensuring they had visual on both of its large entrances. Coda jogged down the metal grating to the man door. He opened it to find a walkway connecting the building with another identical-looking structure.

Streaks of light in the sky rained down like meteors, shooting across the sky in their general direction.

"Sir!" Coda screamed. "Enemy forces incoming!"

Sergeant Haniger appeared at his shoulder, muttering a curse as the first of the enemy drop eggs bounced, rolled, and came to a stop a few hundred meters from their position. From its protective confines, enemy warriors emerged. More drop eggs followed, and within moments, the enemy had assembled a force much greater than their own.

“I don’t like the looks of that,” Coda said.

“Ah, c’mon now, flyboy,” Sergeant Haniger said. “This is when the fun starts.”

As if on cue, the enemy rushed in their direction.

“All right, boys!” Sergeant Haniger bellowed. “It’s time to show your worth.”

Coda turned from the door, walking back toward the center of the building. His father waited there and had taken a seat on the metal grating.

“I feel powerless,” Coda said. “I know they won’t let me help, but...”

His father’s gaze was distant, unchanging.

“Dad?”

Still nothing.

“Hey.” He nudged him with a boot. When his father still didn’t show any signs of acknowledgment, Coda knelt down in front of him. “You all right?”

A shiver went down his spine. He’d never seen that look before, but he knew what it entailed. His father wasn’t with them anymore, not consciously, at least.

“Contact!”

Gunfire echoed throughout the building. Then Coda felt his consciousness pulled too.

# 45

*Baranyk Network*

*New Plymouth, Surface*

CODA FOUGHT THE FORCE PULLING HIM INTO THE BARANYK NETWORK. IT was an odd sensation, almost like fighting a strong desire. His mind was at odds with itself, the logical side resisting, while the animalistic side was compelled, craving the deeper connection the network offered.

He collapsed next to his father, sweat beading on his forehead, breaths coming in ragged gasps. Someone spoke to him, but Coda couldn't make out the words. When he tried to reply, the animalistic side took over, winning the battle of wills. The view of the building's interior vanished and was replaced by the network.

It wasn't visible in the normal sense of the word, no more than a dream or mental image was, though Coda *could* see it. The view reminded him of an expansive starscape, a void of darkness punctuated by millions of distant points of light. But unlike the expanse of space, the network was more navigable, and instead of an empty void, it was accompanied by an oppressive feeling. That feeling was stronger today than it had been in the past. Much stronger.

*Is that what drew me here?*

Coda spun, half expecting the Overlord to be standing over his metaphysical shoulder, but all he found were more distant points of light. Not knowing why he was there or what had drawn him in, Coda tried to leave. He imagined himself disconnecting, the network disappearing back into reality, but when he opened his eyes, it still remained.

Resigned, Coda floated, observing, afraid to do anything more. One of the lights moved toward him, growing brighter as it neared. The sense of caring and comfort accompanied it, and as it drew closer, a fuzzy impression of his father filled his mind's eye.

*It's me*, the impression said. Rather than a voice, it was the idea of a voice, something closer to a feeling.

Coda's animalistic side responded by projecting a mental image of itself as if saying, *It's me, too,* then conveying confusion. *What's going on? Was it you that pulled me here?*

*Yes*, his father said. Then Coda saw the image of cuffs and a feeling of helplessness. *We couldn't be any help there. Here, we can be.*

*How?*

*Captain Coleman is looking for answers. I can get them for him, and you can help me.*

*Me? I don't know the first thing about this place.*

*There are many ways to help. Follow me.*

His father's presence fled, and as if Coda were back in his cockpit following the blue thrusters of his wingmen, he trailed after his father. They didn't have to wait long. Together, their light burned brighter than any of the presences around them, and none of the others seemed to be moving. It appeared they were the only ones actively connected to and exploring the hive mind in this way. That kind of activity drew attention.

The sense of hate and oppression grew, weighing on him like a terrible burden, crushing his spirit. The Overlord was somehow in pursuit and all around them at the same time. How could he run from something like that? How could he hide?

Coda's father must have felt it, too, because he stopped. Coda moved close to him, curious.

The Overlord slammed into him with the force of a thousand suns. He thought his spirit had felt crushed and burdened before, but this was the feeling of true subjugation. He wasn't worthy of bathing in the mucus that dripped from its terrible maw. Coda tried to run, but he was in the Overlord's grasp now, and the terrible being wasn't letting go.

Coda was suddenly transported somewhere else.

It was a red planet, dry and dusty. The sky overcast with thick orange clouds. The heat was unbearable, and the air was thick with the smell of smoke. Each breath was toxic, burning his insides with acrid poison. Coda covered his mouth, realizing that he had a body again, then turned, his eyes growing wide.

No, it wasn't a red planet… it was a *burning* planet. Coda stood atop a hill overlooking what remained of a city. Burning buildings dotted the skyline like flaming refuse. Fallen bridges protruded from poisonous waters like the fingers of a drowning man reaching for the surface a final time before the waters claimed him. What wasn't burning was black, having already been claimed by the fire. Screams echoed from the distance, wails of agony, terror, and despair.

Coda tried to look away, but everywhere he looked, the view was the same. Destruction reigned, and humanity had fallen. He closed his eyes, and through the cries and despair, he felt the presence. Even before he opened his eyes again, he knew the Overlord was with him. *He* had brought Coda to this hellscape. There was no mistaking the implication. The Overlord had brought the apocalypse.

Coda finally turned, ready to confront his oppressor. The Overlord stood in his full glory. Over two meters tall, with a long, powerful body, he stood on four legs, keeping two more forelimbs close to his body. The orange sunlight reflected off his black carapace, highlighting gray-and-white striations. Antennae twitched atop his triangular head, his dark eyes reflecting the world he'd destroyed.

Coda took a reflexive step back and tripped over a rock, falling flat on his back. The Overlord sprang. He moved faster than Coda had ever imagined possible, landing atop him, his two forelimbs piercing Coda near the shoulders, pinning him to the ground. Coda screamed, writhed, and tried to move, but the pain was too great.

Helpless, he spat at the Overlord. Spittle sprayed the black carapace, and Coda felt a surge of satisfaction as a little even got in the Overlord's eye. Though if he noticed, Coda couldn't tell.

The Overlord opened his maw, displaying dozens of razor-sharp teeth, and let a glob of thick mucus drip across the side of Coda's head.

Coda shivered, shaking his head back and forth, but it only smeared the mucus across his face and through his hair. The Overlord chittered, his antennae vibrating.

*Is that laughter?*

"Just do it already!" Coda screamed. "What are you waiting for?"

The Overlord just studied him, waiting—for what?

"Come on! What do you want?"

An image of his father flashed in Coda's mind. In the shock of finding a desolate planet and coming face-to-face with the Overlord himself, Coda hadn't realized his father was nowhere to be seen. He was alone. The realization brought with it a terrible sense of betrayal.

*There are many ways to help*, his father had said. His father had used him as bait.

# 46

*Farming Complex, New Plymouth*
*Surface*

GUNFIRE ECHOED THROUGH THE INSTALLATION. THE METAL ROOFS KICKED it back with nearly the same intensity, rattling Coleman's very being. He stood atop the elevated walkway, positioned near the central stairs, while the rest of the squad was positioned on both ends of the long building, manning its entrances. An open staircase of metal steps connected the upper and lower floors.

The Baranyk moved in a single mass, charging the building as if they were a medieval army storming the walls of a castle. More drop eggs had fallen, giving the Baranyk a horde of reinforcements and a significant numbers advantage. The ground crawled with them, allowing Coleman to fire indiscriminately into the mass, blowing off limbs, heads, and bits of carapace with ease. Yellow Baranyk blood sprayed in the air, coating the bodies of their nearby comrades, the ground, and farm equipment housed in the building.

Still more Baranyk charged, gaining ground. They were already halfway into the building, converging from both sides. They'd tried to jump to the second-story walkway, their powerful legs shooting them high into the air, but fell a meter short. Having failed at that, they'd tried scaling the walls, but the thin metal tore like cloth, sending the Baranyk back to the ground. With their options limited, they'd settled on a strategy that relied on numbers and brute force. Between that and the squad's limited ammunition, it was looking like it would be enough.

"Fire in the hole!" Corporal Abernathy bellowed as a wave of Baranyk neared the stairs then threw a grenade into the mass.

Coleman ducked, shielding his head as the grenade detonated, throwing limbs and deadly forelimbs into the air. Shrieks rang through the building as Baranyk crawled over their fallen comrades. Coleman returned to position, squeezing the trigger, spraying more bullets into the advancing enemy in an effort to keep them from the stairs.

*Click. Click. Click.*

*Out of ammo. Shit!*

Coleman thumbed the release on his rifle, ripped the empty magazine free, and tossed it aside. Fumbling at his belt, he grabbed another before slamming it into place and chambering a round. The brief moment gave the enemy the only advantage they needed. They surged forward, charging up the stairs.

Focused gunfire rained down as other marines rushed to provide support. With the building overrun, their only objective was keeping the enemy from taking the stairs. As long as they held the high ground, they stood a chance.

The lead Baranyk fell, but as quickly as it was eliminated, another took its place. There were too many. It was only a matter of time before they broke through.

"Take out the stairs!" Sergeant Haniger shouted.

"That's our only escape!" Coleman bellowed.

Haniger wasn't listening. "Do it, marine!"

Corporal Abernathy pulled another grenade from his belt then dropped it to the central landing on the stairwell. The explosion ripped a hole in the Baranyk horde and sent the metal stairs crashing down. It also tore a new hole in the building's exterior and damaged the support beams fastening the walkway to the structure.

The metal grating under Coleman's boots lurched. Metal squealed as it tore away from the building.

"Move!" Sergeant Haniger bellowed. He and Corporal Abernathy grabbed Coda and Joseph, rushing toward the man door.

Coleman was right on their heels. The sudden movement did more damage to the wall, shattering more fasteners. The walkway collapsed behind him, dropping a trailing marine into the maw of the enemy below. His screams were cut short as the enemy ripped him to pieces.

Coleman didn't have time to mourn or do anything except push for the door. He threw it open, rushing onto the exterior walkway. More drop eggs fell from the atmosphere, bouncing and shattering open, adding more Baranyk ready to enter the fray.

"*Redemption* actual, it's Captain Coleman. Where's our goddamn dropship?"

"It's en route," Lieutenant Poiu said in his ear. "We had to send a second because the enemy destroyed the first. It's taking a different route to avoid the enemy forces, but it's added time to its ETA."

"How long?"

"Eight minutes."

"Eight *minutes*?" Coleman repeated. "You have to do better, Lieutenant. We don't have eight minutes."

"Working on it, sir."

"Work harder."

Coleman rushed across the walkway and opened the door to the next building. Baranyk streamed up the stairs and raced down the walkway toward him. He slammed the door, throwing his back against it, digging his boots into the metal grating for leverage. Sergeant Haniger rushed toward him.

"What is it?"

"Grenade!" Coleman shouted. "Now!"

"I'm all out." Sergeant Haniger turned to the marines rushing toward them. "I need a grenade!"

The marines grabbed at their belts but came away empty. They were all out.

Sergeant Haniger was already moving to plan B. "Find me something to barricade the door!"

The marines doubled back, but before they'd made it halfway to the other building, a massive weight crashed against the door. It shoved

Coleman forward, and the door opened half a meter before Coleman's weight and leverage won out, slamming it shut again. They were stuck between two buildings. Nowhere to run. No escape. No fallbacks.

"How long until the dropship arrives?" Sergeant Haniger asked.

"Too long," Coleman said. "Too fucking long."

# 47

*Baranyk Network*
*Farming Complex, Surface*

The Overlord wanted Coda's father. Coda laughed bitterly. He hoped his father was accessing the network, making good on his promise to investigate its billions of connections to answer the fleet's most pressing questions. A tinge of doubt had crept into his mind, the last vestige of distrust after years of thinking of his father as a traitor.

"You want my father?" Coda said. "I don't know where he is!"

That part was true, though that didn't seem to matter to the Baranyk leader. Using his needle-like forelimbs, the Overlord lifted Coda off the ground and held him at eye level in front of his triangular head. Coda screamed, his body rigid with pain.

The Overlord's black eyes peered into his, and in an instant, the vision of the burning planet disappeared, replaced by something entirely different. The terrible orange sky and broken human skyline were replaced by an alien world Coda had never seen. It had green skies and a blue landscape with massive stone structures, each of them collapsed. Rubble was strewn across the landscape, and fallen bodies of creatures Coda couldn't begin to describe lay motionless.

The image flickered, becoming a new world. Great coral-like structures jetted from a turquoise sea. Some of the structures seemed healthy, but others were a dull white and brittle. Coda watched as one of the towers collapsed, crashing into the water, sending waves that tore bits away from other nearby structures. Bobbing in the water under Coda, at the Overlord's feet, were strange amphibious beings.

Another image showed tall crystalline structures vaguely reminiscent of human skyscrapers protruding from a rocky ground. Winged aliens littered the rocky terrain, purple blood leaking from bulbous exoskeletons.

More images, more worlds, more death.

It was as his father had told him. The universe was teeming with life, but planet by planet, life-form by life-form, the Overlord was extinguishing it, spreading death and subjugation on a scale the cosmos had never seen.

The images continued. Five more. Ten. Twenty. Each one was different, and each one was the same. Worlds fell to the Overlord. Life was enslaved under his rule. The scenes flickered, moving in rapid succession, becoming more familiar: Fallen human cities. Destroyed buildings. Burning trees and fauna. Collapsed bio-domes. Flooded cities. Broken space stations drifting in space.

"No," Coda said, barely even recognizing that he'd spoken aloud. "No."

Crushed bodies floated in water and drifted through space. What was left of humanity resisted. They fought. Ragged soldiers with guns, starfighters flying in imprecise lines, wounded starships giving the fight everything they had. In every scenario, the human resistance was overwhelmed.

Baranyk warriors tore through bodies, throwing blood and limbs into the air with a carelessness that made Coda sick. Starfighters flying in atmo crashed to the ground in horrible gouts of flame. Starships exploded in space, shattering into a million pieces, spewing their crews into space.

Somehow, Coda's resolve grew. "No," he said, his voice stronger. "We won't be like the others. We've fought you for over a decade. We can win. We *will* win."

The Overlord seemed to pull back.

"Yeah, you can understand me, can't you? Then hear me now, you son of a bitch. You've never fought anything like us before. We're the baddest motherfuckers in the galaxy. We're stubborn, idealistic, self-righteous, capable of terrible evil, but good in our core. Leave us alone, and we'll kill each other, but you've given us a common enemy and woken a monster you'll never defeat. No... you've never fought anything like us before. Everything you've shown me will only strengthen our resolve. We're going to be your downfall."

The Overlord shrieked then flung Coda with his forelimbs, sending him flying through the air. Coda slammed into a rock, his vision flaring white. By the time his vision returned, the Overlord was above him again, raised on his back legs, forelimbs ready to stab downward.

Coda tried to roll, but the pain was too great. Blood poured from the massive puncture wounds under his shoulders.

The forelimbs took him in the chest and *spread* as if the Overlord were trying to rip him in two. Blood flooded Coda's mouth. He choked and spat as blood poured from his mouth and down his chest.

The Overlord lifted him again, and with the movement, the landscape shifted. This time, the image was more familiar: blue skies, tall golden crops, and simple human structures. It was New Plymouth, where they made their stand. Broken drop eggs littered the land, pouring organic Baranyk material over the fertile ground. Smoldering wreckage of fallen Nighthawks billowed black smoke into the air. The ground was trampled by hundreds of legs marching toward the farming installation.

Hundreds of Baranyk raced toward the human structures where half a dozen men fought desperately atop a raised platform connecting two buildings. Two tried to hold a door closed, but Baranyk legs slipped through the open cracks, pushing. It was only a matter of time before they got through. Below the walkway, Baranyk were piling atop each other, creating a hill of writhing alien bodies that other warriors could climb. There was nowhere to go. No escape. The only question was which path would get the enemy to the human survivors first.

The image *pulled back* as if a camera had been zoomed in on a specific location then zoomed out. Coda was in space now, watching as the *Redemption* raced from three Baranyk carriers. The Forgotten resisted but were greatly outnumbered. The battle was lost.

Then they were somewhere else—above a rocky orange planet that

Coda instantly knew was the Baranyk home world. Thousands of ships flew in orbit, larger than any fleet ever assembled against them.

The Overlord was making one thing clear—he was stronger and more powerful. He had greater numbers. And he was coming for them.

"It won't be enough."

Coda blinked. That wasn't his voice.

The Overlord turned, giving Coda a clear view of the person standing behind him. His father. He was as Coda had seen him in the vision. Leaner, his hair less gray, face less weathered. No beard. It was as his father saw himself, Coda realized.

"It won't be enough, because I know your weakness," his father said. "And now I know where to find you. Get ready, you son of a bitch, because I'm coming for you."

The Overlord threw Coda to the side and charged his father. Coda's father didn't move, just watched as the massive creature raced toward him, forelimbs ready to rip him to shreds. As they came crashing down, Coda's father... vanished. The Baranyk shrieked angrily then turned back to Coda.

Stabbed in four different spots, Coda couldn't move. Unable to get his father, the enemy seemed content to settle for killing Coda. The Overlord sped toward him and leaped into the air, angling its forelimbs downward toward his head. Coda flinched, slamming his eyes shut, and was *ripped away*.

*I've got you.* No words, just images of Coda being held by fatherly hands. Safe. *I've got you.*

Coda relaxed, letting himself be carried away. When he opened his eyes, he found blue skies, sunlight, and excruciating pain. He was back, and it seemed his injuries had come back with him.

# 48

*Farming Complex, New Plymouth*
*Surface*

THE CRASH ON THE OTHER SIDE OF THE DOOR WAS NEARLY ENOUGH TO throw Captain Coleman from the two-story walkway. Despite his low stance, which provided him as much leverage as possible, he was pitched forward, slamming against the railing.

Corporal Abernathy rushed to the door as Sergeant Haniger struggled to hold it closed. He shoved his shoulder into it then turned, pushing against it with his back, getting low and using the metal grating to his advantage. They'd found nothing to barricade the door with, so instead, they used the only thing available—human strength.

The door banged again as the enemy made another push. Sergeant Haniger and Corporal Abernathy screamed in defiance, though it did little to prevent their combat boots from sliding across the metal walkway. A black carapace leg reached through the crack, swinging wildly, scraping against the marine's armor.

Below them, the enemy continued to mass, crawling atop each other to create a hill of bodies that new Baranyk climbed, getting closer with every second. More drop eggs fell from the sky. It seemed the enemy had an unlimited supply of those. If something didn't change quickly, they would be overrun.

Coleman rushed back to the door and stuck the barrel of his rifle through the crack. He fired. Shrieks of pain emanated from the other side, and the Baranyk leg withdrew as the alien creature retreated. Coleman continued to fire, knowing there were plenty more to replace it.

*Click. Click. Click.*

Coleman continued to squeeze the trigger, the clicks taking several moments to register. *Out again. Shit!*

"I'm out!" Coleman bellowed. "Give me a magazine!"

That's when the scene took on a different sound. Shrieks and cries sounded from all over—from behind the door Sergeant Haniger and Corporal Abernathy held closed, from the Baranyk below, from the building they'd come from, and from the marines themselves shouting their defiance. What the scene was missing was other gunfire. Nobody else was firing. Looking at the soldiers now, Coleman realized he wasn't the only one who was out of ammo.

Coleman took one look at Sergeant Haniger, saw the same realization on his face, then rushed to provide more help with the door. There was nothing left to do. They would hold out as long as they could, giving themselves every possible second for the dropship to arrive.

A new scream entered the fray. Pained. Human. For a moment, Coleman thought it came from one of the marines, that a Baranyk leg or forelimb had found a vulnerable spot in their armor, but then he saw Coda move. He rolled on the metal grating, rocking back and forth, holding his chest, in clear agony.

"Check on him, sir!" Sergeant Haniger bellowed. "We can hold this."

Coleman darted across the walkway, dropping to where Coda lay. The pilot had been nonresponsive since before they'd blown the stairwell. Coleman hadn't known if he was fighting Baranyk control or had accessed the enemy network, though he'd hoped for the latter. Coda's face was ashen, and blood leaked from his mouth, staining his lips a violent red. He didn't have any noticeable wounds, but something was very, very wrong.

Joseph woke, pushing himself up from the grate. He surveyed the scene, his eyes wide and mouth open.

*Welcome to hell.*

When his eyes fell on Coda, he rushed over then began undoing his flight suit.

"What are you doing?" Coleman asked.

"He's hurt," Joseph said.

"How? He's been with us the whole time. Nothing has gotten to him."

"I don't have time to explain." Joseph pulled open the flight suit then lifted the undershirt. The skin of Coda's chest was pale, with blood pooling under the skin. "He's bleeding internally. We have to get him help."

"Look around, Joseph. We all need help."

"Damn it, Chadwick, you don't understand. He faced the Overlord himself. He knows where the enemy is."

Coleman breathed through his teeth, nodding. He held a hand to the side of his head. "*Redemption*, it's Coleman. Tell me that fucking ship is close."

"It's breaking atmo now, sir," Lieutenant Poiu said. "You should see it any second."

Coleman's gaze went to the horizon, scanning the blue skies and clouds. He didn't see anything.

"Captain!" Sergeant Haniger screamed.

Coleman stood, ready to race to the door and offer more help, but the marine was pointing at something behind him. Turning, Coleman saw Baranyk legs hooked around the railing, pulling itself onto the walkway.

*No!*

They had no grenades or ammunition. His options limited, Coleman picked up a discarded gun by the barrel and rushed over to where the creature was trying to gain purchase. He swung wildly, aiming for central mass. The creature squealed, flailing its limbs. One tore through Coleman's flight suit, cutting him across the chest and neck.

Coleman growled, swinging with more ferocity. Joseph joined him, grabbing at the Baranyk legs and pushing. The alien fell, rolling down the mass of writhing bodies, but already, another one was taking its place. The last marine not at the door rushed to help, using his gun in a similar fashion—swinging, hitting, pushing, fighting to keep the Baranyk from gaining purchase.

A boom echoed from above. Coleman's eyes went skyward, spotting the dropship. It fell like a rock, tearing a hole through the clouds. Two

Nighthawks flew at its wings, and thankfully, nothing appeared to be in pursuit. The Nighthawks blasted forward, taking a new attack vector.

"Push!" Coleman bellowed. "Push them back!"

He stabbed downward, using his rifle for extra reach, stabbing at the climbing Baranyk before they reached the pinnacle of their pile. One hooked his gun with a leg, ripping it from Coleman's hands, nearly dragging Coleman with it. His chest slammed into the railing, feet pulled from the grating, eyes looking straight down. The Baranyk lunged at him, swinging at his face. Coleman pulled away, narrowly avoiding the attack, then stumbled backward.

Cannon fire erupted in the distance as the two Nighthawks tore through the enemy's ground forces. Dirt and limbs flew into the air. The Nighthawks streaked toward Coleman's position, firing controlled bursts into the enemy. The hill of Baranyk didn't retreat or take cover. They were too close to their prey. They grew more desperate, climbing, jumping, flailing.

The marine took a forelimb in the neck and was ripped from the walkway to the ground below. That left only Coleman and Joseph. Sergeant Haniger and Corporal Abernathy still held the door.

The Nighthawks swung around wide to take a more aggressive attack vector that would allow them to hit the enemy at its heart. Coleman ducked, cradling his head as the Nighthawks approached. Cannon fire thundered, rattling every bone in his body.

Wind ripped across their position as the Nighthawks raced past. Coleman looked up, watching them fly by, already sweeping around for another run. The mass of Baranyk had collapsed, but they were already remassing.

The dropship approached then spun so that its rear hatch was facing them, drifting into position a meter from the railing. The hatch opened, and two marines took position on the ramp, guns angled toward their position.

"Come on, sir!" one of the marines shouted.

Two more marines appeared behind them, firing into the Baranyk mass below.

The first marine held out his arm, and Coleman took it, climbing onto the ramp.

"Let's go!" Coleman shouted.

Joseph had taken Coda in his arms and carried him to the edge. The marines took Coda from Joseph and carried him up the ramp. Joseph climbed atop the railing and leaped into the hatch, following his son into the belly of the ship.

"He's bleeding internally," he said over the roar of the dropship's engines.

Coleman watched as Sergeant Haniger and Corporal Abernathy held the door. He waved at them, beckoning them forward. "Come on!"

Corporal Abernathy was first, lunging forward and running down the walkway toward the ship. With less weight holding the door, the Baranyk heaved, sending Sergeant Haniger sprawling. He landed on his face but was on his feet in an instant. Baranyk streamed through the open door, meters from Sergeant Haniger, gaining ground with every step.

"Move, Sergeant!"

The marines on the ramp opened fire, taking careful aim so as not to hit their comrade. Baranyk blood flew into the air as bits of carapace were torn free. Even as the enemy fell, more took their place. But Haniger had some distance now, and Corporal Abernathy was already on the ramp. Sergeant Haniger leaped, a boot landed on the railing, then he propelled himself into the hatch. The marines continued to fire, holding the Baranyk at bay.

"Go! Go! Go!" someone shouted.

The dropship pulled from the building, angling upward and gaining altitude. The Nighthawks swept in behind it, shooting two missiles into the installation, laying waste to the compound and any Baranyk still inside.

Coleman let himself exhale then strode into the ship with the marines. The ramp closed behind them, leaving them in the dark cabin. They had Coda laid across the deck and were administering a shot. He'd stopped moving.

"How is he?" Coleman asked of no one in particular.

"He's beyond my ability to help," the person beside Coda said. She was dressed in a flight suit and had an open medical kit beside her. "Whatever's wrong is internal. We've radioed the *Redemption* to have a medical team standing by. That's all we can do for now."

Coleman nodded, and the woman left to see to the other survivors.

"He's going to make it," Joseph said, holding Coda's hand in his own. "He has to. I'm not losing him again."

Coleman crouched so that he was eye level with Joseph. "What happened?"

Joseph kept his eyes on his son. "We were useless in there. You never would have let us fight, so we did the only thing we could do to be useful. I accessed the Baranyk network and pulled him with me. The Overlord was waiting for us, and he pulled Coda into his consciousness. I don't know everything he did or everything he showed him, but when I found him, he was hanging from the Overlord's forelimbs, bleeding, and near death. I don't know how it works, but even though he was only in a different conscious state, some of his injuries are real. His body is trying to reconcile what happened there."

"Where were you while Coda was with the Overlord?"

"Searching," Joseph said. "He was distracted, and it gave me unhindered access to the network."

"But you didn't find anything," Coleman said, disappointed.

"No," Joseph said. "I found plenty."

"What do you mean? What did you find?"

Joseph met Coleman's eye. "Planets. Moons. An entire system teeming with Baranyk. More than I've ever seen in one place. I found your missing fleet, Chadwick."

"But before, you said..." His gaze fell to Coda.

"I wasn't going to leave him behind," Joseph said. "He's my son, and I'll do whatever I can to protect him."

Joseph had lied to him. Something inside Coleman bristled at that, but at the same time, he couldn't blame the man. He couldn't bring himself to be angry at him. If it had been Aniyah, he would have done the same thing.

"He'll be fine," Coleman said. "He's strong. Determined. More stubborn than anyone I've ever met, including you."

The ship's rocking and bucking subsided as they broke atmo.

"This system you found," Coleman said carefully. "Do you know its name?"

Joseph shook his head. "No, but I can do you one better. I can show you where it is."

"You can show..." The rest of the words died on Coleman's tongue.

"Yes, Chadwick. Give me a star chart, and I'll show you where you can find your lost fleet." His eyes dug into Chadwick's. "I'll show you where you can find the Overlord."

# 49

*Sick Bay, SAS Redemption*
*Deep Space*

The steady beeping eventually brought Coda around. He woke in the medical bay, which was unfortunately becoming a second home to him. Though, in this moment, the familiar sights and sounds offered an element of comfort. His eyes opened slowly, seeming to resist, and the white light burned. But irritating or not, it meant one thing above all else. He was alive.

Wireless electrodes covered his chest and torso. He even felt them on his temples, no doubt monitoring his brain activity in addition to the standard heart rate, blood pressure, and oxygen levels. He tried to sit up, but his movements were uncoordinated and sluggish, and they were accompanied by a stabbing pain on his insides. He groaned.

That seemed to trigger something in the room. He saw movement out of the corner of his eye as someone approached. He exhaled slowly, ready to put on his best face.

"Hey, Doc," Coda said.

A calloused hand took his. "Not the doc, Callan. It's me."

Coda turned his head, surprised to find that even that took

maximum effort and concentration. His father stood there, leaning over him. He spoke in a soft voice, as if concerned that talking too loudly would somehow injure Coda further.

"Dad," Coda said. His voice was quiet too. Maybe his father was just mirroring him.

"Hey, son."

"It sounds good to hear those words."

"It feels good to say them."

Coda smiled and let his eyes close again. He didn't know the extent of his injuries or even how long he'd been out, but with his father nearby, he felt better.

"How are you feeling?"

"Great," Coda said. "Except that I barely have the energy to hold my eyes open and feel like I'm being ripped in two."

His father laughed. "Well, that's about as good as you can hope for at this point."

"How long have I been out?"

He thought he heard his father exhale. "Six days."

Coda's eyes were open again. "Six days?"

"You'll be here for another couple weeks, and who knows how long it'll be before you're in the cockpit again."

"What happened?" Coda asked.

"Later, Callan. You need to rest."

Coda had meant the question to be about the state of his injuries, but his father seemed to have taken it as something else. Memories flooded back. Images of the Overlord, of fallen civilizations, death, and destruction, of the massive Baranyk fleet.

"You used me as bait," Coda said.

"No, son." A weight settled next to him as his father sat on the edge of his bed. He squeezed Coda's hand for emphasis. "Not bait. I'd expected us to search the network together. Find answers together. But the Overlord came, and I used his distraction to our advantage. I figured you'd understand that."

The subtle rebuke made Coda angry. He wanted to argue, but he didn't have the energy for it. The added moment helped him realize something too. He wasn't angry at his father's criticism—he was angry because his father was right. Coda should have known better.

"I thought you used me."

"No, Callan. I'd never do that. You have every right to be angry with me, but don't be mad at me for that. I'd never do that to you."

Coda tried to nod, but the motion left him dizzy and nauseous. "Were we successful?"

"Yes. We did it, Callan. We found the Baranyk fleet and their home system. We sent a stealth probe to confirm, but I already know it's true. I saw it myself."

Coda wanted to be excited, but the truth was that the Baranyk fleet represented a greater threat than anyone realized. There were too many ships. The Sol Fleet couldn't hope to hold them back.

"I saw it too," Coda said. "The Overlord showed it to me."

"Then you know what we face."

Coda grimaced, replaying the images of the Baranyk fleet in his head. "What are we going to do?"

"I don't know. Fortunately, that's not our decision to make. And it's not something I want you to worry about right now. You need to rest." His father squeezed his hand as if to say goodbye.

"Don't go," Coda said. "Please. I'll rest. Just don't go."

"I'm not going anywhere, son. I'll be right here when you wake up. I promise."

Coda moaned and settled into the bed. His father was right. He didn't need to worry about the Overlord or the enemy fleet right now. He'd done his job. He'd brought his father into the fray. In turn, he had discovered where the Baranyk were and the threat they posed. His new priority was to rest, to heal, and when the time came, to be ready to fight.

# 50

*Captain's Quarters, SAS Redemption*
*Deep Space*

Captain Coleman groaned as he sat. He was in the comfort of his own quarters, and damn it, but it had been a long few days. Hell, it had been a long few *weeks*. He leaned back, closing his eyes, his hand absently swirling the snifter of whiskey.

Dr. Rydell had informed him Coda had woken a short time ago. Coleman had thought about going to see him, but Joseph was already there, and he'd already gone back to sleep. Coleman was relieved. It had been touch and go for a while, and even after Dr. Rydell had stabilized his condition, she hadn't seemed optimistic. Whatever had happened to Coda inside that network had left him severely wounded.

Coleman took a deep breath. That was done now. New Plymouth was lost, and the *Redemption* was licking her wounds, but they were safe. He took a sip of his whiskey, letting the alcohol sit on his tongue before swallowing. It burned going down, warming his insides and calming his nerves. He exhaled again, settling into the couch. He sat like that, taking periodic drinks, relishing the peace, knowing that it was only a matter of time before it was interrupted.

That interruption came after he'd nearly finished his drink. The door chimed. It was late, and he wasn't expecting anyone. He stood with another groan, his knees cracking and popping, and made his way to the door, where he thumbed the keypad to open it. The door slid open.

Aniyah stood on the other side.

"Lieutenant," Coleman said, immediately reverting to decorum to mask his surprise. "Is everything all right?"

"Yes, sir." Her tone was soft and vulnerable, quite different from when she had confronted him in the corridor. "I was hoping we could talk."

*I'm not ready for this. Not today. Not now.*

"Of course." Coleman stood to the side, motioning for her to enter. "Come in."

She stepped into the room, eyes scanning its contents.

"Have a seat," Coleman said as the door slid shut. "Do you want something to drink?"

"I'm fine, sir," she said as she took a seat in one of the chairs. "Thank you."

Coleman returned to his spot on the small couch, his eyes on his daughter. An uncomfortable silence extended between them. She looked at him, expecting him to say something, but he didn't know how to begin. What does a person say to someone he hasn't spoken to in years?

"Look—" he began.

"I wanted to—"

Their words crashed into each other.

"Sorry," Coleman said.

"It's fine."

"Go ahead. What were you going to say?"

"No," Aniyah said. "You go."

Coleman smiled. *This couldn't have gotten off to a more awkward start.* "I was just going to say that I'm glad you came by. I've been meaning to come find you, but..." He held up his hands as if to say, "You understand."

"But what?" she pressed, unwilling to let him off the hook that easily.

"But I didn't know what to say," Coleman said.

"How about, 'Hi. How are you doing?' or 'It's been a long time.'"

"You're right," Coleman said. "Can we start over? Let me try again?"

"Sure."

Coleman leaned forward, ensuring he had her attention. "Aniyah… it's good to see you. I wish I had come to see you sooner, but I'm a coward. I'm terrified of my own daughter. Ashamed of my own past. The truth is, I've been waiting for this moment for a long time, and I'm glad you're here."

*Damn, that felt good to get out.*

Aniyah took a shuddering breath and nodded. It was a clipped motion, short and small. She turned away, breaking their eye contact. For a moment, he thought she was mad, that he had said something wrong, then a single tear crested her eyelid and ran down her cheek. She was too stubborn to wipe it away.

"Hey…" Coleman reached for her, taking her hand in his. She didn't pull away. "It really *is* good to see you."

"I know, Dad. It's good to see you too."

*Dad*. He didn't know how long it had been since he'd heard that word directed at him, and he wasn't sure he had the words to describe how great it was to hear.

A heavy quiet filled the room, ripe with implication. Coleman didn't know how long they sat there in silence, but it was different from the awkward silence of before. Something had changed between them. He knew that things weren't good, but they had taken the first step toward healing.

Eventually, they started talking, telling stories of mundane things, sharing histories, and filling in the holes of lost time. They laughed, cried, and laughed some more.

He found out that his daughter was a rabid sports fan and that she could have played college basketball if she hadn't enlisted with the Sol Fleet. His stories were less interesting, but she wanted to know what he'd done since the Nighthawk program had been shut down and why he hadn't returned to Earth or been part of her life.

He'd never had a good answer for that, and when he tried to explain it, his words sounded hollow. The simple fact of the matter was that he didn't have a good explanation, and that was something they were both going to have to get over. Rather than dwell on it, though, they shifted to happier topics and talked well into the night.

He hugged her when she left, holding her tightly, the same way he had always dreamed of. And she hugged him back. It wasn't a perfect moment, but it was close. And when she left, he watched her until she disappeared around the corner. He closed the door and returned to his spot on the couch, a smile on his face. He had the weight of the world on his shoulders, a thousand people under his command and relying on him, but for the first time in a long time, he felt like a burden had been lifted.

The feeling, unfortunately, didn't last.

"Captain?" Lieutenant Poiu said in his earpiece.

Coleman sat forward, immediately on alert. He touched his earpiece, opening the channel to his tactical officer. "Yes, Lieutenant. What is it?"

"The stealth drone has returned, sir. Sending you the information packet now."

His heart already racing, Coleman grabbed his tablet from the table and opened the information package Lieutenant Poiu had sent. What he saw terrified him to his core.

The drone had taken a series of images from the system. As Joseph had said, it was teeming with Baranyk activity. In all, three planets and five moons were inhabited, but what shocked him the most was what orbited the largest planet. It was orange and rocky, and without being told, Coleman knew it was the Baranyk home world. Above it were thousands, maybe tens of thousands, of Baranyk ships.

It was the largest fleet Coleman had ever seen. More numerous than all of the ships humanity had ever assembled combined. *Christ above, how are we supposed to stop that?*

He toggled the last piece of information. It was a video. At first, it seemed to be the same as the images, but Coleman let it play. The drone wouldn't have marked it as important if its onboard computer hadn't thought it worthy of viewing. Coleman downed the last of his drink, then nearly spit it out as the video flashed and hundreds of ships disappeared. With another flash, more ships disappeared. Then again. And again.

In moments, the entire fleet had disappeared. A cold sense of dread washed over Captain Coleman. The enemy was moving. Their fleet was coming. And humanity wasn't ready.

# WINGS OF REDEMPTION

# 1

*Bridge, SAS Redemption*
*Baranyk Space*

"Jump complete, sir," Lieutenant Poiu said. "Sensor data coming in now."

The words were spoken with a tired crispness—as if he'd spoken them hundreds of times before.

Captain Coleman let himself exhale. He stood in his customary position near the base of the battle map, his sweaty hands gripping the railing that circled it. He couldn't remember the last time he'd slept or had anything resembling rest. Couldn't remember the last time he'd spent any meaningful time away from the bridge and its chatter, beeps, and the flashing lights of the *Redemption*'s Condition-1 status.

He couldn't even remember the last time he'd looked at anything other than the imaging display. Blessedly, the battle map was empty. No sign of Baranyk activity.

"Another jump," Commander Garcia said softly. "Another tempting of fate and another lucky draw."

Coleman glanced at him, wanting to nod or maybe even offer a smile in relief, but fatigue stood in the way of anything more than the simple look.

The XO looked how Coleman felt. His hair was in disarray, dark circles surrounded his eyes, and his skin had lost its luster. Even his normally jovial personality had soured. He was an empty husk of himself, worn down, stepped on, and punished by life and the impossible task before them.

They were in a race, and if they lost, humanity and everything it had ever accomplished would be destroyed. The enemy fleet, larger than anything ever assembled, was moving. And Coleman had no idea how fast they were advancing, the limits of their jump drives, or where they would strike first. He could only control what he could control, and right now, that meant making every jump as fast as possible.

That also meant that he was pushing his ship and its crew to their limits. More than one member of the bridge crew had already collapsed from exhaustion. Dr. Rydell had given him a stern reminder of the limits of human physiology but hadn't pressed him too hard. She knew what they were up against and how dire the situation was. Knew what only Coleman and a select few others aboard the *Redemption* knew.

The enemy had found a way to manipulate human behavior, to turn unwitting people into drones controlled by the Baranyk Overlord. In many ways, that was more terrifying than the massive fleet bearing down on the human worlds. He'd had no choice. He'd pressed his crew to their limits. Pushed himself further than he'd ever thought possible.

The jump marked 1,717 consecutive jumps, nearly one every thirty minutes, except when they'd taxed the EmDrive too much and had to allow it time to recover. But every jump brought them closer to a JumpGate that would unlock their return to human-occupied space and the Sol Fleet.

"System clear, sir," Lieutenant Poiu said.

"Thank you, Lieutenant," Coleman said. "Begin initializing jump number one-thousand-seven-hundred-and-eighteen."

"Yes, sir."

Coleman turned to Commander Garcia. The other man had closed his eyes and was leaning against the railing beside him. Coleman told himself he needed to do a better job of staggering shifts and ensuring everyone got some downtime. He needed them alert and in fighting shape. If they ran into the Baranyk in their present condition... He didn't want to think about it.

"I'll be in sick bay," Coleman said. "When I get back, you're ordered to take a three-hour nap."

The smallest of smiles appeared on Commander Garcia's face. "I'd love to argue with you, but that sounds too damn nice."

"We have two hours before the EmDrive will be ready to jump again, and the system is quiet. Have all nonessential personnel report to their bunks."

"What about you?"

"I've got something to see to," Coleman said. "But I'll take a rotation after yours."

"Yes, sir."

Coleman nodded to his XO, strode up the ramp, and exited the bridge. The adjoining corridor was bright, with crisp white light emanating from the walls. It burned his eyes as if he'd just woken from a deep sleep and had a flashlight shone in his face.

He walked the corridor slowly, his footsteps little more than shuffles. Like the bridge, sick bay was nestled deep in the belly of the ship, but despite his slow pace, he made it there in minutes.

The medical bay was alive with activity, which helped him find a reserve of energy he hadn't known he still had. He nodded to nurses and doctors then found Dr. Rydell, the lead physician, at the back of the ward. Seated in front of her, having changed out of the white medical gown and into standard-issue sweats and a tank top, was his CAG.

"Morning, sir." Coda's skin was pallid, eyes dark, and he'd lost a noticeable amount of weight during his recovery, but he was brimming with excitement.

"Good morning, Coda. How are you feeling?"

"If your appearance is any indication, a hell of a lot better than you, sir."

Coleman gave him a half-hearted smile. "That's a pretty low bar, Commander." He turned to Dr. Rydell. "How's he looking?"

"We were just going over that." Dr. Rydell glanced at the tablet displaying his vitals. "The short of it is he's still healing. By all accounts, he should have died on New Plymouth, but he's a stubborn kid. His wounds may have healed, but his body is still recovering. I've placed him on limited duty, and he's to work no more than six hours a day. I've increased his calorie allotment to help him regain what he's lost and prescribed sleeping pills to make sure he gets the required amount of rest. We'll see how he does and reevaluate in a week."

Coda made a face that said he didn't agree with the doctor's assessment. "I'm good, sir. Ready. You say the words, and I'm back in the cockpit."

"You'll get there soon enough, Commander," Coleman said. "But we're all at the mercy of the doctor on this."

That wasn't entirely true, and he was sure Coda saw him hiding behind the words. Physically able or not, Coda wasn't flight ready. Like his father, who was currently lying low aboard the *Redemption*, Coda had a brain defect that made him susceptible to Baranyk influence. Above Kryos, the same planet his father had flown above fifteen years before him, Coda had been targeted by the Baranyk. While under their control, he had shot down several of his wingmen before Coleman's own daughter shot him down. Until they had found a way to protect Coda from the enemy's influence, he would remain grounded.

"Lieutenant Krylov is acting CAG," Coleman said. "He's expecting you."

"Yes, sir." Coda slid from the bed and stood straight, snapping a crisp salute, which Coleman returned, then turned to the doctor. Surprisingly, his face took on a softer expression. Coda and Dr. Rydell had an interesting relationship—one part paternal, another part antagonistic. They were like friends who relished their banter. "Thank you, Doc. For everything."

"Just doing my job, Commander."

"I mean it," Coda said, driving the words home. He held out his hand.

Dr. Rydell took it, a smile splitting her face.

"I almost feel bad for all the shit I gave you." The cocky grin Coleman had come to know so well appeared on his pilot's face. "Almost."

Dr. Rydell slapped him with her tablet. "Get out of here before you require more medical attention."

Coda laughed but did as instructed, slipping through the medical ward to the corridor beyond.

"He's a good kid," Dr. Rydell said. "Cocky and arrogant like all of your fighter jocks, but a good kid."

"How's he *really* doing?" Coleman asked.

Dr. Rydell instantly understood the real question he was asking. "He's not sleeping, and scans show pronounced brain activity, even during REM."

Coleman frowned. "Is it..." He glanced at a couple nearby nurses and their patients to make sure no one else was listening. "Do you think it's an *outside* influence?"

"I don't know," Dr. Rydell said. "I don't think so. Dr. Naidoo is reviewing the data, but she believes its remnants of the Baranyk network. His brain isn't fully disconnecting."

"What does that mean?" Coleman asked. "Is he more vulnerable?"

"It's impossible to say right now. We're keeping an eye on him, but under no circumstances is he to set foot into a cockpit."

"Understood," Coleman said. "I'll talk with Dr. Naidoo and Commander Payton. Maybe there's something they can think of. Thank you, Doctor." He made to leave, but the doctor stopped him short.

"You need some rest, Captain."

"I know, Doc. Believe me, I know."

# 2

*Sick Bay, SAS Redemption*
*Baranyk Space*

For the first time in five weeks, Coda left the medical ward without supervision or equipped with a catheter, IV, or some other kind of medical device. Despite his orders to report to the acting CAG, he paused in the hallway to bask in the white light emanating from the walls, as if he were on a beach, soaking up the sun.

He was *free*.

A smile splitting his face, he closed his eyes, allowing the ship personnel to flow around him like the surf around his feet. They had no idea about the physical, emotional, and psychological hell he'd been through during the last month and a half, and he was fine with that. He was out now, and his mind was sharper than it had been in weeks.

With a purposeful step forward, Coda started for the pilots' section of the ship and his old office. As he approached the door and spotted Moscow in the CAG's office with his flight leaders, Coda realized he didn't know how to address the acting CAG. Moscow was a former rival turned friend, but he was also Coda's superior officer who hailed from a long line of military family members. Best to stick with formality and go from there.

Coda knocked on the open door then stepped inside, snapping a crisp salute. "Commander O'Neil reporting for duty, sir!"

Moscow looked up from the digital desktop. When his eyes fell on Coda, his face came alive, offering a genuine smile Coda had thought he would never see from his former rival.

"Coda," Moscow said with equal parts surprise and recognition.

Squawks and Noodle, who had been sitting with their backs to the door, turned sharply. Then they were jumping out of their seats to attack him—pushing, shoving, hugging, and laughing. If they were at all concerned about injuring someone who was only minutes removed from sick bay, they didn't show it.

"They actually let you out?" Squawks said, eyeing Coda from top to bottom. "I didn't think Dr. Rydell would ever let you out of her sight."

"I didn't think so either," Coda said.

"You look good," Noodle said. "How are you feeling?"

"Great," Coda said. "Aside from just being mauled by you guys."

Squawks and Noodle laughed, but as the moment faded, they seemed to realize they were the only ones who'd jumped up to greet their friend. Coda's eyes found Moscow's, and an awkward silence permeated the room.

"Sorry, sir," Coda said.

"It's okay, Commander. I'm happy to see you too." Moscow cast an amused look at Squawks and Noodle. "Even if I don't need to jump like a kindergartner at recess to show it."

"I always thought I was closer to a fourth grader," Squawks said.

"Nah," Noodle said, "I had you pegged for a freshman. Fifteen, horny, and full of yourself."

"Ah, right you are." Squawks grinned as if his friend had just given him a tremendous compliment. "You know me so well."

"It's good to see some things haven't changed," Coda said to Moscow.

"They're every bit as insufferable as they've always been," Moscow said. "I'd demote them if we had anyone else willing to step into their boots."

"He's saying the rest of the squadron is too smart to go into command. It takes a special kind of stupidity to take on this kind of responsibility."

Coda laughed. He had long since learned fighter jocks had the best kind of self-deprecating humor in the fleet. Any crazy person could climb into the cockpit, but one had to be certifiable to make a career out of it.

"How is the squadron holding up?" Coda asked.

"They're doing well," Moscow said, returning to his seat. "How much has the captain filled you in?"

"He's given me the gist of it," Coda said. "We located the Baranyk fleet, but it's moving, and we're racing to beat it back to human space. But without a JumpGate, we're limited to the range and durability of the EmDrive. It's a race, and we don't know who's ahead."

"That about sums it up," Moscow said. "The last few weeks have been quiet, at least in the sense of battle. We're still operating under Condition-1 and flying a double CAP, but it's the most rest the squadron has gotten in ages. If anything, they've got too much downtime, which is where you come in."

"Anything I can do to help, sir," Coda said.

"The first thing you can do is stop calling me 'sir,'" Moscow said. "In this office, we're equals. Outside it, well, you understand."

"I do."

"Good. The captain said you'd be released to limited duty."

"Correct."

"Okay," Moscow said. "As it stands, we're significantly behind on readiness training and other fleet-issued requirements. I need you to bring everyone up to speed by the time we return to fleet-occupied space. In addition to that, I want you to schedule the CAP and work with the deck chief to ensure ship repairs."

"I'll get it done," Coda said.

Moscow was right. With their original expedited training, the Forgotten had largely avoided much of the required readiness training the rest of the fleet had to complete. Much of it was bureaucratic nonsense mandated by some govie trying to look good to their constituents. And as ridiculous as it sounded, Moscow was right. They couldn't let a little intergalactic war get in the way of sexual harassment training.

"Thank you," Moscow said. "And because I don't want you to be *too* bored, I've got another task for you. I've already programmed the simulators with our latest battles and have been running the squadron through them to keep them sharp. But I want you to think of every cruel machination imaginable that the enemy might throw at us. Situations where we're grossly outnumbered, where we arrive late. Think of new weapons. Scenarios where we lose radio contact. Where the enemy takes control of one of our capital ships. Anything and everything you can think of. We don't know what we're going to step into once we get back, and I need my pilots to be prepared. Can you handle that?"

"Absolutely," Coda said.

"Good," Moscow said. "That's all for now. Squawks, Noodle, show Coda to his bunk. I'll be along shortly."

"Thank you, Moscow," Coda said, nodding.

"It's good to have you back, Coda."

Coda followed Squawks and Moscow out of the room and into the corridor beyond.

"Readiness training?" Squawks asked. "Scheduling? Coordinating repairs? God, I'd go insane. How long until your flight status is reapproved?"

"I have no idea," Coda said. "It's better than sitting on my ass in sick bay, though."

"I guess," Squawks said, sounding unconvinced.

The unfortunate reality was that there were a million tasks aboard the *Redemption* that needed doing, with a thousand just for the strike fighters. The flight calendar alone needed to be updated almost hourly to deal with unexpected illnesses, injuries, or maintenance issues. Then there was coordinating repairs.

The deck chief was a master at making sure their Nighthawks were properly maintained and performed as expected, but he often had different priorities than the pilots strapped inside. Coda would be the middleman between his pilots and the people maintaining their ships. They weren't glamorous jobs, but they were necessary, and until Coda was back in the cockpit, he would do them to the best of his ability to keep his friends safe.

The pilots' barracks wasn't far from Moscow's office, and they arrived quickly. The door opened to a long room with rows of bunks inset in the bulkhead. As they stepped in, Coda received several nods, and a few pilots came up to wish him well. Many others, though, lingered in the distance, watching him uneasily.

*They don't know how to react,* Coda thought. *They don't know if this is a good moment because I'm back or a bad one because I was demoted.*

He tried to put on a good face and nod in the direction of those who seemed the most awkward. All that seemed to do was make them even more uncomfortable. They looked away or tried to occupy their attention with something else.

"Good thing this isn't awkward," Squawks said sarcastically.

"It's okay," Coda said. "It's not like I was expecting a surprise party or anything."

"We *did* talk about it," Noodle said. "Oh well. Come on, there's a free bunk near ours."

Coda followed Noodle across the barracks to the open bunk. He took a seat on the thin fleet-issued mattress. It was harder than the one he'd had in his CAG's quarters, but it would do. He supposed Moscow had the private quarters now—perks of the role and all that.

The room had gone quiet, and Coda began to feel self-conscious. Was everyone looking at him? Why wasn't anyone talking? His friends seem to notice it too.

Noodle offered him a half-hearted smile. "We'll let you get settled."

"Thank you," Coda said.

He cast another look around the room then lay down. He wanted to laugh. An hour ago, he'd thought himself free. How wrong he'd been. He wasn't free. He was like a dog who'd been let out of his kennel but was now trapped in a fenced yard. He had more freedom than before, but more freedom wasn't what he needed. He needed to run. Needed to fly.

"How long until your flight status is reapproved?" Squawks had asked.

*Not soon enough*, Coda thought. *Not soon enough.*

# 3

*Engineering, SAS Redemption*
*Baranyk Space*

"Tell me what I'm looking at." Captain Coleman stood with his chief engineer, Commander Brahm Payton, looking at what Coleman assumed was a readout of the *Redemption*'s EmDrive. Around them, the engineering bay was a hubbub of activity, even more chaotic than the CIC during a battle.

"Well, sir," Commander Payton said with a hint of exasperation, "we've been pushing the EmDrive beyond its limits. We're making jump after jump, and the only time it gets to recover is the time it takes to plot the next jump. It wasn't designed for that, and it's beginning to show signs of degradation."

"What kind of degradation?"

"That's the question," Commander Payton said. "I've got a dozen ideas, but without shutting it down and tearing it apart, I can't know for sure. What I do know is that the green numbers on the readout in front of you are good, and the red numbers are bad."

Coleman scanned the readout again. "There aren't any green numbers."

"Then you understand the extent of the issue."

Coleman took a deep breath. He didn't have the mind of his chief engineer—not many did—but did the man have to flaunt it? Part of him wondered if Commander Payton even did it consciously. He assumed not, which was why he hadn't dressed him down. The man was the best at what he did, personality quirks be damned.

"What are our options?" Coleman asked.

"Well, there are three. One, we shut it down. Full stop. Run a full diagnostic and repair what needs repaired. The second is shutting it down for a short period of time. The heat and pressure readings are the most alarming. It may just need time to cool off."

"And the third option?" Coleman asked, not liking either of the first two.

"We leave it." Commander Payton scratched his cheek nervously. "It's held together this long, and we only have thirteen jumps until we reach the JumpGate. We monitor it, review the readings after each jump, and take it one jump at a time. If anything grows too alarming, we shut it down."

"What does too alarming look like, Chief? You just told me that red was bad, and all I'm seeing is red."

"It's a fair question, sir. What you're seeing are elevated levels. They're not critical yet. The risk is letting one issue become many. A chain reaction leading to complete system failure."

"Complete system failure," Coleman repeated.

Commander Payton made a fist then opened it, spreading his fingers wide, mimicking an explosion.

Coleman's eyes drifted to the engineering personnel occupying the space. He was responsible for the more than nine thousand souls on board, but he also had valuable intel on their enemy, intel that could spell the end of the war if not relayed. He'd sent probes detailing everything in a full report but had no way of knowing if they'd made it.

"If we shut it down, how long are we dead in the water?"

"It'll take forty-eight hours for the system to cool enough to work on. Whether we're letting it take a break or we're running a full diagnostic, that has to come first."

"Forty-eight hours," Coleman repeated. "Minimum."

"Minimum, sir."

"And the repair time will depend on whatever needs to be fixed," Coleman said.

"Exactly, sir."

"We don't have forty-eight hours to spare," Coleman said. "We're in a race against the enemy, and we have no idea if we're winning or losing. Every minute we wait, our lead either shrinks, or we fall farther behind."

Commander Payton opened his mouth to speak, but Coleman held up a hand, silencing him. His comments weren't meant for Payton; they were meant for himself.

"Our intel is only effective if we get it to Fleet Command *before* the enemy arrives. If we don't... How much damage can the enemy inflict in forty-eight hours? Seventy-two? A week? A month?" He looked toward his chief engineer. "Where's the line, Chief?"

"That's a question you need to answer, sir. I'm just giving you the data."

Coleman nodded. Leadership was a lonely bitch. "We'll continue as planned. Push it, Chief, but monitor it and let me know if anything goes critical."

"Will do, sir."

Coleman left engineering. He took his time making his way back to the bridge, striding through the corridors, taking the long way. As he did, he ran a hand along the bulkhead, feeling the smooth hardened plastic. His ship would hold together. It had to.

# 4

*Forgotten Barracks, SAS Redemption*
*Baranyk Space*

CODA WOKE WITH A START. A DARK FIGURE STOOD OVERTOP HIM, PINNING him down. He tried to pull away, but the figure held him firmly. His heart was racing, breathing ragged. Sweat coated his face and back. Coda thrashed, but the harder he fought, the harder the figure held.

"Coda," the figure said. "Hey, it's me."

With his fight-or-flight responses fully triggered, the words didn't register. Coda thrashed harder, grunting with the effort. Suddenly, as if realizing they were doing more harm than good, the figure let him go. Coda slid across the bed and pulled himself close to the wall in a defensive position.

"Coda, it's Squawks. What's wrong?"

When he was no longer restrained, Coda's panic receded, and awareness washed over him. He was in his bed inside the Forgotten barracks. Faint light from the bulkhead illuminated the side of Squawks's face. His friend was shirtless, hair disheveled, and had clearly been asleep.

Coda held a hand to his forehead, trying to catch his breath. "I'm okay." That wasn't true, but he didn't know what else to say. "I'm okay." Maybe if he repeated the words, they'd become a reality.

"You were screaming," Squawks said.

Coda ran a hand across his head. It came away slick with sweat. *Screaming?*

He had been... The images came back to him.

Running.

The Overlord and his warriors chasing him.

Flanking him.

Funneling him toward a specific location.

The Overlord had shown him the end of the world.

"Are you sure you're okay?" There was something in Squawks's voice, not just concern but a tinge of... embarrassment? Squawks looked to the side.

Coda followed his gaze, noticing for the first time the other figures in the distance. Other pilots. They were watching, listening. Like Squawks, Coda must have woken them up with his screaming.

The heat of humiliation washed over Coda's face. "I'm fine."

Coda slid across the bed and stood wearily on unsteady legs. The deck was cold under his bare feet, bringing additional awareness. He nodded his appreciation to Squawks and strode across the room. He passed several bunks on his way, feeling the eyes of his comrades following him. How many had he woken up with his fit? How many had heard Squawks wake him? It was impossible to tell, but even for those who hadn't, word would quickly travel.

*As if things aren't awkward enough.*

The squadron's shared bathroom was nearby and blessedly unoccupied. The lights flickered on as Coda strode in. He paused in front of the mirror, looking at his pale reflection. Finally away from the watchful eyes of others, he let out a long breath.

*What was that? A dream or something more?* It was reminiscent of the times he'd been connected to the Baranyk network, though... fuzzier. Dreamlike. That didn't make the images any less terrifying. The dream had shown him death and destruction on a scale he'd never thought possible. If he had been connected to the Baranyk network, the Overlord was behind it. The question was, was the Overlord showing him something that had already happened or things yet to come?

One thing was for certain—Captain Coleman needed to know.

Coda splashed cold water on his face then checked the time. 0430. The captain wouldn't be awake yet, and Coda had no interest in going back to the barracks. Instead, he showered then wrote the captain, detailing what he'd seen and been through. When Captain Coleman woke and was ready to discuss it, he would find Coda.

With nothing else to do and with a laundry list of to-do items, Coda got to work. The first order of business was scheduling the CAP. The *Redemption* was still in Baranyk space, and though they hadn't seen the enemy in weeks, they'd maintained Condition-1 throughout the ship. That meant a full flight would fly CAP instead of the standard fighter pair. With their reduced forces, that also meant the pilots hadn't gone a full twenty-four-hour rotation without time in the cockpit.

He'd once heard that tackling the day's simplest task first helped build momentum to tackle the next. From a scheduling standpoint, once the flight rotation had been set, little needed updating. Small daily tweaks to accommodate for sick or injured pilots were necessary but uncommon. Finalizing the CAP took all of fifteen minutes, but it was fifteen minutes that Coda didn't have to think about his dreams. Once complete, he sent the schedule to his pilots and made sure it was displayed in the Nighthawk ready room. With the CAP schedule in place, Coda moved on to the next order of business.

The flight deck of the *Redemption* was bustling even during the off-hour. Nighthawks lined the deck. Mechanics performed routine maintenance, while others used yellow roller skids to load the next wave of Nighthawks into the launch tubes that would catapult the next flight of pilots into space.

He found the chief overseeing a hull repair on one of their dropships. Slightly overweight with thinning hair and grease-covered overalls, the chief was clearly someone who preferred to get his hands dirty.

"Good morning, sir," the chief said. "You're up early."

"Lots to do," Coda said. "Looks like things are moving along pretty well here."

The chief wiped his hands on an orange shop towel, his eyes scanning the deck. "The break in action has given us an opportunity to catch up on repairs. Your squadrons should be back to fully operational by the end of the week. Assuming nothing happens in the interim, of course."

"Of course." Images of devastated fleets and floating debris orbiting fallen planets flooded Coda's mind. "Where do we stand today?"

"Forty-four of our forty-eight fighters are flight ready, and two more should be ready by tomorrow. The others"—the chief pointed into the distance where a Nighthawk was getting a full wing replacement—"are undergoing more extensive repair."

"Excuse my ignorance, but I'm stepping into the middle of this without a lot of background. We haven't had a battle in weeks. What's the holdup?"

"The repairs themselves don't take much time. The parts in these Nighthawks were meant to be rip-and-replace, and as you can see, I've got plenty of help. No, the issue is supply."

"The parts themselves?"

"No, sir," the chief said. "We don't store the parts here. We use additive manufacturing to build the parts we need, but even working around the clock, that takes time. Especially with the larger repairs." He motioned once more toward the Nighthawk getting the new wing.

"Makes sense," Coda said. "If you can get me your estimated repair timelines, based on ship type and availability date, I'd appreciate it.

"Will do, sir."

"Thank you, Chief."

Coda nodded and left the chief to his work. Short of getting his hands dirty himself, there wasn't much he could do to speed up the repairs, and he wasn't entirely convinced that would help efforts anyway. His responsibility would be to hold the chief accountable to his timelines, alleviate any bottlenecks, and reprioritize repairs based on anything that came up in the meantime.

Such was Coda's morning—completing what many would have considered mundane tasks. The worst of it was reviewing and organizing the readiness training they had neglected in lieu of their compressed flight training and battle schedule. Scanning through the required trainings, Coda couldn't help but laugh. *What kind of bureaucratic dickwad requires sensitivity training during war? Don't we have bigger issues to worry about?*

He took the question to Moscow, who took the issue up the chain, and the answer Coda got back was no. In their downtime, the Forgotten were expected to complete all required training.

Coda was the first to take it and thus the first to see what the other pilots had to look forward to. They were going to hate it. And they were going to hate him more because it was his responsibility to ensure they completed it. Just another thing driving a wedge between him and his comrades.

A week after scheduling and assigning the trainings, he overheard some pilots referring to him as "HR." If he hadn't already had a call sign, the name might have stuck. As it was, it was already catching on, and even though he outranked every pilot except Moscow, they weren't afraid to say it within earshot.

The only thing that kept him from losing his pilots entirely were his simulations. Moscow had tasked him with developing a new flight curriculum based around new scenarios. Coda had a few initial ideas, including battles in debris fields, enemy cloaking devices, and new enemy weapons, but after the first week, he was beginning to run dry.

He reviewed old battles, seeking inspiration, but those had been the basis for training exercises ever since their time at the flight academies. He was able to repurpose a few of them since those scenarios had been built for training drone pilots, but he still felt like he was failing Moscow.

It was his friends and their dinner conversations that triggered new ideas. What started as a simple vent session turned into a series of "what if" questions.

"What if our communications failed or were hacked?"

"What would happen if we lost sensor data?"

"How would we address gravity fluctuations?"

No idea was too obscure, and each idea was crazier than the last. With them, Coda had everything he needed to build a new training program that would build on itself, growing more difficult by the day.

The Forgotten devoured it. Battle starved, they attacked the new simulations with renewed vigor. The flight leaders held extended training sessions, repeated scenarios, and analyzed them until they were victorious with what Moscow considered acceptable losses.

As the days drifted by, Coda fell into the rhythm of his new life, and his former pilots became less bitter. Seeing Coda surrounded by his friends in the mess hall—friends who were still the Forgotten's flight leaders—helped end the frustrated comments. Coda didn't know if anyone ever addressed the pilots, but as quickly as the HR taunts started, they disappeared.

He doubted he'd reearned their respect, but at the very least, he didn't have their hatred. If only the same thing could be said about his strange dreams. They returned every night with the same intensity, though fortunately, his reactions were less dramatic than the first. He would wake soaked with sweat, with an accelerated heart rate, but he rarely woke those around him. He was suffering but silently.

Captain Coleman ordered him to see Dr. Naidoo, but a series of scans showed no outside influence. If Coda *was* connecting to the Baranyk network, it was by his own volition, and they didn't have a way to test for that. Dr. Rydell didn't seem concerned, chalking it up as posttraumatic stress, prescribed sleeping medication, and extended his restricted duty. When that didn't have an effect, she ordered him to see the ship's psychiatrist.

Coda couldn't help but feel like there was something more. Something they were missing. And his father agreed.

"The Overlord isn't done with you," Joseph O'Neil said. "He's not done with either of us. We have to be ready when he comes."

That was the rub. He and his father were both one step up from being prisoners on their own ship. Coda was running a race, falling farther behind with every lap, and was running out of time to catch up. And he couldn't shake the feeling that when he lost, humanity would lose with him.

# 5

*Bridge, SAS Redemption*
*Baranyk Space*

Captain Coleman tapped his fingernail on the railing that surrounded the bridge's battle map. Like much on the *Redemption*, the railing was made of a composite then coated in a rubber material to make it soft. It wouldn't do to have ship personnel crashing into walls, corners, or railings during the thick of battle. The unexpected consequence was that Coleman's tapping fingernails emitted a deadened sound, not the satisfying tinging he craved.

Thirteen jumps. That was what had stood between them and the JumpGate when Commander Payton had warned him of the damaged EmDrive. Thirteen jumps. Ten of them had gone off without a hitch, but every time Coleman ordered a jump, he wondered if it would be the last.

If the EmDrive suffered a full system failure and exploded as Commander Payton had predicted, would it take out the entire ship or only damage it enough that if left them to suffer a long and slow death?

Ten times crisis had been averted—but not the eleventh.

"The temperature spiked," Commander Payton said directly into Coleman's earpiece.

Coleman cursed silently. They were so close. They couldn't afford to stop now. "Any ideas why?" He kept his voice quiet so that nobody else on the bridge could hear him.

"It could be any number of reasons, sir." Commander Payton was breathless, distracted, and obviously evaluating readings while updating Coleman. "There could be a coolant leak, a damaged pump, or cracked line. Hell, it could even be an issue with the thermostat itself. As we talked about before, there's no way to know without shutting it down."

Coleman slapped the railing. "We're two jumps away, Chief."

"I know, sir."

"Damn it," Coleman said. The words came out soft and defeated, barely more than a whisper.

"What was that, sir?"

"Nothing." Coleman pinched the bridge of his nose. *How does one choose between two terrible options?* He let his eyes drift around the bridge, ignoring the lights and readouts, focusing on his people. Every one of them was an expert at their job, molded through training, dedication, and war. He trusted every one of them, including his chief engineer, with his life.

"Give me your assessment, Chief," Coleman said. "Will my ship hold together?"

Commander Payton sighed. He shared a lot in common with Dr. Naidoo, especially his disdain for conjecture. To them, if it didn't exist on a spreadsheet, it didn't exist at all.

"The temperature readings are dropping, sir. Not back to their previous levels, but no longer critical. Will it hold together? I don't know. It's a calculated risk."

A calculated risk. The words were as close to a prediction as he was going to get, and that gave Coleman a strange confidence. His decisions were based not on blind determination, hope, or luck but on the best information he had at his disposal. Information on a spreadsheet, so to speak.

"Proceed with the jump, Commander."

"Yes, sir."

The line went dead.

"Everything okay, sir?" Commander Garcia asked. He'd sidled next to

Coleman during the conversation. He kept his voice soft, quiet enough that only Coleman could hear it.

"The chief was just giving me an update on our EmDrive," Coleman said. The best kind of lie was the one that was entirely truthful.

Commander Garcia looked skeptical but didn't pry. He knew that if the captain was keeping something from him, he probably didn't want to know anyway.

Thirty minutes later, they jumped for what Coleman hoped was the second-to-last time. His hands were moist against the metal railing as he issued the order. It might have been his imagination, but the world-stretching sensation seemed to last longer than usual. He closed his eyes as he always did during a jump, wondering if he would get the chance to open them again.

One breath.

Two.

*Why haven't we arrived yet?*

Coleman opened his eyes to a world that looked as though he were seeing it through a funhouse mirror. Everything was distorted, elongated, *wrong*. His breakfast threatened to come up, and he had to slam his eyes shut again to keep it down.

*Deep breath. Three seconds in. Hold. Three seconds out.*

"Jump complete, sir."

Coleman let out the breath in a rush. The bridge crew did the same. He suspected they felt his unease. He hadn't done a good job of hiding it today. He nodded to Commander Garcia then made for his captain's chair. He couldn't undo the damage he'd already done, but the ship was only one jump away from their destination. They were going to make it if he had to will it into existence, and he would exude confidence all the way there.

Coleman brought up a direct line to Commander Payton. "Talk to me."

"Temperature and pressure readings are critical," Commander Payton said. The engineering bay was loud, full of shouting engineers and blaring alarms. "Critical but stable. We might only have one jump left in us, sir."

"One is all we need," Coleman said, daring to hope.

"She'll give it to you, sir," Commander Payton said with a strange confidence he hadn't had before.

*One more jump.*

"Begin the jump sequence," Coleman said, this time loudly enough for everyone to hear him. "Let's go home."

The crew answered him with a small cheer.

The jump would take them to the JumpGate on the edge of human space, which would then take them back to the fleet. A different fear wormed its way into Coleman's gut—what would they find when they got there?

# 6

*Control Center, JumpGate Vega-3*
*Edge of Human Occupied Space*

ENSIGN JAMES LARSON HAD DONE THINGS WITH HIS LIFE. GROWING UP IN A small, rural town in the United States' Pacific Northwest, he'd never expected to live a noteworthy life. No fame, riches, glitz, or glamour. After all, his family had raised cattle for six generations. His future had been chosen for him, and he wasn't man enough to look his father, grandfather, and great-grandfather in the eye and tell them that life, *their* life, wasn't for him.

When the Baranyk attacked, slipping through humanity's defenses and killing indiscriminately, life had changed, even in small-town USA. The world was bigger than their ranch and its cattle, and there were more important things than small-minded feelings. Life had been built on what had seemed like an indelible foundation, but when that crumbled, James was left without a present, let alone a future.

Lost and unsure where to turn, James followed in the footsteps of many of his former townsfolk and joined the service. In the same way cattle ranching had been chosen for him, fate, it seemed, had placed him on a different path.

That was what brought him to JumpGate Vega-3 on the edge of human-controlled space. It was also what kept him from complaining about being stationed on one of the most out-of-the-way posts in the system. Every person had a part to play, even a lowly controller in the middle of nowhere, and there was honor in that.

The JumpGates were manned and operated with a skeleton crew of ten who were responsible for everything from operations to maintenance—a perfect job for someone used to working from sunup to sundown and never finishing everything that needed finishing. It was a solitary life, filled with long hours and homemade alcohol, card games, and the occasional fight.

Letting out a long sigh, James let himself look forward to his after-shift drink. His friend and fellow controller, Mickey, had found a new way to cheat in their nightly games, and he was going to figure out how. It was about the only thing worth looking forward to out here, where the silence and lack of anything eventful made it difficult to maintain a steadfast concentration on one's duties.

That was how he nearly missed the blip that appeared on their scans.

"Contact!" James shouted. His thick, callused hands toggled the station, isolating the new ship, bringing up its telemetry data. He felt his CO, Commander Maldari, step closer, likely looking over his shoulder to view the information.

"What is it?" Commander Maldari asked.

"Not sure yet, sir, but it's headed directly for us and coming in hot."

"Bring weapons online," Commander Maldari said. "Track the target, but don't fire. I repeat, do not fire."

"Yes, sir," Mickey said from the station beside James's. He gave James a wicked grin. He hadn't fired the JumpGate's defensive canons since the last maintenance cycle.

"Transponder signal coming in now," James said. "It's... It's one of ours, sir. Designation SAS *Redemption*, sir."

"The *Redemption*?" Commander Maldari asked. "Never heard of it."

"It checks out, sir."

"Get them on the comm," Commander Maldari said. "But keep weapons online. Something doesn't look right."

The commander was right. The *Redemption* was coming in hot, and its starboard hull had been breached. Gases and fluids leaked into space, leaving a trail behind the massive starship. If it had been one of his old farm trucks, it would have been rolling with a broken windshield, nursing a flat tire, and backfiring.

"SAS *Redemption*, this is Ensign Larson of JumpGate Vega-3. Do you copy?"

"We copy, Ensign. It's good to hear another human voice."

"Copy, *Redemption.* Decrease speed to two hundred KPH and prepare to rendezvous with these coordinates." James sent an updated set of coordinates, accommodating their uncharacteristic speed.

"We're working on it, Ensign. Our EmDrive blew, and we're navigating on thrusters. It's going to take us some time to slow down."

"On thrusters?" Commander Maldari repeated.

James was already ahead of him. "Copy that, *Redemption*. In that case, please alter course to the following bearing and try and avoid a fender bender. There's an awful lot of space out here. I'd hate to see us fight over the same parking spot."

"Agreed, Ensign. Altering course now. We'll see you soon."

---

Coda collapsed onto the bed with a groan. It had been another long day of performing mundane tasks and reminding his pilots of things they should have already known and completed. He'd told himself he could handle it if it helped him get back into the cockpit, but damn, it was getting hard.

He missed the speed, the constant movement, the forces pushing him into his seat and shoving him around the cockpit. He longed for the pilot banter, Squawks's bad jokes, and Noodle somehow always finding himself at the butt of them.

More than anything, he missed the feeling of making a difference. It was easy to measure his impact when he could count his kills. It was much less gratifying to measure how many of his pilots had completed their sensitivity trainings.

"You look like hell," his father said.

Coda gave him a short laugh and leaned back on the bed, closing his eyes. They were in his father's quarters, something Captain Coleman had given him after his rescue and their escape from New Plymouth. It was cramped, barely large enough for the bed and a small table fastened to the deck, but they were a large upgrade from the cell Joseph O'Neil had spent his first several rotations in.

"Still not sleeping?" His father wore a worried expression that Coda wasn't accustomed to seeing. In the weeks since New Plymouth, they had grown close, seeing each other almost nightly. After being separated for more than a decade, they had a lot of catching up to do.

"No," Coda said with a resigned breath. Every night was plagued with dreams—or visions; Coda wasn't sure how to refer to them—each similar to the last. Always death and destruction. Fallen worlds. The Overlord was giving him a front-row seat to humanity's downfall. "I went to see Dr. Naidoo again. She assures me I'm not being hit with any sort of outside signal. She's not convinced they're anything more than dreams. And Dr. Rydell thinks it's stress."

"Have you been working on the mental exercises I taught you?" his father asked.

"I'm trying to," Coda said.

"That doesn't sound very convincing."

Coda opened an eye to look at his father. He sat on the edge of the bed with him, his expression firm and unrelenting. His father knew he was lying. *How does he do that? Was it something in my voice?*

"Okay," Coda said. "I tried. But I didn't see any difference, so I haven't done them in a while."

"Callan..." His father often called him by his birth name rather than his call sign. If it were anyone else, Coda might have been frustrated by it, but coming from his father, the name just sounded right. "You didn't learn to fly a Nighthawk in a week. It needs time and practice."

"I know. I'm just—"

"Making excuses."

Coda clamped his mouth shut. He wanted to respond but didn't have anything to come back with. His father was right. He hadn't given the exercises his all.

"The Overlord plagued me after Kryos," his father continued. "It didn't matter how far I was from him. Distance means nothing with the Baranyk network. But I learned how to keep him out of my mind, to only connect with the network when I wanted to, and to only let certain parts of my mind do it. Use the exercises, Coda. They work.

And the sooner you prove that, the sooner you can get back into the cockpit."

Coda had serious doubts that he would ever be allowed back into the cockpit, but it was his ultimate goal. First, he had to prove to Captain Coleman and Dr. Naidoo that he was no longer a liability, that he had control over when and how he accessed the Baranyk network, and that the Overlord had no influence over him.

"You're right," Coda said. "I know you're right. I'll do a better job."

"We can do them together," his father said, not letting him end the conversation there. "At night, when you visit. I'll coach you through them. I should have been doing that already."

"We had other things to discuss."

"Still," his father said. "I was selfish. I wasn't thinking about what you needed. I was just making up for lost time."

"Me too," Coda said. "We're nearly back to human space now."

"I know."

Word had traveled quickly through the ship. The EmDrive was damaged in their last jump, but they had somehow made it to the Jump-Gate. Within the hour, they would be jumping back to the fleet.

Where the prospect of returning home had been a welcome one for most of the crew, it haunted Coda and his father like a ticking clock counting down to his execution. The name Joseph O'Neil wasn't well regarded in the Sol Fleet, and nobody knew what would happen when they returned.

"Listen, Callan—"

"No," Coda said. "Don't."

"When we return, they're going to take me into custody and try me for treason."

"Dad, stop."

"No, Callan, I need you to hear this. At the very least, I'll be convicted of the deaths of my wingmen. My name has been tarnished for too long, and it's going to take years before Fleet Intelligence accepts that the Overlord is controlling us. Years I don't have."

"You have Captain Coleman, who will testify," Coda said. "Dr. Naidoo too. *Me.* You're not in this alone."

His father placed a hand on his shoulder and gave him a wan smile. "I know, son. And I'm not going to give up. Getting you back in my life has been the single greatest gift I could ever ask for. These last few weeks have been some of the best of my life. I'm going to fight, but I want to make sure you understand the battle we have in front of us."

"I understand." The words came out softly. Resigned. Like so much of what he had already said this night, his father was right. They had a battle in front of them. Many of them. With enemies coming from all sides and directions. Coda had no idea how they would keep from being overwhelmed.

His father squeezed his shoulder. "Now, let's practice those exercises. Hopefully, I have at least enough time to leave you with the gift of life without the Overlord."

# 7

*Bridge, SAS Redemption*
*Europa Station, Sol System*

COLEMAN LET OUT A LONG BREATH. WITHOUT EVEN OPENING HIS EYES, HE knew they were back. They weren't home in the sense of familial home but the little part of the galaxy that humanity had claimed as theirs. Despite all odds—weeks spent in enemy territory, servicemen under enemy control, a taxed EmDrive, and a near collision with the JumpGate that had shot them the rest of the way—they had made it back.

Had they made it in time, though?

Opening his eyes, he immediately found the battle map. Readings were already being returned, green wireframe images appearing as more sensor data came in. They quickly filled the entire map, even as the white-and-red glow of Europa filled a good quarter of it.

The moon had been the first human colony established beyond the belt, and it had quickly grown to be the largest in the Sol System. Because it was within jump distance to other occupied celestial bodies and close but not too close to Earth, it had become the Sol Fleet's headquarters. Dozens of warships waited in dock or patrolled the perimeter.

The sight of their fleet triggered a spark of hope. If they were here, they weren't fighting elsewhere, and that meant Captain Coleman had beaten the Baranyk back. Europa had more JumpGates than any other system, making it the best option to move the fleet in a hurry. The fact that the ships were idle and not yet deployed had to be a positive sign.

"Sir," Ensign Richey said, cutting over the din of the bridge, "we're being ordered to dock with Europa Station."

"Make it happen, Ensign."

"Yes, sir." Ensign Richey sent their acceptance back. "There's more, sir. The admiral is onboard as well and requesting direct communication."

Coleman shared an ominous look with Commander Garcia then made for the door to the bridge. "Put him through."

"Patching him directly into your earpiece, sir."

Coleman nodded as he passed Ensign Richey then stepped into the corridor beyond. "Sir, this is Captain Coleman. Do you read?"

"Captain," came the familiar voice of Admiral Orlovsky, "it's damn good to hear your voice."

"Yours too, sir."

"Welcome back."

"Thank you, sir."

"My tactical officer says your ship is a mess."

"She's seen better days, sir. Nothing a few days in dry dock won't fix."

"Glad to hear it, Captain. Once you dock and get your repairs in order, I need to speak with you."

Something in his tone gave Coleman pause. "Of course, sir. I'll take a shuttle over first chance I get. But, sir, can you do something for me first?"

"What is it, Captain?"

"Did our drones make it back? Do you have our reports?"

"They did, Captain," Admiral Orlovsky said. "We do. Thanks to you and your crew, we know the enemy is coming. And when they arrive, we're going to give them a warm welcome."

It felt like a thousand kilograms fell off Coleman's shoulders. They'd done it. They'd made it back before the enemy, and their data on the enemy's fleet had arrived too.

*We have a chance*, Coleman thought. *We have a chance.*

The SAS *Abraham Lincoln* was once the flagship of the Sol Fleet, representing the full might and technological prowess humanity had to offer. But after serving aboard the *Redemption*, Coleman could spot its age. Little things like a scuffed deck that had been worn down by thousands of feet, bulkheads that showed signs of burns or smoke damage regardless of how well they'd been scrubbed, or entire sections of bulkheads that had been replaced but were a slightly different color. It wasn't as different as the *Jamestown* but still a gentle reminder of how good they'd had it aboard the *Redemption*.

He was escorted through the corridors by a marine guard who had greeted him at the airlock. Like all marines, they had little to say and set a brisk pace. The general layout of the ship was similar to the *Redemption,* and Admiral Orlovsky's quarters were near the bridge at the heart of the ship. Once they arrived, the two marines knocked then took up guard beside the door as it opened.

"Come in," Admiral Orlovsky said.

Coleman stepped inside.

Admiral Orlovsky stood with his back to Coleman, looking through the window behind his desk as space traffic flew against the backdrop of Europa. It wasn't a real window, of course, but a digital screen mimicking one. Still, it helped the room feel less claustrophobic.

Coleman snapped to attention. Admiral Orlovsky turned and offered his old friend a weak smile. "At ease, Captain. And take a seat." He gestured at one of the two armchairs on Coleman's side of the desk.

"Thank you, sir." Coleman took a seat.

"It's good to see you, Chadwick." Admiral Orlovsky sat in his thick leather-backed chair. "I must say, there were days I didn't think I'd ever see you again."

"There were days I wondered if I'd ever make it back myself," Coleman admitted. "But I've got a hell of a ship and an even more impressive crew."

"How are they holding up?"

"You saw my ship," Coleman said with a smirk. "The crew's in better shape. Many of them had some downtime on the race back from Kryos.

They know this isn't the end, just the first move in a bigger game. They'll be ready for whatever comes next."

"Good," Admiral Orlovsky said. "Good." He stood and walked to a small bar in the corner of the room. He poured two drinks and offered one to Coleman.

"Thank you, sir," Coleman said, taking the drink.

"You look like you need it." Admiral Orlovsky returned to his seat. "You're wound up tighter than a bull's ass."

Coleman gave him a small laugh. "I guess I'm just wondering what *does* come next. To be honest, I was a little surprised to see our fleet." He took a sip, letting the sharp notes of vanilla linger on his tongue, using it as an excuse to force the admiral into a reply.

"The truth is," Admiral Orlovsky said, "your scans helped, but the drones didn't return much quicker than you. In the little time we've had to prepare, we've done everything we can to ready ourselves for their arrival. Every system is on high alert, every available ship has been mobilized, and any undergoing repairs or new ships near enough to completion have been pushed into production. Not only that, but reserves have been called up, retirees called back, and personnel at the end of their training promoted into service. Your scans showed hundreds of ships. We'll never be able to match that, but we've done what we can to even the odds."

"What about the brain abnormality?" Coleman pressed. "We've seen the damage even a single enemy combatant can do. Imagine a dozen of them. A hundred."

"Medical personnel on every ship, station, and orbital platform are scanning their crews to look for your brain anomaly as we speak. But it takes time."

"Good." Coleman had been afraid Fleet Intelligence wouldn't take that part of his report seriously. Enemy mind control sounded crazy even to him, and he'd seen it firsthand.

"The biggest challenge is not knowing where they'll strike first. That's why I've mobilized the fleet here. Europa Station has more Jump-Gates than any system. The moment we catch sight of the enemy, we can respond in force, and after a few battles, we'll be able to predict where they'll hit next. We're not as flat-footed as we appear."

The admiral's plan was sound, and if they really hadn't had much time to prepare, Coleman wasn't sure he would have planned any differently.

"And," Admiral Orlovsky continued, his voice tinged with a spark of excitement, "we have a few surprises of our own."

"What kind of surprises?" Coleman asked, taking the bait.

Admiral Orlovsky gave him one of his famous smiles, broad and with teeth even whiter than his hair. In that moment, he was the very image of leadership. "Fleet Intelligence has finally countered the Baranyk disruptor weapon. Our drones are operational again."

The admiral obviously meant the news as a grand flourish, but it hit Coleman like five G's to the chest without inertial dampeners. For months, the Forgotten had been doing the impossible and were all that had kept the Baranyk at bay. Humans had returned to the cockpit of starfighters, flying at impossible speeds, risking life and limb on every flight. In a single sentence, all of that was in jeopardy. Again.

Coleman was immediately reminded of a similar conversation with the same man. His old friend had told him the Nighthawk program was being shut down. That the war was moving on without him. That he would never fly again. Though the fleet's drone squadrons being operational again *was* good news, Coleman couldn't help but feel like something was being taken from him. Couldn't help but wonder if he'd flown for the last time without even realizing it.

"How?" was all he managed to get out.

"Something about quantum, fluctuating, variable frequencies or something. It's too complicated for me, but Fleet Intelligence says they'll work, and that's enough for me."

"That's great," Coleman said—and it was. The drones would take some of the stress off his pilots.

"It is," Admiral Orlovsky agreed. "You did it, Chadwick. You and your squadron. We asked for a miracle, and you delivered. But we're not through with you yet. We want to maintain the secret for as long as we can. Funnel the enemy into a large confrontation and unveil them then." He made a fist and punched the palm of his hand. "We mean to hit them hard and where it counts and turn the momentum of this war strongly in our favor."

"Yes, sir," Coleman said. The excitement wasn't gone yet. He hadn't flown his final flight yet. "We'll be ready."

"Good." Admiral Orlovsky stood. "In the meantime, get some rest and patch up your ship. We're going to need you in fighting shape."

"Of course, sir." Coleman stood as well then lingered, not taking the obvious dismissal. "There's... one other thing, sir. Something not in my report."

"Oh?"

"During our investigation, we returned to Kryos." Coleman took a steadying breath. What he was about to do could go in a thousand different directions, most of them bad, and he wasn't ready for any of them. "We found him, sir. We found Lieutenant Joseph O'Neil."

The words hung in their air like a foul stench. Joseph O'Neil. Coda's father. Someone who had long been thought to be a traitor to humanity. Only a small handful of military personnel knew he had evaded capture and had not been tossed out an airlock like the official story claimed.

"What?" Admiral Orlovsky whispered.

"It's a long story," Coleman said. "And I'm not sure you want to get into it now, but we found him on New Plymouth. He's been hiding from the Baranyk as much as he's been hiding from us. I know what you're thinking, sir, but he has information about the Baranyk that's vital to the fleet and was instrumental in helping us find their home world."

"You have a war criminal on your ship, and you somehow forgot to mention it?"

"There's more to his story than anyone knows," Coleman said. "He never turned on his wingmen. He was the first of us to be controlled by the enemy."

Admiral Orlovsky rubbed his hands together nervously. "He's to be taken into custody."

"Please listen to me, sir. He's not a traitor. He never was. He was controlled by the enemy by the same brain abnormality outlined in my report. And he's found a way to resist it. Don't you see, sir? He's got critical information on the enemy. We *need* him."

"I need more time to think about this," Admiral Orlovsky said, rubbing his temples. "But he can't remain on your ship. I'll send a marine guard back with you and have him escorted to my brig."

"Sir—"

"No, Captain. This goes beyond our friendship. Joseph O'Neil is a fugitive and a war criminal. We can't sweep this under the rug because of what he might know. There are protocols to follow here."

"What will happen to him?"

"I don't know," Admiral Orlovsky said. "It will be up to a military tribunal to decide. In the meantime, I just don't know."

*It's not the worst-case scenario.* "I stand behind him, sir. Everything I've learned, everything I've seen speaks to his innocence."

"Then he'll get that chance, Captain. Until then, he'll enjoy the comforts of my brig. Ensure that he returns on your shuttle."

"Of course, sir," Coleman conceded.

"Dismissed."

# 8

*Quarters, SAS Redemption*
*Europa Station, Sol System*

Joseph O'Neil's quarters could hardly qualify as a closet, let alone an accommodation. Still, having a private room to himself at all was something of an unexpected miracle. With just enough room for a cot and a simple chair, it lacked the luxuries of other private rooms, likely because it had, in fact, been a storage locker.

Captain Coleman had said he didn't want to keep him in the brig, not after Joseph had proved his loyalties, but he couldn't have him bunking with the enlisted personnel, either. On a ship where space was at a premium, he'd found a seldom-used storage locker just large enough to house a human being.

Coda had made himself comfortable on the cot while his father sat in the chair. It had been a long day at the end of a long week, full of the same monotony as before—schedule the CAP, check with the chief, ensure that the pilots were completing their required trainings even though they attempted to shirk them at every opportunity, program new battle scenarios, and review previous simulator flights.

The last two items were far and away the most interesting, and the flight reviews gave him time with his friends. Squawks, Noodle, Moscow, and Nails reviewed every flight together, analyzing how their squadrons had done and brainstorming what they could have done differently.

But it was an endless march through uniformity, every day the same, every interaction the same, and all without an outlet. These nightly conversations with his father were as close as Coda ever got to blowing off some steam, and even then, he felt like he was just complaining.

"I would do almost anything to get back into the cockpit," Coda said. His head was at the foot of the bed, nearest his father's chair, eyes locked on the ceiling. If he squinted just right, the dirt and imperfections on the ceiling looked like constellations. "Just one more time. Feel the weight of acceleration, let inertia toss me around, rip through space at speeds most people can't even imagine."

"It's a drug," his father said. "We used to talk about it. The pull. The addiction."

"I've never thought of it that way," Coda said.

"How else can you explain why we climb in the cockpit time after time? Why a man, when given an ultimatum, his fighter or his family, would choose his fighter?"

"I don't know," Coda said. "For me, it was the times I felt the most alive."

"Says every addict who's ever lived."

"I guess." Coda didn't want to think about it too deeply. He missed flying and the comradery with his wingmen. That didn't mean he was addicted. "What about you? Is there any part of you that misses it?"

"No."

"Not even a little?"

The following silence pulled Coda's attention from the ceiling. His father had his eyes on the deck, his face sullen, eyes haunted.

"Sorry," Coda said. "I wasn't..."

His father didn't seem to hear him. It had been a stupid question. Of course his father didn't miss it—he was terrified of the cockpit. The last time he'd flown, he'd shot down his wingmen, killing some of his closest friends.

"It's okay," his father said. "The truth is, I do miss it. There was a freedom in the black. Just you and the enemy, surrounded by nothing but the cold void. There was no hiding. No faking. If you weren't up to snuff, you were done. There's no greater test than that. In a way, it was liberating."

There was a longing in his father's words, an ache in his tone. Maybe he was afraid to admit it to himself, but Coda had the feeling his father missed the cockpit every bit as much as he did.

"Let's find out, then," Coda said.

"Hmmm?"

"Yeah." Coda sat up, swinging his legs around so that his feet were on the deck. "C'mon."

"What are you talking about? They'll never let us in a Nighthawk."

"No," Coda agreed. "But there's no restrictions on the simulator."

His father leaned back in his chair, suddenly understanding where Coda's head was at. "I'm sure they're in use."

Coda shook his head. "They're not. I'd know—I make the schedule." He laughed. For once, the tedious task had worked in his favor.

"I don't know," his father said.

"Why not?" Coda pressed. "C'mon, it'll be fun."

"Dr. Rydell grounded you."

"From flying," Coda said. "She's worried the strain would be too much. The simulator is different."

His father looked at him, his breathing faster. Coda could see the desire in his eyes. The same excitement he felt.

"It'll be fun." Coda stood. "Let's go."

His father's face broke into a smile. "All right, fine. Let's do it."

Coda led his father out of his room and through the ship to the Simulation Room. He set a brisk pace, both excited and worried that his father would back out. Coda wanted this. Needed it. He'd thought he would never get the chance to fly with his father, to share a mutual love the same way so many boys and fathers shared their love of sports.

As Coda had expected, the Simulation Room was empty. The lights turned on automatically as they entered, and he made directly for the control panel. "We can start with a basic survival scenario. Let you get your feet under you again."

His fingers raced across the panel, pulling up the hop that he and every other member of the Forgotten had flown a thousand times. The objective was simply to stay alive for as long as possible while wave after wave of enemy fighters swarmed in in an ever-increasing level of difficulty. The perfect warmup scenario, it was often used if someone just wanted to blow off some steam. The simulator's equivalent of working out or going on a run.

With the scenario selected, Coda turned for the simulator but stopped dead in his tracks. His father stood in front of one of the machines. He grabbed one of the bars and gave it a gentle push. The whole simulator spun, the cockpit in the middle rotating with it.

Coda made his way across the room and stopped beside his father's shoulder. "They're pretty impressive, aren't they?"

"Yeah."

Coda couldn't tell if it was awe or fear in his father's voice. "I remember the first time I ever flew in one. We were aboard the *Jamestown*, and my friend Uno, who had earned the privilege of flying in it first, threw up all over the deck. I guess his anxiety got the best of him. So Captain Coleman, Commander Coleman then, let me take his spot. I'd trained to fly the Hornet drones and thought I knew what to expect, but I'd never experienced anything like it. It was incredible. 'Fucking incredible,' I think my exact words were."

His father remained quiet, watching as the rotating bars slowed to a stop.

"C'mon," Coda said. "I'll help you get strapped in."

"No need. I remember how."

"All right."

Coda strode toward the other simulator. He pulled the ladder into position and climbed the steps to the cockpit. With a hard push, the ladder rolled away. Coda strapped in and closed the hatch.

Pulling on his helmet, he was suddenly transported to a field of stars. The simulation was running. As he turned his head, the field of stars shifted with him, and he found a second Nighthawk off his starboard wing. His heart hammered with excitement.

"You ready?" Coda asked over the comm.

"Yeah," his father said.

Coda hit the flashing green Start icon on his instrument cluster. "Let's do this, then."

# 9

*Simulation Room, SAS Redemption*
*Europa Station, Sol System*

Coda was home. For the first time in weeks, every move, gesture, and maneuver was done with complete confidence. Anxiety, self-doubt, and guilt washed away like soap down a drain. He wasn't just home—he was free, unshackled from every side-eyed look, concern, and tragedy. But even as Coda lost himself in the rhythm of the fight, his father did not.

As the first wave of enemy fighters flew in, Coda let out a yell and plotted an aggressive attack vector. It wasn't until the first two fighters were down and Coda was attempting to get missile lock on a third that he realized his father hadn't engaged. His ship flew in the same direction at the same speed as it had when they'd first plugged into the simulator. Worse, the final enemy fighter was closing in, and if he didn't take evasive action, he would be shot down.

The simulators were programed to provide a sharp electric shock any time a fighter was shot down. Captain Coleman didn't want death to be taken lightly, even during a simulation. That, in addition to whatever else his father was feeling, would surely be enough to prevent him from ever getting back into the cockpit of anything, even the simulator.

"Everything okay back there?" Coda asked over the comm.

His father didn't reply.

Cursing, Coda broke off his attack, performing a hard turn that would have been impossible in a real Nighthawk, and burned hard in his father's direction. "You've got a bogey bearing down on you, six degrees positive-Z. On my mark, cut portside sixty degrees, okay?"

Still no reply.

"Dad, did you hear me? Cut portside sixty degrees on my mark. Acknowledge."

Nothing.

*He'll be all right. When it comes to it, instinct will kick in, and he'll do what he needs to do.*

As the enemy closed in, his father didn't show any signs of altering course. The enemy opened fire.

"Mark!"

His father's ship didn't move. The Baranyk's plasma fire was nearly upon him.

"Dad!"

Joseph O'Neil's ship flared, the blues of its Shaw Drive thrusters burning brighter, and it darted port exactly sixty degrees. Baranyk plasma fire narrowly missed his Nighthawk, disappearing into the black.

The enemy fighter moved directly into Coda's line of fire. He sprayed cannon fire across its path. The enemy fighter broke apart, spewing digital goo into space.

"Splash three!" Coda bellowed. "Well done."

Only one enemy fighter remained, the one Coda had been pursuing before breaking off his attack to aid his father. And it was coming around on Coda's tail. He could easily take it out, but with his father finally getting into the action, Coda wanted to see how far he could push him.

"Looks like I picked up a clinger," Coda said. "Altering course too..."

The entire time they'd been in the simulator, his father had been silent, but his father's laughter suddenly filled the line.

"What is it?" Coda asked.

"Clinger," his father said. "I haven't heard that word in a long time. I had a friend whose call sign was that."

"His call sign was Clinger?" Of all the unfortunate call signs he'd heard, that had to be among the worst.

"Yeah. He was one of those guys that always overstayed his welcome, never knew when to leave, and he'd follow us around everywhere we went, from the gym to the mess to the simulator, wherever. Then one hop, he had an enemy on his tail he couldn't shake, and he radioed for help. 'I've got a clinger I can't wipe,' he said. We were all laughing so hard, he nearly got shot down. But from that day on, we called him Clinger."

Coda laughed. "That's hilarious."

"Yeah," his father's said wistfully.

The enemy in pursuit opened fire, spraying plasma across Coda's flight path. He dove negative-Z then spun, corkscrewing around to reverse course.

"You want to help me wipe this one?" Coda asked as the enemy fighter dove in pursuit.

"Wouldn't be the first time I've wiped your ass."

Coda smiled, watching on his HUD as his father's fighter moved into position. Coda's maneuver had brought the enemy perfectly into his firing range. A yellow indicator appeared on his display and streaked toward the enemy vessel. His father had launched a missile. In moments, it turned the enemy fighter into digital slag.

"Good work," Coda said.

"You could have had him."

"I know, but it was funner to do together," Coda said. "You up for another?"

"Yeah," his father said. "I'm just getting warmed up."

"Good, because here comes the next wave."

There were six enemy fighters this time, and in addition to more fighters with each successive wave, their proficiency grew as well. With Coda and his father coming into range, they split into two groups of three. One fighter plotted a direct course to each of them, while the other two attempted to flank. It was a tried-and-true strategy that the enemy employed in every battle. It rarely worked since the human pilots had long since adopted a fighter-pair strategy, but with his father—

Joseph O'Neil's fighter moved into position off Coda's starboard wing in the dash-2 position. They'd never flown together, let alone fought a battle together. It would be crazy to think they could fight as one, but just like the Forgotten had had to start somewhere, so did they.

"Fighters will be in range in six seconds," Coda said. "Target the intercepting fighter with missiles, then maintain course and rotate ninety degrees to protect your flank."

"Yes, *sir*," his father snapped. Coda couldn't tell if he was being sarcastic or just getting into the spirit of the battle.

Coda thumbed the switch on his joystick, switching from cannons to missiles, and a targeting bracket appeared on his HUD. He let the computer autotarget the lead fighter and waited for it to come into range. Because they were flying on a straight course, it didn't take long. A steady tone sounded through the cockpit, indicating that his computer had achieved missile lock.

"Hawk One," Coda said. "Fox four." He squeezed the firing stud. The cockpit rocked as the digital missile sped away, now indicated by a yellow marker on his battle map. It streaked toward the incoming Baranyk fighter, and in a millisecond, both disappeared.

"Splash four!" Coda bellowed just before his father shouted, "Splash five!"

What remained of the Baranyk formation split apart, one going to their port and starboard flanks, the last two darting above and below the battle plane. With the first two fighters vanquished, Coda used a burst of his nose-mounted navigation thrusters to rotate his fighter to port. After switching back to cannons, he sprayed thirty-millimeter slugs across the enemy's trajectory to the tune of fifty-five per second.

"Splash six!" his father said. Coda thought he heard a hint of pride in his father's voice.

"Splash seven!" Coda said. It wasn't lost on him that his father had vanquished his target first.

Glancing at his HUD, Coda saw that the last two enemy fighters were finishing their loop, but the Nighthawks had rotated to their port and starboard sides, so the maneuver brought the enemy toward their flanks.

Without a command, Coda and his father rotated another ninety degrees so that the enemy was coming in head-on. Coda switched back to missiles and got missile lock just as the enemy opened fire. He squeezed the trigger, pressed his joystick to the right, and yanked back, performing a tight turn away from the incoming plasma fire. To his surprise, Coda's father performed the exact same maneuver.

"Not bad, old man," Coda said. "Looks like you've still got it."

"Just like riding a bike. If that bike was going forty thousand kilometers per hour."

Coda smiled as the new contacts appeared on his HUD. "Well, I hope you're ready to take the training wheels off, because here we go again."

There were eight enemy fighters this time, and instead of coming in with a simple formation, they were broken into two formations of four, each offset by one hundred meters. There was no simple strategy this time; it would be a dogfight requiring equal parts skill and speed.

"Contact in... eleven seconds," Coda said. "Break formation and cut to starboard at least one hundred kilometers. I'll do the same to port. See if we can give ourselves a little room to operate in."

"Sounds good."

"Break in three... two... one... Break!"

Coda fired his thrusters and cut hard to port. Immediately, four enemy fighters moved to intercept him. Another four moved to engage his father.

*Time to see how good you really are.*

Settling into the seat of his cockpit, Coda let the rhythm of the battle wash over him. He fired thrusters, dove, spun, corkscrewed, and looped, and was flipped, shaken, and thrown around the cockpit with a dizzying onslaught of movement. His seat rumbled when he fired his cannons and lurched when he launched missiles.

Through it all, he kept one eye on his father's progress. With every passing moment, he was shaking off rust and showing glimpses of the pilot he'd been. Already, he would have been one of the top pilots of the Forgotten, flying with precision and a subtle hint of flamboyance. Coda was surprised to see shades of his own style in there. It was like he was watching himself walk and talk beside a video of his father, noticing how his gait and facial expressions were the same. The way his father flew wasn't identical—Coda had been originally trained to fly a Hornet drone after all—but there were similarities. He couldn't explain it, but something about that made Coda proud.

They completed the third wave without issue then the fourth. It wasn't until the fifth that they began to struggle. When they completed the sixth, Coda had officially lasted longer than he ever had, whether flying solo or with a wingman. They finished the seventh by the skin of their teeth and were finally blown to hell on the eighth.

Coda took off his helmet, a broad smile splitting his face. Sweat coated his hair and soaked his back, but it was a therapeutic feeling, as if his body was expelling mental, physical, and psychological toxins. He glanced over and saw his dad smiling and sweat stained as well. It was an image he expected to remember for the rest of his life—the first time he'd seen his father truly happy since they'd been reunited.

A single person's clapping echoed through the Simulation Room. Captain Coleman waited near the back of the room. He'd toggled the display wall so that he could watch the encounter. Coda had no idea how long he'd been watching, but considering their success, he hoped it had been a while.

The smile on his father's face faltered a bit at the sight of his old friend, and he gave Coda an uneasy look. Coda thought he understood why. They were back in the real world now. That carefree feeling they'd experienced was as much of a simulation as the enemy fighters themselves. Their real-world issues still awaited them.

"That was a hell of a show." Captain Coleman crossed the room then rolled the ladder into place beside Coda's cockpit.

Coda yanked a lever near his seat, locking his simulator in place, then climbed onto the ladder and stepped unsteadily down its steps.

"How many waves was that?"

"Eight," Coda said proudly.

"Not bad." Coleman rolled the ladder over to the second simulator. "How many was our record, Joseph? Eleven?"

"Twelve," Coda's father said, stepping out of the simulator.

"Twelve?" Coda asked in disbelief. "That's incredible."

"We used to live in these things," Captain Coleman said. "We probably would have slept in them if we could."

"Still," Coda said. "Twelve? How many fighters did you face then?"

"Thirty-two," his father said.

"That's more than an entire squadron," Coda said.

"It's not as impressive as it sounds," his father said. "And you have to realize that we believed that for every minute we spent in here, we'd get better out there. If we could just get to the next wave in here, we could save more pilots out there. It was an obsession, and in the end, it didn't make much of a difference."

"I don't know about that," Captain Coleman said. "There's no telling what would have happened if we hadn't pushed ourselves. If *everyone* hadn't pushed themselves."

Coda's father shrugged, but it felt like some of the air had been sucked out of the room. "You speak with the admiral?" he asked, changing the subject.

Captain Coleman nodded curtly. "We beat the enemy back, and the fleet is on high alert. It's just a matter of time."

"Why do I feel like there's a 'but' coming, sir?" Coda asked.

Captain Coleman winced. His eyes darted to Coda's father, to Coda, then back. "I'm sorry, Joseph. I really am. I tried everything I could. But the admiral ordered me to take you into custody and escort you to his ship."

"What?" Coda said.

His father didn't say anything. He just nodded as if he had known the moment was coming.

"Sir," Coda said, "you can't. My father's not a traitor. He's a hero."

"Coda—" Captain Coleman said.

"Without him, we never would have learned about the Overlord. We never would have found the Baranyk home world and discovered their fleet. You can't let them do this."

"I have my orders."

"Forget your—"

"Stand down, Coda!"

The voice cut Coda short, and it took him a moment to realize that it was his father who had addressed him. He took a deep, steadying breath, imagining his anger and frustration leaving his body with his exhale. It wasn't enough to calm him completely, but it was enough to bring him under control.

"I'm sorry, sir," Coda said. "I just thought that with everything we'd been through, everything he'd done, that the admiral would understand."

"I did too," Captain Coleman said. "And he promises me nothing has been decided yet. But he has to follow his protocols, and *we* have to follow our orders."

The anger was swelling again, threatening to take control.

"We knew this was going to happen," his father said.

"It doesn't make it right," Coda said.

"And it doesn't make it wrong, either." Joseph put both hands on Coda's shoulders. "Everything you've done has given me a chance. This isn't over, Callan. Have faith it'll all work out."

"Faith," Coda spat. "I've never had much of that."

"I haven't either," his father said. "Until my son found a way back into my life. I refuse to believe this ends here. You hear me? I refuse."

Coda swallowed the emotion building in his chest and took a shuddering breath. "I refuse too, Dad."

His father pulled him into a tight embrace. "Thank you, Callan."

For as long as Coda could remember, he'd fought for his family. To undo the wrongs done to and by his father. Those demons had originally been personal, but now, they'd become external and went to the very top of the Sol Fleet. The odds were forever being stacked against him, and in the moment, they felt insurmountable.

"For what?" he asked bitterly.

"For this. For giving me one more chance to hug my son and tell him I love him."

At some point in his childhood, Coda had, without knowing it, hugged his father for what could have been the last time. He wasn't going to make that mistake again. He squeezed his father tighter. "I love you too, Dad."

It felt like his dad held on to him for several minutes, which felt like both an eternity and not enough time.

When the embrace ended, his father gave him an encouraging smile and patted him on the shoulder. "I'll see you soon."

"See you soon," Coda said.

With that, Coda's father walked with Captain Coleman into the corridor, where a marine guard waited. The last image Coda saw before the door closed was his father, head held high and seemingly ready for whatever the world threw at him next, being placed in cuffs.

Years before, Coda had vowed to restore honor to his family name. He'd fought in countless battles and even earned a little prestige, but for some time, he'd known that his job was incomplete. This was proof that there was still work to do.

# 10

*Control Center, Orbital Platform*
*Low Orbit, Morning Sun*

Ensign Richard Black needed a fucking drink. He was tired. No, he was exhausted—the my-eyeballs-feel-like-they're-bathing-in-a-tub-of-alcohol kind of exhausted. He'd been on alert for more than thirty-six hours, and his next sleep cycle wasn't for another six. It wasn't the longest he'd ever been awake, not by a long shot, but those two- and three-day bingers had been fueled by cocaine, methamphetamine, and a whole host of other uppers.

*Those were the days*, he thought.

Life had seemed so much simpler then. He'd lived every day with a singular purpose—to find his next drink, his next hit, his next bump. Things like jobs and responsibilities had taken a back seat to feeding his cravings.

Those cravings were what had forced him into the Sol Fleet to begin with. Not the cravings exactly, but when he couldn't hold a job and he didn't qualify for unemployment, he'd had to find money somehow. The first time he'd been caught stealing, he'd broken into a dilapidated apartment in the housing complex he'd recently been kicked out of. It had only gotten worse from there, until his friend Kevin convinced him that they needed to up their game, that if they continued to steal a couple hundred dollars' worth of items, jewelry, and cash at a time, then they would have to do it regularly. If they went bigger and knocked off a store, then they'd be set for a long time.

In the haze of whatever they'd been on at the time, it had sounded like a great plan. Unfortunately, it was a lot harder to knock off a store than the vids suggested. With a growing rap sheet, the judge had given him two choices: a ten-year prison sentence or enlist in the Sol Fleet. Either way, he would have to get clean and kiss everything that made life interesting bye-bye.

The first two weeks had been the hardest. The sweats, the inability to sleep, and the cravings that made him want to crawl out of his skin would have been unbearable if a ten-year prison sentence hadn't been staring him in the face.

The second week was better, except for the fact that every day was boring, lacking any semblance of goals or outlets. By the third week, the brain fog, something that had been settled for so long that Richard hadn't even known it was there, began to dissipate, and he was reminded of who he used to be and how he used to feel.

When the fourth and final week of the program rolled around, he was actually *proud* of what he'd accomplished and excited for what the future held. That didn't mean the cravings had gone away. Not by a long shot, but at least out here, manning an orbital defensive platform above the planet Morning Sun, temptation was few and far between. Yes, he wanted a drink, but when he'd given up the drugs, he'd also been forced to give up smoking, alcohol, and the occasional bet. He was an all-or-nothing kind of guy, and returning to one meant returning to all.

Sitting in his pod, eyes on the terminal, he battled through the fatigue with a newfound determination. It was also why, when his terminal beeped and a single red indicator appeared on its edge, that he was slow to react. Could he be hallucinating? It wouldn't have been the first time.

A second indicator appeared. Then in an instant, there were a dozen, two, three. The entire terminal went red. He blinked, willing the red indicators to go away, but when he looked at the terminal again, it was only filled with more red.

"Contact," he said, his voice barely more than a whisper. "Contact! Multiple bogeys incoming, four hundred thousand kilometers and closing."

He heard the heavy thump of boots rush up behind him. Commander Hobb peered over his shoulder.

"Get a priority one drone through the JumpGate!" Commander Hobb bellowed. "The fleet needs to know what's coming."

"Yes, sir!" Ensign Card, the communications specialist, said from her terminal.

"How long until they're on us?" Commander Hobb asked.

Ensign Black read the indicators on his terminal. "They're showing no signs of slowing down, sir. If they maintain their present speed, they'll be on us in sixteen minutes."

"Thank you, Ensign," Commander Hobb said. "If something changes, let me know."

"Yes, sir," Ensign Black said. "But, sir, the system only has a single battleship and our orbital platforms. We'll be overwhelmed, sir. What are we going to do?"

"We're going to trust our fleet to arrive on time to provide assistance." With that, Commander Hobb returned to his command chair.

*Yeah, I really need a fucking drink.*

# 11

*Engineering, SAS Redemption*
*Europa Station, Sol System*

There were few places Captain Coleman was truly uncomfortable, but Engineering was at the top of that list. It wasn't just that he had only rudimentary knowledge of how things like the EmDrive functioned or that the men and women who read and relayed sensor data sometimes made him feel like a toddler playing with colored shapes. It was more personal than that. In this realm, he was well and truly out of his element. Useless. Just a broken part gumming up the gears.

The engineers seemed to know it too. He'd tried to stay out of their way as he wound through the engines bay, but he'd collided with more than one who'd had their noses buried in their tablet. They'd looked at him, surprised, as if they'd just run into a wall that hadn't been there before. The current of the engineering department moved in different ways than the currents of his pilots or even the deck crews. Here, he just felt like he was walking into a strong headwind.

Taking a deep breath, he came to the edge of one of the workstations. A brightly painted bar was all that stood between it and a vast chamber at least six decks tall, where the massive EmDrive resided. There were so many moving parts, tubes, pistons, wires, and vents that Coleman couldn't make heads or tails of it. The drive was a far cry from the Shaw Drive that powered the Nighthawks. Those were simple. Those, he understood. The EmDrive, which had opened the stars to humanity, might as well have been a Baranyk invention.

Commander Payton stood on a piece of scaffolding about midway up the engine, listening as one of his engineers gave him an update. Coleman scanned the chamber and its network of metal-grated catwalks, seeking a way to his chief engineer, then started his way.

"How's she looking, Chief?" Coleman asked once he was in shouting distance.

"Ah, Captain." Commander Payton turned to face his approaching senior officer. "We're nearly there. The grunt work is over, and now the real work begins."

*Grunt work*, Coleman thought. *As if removing a six-story tall engine and installing a new one was something that any old mechanic could do.* Five days had passed since the *Redemption* entered dry dock for repairs, and Coleman had quickly acquired a replacement engine. Commander Payton's team had wasted little time getting to work.

"What's next?" Coleman asked.

"Adjustments, calibrations, fine-tuning." Commander Payton waved his hand as if Coleman wouldn't understand any of it. "We've got it operating at ten percent. As we continue to bring it online, we'll slowly ramp up the power output."

"How long do you need?" Coleman asked.

"It's hard to say, sir," Payton said. "This part is more an art than a science."

"And yet artists work on deadlines every day, Chief. How long until my ship is in fighting shape?"

Payton let out a sharp breath. Clearly, he didn't like being pushed. "We'll probably be making adjustments for weeks, maybe even months. But your ship should be operational within a few days."

"A few days," Coleman repeated.

"We aren't talking about swapping out an air filter or a spark plug here, sir—"

"I realize that," Coleman interrupted. "We also don't have the luxury of a few days. We have an enemy fleet bearing down on us, and they're not going to care how much time you think you need. I can't tell you what to do—this is your domain—and you're right, I don't understand. But we need to be faster."

Commander Payton opened his mouth to speak.

"We need to be faster, Chief."

"Yes, sir."

"What's the minimum power output where she'll be operational?"

Commander Payton looked at his new engine. "It depends on a number of factors—"

"Chief," Coleman pressed.

"Twenty-five percent," Payton said. "Twenty-five percent, and she'll be combat ready. But every percent above that will represent a marked improvement."

"Good," Coleman said. "Let me know when she's at twenty."

"Of course, sir."

"Carry on." Coleman left Commander Payton to his work.

# 12

*Baranyk Network*
*Unknown*

For all the time Coda had spent in the Baranyk network, the space still felt just as alien as it ever had. In particular was the way he maintained his sense of self in an otherwise-out-of-body experience. He had no body, no nerves, no brain, but he still felt phantom feelings of seeing, hearing, and touch, the impression of speed and distance. The entire experience felt real yet artificial at the same time.

He drifted aimlessly, another lost soul among a sea of stars. Except he knew the lights around him, burning like distant suns, were actually other forms of consciousness—Baranyk and other alien creatures alike, all a part of the same network. A part of him was still in awe that the universe was full of alien life. In the hundreds of years humanity had traveled the stars, they had only come across one intelligent alien life form—and were at war with them. But his connection to the Baranyk network had shown him a universe even bigger than he'd imagined possible.

The lights of consciousness drifted past him, giving him the faintest impressions of feelings and images. The fuzzy, almost dreamlike qualities would come into focus the closer he got. He ignored each of them, keeping his distance. None of them meant anything to him, though he knew somewhere out there, among the billions of lights, was the one he wished he could talk to, the one that had been taken from him for a second time. He'd returned to the network every night since his father was taken into custody, hoping to find him.

As if responding to his feeling of need, one of the distant lights drew nearer, growing in size and brightness as it closed the metaphysical distance. A sense of knowing and belonging grew with it. Coda moved toward it. When they were nearly upon each other, he felt something else, feelings of concern and frustration. He met it with his own sense of confusion as the glow of the light enveloped him.

Coda was transported to another world.

He didn't know how it was possible, but his father brought him to a place only the two of them would know. A place where the Overlord should never be able to find them. When Coda was a child, his father had been an avid baseball fan and had often taken him to the local minor-league stadium to watch the local boys play on their quest to make the big leagues. It was the same stadium that his father had referenced to help Coda find him in the real world.

They sat as they had in those days, on the first-base side in line with first base itself so that if a ball was overthrown it might land in their waiting hands. No one else was there. No other spectators, players, or vendors shouting about peanuts, cotton candy, or ice-cold beer.

Joseph O'Neil was dressed in the Sol Fleet's standard sweats and T-shirt. His physique appeared more chiseled than his real body. His hair was darker and fuller, and his face showed fewer signs of age and stress. This was how Coda's father saw himself.

"I was afraid I'd find you here," Coda's father said.

"Afraid?" Coda cocked his head to the side in confusion. "You pretty much asked me to come."

He didn't respond, just gave Coda an expression that made it clear he had no idea what his son was talking about.

"You told me you'd see me soon." Coda held up his hands, gesturing to the world around them. "Unless you were planning on breaking out of the brig, commandeering a shuttle, and returning to the *Redemption*, I didn't see another way how."

A small smirk appearing, his father let out a small breath. "That's not what I meant."

"I see that," Coda said. "No wonder you didn't come sooner."

"This isn't the first time you've looked for me?"

"No." Coda shook his head. "I've been here every night since you were taken, waiting. But you never showed up. I was afraid they were somehow preventing you from coming."

"I see," his father said. "No, I didn't come because it is dangerous. This isn't our domain, Coda. We're outsiders here, and if the Overlord is paying attention, he'll be drawn to us. We should go."

"No." The word came out stronger than Coda expected. "The fleet took you away twice. I'm not going to let the Overlord take you away too."

His father eyed him for a moment, then he put his arm around Coda and threw a foot up on the empty seat in front of them. It was a small gesture, but its meaning was clear. His father wouldn't rush them away, and Coda appreciated it.

"I'm sorry," his father said.

"It's not your fault."

"I'm not sure about that."

Coda left his response unsaid. "So, how *are* they treating you?"

"Not bad." His father's eyes were distant, scanning the emerald field in front of him. "The marines brought me to the *Abraham Lincoln* and threw me in the brig. Aside from the marine guard inside the door and the other who brings my food and water, I haven't seen or spoken with anyone."

"That's good, I guess," Coda said. "Could be worse."

"Could be worse," his father agreed. "What about you?"

Coda shrugged. "Same ole same ole. Though now that we're in dock, Captain Coleman has me..."

His father's face had taken on a pained look.

"What is it?"

"Do you feel that?"

"Feel what?" Coda's eyes scanned the stadium. He half expected to see the Overlord or a small army of Baranyk, but the stadium remained as empty as it ever had, almost eerie.

"Pain." He looked at Coda, eyes firm, focused, and scared. "We need to go."

"I don't understand."

"Now, Coda."

The world disappeared, and Coda was back in an infinite sea of blackness, broken up only by tiny dots of light. His father's presence was still beside him, but beyond that, nothing felt amiss.

*Wait...*

Something pulled Coda toward a particular collection of lights. As he drew closer, he realized the bright lights were actually made up of thousands, even millions of smaller lights. Now that he was closer, he could feel distant sensations.

His father was right. Whatever was happening was causing great amounts of pain. And he had the vague sense that some of the lights were disappearing.

"What's happening?" Coda asked.

"They're dying."

"Who's dying?" Coda asked.

"Baranyk."

A chill went through Coda's body. "How?"

"I think," Coda's father said, "the Baranyk fleet has arrived."

# 13

*Bridge, SAS Redemption*
*Europa Station, Sol System*

"REPORT!" CAPTAIN COLEMAN BELLOWED AS HE DASHED ONTO THE BRIDGE. News had come down only moments before. The Baranyk fleet had been sighted, and rumor was swirling that it had attacked one of humanity's larger outer colonies.

"Orders coming in now, sir," Ensign Richey said. "Transmitting."

Coleman's tablet chimed as the orders were relayed to his personal tablet and those of his executive staff across the bridge.

"Looks like our vacation is over," Commander Garcia said, reading the message.

Captain Coleman appreciated his XO's levity, but he'd been dreading this day for weeks, and he couldn't help but feel like he was living a nightmare made manifest. Anticipating a call, he made one of his own, patching through to his chief engineer.

"Commander Payton," Coleman said. "How's our new engine looking?"

"We're still working through a number of anomalies, sir,"

Commander Payton said into his earpiece. "Current output measured at thirty-two percent."

That was well beyond the minimum output Commander Payton had mentioned before.

"We're in fighting shape," Coleman said.

"We'll be stepping into the ring with a swollen eye and a busted nose, but yes, our ship is in fighting shape."

"Great work, Commander. Keep it up. We'll need everything you can give us."

"Of course, sir."

No sooner had Coleman ended the communication than his personal earpiece rang again. He knew who would be on the other side even before he heard the familiar voice.

"Captain Coleman," Admiral Orlovsky said.

"Sir," Coleman said.

"How's that new drive of yours coming along?"

"Just got off with my chief engineer, sir. We're in fighting shape."

"Good," Admiral Orlovsky said. "Rendezvous with the *Oklahoma*, *Montana*, and *Abraham Lincoln* at JumpGate-4 at 1540 and prepare to jump to the Morning Sun."

*The Abraham Lincoln?* That was the admiral's flagship.

"You're coming too, sir?"

"You bet your ass I am, Captain," Admiral Orlovsky said. "I have to see this fleet of yours with my own eyes."

"Of course, sir," Coleman said. "We'll see you at JumpGate-4 at 1540. Good luck, sir."

"You too, Captain." Coleman ended the call.

"Daddy's coming to supervise?" Commander Garcia asked.

"Yes," Coleman said.

He thought back to his last conversation with the admiral, when his old friend had told him of the fleet's preparations. It might have been his imagination, but he couldn't help but feel there were somehow doubts in the fleet about Coleman's report. That some believed the numbers were an exaggeration, that the brain experiments and human control sounded too outlandish, that maybe the whole thing was made up by an old pilot trying to stay relevant.

Admiral Orlovsky had said he believed Coleman, but Coleman

couldn't shake the feeling that more had been left unsaid. The admiral was about to put himself directly in the sights of the enemy. It was a catastrophically stupid tactical decision. The person in charge of their fleet had no business putting himself in jeopardy like this. If the battle went the way Coleman expected it to, the admiral would be in very real danger.

*There will also be no doubting the true threat the Baranyk have brought to bear.*

Was that why his old friend was putting himself in harm's way? To make an incredibly public statement? Too much of military leadership was playing politics—he would leave that to Orlovsky and do his own job.

Coleman turned to Lieutenant Poiu. "Set Condition-1 throughout the ship and plot a course to JumpGate-4."

"Yes, sir."

The lights dimmed, and the familiar soft-amber glow of the heightened status lit the tops and bottoms of the bulkhead.

"Patch me through the entire ship," he said to Ensign Richey. It was time to break the news to his crew.

"You're on, sir," Ensign Richey said.

Coleman nodded and took a deep breath, realizing that he didn't know what he was going to say. The speakers let out a soft hiss of dead air, his breathing faintly audible.

"This is the captain," he said, breaking the growing silence. "For the last few months, we've battled through enemy territory to uncover the secrets of our enemy. Because of your hard work and dedication, we succeeded in that mission. Because of your perseverance, we were able to bring our discoveries home, where our comrades could do something with them. To help us prepare. To give us a fighting chance."

He looked around the bridge from the lower tier near the battle map, feeling the eyes of his crew on him, the eyes of the entire ship. "But we always knew we were in a race against time, that the enemy was on our heels, that whatever respite we had earned would be short-lived. That our worst fears would catch up to us. I'm sorry to say that that day is today. The enemy fleet we uncovered at the Baranyk home world has been sighted and is currently engaged in a battle at the human colony

Morning Sun. We and three other ships, including the *Abraham Lincoln*, are en route to provide aid.

"You all know the challenges ahead. You, better than anyone, know the odds we face. But you also represent the best this fleet has to offer. You've pulled off the impossible more times than I can count, and you will do so again. And through your actions, you will give us a fighting chance. Remain steadfast. Remain vigilant. Trust in yourselves and your comrades. Let's do the impossible. Coleman out."

He pressed his earpiece, ending his direct line to the entire ship, not sure what to do next. Thankfully, he felt Commander Garcia step up beside him.

"You're getting better at those," Commander Garcia said softly.

"Thank you, Commander." *Unfortunately, we both know words alone don't win battles, and even the best words aren't going to be enough to stop what's coming.*

# 14

*Bridge, SAS Redemption*
*High Orbit, Morning Sun*

Unlike many of humanity's colonized worlds, the planet Morning Sun was a close proximity to Earth. From space, it appeared as a beautiful blue marble with streaks of white, and on its three large continents were mountainous peaks, white sandy beaches, and green flora and fauna. It was slightly warmer than Earth, with a tropical climate, making it a comfortable home for its first settlers, who'd largely come from many Asian countries.

Today, it burned.

The Baranyk fleet invaded the system like a swarm of locusts, simultaneously attacking its moon bases, orbital platforms, and the miniscule defense the planet could muster. The Baranyk outnumbered the human ships, vessels, and batteries by an overwhelming margin. Explosions lit the surface and flashed in space in a constant visual symphony of destruction, and still, the Baranyk struck.

"Good god," Commander Garcia muttered as the first readings came back. "We need to do something. They don't have much time left."

Captain Coleman wasn't the superior officer on this mission. He had to wait for his orders, and the flagship hadn't arrived yet. Thankfully, the Baranyk hadn't moved to engage the arriving fleet, likely because they'd arrived so far out of system.

*Not that four ships would do much against a force like that anyway.* Captain Coleman steeled himself, setting his jaw, hoping he looked more confident than he felt. The planet and its moon were lost. The only thing they could do now was save as many lives as possible.

"Active scans," Captain Coleman said, "entire system. I want every ship and fighter logged, categorized, and designated. I need to know how many ships we're facing, their losses, where they're focused, weakest, and strongest. Everything you can give me."

"On it, sir," Lieutenant Poiu said.

Coleman opened a channel to Moscow. "What's your status, Lieutenant?"

"Locked and loaded, sir," Moscow said. "Just waiting for your command."

"This isn't going to be a normal engagement," Coleman said. "We're outnumbered in a way we haven't been outnumbered before. Keep your fighters tight. You're a scalpel here, not a sword, understand?"

"Of course, sir."

"Good." He closed the line.

"All ships have arrived, sir," Lieutenant Poiu said.

"Thank you, Lieutenant," Coleman said. *Orders should be arriving any moment.*

Seconds went by. Seconds that felt like minutes. Hours. Days. Each moment another that ended with additional human loss.

"The *Abraham Lincoln* is hailing us, sir," Ensign Richey said. "Patching them through to your earpiece now."

Captain Coleman didn't move. He remained at the center of the bridge, taking up his customary spot before the 3D tactical display that took up the center of the space, watching the Baranyk fleet ravage the planet.

"Are you seeing this, Chadwick?" Admiral Orlovsky asked.

"I am, sir."

"You were right." Admiral Orlovsky didn't even try to hide his tone of disbelief. Maybe he had believed Coleman, but believing wasn't seeing, and it sure as hell wasn't understanding.

Coleman looked at the count of ships at the top right corner of the tactical display. It was still increasing, but not at the same speed it had originally. The ship's computer was getting close to finishing its count.

"This isn't all of them, sir," Coleman said. "This isn't half of them. Not even a third."

Admiral Orlovsky whispered a sharp curse. "Where are the rest?"

"I don't know, sir," Coleman said. "But I fear this isn't the only attack. It's the only attack we can do something about, though. What are our orders, sir?"

"The Morning Sun is lost," Admiral Orlovsky said after a moment. "That much is clear. We must save as many as we can. The *Abraham Lincoln* will protect the JumpGate. You and the *Oklahoma* will provide additional firepower to the dual rings of the orbital platform and give the evacuees an avenue of escape. The *Montana* will engage the force attacking the moon and give the lunar citizens a chance."

The plan was nearly the same as the one Coleman had been devising. In a situation like this, one could only plan for the broad strokes. Best to keep it loose and flexible and to respond in real time.

"I'm putting you in charge of the planet's defenses," Admiral Orlovsky said. "Get as many people to safety as you can, but do not sacrifice your ship. This is just the undercard, Chadwick. The main event is still coming."

"Understood, sir."

"Good luck and Godspeed."

# 15

*Ready Room, SAS Redemption*
*High Orbit, Morning Sun*

For the second time in his career, Coda was left off the flight roster during a major military engagement. The first time had been his fault. He'd let Moscow goad him and lost his temper. He'd vowed never to let that happen again and had, so far, lived up to his promise, even becoming friends with his formal rival. This time was different. This time, he'd had no control.

Coda sought refuge in the one place that reminded him of everything he'd lost—the Forgotten ready room. This time, he was alone, no Moscow to share his anger and disappointment with. The *Redemption* was outfitted with state-of-the-art visualization equipment. When he'd been grounded on the *Jamestown*, he'd only been able to listen to the battle, but here, he could watch it unfold.

Coda dimmed the lights and took a seat in the front row of the ready room's stadium seating as the first-person view of Moscow's cockpit came onto the screen at the front of the room. He used his tablet to split the screen, bringing up a three-dimensional rendering of the battle map beside it. Lastly, he piped Moscow's comms through the ready room's speakers.

Moscow and the rest of the Forgotten were loaded in the launch bays, going through final preflight checks. Watching the battle rage across the system, he could easily see why the captain had chosen to keep his fighters close, relying instead on the *Redemption*'s antiaircraft batteries and torpedoes as it entered the fray.

This was an invasion at a scale he'd never seen before. The Morning Sun wasn't so much being attacked as being overrun. The Baranyk were an infestation, and nothing they could do would equalize the numbers.

The deck rumbled with cannon fire, vibrating the soles of Coda's boots. The sound echoed distantly through the bulkhead as the *Redemption* and *Oklahoma* burned toward the planet's orbital defense platform—a pair of rings that circled the planet's equator and were armed with heavy antiaircraft cannons. The two human vessels were met with surprisingly little resistance as they approached. Coda had expected enemy fighters and at least a capital ship to engage, but so far, the enemy had let them move into position. It was almost as if the Overlord had rolled out the red carpet to provide them with a front-row seat to the destruction.

The two rings, separated by ten kilometers, had sustained only minor damage. The enemy had focused its attacks on the planet's surface and the neighboring moon. The ten-kilometer gap between the defense platforms left a narrow window for escape, and a group of ships were approaching it now.

The *Redemption* focused its cannons on a swarm of Baranyk fighters moving to engage the incoming vessels. The *Redemption*'s firing crews, aided by computer-aided targeting, fired indiscriminately at broad swaths of enemy fighters, spraying slime, mucus, and other organic Baranyk matter into the black.

In a single moment, more than a hundred Baranyk fighters descended on the two human capital ships. There might have been even more—the ship's targeting sensors were having a difficult time keeping track of all of the moving vessels. But it was clear the Baranyk indifference was at an end.

On the second viewscreen, Moscow's ship launched. He was suddenly speeding through the launch tube. Racing into the black,

Moscow opened fire without hesitation, and it was fortunate he did. If he hadn't, he would have immediately collided with one of the enemy vessels swarming the *Redemption*. More than one human fighter did exactly that, turning to slag before they even had a chance to engage the enemy.

"Nighthawks, break into sections," Moscow said over the comm. "Finger-four formations, and only fire when necessary. We're a distraction here. Our job is to escort as many of these ships to the JumpGate as possible."

Moscow had the right idea. Even heavily outnumbered, they had to preserve their ammunition. If they fired on every exposed enemy in range, they would exhaust their missiles and cannon fire in seconds without doing anything to alter the course of the battle.

The *Redemption* and *Oklahoma* situated themselves just outside the orbital platforms, extending their protection a little farther into space. The Forgotten and the *Oklahoma*'s own squadrons cleared the way, eliminating fighters that moved to engage the convoy. In a short time, the fleet, coupled with the orbital defense platforms, had created a fragile tunnel for escape. But like all tunnels, if a single cog was removed, the whole thing would crumble.

# 16

*Cockpit, Nighthawk*
*Morning Sun*

"Another convoy inbound," Moscow said. "Looks like a big one. Bad Dogs, break off and give these guys a proper escort."

"You got it, Moscow," Squawks said. "Dogs, on me."

Squawks pulled the joystick back and to the left, leading his flight away from the other formations. The flight's designation Bad Dogs still didn't feel right to him. He'd originally wanted to call them Horn Dogs because his pilots would be on the enemy like a pent-up Jack Russell terrier, but Coda had failed to see the metaphor and denied his request. As Tex would have said, Coda could be a right stick-in-the-mud when he wanted to be.

*But Coda isn't the CAG anymore.*

Maybe Squawks could talk to Moscow about it. He might get the humor. Probably not, though. Moscow was twice as serious as Coda ever was, with half the personality. If he wasn't scowling, he was barking. Crazy Russian pride or something. He probably even pissed vodka.

*Worth a shot, though.*

Together, the Bad Dogs and Gold Flight—what a pretentious fucking flight designation—angled toward the planet, meeting the six-ship convoy as they broke atmo. It *was* a big convoy. They would definitely draw Baranyk attention.

"All right, Dogs," Squawks said over their private channel. "Break into sections. Finger-four formations. I got point. Nails, take middle. Noodle, you got the rear where you like it."

"I'm pretty sure that violates at least half a dozen sexual harassment laws," Noodle said.

"Doesn't mean it's not true," Nails said.

"Tell you what," Squawks said, "live through this shit, and you can sue me."

That got more than a few laughs. *Good. That's good.* His pilots were tense. Too reactive. They needed to be loose and aggressive, to fly on instinct. That was when they were at their best.

The three sections formed up on the starboard side of the convoy, with Squawks leading their escape. Nails's section was behind Squawks by nearly a kilometer, with Noodle and his fighters protecting the rear. Moscow's sections did the same on the other side of the convoy. Between the orbital platforms, which launched a continuous volley of protective fire, and the *Redemption* and *Oklahoma* adding muscle to the battle, they'd been able to hold this narrow crevice long enough for dozens of ships to slip through.

Squawks smirked. His friends liked to complain about the shit that came out of his mouth. If they only knew what went through his head.

The moment they were beyond the range of the orbital platforms and *Redemption*'s defensive fire, the Baranyk attacked. The convoy was comprised of civilian vessels without weapons, so their survival depended on the Dogs.

A host of Baranyk fighters swarmed in, opening fire immediately. Outnumbering their enemy by a massive, unknown number, the Baranyk didn't need to be precise with their targeting and instead sprayed plasma fire across a wide swath of space.

"Evasive maneuvers!" Squawks bellowed.

His pilots took immediate action, darting away in a series of dangerous high-G maneuvers. Squawks's G-suit tightened around his limbs and torso, preventing his blood from being pushed to his feet, while his mask forced extra oxygen into his body. Blackness still creeped in from the edges of his vision.

Once he leveled out, it took half a moment to regain his bearings. The plasma fire hadn't hit a single fighter, and the angle of the attack had left the convoy unharmed. Even better, the Bad Dogs were in a great flanking position.

*Time to jump on them like a pent-up Jack Russell terrier.*

Squawks had the computer divide the swarm into thirds, then he launched an equal number of missiles. They hit the swarm just before the enemy fighters changed course. Being outnumbered like this was a real bitch, but it also meant the enemy was clumped up, allowing his missiles to inflict maximum damage.

The swarm disintegrated, replaced by Baranyk goo and a couple dozen straggling fighters that struggled to regroup. His fighters made quick work of them.

"Well done," Moscow said. "But conserve your weapons."

*Conserve?* It was hard to conserve anything when they were under near-constant bombardment.

"Doing what I can," Squawks said.

The enemy attacked at will now, swarm after swarm engaging and disengaging. The Forgotten were being hit from all sides in a relentless assault, and since they were in the dead zone between the safety of the orbital platforms and the JumpGate, they were truly on their own.

Squawks grunted as he nearly took a splash of plasma fire to the cockpit. "This isn't working. We need to be nimbler. Break into fighter pairs."

They would lack a cohesive strategy in fighter pairs, but Squawks trusted his pilots to do what was best in the moment. They didn't have time to think. Only react. And working in sections wouldn't enable that.

"Nails, where are you?"

"Forming up," his wingman said. "Why do you think you're still alive?"

"Ha!" Squawks barked. He risked a quick glance at the battle map and saw Nails was already flying just off his wing. "Glad someone is looking out for me. Guns only. Save your missiles for large swarms."

"You got it."

"The *Abraham Lincoln* is only six minutes—"

"Squawks," Moscow interrupted, "another convoy is headed our way. I'll take my flight back and give them an escort. After you see these ships through, double back and give us a hand."

"Affirmative," Squawks said. "Go get 'em, Moscow."

He watched the green indicators on his HUD as Moscow's flight broke away from the convoy and doubled back toward the planet. In a single moment, their numbers had been cut in half.

"All right, Dogs. It's just us now. The *Abraham Lincoln* is only five minutes out. Keep these vessels flying until then."

His fighters didn't have time to respond. Several formations of Baranyk fighters darted in, going straight for the open flank where Moscow's fighters had been. Squawks and Nails flipped and burned, coming at a dozen enemy fighters from under the convoy. Noodle and his wingman came from the opposite side, and the four of them used controlled bursts of cannon fire, knocking out several fighters, but not before the enemy unleashed a barrage of plasma fire.

If the enemy attack had hit the *Redemption* with its reinforced hull, it would have only caused minimal damage, but these weren't military vessels. These were private civilian ships, luxury liners, and industrial ships meant for hauling cargo. The plasma fire tore through their hulls like molten lava. Hulls depressurized, venting oxygen, fluids, and human lives into the void.

The remaining Baranyk fighters stayed on a tight attack vector, strafing the convoy, firing more plasma fire along the full length of the fleeing vessels. Squawks and Nails followed. Noodle and his wingman did the same. The remaining enemy fighters were relentless, though. Blue fire peppered the hulls of the human ships like someone had flung paint from a paintbrush. Everywhere it struck, fire burned, and precious life support escaped.

"Missiles!" Squawks thumbed the trigger from cannons to missiles, allowing the computer to autotarget the farthest ship, trusting that Nails and the other fighters would take the ones trailing behind.

He squeezed the trigger. His Nighthawk rocked as the missile detached and sped forward, quickly disappearing from view. The yellow indicator on his HUD caught up to the lead Baranyk ship, turning it to slag. Several other missiles did the same, taking out the strike force.

Squawks performed a quick scan on their immediate battle space.

The battle raged around them, but for the moment, their small convoy was unmolested. He let out a short breath.

"Squawks!" Noodle bellowed.

Squawks double-checked his battle map, expecting to see another wave of inbound fighters. Before he could determine what had spooked his friend, a blinding flash enveloped everything.

Squawks was shoved against his seat, his G-suit constricting around his appendages. He couldn't see anything but blackness, and for several terrifying seconds, he thought he was either in the void or had lost his vision.

Emergency claxons wailed. That was a good sign. The blackness was slowly replaced by bright afterimages of whatever the terrible light had been. That was when he realized he was flipping out of control. On instinct, Squawks countered the spin with subtle movements until it dissipated. By the time he had his spacecraft under control, his vision had partially returned.

"What the hell was that?" Squawks asked.

"The ship's reactor blew." Noodle sounded as breathless as Squawks did.

Squawks almost asked what ship, but the battle map told him everything. The ship hit hardest from the Baranyk's attack run had gone nuclear. Worst of all, it had taken out the two ships closest to it.

"Get the ships to the JumpGate," he'd said. They'd failed.

*No*, Squawks told himself. The blast had taken out the Baranyk fighters too. *There are still other ships. We can still get them to safety.*

"Bad Dogs," Squawks said, making his voice as strong as possible, "form up. We're nearly there. We can still do this."

Affirmatives rang through the radio, but not as many as he'd expected. Another look at the battle map told him why. The explosion had knocked out four Nighthawks.

His first thought was to do a quick roll call or have his computer provide a report of the fallen pilots, but he pushed the thought to the back of his mind.

"You still with me, Nails?" He could afford himself that one question.

"Shaken but still here." Her voice was breathless. She'd probably been thrown like he had, but she was tougher than anyone had a right to be.

"Good."

The explosion had thrown him off course, but once he and Nails formed back up with the remaining convoy, he had his computer recalculate their time of arrival. The *Abraham Lincoln* was only two minutes away.

*Come on.*

This close to the JumpGate, the Baranyk launched one final attack, sending in two waves of fighters and coming at them from the rear. This time, Squawks was ready.

"Bad Dogs, cut them off. Do whatever you have to do. Nothing gets by us."

He targeted the lead fighter, squeezing the firing stud. The fighter broke apart into a series of organic fragments, taking out the nearest fighter behind it. Nails launched a missile, aiming for center mass of the swarm. It took out several more, but half a dozen still remained, and they were incoming fast.

Screaming in defiance, Squawks pressed the firing stud, holding it down, spraying cannon fire across the fighter's incoming trajectory. There were more flashes of light, more organic debris. Noodle joined in the cacophony as Squawks watched his available rounds rapidly decrease. They had to get these refugees to safety—nothing else mattered. It was the only objective. The only mission.

It wasn't enough. Two Baranyk fighters slipped through.

"No," Squawks whispered. Then again, stronger, he said, "No!"

He slammed on his front thrusters. His flight harness dug painfully into his chest and shoulders, then he flipped his fighter nose to tail and punched the throttle. Something in his body twisted, and pain exploded across his chest and abdomen.

Eyes watering, Squawks targeted the Baranyk fighters, waiting agonizing seconds for the computer to lock on, then fired two of his remaining missiles.

"C'mon," he said, encouraging the missiles. "C'mon, c'mon, c'mon!"

The two ships erupted in a flash of light. Squawks let out a whoop then an agonizing cry, as the movement made the pain even worse.

*We did it. We fucking did it.*

"*Abraham Lincoln*," Squawks said as fighters from the capital ship flew past his wing, "look after the convoy and make sure they're seen safely home. The Bad Dogs are rendezvousing with the rest of the Forgotten."

"Well done, Lieutenant," the voice over the comm said. "We'll take care of them. Good luck out there."

"Thank you."

With a slight nod toward the convoy and a long breath, Squawks pulled back on the joystick and moved into an attack vector that would take him back into the heart of the battle. Their first objective was complete, but the battle was far from over.

# 17

*Bridge, SAS Redemption*
*Low Orbit, Morning Sun*

"The first evacuees are away, sir," Ensign Richey said.

Captain Coleman let out a thankful breath. The battle was lost. Hell, it had been lost before they'd ever arrived, but looking at the Baranyk's numbers, he realized that even the full might of the Sol Fleet wouldn't have been enough. They needed to evacuate all outer systems to prevent a catastrophic loss of life. He wasn't sure why the fleet hadn't done that already.

"Moscow's Gold Flight is enroute to the JumpGate, but he's reporting he's down another fighter," Ensign Richey continued. "Do you want Squawks's Bad Dogs to reinforce?"

Coleman stared intently at the battle map. The four capital ships and their fighters were single beacons of light in an otherwise-endless sea of enemy red. The steady rumble of cannon fire through the deck was a constant reminder of the odds they faced. How long could they keep it up? How long could they hold out? A series of blue wireframe images joined the melee, flying up from the Morning Star's surface. More evacuees.

"No," Coleman said. "Have them return to our position and escort the new ships to the JumpGate."

Every human life they saved was a small victory in and of itself.

"Yes, sir." Ensign Richey's voice softened as she relayed orders.

Coleman didn't take his eyes off the battle map. Something felt off. The Baranyk were focusing their forces on the planet and moon themselves, assaulting the major cities with devastating plasma fire, inflicting as much death and destruction possible. Baranyk fighters attacked the defense platform and the *Redemption* and *Oklahoma*, but the larger capital ships stayed on the outskirts of the battle.

He had no doubts that if the enemy focused their attacks on the human vessels, they would be overwhelmed in moments. It was almost as if they were intentionally avoiding a heavy engagement but doing just enough to keep the stronger human warships occupied. But why? The Overlord was a showman—did he want them to see firsthand the devastation he wrought? To show humanity how powerless they truly were?

*Is that sonuvabitch here?*

Another, simpler thought came to mind. The enemy didn't engage the human vessels because they didn't have to. The human resistance was little more than an annoyance to a fleet of this size.

*And this isn't even their full force.*

The thought left a pit in Coleman's stomach. They were virtually powerless to prevent this—how bad would it be when the enemy assaulted with its full force?

"Sir!" Lieutenant Poiu's voice cut through the bridge's chatter. "The *Montana*'s reactor is going critical!"

Coleman squeezed the metal railing surrounding the battle map, watching the green wireframe above the digital moon. Unlike the planet, the moon didn't have an orbital defense platform, so where the *Redemption* was operating more as a defensive force, allowing ships to escape the planet, the *Montana* was attacking, trying to create a path to escape.

He hadn't focused on that part of the battle, so he wasn't sure how many lives the *Montana* had been able to save. He prayed it was worth their sacrifice.

The wireframe disappeared.

"The *Montana* is gone, sir." Lieutenant Poiu's soft voice seemed to echo across the bridge as if he'd yelled the news. Silence followed in its wake, broken only by the soft beeping of consoles, the heavy breathing from the bridge personnel manning them, and the distant, ever-present canon fire.

"Damn it," Coleman grumbled. "How many ships are still on the planet?"

"Hard to say, sir," Ensign Richey said. "It's an unorganized evacuation, and many are flying without transponders."

"Tactical," Coleman said. "What do you see?"

"Not much more than Ensign Richey, sir," Lieutenant Poiu said. "The ships don't appear on our sensors until they're entering atmo, and even then, the enemy is on them."

"They're attacked into atmo?" Coleman asked.

"Yes, sir. There are swarms of Baranyk fighters patrolling the skies, attacking the fleeing ships until they reach firing range from the orbital platform."

Coleman let the explanation wash over him. There was something he was missing. Something he didn't understand.

"Sir!" Lieutenant Poiu said.

No longer engaged with the *Montana*, a large force of enemy fighters left the moon, burning hard toward the JumpGate and the *Abraham Lincoln*.

"I see it." Coleman channeled a direct line to the admiral. "Sir, you've got a large force of enemy fighters inbound."

"We see them," Admiral Orlovsky said. "We can't last much longer, Chadwick."

"I know." The words were bitter. Coleman hated to admit defeat.

"We'll see the newest convoy through the JumpGate, but the moment we're gone, we have to pull back. We won't have time to use the JumpGate, though, so jump to the Iridium System and use the JumpGate there to rendezvous back in the Jovian System."

"Yes, sir," Coleman said, words cold, emotionless. He couldn't help but think of the millions of souls they were leaving behind. The billions. It was unfathomable. That kind of loss of human life hadn't been seen since the early parts of the war.

"Sir," Lieutenant Poiu said, "I'm picking up multiple evacuees. A swarm of Baranyk are on their tails and not breaking off."

"Where's Squawks's Bad Dogs?"

"En route, sir," Lieutenant Poiu said. "Twenty seconds out."

The evacuees' wireframes were just appearing on the battle map. There were nearly a dozen ships, but all smaller, private vessels likely owned by some of the richest families on the planet. He wasn't sure, but he thought those ships could fit in the *Redemption*'s hangar.

"Squawks," Coleman said, "there's another convoy inbound, and they have a Baranyk force hot on their tails. I want you to escort them to the *Redemption* and see them land safely on our deck."

"Yes, sir," Squawks said. There was a slight hesitation to his voice, a weariness that Coleman wasn't accustomed to hearing. But if Squawks was slow in receiving his orders, he wasn't slow in obeying them. His fighters moved into a crisp delta squadron, knifing through the atmo toward the human vessels attempting to escape.

Coleman put himself in Squawks's shoes. As a pilot, he'd hated flying in atmo. Compared to spaceflight, it was rough, bumpy, and slow, lacking the freedom of movement zero-g provided. It took a very different kind of pilot to fly in atmo, and for all of the missions the Forgotten had flown, only a handful had ever ended up there.

*Just get them aboard, Squawks. No hero shit.*

Trusting his pilots, he shifted his attention back to Moscow and the JumpGate. Their fighters were nearly there and would beat the enemy by several minutes. Just long enough for the civilian ships to get away.

"Order Moscow to dock on the *Abraham Lincoln* when the last of the civilian vessels are away," Coleman said.

"Yes—"

"Sir!" Ensign Richey bellowed. "I'm picking up a high-intensity signal from the Baranyk capital ships."

"What kind of signal?" Coleman asked, already dreading the answer.

"It matches the frequency of the Kryos Signal," Ensign Richey said.

The Kryos Signal. The same signal that had exploited the genetic defect in Coda's and his father's brains, allowing the enemy to use them like puppets.

"Can you tell where it's directed?" Coleman scanned the bridge, looking for any signs that his bridge personnel were under enemy influence. Doctors Rydell and Naidoo had scanned the entire ship, looking for anyone else who suffered from the same brain anomaly, but hadn't found anyone. Based on their limited intelligence, nobody else aboard the *Redemption* should have been susceptible to the Baranyk attack.

"Not precisely, sir, but it's aimed in our general direction."

"Overlay it on the battle map," Coleman said.

An orange funnel representing the signal appeared a moment later. It originated from one of the capital ships on the outskirts of the battle and enveloped the *Redemption*, the *Oklahoma*, and a section of the orbital platform. Fortunately, the fighters Coleman had just ordered to enter atmo were spared.

"Captain Williams," Coleman said, opening a line with the captain of the *Oklahoma*. "Listen to me. We're picking up a strange signal from the Baranyk capital ships. We've seen it before. The signal exploits a brain defect that allows for enemy control. You may have an unwilling enemy combatant in your midst."

"It's not directed at us, Captain," Captain Williams said.

*What is he talking about?*

"Sir!" Lieutenant Poiu looked up from his terminal, his dark face ashen. "The orbital platform is firing on the *Oklahoma*."

# 18

*Control Center, Orbital Platform*
*Low Orbit, Morning Sun*

Terrible screeching pierced Richard Black's head. He cupped his ears and squeezed his eyes shut, praying for it to end. When none of that helped, he clawed at his face, his nails raking across his cheeks, gouging trails across his skin. But the pain was only a distant distraction to the terrible pain in his head.

It continued for what felt like an eternity, then, as quickly as it had begun, it stopped. He sat dazed for several moments, eyes unable to focus. He tried to flex his jaw and open his eardrums, but his body didn't respond. His first thought was that he was still in a state of shock, still recovering, his body protecting itself from further abuse. But then his hands and arms moved under their own volition.

At first, he believed that the movement was some sort of neurological response, almost like a muscle spasm, but the movements were too precise. His hands returned to his controls, one on the firing trigger, the other cycling through the computer's targeting system with practiced precision. In a few quick taps, he'd bypassed the system's internal safety systems, manually taking fire control.

*This can't be happening. This can't be happening. This can't be happening.*

It was an out-of-body experience unlike any he had ever experienced, not even during his drug-filled days. A nightmare he lived in in real time.

He didn't know what was happening to him, but he'd fought too long, overcome the most powerful drug addiction in the world, lost or intentionally said goodbye to the people closest to him, and remade himself at a point in his life when it would have been easier to just give up. He wouldn't give up now.

Richard resisted with everything he had, trying to hold his hands back, tried to scream, to do something to warn his comrades that something was truly wrong. When that all failed, he tried to stand up from his station and remove himself from the situation. Every action was met with inaction, his body refusing to listen.

He would have done anything to stop himself, but he had no control.

---

"All engines, full burn!" Captain Coleman ordered. "Get us away from that platform!"

It was happening again, and just like before, Coleman was powerless to stop it. At least he knew what was happening and could respond. The *Oklahoma* took several direct hits from the platform's nearest turret before it moved to counter. Only instead of retreating, it was moving into an attack angle.

Coleman reopened a direct channel to the *Oklahoma*'s captain. "Captain Williams, someone on that platform is an unwilling enemy combatant. I repeat, an *unwilling* enemy combatant."

Captain Williams didn't respond. The *Oklahoma* continued to move into an attack vector, angling its reinforced port-side hull toward the platform even as it continued to take a pounding.

"Captain!" Coleman bellowed. He might as well have been talking to himself.

"The *Oklahoma* is firing, sir!"

The battle map was good for many things, particularly showing strategic positions and tracking missiles and other heavy bombardment, but it didn't display cannon fire.

"If they destroy that platform, we're sitting ducks out here," Commander Garcia said, echoing Coleman's thoughts.

"Captain Williams," Coleman said. "Cease fire. I repeat, cease fire. If you destroy that platform, we lose all fire support, and you're liable to take us out too."

"It's been compromised," Captain Williams said.

"There's another way." Coleman had only a vague idea of what that other way looked like, but he didn't tell the other man that.

He didn't get a chance to flesh it out further. Two missiles appeared on the battle map. With their close proximity to the platform, Coleman didn't have a chance to issue a deactivate order.

The yellow indicators struck.

"Damn it!"

The platform was made up of two separate rings and was armed with thousands of turrets, but they were all controlled by the central command center that had just been destroyed. If Captain Williams had just let them contact the platform's command, they wouldn't have lost the entire thing.

But the orbital platform was destroyed. Its rings had shattered and were now flying dangerously into space or the planet below. Worse yet, their combined firepower had kept the enemy at bay, and already, Coleman could see the tides of the battle shifting.

"How long until the Bad Dogs are aboard?" Coleman asked.

"We're burning hard away from them," Lieutenant Poiu said. "And they're engaged with another Baranyk swarm. Current ETA in... eight minutes."

"We're not going to make it eight minutes." Coleman channeled Squawks directly. "Lieutenant, things have taken a turn for the worst up here. Increase speed and return to base."

"Negative, sir." Squawks's voice was pained and breathless. "We've drawn heavy fire. Without us, these civies will last as long as a sophomore on prom night."

"Issue the order for maximum burn and prepare for emergency landings," Coleman said. "You have three minutes."

"Sir—"

"Three minutes, Lieutenant."

"Yes, sir."

Coleman closed the line. On the battle map, two massive swarms were inbound. Coleman's initial assessment was correct—Squawks and his pilots didn't have eight minutes. Coleman wasn't sure they even had three.

# 19

*Cockpit, Nighthawk*
*Morning Sun*

*I* AM NOT *LEAVING THEM BEHIND*. SQUAWKS ANGLED HIS NIGHTHAWK, USING the drag of atmo to his advantage, and fired another cannon burst, destroying a pair of Baranyk fighters. Nails corkscrewed then looped around his port side to take out another fighter pair coming in on Squawks's flank.

"Thanks, Nails," Squawks said. He hadn't seen the enemy fighters closing in on him.

Nails grunted a reply. She didn't have time for a proper response—more fighters were already harrying the convoy.

"Communications," Squawks said, "patch me through to the leader of the convoy."

"Copy," Ensign Richey said over the comm. "You're on."

"Captain, things are getting hairy out here," Squawks said. "Our ride leaves in three minutes. I need all ships burning at one hundred and twenty percent and prepared for a bumpy landing."

"Some of the ships are already at maximum," the ship's captain said. "We go any faster, and we'll leave them behind."

"You worry about your ship," Squawks said. "We'll take care of any stragglers."

The captain didn't respond, but their engines flared, and they began to pull away from some of the ships behind them. Squawks checked his altimeter. He didn't know this planet well enough, but they had to be getting close to the Karman Line, the boundary where the planet ended and space began. Already, his vision was closer to a hazy view of stars than it was of clouds.

"Bad Dogs, mission's changed," Squawks said. "On my wing and increase thrust. Only engage when necessary. We're going to cut through any incoming swarms and let them get on our six. It'll be a merry chase back to the *Redemption*."

"We're leaving the convoy behind?" Noodle asked.

"Not if we can help it," Squawks said. "Most of the enemy fighters are coming in from orbit, not the surface. Once past us, they'll have to slow down before reversing course or risk burning up in the atmosphere." He spoke with a confidence he didn't have. "We don't need much time anyway. We rendezvous with the *Redemption* in less than three minutes."

His flight moved into a small delta formation at the tip of the convoy. They were the tip of the spear, cutting through the outer layers of atmo, their ships bucking and shaking less and less, bodies growing lighter as gravity's pull grew weaker. Three new swarms of Baranyk fighters hurtled their way.

"Enemies inbound!" Squawks bellowed. "Dashes one through three, target dead ahead. Four through eight, offset ninety degrees and protect our flank. Use missiles, aim for center mass, maximum casualties. Anyone returning with unfired missiles will owe me a drink for every unused weapon."

"He says that like he doesn't brew his own moonshine," Noodle said.

"I meant back on Europa, jackass," Squawks said. "That swill burned away my taste buds. I'm ready for a real drink."

Noodle laughed. "Tell you what. Get us out of this, and I'll buy you as many as you want."

"You hear that, ladies?" Squawks said. "That's a real friend."

As Squawks expected, the three incoming swarms moved together. The smallest angled directly toward them while the others darted to the sides to flank the human convoy.

"Fire!"

His Nighthawk bucked as the missile unlatched and burned into the black. It rocked again as a second sped from his other wing. He watched on his HUD as the two missiles, now accompanied by missiles from two other fighters, raced toward the swarm of fighters. They exploded, taking out a wide swath of the middle formation. Blood and organic material smeared across his fighter.

"Dashes four through eight," Squawks said. "Fire!"

Another wave of missiles launched toward the remaining enemy formations, carving deep rents into their numbers. Then... chaos.

The three swarms dove in and were met with a hail of gun- and missile fire. Coming from above, their speed was significant, and they shot past the convoy just as Squawks had anticipated. The atmosphere was thinner than Squawks expected, though, and they changed course much faster than he had anticipated. He'd hoped to have a lead of several seconds on the enemy, but he had nowhere close to that.

The enemy fighters were able to right their course in time to come up directly behind the slowest ships in the convoy. They peppered the rear of the civilian ships with plasma fire, and Squawks had to watch in horror as two human vessels exploded.

He was about to order his fighters to engage when something streaked past his cockpit window. It was large, bigger than even his Nighthawk, leaving a trail of fire as it hurtled past him and slammed into the nearest civilian vessel. The following explosion sent Squawks's fighter hurtling away and left another civilian ship destroyed.

Squawks glanced at his HUD, trying to make sense of the object. It wasn't an enemy fighter. There were no other Baranyk fighters inbound.

Another object burned past his fighter. This looked almost metal as if it were a part of a ship. No, not a ship—this had the wrong coloring. That was when he saw it. The planet's orbital platform, once a protective ring that circled the planet, had been destroyed. Huge chunks of it were caught in the planet's gravity well and fell like iron rain.

"Evasive maneuvers!" Squawks shouted. "The orbital platform is raining down on us."

A particularly large chunk hurtled toward him, its dark metal glistening faintly as it caught the sun's light, and headed straight for the convoy.

Squawks ripped his fighter left and right, his body screaming as it was thrown around the gel seat, flight harness digging into the already-tender parts of his body. Molten metal screamed past his fighter, and he did his best to dodge it. The ships behind him weren't so lucky as what remained of the orbital platform tore through the human vessels and Baranyk swarms without prejudice.

His first thought was to fly adjacent to the debris field, to somehow get around it, but whatever had destroyed the platform had done so with enough force that debris was blasted over a thousand square kilometers. They couldn't go around it.

"We have to go through it!" Squawks bellowed.

"There's too much!" Noodle said.

Squawks opened his mouth to respond but couldn't spare the little focus it required. Screams, confusion, and maydays filled his radio. And still large chunks of wreckage rained down, metal burning, cables whipping, larger chunks hurling. Squawks dipped, dodged, turned, and corkscrewed, maneuvering his Nighthawk without thought, relying purely on reflex and instinct.

Explosions lit the black like tiny fireworks as falling debris struck Nighthawks and civilian vessels alike. He didn't know how long it took, but when he was through the debris, he saw what remained of the orbital platform. A large chunk of its ring was missing. What had once looked like a glittering ring of human might protecting the planet was now nothing more than dead and lifeless metal.

In the distance, the *Oklahoma* was engaged with a horde of Baranyk fighters. They swarmed its dark hulls, darting in and out like a cloud of bees, biting, stinging, leaving gouts of flame in their wake. The ship's antiaircraft batteries loosed a constant barrage of firepower, destroying fighters by the hundreds, but it did little good.

The *Redemption* was less than a minute away and engaged in a battle of its own but had somehow avoided getting caught in the middle of an enemy cloud. Before long, they would be in a similar situation.

"Status check," Squawks ordered. His fighters should be through the debris field now, free and clear for a full burn back to base.

Squawks's initial elation at getting to safety was short-lived as he looked at his battle map and the roll call came in. Less than a quarter of the convoy remained, and his flight had taken heavy casualties. One voice in particular was missing.

"Noodle," Squawks said. "Noodle, come in."

Silence answered him.

"Noodle?"

Still nothing.

"Goddamn it, Lieutenant, come in."

His wingman, Wrath, answered. His voice was firm. "He's gone, Squawks."

"No," Squawks said. *No.*

"A chunk of debris hit his fighter," Wrath said. "He didn't... I... There was nothing any of us could do."

Squawks was numb. How could one of his best friends die without him knowing about it? Their final exchange floated back to the center of his consciousness. Noodle screaming as if he saw his future, telling Squawks he couldn't make it—and Squawks ordering him ahead anyway. He'd killed his best friend. For the first time in his life, Squawks was speechless. There was nothing to say.

# 20

*Bridge, SAS Redemption*
*Low Orbit, Morning Sun*

"The Forgotten are reengaging, sir!" Lieutenant Poiu said from his station.

"They're what?" Coleman bellowed.

"Sir!" Lieutenant Poiu looked up from his station. His eyes were wide, hair frayed, his troubled thoughts clearly visible on his young face. "I said our squadrons have reengaged with the Baranyk forces."

Coleman couldn't believe the words. His eyes found the battle map, and as his tactical officer had said, the green indicators representing his fighter squadrons were altering course to take on the horde of the enemy vessels. He channeled a direct line to his flight leader.

"Squawks," Coleman said, filling his voice with every ounce of command he could muster. "You were ordered to RTB. What the hell is going on out there?"

Squawks didn't respond immediately. Sounds of heavy breathing echoed in Coleman's ears. Hollow breaths of pain and loss.

"Lieutenant?"

"They killed him."

Coleman sighed. There was no telling who Squawks was talking about, and in the end, it didn't matter. Grief was grief. And his flight leader was letting his personal grief endanger the entire squadron. Coleman cursed himself for ordering Moscow to rendezvous with the *Abraham Lincoln.*

Squawks may have been a flight leader and one of his most experienced pilots, but he hadn't been put into a higher level of command for a reason. The man was too emotional.

"Squawks," Coleman said, his voice softer this time. He knew exactly what the other man was feeling. He'd felt it on too many occasions himself. "The fleet is retreating. If you and your squadron are not aboard in ninety seconds, you'll miss your bus back, and the enemy will kill a lot more."

"They killed him, sir." The words were hardly more than a whisper.

"I know, Squawks. Death is always our companion. He's been flying your wing since the moment you stepped into the cockpit, just as he has mine. I know the pain you're feeling now. The anger. I've seen it and felt it more times than I can count. And I promise you this: you'll get your chance to say goodbye. To exact revenge. But this isn't the way. This isn't the time."

Squawks's breathing became more ragged. Coleman feared the man had fully broken.

"Lieutenant..."

"I know."

"Then I need you to get your ass back to the ship."

"Okay." His voice was stronger. Firmer. "Yes, sir."

Coleman turned off the communication.

Commander Garcia was watching him from the other side of the bridge. His face was expressionless, but his eyes betrayed the truth. He knew what had happened. They all did. His pilots had been fighting combat missions for fourteen straight months with barely any respite. They were at their breaking point. Maybe beyond it. Sprinkle in their relative inexperience, and it was a piss-poor recipe.

"Sir, they've broken off their attack," Lieutenant Poiu said. "ETA in forty seconds."

*Good.* Finally, something was under control. Squawks's reckless assault had kicked the hornets' nest, though. If the Baranyk fighters hadn't focused on the Forgotten before, they were now. Enemy fighters were coming in from every direction.

"All batteries, open fire," Coleman said. "Get our boys home."

Lieutenant Poiu relayed the order into his headset. The batteries were largely automated, but like most computer-aided systems, they needed to be guided by a human hand.

Eyes locked on the battle map, Coleman watched as the green indicators methodically moved toward the *Redemption*. The *Oklahoma* and *Abraham Lincoln* disappeared, jumping to the rendezvous point Admiral Orlovsky had sent out.

Enemy ships, too many to count, came from every direction. The battle map couldn't display them all. The constant rumbling through the deck told Coleman that the batteries were firing nonstop, but it made no difference. For every enemy fighter they destroyed, three more took its place.

The Nighthawks unleashed everything they had, firing a full barrage of cannon fire, loosing every missile, even dumping chaff, which proved incredibly effective. The combined might and desperation kept the enemy at bay, but just as Coleman was about to let out a relieved breath, the civilian ships began disappearing.

His pilots had hope. An escape. A path to survival. The inhabitants of the Morning Sun did not.

Coleman watched as more ships disappeared, knowing each one represented the lives of hundreds, perhaps thousands of people. And there was nothing he could do.

"I'm sorry," he whispered.

He felt the eyes of his command staff turn to him. He hadn't meant to speak the words aloud, but his pain was their collective hurt. His words, their words. A quiet pall fell over the bridge, broken up by only the chirps and beeps of the sensor data and the rumbling of the antiaircraft batteries.

It was the *Redemption*'s version of a ten-shot salute, the best honor they could give the people they were about to abandon. But like Squawks, he took solace in the fact that living for another day would give them a chance to exact revenge. To scour the galaxy of the Baranyk so that humanity might one day live in peace.

Lieutenant Poiu broke the silence. "All ships are aboard, sir."

"Jump," Coleman said.

# 21

*Ready Room, SAS Redemption*
*Rendezvous Point, Human Controlled Space*

Coda stumbled out of the ready room and into the corridor, dragging his hand against the bulkhead for support. His steps were slow, aimless, adrift, as if he were in his fighter without any controls. Lost in the blackness of his sorrow.

Squawks's words echoed through his memory. His pain. His grief. They might as well have been Coda's own.

"He's gone, Squawks," Wrath had said. "There was nothing any of us could have done."

Squawks hadn't believed that, and Coda didn't, either. Guilt was an angry mistress capable of crushing even the strongest man, and it weighed on Coda's shoulders, threatening to buckle his knees. He should have been out there. He should have been with his squadmates. His friends.

He found himself in the hangar as the Nighthawks landed. The nearest one had markings on its wing, telling Coda that it was Squawks's fighter. Coda closed the distance, dodging mechanics and forklifts that were already moving the fighters into a more organized line, where they could be worked on.

The cockpit canopy opened, and a technician rolled over a ladder, but Squawks didn't move. He didn't even take off his flight helmet.

Coda climbed the ladder, his heavy boots clanging against the metal grating, and froze when he made it to the top. He knew he needed to be with his friend, that the other man needed him too, but now that he was here, he had no idea what to say.

"Squawks."

His friend looked up then slowly slid off his helmet. His face had lost all color, making his bloodshot eyes even more piercing. "He's gone."

"I know."

"It's my fault." Squawks's voice was quiet, barely audible over the din.

"No," Coda said. *It's mine.*

"I should have... I ordered him..." He didn't finish the sentence. There was nothing to say. Squawks had been with the Forgotten long enough to know that.

"There's nothing you could have done," Coda said.

Life returned to Squawks's eyes. "You should have been out there," he said angrily.

The words hit Coda like a truck. It was one thing to blame himself. It was quite another for someone else to share the same feelings. Coda opened his mouth to speak, but the words dried up on his tongue.

"We needed you," Squawks said. "*He* needed you. If you'd been out there..."

"If I'd been out there..." Coda said. "Then Noodle would still be alive."

Squawks didn't say anything, instead unbuckled his flight harness.

"I know," Coda said, agreeing with him. "Noodle died because of me and my weakness."

The anger faded from Squawks's eyes. "I don't... You don't... That's not true either."

They were the words and tone of a broken man. The anger faded from Coda as he realized he was looking at a mirror of himself. Two men, two friends, one with their grief. But Squawks was right. Coda was the best of them. If he'd been out there, the squadron would have been stronger for it. He would have been able to protect him. If it hadn't been for his weakness, they never would have reorganized the fighter pairs. Nails would have been flying with Coda and Noodle with Squawks. If Coda had been out there, Noodle wouldn't have been in the path of that falling debris. It was really quite simple when he boiled it down.

Squawks must have seen something in his face, because it was his turn to look concerned. "I'm sorry."

"Me too," Coda said, though he had a suspicion they were talking about different things.

# 22

*Bridge, SAS Redemption*
*Rendezvous Point, Human Controlled Space*

It was a broken fleet that arrived at the rendezvous point. Of the four ships that had left for the Morning Star, only three returned, and of them, only the *Abraham Lincoln* had avoided serious damage. Worse were the handful of civilian vessels with jump capabilities who had retreated to the rendezvous point with them. Maybe a handful of other vessels had escaped through the JumpGate, but all told, the thousands they'd saved was a pitiful percentage compared to the billions they'd left behind.

The time for mourning would come. Right now, Coleman was furious. As soon as he was sure his ship repairs were underway and that nothing critical would require his attention, he opened a line to the *Abraham Lincoln*. To his surprise, the communications officer told him the admiral would take his call and put him on hold.

Coleman excused himself from the bridge, giving temporary command to Commander Garcia, and retreated to the privacy of his personal quarters. He was nearly there when Admiral Orlovsky's voice came through his earpiece.

"Captain, we need to talk."

Coleman bit back an angry curse, falling back on decorum to both mask and express his anger. "Yes, sir."

"In person."

"Even better, sir."

"How soon can you be aboard?"

Coleman had stopped in the corridor directly outside his door. "Right away, sir."

"Good," Admiral Orlovsky said. "I'll see you shortly."

---

"SAY IT," ADMIRAL ORLOVSKY SAID.

"Say what, sir?" Coleman asked.

"That was a colossal clusterfuck, and you knew it would be."

Coleman let out a breath. Having the other man speak his thoughts aloud eased some of the tension. "It was worse than even I feared."

"I need a drink." Admiral Orlovsky turned from Coleman, strode across his personal quarters to a decanter in the corner filled with a brown liquor, and filled two glasses. He returned and handed one to Coleman before unbuttoning his uniform jacket and taking a seat on a nearby chair. Coleman followed his lead and did the same.

After he'd arrived on the *Abraham Lincoln*, a young ensign had met him in the hangar and escorted him to the admiral's quarters. All told, Coleman had only been onboard for a few minutes.

"How many did we save?"

"Not enough." Admiral Orlovsky took a sip then leveled his gaze on Coleman. "I have your report. I knew what was possible, but part of me didn't believe it. Didn't want to believe it."

Coleman kept his thoughts to himself. The admiral was coming to terms with the situation. Given time, he would arrive at the place where Coleman had been for months. Coleman just had to make sure the admiral got there.

"We'll order a sector-by-sector retreat," Admiral Orlovsky continued. "Centralize our forces. We can't fight on their terms. Can't afford to be spread thin. There's too many of them."

"It's a good start, sir."

"Stop with the 'sir,'" Orlovsky said. "We're licking our wounds and drinking to the dead. We're human right now. Nothing more. Nothing less."

"Then let me say this," Coleman said, taking the opening. "Consolidating forces won't be enough. As you said, there are too many of them. Even with our drone squadrons, the best we can hope for is stalling them. And that's assuming anyone susceptible to Baranyk control are accounted for and relieved of duty. Even picking the battlefield is fighting a battle on their terms. It'll never work."

"What are you suggesting?"

Coleman slid to the edge of his seat. "We take the fight to the Overlord. You saw the power he has. The damage a single person on the inside can inflict. How many more like him are there across the fleet? How many more weak points do we have?"

"The fleet is screening all active personnel," Orlovsky said.

"Yes, but how long will that take? And what happens when the Overlord gets closer to civilian populations? Imagine the damage he could instigate on the surface of Europa or our stations in the belt. Imagine the damage he could inflict on the surface of Mars. Or, god forbid, Earth. There's no getting away from it. We have thousands, maybe millions, of vulnerabilities. They have one." Coleman let the words hang in the air. "But..." He held up a finger for dramatic effect. "That's both our greatest weakness and our greatest advantage."

"I don't follow." Orlovsky slid forward in his seat too. Coleman had his attention.

"The Overlord is more than a king," Coleman said. "He doesn't just rule the Baranyk; he controls them. Eliminate him, and you eliminate his influence across billions of enemy soldiers."

"And what? They'll die?"

"Maybe," Coleman said. "Maybe they'll go brain-dead the same way our drones do when you remove the signal that controls them. At the very least, they won't be under his influence anymore."

"And maybe another advanced Baranyk takes control."

"Who maybe has other desires."

"Maybe, maybe, maybe." Orlovsky slid back in his chair. "There are too many maybes. We're not going to win this war with wishes and speculation."

"It's not speculation."

"Where's it coming from, then?" Orlovsky asked. "What are you basing the lives of billions on?"

"Joseph O'Neil."

Orlovsky laughed. He *actually* laughed. Coleman wanted to slap him but continued before the admiral had a chance to dismiss the idea entirely.

"You saw what happened out there. You saw what happened on the orbital platform. We detected the same Baranyk signal moments before the platform opened fire on our ships. The same thing happened twenty years ago with O'Neil. You're just allowing twenty years of anger to cloud your judgment."

Admiral Orlovsky gave him a steady look. Coleman's friend or not, Orlovsky was still the admiral, and he wasn't used to being challenged. He stood without a word, drained his glass in a single pull, and retreated to the decanter. He didn't offer to top off Coleman's own drink.

"So what?" Admiral Orlovsky said. "He knows the enemy's deepest secrets?"

"No," Coleman said, refusing to meet a flippant question with a flippant response. "But he is the foremost expert in how they communicate. How they think."

Admiral Orlovsky filled his glass but didn't move. Didn't even drink.

Coleman kept pushing. "Think about it. The Baranyk throw their lives away with reckless abandon. We've never been able to make sense of it. Fleet Intelligence says they are capable of individual thought. The truth has stared us in the face ever since the beginning. We're not fighting an entire species. We're fighting a single, power-thirsty dictator just like we've fought so many times throughout history. Kill him, and we win the war."

Admiral Orlovsky remained silent for several moments—long enough for Coleman to take a sip of his own to break the uncomfortable moment.

"Say that you're correct," Admiral Orlovsky finally said. "Say that if we eliminate him, we win the war, there's still one glaring problem with your idea."

"Which is?"

"The universe is a very large place. You're not just looking for a single grain of sand on a beach. You're looking for... I don't even know what an apt metaphor is."

"We have O'Neil."

"So? You said it yourself that his intelligence is limited."

"It's not about that. There's something personal between them. The Overlord *wants* him, and he'll do anything to get him."

"You want to use him as bait."

"Not in the way you're thinking. He doesn't have to be present in the physical sense. He just has to be connected to the Baranyk network. From there, he can use the Overlord's strange obsession with him against him. Find out where the Overlord is hiding and relay that information to us."

"Which would require us letting him out of our custody," Admiral Orlovsky said. "Something I'm never going to let happen."

Coleman was prepared for this. "What if you didn't have to?" He spoke the words slowly, maximizing their effect.

Orlovsky froze with his glass touching his lips. "Explain," he said over the rim of the glass.

"Joseph was able to use the Baranyk network to communicate with his son across the galaxy. That's how we found him in the first place, and it's the same way the Overlord controls his soldiers. Once connected, they're able to reconnect. Whatever information Joseph gleans, he can relay to the *Redemption* through the same network."

Coleman could see the spark in Orlovsky's eyes. He felt that same spark in his own heart—the spark of hope. "Joseph can remain in your custody, observed and studied by whatever security and intelligence personnel you want, and we, on the other side of the galaxy, deep in Baranyk territory, won't be flying blind."

Admiral Orlovsky finished the sip he had been about to take then returned to his seat, letting out a long sigh. "I'm not going to lie to you, Captain. You have my attention. Command isn't going to like it."

Coleman opened his mouth to speak but was cut off.

"But it's a relatively low-risk, incredibly high-reward tactic." Admiral Orlovsky tapped the side of his glass with a fingernail, deep in thought. "Aside from the obvious security concerns, they'll want your ship on the front lines. And there's obviously no assurances that eliminating the Overlord will even do as you say."

"And yet," Coleman said, unable to stay silent, "you know one ship isn't going to make a difference."

Admiral Orlovsky held up a hand, stalling further objection. "I said the concerns would be theirs, not mine. You've given me a lot to think about."

Coleman relaxed enough to take his first sip. The admiral might not know it yet, but Coleman had just secured one of the first victories in their escalating war against the Baranyk.

# 23

*Hangar, SAS Redemption*
*Europa Station, Sol System*

There was no funeral for Noodle or any of the other fallen pilots. Coda hadn't expected one. It wasn't standard procedure, nor was there time. In the aftermath of the battle there were too many debriefings, repairs, trips to the infirmary, and a never-ending list of tasks that needed to be accomplished to return to fighting shape.

But Coda had thought there would at least be a small memorial among him and his friends, like there had been when Whiskey and Tex passed. The busy schedule was a valid excuse, but still an excuse, and in the absence of saying goodbye, Coda couldn't help but wonder if they'd just grown more callous over the months.

Captain Coleman had often said that death was part of being a fighter pilot. That if they flew long enough, they'd eventually buy it themselves. But until that day came, death would fly their wing like an invisible wingman and take enough of their friends and comrades that it would scar their very souls.

Three days after the battle and two after they'd returned to the Jovian System, Coda found himself alone in the cockpit of his Nighthawk.

Feeling the familiar gel seat, he gently ran his hands over the controls like a former lover, smelling the familiar scents of sweat and determination. His losses hit him all at once.

When he'd made the Forgotten, he'd thought he'd finally found the place he was supposed to be. He'd made new friends, become a part of something bigger than himself or any individual, fought in battles, and made a difference. And through it all, he'd returned a sliver of honor to his family's name. But despite Captain Coleman's repeated warnings, he'd held on too tightly.

Part of him had always thought the Forgotten were different. That they were special—or at least that their time as fighter pilots would be too short-lived to feel the worst horrors that came with it. Captain Coleman had been right, though. His prophetic words were becoming more and more real every day.

Coda had lost friends in battle. He'd lost comrades during training. He'd even had to say goodbye to Uno, who hadn't made the squadron. But deep in his sorrow, Coda realized it went deeper than that. He'd lost others even earlier. To join the Forgotten, he'd left behind his future as a drone pilot, knowing he would probably never see his old friends or squadmates again. In some ways, his old friends like Buster from the Terran Fleet Academy were every bit as dead to him as Noodle or Tex.

*Why do I do this?*

It was a stupid question. He knew why. He'd always known why—the hardships he faced would be experienced by billions more if people like him weren't on the front lines. His sacrifice gave others hope.

*But where do* I *find hope?*

Under normal circumstances, he would have turned to his friends. But Moscow was run ragged and didn't have the time to deal with an emotionally wrecked former pilot. Squawks had shut down and was avoiding everyone. And Noodle, the person who'd always brought them together, was gone.

Coda closed his eyes and let himself sink into the gel seat. He couldn't fly anymore, but the cockpit was still the closest thing to home he'd ever felt. It was almost like he was in the arms of an ex-lover. If he just let himself go and didn't think about their past, maybe they could be together again. Maybe they should never have broken up to begin with.

He sat there quietly, eyes closed, mind wandering, for what could have been minutes or hours. For the first time in a very long time, he just let himself *be*.

"I used to do the same thing."

The voice brought Coda out of his meditation. Captain Coleman stood on the hangar deck at the foot of the ladder.

"Sir!" Coda went to stand, but the harness yanked him back into the seat.

"At ease," Captain Coleman said before Coda could unfasten the harness. "I interrupted you."

Captain Coleman climbed the ladder then took a seat at its top. They were mostly eye level with each other, but Captain Coleman didn't look at Coda. Instead, his gaze travelled over the hangar activity.

In Coda's meditation, all the sounds had whispered away.

"When the Nighthawk program shut down, I must have spent days just sitting in my cockpit," Captain Coleman said. "I never thought I'd fly again, and I didn't know how to say goodbye."

Coda didn't say anything. The words struck too close to home, and he didn't trust himself to control his emotions.

"For years, I missed the rumbling of the seat. The G's. The speed. Being on the edge of death itself and laughing as it reached its dark fingers for me. Those were the only times I ever felt truly alive."

Coda nodded. He knew the feeling well and had heard other pilots talk about flying the same way.

"I've heard it compared to a drug," Captain Coleman continued, his eyes finally finding Coda's. "And I was addicted."

Coda looked down at his thumb rubbing against the joystick. "It's different for me. My whole life, I've been an outcast, my father's shadow hanging over me and anything I've ever wanted to do. This gave me an outlet. Gave me something that was mine. Which doesn't really make sense because he was a pilot too. It's almost as if I had to get closer to him to break away."

"Your fates have always been intertwined. They probably always will be."

Coda sucked on his teeth. He'd long since come to terms with that idea, and ever since he'd learned the truth about his father's past, he'd lost some of that desire to forge his own path. He'd taken on a new purpose. It wasn't about undoing his wrongs but proving they weren't his to begin with.

"For what it's worth," Captain Coleman said, "I'm sorry."

"For what?"

"For taking it away from you."

Coda looked up, meeting Captain Coleman's eye. There was true pain there.

"I knew what this fighter meant to you, because it meant the same to me."

"You didn't take it away from me," Coda said. He'd truly never blamed the captain. "I did."

It was the first time Coda had ever spoken the words aloud. He'd expected a sense of catharsis and was surprised to find they felt... empty.

"I hope you don't believe that," Captain Coleman said.

"I..." *What* do *I believe?* "I don't know. It's my weakness the Overlord exploited. The reason my friends are dead."

"A weakness is something you have control over, Coda. Something you can improve. Shore up. What the Overlord did to you was not a sign of weakness. It was a sign of evil. We've made enough of our own mistakes in life, and we have enough to blame ourselves for. Don't lay this at your feet too. Do you hear me?"

Coda nodded.

"Good." Captain Coleman's gaze went oddly distant for a moment. "You once asked me if by joining the Forgotten, you'd get to kill Baranyk. Do you still want that?"

"With every fiber of my being, sir."

Something Coda hadn't felt in days blossomed in his chest. Hope. Coleman's words were like a hand lifting him from the darkness.

"I'm offering you that chance again."

Coda unfastened the harness and stood. "Well, just like that day, sir. I'm ready. Just tell me what to do."

"It's really simple, Commander," Captain Coleman said. "Just come with me."

# 24

*Corridor, Europa Station*
*Europa Station, Sol System*

Europa Station was a hubbub of activity. Military personnel rushed from place to place, noses buried in tablets while more senior leadership remained among the edges of the crowd, talking in hushed voices and watching the rest with an anxious eye. Captains, officers, CAGs, and drone squadron leaders from every ship in the fleet were aboard, ready to hear the admiral's address.

Captain Coleman led Coda and Moscow out of the crowd, stopping outside a set of double doors guarded by a pair of armed marines. They all were dressed in their full dress uniforms. Coda had changed after Captain Coleman summoned him from the cockpit of his Nighthawk. They wore light blue and white, colors meant to represent the free skies of Earth. Their rank, medals, and decorations were polished to a golden shine and proudly displayed on their chests and shoulders.

A nervous shiver ran down Coda's spine. The uniform felt like something his mother would have picked out for him, something "respectable" to take a picture in. The Forgotten pin on his chest was the only thing that helped him stand tall—the only thing to give him a shred of confidence. He was a pilot, through and through. And not only that, he was part of the best squadron in the fleet.

The people around them seemed to notice, casting glances and talking in hushed voices as the three of them passed. Having been in the thick of the fight, Coda had been insulated from the attention and the true impact of their efforts. Seeing it now, he understood the Forgotten were respected. More than that—relied upon. Treasured. He stood straighter, holding his chin higher. Nothing the Overlord did could take that away from him.

The captain was also in full dress uniform. He had picked and fidgeted with it in the shuttle, clearly as uncomfortable in the attire as Coda. He was a fighter pilot at his core too. The cockpit was his home; the G-suit was his comfort clothes. Anything outside that was alien. The only person who looked comfortable in the formal dress was Moscow. He wore the uniform like a second skin, as comfortable in it as he was his flight suit.

Captain Coleman pulled them to the side of the corridor a small group of personnel had just vacated. "The admiral will begin his briefing in twenty minutes," he said. "I have something I need to see to. When they begin seating everyone, go in with the rest. I'll meet you in there."

"Sir," Coda and Moscow said in unison, snapping to attention.

Captain Coleman gave them a small nod and strode down the corridor. The station was an older design, using centrifugal force to create artificial gravity instead of the newly designed gravitational field systems R&D had created. That meant the deck rotated upward in front and behind them, the ceiling blocking his line of sight and restricting his view. Rooms and hallways branched off the main corridor. The automated doors were shut and guarded by armed marines.

It gave the illusion of security, though Coda knew they were one attack, one Baranyk-controlled human, from every leader of the fleet being killed and the fleet decimated.

"They're taking a hell of risk, bringing us all together like this," Coda said, voicing his concerns.

Moscow shrugged. "We're nowhere near the front. If we're not safe here, we're not safe anywhere."

It was true. There were a dozen systems between them and the last place the Baranyk fleet had been sighted, but Coda didn't understand why they couldn't have held the meeting virtually.

"How is Squawks doing?" Coda asked, changing the subject.

Moscow turned his eyes from the crowd, shooting Coda a surprised look. "I was about to ask you the same thing. He hasn't talked to you?"

"No..." Coda said slowly. "Was he supposed to?"

"I just assumed... You were both friends with Noodle after all."

Coda let out a frustrated groan, which he instantly regretted.

"Look," Moscow said defensively. "We've been through enough. He knew the risks. He'll be fine."

Coda wasn't so sure, but he kept the thought to himself. Moscow had only spent a few weeks as the CAG and had only overseen one battle. There was more to it than preparation and battle planning. There was a personal element too. It was up to the CAG to keep his pilots in fighting shape.

Judging by his tone, Moscow knew that too, but like most people, he was masking his personal frustration by projecting onto everyone else. Coda made a mental note to talk to Squawks. He should have days ago, though his friend hadn't made it easy. Coda would just have to force the issue, even if he had no idea what to say.

They fell into a companionable silence, watching the various military leaders. More than one came to speak with them, gifting them praise and encouragement, and quite a few more nodded or pointed. Coda was surprised it made him uncomfortable.

Ever since signing up for the Sol Fleet, he had dreamed of moments like this, moments where people pointed at him not because of what his father had done but because of his own accomplishments. Now, he felt like a fraud. He still wore the wings of the Forgotten on his chest, but he wasn't part of the squadron anymore. Not in the same way.

*Why am I here?* The thought kept pounding in his head. He hadn't seen anyone of a lower rank than a flight leader. Coda wasn't even on active flight duty, so he wasn't sure why Captain Coleman had brought him along.

They waited there for nearly twenty minutes, talking periodically, Coda stewing on his thoughts, until the doors to the amphitheater opened.

"Everyone's going inside," Moscow said. "I don't see the captain anywhere. Do you?"

Coda craned his neck to see past the gathering personnel, but between them and the ceiling of the corridor restricting his view, he couldn't see much. "Not yet."

"Should we head inside, then?"

"I guess," Coda said.

Together, Coda and Moscow entered the amphitheater, ready to hear Admiral Orlovsky's battle plan.

# 25

*Brig, Abraham Lincoln*
*Europa Station, Sol System*

THE BRIG WAS MUCH LIKE EVERY OTHER BRIG COLEMAN HAD SEEN throughout his career—a single room divided into six separate cells. They were of a traditional style, little more than a narrow bed and a very public toilet, all wrapped by deck-to-ceiling steel bars.

Coleman had, fortunately, never been inside one of those cells, but he'd visited more than one rowdy friend who'd earned a night in the ship's most accommodating resort. In fact, this wasn't the first time he'd found Joseph in one.

His friend wore the orange jumpsuit of an inmate and was lying on the bed, his back to the door, so he didn't see Coleman come in. Coleman's boots thumped against the deck as he strode through the room. Oddly enough, Joseph didn't so much as stir, showing no sign that he'd heard Coleman enter the room.

*Strange behavior for someone who likely doesn't get many visitors.*

Coleman stopped outside the cell, resting his hands on the steel bars. "I like what you've done with the place." He'd hoped to come up with something witty, maybe ease the tension in the room. Instead, the words sounded hollow, dying without so much as a chuckle.

Joseph didn't give any sign that he'd heard him.

"Hey, you asleep? I need to talk to you."

Joseph twitched then inhaled sharply like a diver emerging from the water and taking his first breath in minutes. Something was decidedly off about him, and Coleman was about to call the guards when Joseph rolled over, his eyes finding Coleman's. They were distant and unfocused, as if he'd just woken from the dead of night.

"Chadwick," he said, his voice thick and raspy. He sat up. Even his movements were sluggish.

"You okay?" Coleman asked. "You need me to send for the doc?"

"No." Joseph held his head in his hands but waved away the suggestion. "Just give me a minute." Then after he'd collected himself, he smiled and stood. He was still slow, but within the span of a few seconds, he had nearly transformed back into the man Coleman had expected. "It's good to see you."

"I'd say the same about you," Coleman said, "but you look like hell. It's illegal to mistreat a prisoner. If I need to—"

"No," Joseph interrupted. "It's nothing like that. I was just... out."

"You sure?" Coleman asked, not quite following Joseph's meaning.

"I'm sure."

"Okay." Coleman took a moment to collect his thoughts. The meeting had gotten off to a very different start than he'd been planning.

"What are you doing here?" Joseph asked. "Shouldn't you be aboard the *Redemption*?"

*No pretense. Straight to the point. God, I love being around fighter jocks.* "Admiral Orlovsky is about to outline his battle strategy to the fleet."

Joseph's lower jaw shifted to the side, and he tapped his teeth together, making a face Coleman had seen a thousand times—a face that meant he'd arrived at a conclusion ages ago and the world was finally catching up. "The Baranyk have arrived."

It wasn't a question, but Coleman answered it anyway. "They have."

"And it's not going well."

"It's not."

Joseph leaned forward, resting his elbows on the steel crossbeam.

"And the admiral wants to consolidate forces, meet them in a predetermined location, and fight them head-on."

"You know I can't confirm—"

"Gah!" Joseph said, disgusted. "That man has no imagination. He never did."

Coleman shot an uneasy look toward the corner of the room. There were no visible cameras, but he knew the brig was monitored, and all conversations were recorded. In fact, he was counting on it.

"That's why I'm here," Coleman said. That seemed to get Joseph's attention. "I need to know a few things."

"Okay..."

Joseph had gone straight to the point, so Coleman did the same, trusting that the other man would appreciate it. "Coda said you contacted him through the Baranyk network. I need to know if you can do that again."

Joseph's posture stiffened. "Why?"

"I just need to know if it's possible."

Joseph eyed him suspiciously, as if weighing his words. "It's possible," he said, but his body was still coiled like a cat about to spring.

Coleman nodded and let out a breath. The words brought him an element of comfort. "Good... Good."

"Why?"

It was a simple question wrought with a dozen consequences. Joseph was a prisoner of the fleet—actually, Coleman wasn't sure if he was technically part of the fleet at all anymore. Either way, he wasn't privy to battle plans or anything else that might jeopardize the safety of the fleet or its personnel. At the same time, locked away on a foreign ship, facing God knew what, his friend might not be as forthright as Coleman needed him to be. After all, it wasn't just information he needed.

"Let's just say I have an idea," Coleman said. "But it's just that. An idea. I don't even know if it's possible. But if it is, the admiral has given me leave to pursue it."

The tension melted from Joseph's body in an instant. Even after everything, Joseph still trusted him. "What kind of idea?"

"One with imagination," Coleman said.

That actually brought a smile to Joseph's lips, and the entire atmosphere in the room changed. "What do you need to know?"

"More about the Baranyk network," Coleman said. "For instance, are there any limits with your ability to communicate in it? Time limits? Distance? Anything that could get in the way of relaying information?"

"Not that I know of," Joseph said. "Except that both of us would have to be actively connected to it at the same time."

"At the same time? I thought once you were connected, you stayed connected."

"In a way," Joseph said. "Connecting to the Baranyk network isn't much different than connecting to, say, Wi-Fi. We can connect and disconnect as we please, and once connected, it's far easier to reconnect. But communicating through the network is closer to the old wired telephones. I can call, but he has to be on the other end to pick up."

"I think I understand," Coleman said. That threw a wrench into his plan, but it wasn't unworkable. "But as long as you're both connected at the same time, you could communicate... consistently."

"Yes."

Coleman rubbed his face, his mind racing. There was so much he didn't know and even more that he had only a rudimentary knowledge about. The difficulty was determining what he truly needed to understand at a detailed level and what he could lean on others for. "Tell me how you found the Baranyk home world."

Joseph's eyes went distant, almost as if he were reconnecting to the Baranyk network in that moment. "Imagine space. The void, its infinite blackness. But instead of distant stars like pinpricks of light, each pinprick is a consciousness. And like space, there's billions of them. Each a tiny flame among a sea of nothingness. When you get close to one, you get a sense of them. Who they are. *What* they are. Maybe even where they are or what they're doing in the physical world. It depends how deep their connection to the network is."

"Billions?"

"If not more," Joseph said.

"Then how'd you find the Overlord? Or even Coda?"

"Every being has its own presence," Joseph said. "A... signature. All of the races the Overlord has subjugated have their own, but there's a uniformity about them. Only a few are different. If you're looking properly, they're relatively easy to spot."

"So that's how you found the Overlord."

"That's how I found my son. He stood out to me like a beacon on a foggy shore. It's also how the Overlord can find us so easily. Time and distance mean nothing in the network. If he's looking, he will find us, so we have to take care not to connect too often. The more he finds us..."

"The more often he's going to look."

"Exactly."

Coleman remained silent for a moment, taking it all in. "You said that's *not* how you found the home world?"

"It's not," Joseph said. "Not exactly, anyway. As I already said, there's no such thing as distance in the network, but what I mean is that there's no correlation between space in the network and space in the real world. Just because something is fifty light years away in the physical world doesn't mean it's the same distance in the network. In fact, it's not nearly that far, and it's much faster to traverse."

Joseph spread his hands apart then brought them together. "But there is a correlation with proximity. Gather enough creatures together, and their presences will burn like a galaxy for all to see. That narrowed my search to a few thousand locations. From there, I looked for the Overlord's signature. Once I found that, the visual impression I got from the creatures located with him were of an invading fleet, and they happened to be massing at their home world."

"Could you find him again?"

"The Overlord?" Joseph asked. "Of course. But I don't need to. He never left."

"What?"

"He never left," Joseph repeated. "He stayed behind. He coordinates his forces through the network. It's not much different from you coordinating your squadrons from the bridge. His bridge just happens to be a few hundred light years away."

"Because there's no concept of distance in the network," Coleman said.

"Exactly."

Coleman ran his hand over his head and rubbed the back of his neck, the final piece of his plan clicking into place. "The Overlord is still on the home world."

"Yes, and guarded by a token force that would still rival many of our fleets. But yes, he's there."

"Thank you, Joseph." Coleman offered his hand through the bars, not even trying to keep the smile from his face.

Joseph looked at the hand then at Coleman's grinning expression, clearly confused. "For what?"

"For giving us a chance."

"I don't understand," Joseph said but finally took his hand.

"You will." Coleman gave his friend a firm shake. "You will."

# 26

*Amphitheater, Europa Station*
*Europa Station, Sol System*

The amphitheater was circular in design, with a central dais where Admiral Orlovsky and his command staff would be presenting. The folks from the corridor filed into the room, continuing their conversations and slowly taking seats.

Coda watched everyone, feeling out of place. Captain Coleman hadn't told Coda why he'd been invited, and trusting his judgment, he hadn't thought to ask. The unknown made him uncomfortable, but even deeper than that was something as equally unsettling that he couldn't put his finger on.

Once everyone was seated, the lights dimmed, and a spotlight lit the central dais. Admiral Orlovsky emerged from a hidden stairwell and climbed the dais, taking a moment to survey the scene. As he did, the entire amphitheater rose and saluted their commanding officer.

"At ease," Admiral Orlovsky said. He paused as the several hundred command staff retook their seats. "Seeing you all assembled here is an incredible sight, though I wish it was done under better circumstances. The fact is the war against the Baranyk has taken a terrible turn. After a slight reprieve, the enemy is back, stronger and more numerous than ever. Four systems have fallen already, and we've issued a full-scale retreat from nine more. Make no mistake about it, ladies and gentlemen, the enemy has us on our back foot."

The admiral's words echoed throughout the chamber as he stood, surveying the silent crowd. Coda followed his gaze, wondering if he was looking at anyone in particular or simply engaging his audience. He couldn't make out any patterns, so he assumed the latter.

"But I look at the collection of men and women in this room, and I have hope. Never before has the human race assembled so many capable fighters under a single banner. Never before have they fought together on a mutual battlefield. That ends today."

Coda shifted in his seat, unable to shake the feeling that they were one Baranyk-controlled enemy insider-turned-bomber from losing every member of their command staff. Why hadn't the admiral just issued instructions as he normally would have?

"It is a pretty incredible sight, isn't it?" Moscow said softly.

Coda just nodded. But Moscow's remark helped him see through a clearer lens. This wasn't for the admiral. It wasn't even for the individual captains and commanders. It was for their collective. Alone, humans were weak, impressionable, and prone to failure. But together, fighting for a mutual cause against a mutual enemy, they were capable of incredible feats. Looking around the room again, Coda saw rapt attention, slight nods, and a firmer resolve. Even knowing the odds they faced, it gave him a renewed sense of hope.

Admiral Orlovsky pressed a button on his indicator. At his gesture, a star chart appeared above the dais, very similar to the 3D battle maps equipped on all of the capital ships. "The enemy has followed a direct route through the heart of our outer systems. Based on fleet intel, we predicted they would attack the Indirian system next." He took a breath for effect. "And unfortunately, our predictions were correct. Just an hour ago, we received word of a full-scale assault. Early indications suggest it's a total loss."

As if to punctuate his words, a series of images replaced the star chart, showing the breadth of the destruction. Initially, they showed a distant view of a planet and its three moons entirely encompassed by enemy forces. Then closer. A broken orbital platform. Shattered remains of a defensive force. All coalescing to form a ring of debris around the planet, the graveyard of a fallen civilization.

As if to drive the point home, Orlovsky zoomed in, and the images became more personal. Buildings, fifty stories high, had collapsed, crashing into each other. Glass and shrapnel littered the streets. Bridges had collapsed into rivers. Cars and other equipment were little more than burnt exoskeletons, clogging transportation arteries. The entire planet was a visual representation of death. Of a fallen people. Of what would happen if they failed to stop the enemy fleet.

"Due to an early full-scale evacuation order," Admiral Orlovsky continued, "the loss of human life was minimal. But this is the threat we face. And if we are unsuccessful, this will be every world, in every system, including Earth. The continued existence of our very race depends on us. On our actions."

The image on the display zoomed way out, showing a view of human-occupied space. Each system was labeled. Overlayed on this was a red line showing the Baranyk advance, ending with Tau Titus.

"Based on our projections, the Baranyk fleet will continue on its current path until it reaches Tau Titus. From there, it's difficult to predict, so it's there that we'll make our stand."

A series of dotted red lines cut through the image, ending at a particular system. The image then zoomed in to show an inhabited orange planet orbited by three moons.

"The lone populated planet makes it simpler to defend, and the proximity of the moons provides us certain strategic advantages. Our main force will assemble here, roughly four hundred thousand kilometers from the planet and thirty thousand kilometers from its nearest moon. Our goal is to funnel the attack this way, where the enemy will trigger a newly devised space minefield that'll decimate the lead fighters. When the bulk of their forces make it through the minefield, we'll order an organized retreat. The objective is simple: get them to chase, at which time our secondary force, hidden on the dark side of the moon, will flank the incoming ships. These tactics alone will not win the battle. The goal is simply to even the odds. Because then the real battle will begin, and we'll unleash our biggest surprise. Our drone fleets are operable again."

This elicited a cheer from the crowd.

Admiral Orlovsky held up a hand to ask for a moment. "Which is what makes Tau Titus another strategic choke point. The drone manufacturing facility on its moon is as large as six of our largest capital ships, and hundreds of fully operational Hornets are waiting, unused, in its warehouses. And work is underway to increase that. By the time of the battle, we aim to have a full ten squadrons that can launch from the moon installation itself."

Coda and Moscow exchanged a look. Ten squadrons was two hundred and forty individual fighters. Quite a force. Added to the rest of the fleet's firepower, Coda was beginning to believe they had a chance. Seeing the enthusiasm spreading through the room, he longed to get back into the cockpit. But that longing quickly turned into an ache as he was reminded that it would never happen again.

He wondered if the captain would allow him to fly a Hornet drone. The *Redemption* was outfitted with a full complement of drone squadrons, after all. Flying a Hornet wasn't the same as flying a Nighthawk, but it was better than nothing. He promised himself that he would talk to the captain about it. He wouldn't be left on the sidelines of the most important battle humanity had ever fought.

"Our drone fleets may even the odds," Admiral Orlovsky said, "but they are not the silver bullet. We will still be vastly outnumbered, outpowered, and outgunned. But we have one thing the Baranyk will never have. The ingenuity, creativity, and strategic brilliance of the men and women in this room. It's not our weapons or our technology that we put our faith in. It's you."

There was another round of applause, this one more energetic than the last. Coda found himself caught up in it. He cheered and clapped with the rest of them.

"A full battle plan has been provided to each of you. Over the next hour, familiarize yourself with it. My staff and I are here for any questions. If I don't speak with you individually, then Godspeed and good luck."

# 27

*Corridor, Europa Station*
*Europa Station, Sol System*

THE BUZZ IN THE CORRIDOR SEEMED TO VIBRATE THE DECK. CHATTER WAS at an all-time high, significantly more energetic than before, voices loud and excited as groups of three to four captains spoke among themselves. Walking out of the amphitheater and through the corridor, Coda picked up fragments of conversation.

Most were centered on how the newly available drone squadrons could turn the tide of the Baranyk advance. Others were focused on the battle tactics themselves. The general consensus seemed to be that the strategy was sound, though there were concerns of the Baranyk dividing its forces between the planet and the nearest moon, where the human's flanking force was hidden. By doing so, they could negate the fleet's most decisive blow.

It was a risk—hopefully a calculated one based on previous Baranyk battle tactics—but battles were always rife with risks. Sometimes, the difference between winning and losing was choosing which risks to accept. Unfortunately, too much of war was decided by luck.

Coda scanned the corridor, looking for Captain Coleman, who still hadn't returned. The amphitheater was large, and Coda's attention had been on the presentation, so it was possible he had snuck in shortly after it had begun. If that had been the case, though, Coda suspected Captain Coleman would have rejoined them already.

"I don't see the captain," Moscow said. "Do you?"

"No. I haven't seen him since he left. Should we go back to the ship?"

"Maybe." Moscow drew out the word then stepped out of the main pathway, putting his back to the bulkhead. He clearly had no intentions of going back to the ship without the captain. "Where would he have gone?"

"I don't kn—"

"Coda?" The voice cut through the corridor's chatter like a sharp note in a symphony.

Coda tore his eyes off Moscow, scanning the corridor. There was something about that voice.

A man walked toward him, his powerful build making purposeful strides through the crowd.

"Buster?"

A smile a country mile wide split the other man's face, and his step found an extra gear. He crossed the last few meters between them in an instant then crashed into Coda, giving him a tight hug and slapping him on the back, laughing all the while.

"Holy shit," Buster said. "It is you!" He held Coda by his shoulders, appraising him as if he were a distant relative he hadn't seen since he was a child. "What are you doing here?"

"Me?" Coda asked in disbelief. "What are you doing here?"

"I'm..." Buster's gaze went to Coda's lieutenant commander insignia, and his eyes grew wide. "I'm sorry... sir. Please excuse my lack of decorum."

Coda glanced at his uniform then Buster's. It wasn't until then that he noticed Buster's insignia. He had the gold wings of a squadron leader and the lapels of a lieutenant, which meant Coda outranked him. A remnant of his days as CAG.

"Don't," Coda said, finally understanding why so many of his superior officers quickly did away with decorum the first chance they got. "None of that. We're friends."

"Of course, sir," Buster said with a straight face, no sarcasm at all.

"Shut up." Coda gave his old friend a playful shove, the kind he would have given him during their time at the Terran Fleet Academy. Buster had been his best friend, his fellow flight leader in Dragon Squadron, and the first person Coda had celebrated with when they'd become the Ace Squadron in their academy. "Seriously, what are you doing here?"

Buster seemed to stand straighter. "I'm CAG on the *Olympia*."

"CAG?" Coda said. "I thought you were on the *Abraham Lincoln*."

"Reassigned and promoted," Buster said with a smile.

"Congratulations," Coda said.

"You too." Buster's eyes drifted to Moscow, who had been quiet during the exchange. Like Coda, he and Moscow had been rivals during their time at the flight academy. But unlike Coda, Buster hadn't gotten over it. "Both of you. The Forgotten have been the talk of the fleet for months. And my old friend, my CAG, is the leader. Unbelievable."

Coda gave him a half smile, glancing at Moscow, and waited for him to say something, to correct their former academy mate and put Coda in his place. When he didn't, an awkward pause filled the conversation.

"It's been unbelievable," Coda finally said.

"I bet!" Buster hadn't lost any of his enthusiasm. "We used to study Commander Coleman's battles, remember? Hell, we used the Coleman Diamond in our final battle... Sorry, Moscow. And now you're flying with him. What's he like?"

"He's... exactly what you'd expect him to be. A living legend. But also one of us. A fighter jock to his core."

"Incredible," Moscow said. "So much has changed since Dragon Squadron, hasn't it?"

Coda couldn't help but think of all the people he'd flown with. The battles tended to jumble together, but he never forgot the people.

"It really has." Coda couldn't help but hear the melancholy in his own voice. He hoped Buster didn't notice.

"And now our drone squadrons are operational again. We're back in the fight. Maybe I'll see you out there. Just like old times."

"Yeah," Coda said. "That would be something."

"Yes, it would." Buster's smile finally waned. The conversation had taken a turn, and he'd noticed it but obviously didn't know why. Coda couldn't help but feel like he was being unfair. Knowing Buster, his old friend would think it was something he had done. He wouldn't know that Coda was the problem, that he was keeping secrets from him.

But what made Buster an amazing person was his ability to shine even when he was surrounded by darkness. As quickly as his smile faded, it returned, bigger and brighter than ever. "Damn, Coda, it's good to see you."

"You too, Buster." Coda pulled his old friend into a hug. "You too. More than you know."

"I'll see you around." Buster slapped him on the back. "Good luck out there. Both of you."

Just as quickly as Buster had returned to Coda's life, he was gone, disappearing into the crowd. Coda watched him go, his melancholy becoming full-blown sadness. Seeing his old friend had been great, but in too many ways, it reminded him of what he had lost.

"Thank you for not telling him," Coda said.

"It wasn't my place," Moscow said.

Coda didn't disagree. Still, he couldn't help but think that the old Moscow wouldn't have let the opportunity pass him by. Buster had been right when he'd said so much had changed. "Still."

Moscow turned to face him. "I know things are awkward between us, but I'm still your friend. I hope you know that."

"I do."

"Good. Now, where the hell is our captain?"

It didn't take them long to find out. He appeared out of the crowd, spotted them, and immediately made for them. "There you are. You ready?"

"For what, sir?" Moscow asked.

"To return to the ship."

"Yes, sir," they both said.

Then Coda added, "Sir, you said you needed my help with something."

"Turns out I didn't," Captain Coleman said.

"Is that a good thing or a bad thing, sir?"

Captain Coleman shrugged. "That's still to be determined. But for now, let's say it's a good thing. Come on, let's get back to the ship. We have a lot of work ahead of us."

---

CODA STEPPED OFF THE SHUTTLE RAMP ONTO THE DECK OF THE *Redemption*. The hangar was always a hive of activity, and today was no exception. As Coda had learned recently, there was no shortage of work to do aboard a ship. Even when the technicians weren't repairing battle damage, the Nighthawks required constant maintenance to perform at their best. In that way, they weren't unlike the pilots themselves.

Coda followed Captain Coleman, with Moscow trailing him. The flight back from the admiral's address had been a quiet one. Captain Coleman hadn't said much since returning to the shuttle, and he hadn't provided any information about what he was doing while Coda and Moscow were attending the briefing. Coda hadn't pressed for answers, deep in his own thoughts.

"Can I have a moment, sir?" Coda asked.

Moscow glanced at him and, apparently realizing the question wasn't directed at him, continued through the hangar.

Captain Coleman stopped and turned to Coda. "Of course."

"Thank you, sir." Coda took a deep breath. "During his briefing, the admiral said that the Hornet drones were operational again. I know I'm grounded, sir, but I thought... maybe... I could join the drone squadrons we have on board the *Redemption*."

His idea had come shortly after this reunion with Buster, his old friend's words echoing over and over again in his brain. *Maybe we'll see each other out there.*

Captain Coleman leveled a thoughtful gaze on him. "I know you miss it, Coda." His words were slow, as if he didn't know what he was going to say next. "But it's my job to ensure the success of the mission while minimizing the loss of human life. I'm sorry, but my position hasn't changed. As long as you're susceptible to the Baranyk signal, you'll remain grounded."

If Coda had had any hope, it would have been sucked away like oxygen in a breached hull. The most he'd allowed himself was the idea of hope. Still, to know his lot wouldn't change, that he'd sit on the sidelines while his friends fought and died, was enough to crush him.

"I understand, sir." The words were robotic, emotionless. Despite their relationship, Coda couldn't argue with the captain. Not that he'd had much of an argument to begin with. The idea had never been much more than a fool's hope.

"Your father learned to resist it," Coleman said. "He said he has been teaching you the same techniques. Have you made any progress?"

"No," Coda admitted.

He'd tried to follow his father's instruction during their journey back. Although it had been easier when he was still onboard, the exercises had been mentally taxing even then, and he could only take so much of it. Since he'd returned to active duty, the exercises had become even more difficult. Then when his father was taken into custody, Coda had largely abandoned them. It was an odd form of self-sabotage, and he knew it.

"Keep working at it," Captain Coleman said. "If he can do it, you can as well. And that's your path to flight status."

"Thank you, sir." Coda nodded to him then looked elsewhere, breaking eye contact. Feeling the captain's eyes on him was hard enough, but when he looked into them, he couldn't help but see an indictment of all his failures. Coda waited to be dismissed, but Captain Coleman didn't make any motion toward the hangar's exit.

"That said, Coda, the admiral's plan is not my own. We have our own mission, and for that, I don't plan on keeping you on the sidelines."

"Sir?" Coda said.

"I can't say too much," Captain Coleman said. "I'm still working out the details, but in order for our plan to succeed, you'll need to play a key role."

"I... don't know what to say, sir."

"No, I don't imagine you do. It's hard to have something to say when you don't know what you'll be doing, isn't it?"

The smallest of smiles split Coda's face. "Whatever it is, sir, I'll be ready."

"Of that, I have no doubt. Now, if you'll excuse me, I have a lot of preparation ahead of me. But remember what I said. Keep working, and be ready."

"I will, sir." Coda saluted the captain.

Captain Coleman nodded and strode away. Coda had done everything he could to stifle his hope, dousing it any time he'd felt its spark. But with the captain's words, and despite all of his efforts, he could feel it catching in his chest.

# 28

*SAS Redemption*
*Europa Station, Sol System*

Captain Coleman's summons didn't come that day or even the next, and for all intents and purposes, life aboard the *Redemption* returned to normal. The rest of the ship personnel hadn't been at the admiral's briefing, but word spread. There was a buzz for the first time in as long as Coda could remember. The Sol Fleet was going on the offensive, and in some form, the years of constant vigilance would come to an end.

The ship's personnel went about their daily tasks with more vigor. No longer were they the mundane daily tasks that needed to be completed, another box checked. Instead, they were of vital importance, a critical cog in the war effort.

The one command Coda received from Captain Coleman was a new set of training scenarios he wanted programmed into the simulators. At first, Coda expected a grand display of military might, a great battle with tens of thousands of bogeys, fought in the location the battle would be waged.

To his surprise, he received instructions for an alien world he'd seen only once, via a drone recording. The barren planet of yellow rock with three moons was a hellscape if he'd ever seen one. The Baranyk home world.

Coda didn't understand, and he didn't ask questions. Captain Coleman had said his mission wasn't that of the rest of the fleet, but Coda hadn't expected anything like this. Every scenario involved an assault on one of the four celestial bodies—the planet and each of its moons.

Based on the intel they'd received, each of the landscapes were markedly different, with the planet itself most similar to Mars. It had a thin atmosphere with drastic temperature variance and was plagued with high-speed winds on the surface that could kick up debris and cause issues with their computers. It was here the captain wanted them to spend the most time preparing.

*We're going to assault the Baranyk home world*, Coda thought. *But with what?*

The fleet was staying behind, preparing for the Baranyk invasion force. Every ship was needed, so anything sent into Baranyk territory would be incredibly small in number.

Not an invasion force, then. A ship of assassins. The idea seemed a special kind of crazy, which, if Coda was being honest with himself, also brought a special blend of excitement.

*What is my role in all of this?*

Try as he might, even though Captain Coleman had told him he would have a role to play, he couldn't place it. He couldn't even come up with a plausible idea. Then, finally, the order arrived. Coda was simultaneously excited and dismayed.

The briefing was to be held in the command quarters just off the bridge at 1800 hours. Coda arrived a few minutes early and found the room already nearly full. The usual suspects were in attendance, including Captain Coleman, Commander Garcia, Commander Payton, and Dr. Naidoo. New to the proceedings was Lieutenant Cahill, call sign Phantom, the *Redemption*'s Hornet CAG. Moscow, the last to arrive, was clearly surprised by Coda's presence.

The room itself was moderately sized, mostly occupied by the single old-fashioned table bolted to the deck. A wall of digital displays along the bulkhead parallel to the entrance showed a live view of the ship's exterior. The red glow of Jupiter lit the space station, and lights from various ships flashed in the dark. Preparations were underway for every ship in the fleet.

"All right," Captain Coleman said. "Everyone's here. Let's get started."

Coda went to take his usual seat with the rest of them, then he realized it was the CAG's chair. He shot a glance at Moscow while in an awkward squatting position and found that the other man had already taken a spot down the table.

Not knowing what else to do, Coda fell farther into the chair. Moscow didn't seem to care, and it was too late to swap seats without making a show of it, which he hardly thought Moscow would appreciate.

The only person who didn't sit was Captain Coleman himself. He remained standing at the head of the table. "By now, you've all read the admiral's orders."

There were a series of nods and nonverbal confirmations around the table. No longer a part of the command staff, Coda hadn't received the orders. He'd seen the address in person; that would have to be enough.

"Good," Coleman continued. "Then I don't need to review the mission. Since the orders came through, the Baranyk trajectory has remained unchanged. They continue to cut through the very heart of our systems."

Captain Coleman tapped a button on his tablet, dimming the lights in the room and calling up a display. It resembled the same one the admiral had shown, with indicators for the Baranyk force and an arrow through the various human-occupied systems.

"Judging by our estimates, the Baranyk force will arrive at Tau Titus within thirty-six hours."

Coda shifted as a cold chill went down his spine. If the battle went poorly, the future of the human race could be measured in hours. Not centuries. Not millennia. Hours.

"We..." Captain Coleman let the word hang in the air. "Will not be there to welcome them."

This time, confusion spread through the room. Commander Garcia's face twisted into a scowl. It appeared he was just as surprised as the rest of them and hadn't appreciated being kept in the dark.

"We have a mission of our own." Captain Coleman toggled another button, replacing the macro view of the universe with a single image: the barren yellow rock, pitted and windswept. "The Baranyk home world."

Someone on the other end of the table was tapping their nails against its surface, but Coda didn't bother to look to see who it was. His eyes were fixed on the planet, remembering a dream from several weeks before. Being pursued by Baranyk warriors. Chased. Running through what he'd thought was a ruined landscape. It wasn't until that moment that he realized he'd dreamed of the surface of the Baranyk's planet.

An angry hand seemed to squeeze his heart, freezing it, as he remembered the fear from the dream. Of all the places in the universe, that was the one place he wished like anything to avoid.

"Early intelligence suggests the planet is made up of a series of tunnels and chambers, providing shelter from the extreme temperatures and high-speed winds. Light measurements suggest water and a relatively limited biosphere."

That the Baranyk lived underground wasn't much of a surprise. The planet clearly made living on its surface difficult, and even when the Baranyk had occupied or colonized other planets, they had done so by creating their own tunnel systems.

"May I ask a question, sir?" Moscow asked from the other end of the table. His index finger was pressed onto the tabletop, his eyes on it instead of the captain.

"Please," Captain Coleman said.

"How many other ships will be joining us on this mission?"

"None."

Moscow's eyes came up from the table, meeting Captain Coleman's. "That's what I expected. But it begs the question: we're one ship, not an invasion force. How could we possibly assault a planet, let alone an entire system?"

Captain Coleman seemed to have anticipated the question. Moscow wasn't halfway through it by the time he replaced the image of the planet with another of a black Baranyk warrior with gold stripes. For the sake of scale, the Baranyk was next to a normal Baranyk warrior. The warrior was nearly twice its size.

"Following our assault in Kryos, we learned of a special kind of Baranyk," Captain Coleman said. "Bigger and faster than the normal warriors, this one also communicates telepathically with the rest. Like a queen ant, this Baranyk, this *Overlord*, controls the hive. This creature is who's been directing the enemy forces. This is who we have been at war with. This is the true face of our enemy."

Coda had lived with the knowledge of the Overlord for so long, he had to remind himself that it was still classified information known only to a small number of people. Looking around the room, he could see who had been privy to that secret and who had not.

"We're not assaulting the planet," Captain Coleman continued. "We're there for one reason and one reason only. To blow the Baranyk Overlord back to whatever special hell he crawled out of. If we do, the enemy forces will be leaderless, confused, defeated. If we do this, we will win the war."

Coda felt Moscow's eyes on him. He could only imagine what the other man was thinking.

"But still, your question is valid," Captain Coleman said. "From what we know, a defensive force remains on the planet, but early numbers estimate it's a fraction of what we originally uncovered. Like us, they seem focused on the battle at Tau Titus. We also have the element of surprise—not only with a surprise attack but with a fully operational drone squadron, including a full outfit of drone bombers."

Coda steepled his fingers, staring at the image of the Overlord. "Sir, from what I remember, the home world is smaller than Earth, maybe half its size. But that's still a lot of planet to cover when we're looking for a single Baranyk. How are we supposed to find him? And to Moscow's point before, even if we're able to find him, those tunnels will make for a hell of an assault."

Captain Coleman smiled. "That, Coda, is where you come in."

"Me, sir?"

"Well, more specifically, your father. Using the Baranyk network, he's confident the Overlord remains on the planet. Because time and space mean little inside the network, the Overlord is able to command his forces from half a universe away. Which means he might not see us until it's too late. Even if he does, your father has agreed to use the network to learn everything he can about the planet and the Overlord's whereabouts. R&D also equipped us with an allotment of new autonomous surveillance drones that will scout the tunnels and map it for us."

And just like that, the final piece clicked into place. Coda finally understood his role in all of it and why he had been invited to the briefing. "I'm supposed to be your translator."

"I thought of you more as our communications specialist, relaying information from your father," Captain Coleman said. "But I suppose that's an apt description as well."

Coda sat back in his chair, strangely disappointed. The captain had said he wouldn't be on the sidelines for this, and so far, he had held to that promise, but Coda had hoped for something more than being a glorified telephone.

"I have a hard time believing Joseph O'Neil will be our savior," Commander Garcia said.

Captain Coleman started to say something, but Commander Garcia held up a hand. "But"—he emphasized the word as if to say that this wasn't his main point—"say we are successful mapping out the tunnel system. And say he's successful locating the Overlord inside them. Sir, we only have one platoon of marines stationed aboard the ship. And to Coda's point before, that's a lot of ground to cover."

"We're not going in with marines, Commander." With a final click of the button, the Overlord disappeared, and an image of the mouth of a tunnel appeared. "The Baranyk do nearly everything underground. And that includes the manufacturing, or whatever it is they do, of their ships. *All* of their ships. The tunnels aren't like you and I think of them. They're big. Massive. Some larger than the *Redemption* itself."

Another click superimposed a squadron of Nighthawks over the image of the cave mouth. "We're going in, all right. For a good, old-fashioned tunnel run."

# 29

*Briefing Room, SAS Redemption*
*Europa Station, Sol System*

Commander Garcia laughed. It was a great booming laugh that came deep from his gut. "A tunnel run," he said between breaths. "And here I thought you were crazy."

The rest of the room's occupants looked at each other uncomfortably, but contrary to their expectations, the outburst didn't make Coleman angry. In reality, that was one of the things he appreciated most about his XO—his no-bullshit attitude. When the captain wasn't safe, no one was.

"I'm a fighter pilot," Captain Coleman said. "Always will be. We're a special kind of crazy." He tapped his tablet, zooming out on the image, showing another image of a battle being waged above the skies of the home world. "When we have the tunnels mapped out, we'll begin the assault. The bulk of our squadrons will occupy the defensive force above the surface while a reserve force of Hornets will slip in and make for the Overlord."

"Why the Hornets?" Moscow asked. "Seems like a job for a real pilot."

"Real pilot?" Phantom asked. The Hornet squadron leader's dark face was hard.

There had always been a large amount of tension between the two groups of pilots. The old guard had been replaced by the Hornet squadrons and felt a deep animosity toward them, almost as if they were the new husbands who had stolen away their wives and were taking care of their kids. And despite their success earlier in the war, Coleman suspected the drone pilots felt a sense of inferiority since they didn't assume the same level of risk as the Nighthawk pilots. Those feelings had become even more exacerbated since he'd built the Forgotten.

"Poor choice of words," Moscow said. "You know what I meant."

"I'm not sure I do," Phantom said, clearly not ready to back down.

"Many of the tunnels are incredibly large," Coleman said, stepping in before the situation could get worse. "But the farther inside we go, the narrower they get. The Hornets are half the size of the Nighthawks, providing more room to maneuver."

"And we have more of them than we do of you," Commander Garcia added.

"That too," Captain Coleman agreed. "Plus we have the raw material to make more."

That seemed to quell Moscow's initial objections, though it did little to ease Phantom's frustrations. The man continued to glare daggers at Moscow.

"You're not worried about latency issues?" Coda asked.

It was a good question, and it made sense coming from someone who had trained to fly the Hornet drones long before he'd ever joined the Forgotten. The biggest problem was basic physics. Light, and thereby communication, could only travel so fast. That meant that any commands issued by the drone operators aboard their respective capital ships were delayed by the time it took to make it to the drone itself.

The reverse was true as well. Any images the Hornet pilots saw in their VR helmets could be anywhere from a sixteenth to a half a second late. The fleet did everything it could to keep the latency as low as possible, but operations were never as clean as they could be. What they lacked in precision, they had made up for in sheer numbers. That had always been the tradeoff.

"The *Redemption* should be close enough to avoid any major lag," Coleman said. "But it is something we'll monitor. Any other questions?"

Coleman scanned the room's occupants.

"Jump in," Moscow said. "Scout the area, create a diversion, then slip in and kill the Overlord. Sounds simple enough. I'm assuming we'll update the training scenarios for the Forgotten to include the tunnel run as a precaution?"

Moscow was like a dog who wouldn't drop his bone. Coleman had already made it abundantly clear the Hornets would be going in, not the Nighthawks. Still, he appreciated the added strategic redundancy.

"Yes," Coleman said. "The moment we get our first scans back, we'll turn them into a training scenario that *both* of you can run your pilots through."

"Thank you, sir," Phantom said.

"Sounds good, sir."

"When do we ship out?" Commander Garcia asked.

"That is entirely dependent on the Overlord," Coleman said. "Our goal is to remain undetected for as long as possible. Our best chance of doing that is when the Overlord is distracted, so we won't jump in until the larger battle has started."

"So, thirty-six hours or so," Commander Garcia said.

"That's my best guess," Coleman agreed. "If any of you have anything pressing, get it done soon, because there's no telling when you'll get another chance. Anything else?"

His command staff looked at each other, but nobody spoke up.

"All right," Coleman said. "Prepare your people. We're about to embark on the most important mission any of us have ever fought. We need to be at our best. Dismissed."

Everyone stood and began filtering out of the room.

Commander Garcia lingered. "When you get a moment, I'd like a word, sir."

He wouldn't be happy about being left in the dark again. Coleman couldn't blame him. It wasn't normal operating procedure, but the plan had come together too quickly. He hoped his old friend would understand that.

"Of course," Coleman said. "Give me twenty minutes."

"Thank you, sir." He turned to go.

Making up the last of the fleeing occupants were Dr. Naidoo and Commander Payton. "Hold up a moment," Coleman said, stopping them. "There's one last thing that involves you."

"What is it, sir?" Dr. Naidoo asked.

Coleman glanced at the door, where Coda and Moscow were stepping out. Once they'd left the room, Coleman returned his gaze to the room's final two occupants. "Based on what you know of the Baranyk signal, how difficult would it be to block?"

"Block?" Commander Payton asked. Always the engineer, he needed specificity.

"Yes," Coleman said. "Block. Prevent it from reaching its destination. Or at least prevent it from allowing the Overlord to take control of his host."

"It's a basic extreme low-frequency signal," Commander Payton said. "In theory, it should be simple enough to create a countersignal that would negate the source. The issue is range. The signal we've encountered is incredibly powerful. In order to keep it from washing over the entire ship, we'd need to amplify to massive levels, and I'm not sure we have the correct tools."

"What if it didn't have to protect the entire ship?" Coleman asked. "What if it only needed to negate the signal enough to protect one individual?"

Commander Payton rubbed his chin, his index finger tapping his lip. "That... might actually be possible."

"What would it look like?" Coleman asked. "A helmet the subject would wear? An implant? Or do we stick him in a room where the countersignal is broadcast?"

"Some sort of helmet device would be quickest and simplest," Commander Payton said, "but clearly impractical. A simple transmitter attached to the temple region should do the trick."

"What do you think, Dr. Naidoo?" Coleman asked. "If we were able to negate the signal before it ever reached its host, would that prevent the Overlord from being able to take control?"

"In theory, yes," she said. "But I'd want to run some experiments first."

"Of course," Coleman said. "How soon could you have something mocked up?"

"We're still optimizing the new EmDrive," Commander Payton said. "But I can get a team started on it—"

"No team," Coleman said. "Just you if possible."

"Sir, I've got a thousand responsibilities and projects demanding my attention. If you need this ship to be battle ready in thirty-six hours, I don't have the bandwidth to—"

"A team, then," Coleman said. "Could it be ready before we jump?"

"The preliminary design? Probably."

"Okay," Coleman said. "Make it happen. But keep it quiet, and don't tell the team what they're working on. We have to keep this one between us. Understood?"

"Yes, sir."

"Of course, sir."

"Let me know when you begin your tests."

"Will do, sir."

Coleman let out a long sigh as Dr. Naidoo and Commander Payton left the room. All things considered, the briefing had gone well. The plan was falling into place better than it had any right to.

It wasn't until then that he realized he'd just added another item to the list of things he was keeping from his XO. He would let Commander Garcia in on this one. It involved his ship's personnel after all. And if it worked, it would give them another weapon they hadn't had in a long time.

For Coda's sake, he hoped it did.

# 30

*Storage Locker, SAS Redemption*
*Europa Station, Sol System*

Captain Coleman had said to take care of things that needed taken care of before it was too late, so Coda resigned himself to doing something he had been putting off for far too long.

The unfortunate reality was that he should have done it long ago. Squawks was hurting. He needed help. Support. A friend. But Coda had abandoned him, and the longer he hadn't gone to talk to him, the harder it was to rebuild that bridge.

His father used to tell him that the harder something was, the more important it was. When it was the hardest, that was when you were needed most. With that in mind, Coda searched the barracks, gym, and Simulation Room, coming up empty each time. He resisted the urge to turn back, to say he'd tried, give up, and wait for Squawks to come to him. The truth was, though, Coda knew where Squawks was—where he had always been.

Dating back to their time aboard the *Jamestown,* Squawks had always been the one tending to the still. Alcohol was an incredible drug, made more special by its lack of availability when traversing the impossible distances between civilizations. For as long as there had been space travel, no, since humanity had traversed the skies and the seas, unsanctioned stills had been a place of community. A place where soldiers, sailors, and all forms of military personnel congregated to drink whatever piss-flavored alcohol flowed.

Tex had taught Squawks, and Squawks had kept the tradition alive. The still was "found" from time to time, usually by an upstart officer or after someone had gotten on their superior's bad side. Then it would have to be built again somewhere new. These days, it was in a storage locker off the hangar, which, coincidentally, was where the heaviest drinkers seemed to be.

It was located in the corner of a locker, roughly the size of a small bedroom, between racks of seldom-used spare parts. The special kind of place that was a room off a room, that everyone knew existed but rarely ventured into.

Coda stepped through the door immediately off the hangar and thought he heard hushed voices. At the *whoosh* of the automated door sliding shut, the voices cut off. It was one thing to drink in a place everyone knew existed. It was something else to flaunt the infraction in front of leadership.

He waited a second to see if they picked back up, and when they didn't, he turned to go. He'd hoped Squawks would be alone. The door opened.

Coda didn't go through. He waited, chastising himself. He couldn't run away. Squawks needed him.

The door closed again, and thinking that whoever had entered had ventured back out, the voices returned. Coda slipped through the room toward the second door that led to the equipment locker then stopped as the voices became clearer.

"You have to stop beating yourself up," a firm female voice said. Coda didn't have to see her to know it was Nails—Captain Coleman's daughter and Squawks's wingman.

Squawks said something Coda couldn't make out. Coda pushed on the door, ready to go in, when Nails erupted.

"I can't do this anymore," she said sharply. "I'm not going to play the blame game with you. We're fighter pilots, Squawks. We fly at speeds that alone are enough to kill us. We're one rock, one grain of sand, one piece of debris away from tearing a hole through our canopies. One technical malfunction away from becoming human soup in our cockpits. Oh, and there's the little detail of aliens trying to fucking kill us." Nails was breathing heavily. "There is no blame in Noodle's death, the same way there's no blame in any of the other pilots we've lost. It's part of the game, Squawks. You know this. You've always known this."

Coda could almost feel the intensity from the other room, the fire in her caramel-colored eyes, see the sharp, you-better-fucking-listen expression she had inherited from her father on her face.

Squawks said something inaudible, something that Nails immediately shut down.

"Fine," Nails said. "You want to play the blame game? Let's do it. The admiral is responsible for Noodle's death. After all, he sent us there. He didn't take the captain's warnings strong enough, which left that planet basically defenseless. He's at fault."

Squawks must have made a skeptical face, because Nails pivoted.

"No?" Nails said. "You don't like that one? Fine, it's my father's fault. Despite having a broken-down ship and holes in our ranks, he probably asked the admiral to go. And even if he didn't, he trained you. Trained Noodle."

Nails was finding a rhythm now and didn't let up. "How about our engineers, in all their collective genius, who couldn't figure out how to counter the signal that made our drones useless? If they'd been smarter, faster about coming up with a solution, we never would have reinstated the Nighthawk program. No, it's Moscow's fault for not coordinating the battle better. Coda's fault for forcing an unproven CAG to step into the role. Coda's fault for not being there. For having a fucked-up brain that the Baranyk could exploit. His father's fault for passing *his* fucked-up brain to his son."

"Stop," Squawks said, the word barely audible through the door.

Coda was thankful for it. Nails's comments hit too close to home. The same irrational way Squawks was blaming himself, Coda was too. He was just compartmentalizing it better.

"No, Squawks," Nails said. "We're going to see this through. I'm going to *show* you how pointless this blame game is, because we're not done. It's his wingman's fault for not being there. I've watched the flight vids. If they'd been in proper formation, Noodle wouldn't have drifted. It's the sorry-ass technician who manned that orbital platform's fault for having a fucked-up brain. *His* parents' fault for passing it to him. *His* fault for having such a sorry-ass life to be stationed in some backwoods, forgotten-about post to begin with."

"Stop," Squawks said again, more forcefully this time.

"It's Noodle's fault for signing up for the Forgotten to begin with," Nail said, voice suddenly softer. "And for not bailing the moment he realized what the fuck it was he signed up for."

The words hung in the air between them. They were harsh and unsympathetic but honest in a way that only a brutal truth can be.

"There are no faults in war. There's only life and death and the terrible aftermath."

"I know," Squawks said. "It doesn't make it any easier, though."

"No," Nails agreed then grew softer. "No, it doesn't." It was quiet for a moment. "Do you want to know something my father used to tell me? He said that death was every pilot's wingman. It's always there, on your six, and as much as we try and shake it, death always catches up. Our only chance is to keep moving. The moment we slow down, the moment we stop, that's when death catches us."

There was another pause, and Coda could almost see Nails leaning forward, making sure she was looking directly into Squawks's eyes. Maybe even grabbing his hand.

"You have to keep moving, Squawks. We need you. *I* need you." Nails must have stood, because the next moment, she was walking toward the door. "I need my wingman back."

Coda scrambled backward, triggering the motion detector to automatically open the outer door. With any luck, Nails would believe Coda was walking in and hadn't been eavesdropping on their conversation.

The inner door opened, and Nails stopped, wiping away tears with the palm of her hand.

Coda didn't know what to do. They just stood there, frozen in place, one emotionally raw, the other guilty for violating what had been a deeply personal moment.

"Are you okay?" The words stumbled out of his mouth, lacking any form of sincerity.

"I'm fine." Nails strode past Coda with a huff and slipped back out into the hangar.

Coda remained rooted in place. Truth be told, he didn't know how to follow up Nails, and he wasn't even sure he had to.

"How long where you listening?" Squawks asked from the other room.

*Busted.*

Shaking his head, Coda walked into the storage locker. The still sat in the corner, and Squawks held a spare part that had been retrofitted into a drinking cup. If he'd been drinking, he didn't show any of the physical signs.

Coda took a seat on a latched cargo box that had been strapped to the deck. "Long enough."

"And you just let her rail into me?"

"I didn't want to interrupt," Coda said. "And... she's not wrong."

Squawks barked a bitter laugh and downed his drink. "You too, huh?"

"Yeah."

Squawks refilled his drink. Coda had made the flight roster that morning. Thankfully, Squawks was off for the next few rotations.

"I just miss the goofy sonuvabitch," Squawks said.

"I do too," Coda said.

Squawks swirled his drink, watching as the fluid circled the cup, coming closer and closer to the rim. "Do you remember that time on the *Jamestown*, during training, that everyone talked about why they joined the Forgotten?"

"Yeah," Coda said. "Tex had always wanted to fly, but they shut the Nighthawk program down before he got a chance. Noodle was supposed to go into advanced manufacturing but thought the drones were just too damn cool. And you... Actually, I don't remember what you said."

"Because I didn't. Truth is, I was embarrassed. Tex talked about how his family was against him joining up. You guys too." He took a steadying breath as if preparing himself for a great undertaking. "I don't have a family, Coda. I've never had anyone care about me enough to try and stop me from doing something."

"What do you mean?"

"Just that," Squawks said, as if it were the simplest thing in the world. "I don't have a family. I don't know who my parents are, what they were like, if they were heroes or pieces of shit. My entire life has been a mystery."

"I..." Coda stammered, not knowing what to say.

"I know," Squawks said. "That's why I never said anything. Didn't want things to get awkward."

"It's not awkward," Coda said. "I just... I'm sorry, Squawks."

Squawks waved the words away with his hand. "That's not what I meant. I don't want your pity, just want to help you understand where I'm coming from." He looked up from his cup, tears in his eyes. "I never had a family. Until now."

It seemed as if all the air was suddenly sucked out of the room. Coda's throat grew tight as understanding washed over him.

"Noodle wasn't just my friend," Squawks said. "He was my brother." He took a shuddering breath. "I've never had a brother before, so I didn't know what it was like to lose one. Hurts like hell."

"Yeah," Coda said. "It does."

"You're my brother too, you know."

"I know," Coda said. "You're mine too. The only one I have."

"I can't lose you too."

"You won't," Coda said. "But we need you. We need the Squawks who talks faster than he flies. The loud, egotistical, walking HR violation."

Squawks laughed, a tear dripping from his nose into his cup. "I can do that."

"Good," Coda said.

Squawks met his gaze, and for the first time in a long time, Coda saw the mischievous spark of life return to Squawks's eye.

"Now, are you going to offer me a drink or what?"

"Ha!" Squawks grabbed one of the spare cups, filled it, and handed it to Coda.

He studied the clear contents. "What is this?"

"It's best not to ask," Squawks said. "Or smell."

It was too late. Coda was already taking a whiff. He flinched back as if punched. "God! It smells like... like..."

"Like Baranyk piss. I know. Isn't it great?"

"That wasn't the word I was going to use."

Squawks laughed again.

*Damn, it's good to hear that sound.*

"It gets the job done," he said.

"I guess." Coda held up his cup. "Let's get this over with. To Noodle."

"No," Squawks said. "To our brothers."

"I like that better," Coda said, thinking of Noodle, Tex, Uno, and everyone else they'd lost. "To our brothers."

They tapped cups, and Coda downed the foul drink in a single gulp. It burned his mouth, his stomach, and everything in between. But it was a good burn. One that felt earned and brought him closer to his friend.

To his brother.

# 31

*Drone Operation Center, SAS Olympia*
*Tau Titus*

Buster had been trained for a war he'd never been able to fight, but he'd always heard the worst part of battle was the waiting. The long minutes, hours, and days leading up to the first shot, before all hell broke loose and there wasn't time to think, let alone worry.

On the eve of his first real battle, those old words felt all too accurate. He paced anxiously on the observation deck in the drone operation center. Around him, the *Olympia*'s four squadrons under his command were already plugged in, donning their VR helmets that would give them a first-person view of the inside of their Hornet's cockpit. The operation center wasn't too dissimilar from the Coliseum back at the Terran Fleet Academy, though smaller in scale since it was designed solely for the drone pilots and not a crowd of spectators.

Those pilots rose up around him in rings of stadium seating, each of his four squadrons occupying a different quadrant in the room. Above him loomed the battle map. Larger than the similar one on the bridge but considerably smaller than the one at the Terran Fleet Academy, the battle map displayed photo-real images of the battle. And since Buster was the conductor of the battle, controlling its pulse, tempo, and rhythm, he could zoom in or out as much as needed to ensure his pilots were best positioned.

Right now, he had it zoomed out to provide a macro view of the battlespace. The might of the Sol Fleet floated through space in a rectangular shape, taller and wider than it was deep, made up of nearly every ship humanity had to throw at the invaders. Nighthawks flew through their ranks, twisting and turning between the ships, flying the perimeter, and circling the moon.

It was a jaw-dropping, pump-your-fist-in-the-air, blast-the-fight-song-of-the-Sol-Fleet kind of sight. Buster had never felt so proud to be a part of it, never more confident in their ability to prevail. If the enemy would just hurry up and arrive.

The battle map beeped as if granting his wish and zoomed way out to display a universal view of the battlespace. A single bogey, so tiny in the void that it was little more than a miniscule dot, appeared. The indicator was enclosed by a red circle and flashed red, denoting the enemy signature. The enemy vessel didn't appear to be moving, but Buster knew that was more of a byproduct of the distance between it and the waiting fleet.

A second signature appeared. And a third. Fourth. Fifth.

Soon, the edge of the battle map was teeming with them. A soft murmur rose in the operation center, nervous chatter between his pilots. Still, the enemy continued to roll in.

Seventy-five ships.

One hundred.

Then it outnumbered the Sol Fleet.

Doubled it.

Tripled it.

Then Buster couldn't keep track.

He needed to say something, instill confidence, not stand there like a slack-jawed jackass. He tapped the new implant in his ear, opening a line to his air group.

"It's a hell of a sight, isn't it? It's nothing we didn't expect. Stay steady. Trust in your training and the pilot next to you, and we will be victorious."

They were hollow words, but they seemed to do the trick. The chatter died down, turning into a quiet anticipation. Their time would come, but they had to wait. The drones were the ace up the admiral's sleeve, the lynchpin of their battle strategy. What had once been the might of the Sol Fleet had been relegated to the sidelines over the last year. But those were days of the past. The Hornets were operational again, more numerous and deadly than ever. And the enemy was about to feel their sting.

The enemy fleet drifted slowly across the empty space on the battle map. The human forces made no effort to engage, forcing the enemy to come to them. Half of the human vessels had a full complement of Nighthawks that they had so far kept within the bowels of the ship.

Buster absently thought of Coda and their short reunion at the admiral's briefing and wondered where he was in all of this mess. He hadn't seen the *Redemption* in the formation, and his eyes were now too focused on the hundreds of red indicators methodically drawing closer.

Growing up, Buster had been a fan of boxing. At the start of every bout, the two fighters would start in their corners, getting last-minute instruction and pep talks from their teams. Then the bell would ring, and one of two things would happen: either the fighters would show their respect and sportsmanship by quickly touching gloves, or they came out swinging.

The Sol Fleet was in its corner. There would be no touching of gloves, and there was no referee. It would be straight to violence.

The Baranyk threw the first jab, launching fighters as the two fleets were still a great distance apart, likely expecting the human vessels to do the same. This wasn't a normal battle, though. Humanity was against the ropes, fighting to survive. With no referee, there were no rules, and they could fight dirty.

Thousands of enemy fighters zipped across the battlespace, racing ahead of the capital ships, completely unaware of what awaited them in that dead space.

Ancient armies had dug holes and trenches, traps designed to trip, snag, or kill horses of a mounted charge. More modern warfare used razor wire to slow an enemy's advance and mines to thin superior numbers or heavy artillery.

In space combat, speed kept you alive. It was also your greatest weakness. It doesn't take much to punch a hole through a ship when it's flying thousands of kilometers per hour, which was why capital ships had heavy plating. But starfighters needed to be quick and agile. They didn't have the same kind of protection.

One moment, the enemy was a horde beyond counting, then it was decimated into a mess of organic matter. At thousands of kilometers an hour, even a grain of sand could be a weapon, especially if it was deployed in a cloud.

The incoming fighters were cut down by a third then a half. Then more. Shouts of excitement replaced the nervous chatter from before. The plan was working. They'd struck first, drawn enemy blood, and hadn't even fired a shot.

There was a distant rumble, and the deck vibrated as the captain ordered the *Olympia* to its secondary position. To the unknowing eye, it would look like a retreat, but the ships were just moving to a safer distance from the debris cloud, allowing their Nighthawks and Hornets, when they were eventually deployed, more room to operate. Because the problem with a debris cloud was just like a twentieth-century mine: it would kill indiscriminately.

Even with the debris cloud decimating the horde of enemy fighters, many still got through. Dozens. Maybe hundreds.

The deck thunked as the *Olympia* opened its cannons. Green indicators appeared on the battle map. The Sol Fleet had launched its Nighthawks. They immediately moved to engage the incoming fighters. Even though their ranks had been decimated, the enemy still outnumbered the Nighthawks.

The battle was going according to plan. Now, it was time to see how much difference that plan would actually make.

# 32

*Commander's Quarters, SAS Redemption*
*JumpGate, Sol System*

"Tell me what I'm looking at," Captain Coleman said.

He stood with Commander Payton and Dr. Naidoo in the commander's private office, looking at a series of images on the display board. Similar to the display board in the CAG and captain's office, this one was a dual touchscreen inset into the bulkhead, taking up the majority of the wall nearest the commander's desk.

"We've isolated the Baranyk signal, sir," Commander Payton said. "Both its amplitude and wavelength, which is what you're seeing here. As I said before, it's an extreme low-frequency wave, electromagnetic, clearly capable of traveling through vacuum, not very much unlike the one that attacks our drones. Except this one doesn't change. Every time we've encountered the signal, it's been identical. No variance. We checked."

"Then double- and triple-checked," Dr. Naidoo said.

"Which should make it easier to counter," Commander Payton said. He brought up a new image on the display board. It was another wave, blue in color compared to the Baranyk wave's red, and looked nearly identical. It hovered above the Baranyk signal. "This countersignal represents the Baranyk signal's opposite. Where theirs peaks, ours troughs. Where theirs troughs, ours peaks. And at equal amplitude, which should render the net zero."

As if for effect, Commander Payton dragged the new signal overtop of the Baranyk representation. As Commander Payton had said, they lined up perfectly, except that they were equal and opposite.

Coleman rubbed his chin, not taking his eyes off the display, working through the commander's explanation. "So, if I understand correctly, the Baranyk signal never changes—"

"Not never," Dr. Naidoo said. "Just hasn't."

"Hasn't changed," Coleman corrected. "And as long as that remains true, you can broadcast this signal to attack the Baranyk signal?"

"Actually, nothing that complicated," Dr. Naidoo said. "We don't have the broadcast capabilities to counter the signal's strength at a macro level, but at an individual level, we built a device that steadily emits this signal. If the subject encounters the Baranyk signal, this one, which is already emitting, will thereby negate the new one, never letting it take hold."

"One minus one equals zero," Commander Payton said.

"In theory," Dr. Naidoo said.

"In theory," Commander Payton agreed.

Coleman tapped his lips with his finger. The benefits of the signal were clear. If this new version could keep the other at bay, then they could avoid all of its effects, and he would get his pilot back. It almost seemed like too much to hope.

"You said 'individual,'" Coleman said. "Could this device be fitted into an earpiece?"

"Eventually, yes," Commander Payton said. "We'd obviously want to ensure it worked before it came to that, but yes."

"In the meantime," Dr. Naidoo said, turning and plucking a small device off a nearby tray, "we've created these." They looked like two quarter-sized metallic devices, dark in color, with a single green light already illuminated, showing that the device was functioning properly. "We'll secure these to the subject's temple region, which should create a protective web around his head."

"It's ready for testing?" Coleman asked.

"Yes, sir," Commander Payton said.

Dr. Naidoo handed the devices to Coleman. He held them almost reverently. He longed to return to the cockpit himself—the captain's chair would never be an equal replacement for him—but settled for knowing he might be able to give Coda his wings back.

"The moment we jump to Baranyk space," Coleman said, "I want Coda in sick bay, monitored and controlled in case this doesn't work as expected. Brief Dr. Rydell and let her know what we plan to do. She's seen firsthand what can happen when someone is hit with that signal."

Before Coda had ever been hit with it, they'd found a few survivors on a ravaged human colony, and after they'd been brought aboard the *Redemption*, one had been hit with the signal. Under Baranyk control, they had fought against their binds, eventually ripping free and killing themselves. Dr. Rydell had seen the horrors of war, but the event had shaken her in a way Coleman had never seen.

"Yes, sir," Dr. Naidoo said.

"Great wor—" Coleman's earpiece chimed. He placed a hand to his ear, tapping the top of the ear against the side of his head, activating the device. "Coleman."

"Sir, we've received reports," Ensign Richey's voice said through the earpiece. "The battle has begun."

"Very well," Coleman said. "Let the JumpGate crew know we're ready to go, and get the process initiated. I'm on my way."

"Yes, sir," Ensign Richey said.

Coleman tapped the device again, ending the communication. "The battle is underway," he said to Commander Payton and Dr. Naidoo. "Get Coda to sick bay. It's time."

# 33

*Drone Operation Center, SAS Olympia*
*Tau Titus*

Buster watched the Sol Fleet fall back on the battle map. The maneuver served two purposes: to give the Nighthawks, and eventually the Hornets, more room to operate without the debris field inflicting collateral damage and to draw the Baranyk fleet into pursuit. Once they'd advanced far enough, the ships Admiral Orlovsky had placed on the far side of the moon could swoop in behind the Baranyk and box them in.

At first, the plan seemed to work. The Baranyk fleet continued its pursuit, but as the debris field wreaked havoc on the Baranyk fighters near the back of the formation, the capital ships slowed.

"Come on," Buster said. "Don't stop now. Keep coming. You've got us on the run."

If somehow the Baranyk heard him, they didn't listen to him. They continued a full-reverse burn, coming to a stop just outside the debris field. They might have been taking sensor readings, determining what had destroyed so many of their fighters, and assessing the potential damage it would inflict on their larger ships.

"Not much," Buster answered. "It doesn't pose any threat to you as long as you go slow."

The debris field was specifically designed for that purpose. The fighters, coming in much faster, wouldn't see it and wouldn't be able to avoid it. But the larger vessels with their stronger hulls would be fine.

"Come on," Buster coaxed.

With the Baranyk fleet at a standstill, Buster's attention shifted to the battle between the Nighthawks and what remained of the Baranyk fighters. Zooming in on the battle map, he watched the images of the Nighthawks and wondered if Coda was out there. Part of him wished he was, trusting in the reputation of the Forgotten to lead them to victory, but he also feared his friend being alone, relying on his own abilities and tactical ingenuity.

He keyed in on a particular fighter pair that seemed to be having a better time than others. They knifed through Baranyk formations, using missiles when they were clumped together and picking them off with their cannons when the formations broke apart.

Their fighting style couldn't have been more different from the Hornets. The Hornets, restricted by lightspeed communication, lacked the ability to react immediately and relied on formations and attack waves. But the Nighthawks twisted, turned, and dove on a dime. The Baranyk fighters moved with them, flying in larger formations and fighter squads, but were individually overmatched.

Where the Nighthawks struck, devastation reigned. In one impressive maneuver, they attacked the flank of a Baranyk formation, opening cannon fire to cut a hole in the center of their swarm before darting away. The Baranyk, thinking they had an opportunity for pursuit, split their formation, with the rear half moving to engage the Nighthawks' six. But the pilots had anticipated this. Maybe wished for it.

The moment the Baranyk moved into a pursuit vector, the fighter pair flipped noses to tails and launched a pair of missiles. The lead Baranyk fighters didn't have enough time to disengage before the missiles turned them into a small-scale debris field of organic material that took out the ships nearest them.

The Nighthawks accelerated, diving into what remained of the pursuit. By then, the last of the Baranyk fighters in the formation scrambled to disengage. Once the hunted, the Nighthawks had become the hunters. They had the momentum and were quickly able to get into an attack vector, swinging around behind the enemy fighters. With a quick cannon burst, what remained of the Baranyk formation had been eliminated.

Buster zoomed out on the battle map. The smaller battle was indicative of the larger one. The Nighthawk squadrons now outmatched the remaining Baranyk fighters. Finally, with superior numbers they pushed the advantage, and within a few minutes, they had eliminated what remained of the Baranyk vanguard.

A cheer went up in the control room; the pilots were no doubt watching the battle on their HUDs too.

Buster grabbed the back of the seat in front of him, squeezing the gel material until his knuckles went white, never taking his eyes off the battle map. "Come on, we're right here."

It was an old-fashioned standoff, neither force making a move. Perhaps sensing the battle walking the razor's edge, the admiral ordered the Nighthawks in. They didn't venture all the way through the debris field but far enough to launch their heavy CapKillers. The specially designed missiles had one mission and one mission only—to pack a big fucking punch.

Unlike normal missiles that were explosive, nimble, and packed with a full supply of fuel to continue pursuit even if a target tried to shake it, the CapKillers relied on mass and kinetic energy. Made primarily of tungsten and depleted uranium, two of the heaviest metals known to man, and equipped only with enough fuel to maximize kinetic destruction, they were the perfect weapon to fly through the debris field.

Twelve CapKillers zipped through the debris field, blowing through the small bits of rock and metal like bulldozers. Even the antifighter artillery did little to slow them down or knock them off course. They hit with a silent thud, no explosion, just disappearing into the enemy, tearing through hulls, decks, and anything that got in their way.

More than one shot clean through its target, striking another ship behind the initial target. Gasses, fluids, and organic material poured into space. One enemy vessel exploded, the CapKiller having hit something critical inside. The explosion took out two other vessels near it.

Another cheer erupted in the control room, but Buster wasn't ready to get in on it yet. There were hundreds of capital ships, maybe more, and he suspected each had at least one squadron of fighters. By destroying three ships and a wave of fighters, they'd effectively stepped on a handful of ants from an anthill. If the enemy continued its pursuit, that gave humanity the best odds.

But still, the Baranyk didn't engage.

Another wave of Nighthawks swooped in, launching another volley of CapKillers. Again, the Baranyk used standard antiaircraft strategies to destroy or deflect them with minimal results. Several more Baranyk vessels were torn apart, three more going critical and creating a cascade of destruction, eliminating other ships closest to them.

The admiral didn't wait to see the enemy's response. Another wave of fighters swooped in, launching a third volley of the devastating weapons, baiting the enemy into action.

It worked. The Baranyk drives flared to life, spurring their gargantuan vessels into motion. Slow at first but gaining speed, the enemy ships parted the debris field like a ship through water, pushing aside the tiny bits of rock and metal.

The human fleet continued to withdraw, moving farther into the system, closer to the planet itself. When the enemy vessels were finally clear of the debris field, they launched a fresh wave of fighters. Buster didn't know the full count, but it appeared to be at least twice as large as the initial one.

Buster finally let himself grin. That grin turned into a full-fledged smile as the deck thumped and more Nighthawks appeared on the battle map. The admiral matched the Baranyk force, unloading several more squadrons. It was a mighty force that left plenty in reserve. And if the Baranyk were wary about the debris field and CapKillers, then they were *not* going to like what these fighters were equipped with.

# 34

*Drone Operation Center, SAS Olympia*
*Tau Titus*

THE BARANYK FIGHTERS RACED IN. THEIR NUMBERS DWARFED ANYTHING humanity had ever thrown at them. That had always been the way of this war—humanity woefully outnumbered, their only chance of survival tied to human ingenuity and technical advancement.

Even though he knew what was coming next, Buster still felt sweat drip down his spine. His flight suit was wet with it. The waiting and anticipation killed him. Once he finally got the order to plug in, then all of the fear and worry would disappear, replaced by a singular focus. Distraction had long since been trained out of him. Distractions meant death.

But Buster wasn't flying yet, which meant he was left to sweat.

The Nighthawks moved into a rare, two-dimensional, rectangular formation. If they maintained it, every fighter would be vulnerable, but Buster knew they wouldn't hold it for long. They were currently out of range anyway. The formation was designed for a very simple reason—to give every pilot a clear shot at the incoming enemy.

The time to engage ticked down in the form of kilometers. Buster could almost feel his hand tighten around the joystick, his palms slick, index finger massaging the firing stud. He wondered if the Nighthawk pilots were experiencing the same.

Twenty thousand kilometers.

*Almost there.*

Fifteen.

*Here we go.*

Ten.

"Fire," Buster whispered.

And as if upon his command, the Nighthawks launched a volley of missiles.

At five thousand meters, the Baranyk fighters barely had time to take evasive action. They tried, but the missiles weren't like any they had encountered before.

Just as the first Baranyk fighters passed the incoming wave of missiles, the missiles exploded, unleashing a hidden package inside. Thousands of marble-sized tungsten ball bearings shot out with enough force to crack a hole in a six-foot-thick reinforced hull. The hulls of the Baranyk fighters were no match.

The same way the CapKillers had decimated the capital ships, the new missiles annihilated the swarm of enemy fighters, leaving trails of slime in their wake. Dozens of enemy fighters exploded. Others disintegrated. But many were simply damaged, thrusters and navigation equipment destroyed, sending them careening into nearby fighters.

A single wave of missiles destroyed nearly a quarter of the incoming force. Even more devastating, the enemy formation was in shambles. The Nighthawks wasted no time engaging and swooped in aggressively. By the time they were in the fray, the ball bearings had long since hit their targets or been shot harmlessly into the endless void of space, giving the human pilots free rein to engage.

They easily picked off stray fighters first and used traditional missiles to inflict maximum damage when the swarm or formations drew too close to each other. Again, Buster picked out a single fighter pair, watching as they cut through the confused enemy.

Every enemy fighter that drew their attention met its end. The Nighthawks were a scalpel—sharp, precise, and steady. And the Nighthawks around them were equally devastating. When the battle was solidly turning into the Sol Fleet's favor, the Nighthawks pressed their advantage.

Not all of them were equipped with CapKillers, since the heavy missiles greatly reduced their maneuverability, but those that were zipped away from the main battle toward the incoming capital ships to unleash humanity's devastating creations. They took out six more capital ships and still hadn't lost a single ship of their own.

Buster could almost sense the enemy commander's rage. It mirrored his own excitement. The battle was going better than he'd even dared to hope. They had a chance. A real chance.

But the enemy had numbers humanity could barely fathom, and the enemy commander finally unleashed them. Swarms upon swarms of enemy fighters streamed out of their capital ships, zipping toward the Sol Fleet with malicious intent. Thousands of them. Maybe more.

"Are you watching this, Lieutenant?" Captain Lozada's voice came through Buster's earpiece.

"I am, sir."

"Then you know what comes next. Are your squadrons ready?"

"We are, sir."

"Good. Plug in and prepare for flight."

"Yes, sir."

Buster took one last look at the battle map, watching as a fresh wave of Nighthawks launched from their own ships. They were the jab, jab; his pilots were the right hook.

"It's our time," Buster said, his deep voice booming in the control room. "Crush the enemy like the vermin they are."

His pilots cheered as he sat in the gel seat in his drone command console and put on his flight helmet. His view of the control room was replaced by the inside of his Hornet. It was just a virtual representation of what he would see if he were actually sitting there, but it still had a disorienting effect.

"Radio check," Buster said. "All Hornets report in."

Buster listened as his pilots checked in, confirming their radios functioned properly, and called up the battle map on his HUD. The newly launched Nighthawks avoided the main conflict, moving to the edge of the battle plane, out of enemy range and ready for the new horde of incoming fighters.

Once they were assembled into two separate tight formations, they rocketed directly toward the enemy. They might as well have been a young boy standing with his father's rusted sword, trying to stare down a dragon. They had to be outnumbered fifty to one. Sitting in the safety of his VR cockpit, Buster saluted their bravery. The courage it took to face those kinds of odds, to face one's death itself, was indescribable.

The Nighthawk pilots were truly a rare breed. When he'd first heard that Coda was part of the legendary squadron, Buster had been envious, feeling somehow inadequate despite the fact that he'd been placed in a prime position, where Coda had nearly been kicked out of the Terran Fleet Academy, not even allowed to attend his graduating ceremony. But now that he was here, now that he saw what the Forgotten had faced in all those battles while the Hornets were inoperable, he knew he didn't have what it took.

*Commander Coleman recruited the right man.*

"Hornets," came a voice on the squadron's radio. "Prepare for launch."

Buster settled into his cockpit seat, grasping the controls. Without any further warning, his Hornet catapulted through the launch tube. It bucked as it left the artificial gravity bubble behind, entering the zero-g of space. Around him, dozens of other drones shot from the *Olympia*, hundreds more from their own ships.

They split into three formations. Buster led his formation and ordered another to assemble behind the two new Nighthawk formations, while the third waited near the capital ships in reserve.

The new swarm of enemy fighters rushed in, and the two Nighthawk formations raced in to meet them, launching successive waves of missiles. Just like the previous wave, they inflicted overwhelming casualties, wiping out the head of the enemy charge. For every Baranyk fighter they destroyed, though, it seemed as if three more took its position.

The Nighthawks launched a second volley of missiles, inflicting similar damage, then, before they were consumed by the enemy swarm, veered off, clearing the road for the Hornets that were right behind them and coming in hot.

*Jab, jab.*

"Our turn," Buster said into the comms.

*Right hook.*

The two Hornet groups split into its four squadrons, ninety-six Hornets in total, and knifed into the incoming swarm. Hundreds more from other human vessels did the same.

*Finally*. Buster squeezed the firing stud, loosing a barrage of cannon fire from the nose of his Hornet.

He'd trained for years at the Terran Flight Academy, honing his skills, fighting among some of the best pilots humanity had to offer, but he'd never fought in a real battle, inflicted real damage, truly protected his own, and done his part. That changed in a single burst that cracked the hull of an enemy fighter like a hammer to a melon.

*Splash one.*

His pilots on his wing did the same, firing in controlled bursts, carving a path through the swarm. He barely let off the firing stud. Doing so would have resulted in a high-speed collision. They might as well have been driving through a swarm of locusts, bugs zipping past their windshields like flakes in a snowstorm. The enemy numbered so many, Buster could barely see the blackness of space. And they didn't appear to be altering course, choosing to ignore the waves of Hornets cutting through the belly of their formation.

*They're going after our capital ships.*

It was a tried-and-true strategy. Not only were the capital ships the largest and most powerful ships either side had to offer, but destroying those left the drones and Nighthawks with nowhere to return. It was a death sentence for any pilot in the void. Destroying the capital ship would render the drones inoperable by killing their pilots.

*Squeeze and fire. Squeeze and fire.*

Buster's trigger finger never fully relaxed. He was an exterminator taking care of an infestation, killing dozens of enemies before they could do the same to him. He glanced at the battle map, judging where they were in the enemy formation, but all it showed was a solid sphere of red, unable to distinguish between individual fighters.

He tightened his hand around the joystick, continuing his barrage. The ammunition counter on the top-right corner of his HUD ticked down. The Hornet was armed with a thousand rounds, and he'd already exhausted more than half of that. He thought about launching a couple missiles, but at their speed and proximity to the enemy, doing so would likely result in too much collateral damage.

There was a sudden flash of light to his right as one of the Hornets collided with a Baranyk fighter.

"Damn it," someone said over the comm. "I'm out."

"Me to," someone else said. There must have been an explosion behind Buster, because he hadn't seen another go down.

His Hornet bucked as the fighter in the dash-2 position exploded. Two more went down, and he ordered the remaining pilots to tighten the formation. The maneuver narrowed their focus but reduced their casualties. If the Nighthawks had been a scalpel, the Hornets were a needle, plunging into the heart of the formation.

Buster didn't know how long it took them to carve through the entire formation, but one moment, fighters were racing past him, blotting out the blackness of space, and the next, he was free. The sound of the cannon receded as he relaxed his firing finger, leaving nothing but the sound of his own heavy breathing. Beads of sweat trickled down his back. He'd thought he was sweaty before, but it was nothing compared to the swamp of his lower back now.

He banked hard to port, turning back toward the *Olympia* and the rest of the human vessels, careful to remain on the outskirts of the swarm. "Missiles free!" he ordered. "Missiles free!"

The Hornets weren't equipped with the new missiles the Nighthawks were, but they still carved deep rents into the enemy formation. There was no point in conserving ammunition. As long as the enemy was going to let them kill them indiscriminately, Buster was going to take full advantage. Every Baranyk fighter they destroyed now was one they wouldn't have to face later.

The drones remained on the outskirts of the enemy swarm, launching missile after missile into their flank. And because the other squadrons had knifed through the enemy formation from the opposite angle, they were doing the same from the other flank. They eliminated dozens of enemy fighters. Hundreds. But the enemy outnumbered them so greatly that it didn't seem to matter.

Buster fired his final missile as the head of the swarm entered firing range. If he'd thought the Nighthawks' missile barrage was impressive, then the enemy's response was downright terrifying.

An ocean of plasma fire erupted from the Baranyk swarm. It crashed into the reinforced hulls of the human capital ships as if they were being sprayed with a firehose. Explosions lit the black like fireworks as the plasma tore deep holes in the human ships. Oxygen and other critical gasses and fluids emptied into space. Two human vessels went critical, exploding in a terrifying flash of white light. Unlike the Baranyk formation, the human vessels had kept their distance from each other, minimizing collateral damage.

Buster exhausted his remaining cannon fire, ordered his pilots to do the same, then triggered the computer's autolanding procedure. His fighter would return to the *Olympia*, where it would be rearmed and refit, and he would be given a fresh Hornet and reenter the fray. When the last of his pilots exhausted their ammunition, he ordered the reinitialization sequence.

One moment, he was in the thick of the battle. The next, he was back on the *Olympia*, sitting in a fresh Hornet inside the launch tube. The sudden change was jarring, but it gave him a brief respite. His heart hammered, body trembling as adrenaline coursed through his veins. He closed his eyes, willing himself to go through a calming routine. But it was too much. Every time he closed his eyes, he saw the yellow carcasses of the enemy fighters. The blue of their plasma fire. He abandoned the exercise, succumbing to the emotion of the battle.

"Come on," he said to no one in particular. "Get us back out there!"

It was the launch technician who answered. "Loading the final drone now. Launch in T-minus twenty seconds."

*Twenty seconds.*

*How long was I out there?* It had felt like hours, but if the *Olympia*'s launch crew hadn't even had enough time to prepare for the second wave of Hornets, it couldn't have been more than a few minutes.

With a few seconds to spare, Buster eyed the battle map. The red wave had engulfed the fleet's position. He could only imagine what that looked like in reality. If the steady rumbling of the deck from the antiaircraft batteries and distant booms of plasma fire striking the *Olympia*'s hull were any indication, it was a mess.

And the enemy capital ships were still inbound. Moving slowly and methodically, they were just emerging from the debris field, finally clear of the moon. Newfound hope bloomed in Buster's chest as a handful of new readings appeared on the HUD. From behind the moon, ten more human capital ships appeared, burning hard. And around them, a full bloom of green as hundreds of Hornets flew with them. They flew in hard against the unprotected rear of the enemy formation.

"Launch sequence initiated," the launch technician said. "Prepare for launch in five, four, three..."

Buster shifted in his control seat, hands tightening on his controls, ignoring the rest of the countdown. The battle was just beginning. And since the Baranyk had almost willingly stepped into their plan, they still had a chance.

His Hornet lurched, zipping through the launch tube. It was time to reenter the fray.

# 35

*Sick Bay, SAS Redemption*
*JumpGate, Sol System*

"YOU WANTED TO SEE ME, DOC?" CODA SAID. THE DOOR TO SICK BAY closed with a hiss behind him.

Dr. Rydell looked up from her patient, someone from engineering suffering from burns on their hands and arms. She held a gun-like device that he knew administered shots, usually to ease pain—something the patient seemed to be suffering from quite a bit.

"Ah, Coda, you made it. Go ahead and head on back. Doctor Naidoo is waiting for you." She nodded toward the rear of the medical bay, where a curtain had been drawn.

"All right," Coda said uncertainly and made his way to the cordoned-off area.

He hadn't been given any explanation why he was wanted in sick bay, though now that he knew Dr. Naidoo was present, he had a pretty good idea. She was the foremost expert on Baranyk physiology and had been leading the study of the Baranyk signal that plagued him.

He pulled the curtain back to find Dr. Naidoo studying something on her tablet and the wall display. "Coda," she said, looking up. "Good.

You're here." She motioned to the end of the hospital bed in the center of the makeshift room. "Please sit."

Coda took a seat on the edge, resting his foot on the steel supports. "What's this all about, Doctor?"

Dr. Naidoo had gone back to her tablet, tapping and dragging her finger across its surface. "We've received word that the battle has begun. We're loading into the JumpGate now, preparing to jump to the Baranyk home world."

"And you can't risk me acting on the Overlord's behalf," Coda said. "I'm surprised you didn't just lock me up in the brig."

"The danger of ignorance, Commander, is when you don't know what is going on and react anyway." Dr. Naidoo slid her tablet into her lab coat. "You're not here because you're a danger to the ship or even a danger to yourself. You're here to receive treatment for your condition."

"Treatment?"

"Of a sort," Dr. Naidoo said. "The captain has taken it upon himself to protect you. Sit back."

Coda slid farther onto the bed, resting his back against its elevated portion. His polished boots were a stark contrast to the white of the bedding. "How?"

Dr. Naidoo grabbed something from a nearby chair. "Using these."

She held a pair of circular devices made of dark metal. "I don't understand."

"Commander Payton and I have constructed a countersignal to the Baranyk's that we believe will prevent it from interacting with your brain. These will continuously broadcast the countersignal, providing uninterrupted protection."

He gestured to the device in her hands. "May I?"

"Of course." Dr. Naidoo handed them over.

They were light, but he couldn't help but feel the weight of their importance. His thumb brushed against its smooth exterior, stroking it as if it held the promise of a lover. "You really think it'll work?" He almost feared the answer.

"There's only one way to find out," Dr. Naidoo said.

"What do I have to do?"

"We'll adhere them to your temples." She tapped her own for effect. "You just need to wear them."

"That's it?"

"And don't take them off."

Coda was being given the promise of life. He had no intention of taking the devices off if he could help it.

---

CAPTAIN COLEMAN TOOK A DEEP BREATH AND TAPPED HIS EARPIECE, opening a shipwide channel. He heard the soft static of the ship's speakers and made eye contact with each of the bridge personnel. He wasn't one for speeches, but they were about to venture into the hostile unknown, a place no other human had ever set foot, and he needed his crew to know that he believed in them.

"This is the captain. By now, our forces at Tau Titus have engaged the enemy. We have not received any reports about how the battle is progressing, but I do know that we have a few surprises waiting and that the men and women of the Sol Fleet will put up a hell of a fight. You should also know that is not our fight. As your commanding officers have already briefed you, we have a different objective."

He let the words linger as he scanned the room. The eyes of every member of the bridge crew were firmly on him, and he caught more than one nodding. Commander Garcia pumped his fist at his side in what Coleman thought was a sign of encouragement.

"In a few minutes' time, we will venture into deep Baranyk space. Farther than anyone has ever gone before. To their very home world. I do not know what will be waiting for us or what we'll find. But I know what we seek. The enemy is led by a terrible leader. Someone driven by hatred. Someone that seeks to dominate all living species. We will not let that happen. Our mission is to take him out, whatever the costs. And like our fleet, we have a few surprises of our own."

Coleman drew in a deep breath and held it for several seconds before letting it out. "But none of them mean as much as you. We were selected for this mission because we have the strongest crew in the fleet. Because the men and women of this ship have seen and done more than any other out there. You are uniquely equipped for whatever the enemy throws at us. Together, we are stronger. Together, we will prevail."

He held up a fist. Only his bridge crew could see it, but he hoped the rest of the ship could hear the conviction in his voice. "We all know what's at stake. Our very survival as a species hangs in the balance. I don't just need your best. Humanity needs it and more. As long as there is a chance, we fight. For as long as there is hope, we fight. For as long as our hearts beat and we have breath in our lungs, we fight. Failure is not an option."

He locked eyes with Ensign Richey, her dark eyes radiating conviction. Her dark hair was pulled back into a ponytail. He nodded to her, giving her a silent command. She immediately said something into her headset.

"Prepare to jump," Coleman said.

He closed the broadcast. Commander Garcia gave him another encouraging fist pump. He nodded his approval and gripped the railing that surrounded the top level of the bridge. No sooner had his hands cupped the padded railing than the world stretched.

The world snapped back into focus. His hands tightened around the railing as the usual disorientation hit him. He forced his eyes to stay open and swallowed the excess spit in his mouth, hoping he wasn't visibly sweating.

"Report," he said.

"Sensor data coming in now, sir." Lieutenant Poiu's hands were like lightning across his terminal.

Coleman watched as the battle map began to update. Within moments, it showed a single barren planet surrounded by even-more-barren moons.

*We made it.*

They were on the edge of the system, several hundred thousand kilometers from the nearest moon. They waited for several minutes, watching for any sign that the enemy knew they had arrived. If the Baranyk knew they were there, they weren't showing it. There was no enemy activity of any kind.

"Good work," Coleman said. "Deploy the Dragonflies. Let's see what the enemy has waiting for us down there."

"Yes, sir," Lieutenant Poiu said. "Deploying reconnaissance drones now."

A dozen new signatures appeared on the battle map. In reality, they were barely larger than Coleman's hand, equipped with full sensor systems and video that would be automatically sent back and logged by the *Redemption*'s computer. They flew toward the planet. It would take hours, maybe longer, for them to arrive and complete their initial scans. As he waited, Coleman found himself thinking back to Tau Titus, wondering how the battle was progressing.

# 36

*Drone Operation Center, SAS Olympia*
*Tau Titus*

Another explosion lit the black as another human capital ship went critical. It started as a brilliant flash of white light, followed by plumes of fire and debris. Gas and fluids spilled into the void as more explosions wreaked havoc on the hull. Then, in a single explosion that made the rest look tiny by comparison, the ship was cut in two, both pieces drifting aimlessly in opposite directions.

Buster cursed. It was the fifth capital ship they'd lost. Each one left a hole in their defenses that was difficult to fill. Not only did they lose the firepower of each ship, but they lost the cover fire provided by their anti-aircraft batteries. Most importantly, they lost the ability for those ships to launch new fighter drones. Eliminating a single capital ship was the equivalent of wiping out an entire fighter group.

"We need to get them off our capital ships!" Buster bellowed.

"Agreed," a voice on the radio said. It was his second-in-command and Bravo Flight Leader, Slides. "How?"

That was the question, wasn't it? One the entire fleet was trying to answer. The Baranyk fighters outnumbered them by immeasurable odds and barely seemed to be paying their drones or Nighthawks any attention, focusing instead on the larger human vessels.

The enemy fighters fought as a swarm, engulfing ships in a cloud of constant and unrelenting fire. Fire and flee, fire and flee, back and forth, blasting the hulls with blue plasma fire that melted the steel like lava on rubber. The antiaircraft batteries destroyed dozens of ships with every attack run, but the Baranyk overwhelmed them so considerably that they were able to absorb the losses.

Buster let out a frustrated breath. They'd abandoned larger formations to fight in a style more reminiscent of the Nighthawks. It was their best way of maximizing damage while also absorbing losses. Each time a drone fighter was shot down, it required them to fill the formation's hole. And when that pilot was provided a new drone, they had to rendezvous with the formation and resume their position. It simultaneously left them weaker and slower. Buster himself was already on his third drone.

Ten friendlies glowed with brilliant green on his HUD, ten squadrons of Nighthawks at their tip, burning hard for the open flank of the enemy's capital ships. As soon as they were in firing range, they launched a deadly wave of CapKillers. The specially designed munition laid waste to the unprotected rear of the enemy formation, destroying several of the Baranyk vessels in a flash.

Just behind the Nighthawks, hundreds of fresh Hornets launched from the moon's underground base and rushed in. In a few short moments, the Nighthawks and Hornets completely engulfed the enemy vessels, destroying several.

Buster let out a loud hoot, expecting the fighters that engulfed the human vessels to break away and provide aid to their own. His hope was quickly dashed as more fighters emerged from the bellies of the distant enemy vessels.

*How many fighters do they have?*

Buster's heart was in his stomach. No matter what the fleet threw at the enemy, they threw more fighters back at them.

*We're not going to make it.*

Buster hated that the thought had even entered his consciousness. If it had entered his, it had certainly entered others'. As if the words were made manifest, the *Olympia* gave a shuddering shake. A piercing metal-on-metal noise cut through Buster's helmet and radio chatter. They were going to die like baby birds in a nest, unable to fend off a hungry predator.

*No*, he told himself. *I will not give in. I will not give up.* And he couldn't let anyone else in his fighter group give up, either.

"As long as we have a ship, we have a chance," Buster said. "Don't give in. Don't give up. We are the sword that'll pierce the enemy's heart. Stay strong. Don't hold back. Give them everything you have."

The words strengthened Buster's resolve. He settled into his seat, hands tightening around the controls, eyes reassessing the battle map as a deep focus enveloped him.

The Baranyk surrounded them with a spherical formation of fighters that was in constant movement. Ships darted in to attack while others filled the hole in the formation.

"We can't win this by going on the offensive," Buster said. "This is now a defensive battle."

"What are you getting at, sir?" Slides asked.

"Our ships are vulnerable. We have to protect them at all costs. Every available Hornet, close in on the *Olympia.* Encase her with our drones. Give her an extra layer of protection. When a swarm makes its attack run, fight back and chase them away. We are crows in this, fighting off a hawk."

He made for the *Olympia*, taking out a few enemy fighters along the way. He took up position only meters from the *Olympia*'s hull, positioned between a pair of antifighter batteries. Around him, his drones did the same, and within moments they had the entire ship encased.

"Buster," Captain Lozada said over the comm. "What are you doing?"

"The enemy fighters are getting through our defenses, sir," Buster said. "We're tightening the line."

"You're nearly attached to the ship's hull."

"That's the idea, sir. Every meter we occupy is a meter they can't harm. When they attack, we'll drive them off. It'll work, sir."

The hiss of the radio extended for several moments.

"Carry on," Captain Lozada eventually said.

"Thank you, sir." Despite his bluster, Buster wasn't convinced the strategy would pay off. They weren't fighting to win the battle anymore—they were fighting for time.

The effectiveness of the formation was quickly put to the test.

Baranyk fighters dove in, seeking to strafe down the *Olympia*'s length. Buster's Hornets maintained position but were angled so they faced the incoming enemy and opened fire. Their cannons and missiles mixed with the antiaircraft batteries, cutting through the incoming wave. The enemy's formation was in shambles by the time it finished its run, and as they zipped past the bow of the ship, a few Hornets darted after them, taking them out from behind.

As soon as that wave was complete, another was inbound. These were directly in Buster's sights. He launched a missile, taking out the lead fighter and letting the debris take out the two nearest it, then used his cannons to eliminate two more. The moment they were out of his range, they entered someone else's, who inflicted similar damage.

Another run ended with similar results.

"It's like they don't know we're here," Slides said.

That was when Buster realized it. "They don't. We're so close to the ship's hull, they can't see us."

It was just like their own computers. The Baranyk overwhelmed them by so many fighters, it didn't even try and distinguish between them anymore. Maybe the Baranyk systems only saw what they thought was a single unprotected ship.

"It's working, sir," Buster said. "The enemy can't distinguish between us and the *Olympia*'s hull. Their attacks are picking up in frequency, but we're inflicting heavy casualties."

"Interesting," Captain Lozada said. "You're sure they can't see your fighters?"

"It appears that way, sir," Buster said. "Might be worth trying with a few other ships and following their results."

"I'll take it under advisement," Captain Lozada said.

"Yes, sir," Buster said.

Even with the strategy working, it felt wrong sitting still during a battle. It went completely against everything he had ever been taught, but Buster couldn't argue with the results. They were inflicting more damage and losing fewer ships in the process. Most importantly, the *Olympia* was taking less fire.

Another wave of fighters flew in, and again Buster's Hornets held them at bay, except this time, he lost one to the ship's antiaircraft batteries. Losing a ship to friendly fire pained him, but if they could coordinate their attacks so that the batteries stopped firing when the Hornets went into pursuit, then—

Something caught Buster's eye. On the HUD, it appeared as a small change, but it represented a significant shift in the battle. The last of the green indicators at the rear of the enemy's formation disappeared. What happened? How had the enemy eliminated them so fast?

Worse yet, the Baranyk capital ships that had broken away from the main formation were not returning to their previous positions. They were moving toward the moon.

*Oh no.*

Without the human ships, the moon would be almost completely undefended. Its orbital platforms and drone squadrons were all that was left to fight the enemy, and they weren't going to be enough.

Buster cursed. Those ships were supposed to be the decisive blow, the move that shifted the tides of the battle into humanity's hands. Instead, it had shifted the odds even further in the enemy's direction.

As if sensing blood, the Baranyk attacked with more frequency and greater fervor. It took everything Buster could do to keep the fighters off the *Olympia.* They swooped in, spraying plasma fire down the *Olympia*'s length, taking out both Hornets and antiaircraft batteries alike. Hornets flew in pursuit, laying waste to formations and eliminating Baranyk fighters by the dozen, but the attacks came in so fast that the Hornets were unable to return to their position before the next wave was inbound.

It left the drones in a helpless position, and within moments, Buster's air group was down half a flight's worth of drones.

"Buster," Slides said, an urgency in his voice that Buster hadn't heard before. "The moon."

Buster didn't bother to look at his HUD. He angled his fighter so that it faced the moon itself. The Baranyk carriers were already in orbit, assaulting the moon directly. He was too far away to make out the Baranyk's attacks, but the moon, normally a slate gray, was dotted with orange plumes.

"Fuck," Buster said.

"Yeah," Slides said.

They'd spent so much time protecting the *Olympia*, knowing that losing the ship meant they were gone too, but the moon base housed the equivalent of five ships of drones. Losing it was enough to knock them out of the fight altogether.

The orange plumes grew in size, expanding outward, engulfing the surface of the moon. Rock and debris shot up from its surface, escaping its low gravity and catapulting into space. The Baranyk carriers continued the onslaught, the moon's orbital platforms long since dealt with and Hornets consumed by the horde of Baranyk fighters.

The moon and everything on it was lost.

New flashes of light pulled Buster's attention from the moon. It was more plasma fire, but this was larger, thicker, more deadly. Buster's heart sank even deeper. The Baranyk capital ships had entered firing range.

"What do we do?" Slides asked. He hadn't even bothered to keep the channel private, asking the question so that the entire flight group could hear.

*I don't know.* Buster didn't know what to say.

Fortunately, the captain saved him.

"All fighters, return to base." Lieutenant Mitchell was the *Olympia*'s communications officer. His word was the captain's. "I repeat, all fighters return to base. This is a full-scale retreat."

Buster remained still, dumbfounded. The early parts of the battle had been promising. They'd inflicted more damage than ever before. Destroyed more Baranyk ships and fighters than in any single battle in the war's history. And it hadn't been enough. Not nearly enough.

An explosion unlike Buster had ever seen lit the night sky. It was equal parts orange and white and followed by a concussive blast that he couldn't tell if he heard through his radio or with his own ears. Massive chunks of rock exploded from the moon's surface, and to Buster's horror, the moon *cracked* like a broken egg.

*They destroyed the moon.* He couldn't believe it. It was destruction on a scale he hadn't known was possible. *How many souls were down there? A hundred thousand? A million? More?*

He felt hollow. Empty. Lifeless. What could they do in the face of that kind of firepower? He'd heard the word *helpless* before. Known in theory what it meant. But had never truly understood the full gravity of the term.

Helplessness wasn't a feeling. It was a power that infested a person's very soul, removing all semblance of control, shaking the very foundation on which they stood. To be helpless wasn't to lose hope. It was to experience a life where hope had never existed in the first place.

"Buster."

The word barely registered. All of his attention was focused on the expanding ring of debris that shot out from the moon.

"Buster."

He blinked. The images of the moon were replaced by the incoming Baranyk vessels. They were close enough now that he could see them with his naked eye. He watched as the blue plasma fire pummeled toward them like a tsunami. There wasn't a human force anywhere in the world strong enough to withstand that.

"Buster," the voice came again. "Goddamn it, do you hear me?"

"I hear you."

"We need to RTB."

*We.*

Something about that word shook him, knocking him out of his daze.

*We.*

He glanced at his HUD, realizing that Slides hadn't returned to base either.

"Buster."

"I know."

"Then let's get our fighters onboard. Ships are retreating."

So focused on the moon and incoming vessels, Buster hadn't realized that their own forces were abandoning their positions. More than a third of their fleet had already disappeared, jumping to the predetermined fallback position.

"Do you think they'll break the planet the same way they broke the moon?"

Slides let out a long sigh. "I don't know. I hope not."

"I hope not too." It felt like a foolish thing to say. The words were almost meaningless when compared to the horror they'd just witnessed.

Buster keyed in the automated RTB sequence and pulled off his VR helmet. Somehow, even seeing the drone operation center with his naked eyes again, all he could see were the images of the moon breaking apart. He wiped the sweat off his forehead.

It had been a hard-fought battle. They'd inflicted heavy losses and made the Baranyk bleed. The enemy, in turn, had made the world burn.

# 37

*Briefing Room, SAS Redemption*
*Distant Orbit, Baranyk Homeworld*

"I CALLED YOU ALL HERE," CAPTAIN COLEMAN SAID FROM THE HEAD OF THE table, "because our reconnaissance drones have completed their initial sweep."

Coda sat on the far end of the table, where Moscow had sat previously. He'd made it a point to give the acting CAG the chair nearest the captain. The rest of the executive staff—Commander Garcia, Commander Payton, and Dr. Naidoo—occupied their normal positions, and Phantom, the drone air group's CAG, also joined them.

Coda absently ran a hand over the side of his face, touching the transmitters adhered to his temples. They felt weird, and he looked ridiculous, but they'd let him out of sick bay, so he couldn't help but feel like they were worth it.

"We've encountered other Baranyk structures on other planets," Captain Coleman continued. "And while this has many similarities, there are a few stark differences as well." His eyes fell to Dr. Naidoo. "Doctor?"

"Thank you, sir." She remained in her seat as a holographic projection appeared in the center of the table. White in color, the structure looked almost like a piece of sea coral and was nearly as wide as it was tall. "The Baranyk are ground-dwelling creatures, living in a complex hive made up of a series of tunnels and chambers. Like many insects found on Earth, they seem to be caste based, with workers, soldiers, harvesters, and many other types of roles. Their habitats are a direct reflection of these roles."

She reached toward the hologram, her hands going directly into the middle of the projection, and stretched them apart. The image expanded, zooming in on a specific area of the structure near the top.

"The entrance to the structure is on the surface," Dr. Naidoo continued. "Easily disguised as a small hill, this mound is actually the excess rock and soil dug from the chamber itself. Unlike other habitats we've encountered that seemed to be dug directly into a mountainside, similar to a human mine, these go almost immediately downward and branch out in multiple directions."

She collapsed her hands, zooming out to the image's original perspective, then found a different location to home in on. "So far, we've discovered what we think are chambers used for food and supply storage, new tunnels for the expansion of the habitat, egg storage, chambers for larvae and pupae, even nurseries for newly hatched Baranyk. Other chambers appear to be for nothing but waste. What we haven't found is the Overlord himself or, quite honestly, any sign of him."

Coda looked around the table. Most of the occupants were looking at the image, but a few others, like him, were interested in what the others made of the information first. Coda had his own set of questions but felt more like an outsider than he cared to admit. He wasn't here to ask questions or come up with solutions. It was to understand the information and relay it as necessary.

"You said the structure was different from others we've encountered," Moscow said. "How?"

"A couple different things immediately stand out," Dr. Naidoo said. "First and foremost, the size of the structure is unlike anything we've ever seen. It dwarfs anything we've uncovered. This image doesn't do it justice. What you see here represents thousands of kilometers of tunnels and chambers. The chambers themselves are the size of small cities, and, as you can see, there are dozens of them."

Commander Garcia's chair creaked underneath him. "Thousands of kilometers," he repeated. "Chambers the size of cities. That must mean there are millions of Baranyk in there." He looked around the table as if expecting someone to take his meaning.

"The structure is capable of housing millions of Baranyk," Dr. Naidoo said. "Likely hundreds of millions, and I wouldn't be surprised if this is only one habitat out of hundreds. But initial population estimates based on our scans come in significantly below that."

"There're fewer than we expected?" Commander Payton said.

"Yes. At least fewer fully matured Baranyk."

"Where'd they go?" Moscow asked.

"We have no way to be certain," Dr. Naidoo started, "but—"

"They're attacking our forces at Tau Titus."

Silence filled the room. The Baranyk had withdrawn from several systems, leaving behind planets and moons. The belief among Fleet Intelligence was that the enemy was consolidating their forces to assemble an overwhelming invasion fleet. Nobody had expected the enemy to throw nearly every living being at the Sol Fleet. If that were truly the case, that force had to be even larger than their most pessimistic approximation.

After several seconds, Dr. Naidoo continued. "Which is the other difference from other populations we've encountered. Most of those were evenly split between the working caste and the warrior caste. Here, we've uncovered almost no warrior caste. And even the worker caste is focused less on resource accumulation or habitat expansion than we've seen elsewhere. These workers are focused almost exclusively on replenishing their population."

"Which may explain why our presence has so far gone unnoticed," Captain Coleman said. "Between the battle at Tau Titus and the workers focused on their purpose, it seems the enemy is either distracted or doesn't have the same resources to discover our presence."

"How much longer until our scans are complete, sir?" Moscow asked. "I'd love to use this time to start running our pilots through various simulations."

"The initial scans have already been uploaded directly into the simulator," Captain Coleman said. "You can start running training scenarios and get your pilots used to flying through the tunnels now. But to your question, it could be some time. Days at least."

Commander Garcia tapped his finger on the tabletop. "You said their warriors are with the invasion force. So, what's stopping us from launching an offensive now and ending this thing?"

"We don't know where the Overlord is hiding," Captain Coleman said, "or even if he's in this habitat. It may also be smaller than expected, but they still have a fighting force. And their workers are deadlier than I think the doctor is suggesting. As hard as it is, we need to be patient. As long as we remain undetected, we'll use the time to plan the best possible strategy."

Commander Garcia winced, and his tapping finger grew more urgent. "I don't mean to contradict you, sir. But you know what our forces are up against. Every minute we wait, another human colony will fall. We don't know how long our fleet can hold out."

Captain Coleman stepped forward and placed his palms on the table. Coda expected him to be angry, but if anything, he seemed more resigned. "I know, Jaime. We know better than most. Which makes our mission here even more important. We may only get one shot at this. We can't afford to screw it up."

If Commander Garcia disagreed, he didn't show it. Sometimes, Coda wondered if the Commander just voiced questions to voice them, not necessarily because he believed in them. This scenario was different, though. They all knew it because they all felt it. They were straddling the line between caution and aggression. Moving fast enough to save lives but not so fast that it would cost even more. Like many decisions in war, it was an impossible one.

"I've got a stupid question, sir," Coda said. "But how long does it take for a Baranyk to grow?"

It was Dr. Naidoo who answered. "The complete metamorphosis takes about three months from egg to pupal stage. Then another three to mature into what we could call an adult."

"And you said they were primarily focused on repopulating their habitat," Coda said. "I'm assuming, then, that they have Baranyk at every stage of their metamorphosis?"

"Yes."

"How many would you estimate?"

"I haven't seen any hard data around it," Dr. Naidoo said. "But if I had to guess, I'd say thousands. Maybe more."

Coda's eyes found Captain Coleman's. The man stood straighter, grimacing. It seemed he came to the same conclusion Coda had. "So what you're saying, Doctor, is that thousands of Baranyk are maturing as we sit here talking about it, with thousands more right behind them. And since most of their warriors are in the invasion fleet, there's a high likelihood that those maturing Baranyk are warriors themselves."

Dr. Naidoo sat back in her chair, her eyebrows knitted together. "I suppose that's correct."

Coda glanced around the table. Judging by the expressions on the rest of their faces, they had all arrived at the same conclusion. "Then it's not only the Sol Fleet we need to be worried about. In days, we may be outnumbered ourselves."

Captain Coleman folded his arms. "Thank you, Coda. But ticking clock or no, the plan remains the same. We let the drones complete their scans, locate the Overlord, and plan from there. In the meantime, Moscow and Phantom will run their pilots through the initial scans already loaded into the simulators. And you, Coda, have an assignment of your own."

Coda nodded. It was time for him to play telephone. Hopefully, his father could help them locate the Overlord's whereabouts and give them an update on the battle's progress. With any luck, the human fleet was holding the Baranyk at bay, giving the *Redemption* the necessary time to be successful.

# 38

*Sick Bay, SAS Redemption*
*Distant Orbit, Baranyk Homeworld*

Coda lay on the hospital bed in the cordoned-off area of the medical ward, trying to act as if the nylon straps being fastened around his arms and legs didn't bother him. His freedom, it appeared, was a thing of the past.

"We're lucky accessing the Baranyk network isn't like falling asleep," Coda said. "Otherwise, I don't think I'd be successful." He pulled on the straps for full effect.

"Stop complaining," Dr. Rydell said. "You know we hate to do this as much as you do."

"I'm not sure that's the case."

"You know what I mean."

He did and let the matter drop. It wasn't the doctor's fault, and he knew it. If he were being honest with himself, he didn't even disagree with the decision, either. His father said there was no such thing as distance in the Baranyk network, but accessing it this close to the Overlord was testing that theory. For all they knew, he would be able to locate

Coda more easily, maybe get to him even faster. Coda had no idea what the consequences would be if something like that happened.

"What time is it?" he asked, changing the subject.

Dr. Rydell looked at the digital clock in the corner of the room. "You have four minutes."

"Okay." Coda had a notion to join the network early but knew that was a mistake. His instructions were clear: join the network at the designated time and not a moment before. They needed to take every possible measure to reduce the likelihood that the Overlord would discover them.

Bound to the bed, electric diodes stuck to his head and chest monitoring his every move, Coda felt his heart begin to race. It wasn't the anxious energy he usually got before a flight. This was different. This was fear of the unknown. He closed his eyes and steadied his breathing, willing his body to relax. Someone had once told him that if he could control his breathing, then he could control his body. It wasn't as simple as that, but it helped.

When he opened his eyes, Dr. Rydell was holding a needle and filling the syringe with a clear fluid. That was certainly *not* helping.

"What's that?" Coda asked.

"Propofol," Dr. Rydell said. "Just a general anesthesia in case something happens while you're... gone."

She placed the syringe on the metal table beside his bed and gave him a reassuring smile. "Ready?"

"No," Coda said, half joking.

"You'll do fine, and if anything goes wrong, I'm here."

He didn't know what she would do if something went awry, but knowing that he wasn't alone was comforting.

"Thank you," Coda said then closed his eyes.

Joining the Baranyk network didn't require falling asleep, but the act of connecting was similar. Reducing visual and auditory distractions was helpful. Exhaling, he let his body relax, his eyes rolling to the back of his head. Then he just... let himself go.

One moment, he was strapped to the hospital bed. The next, he was elsewhere. His consciousness swam in what looked like a sea of stars, except Coda knew that every one of those lights was actually another consciousness. Even the larger stars reminiscent of distant galaxies were actually collections of consciousnesses.

There was a certain kind of uniformity in the Baranyk network since it was made up predominantly of Baranyk. As he had learned to do, Coda sought the ones that didn't belong. In a way he didn't understand, he was given a sense of direction. Trusting in that feeling, he followed it and found a distant light doing the same. Without knowing how, Coda knew that other light was both his destination and his contact.

As they came together, something more familiar replaced the image of the network. He was aboard the bridge of a ship reminiscent of the *Redemption*, though showing more signs of age. The bridge was a three-ringed structure, with its center occupied by a large battle map. The various stations were lit up with green, yellow, and red indicators. Even the battle map had images on it.

Coda decided this was the *Abraham Lincoln*. It made sense since that was where his father was... *stationed* wasn't the right word. *Held? Imprisoned?*

"You made it."

Coda spun, finding his father behind him. He looked better and more rested in the network than when Coda had last seen him. The dark circles were gone, and he was less gaunt. Despite everything they had been through, he wore a warm smile, which Coda returned. In that moment, all of his anxiety disappeared.

Coda gave him a big hug, slapping his father on the back for full effect. "It's good to see you," he said into his ear. "How are they treating you?"

"As well as can be expected. And you? You made it to the home world." It wasn't a question. Somehow, his father already knew—a byproduct of the network? "Were you detected? Tell me everything."

"No," Coda said, then he quickly recounted their jump and initial actions since entering Baranyk space, including the drone deployment and their initial scans.

"Then it worked." Joseph sounded surprised.

"So far," Coda said. "Tell me how you've been. You said they're treating you okay—are you still in a cell, or did they give you your own quarters?"

His father waved away the questions. "I'm sorry, Callan. We don't have time. I won't risk an extra second here if we can avoid it. Tell me about the scans."

"But—"

"The scans, Callan. Everything you can remember."

Coda let out a frustrated sigh, but he recounted the general design, population numbers, and structure of the hive.

"Interesting," Joseph said. "These... chambers. They're vertical? As in the deeper the chamber, the more mature the Baranyk?"

Coda thought back to the image. They hadn't talked about that explicitly, but as Dr. Naidoo had explained the drone findings, he thought that was what she had alluded to. "I believe so. Why?"

"That makes sense." He said the words almost to himself. He sat in a nearby chair behind one of the terminals, his eyes distant. "The eggs are the easiest to replenish, then the larvae and pupae. The layers add protection."

"What are you talking about?" Coda asked.

Joseph leaned forward, resting his elbows on his knees. His eyes met Coda's. "I've tried to determine where the Overlord is but can't find anything. I know he's there, but it's like he's hiding from me. If what you're saying is correct, though, he's going to be well below the surface."

"How do you know that?"

"Look around, Coda." He gestured at the bridge around them. "Where is the ship's bridge located?"

Coda followed his gesture, taking in the sight. He hadn't spent a lot of time on the bridge, but unlike the ready room and barracks, the bridge wasn't located near the exterior of the ship.

"It's in the center of the ship," Coda said.

"Why?"

"I..." The ready room and barracks were located next to the hangar bay, allowing the pilots to man their ships and take flight as fast as possible. The bridge was located in the center of the ship... "Because that's where it's the most protected."

"Exactly." His father began to pace the upper ring of the bridge. "We're in the bowels of the ship, protected by dozens of floors, quite literally as far from enemy fire and vacuum as possible. If we apply the same logic to the Baranyk, that means the Overlord is going to be in one of the lowermost chambers."

"If that's true, then it's going to be a hell of a lot more difficult to get to him," Coda said, thinking about flying through the tunnels. They may have been large enough to allow for hundreds of Baranyk to move through them at once, like an underground highway of sorts, but even a "large" tunnel would be challenging to navigate when flying at hundreds of kilometers an hour.

"Which is precisely the point." Joseph placed his hands on Coda's shoulders and gave him a smile. "Thank you, Callan. I'll use this and see if it helps me find him. Now, we need to go."

"Go?" Coda said. "We just got here."

"Like I said, I don't want to be here for an extra second if it can be avoided. You gave me what I needed. Now, we need to leave before we're detected."

"But..." The whole situation felt incredibly unfair. He could attend briefings, but he didn't have any authority. They could block the Baranyk signal, but he couldn't fly. He could see his father, but he couldn't spend any real time with him. "You have what you need, but I don't."

"Okay, Callan." His father took a step back and crossed his arms. "What do you need to know?"

"Several things," Coda said. "How'd the battle go, for one?"

"Not good," his father said with a grimace. "We came out swinging and bloodied their nose, but their numbers were too much. The fleet has retreated. The Tau Titus system is lost."

"Retreated?"

They had been able to scout the tunnels and chambers without detection in part because the Overlord had been distracted. If the battle was already lost, what did that mean for the *Redemption*?

"We haven't lost yet," his father clarified. "The fleet is regrouping, preparing to fight at another location. I don't know if it'll be enough, but we can slow them. Which is why it's so critical the Overlord doesn't find us. Every moment his eye is directed elsewhere is another moment we can take advantage of. Is that everything you need to know?"

Coda wanted to get his father's take on the countersignal the captain had devised but decided against it. He wasn't convinced his father would have anything more than a guess, and his father was paranoid about the Overlord secretly listening in on their conversation. If that were the case, this was an ace he wanted to keep up his sleeve.

"Yes," Coda said reluctantly. He hated to leave so soon, but there was little he could do to keep his father around. Better to end on good terms than push and have it end poorly. "It was good to see you."

"It was good to see you too, son. I'm sorry to be so short. This is the way it must be. Short and to the point now, to give us more time in the future."

"I know."

"Don't ever forget that, Coda. We fight to give everyone the same thing that's been taken from *us*."

"I won't."

"Good." Joseph gave him another smile then brought him in for a final hug. "I'll see you tomorrow. Hopefully, I'll have better news."

"Sounds good," Coda said. "Goodbye, Dad."

"Goodbye, son."

Coda disconnected from the Baranyk network and opened his eyes. The harsh white light of sick bay burned his eyes, and it took several moments for him to blink away his disorientation. When he came to, Captain Coleman was standing beside the doctor.

He tried to sit up, but the binds held him firmly in place.

"Coda?" Captain Coleman asked.

"It's me, sir," Coda said, his voice oddly strained. "Forgot I was bound."

"Release him," Captain Coleman said.

Dr. Rydell started on the binds, beginning with the ones around his arms and chest first. Once they were off, Coda sat up, rubbing the raw skin of his wrists.

"Were you successful?" Captain Coleman asked.

"Yes, sir," Coda said. "He hasn't found the Overlord yet, but our intel was helpful, and he hopes to have a better update tomorrow."

The captain's face remained hard, as if chiseled from granite. Coda knew he was disappointed, his stress factor going up by a factor of ten, but the captain internalized it better than anyone he had ever met. "And the battle?"

"Lost," Coda said. "Our forces were overwhelmed. They retreated and are reassembling to prepare for another stand."

He thought he saw an almost imperceptible shake of the head. "Thank you, Coda."

"Is that all, sir?"

"For now," Captain Coleman said. "Get some rest. There's no telling how much opportunity you will get in the coming days."

# 39

*Mess Hall, SAS Olympia*
*Rendezvous Point, Human Controlled Space*

Buster sat alone in the mess hall. It was alive with more conversation than usual, though he didn't take part in any of it.

The fallout from the defeat at Tau Titus had hit the *Olympia* hard, and in the days since, Buster had realized there were two common responses to a defeat like that. Some wallowed in the loss, overwhelmed by negative thoughts and feelings, overcome by the sheer impossibility of the situation. Others became loud and boisterous in attempt to make up for the feelings of defeat from the others. They were two ends of the spectrum in a constant battle with each other.

Buster was closer to the former, though he thought of himself as introspective rather than defeated. Overcome with what-ifs. Brainstorming ways to learn from the past to better prepare for the future. The process had so far netted nothing of substance. So it was that he sat alone and quiet in a room full of people and conversation.

"Orders are coming soon," Kane said. He was a fellow pilot. Not anyone of any particular renown, a solid if unspectacular pilot who would always have a spot in the fleet's drone squadrons.

"Who'd you hear that from?" Casper asked. Like Kane, he was a pilot in Buster's squadron. His complexion, or the complete lack thereof, had inspired his call sign. It was one step north of albino, and the squadron often gave him shit, saying if he wasn't careful, he would get a sunburn from the ship's interior lights.

"Everyone is talking about it," Kane said as if that answered everything.

"I haven't heard anything."

"Everyone important."

"Fuck off."

The other pilots at the table laughed, though more than one looked in Buster's direction as if silently waiting for him to confirm or deny the rumor. He remained silent, letting the two pilots who seemed to be in the middle of most things see the conversation through to its end.

Kane set down his fork on the plastic tray and looked at Casper, who sat across the table. "Think about it," he said as if it were the most obvious thing in the world. "The admiral's brass may have positioned the last battle as exactly that... the last battle. But he knew what we were up against and would have had contingencies. He didn't just prepare for a loss. He planned for it."

"Then what the hell happened at Tau Titus?" Casper pressed. "You going to say that was part of the plan too?"

"Of course not," Kane said. "But that was just the opening round to a five-round fight. We got bloodied a bit, but we landed a couple good blows too, and the fight is just beginning."

"I don't know," Casper said.

Buster had heard a hundred such conversations echoed in the corridors, mess hall, ready room, gym, and other communal spaces, always refusing to take part in any of them. On one level, it was his job to keep his pilots in fighting shape, but on another, his pilots needed an opportunity to vent, to comprehend, and to process what they were up against. The same way he was.

"I heard the Baranyk tore through the Molaran and Elea systems." The voice came from Leather this time, who sat at the other end of the table. Having grown up on a ranch, her skin was thick and shared the same color as her call sign's namesake.

"Rumor is the Sutalia is gone too," Tiny said. His voice was deep, the spoon he held in his hand small. His was the best kind of call sign: ironic, sarcastic, and completely at odds with his physically imposing frame.

"Where'd you hear that?" Leather asked.

Tiny shrugged. "Around."

They all seemed to take that as gospel. Truth be told, there were enough rumors aboard the ship that if they were sperm, everyone would have been impregnated.

"Whatever," Kane said. "We're going to stop them this time. I'm telling you."

He was met with halfhearted agreement before a second silence fell over the table. That had been the rhythm of conversation since the battle at Tau Titus. Truth and rumor, followed by bravado and contemplation. Everyone knew the odds they faced, and nobody truly believed they'd overcome them. Not without anything short of a miracle.

Buster dropped his fork onto his tray and stood. Though no one had voiced it, they should have received their orders already. Every minute they waited, another system fell. Even if they somehow slowed the Baranyk or even stopped them, they'd still lost half their systems. It would take decades to recover. And the longer the admiral let the rumors persist, the worse the morale would become.

The others seemed to think he knew more than he was letting on, and he could feel their eyes as he walked away. It was a difficult place to be. His pilots looked to him for answers that he didn't have and encouragement he wasn't sure he felt. He just felt... lost.

The Baranyk's show of force was unlike anything he'd ever seen or witnessed. It caused terror on a scale he hadn't known existed.

Buster emptied his tray into the compost and recycling receptacles and exited the mess hall. The immediate quiet of the corridor was refreshing and better matched his introspective mood. He chose a direction and went, no destination in mind, just content to be moving. Since the battle at Tau Titus, he couldn't sit still for too long. The Forgotten talked about speed being life. Stillness was death. So as long as they kept moving, they had a chance. Such a simple thought yet impossible in reality.

Buster didn't need to receive the new orders. He already knew how the rest of the war would be fought. Minor skirmishes would draw the enemy fleet farther into human space, cutting them off from resources and supply lines. Then they would flank the enemy with a series of hit-and-run maneuvers, whittling down their strength while incurring as few losses of their own as possible. Death by a thousand cuts. Until the forces were more equally matched and humanity could present a last stand. Did they have enough ground to give up for the tactic to work, though?

Unsurprisingly, Buster's feet led him to the drone operation center. No simulations were scheduled for the moment, but the room was full, nearly every seat taken. Buster stepped into the room, letting the door close behind him, but didn't venture farther.

On the battle map, dozens of Hornets took on a force fifty times its size. For several minutes, Buster watched as the Hornets cut, swerved, dove, and sliced through enemy formations, laying waste to enemy fighters with cannon fire, missiles, and sheer bravery. For every drone they lost, they eliminated ten enemy combatants. By the time the simulation was over, they'd cut the enemy force in half. The pilots who'd been plugged in removed their helmets, smiling as they wiped sweat-slicked hair back, and talked animatedly about what they'd learned and what the spectators had seen.

The simple scene knocked the breath from him. Humans may bitch and complain, talk, shout, and argue, sink into a morose state, and attempt to overcome it with overconfident bravado, but they never gave up. There was a spark that could never be extinguished. And as long as they had that spark, they stood a chance. They were still moving. They were still alive.

Buster straightened his back and took a purposeful stride forward. "That was impressive. One of the best displays I've seen. How did you do it?"

The pilots were excited and talked over each other. That made it hard to get a cohesive story, but Buster wasn't about to negate their enthusiasm. Over the course of several minutes, he stitched together what they'd done.

They'd used a combination of formations to attack the heart of enemy swarms, plunging in like a knife digging into the chest of an enemy. Then they would twist, increasing the damage. And they had other ideas—ways they could feint, counter, and press advantages.

Buster didn't tell them to keep it up; he didn't have to. They were already too eager to try.

Buster stayed with them well into the night, watching simulation after simulation, participating in more than a few. By the time he turned in for the night, he felt more optimistic than he had at any other point.

Shortly after he closed his eyes, he received an emergency communication. They'd received their orders. Their next battle would occur the following day at 1800 hours.

# 40

*Drone Operation Center, SAS Redemption*
*Distant Orbit, Baranyk Homeworld*

Coda stepped into the *Redemption*'s drone operation center with Moscow, Squawks, and Nails, ready to watch the drone pilots run through their first training scenario. Rings of individual operation bays rose from the deck to the ceiling, circling a large display at the center of the room.

Moscow stood under the display, with Phantom at his shoulder. He was a large man, over two meters with broad shoulders and a thick chest that made Moscow look small by comparison. It was the type of physique that never would have fit inside a real cockpit. The pilots, ninety-six of them in all, were already settled into their bays, ready to plug in after the CAG's address.

"The geographic information has already been uploaded into the simulator," Phantom said. "It's still based on preliminary scans, so don't expect this to be your flight path in the real mission. The goal is to get used to flying in atmo and confined spaces. For the purposes of this training scenario, our objective is to destroy Target Designation Alpha at the end of a series of tunnels and chambers, using traditional missiles.

You will be flying your own mission, nobody on your wing and no formations. The pilot who destroys the target the fastest and escapes with their drone intact will be the winner of the training hop. Any questions?"

Phantom scanned the room as if looking for a hand or someone standing. He didn't have to wait long.

"Sir," a voice said from the third tier of fighter bays. "Will there be enemy contacts in this scenario?"

"No," Phantom said. "As I said, the purpose is to get you familiar with the specific challenges of the mission. We'll add enemy fighters to future simulations."

"Thank you, sir."

"We're simulating a drone control distance of two hundred fifty thousand kilometers from the planet, which equates to just over eight-tenths of a second of lag time. This has already been calculated in the scenario."

Coda looked for any signs of frustration, but the pilots took the words as a statement of fact, nothing to get worked up about. Dealing with lag time was just part of flying a drone fighter, the same way managing G's was for a Nighthawk pilot. If he had to choose, he would choose G's every time.

"And while this is a competition of sorts," Phantom continued, "I want you to approach the scenario as preparation. Experiment. Push yourself. But do so gradually. I want to know what speeds you're comfortable at and how far you can push it. We can't measure our improvement if we don't know our baseline. And we can't improve if we don't know our weaknesses. Let's get started."

They drilled for two hours before taking a break. By then, Coda had taken up station in one of the seats that surrounded the battle map but wasn't a part of an operation bay. From his vantage, the pilots seemed to be flying tentatively. Their commander had given them an opportunity to play it safe, and they had done just that.

"They look like they're flying with training wheels," Squawks said quietly but not so quiet that those nearest him couldn't hear.

"They're stuck in first gear," Nails added.

"They've barely been trained for this," Coda said. "Give it time."

Phantom pulled up the results from each pilot, displaying it on the battle map. He sorted the information by call sign, quickest time to target, and average attack time. All were significantly below the target time.

"That's not good enough," Moscow said to the other Nighthawk pilots. "If there'd been enemy fighters or defensive turrets, they'd all have been destroyed before they ever made it to the target."

Phantom cast a wary eye toward the group of Nighthawk pilots, clearly worried about their opinions. He tried to remain positive. "Okay, we have a baseline. It's time to push it. The target time for this hop is nine minutes, and nobody came in under twelve. We have to do better."

If the pilots had been expecting a longer break, they were sorely disappointed. For the next hour, they repeated the training scenario. It was clear they were flying with more urgency now, and those who completed the scenario did so faster than before. The consequence was more fighters crashed into the tunnel walls as well. And none came close to the target time Phantom had set.

Moscow groaned when Phantom put up the performance numbers again. This time, the other CAG had had enough.

"Do you have something you want to say, Lieutenant?" Phantom asked.

"Nothing you haven't already said," Moscow said, taking the diplomatic route.

"Which is what, exactly?" Phantom asked, not ready to let him off the hook.

"They're not fast enough," Moscow said. "Even in atmo, the Hornets are capable of much faster speeds. What's the issue?"

There were quiet grumblings throughout the operation center, but nobody braved an answer.

"I'm serious," Moscow pressed. "I haven't flown a Hornet in a while. What am I missing?"

"It's the lag time, sir," one of the pilots finally said. "It's too much."

Moscow turned toward the voice. "Two hundred fifty thousand kilometers is nothing. You've faced worse."

The statement wasn't exactly true. Most of the drone pilots aboard the *Redemption* were first-year pilots fresh out of the academy. But to Moscow's point, they at least would have trained for more difficult situations.

"Yes, sir," the pilot said. "But that was in the emptiness of space. This is different. There are too many turns and choke points. If this was our flight path, then yes, I'd feel confident we could learn and adapt. But if your goal is to understand the limitations, I'm telling you lag time is an issue."

Moscow frowned and looked at Phantom for his assessment.

"Is it possible to get closer?" Phantom asked.

"Anything closer, and we'll be inside the moon's orbit," Moscow said. "Strategically, it creates a blind spot and exposes our flank. But let's see what it does."

Phantom gave the pilots a twenty-minute break while he and Moscow updated the scenario so that the *Redemption* was one hundred fifty thousand kilometers from the planet. Then he ran the pilots through another hour's worth of exercises. It was clear the shorter lag time made a difference, but they were still slower than expected.

Moscow raked his fingers through his hair, clearly frustrated. He looked to Coda, Squawks, and Nails for support, but if anyone had any new ideas, they kept them to themselves.

"That was obviously better," Phantom said. "Times are down across the board, but we're still not where we need to be. Tell me what you're seeing. What you're feeling."

"The lag time is still too much," the same pilot said. "At five hundred kilometers an hour, we're covering one hundred forty meters in half a second. That's longer than some of these tunnels. We quite literally can't navigate our fighters in time if we move too fast."

Phantom and his pilots began talking about reprogramming the scenario with a distance of fifty thousand kilometers. It didn't matter that the majority of Baranyk fighters were with the invasion fleet; the captain would never agree to such a close orbit. Being that close to the planet would expose them to the entire might of the Baranyk's defensive forces. They needed another way.

"This is a job for the Forgotten," Coda said, finally voicing what he'd been thinking all along.

"No shit," Squawks said.

"You just now realizing that?" Nails chided.

"No," Coda said. "But at least now we know for sure."

"And wasted a full afternoon," Nails said.

"It's not a waste if they've proven they can't do it," Coda said. "All the captain needs is a frame of reference."

"What do you mean?" Squawks asked.

Coda smiled, the idea crystalizing in his mind. He had another meeting with his father in a few hours and a briefing with the captain after that. If they were correct, then he would have his frame of reference, and the captain would be reminded of what the Forgotten were truly capable of.

"Follow me," Coda said.

# 41

*Simulation Room, SAS Redemption*
*Distant Orbit, Baranyk Homeworld*

"Clear the room," Moscow said as they entered the Nighthawk simulation room.

Only a handful of pilots were in the room. None of them were in the simulators. Hearing the no-nonsense tone in Moscow's voice, they vacated the room quickly and without a word.

Coda wasted little time making for the control terminal on the wall near the display. "Who wants to go first?"

"This was your idea," Moscow said.

"I'm not on the flight roster," Coda said.

"Irrelevant," Moscow said. "If your point is that the Nighthawks can perform the mission faster and cleaner, then it doesn't matter if you're on the roster or not. And that is your point, isn't it?"

"Yes."

"Then get in the simulator," Moscow said.

He and Moscow often skirted the line between friend and subordinate, but there was no mistaking Moscow's tone. It was a direct order, and Coda had no intention of disobeying.

"Yes, sir." Coda failed to keep the excitement out of his voice. He knew that posting the best time wouldn't get him into the cockpit any sooner, but it felt good to be doing something other than playing telephone.

There was no question who would occupy the other simulator. Moscow strode toward it, clearly ready to take on Coda for old times' sake. Nails and Squawks rolled the two ladders into place and helped Coda and Moscow get set up.

Coda ducked between the rotating arms of the gyroscope, stepping into the cockpit at the center of the simulator, and settled into the gel seat. It was a far cry from the seat of his Nighthawk, but he had cut his teeth in these simulators and earned his position among the Forgotten. It was home in the way a childhood house was home. Something he would always look back on fondly, even if he had moved onto bigger and better things.

"Just like we said to the drone pilots," Coda said, "don't worry about time—not yet. More than anything, I want to know if this is even possible."

"Forget that," Squawks said. "Speed is life, and there's no way the two of you are going to do this without a little competition."

Coda waited for Moscow to correct him. When it didn't come, Squawks's smile consumed his entire face. Coda knew that smile too well—nothing good ever came after it.

"Moscow, what do you say to a little bet?" Squawks asked.

"What do you have in mind?" Moscow asked, sliding on his flight helmet.

"Well, my money is on Coda," Squawks said. "And if I win, I don't have to fly CAP for a month."

"Their wingman either," Nails said, making sure she was included in any of Squawks's winnings.

Moscow barked a laugh. "Well, if I win, you're doing my sensitivity trainings for me."

"You sure that's a good idea?" Nails asked.

"Deal," Squawks said before Moscow could think twice, then winked at Coda.

Coda couldn't help but laugh. The fact that Squawks was betting on his rusty abilities hadn't gone unnoticed. Though he'd told his friend they needed the fast-talking, fast-flying version of Squawks back, he didn't know how much of this was Squawks's natural bravado and how much was him forcing the issue. Either way, it was nice to see his playful side coming back.

"All right," Coda said. "Let's see what we can do."

"You better win," Squawks said.

"No pressure," Nails added.

Coda slid on his flight helmet and punched the button to begin the simulation. It started the same way the Hornet simulations had. Coda's Nighthawk raced across a rocky landscape, flying low enough to kick up dust and debris. His seat vibrated, simulating the feel of the engine. The ground was the color of dead grass, with no sign of vegetation anywhere. The cloudy sky had a yellow hue. It was as if the planet itself was dead, a yellow version of Mars before humanity had terraformed it.

Ahead of him was what looked like a large round hill, though he knew otherwise. Like a mole- or anthill, it was the dirt and rock that had been dug out of the landscape to create the tunnels and chambers underground. Coda couldn't help but reflect on how large the underground habitat must be for that much rock and soil to have been dug out.

Coming to the base of the hill, Coda pulled back on his joystick, raising the nose cone to the sky, and raced to the summit. Once clear of the top of the hill, he performed an inverted dive and spun into the entrance. He couldn't see it, but the gyroscope rotated, simulating the move. It left him facing toward the deck, hanging, held in place by his flight harness.

Blood rushed into his face, and his breath became more restricted as darkness washed over his Nighthawk. The four headlamps, two mounted on either side of the Nighthawk's nose cone and two more on the edges of Coda's wings, did little to penetrate the darkness, barely lighting the area immediately in front of them.

Toggling the appropriate setting on his HUD, Coda activated his computer-aided sight. His fighter's computer took constant readings from the ship's radar and lidar systems and turned them into a visual in the same way infrared showed heat.

The tunnel's rough walls were pockmarked, worn by time and water, and of varying widths and depths. Stalagmites and stalactites lined the tunnel's ground and ceiling, sometimes reaching into the middle of the tunnel itself.

With his vision improved, Coda pushed the throttle and ripped through the tunnel. Weaving around obstacles, he grinned as his simulator swayed and spun, speeding ever downward. He barely had time to register the solid wall in front of him. Relying more on reflex than anything, he engaged the air brakes, increasing drag and reducing speed, then pulled back on his joystick.

The harness dug into his shoulders again, simulating the feel of dramatically reducing speed as his fighter rocketed through the tunnel and into one of the large chambers. Coda let out a strained breath as the harness relaxed, glancing at the map as he sped through the chamber. Although the tunnel had been going downward, the chamber extended horizontally.

Coda punched the throttle, accelerating through the chamber, which was the length of a small city. The simulation was programmed to include only the tunnels and chambers themselves. Coda thought back to the purpose of this particular chamber. Some sort of communal area? The other chambers for supply storage, egg storage, and nurseries were deeper in the habitat.

"Pick up the pace, Coda," Squawks said. "You're losing."

Coda had no idea if Squawks was telling the truth or not, but he pushed the pace anyway. He may not have anything on the line, but he hated losing. And to Moscow most of all.

Coming up on the far wall of the chamber, Coda spun his Nighthawk so that his cockpit faced the ground, then he pulled back on the joystick as he came to the next tunnel's opening. The maneuver brought him into the tunnel without shedding speed. This one was narrower and more rugged than the previous one, and Coda darted around obstacles, trusting his instincts.

He continued like that, zipping through tunnels, emptying into chambers, increasing thrust when he could, slowing down only when he had to. He cut through switchbacks, swerved around stalagmites, and dove ever downward, venturing deeper and deeper into the tunnel system, until finally, he reached his destination.

His objective was little more than a massive Baranyk skeleton that wasn't even programmed to move. Coda fired. His cockpit bucked as the digital missile rocketed away, streaking smoke toward the Overlord. It connected with a massive explosion that rocked his cockpit, but he was already shedding speed, attempting to swerve around and exit the way he had entered before the explosion consumed his fighter.

The image dissolved, the simulation over.

"What happened?" Moscow said. "The mission wasn't over."

"Coda won," Squawks said, triumph in his voice. "The target was destroyed. And *I* don't have to fly CAP."

Coda removed his flight helmet and wiped his sweaty forehead with the back of his arm. "How'd we do?"

"A full one minute and seventeen seconds faster than the fastest Hornet," Nails said.

"Not bad," Squawks said. "I'm sure I could have done better, but at least you didn't embarrass yourself like Moscow. He looked like he was flying with his eyes closed."

"Careful. I am still your commanding officer," Moscow said, though there was no mirth in his voice.

"You think that was enough to take to the captain?" Nails asked.

"Maybe," Moscow said. "We've proven we can fly faster than the Hornets. Let's see what a couple more runs can do."

"Agreed," Coda said. Every moment he spent in the simulator, flying with his squadron mates, was a blessing, and he wasn't about to give it up.

"Double or nothing?" Squawks asked as Coda slipped his flight helmet on again.

"Keep talking, and you'll be my latrine queen," Moscow said.

Coda laughed as he hit the button to initialize the simulation.

# 42

*Baranyk Network,*
*Unknown*

"We don't have much time," Coda's father said the moment their meeting began.

"Why?" Coda asked. "What's wrong?"

His father looked over his shoulder as if expecting the Overlord to appear at any moment. The action sent a chill down Coda's spine. He checked their surroundings too, scratching the back of his neck nervously.

They were back at the baseball stadium where they'd first reconnected. It was a smaller venue with only fifteen to twenty rows of seating rising from the field. The kind where the local team lived and played in the community, the proximity to the field making it feel like the spectators were out there with them. But without spectators, the empty seats and press boxes left an eerie feeling, casting long shadows that played games with Coda's imagination.

"The fleet is moving," Joseph said. "The next battle will begin within the hour."

"Already?" Coda had spoken with his father twice since their initial meeting, but he hadn't said anything about the next battle being imminent. "At least that'll give us a chance to scout more."

"No need for that," his father said. "I found him."

"You—"

"Yes." His father's eyes kept darting around the stadium. "No talking. No questions. Just listen." Even his words were sharp. "In the northern hemisphere around the forty-fifth parallel is another hive. He's there. But, Coda, it's one of their oldest colonies, deeper than anything you have explored, and well defended."

"How do you know?"

"We don't have time for that." Joseph shot a look over Coda's shoulder then spun, looking behind himself. His breathing was quick, and Coda thought he saw the shine of sweat on his forehead. He hadn't known it was possible to sweat in the Baranyk network. "I think he saw me. He knows I found him."

Coda took an involuntary step back. "Then he knows we're coming. He might move. Might hide."

"Like I said, we don't have much time."

"I have to—"

Joseph held up a hand, cutting Coda off, then spun.

Coda followed his eyes, hearing before seeing anything.

*Click. Click. Click.* Slow and menacing, it was the sound of something hard on concrete. *Click. Click. Scraaaaape.*

His father took a step back, his hands finding Coda and pushing him behind his back, protecting him in the way a father does.

Then the sound was behind them. *Click. Click.*

Coda spun, placing his back to his father's. Rising from the stairs was a hulking black mass, sharp mandibles jutting forward as if reaching for them, and a triangular head appraising its prey.

"Coda..."

"We're surrounded."

"Get out!" his father yelled. "Disconnect!"

Coda slammed his eyes shut, trying to let his consciousness wash away, but the fear was too strong. "I can't!"

"You have to!"

"I can't!"

Coda opened his eyes. A second Baranyk warrior was climbing the stairs now, directly behind the first. They fanned out, taking away any hope of escape. Coda risked a glance behind him, and his blood went cold. The Baranyk approaching from the other side was twice the size of the others, with silver streaks across its dark carapace.

The Overlord.

"It's not real," his father said. "The fear. The adrenaline. The blood pounding through your veins. It's not real. Just let yourself go. I'm right behind you."

Coda whipped his head back around just as the two Baranyk warriors lunged, mandibles pointed directly at his chest. He dove to the side without thought, landing hard on his shoulder, and rolled down the aisle toward the field. Coda scrambled to his feet, surprised that the two Baranyk warriors hadn't pursued him down the aisle.

His father screamed.

*No.*

The Baranyk warriors that hadn't followed Coda down the aisle had attacked the unprotected back of Coda's father. Two mandibles had torn through his back and chest and held him a meter off the ground. His father flailed, legs kicking in agony, bloody spittle coating his lips.

The Overlord continued his meticulous approach, his triangular head tilting to the side as if appraising its prey. Joseph let out a defiant roar and spat in his direction.

Coda stood frozen in place. He couldn't just leave his father to his fate, but there were four Baranyk warriors plus the Overlord, and Coda didn't have any sort of weapon. He wasn't just outmatched; he was hopelessly outnumbered... just like their fleet.

"Go!" The word was little more than a growl. Spoken in the Overlord's direction, it took Coda a moment to realize it was directed at him. "Go."

Coda stepped backward involuntarily. It took everything he had to take a second step and a third, slowly moving away from the scene. His father was being left behind again. Only this time, it wasn't the fleet abandoning him. It was his own son.

Joseph didn't so much as look at him. Deep down, Coda knew it was to keep the Baranyk's attention off him for as long as possible and give him a chance to escape, but it still hurt. He took a shuddering breath, willing his body through a relaxation exercise as he slowly descended the stairs.

Another step.

His foot slipped on the edge of the stairs with an audible scrape.

The rearmost Baranyk warrior whipped its head around and charged.

Coda let out a resigned breath and closed his eyes, letting himself go. The last thing he heard was the clicking of the Baranyk's legs as it raced down the concrete stairs.

# 43

*Sick Bay, SAS Redemption*
*Distant Orbit, Baranyk Homeworld*

Coda's eyes snapped open. The light was blinding. He blinked, trying to force his eyes to adjust. Something held him down. He fought. Flailed. Screamed.

"Easy, Coda." The voice came from a dark shadow that loomed over him.

"No!" Coda screamed. "No!"

"Easy." The voice was soft and consoling but tinged with worry.

"They have him!" Coda said.

"It's okay, Coda. You're safe now."

"You don't understand!" Coda strained his arms and legs, trying to pry himself from the hospital bed they'd strapped him to. "They have him!"

*Why isn't anyone listening?*

The shadow moved. "We need to sedate him," the shadow said. Female. Dr. Rydell.

"You think he's under their control?"

"I don't know, but we have to be sure."

"No!" Coda screamed. "You don't understand. They have him. They have my father."

Something about the room's dynamic changed. The chatter silenced, and an eerie quiet settled over the room. The shadow returned. Coda's eyes had adjusted enough to make out Dr. Rydell's features.

"What did you say?" Dr. Rydell asked.

Coda forced himself to take a breath, to bring himself under control. "I said they have him. The Overlord appeared and attacked us. The captain has to know."

Dr. Rydell looked up to the second occupant in the room. Coda tried to follow her gaze, but his angle on the hospital bed made it impossible.

"Get Captain Coleman on the line," Dr. Rydell said.

---

Captain Coleman marched into sick bay. As usual, they had Coda segregated from the rest of the patients in a cordoned-off area at the back of the room. One of the curtains had been pulled half open, allowing him a glimpse of Dr. Rydell, who stood at Coda's feet. Oddly, he still looked to be restrained.

"What happened?" Captain Coleman asked as he stepped through the opening.

Coda lay flat on his back, thick straps fastening his ankles, wrists, chest, and head to the hospital bed. His eyes were wide, red, and frantic, darting to Coleman the moment he stepped into his view.

"Why is my pilot still restrained?"

"Sir," Dr. Rydell said, "he came out of the network... *distressed*. We kept him restrained to protect him."

The undertext of Dr. Rydell's words was clear. They didn't know if he was under his own control or not.

"He appears himself now," Coleman said. "Remove the binds."

"Sir, we haven't completed our scans yet," Dr. Rydell said.

"For God's sake," Coleman said. "He's not under Baranyk control. I can see it in his eyes. Now remove his binds." To further spur them into motion, Coleman started on one of the ankle straps himself. "Report."

"Yes, sir," Coda said as Dr. Rydell worked on his binds. "The meeting occurred as planned, sir, but from the moment it began, my father was nervous. I don't know what it was or how he knew, but something had him on edge. He kept saying we didn't have much time and, sir..." He swallowed the emotion in his throat. "Sir, the Overlord ambushed us. I don't know how he found us, but he did, and he had four Baranyk warriors with him. We were defenseless."

Coleman's blood went cold. Joseph O'Neil was a vital cog in their battle plan. Not only could he uncover the Overlord's location, but he was their only connection to the rest of the fleet. Without him, they had no way of knowing when to attack or if their efforts were successful.

"What happened?" Coleman asked.

Dr. Rydell removed the bind from Coda's forehead, and the pilot sat up.

"They took him, sir."

"Took him?" Coleman repeated. "They didn't kill him?"

"I don't know for sure," Coda said. "I got out of there as fast as I could, but it didn't look like it, sir."

"Why not?" The question wasn't directed at anyone in particular. Coda didn't have an answer, not even a guess.

Surprisingly, it was Dr. Rydell who spoke up. "The Baranyk are clearly capable of complex thought. The question is, are they capable of complex emotion? Joseph O'Neil is the only person to have successfully fought back against Baranyk control and achieved some level of autonomy. It could be that the situation with the Overlord has, as they say, grown personal."

Coleman chewed on the words for a moment. Much of the Overlord's tactics, including the surprise assault on New Plymouth when he and Coda had found him seemed to support the doctor's argument.

"Or..." Coleman said simply, "he's going to use Joseph the same way we did. To extract as much information about our forces, location, and plans as possible."

"Can he do that?" Coda asked.

"I was going to ask you the same question," Coleman said. "But we need to prepare as if he can."

"Sir..." Coda said slowly. "That would mean the Overlord knows we're here."

"Yes," Coleman said. "And whatever information your father knows about the battle plans with the rest of the fleet."

"And we have no way to warn them."

"No, we don't," Coleman said. "Which means our attack window just got a lot shorter. You said the meeting occurred as planned. I need to know what your father told you."

"He said..." Coda's eyes went distant with thought for a moment, then they snapped back to focus. "He said he found him."

"He *what?*"

"Just before the Overlord arrived, he said that the fleet was about to engage the enemy forces but that we didn't need to search for him anymore because he'd found him."

Coleman took two powerful steps forward, his steps thumping against the deck with every ounce of authority he commanded. "Where?"

"He said there's another hive in the northern hemisphere around the forty-fifth parallel. It's one of their oldest colonies, deeper than anything we've explored, and well defended. He said he's there."

"You're sure?"

Coda gave him a curt nod. "Positive, sir."

Coleman wasted no time. He pressed the top of his ear to the side of his head, activating his earpiece. "Commander Garcia," he said without preamble, "have our advanced scouts located any signs of a Baranyk colony in the northern hemisphere around the forty-fifth parallel?"

"Forty-fifth parallel," Commander Garcia said. "Checking now, sir."

Coleman tapped his boot against the deck, the seconds feeling like hours.

"Yes, sir. But it wasn't more than a preliminary scan."

"Redirect all reconnaissance drones," Coleman said. "He's there, Commander. I want to know every nook and cranny of that hive within the hour."

"Yes, sir."

Coleman ended the transmission and turned to Coda. "Good work, Commander." With that, he strode from the partitioned section of the room.

"Sir!" Coda shouted, stopping him before he'd taken two steps.

"Is there something else, Coda?"

"Sir, I left him there. I left him with the Overlord, and I'm the only one who can get him back."

Coleman's head was shaking before Coda had even completed the thought. "I know what you're asking, Coda, and the answer is no. I can't risk it."

"Sir, the only reason I returned was because you needed this information. But now that you have it—"

"You have vital intelligence about the whereabouts of this ship, our battle capabilities, and that we have critical intel of the Overlord's location. We can't risk you falling into enemy hands and delivering that information. I'm sorry, Coda, but your request is denied. We'll find another way to get your father back."

Coda's body seemed to deflate. He let out a long breath, his posture faltering, and nodded. "Yes, sir."

Coleman prepared to leave and was stopped a second time.

"It should be said," Dr. Rydell said, "that while Joseph's mind is in the Baranyk network, his body still resides on the *Abraham Lincoln*. It's possible that if we are successful and the Overlord is defeated that the Overlord's grasp on him will falter and he'll be able to return."

Coda sat straighter with that. He must have known it was the best they could hope for. "Then let's get him."

Coleman gave him a crisp nod. "Agreed, Coda. Updated scans should be coming in within the hour. I need my pilots ready."

"Yes, sir," Coda said, adding a sharp salute.

Coleman returned the gesture and turned to leave. His earpiece chimed as he did. *What now?* He tapped the earpiece, opening the channel. "Coleman."

"Sir, we have enemy contacts approaching," Commander Garcia said. "Three hundred thousand kilometers and closing."

Coleman cursed under his breath. The situation had gone from stable to shit show in minutes.

"Sir?" Commander Garcia said, likely having heard the curse.

"Deploy fighters," Coleman said. "I'm on my way."

He closed the transmission. Coda's and Dr. Rydell's eyes were on him, obviously having heard his side of the exchange.

"It seems we're going to get that chance, Coda," Coleman said. "The Overlord knows we're here, and he's sent a welcome party."

# 44

*Bridge, SAS Redemption*
*Distant Orbit, Baranyk Homeworld*

"WHAT'S THE SITUATION?" CAPTAIN COLEMAN BELLOWED, STEPPING ONTO the bridge.

Commander Garcia looked away from the battle map. "Sir, enemy forces en route, just under three hundred thousand kilometers and closing."

"How many are we talking about?" Coleman asked.

"One carrier," Commander Garcia said.

"*One* carrier?" Coleman checked the battle map for himself. Assuming the readings were correct, and he had no reason to doubt them, then a single ship was indeed plotting an intercept course. It was a far cry from what he'd expected. Did that mean the reserve force was truly that small, or was the Overlord playing at something else?

"Yes, sir," Commander Garcia said. "We've launched fighters but are keeping them tight." The green indicators of twenty-four Nighthawks shone brightly, flying in a simple formation around the image of the *Redemption*.

"What's the status of our reconnaissance drones?" Coleman asked.

"They haven't arrived yet," Commander Garcia said. "They should be arriving in… eleven minutes."

"And the ETA of that carrier?" Coleman asked.

Commander Garcia looked from Coleman to Lieutenant Poiu, who sat behind his terminal.

"At this rate of acceleration, sir," Lieutenant Poiu said without looking up from his readings, "they'll be in weapons range in two hours."

*Two hours.*

Coleman chewed on the words. Two hours would give them critical time to scout the Baranyk hive before that carrier arrived.

*That's if we sit here waiting to welcome them.*

If that truly was the bulk of the Baranyk reserve force, then the odds were more in Coleman's favor than he'd ever dared to hope.

"Prepare the Nighthawks to land," Coleman said. "Prepare our Hornet squadrons, and plot an intrasystem jump that'll put us in high orbit."

"Sir?" Commander Garcia said.

"You heard me," Coleman said. "The moment the Baranyk forces are within firing range, we are to jump. I want us in geosynchronous orbit directly over the Overlord's colony. When he looks up, I want him to see us pissing down on him. It's time we took this fight to him."

---

Coda was in the Simulation Room with Moscow, Squawks, and Nails when the scans from the first reconnaissance drones came back. The other flight leaders were still flying CAP, waiting for the incoming enemy. Moscow, Squawks, and Nails were on standby and had already donned their flight gear, but they knew they weren't going to be needed for this first round of the fray. Their efforts would be better leveraged in providing Captain Coleman with a battle plan and ensuring the drone pilots were prepared to execute it.

The image on the screen was pixelated, as if it were a broadcast with a weak signal, but was growing clearer by the second. Every reconnaissance drone, each barely the size of Coda's fingertip and equipped with the most advanced camera Fleet R&D could build in such a small application, took a narrow reading that the ship's computer would assemble into a cohesive image as if it were a puzzle.

The drones' size made them nearly undetectable, especially since their propulsion systems were incredibly limited. Using a tiny version of the EmDrive that the capital ships like the *Redemption* used, they generated thrust by reflecting microwaves within the engine itself. Because of that and their small size, they were incredibly difficult to detect. That was the theory, anyway.

The drones floated through the hive opening, a mountain of rock and dirt shaped like a giant molehill. They moved with a natural course as if they were dust motes floating on the wind, pouring ever deeper into the colony. The hole quickly closed in size, forming a long shaft that burrowed deep into the ground.

Coda had seen vids of Baranyk pouring out of similar shafts and tunnels by the thousand, as if the very ground were infested with them. And those had been smaller hives. This one had to house hundreds of thousands of Baranyk. Maybe more.

"The tunnel walls are wider than the other hives," Moscow said.

"That'll make them easier to navigate," Nails said.

"What are those stalactite-looking things?" Squawks asked.

"Probably stalactites?" Nails said sarcastically. Their training simulations had included them as well.

Squawks didn't appear to be in a joking mood. He stepped closer to the image and squinted as if that would make the image clearer. "No, these are different. There's an opening on the end, and look at how they connect to the tunnel. It almost looks like they can swivel."

The rest of them stepped closer to get a better look at what Squawks was talking about.

"I don't know," Coda said. "It might just be a shadow or an artifact from the scan."

"Switch to infrared," Squawks said.

Moscow tapped a series of commands into his tablet, changing the view of the chamber. The grays of the tunnel walls were replaced by the blues, greens, yellows, and oranges of the infrared image. The majority of the image was mapped out with the cooler colors of blues and greens, but the stalactites themselves were yellow and a deep orange at their center.

"What the hell is that?" Moscow asked.

"Some sort of surveillance device?" Nails suggested.

*But why would that give off a heat signature?*

"Something's happening," Squawks said, pointing at one of the stalactites. It was directed toward the tunnel's entrance. The orange color at its core flared red, and a moment later, the entire stalactite was burning. Fire flared from its tip as a wave of heat belched forth, washing the entire image with the same color.

"Whoa! What just happened?" Nails asked. "Where's the image?"

Moscow punched in another series of commands, switching the view from infrared back to a standard image, but it was black. His eyes narrowed as he read something else on his tablet.

"What is it?" Coda asked.

"I don't have everything from the bridge," Moscow said. "But I think the drones were destroyed."

"Destroyed?" Nails asked.

"Play it back," Squawks said. "Not in infrared."

Moscow started the vid from a few seconds before the wave of heat had hit the drones. Back were the various grays and yellows of the tunnel walls, but their attention was focused solely on the inconspicuous stalactite. As Squawks had said, it was angled outward, toward the entrance of the tunnel, and the wall around it had been worn smooth, as if it could turn and pivot. From within the dark interior, a bright-blue light appeared.

"Freeze it!" Squawks said.

Moscow punched a button on his tablet, freezing the image as a massive wave of blue light exploded from the stalactite.

"They're not stalactites," Squawks said. "They're turrets. They just hit us with a wave of plasma fire."

The four of them looked at each other in wide-eyed astonishment. None of the other hives had similar defensive measures. It seemed the Overlord valued his life above all else. Not surprising since the other creatures were little more than minor appendages that could be regrown at will.

"Okay," Moscow said. "Step one, locate and destroy all defensive turrets."

Nobody voiced step two.

*Determine what other surprises the Overlord has in store for us.*

# 45

*Briefing Room, SAS Redemption*
*Distant Orbit, Baranyk Homeworld*

"Here's the situation," Captain Coleman said. He stood at his usual spot at the head of the table in the briefing room. Commander Garcia, Dr. Poiu, Commander Payton, Moscow, and Coda were in attendance, as were Phantom and Sergeant Haniger from the Marine contingent aboard the *Redemption.*

"Enemy forces are inbound," Coleman continued. "A single carrier, and they haven't deployed fighters. It'll be within firing range within the hour."

There were a couple glances around the table, but the news hadn't come as a surprise. By now, the command personnel had known about the incoming vessel.

"But"—Captain Coleman held up a finger, emphasizing his point—"we will not be here when it arrives. We have lost communication with the fleet, but they should have engaged the enemy by now, and we'll use that confusion to mount our attack. Our sights are on the planet. Or more specifically, the hive where the Overlord is located."

He turned down the lights and called up the holographic image above the center of the table. It showed a distant image of the barren landscape of the Baranyk home world. Then he zoomed in to a single location in the northern hemisphere until the image showed what looked like a small hill without a mountain range beyond.

"Our Dragonflies have been largely ineffective," Coleman continued, "having only surveyed the entrance to the Baranyk hive before the enemy discovered their presence, so we'll be going in blind. But with the enemy focused on the larger battle, this is our best opportunity to strike. The Overlord will be forced to manage two separate fronts at once, and as you'll see, one of our aims is to sow as much confusion as possible."

Tapping another button on his tablet, Coleman pulled up the next image. "Our forces will take a multiwave approach, the first made up entirely of Hornets."

Phantom sat up straighter, his eyes finding Coleman's.

"Our Dragonflies couldn't complete their scans, but one thing they did discover was a series of plasma turrets lining the interior walls of the tunnel entrance." Red brackets encased the defensive turrets the nanodrones had discovered.

"They look like natural stalactites, but they pack a hell of a punch. Based on previous attacks and heat signatures, we're confident we've identified all of the initial turrets in this main entrance tunnel. Your first objective, Lieutenant Cahill, is to take them out. But beware, the plasma turrets, when fired together, act as a flushing system, washing the entire tunnel in plasma and eradicating anything that's not supposed to be there."

Phantom placed both elbows on the wooden table and intertwined his fingers. "We'll need speed. Approach the summit of the hive at full speed then perform an inverted dive directly into the entrance, shedding as little speed as possible. The first few turrets should be simple. After that, it'll depend on the Baranyk's response time."

"Agreed," Coleman said. "Which is why we're taking a multiwave approach. We expect heavy losses as we eliminate their initial defense systems. The Hornets will be staggered so that the moment the plasma fire vents onto the surface and the chamber is clear, the next wave will be entering the tunnel and moving to eliminate the next section of defensive turrets. That staggered approach will continue until our forces enter the first chamber, at which time they'll be joined by the attack force Alpha."

Several more images of Hornets appeared on the screen, each representing a full squadron instead of individual fighters.

"Based on initial intel, we believe there are other turrets in the hive's chambers and tunnels but not nearly at the same frequency. The Hornets will continue deeper into the tunnels, surveying and eliminating any defensive measures the Baranyk employ."

Phantom slid his elbows off the table and leaned back in his chair, his eyes focused on the image above the table. "What kind of enemy response do we expect?"

Coleman bit back a wince. "We don't know. Our scans didn't turn up any Baranyk fighters or warriors, but we'd be stupid not to expect them. We are, after all, kicking the proverbial hornet's nest."

"That hive houses several hundred thousand Baranyk," Moscow said, joining the conversation for the first time. "Based on other scans taken from the home world, some of the chambers can be many kilometers in length. If we are engaged by enemy fighters, there will be plenty of room to operate."

"Correct," Coleman said. "But we must not forget the true mission. We're here for the Overlord. Even if engaged, the Hornets are our eyes and ears. In addition to removing any more plasma turrets, we need to find the location of the Overlord's command chamber. That's the primary objective."

Phantom gave him a sharp nod. "Understood, sir."

"Good." Coleman returned the nod. "The first objective is to kick in the door. The second is here." The image dove deeper into the Baranyk tunnels to a massive chamber. The ground was littered with even more alien-looking Baranyk. Lacking size and fully formed extremities, they were something out of a horror story. "Dr. Poiu, this is your territory."

"Thank you, sir." Dr. Poiu remained seated and surveyed the table. "The Baranyk follow a four-stage metamorphosis life cycle, beginning as an egg before developing into a pupa, a larva, and finally, a mature adult. The chamber you see here is what we call the nursery, which is where the larvae are cared for by other Baranyk as they mature into adulthood."

An uncomfortable silence hung over the table. Coleman could see the implications of the second objective were clear. Killing Baranyk that were trying to kill you was a simple undertaking. But taking the life of an unformed lifeform was another story altogether. Alien or not, enemy or not, it wasn't something most people were comfortable with.

"Adulthood," Commander Garcia said as if echoing the thought on everyone's mind. "These pupae, then, are what? Children?"

"No," Dr. Poiu said. "Insects, and the Baranyk, as we know them, do not have children. They have pupae that are unable to survive on their own."

Commander Garcia made a disgusted look. "Not children, then. Babies. You're talking about killing baby Baranyk."

"No," Dr. Poiu said, this time more forcefully. "They're pupae. You wouldn't think twice about sweeping off a spider's nest from your porch or cracking a chicken egg for breakfast. This is no different."

Commander Garcia started to respond, but Coleman cut him off. "I understand your hesitation, Jaime. We don't have to like our task, but it has been handed to us. The Overlord is fighting a battle on multiple fronts, and I intend to create even more here. Wreak havoc. Confuse him. And in the event that we're not successful in eliminating the Overlord, render his ability to reproduce nearly impossible so that the fleet can come and finish the job."

*Assuming they win their own battle with them first.* But he kept that thought to himself.

Commander Garcia met his eye, and it was clear he would never agree with the order, but he fell in line like a good soldier.

"Once the path is clear, we'll drop you and your marines, Sergeant Haniger," Coleman said. "It'll be your task to see the operation through."

"Yes, sir," Sergeant Haniger said. "I have a squad of Firestarters that'll make hard-boiled eggs out of the little buggers. Leave it to us."

"We expect heavy resistance once you begin your assault. Coordinate with Phantom and Moscow on air support."

"Oorah, sir."

Coleman turned back to Phantom. "When you're not providing air cover or eliminating defensive turrets, your next objective is finding the Baranyk queen. Our secondary mission is eliminating the Baranyk's ability to reproduce and reinforce. Once found, you are to eliminate her."

"Of course, sir," Phantom said.

Coleman took a long breath. "All right. I've said it before, and I'll keep saying it until the mission is complete. Our primary objective is the Overlord." He keyed the next sequence into his tablet. The image pulled back, providing a macro view of the Baranyk hive. "This is a speculative rendering based on previous hives and what this one *could* look like. As you can see, it's made up of dozens of chambers and tunnel structures. Some, like the nursery, have dedicated functions. Others are used for storage. Some tunnels are for ventilation. We expect the Overlord to be in the safest spot in the hive, which we speculate is in the lower chambers. Find him, and we'll call in the bombing squadron to drop a Reaper down his throat."

A Reaper was a four-thousand-kilo, twenty-megaton nuclear weapon designed to eradicate all life and structures in a two-hundred-kilometer radius. Depending how deep the Overlord's chamber was located, Coleman wouldn't be surprised if the detonation cracked part of the planet away.

"What about the marines, sir?" Commander Garcia asked.

"Once the Overlord's chamber is identified, they'll send for immediate extraction." Coleman turned to Sergeant Haniger. "I can't promise more than a few minutes to disengage and hightail it to the surface."

"It'll be enough, sir."

Like every marine he'd ever met, Sergeant Haniger was a crazy sonuvabitch, though Coleman wondered how much of his bravado was real. As long as he performed as expected, Coleman didn't care. Every job in the fleet was risky. He knew that more than most.

"Any other questions?" Coleman asked.

"Just one, sir," Phantom said. "Say all of this goes according to plan, how will we know if we're successful?"

"A good question, Lieutenant." Coleman looked to Dr. Poiu. "Doctor?"

She met Commander Garcia's eyes. "The Baranyk are under the control of an advanced being that we refer to as the Overlord. That means their movements are an extension of his will, the same way our arms and legs are an extension of our own. It's our belief that when the Overlord is eliminated, the rest of the Baranyk will no longer be under his control. So it stands to reason their behavior will change."

"What she's saying," Coleman added, "is that even if the Baranyk do not withdraw, their efforts will become confused. Fractured. Leaderless. Our expectation is that free of the Overlord's influence, the surviving Baranyk will withdraw and retreat. But there's no way to know for sure."

"Understood, sir," Phantom said.

The skepticism in Phantom's tone was clear. Coleman found his gaze sliding to Coda. His pilot had remained silent for the entire briefing, but he had even more riding on the mission.

"We have... other ways of identifying the effectiveness of the mission," Coleman added. "But that information is known only to the senior-most officers on this ship. Rest assured, Lieutenant. If the Overlord is eliminated, we will know."

"Of course, sir."

"All right, ladies and gentlemen. It's almost showtime. Get your teams prepped and ready. The battle begins within the hour."

# 46

*Bridge, SAS Redemption*
*Distant Orbit, Baranyk Homeworld*

"The Baranyk carrier has launched fighters, sir," Lieutenant Poiu said, looking up from his terminal. "Two minutes from firing range."

There might have been a time, months ago, when Coleman would have detected an anxious tenor to his tactical officer's voice, but not now. He had been battle hardened like the rest of them. It would take something truly catastrophic to shake any of his bridge crew.

"Very good, Lieutenant," Coleman said. "Is our EmDrive charged and ready for jump?"

"It is, sir," Lieutenant Poiu said. "Coordinates are set. We're ready to jump on your mark."

Intrasystem jumps were always risky and seldom used. At these distances, precision was paramount. Miscalculations of even the smallest degree could land them in the planet's atmosphere or worse. He'd had the computer calculate the jump twice then a third time for good measure. Then he'd asked his navigation crew to confirm it by hand. It had taken the two hours, each minute the enemy drawing closer, but this wasn't a time for mistakes.

"Thank you, Lieutenant." Coleman sucked in a deep breath and let it out slowly. If there was ever a time when he felt the nerves, it was in this moment. The short time between planning and execution. The space where the prep was done and all that awaited was the execution, but the lingering doubts persisted. Had they done enough? What had they missed? Should they step back and reassess?

"They've entered firing range, sir," Lieutenant Poiu said. "They're opening fire!"

"Jump."

The world stretched out in front of Coleman. He'd once wondered if distance played a role in the duration of the jump sensation, but in his experience, it didn't. Intrasystem jumps took just as long as the interstellar variety, which likely meant the sensation was created by the warping of space itself rather than the distance traveled.

Coleman swayed as the world snapped back into place. His eyes immediately went to the battle map. It had gone blank but was repopulating with images as new sensor data came in.

"Lieutenant Poiu," he said, "I need to know if anything on the surface moves, launches, or even squirms."

"Yes, sir," Lieutenant Poiu said without looking up from his terminal.

"And don't lose sight of the Baranyk carrier. The enemy is capable of intrasystem jumps as well. It'll just take some time to plot."

"On it, sir."

*I know you are, Lieutenant.*

"Launch fighters," Commander Garcia said.

"Yes, sir," Lieutenant Poiu said. "Launching fighters."

Coleman watched as forty-eight green contacts appeared on the battle map. Immediately, they split into two delta squadrons and made for the planet's surface.

As Coleman had ordered, they were in geosynchronous orbit directly over the Overlord's hive. The extracted dirt, forming what looked like a small hill with an opening at its peak, wouldn't be visible from space, though Coleman liked the idea of looking down on it, as if the hive was something he could crush beneath his foot.

*I'm coming for you.*

"Sir!" Lieutenant Poiu said urgently. "I've got movement on the surface."

"What is it?" Coleman strode to Lieutenant Poiu's terminal and peered over his shoulder. On his terminal was a smaller version of the battle map, though zoomed in to provide a narrower focus.

"I'm not sure, sir," Lieutenant Poiu said. "It looks like a vent of some kind but..."

"Communications?" Coleman asked, turning to Ensign Richey.

"It's just static, sir," Ensign Richey said. "Whatever it is, it's not organic."

"Sir, I've got something!" Lieutenant Poiu said.

Coleman snapped his head around, looking back at Lieutenant Poiu's terminal. It was an image of the planet's rocky surface, now infrared, with a white-hot blotch dead center.

"There!" Lieutenant Poiu said, pointing at two new heat signatures. "I'm getting more."

"Overlay them with the Hornets' trajectory."

"Already on it, sir."

Within moments, Lieutenant Poiu had the Hornets' flight trajectory overlaid on top of the infrared image. The vents that burned the hottest were either directly below or slightly in front of the drone squadrons' flight path.

"Those aren't vents," Commander Garcia said. "They're more plasma turrets."

Coleman opened an immediate channel to his Hornet CAG. "Phantom, it appears the Baranyk have ground-based antiaircraft turrets disguised as vents. Tell your pilots to maintain elevation and take evasive maneuvers until they enter the hive. Sending you the data now."

"Yes, sir," Phantom said. "Thank you, sir."

The problem, Coleman soon realized, was that the drones were still entering the planet's atmosphere. They didn't have the ability to alter course. If they did, their entrance vector would create too much friction, causing them to burn up.

*They're sitting ducks.*

But hitting a target moving at the speed of reentry nearly ten thousand kilometers away proved easier said than done. The first wave of plasma fire missed by almost nine kilometers, blasting through the atmosphere before jetting harmlessly into space. The second was closer, and the third narrowed the gap even more. It wasn't until the fourth that there was any real threat.

It cut through the rear of the formation, shooting through the middle of their V formation without hitting anything. But the enemy had the range and calculations now.

"How long until they're out of atmo?" Coleman asked.

"Thirty seconds, sir," Lieutenant Poiu.

"And the plasma's rate of ascent?"

"If my readings are correct, about thirty-two thousand kilometers per hour, though it slows as it gets farther from the surface."

"Which means?"

"It's going to be close, sir."

Coleman looked up from his tactical officer to the battle map. He was helpless, unable to do anything, which was the worst feeling he could ever experience.

*This is why I belong in the cockpit, where I'm in control.*

"Switch from infrared," Coleman said. "Give me actuals."

The *Redemption* was close enough that its exterior cameras could give him a live image. The battle map updated from the infrared image to the live visual. The hulls of the Hornet drones burned red and orange in reentry, but from the *Redemption*'s distance, they appeared as little more than dark objects against the yellow backdrop. Somewhere under them was a bloom of blue death ready to tear through their hulls.

"Ten seconds, sir," Lieutenant Poiu said.

"Come on," Coleman whispered. "Come on."

A small blue dot appeared below the Hornet formation. It grew by the second until it was nearly as big as the Hornets themselves. If it struck one of the lead fighters, the shrapnel from the blast alone would take out the majority of the formation.

"Two seconds," Lieutenant Poiu said. "One."

The Hornets veered hard, splitting into opposite directions. The blue blast erupted into visual, slicing between two Hornets, missing them by mere meters. A cheer went up on the bridge, and Coleman let out a nervous breath. They'd cleared the first hurdle, one they hadn't even known existed, but they'd topped it with barely a stumble. The rest of the plan could move forward.

"Sir!" Lieutenant Poiu said suddenly. "I'm picking up more readings, sir. Almost a dozen of them."

Coleman's throat dropped into his stomach. "Where?"

"Headed toward us, sir," Lieutenant Poiu said. "The planet's turrets have fired at us. At the *Redemption*."

# 47

*Drone Operation Center, SAS Redemption*
*High Orbit, Baranyk Homeworld*

MOSCOW STEPPED INTO THE DRONE OPERATION CENTER. HE WAS DRESSED in his flight suit, holding his flight helmet under his arm. He'd just completed his own briefing, and the first wave of Nighthawks were ready to launch at the captain's command. He still longed to be out there, itched to be in the fight, but for now, this was the closest he was going to get.

He stood off to the side, letting the door slide closed behind him, and scanned the room. The ninety-six drone pilots manned their operation bays, though only half were plugged in and wore their VR helmets. The rest watched the battle map, which showed a live view of the battle on the surface.

The two squadrons were separated by a thirty-second interval and flew higher above the ground than they'd simulated. It took Moscow a minute to see why, though when the first plasma blast erupted past the fighters, he quickly understood. The added elevation gave the pilots time to take evasive actions, and thus far, they hadn't lost a single fighter. They all knew the real test would come soon, though.

"Azure Squadron, we have visual on the target." Phantom's voice echoed through the vaulted ceiling of the operation center. "Prepare to break into Azure and Bronze flights, fifteen-second intervals. Crimson Squadron, circle the target and wait for my mark. And stay clear of the entrance. We can't afford to have you get caught in a plasma blast."

Affirmatives echoed through the room.

"Break!"

Azure Squadron's delta formation broke, with twelve fighters separating from the rest then breaking into two smaller flights of six. The lead six raced ahead, while the second lagged behind, creating a fifteen-second delta between them. What remained of the squadron did the same, creating a force of four separate flights of six fighters, each staggered by fifteen seconds, and a full squadron behind them in reserves.

The lead flight dove straight toward the rocky surface below, cutting through the cloud cover. The hill marking the hive loomed large, its entrance a black dot like an angry maw of a terrifying monster growing ever larger.

"Deploy flaps," Phantom said.

Flaps along the wings and fuselages of the Hornets extended outward, creating drag, and slowed the fighters to a more manageable speed.

"Remember," Phantom said, "our objective is the plasma turrets. We're the battering ram that'll allow our forces to storm the castle. Contact in five seconds. Good luck."

The mouth of the hill raced toward them. Moscow shifted from foot to foot nervously.

Then... darkness.

The image on the battle map shifted to show Phantom's first-person view. He'd shifted his view from standard to computer-aided for better visibility. The walls of the tunnel screamed past his cockpit. Red targeting brackets appeared around known plasma turrets, and without hesitation, Phantom fired two missiles. They exploded in a wave of rock and debris, peppering the hull of his Hornet.

On the other side of the tunnel, the Hornet in the dash-two position unleashed a missile, eliminating another plasma turret. A large chunk of debris struck its portside wing, sending it careening into the wall of the cavern in a ball of flames. The explosion took out the Hornet immediately behind it then caused two more behind to collide as they tried to avoid the carnage.

In the span of a second, the flight of six fighters had been cut in half. The remaining three Hornets raced onward, taking out four more turrets before disaster struck. Deeper into the tunnel, a blue image of burning plasma raced toward them.

"Evasive maneuvers!" Phantom bellowed.

The wave of plasma fire filled the tunnel like water in a pipe, extending from wall to wall, giving the Hornets nowhere to hide. It washed over them in a flood, destroying the remaining fighter drones in a flash.

"Bronze Flight, engage," Phantom said. "Crimson, you're on deck. Delta, standby. Keep pushing."

"Yes, sir!"

The image was replaced with the image of the lead fighter of Bronze Flight. They were closing on the tunnel entrance but at an angle that kept them safe from the plasma fire that now vented from the tunnel mouth. It burst from the hole like lava erupting from a volcano, venting into the atmosphere before gravity pulled it back to the surface. Steam rose from the rocky ground, yellow rock turning a glassy black.

As soon as it was clear, Bronze Flight dove into the tunnel. With the first set of turrets already destroyed, they increased their speed and had missiles away in moments. The next set of turrets were reduced to rubble in a blink, and the exploding debris missed the Hornet formation.

A third layer of turrets were already priming, their bowels burning white hot with plasma, but one of the weaknesses of the plasma turrets was that unlike the *Redemption*'s munitions, these couldn't be fired at will. Each round required a charging, and that took time. Before they could unleash their next wave of plasma fire, the Hornets attacked, leaving nothing but a cloud of dust in their wake.

As if learning from their mistakes, the Baranyk sacrificed the next layer of turrets, choosing instead to charge the ones near the back of the tunnel. The wave of plasma fire that followed enveloped Bronze Flight, but not before they reduced another layer of plasma turrets.

"Crimson Flight, wait for the plasma to vent and then give it a ten count before starting your next run. We can't allow our attacks to become too predictable."

"Yes, sir."

Plasma erupted from the mouth of the hive in a brilliant blue explosion. Crimson Flight was well above the fire and protected from its heat. They continued to circle the entrance to the hive, waiting—and were rewarded for their patience as a second eruption of plasma fire vented a split second later.

"*Redemption* actual, this is Phantom. We've nearly punched through. Launch the additional squadrons."

"Copy, Phantom. Launching squadrons."

Somewhere in orbit, another two dozen Hornets were exploding from the hull of the ship, ready to rip through atmo and join the fray. By the time they arrived, Moscow hoped the initial wave of fighters would be well inside the hive.

When a third eruption of plasma fire didn't immediately follow, Crimson Flight began their attack run and disappeared into the tunnel.

They were met with an immediate wave of plasma fire that destroyed the entire flight before they could launch a single missile.

*Shit!*

The enemy was onto them now. Moscow had expected it, though he'd hoped the Hornets would get at least one more attack run before being forced to change tactics. Fortunately, there was only one more layer of plasma turrets, and those were located near the rear of the tunnel.

Phantom, no longer piloting one of the drones, called up Bronze Flight's attack run and had his computer locate the remaining turrets and calculate their distance in the tunnel. The relative verticality of the tunnel made calculating the depth easy.

"Boomer," Phantom said, calling on the flight leader of Delta Flight, "we're nearly through. Time to introduce our friends to a little Welcome Party. Depth, eighteen seconds."

Boomer laughed over the radio. "On it, sir. Time to show them some hospitality."

Two Hornets broke away from Delta Flight and circled the mouth of the hive at a lower altitude, just above the lip of the tunnel. Once above its entrance, they dropped two of their bombs dubbed the Welcome Party then rejoined the rest of their flight in formation.

Moscow could see that Phantom hoped the smaller, slower munitions would go unnoticed and possibly mistaken for falling rock or other debris. He watched the countdown he'd pulled up on the battle map.

*Ten seconds.*

*Five.*

No plasma fire or explosions. That was a good sign.

Then a pair of deep, resounding booms registered. Dust billowed from the mouth of the hive but no plasma fire.

"Delta Flight," Phantom said, "go! Go! Go!"

Boomer sped into the hive. The tunnel was filled with smoke and dust, but there was no enemy fire. By the time they got to the back of the tunnel, they discovered the turrets had been reduced to nothing more than molten rock.

"All Hornets, engage!" Phantom bellowed as Boomer's flight came to the end of the tunnel, spun, and angled into the adjoining chamber. The remaining Hornet fighters dove into the tunnel, hot on Delta Flight's heels. "*Redemption* actual, we're in. I repeat, the front door is open. Send in the cavalry. It's time to storm the castle."

# 48

*Bridge, SAS Redemption*
*High Orbit, Baranyk Homeworld*

THE PLASMA BLAST RIPPED PAST THE *REDEMPTION*, MISSING BY LESS THAN ten kilometers. If Coleman hadn't taken immediate action, it would have hit them directly in the starboard side. Larger than the plasma blasts from the Baranyk fighters, its destructive power was undeniable. At the bare minimum, it would have punched through the *Redemption*'s reinforced hull, and that was if it didn't skewer them altogether. And more were already on their way.

"Forward thrusters!" Coleman bellowed. "Full reverse!"

They hadn't gained much speed yet, roughly twelve thousand kilometers an hour to maintain their geosynchronous orbit, but even in vacuum, it took a lot of power to navigate the *Redemption*. Even more to slow it down.

*In a world where speed is life, we're too slow.*

His navigation officer repeated his full-reverse order, and within moments, the ship rumbled. Coleman staggered as the forward thrusters fired, countering the ship's momentum to slow their course.

Coleman watched the battle map as it updated with the

*Redemption*'s change in speed. A red dotted line showed the incoming plasma blast's trajectory, which now appeared in front of the green dotted line that represented the *Redemption*'s current course. If everything went as projected, the blast would miss them by less than five kilometers.

*They're getting closer*, Coleman thought. *It's only a matter of time until one of those hits us.*

They weren't able to maneuver the same way as his old Nighthawk, but they did have two advantages, and both played into his hands. The first was the sheer distance. They maintained a geosynchronous orbit almost forty thousand kilometers above the surface. That gave them time to get the giant hunk of steel moving. And because the plasma blasts mimicked basic ballistics, which had no way of changing course once fired, their maneuvers, up until this point, had been successful.

"The Baranyk are launching additional plasma blasts, sir," Lieutenant Poiu said.

New red indicators appeared on the battle map, each accounting for the *Redemption*'s new course.

"We can't keep this up," Commander Garcia said. "We're sitting ducks up here. We have to take out those turrets."

"I know," Coleman said. "Lieutenant Poiu, what's the status of our drone squadrons? Have they got through atmo yet?"

Coleman had ordered them out as soon as Phantom punched through the Baranyk's tunnel defenses.

"Almost, sir," Lieutenant Poiu said. "They should be through the last of it in thirteen seconds."

"Good," Coleman said. "Have Phantom carve off a bombing flight and carpet those ground turrets."

"On it, sir."

Coleman let out a long breath. Eliminating the ground turrets would give them more time, but it wouldn't help with the plasma fire the enemy had already launched.

"They're getting smarter," Commander Garcia said.

Coleman agreed. The first blast had been launched directly at them and made Coleman commit to a direction. The second would have hit them had they continued on that trajectory. But now their options were limited, and the Baranyk had them boxed in. They'd launched three more successive blasts, each anticipating different speeds and maneuvers.

If they continued slowing down, the first new blast would hit them. Speed back up, and the second would hit its mark. Maintain current speed, and the third would land.

The safest bet was to jump deeper into the system. The computer had already plotted a fallback position, but doing so would increase the lag time with the Hornets and make their mission more difficult. He could let one of the blasts hit, trusting the reinforced hull to minimize damage and give his bombers time to take out the ground turrets. But that had obvious risk.

*Too much*, he decided.

"Fire starboard thrusters," Coleman ordered. "Rotate us ninety degrees."

"Taking a page out of your old piloting days?" Commander Garcia asked.

"Something like that." Coleman gave him a confident smile.

The rumbling in the deck changed as the forward thrusters stopped firing and were replaced with those on the starboard side. As he'd said, the maneuver would rotate the ship ninety degrees. More importantly, given the ship's rectangular design, it would provide the smallest surface area to hit. If the previous blasts just had to hit the target, this one would have to be a bull's-eye, and Coleman was trusting the Baranyk weren't that good.

"Hornets are through atmo, sir," Lieutenant Poiu said. "Bombers en route. ETA four minutes."

"Thank you, Lieutenant."

Coleman kept his attention focused on the incoming plasma blast. It would arrive before the bombers, and if the plasma struck, it could render the entire mission a failure. And the computer's estimated course had that blast right on target.

Coleman leaned forward against the padded railing, his sweaty hands squeezing its rung. There was nothing left to do but wait. Wait and hope.

The seconds felt like hours as the blast rocketed toward them. Ten seconds before impact, the starboard thrusters cut out and the portside fired, keeping the *Redemption* from overrotating. Coleman had done everything he could do—everything except the one maneuver that guaranteed their safety.

*Please, God, let this work.*

Warning claxons sounded as Coleman braced for impact.

The *Redemption* shuddered violently as a terrible screech ripped across its bow. The lights flickered, sparks flaring. Coleman forced himself to keep his eyes open, to stand proud and confident. If this was the end, the last thing his bridge crew would ever see was a confident man standing defiantly against the odds, doing everything in his power to give humanity a chance.

In the wake of the terrible screech came a quiet calm. No rumbling through the deck. No additional warning claxons. Red warning lights flashed, bathing the bridge in a bloody hue.

"Damage report!" Coleman said.

"The blast struck the portside, sir," Lieutenant Poiu said. "It looks like it carved through the entire length of the ship, but..." The tactical officer trailed off as he read the incoming data.

"But what, Lieutenant?"

"It looks like it was a glancing blow. We lost sensors and turrets on decks thirty-six through fifty, sir, but no reported hull breaches."

Coleman released his grip from the railing. They hadn't escaped the blast unscathed. The loss of their sensors and half their antiaircraft batteries would be a massive blow, but they were still alive. They were still in the fight.

"Thank you, Lieutenant," Coleman said. "That's great news."

Coleman returned his attention to the battle map, where the Hornet bombers were preparing for their attack run. They flew in standard formation, six fighters shaped like a V, ready to turn turret to rubble.

The first bombs hit the surface in a fiery explosion, but the ones that landed inside the turret openings did the most damage. The surface ballooned upward then exploded into a fireball of rock, debris, and plasma that set off a chain reaction of destruction. Within seconds, the entire valley was aflame.

The Hornets circled the destruction, checking for signs of activity, that any of the turrets were still active and operational. All they found was destruction.

A triumphant cheer rang through the bridge. Commander Garcia slapped Coleman on the back, hard enough to knock him to the side.

"Congratulations, sir," Commander Garcia said. "It worked."

Try as he might, Coleman couldn't keep the smile off his face. "We're still in the fight, Jaime. Still in the fight." He turned back to his tactical officer. "Have those bombers return to their squadron. They have a job to fin—"

"Contact!" Lieutenant Poiu bellowed.

*Contact? Where? Did another Baranyk ship arrive?*

A quick look at the battle map answered all of Coleman's questions. Not another Baranyk ship. The same one. Except it had followed the *Redemption*. He cursed silently—he himself had said the enemy was capable of intrasystem jumps, and he'd just proven himself correct.

"It's launching fighters, sir," Lieutenant Poiu said.

A wave of red washed over the battle map, crashing toward the lone green wireframe image of the *Redemption* on the display.

"Rotate starboard ninety degrees and open fire!" Coleman ordered.

The deck roared beneath him as the ship rotated its good side toward the new enemy. It wouldn't be enough. There were hundreds of enemy fighters. And with only one fully operational side, there was no way they could fight them all off.

"Launch fighters," Coleman said.

It was time for the Nighthawks to enter the fray.

# 49

*Cockpit, Nighthawk*
*High Orbit, Baranyk Homeworld*

Moscow rocketed down the launch tube. For the first time in hours, his nervousness was finally abating, and he felt like himself. Something about the weight of three G's and an impending life-or-death struggle had a way of centering a man.

Like bullets from a revolver, the squadron of Nighthawks shot from the *Redemption* and formed into their various flights, each in a six-fighter delta formation. The incoming enemy had no semblance of order. They were a swarm of fighters, hundreds strong, all bearing down on the *Redemption*.

"All fighters, listen up," Moscow said. "We have one objective. Keep those fighters away from the *Redemption*. Every minute we keep them off her is another minute our squadrons on the surface have to find the leader of the Baranyk. So stay tight. Nothing fancy. And let's remind the enemy who we are."

The *Redemption*'s antiaircraft batteries fired in full force, cannon and tracer fire ripping past the Nighthawk formations with terrible intentions. The enemy was too far away to make out individual kills, but Moscow knew at least some of the defensive fire met its target. As soon as the Nighthawks engaged, the *Redemption*'s computers would have to be more selective with its defensive fire lest it inflict friendly fire. Moscow would have to give them a window to continue the onslaught.

"On my mark, accelerate at twenty-five percent thrust," Moscow said. "Maintain delta formations and lay down a carpet of cannon fire. Missiles where the fights clump together. Then veer off forty-five degrees positive and negative-Z, standard cadence. Let's see if we can get a few of these bastards to chase us."

Moscow waited another few seconds as the affirmatives from his flight leaders rolled in. Then, after a series of short, aggressive breaths, he tightened his hands around the controls. "Engage!"

The Nighthawks zipped forward, maintaining their four delta formations with a crispness the captain had to appreciate. Moscow steadied the throttle at twenty-five percent thrust and did a quick check that nobody was falling out of line. They weren't. They were too well-oiled. Too well practiced. Not just the best of the best but the uncommon among the uncommon. The very pinnacle humanity had to offer.

The enemy was close enough now that Moscow could make out individual fighters. He let the computer autoselect targets based on the same parameters he'd given his fighters—identify groups and clusters—and a series of red brackets appeared. He squeezed the trigger twice, paused, then squeezed a third and fourth time.

His Nighthawk bucked as multiple missiles disengaged from his wings and rocketed toward their targets. Dozens more from the Nighthawk formations appeared half a second later. They were all quickly lost in the black, but Moscow watched on his HUD as they tracked their targets, disappearing at the same time as a distant series of flashes.

"Splash one!" Moscow bellowed.

"More like splash fifty," Squawks said over the radio.

Moscow grinned. Squawks was right. Their computers had done a great job of targeting groups of fighters where their missiles could inflict maximum damage. Not only had they taken out those select groups, but the debris had crashed into other nearby fighters, taking them out of the fight as well.

Moscow settled into his seat. It felt good to be back out where he could be making a difference. A *real* difference.

"Cannons!" Moscow ordered. He thumbed the switch on his joystick from missiles to cannons then squeezed the trigger in a series of short bursts. His fighter rumbled with each one of them, the only sign that its nose-mounted cannon was indeed firing. That was, until the lead Baranyk fighters exploded into a mess of organic matter.

Sparks flew from noses of the lead Nighthawks to either side of him as they continued the onslaught. If the enemy had been flying in any sort of formation, it would have long been broken, but massed as they were, and outnumbering the human fighters at least six to one, they glided forward unfazed.

Blue streaks of plasma fire slid past his fighter.

"Offset forty-five degrees on my mark," Moscow said. "We're going to create a lane for the *Redemption*'s battlements and see if we can draw a few of these guys off her. Break!"

The six flights broke in six different directions. Those on either end of the formation shot north of the orientation line, the next ones south, and the two middle flights north and south as well. The maneuver left a clear lane for the *Redemption* to fire, and that was exactly what she did.

Opening up her full array of antiaircraft batteries, the *Redemption* fired with everything she had. Dozens of ships in the middle of the incoming Baranyk mass exploded in a sea of yellow slime, pieces of carcass destroying even more of their formation.

Moscow grunted under the stress of the maneuver. His G-suit tightened around his limbs, keeping his blood from pooling in his extremities and causing blackout. It kept him conscious, but it wasn't enough to keep the black spots from appearing in the corners of his vision.

Leveling out, he saw that several dozen Baranyk fighters had broken from the main horde, following the six flights that had veered away from their original trajectory. Those that remained now swarmed the *Redemption*, which fought like hell to swat them away.

"Fighter pairs!" Moscow ordered. "Do what you can to eliminate the stragglers. But don't lose sight of the objective. The *Redemption* comes first!"

Moscow's flight broke into three fighter pairs, each veering off in different directions. The pursuing enemy fighters did the same, following what they thought were easy targets.

"All right, Dumper," Moscow said to his wingman. "Let's do this."

"Hell yeah, sir."

Dumper, named after his generous backside, was Moscow's third wingman since joining the Forgotten, and he'd only just started flying with him. They weren't as fluid as they should be, but Moscow was confident he could pick up the slack.

Still veering off from the other fighters, Moscow and Dumper spun one hundred and eighty degrees so that they were facing the incoming enemy fighters even though their movement had them going backward. The maneuver wreaked havoc on his spine, and the only thing that kept him from being ripped out of the cockpit was the harness digging into his chest. It also brought the enemy directly into their sights. A couple short bursts of cannon fire later, the pursuing enemy was reduced to space sludge.

Several more Baranyk fighters engaged, and each met a similar fate.

"Back to the *Redemption*," Moscow said.

Dumper voiced his affirmative and took position on Moscow's wing. Because they had deviated from the main formation, they had a clear path to their ship. They looped around and came in at the front of the *Redemption*. Flying its length from bow to stern, they kept their fighters level so that any overshot didn't hit the ship.

Moscow squeezed his trigger, firing burst after burst. He took out half a dozen fighters, Dumper doing the same, then, with the attack run complete, looped around preparing for another. Their tactic had caught the attention of a few fighters who broke away from the main horde in pursuit. Plasma fire shot past their cockpits.

"Shit!" Moscow zigged and zagged, spun and dove, but couldn't shake the enemy fighters. Dumper had similar issues. They might have been toast if it hadn't been for Squawks.

"Looks like you have a couple clingers," he said. "Need me to wipe them for you?" Squawks didn't wait for a response. "Break twelve degrees starboard in three, two, one, break!"

Moscow threw his joystick to the right, angling his fighter starboard. Squawks and Nails dove in at a perfect attack angle, ripping through the enemy fighters like a knife through bread.

"Thanks, Squawks," Moscow said.

"Nothing to it," Squawks said.

"Don't listen to him," Nails said, chiming in. "He'll make you buy him a drink next chance he gets."

Moscow couldn't help but laugh. The cockpit was like a second home to him, and the banter was a big part of that. Dumper reappeared at his wing, and the two of them swooped back around. Just seconds behind, Squawks and Nails were cutting across the *Redemption* in a similar maneuver that Moscow and Dumper had just completed.

Still, blue plasma fire coated the *Redemption*'s hull, burning through steel and leaving massive pockmarks in its wake. Moscow couldn't tell if any had breached the hull yet, but it was only a matter of time. Worse yet, the enemy seemed to realize that an entire side of the *Redemption*'s batteries were inoperable and focused their attacks there.

Moscow and Dumper followed in Squawks and Nails's wake, destroying the ships that had filled the void left by Squawks and Nails. It was a game of cat and mouse. The only problem was Moscow didn't know which they were.

# 50

*Bridge, SAS Redemption*
*High Orbit, Baranyk Homeworld*

"Hull breach!" Lieutenant Poiu shouted after a particularly vicious shudder. "Decks seventeen and eighteen!"

"Get containment and maintenance teams down there now," Commander Garcia said.

"On it, sir!"

Coleman let his XO handle the ship's issues. His attention was focused solely on the battle at hand. It was progressing, maybe not exactly as planned, but within the bounds of expectation.

"They're focused on us," Coleman said loudly enough for Commander Garcia to hear, though it was more of an audible thought than anything.

"Remove us, and they all but win the battle," his XO said.

"I'd hoped they'd engage the Nighthawks," Coleman said. "It would give us more time. Instead, we're taking a beating. I don't know how much longer we can hold out."

As if some malevolent God were listening, the *Redemption* took another direct hit, causing the ship to shake hard enough that Coleman had to grip the bridge's railing.

"Lieutenant Poiu, remind the Forgotten their primary objective is to protect the *Redemption*," Coleman said. "If they can't keep the Baranyk fighters off us, we'll be forced to pull back."

"Yes, sir."

Coleman returned to his captain's chair at the top ring of the bridge. He rarely sat in the thing, feeling more comfortable on his feet, but set within the chair's armrests was the battle map's control panel. His fingers raced across its glassy surface, replacing the image above with that of the battle below.

Escorted by a fresh squadron of Hornets, the *Redemption*'s drop ships, commonly referred to as Storks, were just about to enter the hive's entrance. In their bellies was a full platoon of marines, including a squad of what Sergeant Haniger had called Firestarters. Coleman had only seen them once. Seven feet tall, encased in full battle armor, and armed with a flamethrower that could launch napalm one hundred meters, they were the living embodiment of hell.

If the Storks could land in the nursery and the Firestarters could unleash their inferno, then maybe the Baranyk would be forced to split their forces and come to the hive's aid.

*Maybe.*

Coleman hated maybes. They were foolish hopes that ended in pain.

"Lieutenant Poiu," Coleman said. "How many Hornets do we still have onboard?"

"That haven't been flown, sir?" Lieutenant Poiu asked.

"Yes, Lieutenant. How many in reserve?"

"Forty-eight, sir."

Two squadrons' worth. Coleman had intended to keep them in reserve, to use them in the Baranyk hive to scout and destroy plasma turrets. But good intentions were never enough.

"Launch another squadron," Coleman ordered. "Give our Nighthawks some added firepower."

Lieutenant Poiu voiced his affirmative, and moments later, the ship's deck rumbled with the telltale sign of the fighters being launched. Coleman let himself lean back in the captain's chair. This had been the hardest part of assuming responsibility of the *Redemption*. He was used to being *in* the shit. Not directing it. Like a master chess player, he'd put his people in position. Now it was their time to execute.

"Sir!" Ensign Richey shouted. "I'm picking up a new Baranyk signal."

Coleman rushed to her terminal. "What is it?"

She'd isolated it on her terminal. Coleman couldn't be sure, but he thought the wavelength looked familiar.

"It's the same signal as Kryos, sir," Ensign Richey said.

*The mind-control signal.*

The Baranyk were searching for anyone on the *Redemption* with a brain abnormality that would allow the Overlord to control them as he controlled the rest of the Baranyk. Dr. Rydell had scanned the entire crew twice, confirming and reconfirming that nobody was susceptible to the Baranyk signal. Nobody save one.

*Coda.*

---

"ISOLATE THE SIGNAL!" DR. NAIDOO SAID AS SHE AND DR. RYDELL RUSHED to Coda's gurney.

Strapped down tightly, Coda couldn't see the commotion around him, but by the way the shadows darted around him, he could tell the medical staff was working urgently.

"Okay, good," Dr. Naidoo said. "Now, overlay the baseline." The technician must have done it because the next thing Dr. Naidoo said was, "Good. It hasn't changed."

There was more than a hint of relief in her voice. "Now, overlay the countersignal and give me the projected outcome."

A tense silence, broken only by the beeps and chimes from the medical equipment, filled the space. A quiet that tense might as well have been a scream. Unable to see what was happening, Coda felt his heartrate spike. Adrenaline pumping, his restricted limbs clawed to break free.

"It's working," Dr. Naidoo said.

"What is it?" Coda asked. "What's working?"

Coda couldn't explain it, but he could almost *feel* their eyes on him. Something was happening, something they weren't telling him. Something about *him*.

*The signal,* he thought. *The Overlord is hitting us with their signal.*

There was movement on the edge of his vision, and a shadow creeped over him. It took Coda a moment to recognize the friendly face of Dr. Rydell, the white lights of the medical ward above her.

"Coda, can you hear me?" Dr. Rydell pulled a small penlight from her smock and shone it in Coda's eyes. She seemed pleased with the result. "Coda, I need you to answer me. You're being hit with the Baranyk signal, but it appears the countersignal is nullifying its effects. Can you hear me?"

Coda tried to blink away the black splotches caused by the penlight. "Yes. It's okay. I'm okay."

Speaking the words aloud brought tears to his eyes. He was *free.* They had given him his life back. "I'm okay, Doc," Coda said. "Thank you."

Dr. Naidoo appeared beside Dr. Rydell, and together, they ran him through a series of physical tests. Coda did as instructed, never so happy to move his fingers and toes in his life.

"Good," Dr. Naidoo said. "His physical response looks promising."

Over the next several minutes, Dr. Naidoo and her staff ran even more tests on him. From moving his limbs to repeating complicated phrases, they did everything they could to prove that Coda wasn't under the influence of the Baranyk. Even in the end, Coda could see it in their eyes that they weren't entirely convinced.

*After all, how can one prove that they're themselves?*

But Coda already knew the truth. They'd done it. He'd escaped the Overlord.

---

THE *REDEMPTION* SHOOK AGAIN. DISTANTLY, CAPTAIN COLEMAN HEARD Lieutenant Poiu's report and Commander Garcia's reply, but his attention was squarely on the battle reports coming in. His Nighthawks were doing everything they could to keep the enemy off them, and the newly arrived Hornets were helping with that. The plasma fire hitting the *Redemption* was coming fewer and farther between now, and there were early signs that the battle was swinging in their favor.

The marines had landed in the first cavern and were laying waste to the pupae with terrible efficiency. It hadn't taken long before they'd been met with a fierce resistance, but the Firestarters with their massive flamethrowers and the traditional squads made for a devastating combination. Baranyk from all parts of the hive continued to pour into the cavern to protect their young, but the marines held their ground. Any time Coleman feared they would be overrun, the Hornets provided air cover, beating the enemy back enough to allow the marines to advance.

The Hornets themselves continued their push into the hive. Already, they'd discovered several other chambers, including other nurseries with pupae and another with larvae, as well as several supply chambers. The plasma turrets were less common deeper in the hive. But any they found, the Hornets destroyed.

All in all, the battle was going well. Too well, in fact. Coleman couldn't help but feel like he was missing something.

"Captain," Ensign Richey said. "I've got Dr. Naidoo on the line. Sounds urgent."

The doctor had the ability to reach out to him directly via his earpiece but clearly knew better than to disrupt his attention during a battle.

"Put her through," Coleman said.

"Captain," came Dr. Naidoo's voice in his ear.

"What is it, Doctor?"

"The patient appears to be doing well, sir," she said. "We are reading zero negative effects from the Baranyk signal."

Coleman's body tensed. "It's working?"

"It appears that way, sir," Dr. Naidoo said. "We have completed our physical examination and brain scans, and all appears normal. Beyond that... there's no way to know for sure."

"Is he alert?" Coleman asked.

"Yes."

"Put him on."

"Yes, sir."

After a brief pause, another voice came on the line.

"Sir?" Coda said.

"How are you feeling, Commander?" Coleman asked.

"Like myself, sir."

Coleman tapped his finger on the side of his chair. Did he dare to hope? When everything was going so well, did he dare to push? Why perform a risky maneuver when he didn't need to? Because it was in a fighter pilot's DNA to push the envelope. To take risks. To take every potential advantage.

"Back at the Terran Fleet Academy, when I invited you to train with the Forgotten, you asked me a very important question. Do you remember what that was?"

"I do, sir," Coda said.

"What was it?"

"'Will I get a chance to kill Baranyk?' sir."

"And what did I tell you?"

"You said yes, sir."

Coleman inhaled slowly. The doctors could run all the tests they wanted to, but Coleman knew that voice. Knew that tone. His pilot was back.

"Get your ass down to the drone operation center," Coleman said. "It's time to make good on that promise."

# 51

*Corridor, SAS Redemption*
*High Orbit, Baranyk Homeworld*

CODA *RAN* THROUGH THE CORRIDORS. DRESSED IN HIS FLIGHT SUIT, HE barely received a second glance. They were in the middle of a battle, after all.

Slowing as he came to the double doors of the drone operation center, Coda gathered his breath and strode in. The two-story room, easily one of the largest on the *Redemption*, was alive with activity. The room smelled of sweat and determination, and the curses and battle chatter that Coda was accustomed to hearing over the radio echoed off the room's bulkhead.

Coda quickly found Phantom, who was conveniently removing his flight helmet and sliding out of his operation bay. Coda's orders had been simple: report for duty and fight wherever Phantom told him to fight.

Coda snapped to attention and gave Phantom a sharp salute. "Lieutenant Commander O'Neil reporting for duty, sir."

Phantom returned the salute. "Coda, I just got off the line with the captain. It seems he wants you fighting a real war machine."

Coda smiled. The competition between the Nighthawk and Hornet pilots was little more than a sibling rivalry, but that didn't mean they didn't take every chance they had to enter into its pissing contest. "Something like that, sir."

"Good. We could use you out there." Phantom glanced up at the battle map, which showed the familiar terrain of the Baranyk hive. "We're fighting on two fronts and dropping like flies any time we encounter those turrets."

"Sorry to hear that, sir," Coda said, not knowing how else to respond. "How can I help?"

"Take my bay," Phantom said, indicating his operation bay. "I'm better suited out here, where I can coordinate the larger strategy more effectively."

"Yes, sir." Coda failed to hide the glee in his voice.

He sat down in the drone operation bay, feeling an overwhelming sense of familiarity. Each cockpit, from the Terran Fleet Academy to the various ships in the Sol Fleet, had a similar design. The bay was equipped with a panel in front of him complete with the various buttons and levers required for flight. The seat was clearly modeled after the Nighthawk's gel seat but lacked the flight harness that would normally hold a pilot in place. The stick between his legs was similar, though it didn't have the resistance and weight of his fighter. And of course, there was no motion. Just him, his seat, the stick, and the panel.

"Another flight is about to launch," Phantom said from behind. "You'll be in the dash-five position."

"Thank you, sir," Coda said. "Where are we headed?"

"The hive."

"Hell yeah, sir."

Phantom barked a quick laugh and gave him a sharp nod. "Good luck out there, Coda."

"Thank you, sir."

Phantom strode away, and Coda slid on the VR helmet. His view was immediately replaced with a first-person view from the seat of the drone's would-be cockpit. He barely had time to collect his bearings and settle into the seat before the fighter was fired through the launch tube. One moment he was in the *Redemption*, then he was in the black.

*I'm back.*

His change in fortune had been so abrupt, he hadn't had an opportunity to reflect on it. Within minutes, he'd gone from being restrained on a gurney to piloting a war fighter. He didn't have time to reflect beyond that. A battle raged around the ship.

Baranyk fighters swarmed in, targeting the *Redemption*, while Hornets and Nighthawks alike fought to keep them at bay. As it always seemed, the human forces were outnumbered, though clearly, the enemy was more interested in the *Redemption* than the rest of the fleet. It made the enemy fighters easier targets, but the ship was taking a beating. There were several pockmarks where there'd been breaches in the hull, and in the brief moments Coda watched, the *Redemption* took two more direct hits that rocked the deck under him.

Coda fought every instinct he had to aid, and instead took his position in the formation and followed as the rest of the Hornets made for the planet. He tightened his grip around the joystick, willing himself to focus. Squawks, Nails, Moscow, and the rest of the Forgotten were out there, protecting the *Redemption*. He couldn't let himself be distracted by their task. He had his own.

They cut through the atmosphere and made directly for the hive's entrance. It looked exactly as it had in their simulations, and Coda was grateful that he and the rest had flown their own training hops. He didn't miss a beat as the formation crested the hill, spun, and dove into the tunnel.

Without slowing down, the flight screamed through the tunnel, past its ruined plasma turrets then into the first chamber. Where the entrance tunnel had been empty and devoid of all life, the chamber was its opposite.

The ground itself was *crawling*. Thousands of Baranyk charged the brigade of marines who were already on the ground. A squad equipped with massive flamethrowers laid waste to everything in front of them, while more marines behind and stationed on the high ground the rocky surface provided offered cover fire.

Grenades exploded in the writhing mass of Baranyk, sending yellow blood and limbs into the air, but for every Baranyk they killed, three more took its place. The marines were putting up a hell of a fight, but if they didn't get cover fire soon, they would be overrun.

"Crimson Flight," Rascal, Crimson Flight's flight leader, said over the radio. "Follow my mark and provide cover fire for our marines below."

A series of affirmatives echoed across the line, then they were banking hard to starboard and racing toward the marines' position. Coda's hand tightened around the stick, his thumb ensuring he had his cannons selected, then squeezed the trigger. His joystick vibrated as rounds erupted from the nose of the Hornet. They tore through Baranyk as if they were nothing more than paper targets.

Crimson Flight ripped through the heart of the mass, tearing deep gouges through their ranks, then angled around for another pass, this time cutting across diagonally. The drones weren't equipped with exterior auditory sensors, but Coda thought he could almost hear the high-pitched squeals of the dying enemy.

Any normal enemy would have retreated or taken cover under the onslaught, but not the Baranyk. Not under the Overlord's control. The enemy warriors continued to push. The flamethrowers were proving incredibly effective, though, and coupled with the marines' discipline, the human forces didn't just hold their position but advanced.

Refusing to allow the enemy to gain any footing, Crimson Flight carved three more rents through the enemy mass, even expelling a handful of missiles to soften their ranks, before disengaging to make for deeper parts of the hive.

While isolated in the medical ward, Coda hadn't heard anything about the battle. He soon learned that the drone squadrons had found more than half a dozen chambers, with more than three times the number of tunnels. Some were used for storage, but others housed the Baranyk colony. Many of those chambers were strangely vacant.

A good part of their population, Coda expected, were attempting to fight off the marines, but from what he'd seen of the hive so far, it had housed hundreds of thousands—far more than were currently engaged with the human ground forces. Did that mean the bulk of the missing Baranyk were warriors with the fleet? Or pilots flying their organic ships? Or was something else at play?

They continued deeper underground, following tunnels and discovering new chambers, often coming to dead ends. As frustrating as each was, Coda took it as a sign of progress. Dead ends meant they were finding the limits of the hive. It was only a matter of time until they discovered a tunnel that led to the Overlord's chambers. Instead, they found where the missing Baranyk had gone.

After successfully eliminating another set of turrets in a short tunnel, Coda came out into another chamber. This one was wider and longer than the others, but its ceiling hung lower, and light shone through hundreds of small holes. Based on the ground's topography, this chamber was somehow closer to the surface. Dark shapes, slightly larger than the Hornet drones, hung ominously from the tunnel's ceiling.

"What are those?" someone asked over the radio.

Coda's first thought was a large alien bat, but as he slowed and shone his fighter's headlamps onto one, his blood ran cold. He knew that shape. He'd seen hundreds of them. Thousands. More.

"Baranyk fighters," Coda said.

Then, as if the enemy had heard him, they dropped from the tunnel's ceiling.

"Evasive maneuvers!" Phantom yelled.

To Coda's left, a ball of orange flame lit the corridor. Before it burned out, another flashed to his right. The enemy fighters had fallen directly onto two Hornets, destroying them without ever firing a shot.

Coda didn't wait for an order to open fire. He angled his fighter close to the chamber's ceiling and flew its length, squeezing the trigger, destroying enemy fighters before they had a chance to disengage from the ceiling. Around him, several pilots did the same, but there were too few Hornets. For every fighter they eliminated, two more dropped, and in moments, the chamber was alive with activity.

The Baranyk fighters massed into a swarm as Coda reached the end of the chamber then banked hard to make a pass in the opposite direction. To his surprise, most of the swarm, hundreds of Baranyk fighters in all, flew out of the holes and above ground. What remained was a force only slightly larger than their flight.

What remained of Crimson Flight's squadron broke. The drone pilots liked to employ large formations and collective firepower to make up for their biggest disadvantage: the lag time. But the *Redemption* was close enough that it was minimal, allowing Coda and the rest to operate their drones almost as if they were Nighthawks. The chamber's narrow confines would have made formations difficult anyway.

A Baranyk fighter zipped across Coda's trajectory on the six of one of the drones. Coda banked hard, moving into firing position behind it.

After a moment, he got missile lock, squeezed the trigger, and eliminated the target before it had a chance to destroy its prey.

Coda whooped. He'd known deep down that there were other ways to make a difference, that he had more to offer than death, but this was what he'd been trained to do. His short time in leadership had taught him that it was best to put people in positions where they could be most effective. And this was that for Coda.

He fell into the rhythm of the battle, allowing its underlying beat to influence him. Moving almost on instinct, he banked and swerved, toggling between guns and missiles, focusing first on providing backup. It was a tactic he'd long since developed as a Nighthawk pilot when a downed fighter also meant a pilot's death. When he didn't do that, he used the chamber's natural terrain to his advantage, often flying between its stalactites and natural rock formations for cover then coming out and reengaging from an unexpected angle.

He relished the moment. His face hurt from the smile he hid under his helmet. He'd longed for this moment for so long, he wasn't going to let any of its details escape him. He savored the speed. Lived for the drag on his fighter's wings. Embraced the challenge the planet's gravity presented to his fuel and navigational thrusters. Most of all, he treasured every kill. Each downed fighter was one less enemy that could hurt him or his friends above.

He was ruthless and efficient. By the time the skirmish ended, only three fighters remained. Coda's breathing was heavy with the exhaustion of a job well done as Phantom's voice came over the radio.

"Reinforcements en route," he said. "Crimson Flight, hold position until they arrive."

"Yes, sir," Coda said.

"Where did the rest of those fighters go?" someone else asked. Chipmunk, based on the icon next to her fighter.

"Skyward" was all Phantom said. It was all he had to say. They all knew what that meant.

They were headed for the *Redemption.* If it was destroyed, the battle was over.

# 52

*Bridge, SAS Redemption*
*High Orbit, Baranyk Homeworld*

"Sir, I'm picking up multiple contacts accelerating from the planet's surface," Lieutenant Poiu said.

"Are they the fighters Lieutenant Cahill warned us about?" Coleman asked. Word had come from his drone squadron CAG moments ago.

"No, sir," Lieutenant Poiu said. "Well, yes, but I'm also picking up readings from other parts of the planet."

Coleman exchanged an uneasy glance with Commander Garcia. The fresh fighters from the surface already represented a large threat. What else could the enemy be preparing?

"Put it on the map," Coleman said.

"Yes, sir."

The battle map focused on the planet itself. The yellow planet had five separate red beacons shining where his tactical officer was picking up readings.

"Those are the other hives," Commander Garcia said.

"Yes they are," Coleman said. "Lieutenant Poiu, what am I looking at?"

"Enemy fighters, sir," Lieutenant Poiu said in a resigned tone. "Preliminary readings estimate... nearly four hundred, sir."

"Four *hundred*?" Coleman repeated.

"I thought we weren't expecting a large defensive presence?" Commander Garcia said.

Coleman did his best to keep his face stoic. He wanted to pace, to massage his forehead, anything to help him process the information faster. Four hundred fighters was larger than the entire force on the *Redemption*. There was outnumbered, then there was *outnumbered*. They couldn't contend with that.

As if to echo his thoughts, the ship shook under a massive impact then four more in quick succession. Red alarm claxons flared on the bridge.

"What the hell was that?" Commander Garcia asked.

"Multiple hull breaches," Lieutenant Poiu said. "Decks seventeen—"

"That wasn't a normal impact," Commander Garcia said. "What did they hit us with?"

"Unknown, sir," Lieutenant Poiu said. "Containment teams are on their way."

Coleman let the exchange wash over him. He was still focused on the incoming enemy. "Why now?"

"Hmmm?" Commander Garcia asked.

"Why wait until now to deploy their full force?" Coleman asked. "It doesn't make sense."

"They wanted to draw us in," Commander Garcia said. "Make us commit our resources then strike where we're weakest."

"Yes," Coleman agreed. "But there's something else. Something we're missing. It's like they never thought we were a threat to begin with. The Overlord is planning something, Jaime. I can feel it."

"I hope you're wrong, sir," Commander Garcia said. "Either way, we have to do something about those incoming fighters."

They were close enough now that the battle map was registering individual fighters flying from the planet, not just shining red beacons on the surface.

"How long until they arrive?" Coleman asked.

"Eight minutes, forty-three seconds, sir," Lieutenant Poiu said.

Coleman cursed silently. That wasn't enough time. Not nearly enough time. There was zero chance they could hold the enemy back. But what could he do? He couldn't just sit idle as a wave of enemy fighters were inbound. Withdrawing their forces meant allowing the enemy to regroup. Allowing the Overlord to hide. Retreat. Disappear. And without Joseph, they had no chance of finding him again.

This was their chance. Their *one* chance.

They couldn't disengage. And the *Redemption* couldn't hold its position. That left only one option.

"Lieutenant Poiu," Coleman said. "I want every available drone fighter on the surface. We're going after the Overlord with everything we have."

"What about the ship, sir?" Commander Garcia asked.

"We're falling back," Coleman said.

"You know what that'll do to the drones' lag time," Commander Garcia said.

"I do," Coleman said. Their fallback position was a little more than four hundred thousand kilometers from the planet, which meant the lag time was a little under two seconds. That would create massive challenges in the hive. "We don't have a choice, Commander."

"What about the Nighthawks, sir?" Commander Garcia asked.

"No," Coleman said, shaking his head.

"They're your best asset, sir," Commander Garcia pressed.

"Which is why we can't risk them. You saw what those turrets did to the drones, Jaime. No, they'll have a part to play in this. It's just not yet."

"Yes, sir," Commander Garcia said in a tone that said he disagreed but was powerless to do anything about it.

Coleman opened a line to Moscow and Phantom. "Gentlemen, it's Coleman. We've got a large force of enemy fighters inbound and are being forced to retreat. Phantom, I'm sending every available Hornet your way, but you'll be significantly hampered by lag time. Continue with your objective. Find the leader of the Baranyk."

"Yes, sir," Phantom said. "We're ready, sir. We've trained for this."

"Moscow, you're wasted out there," Coleman continued, "Prepare to RTB for rearm and refit."

"Sir—"

Coleman heard the objections in Moscow's tone the moment he

opened his mouth and shut him down just as quickly. "I know, Moscow. You'll get your chance. In the meantime, prepare to RTB."

"Yes, sir."

Coleman let out a quiet breath. The plan was decided. The Hornets would continue their assault. The marines would continue their raid. The Nighthawks would prepare for what came next. And Coleman would bide his time, wait for the exact moment to commit his most prized assets in a do-or-die gambit.

He watched as the last of the Hornets launched from the ship and raced toward the surface, then the Nighthawks broke off their attacks and landed back on the ship. Without fighter support, the *Redemption* took a beating. Plasma fire carved deep holes into her hull, and the ship bucked several more times with those terrible impacts.

*What the hell are they hitting us with?*

As soon as the last Nighthawk was aboard, Coleman gave the order to jump. He nearly fell into his chair as the world stretched in front of him. A collective calm washed over the bridge as it snapped back into focus. The Nighthawks weren't the only ones who needed to rearm and refit. His bridge crew needed a breather as well.

"Jump complete—"

"Sir!" Ensign Richey had her hands over her ears, listening to something in her earpiece. She looked up, terror marring her young face. "We have enemy hostiles onboard!"

"*What?*"

That's when he heard the distant gunfire.

"How the hell did the enemy get onboard?" Commander Garcia asked.

Then it all clicked into the place. "The impacts," Coleman said. "They weren't hitting us with a new weapon. They were landing raiding parties."

The enemy was on the ship. And most of their marines were on the surface, nearly four hundred thousand kilometers away.

# 53

*Corridor, SAS Abraham Lincoln*
*Rendezvous Point, Human Controlled Space*

ADMIRAL ORLOVSKY MARCHED THROUGH THE *ABRAHAM LINCOLN'S* corridors, careful to keep his back straight and expression firm, exuding every ounce of confidence he *didn't* feel. Knowing he was a living, breathing, walking lie, he did his best to avoid eye contact with the others in the corridors. When he failed, he could see his lie reflecting back at him through the mirrors of their eyes and hear their unspoken questions on their lips.

*What are we going to do next?*

It was an impossible question without an answer. It was the worst part about leadership. The unspoken reality that everyone looked to him for answers—especially when he didn't have them.

The reality was since their battle at Tau Titus, five human systems had fallen, and in the aftermath, the enemy had simply disappeared. Admiral Orlovsky hadn't believed the reports. The enemy had hit them like clockwork, following their pattern with precision, until they didn't. Since then, he had sent every reconnaissance drone in the fleet to scout nearby systems, and each and every one of them had come back emptyhanded.

The enemy hadn't disappeared—they'd vanished. He'd widened their search, but with each returning drone, the feeling of helpless dread coiling in his core stretched outward.

They were ghosts. The irrational part of him wanted to believe their sudden change in strategy had been the direct result of something Captain Coleman and the *Redemption* had done. Maybe they had the Overlord in their sights and the enemy fleet was hightailing it back to their home world to protect him.

*No*, he told himself again.

Even if it were possible for the Baranyk to jump halfway across the galaxy, which it wasn't, Coleman's chance of success was so small, it was barely worth thinking about. More likely, Orlovsky had fallen into some bait-and-switch strategy.

*Or they discovered a new piece of information they didn't have before, which caused them to alter their strategy.*

He couldn't shake that terrifying thought, and it was impossible to confirm. But he had an idea.

The sick bay door opened with a hiss as Orlovsky stepped into the medical ward. The beds lining the bulkhead were all occupied, and medical personnel scrambled from patient to patient. Often secluded on the bridge, he could easily forget the true cost of war. The painful cries of the wounded were stark reminders.

He found Dr. Sullivan near the back of the ward, where she was helping a wounded pilot. She had her thin blond hair tied back in a bun. Worry lines carved deep trenches in her skin. She was the best kind of doctor—one who cared. He'd met too many physicians who had become cynical after seeing thousands of patients and administering years of treatment, lacking the comforting bedside manner a doctor was meant to possess.

Dr. Sullivan was the opposite. If one could say anything negative about her, it was that she cared too much and took on too much of the pain herself.

She laid a hand on the pilot's leg as her medical assistant prepared a shot. The pilot still wore his flight suit, but much of it had been burned away, leaving red-and-black blistered skin below. He thrashed and screamed, the agony of plasma fire burning without remorse. Once burned by the enemy weapon, there was no escape. Not until the dead skin had been removed and new skin had replaced it. Even then, its victims often complained of its phantom pain.

"What is it, Admiral?" Dr. Sullivan asked without looking up. She sank a needle into the pilot's shoulder, providing the temporary promise of relief. "As you can see, I'm a little busy at the moment."

Orlovsky bit back a smile. It didn't matter how far he'd risen through the ranks, the doctor of his ship was always the one with the most power.

"I need to see O'Neil." He glanced around the ward and didn't see the former fighter pilot.

Dr. Sullivan let out a frustrated sigh. "I'm sorry, Admiral, but I have more pressing needs."

She turned back to her patients but hesitated when Orlovsky placed a gentle hand on her shoulder. "I assure you, Doctor. There is nothing more important right now than O'Neil."

She peered into his eyes and must have seen something in them, because she gave a quick order to her assistants then said, "Follow me."

Dr. Sullivan led him through a door and into a separate room just off sick bay that usually stored their various medications and extra medical equipment. It had been turned into a makeshift isolation ward with Joseph O'Neil's comatose body lying on a gurney at the room's center. Various probes were attached to his chest, arms, and head, and several monitors surrounded him, displaying his heart rate, blood pressure, oxygen levels, and brain activity.

"There's unfortunately been no change," Dr. Sullivan said. "His vitals remain spiked. His heart rate is well over one hundred beats per minute, his breaths quick and shallow, and the adrenal medulla is working overtime, pumping his body full of epinephrine at an alarming rate."

"Which means what exactly?"

"It means his body is in a steady state of fight-or-flight."

"And you have no idea what's causing it?"

Dr. Sullivan shook her head. The entire ordeal was strange. One moment, O'Neil was following the plan, meeting with his son in the Baranyk network at their scheduled time, and the next, his body had spasmed and his vitals had spiked. Ever since, he'd been in this state.

"My *guess*," Dr. Sullivan said, "is something happened to him in the

Baranyk network. Drs. Rydell and Naidoo's report cited evidence that injuries sustained in the network manifest physical reactions in the real world. Either way, his body can't sustain this forever."

Orlovsky grimaced. He'd provided the doctors' reports, as well as Captain Coleman's own, to Dr. Sullivan before O'Neil first connected to the network from his ship. He needed his fellow leaders prepared. Unfortunately, her thoughts echoed his own. Something had happened to him, and they had no way of determining what.

"What are they doing to you?" Orlovsky asked.

The situation was eerily similar to what Coleman had described when the host was under the Overlord's control. Only in those instances, the host was forced to act against their will.

"Could the Overlord be forcing him to remain connected to the network?" Orlovsky asked.

"I think it's safe to assume he's doing exactly that," Dr. Sullivan said. "The question is why?"

"To torture him?" Orlovsky asked. "Captain Coleman said there was something oddly personal between them."

"Torturing him for the sake of torturing him?" she asked.

"Sure," he said, but while it wasn't out of the question, it felt too simple. "Or to question him."

"Lieutenant O'Neil was out of the Sol Fleet for almost twenty years," Dr. Sullivan said. "His military intelligence is sorely lacking."

It was true. Any military intelligence O'Neil possessed would be so outdated it would be next to useless to the Overlord.

"Unless..." he said, a thought coming to him.

"Unless what, sir?"

"Unless there's something that O'Neil himself knows. Or rather, something only a human would know."

"Like what?"

"Military bases. Population centers. Or..." Orlovsky's blood ran cold. "Good god, it all makes sense."

"What makes sense?" There was fresh urgency in Dr. Sullivan's tone.

But Admiral Orlovsky had already moved on. "Find a way to break the connection. Drug him. Put him into a medically induced coma. I don't care, but do whatever you can to get him out of the Baranyk network."

"That's dangerous, sir," Dr. Sullivan said.

"Not as dangerous as the alternative."

She knew better than to ask, so all she said was, "I'll see what I can do, sir."

Orlovsky stormed from the room, through the adjoining sick bay, and back into the corridor. Like sick bay, the bridge was located in the belly of the ship, and he would be there in moments, but he opened a direct channel to his XO anyway.

"What is it, sir?" Commander Yoshida asked through his earpiece.

"Prepare the fleet to jump."

"Sir?"

"I'm on my way to the bridge," Orlovsky said. "I'll be there in two minutes. I want the order to go out and the ships moving toward the JumpGate by the time I get there."

"Yes, sir," Commander Yoshida said. "Where are we jumping, sir?"

Orlovsky hesitated, as if vocalizing the thought would somehow make it a reality. Like them, the enemy was prepared to strike humanity where it hurt most. Their home world.

"Earth. We're jumping to Earth."

# 54

*Bridge, SAS Redemption*
*Distant Orbit, Baranyk Homeworld*

"Enemy contact!" Lieutenant Poiu bellowed. "Decks nine, thirteen, seventeen, twenty-two, and thirty-five. Personnel requesting immediate assistance, sir."

"Deck thirty-five," Commander Garcia echoed. He looked at Coleman, concerned. "That's where our drone pilots are located."

Coleman gave him a gruff nod of acknowledgment. "How many onboard?"

"Unknown, sir," Lieutenant Poiu said. "I'll have numbers and live locations in two minutes."

"Let me know the moment you have something."

Coleman suppressed a curse. He hadn't planned for enemy boarding parties. His marines were on the planet's surface. Thankfully, the ship was equipped with a security force. More than that, he had an entire ship full of military personnel.

"In the meantime, close the blast doors and shut down all elevators on the infiltrated decks," Coleman continued.

"That's casting a death sentence to everyone down there,"

Commander Garcia said quietly enough that only Coleman could hear him.

Scanning the bridge, Coleman knew Garcia wasn't the only one thinking it.

"We can't let them reach the drone operation center," Coleman said. "Get with the master-at-arms and lead a team of security and nonessential personnel to sweep the other decks, beginning with twenty-two. But listen to me—no matter what happens to the rest of the ship, we can't lose our drone fighters or our ability to jump back to the planet."

Coleman expected his XO to exude some level of concern, but to the man's credit, his resolve seemed to harden. Back stiff, he snapped a salute with a crisp, "Yes, sir" and strode from the bridge, already using his earpiece to assemble a resistance.

"Where are we at with those scans, Lieutenant Poiu?"

"Coming in now, sir."

"Put it on the battle map."

The image on the battle map changed from the macro view of the planet to a single wireframe image of the *Redemption*, sixty-three levels at its tallest point. Each level was displayed with surprising detail. Red circles indicated the enemy's entrance points, while red dots moving through corridors represented the enemy forces on the ship.

"Scans indicate twenty Baranyk warriors onboard, sir," Lieutenant Poiu said. "Four per infiltrated deck."

Not an overwhelming force, but left unimpeded, twenty Baranyk could inflict catastrophic damage on the ship.

"Provide Commander Garcia with a live feed."

"Yes, sir."

*Good luck and Godspeed, gentlemen. Do us proud.*

---

THE SHIP WAS EERILY QUIET AS COMMANDER GARCIA LED HIS FIRETEAMS toward the beacon. He and the rest of their ragtag group had been outfitted for the battle by the master-at-arms. They wore full tactical gear, including a pair of clear tactical glasses under their combat helmets that gave them a live view of the enemy's movements. Since the captain had closed the blast doors and shut down all movement between decks, the enemy was still contained on the original infiltrated decks.

The beacon was a red symbol located in the middle of deck thirty-five and moving toward the center of the ship, where the drone operation center was located. Commander Garcia didn't know if the Baranyk were aware of that, but their movements indicated they were.

"We've arrived at the blast doors, sir," Commander Garcia said.

"Good work, Commander," Captain Coleman said through his headset.

Unlike much of the Sol Fleet, the fleet's ground forces still wore bulky headsets designed more than a hundred years ago. Their range was longer, the communication was crisper, and they were supposedly more reliable. When it came to noise suppression, though, humanity hadn't found a better design than the good old-fashioned over-the-ear design.

"Opening the door now."

Commander Garcia nodded to his fireteams and stepped back, raising his rifle. His men were already fanned out across the corridor, four having dropped to a knee, with Garcia and three others behind them, eight in all against four enemies within a confined space.

*I should have stayed retired.*

The interlocking segments of the blast door separated and slipped into the bulkhead, opening a passage beyond. Garcia's finger rested against the trigger of his rifle, but no enemy waited for them on the other side.

Garcia stepped out from behind the security guard and strode into the infected deck. The corridor on this side of the blast doors couldn't have been any more different than the one they'd left behind. The normal soft white glow of the bulkhead was dimmer and flickered where panels had been destroyed, creating long shadows. Sparks flashed, and electrical currents hissed as exposed wires brushed against metal surfaces.

The dead littered the deck—fallen bodies, torn to pieces. Blood smeared the white bulkhead and pooled across the deck. The poor souls had tried to escape but had come to a dead end of their own leader's creation. Unarmed and with nowhere to run, they hadn't stood a chance. He could almost see them banging against the blast doors, screaming, begging, pleading for someone to open them. They would have tried to pry open the doors as the enemy advanced on them. Salvation hadn't come, and there was nothing Garcia could do for them now except exact revenge and prevent as many more meaningless deaths as possible.

The red indicators on his tactical glasses showed that the enemy force was moving in the opposite direction, toward the center of the ship. Garcia waved the squad forward, and they advanced through the corridor, keeping their rifles trained forward, not trusting the ship's readings, refusing to be taken unawares.

A woman's scream cut through the corridor ahead of them. Garcia took one look at his team and darted forward double time. Rounding a corner, they came on the enemy and the pathetic resistance of the trapped personnel. A pair of men in bloodstained uniforms wielded fire extinguishers, swinging their bulk when the enemy warriors lunged at them.

The corridor's straight design left the enemy between the two human groups but also left the survivors in the line of fire. Garcia hadn't fired a weapon in years, but he didn't have a choice. He opened fire, shooting controlled bursts into the enemy's flank. His squad followed suit, and the corridor erupted into rifle fire.

High-pitched shrieks washed over them like a warm blanket as bits of Baranyk carapace and yellow alien blood splattered against the bulkhead. The two enemy warriors in the rear turned and charged Garcia's fireteams. One leaped and spun, landing on the bulkhead. Its sharp legs dug into the panels, keeping it suspended on the bulkhead as if it were in a tunnel. Panels of light shattered in its wake, and as the enemy warrior advanced, darkness followed.

They moved with terrifying speed, their size nearly filling the narrow corridor, but the squad's combined firepower was too much. The enemy shrieked as dozens of rounds peppered its carapace. When the advancing force finally fell lifeless to the deck, Garcia released a breath he hadn't realized he was holding and looked beyond the fallen enemy. The human resistance had been slaughtered, their bodies hardly recognizable. Their attackers had vanished.

Garcia cursed. The red dots were moving directly toward the drone operation center, and they seemed to be moving with more urgency.

"Move!" His legs pumping under him, Garcia opened a line to the ship's tactical officer. "Lieutenant Poiu, we've engaged the enemy, but a contingent has broken off and is making for the drone operation center. We're in pursuit but unlikely to arrive in time to halt their advance. Advise."

"Understood, Commander," Lieutenant Poiu said. "The captain has already ordered the drone operation center's doors sealed. They're not as thick as the blast doors, but they should hold long enough for you to engage."

"Roger." Garcia closed the line.

The remaining two Baranyk enemies were too big, too fast and powerful to keep up with. With every step, the enemy force created more space between them and their pursuers. And in their wake, they destroyed bulkheads and the light they provided.

Garcia's squad passed more than one frightened crew member and others that had been injured in the enemy's passing. He resisted the urge to drag them to safety and order a member of his team to provide medical assistance. He had his orders, and the sooner he completed them, the sooner medical personnel could arrive on the deck.

The red enemy dots on his tactical glasses stopped moving.

*They've arrived.*

Grinding his teeth, Garcia pushed harder. He was already tired and winded. Combined with his lack of recent firearms training, it wasn't a good combination. Worse yet, he and his squad were still at least another fifteen seconds out. Would the operation center's reinforced doors hold for that long?

When they finally came upon the enemy, the two warriors were scratching at the doors with terrifying violence. The reinforced windows in the middle of the doors had been shattered, and the scared pilots beyond watched in horror as Baranyk limbs reached through, scratching and clawing, trying to find purchase. A couple drone pilots had left their bays and were trying to repel the enemy by any means necessary.

Garcia registered all of this in the blink of an eye and opened fire in the next. Painful cries followed, but the enemy didn't turn to engage. Their efforts increased in intensity, movements becoming desperate. And because they didn't turn to engage, they kept their flank facing the squad, protecting their vital organs. That meant they took longer to kill.

Garcia's rifle clicked. Out of ammo.

*Shit!*

He released the magazine, ripped a replacement off his belt, fumbled with it, dropped it, picked it up, and snapped it into place. By the time he chambered a round, the enemy had fallen. The doors still held.

Garcia advanced cautiously. If the enemy had turned on him while he made a mockery of replacing the magazine, he would have been torn to bits. The Baranyk to his left still moved, its limbs reaching for the door to continue its efforts. He circled its body, finding the triangular head at its front.

*What would Sergeant Haniger have said if he was the one who had slain the beast?*

"Oorah, motherfucker." Garcia squeezed the trigger, sending three quick rounds into the enemy's head.

# 55

*Drone Operation Center, SAS Redemption*
*Distant Orbit, Baranyk Homeworld*

"Enemy forces on deck thirty-five neutralized," Commander Garcia said. "I repeat, deck thirty-five is secure."

There were so many improbable things about the situation that it took several moments for Coda to register. Commander Garcia looked like a bratwurst shoved into a too-small bun. His tactical vest barely covered his round chest, and his helmet was so small that it wasn't even latched at his chin. Still, he was covered in yellow blood and had just saved Coda and the rest of the Hornet pilots.

"Moving out," Commander Garcia said.

"Wait," Coda said. "Sir, please.

The words were breathless and nearly inaudible above the sound of Coda's hammering heart. He was still on the other side of the operation center's doors, but the glass in the windows had been shattered, and he could hear the commander's conversation on the other side. Before that... the Baranyk had nearly forced their way in.

"What the hell's going on?"

"Enemy boarding parties," Commander Garcia said, looking down at the lifeless bodies of the two Baranyk warriors at his feet. "It's under control."

"Under control? Didn't you just say there are other Baranyk on the ship, sir?"

"We're working on it." Commander Garcia spun his finger in the air, signaling for his team to form up and move out.

"What if they come back, sir?" Phantom asked. He had been part of the group who'd tried to fight off the enemy on this side of the doors. They weren't armed, so they'd been forced to use anything that wasn't bolted to the floor.

"The captain has them locked on the affected decks," Commander Garcia said. "Now, if you please... I have a job to do."

Phantom nodded, but his gaze fell to the fallen Baranyk warriors as if he were afraid that they were playing dead and would rise again the moment the marines were gone. That fear, fortunately, wasn't realized as the security force disappeared down the corridor.

"What the hell's going on?" Phantom asked, turning to Coda. "Enemy boarding parties? I've never heard of that."

It wasn't quite a question, but Coda heard the uncertain tone in it. He and the rest of the Forgotten had seen more action than any other unit or squadron in the fleet. More than that, they'd flown deeper into Baranyk space than anyone else ever had. If anyone had seen nonstandard enemy tactics, it would have been them.

"I haven't either," Coda said. In reality, the battles were fought in the black, often times hundreds of kilometers away from the capital ships themselves. The enemy rarely got close enough to attack the larger ships and certainly not close enough to land a boarding party.

"What does it mean?" Phantom asked, clearly shaken.

"It means we're getting close," Coda said.

Phantom took a shuddering breath then turned to face the rest of the operation center. In the chaos of the fight, they'd forgotten about the battle on the planet. Some had removed their flight helmets midbattle. Others, like Coda, had been so distracted that their drone fighters had been shot down. They were now looking to their commander for orders.

Coda ignored them and focused on the live feed on the battle map. Their forces had done an admirable job of exploring its depths, uncovering chamber after chamber below the surface. Seeing the hive at a macro level, he realized just how expansive it was. Not just its depth but how wide it was too. Separated from the battle and finally with a moment to breathe, Coda found himself studying it.

"We're getting close," he repeated. *But to where?*

Phantom suddenly cocked his head to the side and reached for his ear. He was getting a communication. "Roger." After the communication ended, he added, "Shit."

"What is it?" Coda asked.

Without responding, Phantom changed the view on the battle map to show a more distant view of the planet itself. Green indicators represented their available drones—just before jumping, the captain had launched all available drones, using their onboard computers to navigate the fray and take up station in the planet's orbit. It left them as sitting ducks, but it was better than being several hundred thousand kilometers away.

That wasn't what Phantom was looking at, though. Farther away from the planet, the Baranyk fighters that had been engaged with the Forgotten and the *Redemption* itself weren't sitting idle. They raced toward the planet.

"Lock in!" Phantom bellowed.

His pilots moved without hesitation, donning their flight helmets and turning back to their operation bays.

"Wait," Coda said.

"We don't have time. The enemy fighters will be on us in minutes."

"They're headed toward the planet," Coda said. "We have no indications they're making for our drones."

"Those are the only drones we have left," Phantom persisted. "We can't take that risk."

"Just wait," Coda said. "Two minutes. That's all I ask."

Phantom shook his head in frustration but did as Coda asked.

Coda was right, and he knew it. They were close to the Overlord's doorstep. Really close. And regardless of whether they powered up those drones now or not, this would be their last chance. They couldn't afford to search aimlessly in the dark.

Studying the battle map, he realized their entrance point wasn't the main entrance to the hive. Several dozen kilometers to the north, closer to the mountains, was an entrance centralized to the rest of the dwelling.

The hangar they'd discovered was in the opposite direction, on the outskirts of the hive and near the surface. That made sense since they needed to get airborne quickly, and they wouldn't want such a prime military target close to the rest of the hive.

His eyes kept returning to those mountains. Just like engineering, the bridge, and the drone operation center were protected in the heart of the ship, the Overlord would be too. And what better way to protect himself than with a mountain range. Even back on Earth and Mars, critical bunkers meant to protect the world's leaders had been built deep below mountains. They often had hidden emergency exits too.

"There," Coda said. "Those mountains. How much of the hive have we searched under them?"

Phantom zoomed in on the area. "Not much. The little we found appeared to be domestic areas. We encountered moderate resistance, but it appeared to be of little tactical importance."

"That's it." Coda knew deep down, with every cell of his body. "That's where we need to focus."

"There was no—"

"Think about it," Coda said. "That area is protected by the largest mountain range on the planet. That's almost ten thousand meters of rocky protection above ground, not counting what's below it. And what better way to rule your minions than being in the middle of them? Remember, the Overlord isn't just their king. He's their emperor. Their ruler. I'm telling you—that's where we'll find him."

Phantom looked back at the battle map, his eyes narrowing, almost as if he were seeing it in a new light. "There's only one flaw with that line of thinking."

"What's that?"

"You say he's like a god to them," Phantom said. "That he's basically an Olympian looking down at all of his peasants from Mount Olympus."

"Yeah."

"Well, that's just it, isn't it? Gods don't look up to mortals. They look *down* on them."

It clicked.

"Holy shit, you're right! He's not using the mountains because they provide *more* protection. He's there because it offers *enough* protection and allows him to rule from above. We've been searching all wrong. Are there any chambers in the region we've found that go *up?*"

Phantom was already zeroing in on the area. Within moments, he'd found what he was looking for. He looked at Coda, true excitement burning in his eyes. "We thought it was a ventilation shaft, but looking at it again..."

"It's directly over the main habitat."

Coda clapped his hands then pointed at the screen. "That's it. Relay the information to the captain, and let's go get the sonuvabitch."

If Phantom had any issues with being ordered around by someone technically under his command, he didn't show it. He radioed the bridge and began his report.

Coda left him to it, returning to his operation bay. *I'm coming for you. I hope you're ready.*

# 56

*Drone Operation Center, SAS Redemption*
*Distant Orbit, Baranyk Homeworld*

FORTY-EIGHT FRESH HORNETS CUT THROUGH THE BARANYK HOME WORLD'S atmosphere, burning a fiery tail like a comet about to make impact. They flew in a revised delta formation that was more diamond in shape than the traditional V.

Coda couldn't help but anticipate the bumps and shakes that came with breaking atmo. Tucked in the belly of the *Redemption* hundreds of thousands of kilometers away, he felt none of it. Strangely, he missed it. Having trained to fly the Hornet at the Terran Fleet Academy, he was more than capable, but after spending the last year in a Nighthawk, he couldn't help but long for his old cockpit and everything that came with it.

There was something about *feeling* the movement, experiencing the flight, that he thought made him a better pilot—even if the Hornet was capable of performing maneuvers that the Nighthawk could not.

"The enemy formation has spotted our reserve force," Phantom said over the radio.

Coda glanced at the battle map on his HUD. The red indicators of the incoming enemy force moved toward the leftover Hornet drones. When Captain Coleman had ordered every available Hornet launched before the *Redemption* jumped away, they'd thought that they would be able to keep a reserve force on standby. That would have allowed shot-down pilots to reenter the battle in fresh fighters. Unfortunately, the enemy appeared to have spotted them.

The massive force that had launched from the planet's surface before descended on the reserves, laying waste to them with deadly efficiency. In moments, they were beyond and in full pursuit of the formation.

*This truly is our last chance.*

"Enemy in pursuit," Phantom said. "We won't be able to stagger our attack runs the same as we did before. Keep it tight."

Coda shifted in his seat, his hands tightening around the controls. They were flying at over two thousand kilometers per hour, but as soon as they neared the hive's entrance, they would be forced to slow down. With the *Redemption* so far away, they estimated the lag time to be nearly two seconds. To the uninitiated, that didn't sound like much, but when flying at several hundred kilometers an hour and within a tight space, even a split second of delay could be catastrophic.

*No time for excuses. This is what we trained for.*

The white haze of atmo washed away, leaving a clear picture of the planet's surface. They'd come in on a steeper approach, enabling them to dive directly toward the entrance. The giant hill loomed up at them as if it were the mouth of a giant worm, preparing to swallow their fighters in a single, massive bite.

"Deploy flaps and slow to three hundred KPH," Phantom said.

Coda flicked the switch on his terminal, and his fighter immediately bucked. Had he been in the cockpit, he would have been thrown violently against his flight harness.

*There are benefits to the* drones, he admitted to himself.

The enemy rushed in, making up ground by the second.

"Emerald Flight," Phantom said, "decrease speed to one-seventy-five and circle the hive's entrance. You're to come at the incoming enemy from its flank. Stall them for as long as possible. Every second counts."

"Yes, sir," their flight leader said.

"The rest of you, prepare to enter in five seconds."

As they neared the entrance, the formation flattened out, shifting from a diamond to a spear shape. Bringing up the rear, Emerald Flight broke away and flew toward the mountain range.

Darkness washed over Coda's fighter as they dove into the entrance, and he immediately switched to his computer-aided view. Inside the hive, they slowed. Compared to their previous attack runs, it felt like they were crawling, but the reduced speed gave them time to see the corridor's end and make the necessary course adjustments.

It was an odd sensation to see the incoming obstacle and turn the stick, only to have the image on the display continue on its previous course. Then, a couple heartbeats later, the image shifted as the signal finally made it to the drone.

The crisp lines of their formation grew ragged, and at least one fighter misjudged the timing. The craft exploded into a ball of fire and molten metal, leaving a blackened splotch on the yellow-tinted walls. As they exited the tunnel and entered the first chamber, they increased speed again, flying its length before deploying flaps again. They moved like that through several tunnels and chambers, making for the hive's center.

When they came upon it, Coda couldn't help but feel awed. Phantom had said the chamber was primarily a residential area. What he hadn't said was that it was at least ten kilometers deep and an equal distance wide or that it had a strange alien beauty.

Dug into the ground were various holes and chambers, almost honeycomb in design, while fissures and stalagmites had been hollowed out to create buildings and structures above ground. Even the walls of the chamber had been gouged out to create tunnels for individuals. Long, flat strips were cut through the honeycombs in what must have been streets, and soft blue light emanated from several of the structures.

For the first time in his life, Coda realized the Baranyk were much more than an enemy of bugs. They were a race complete with soldiers, workers, families, and who knew what else. They had built a civilization, something worth remembrance. He couldn't help but wonder how much of this had existed before the Overlord. Had their civilization thrived before him? How much had they lost under his rule? Coda didn't have long to think about it. Their objective was dead ahead.

At the center of the city was a circular clearing. The ground rose up gently in its center. Anyone who stood at its peak would be visible to everyone around them. A hundred meters above the small hill was a massive stalactite reaching toward the ground like a finger pointing downward. They flew a small circle under it, getting a better vantage. As he'd expected, the formation was hollow.

"Crimson Flight, you're up," Phantom said. "We need eyes in there. Show us what we're dealing with."

The affirmative came over the radio, and twelve fighters broke away from the formation. They approached the entrance then banked hard, flying upward into it.

Coda called up a new image on his HUD. In the top left corner, the new visual appeared, taken straight from the lead fighter in Crimson Flight. The inside of the tunnel looked much like the others, except this appeared to have row after row of teeth.

*Not teeth. Turrets.*

And they were already glowing hot.

Without waiting for Phantom's order, Crimson Flight struck first, firing a wave of missiles. Explosions littered the inside of the tunnel, destroying the nearest turrets, but within moments, a wall of plasma fire erupted downward, washing over the fighters and onto the clearing below. In a single destructive second, every fighter in Crimson Flight was eliminated.

"All right," Phantom said. "If there was any doubt this is where the Overlord is holed up, that's gone now. Break into subflights and wait for my mark. We're going to have to take out those turrets one by one. Azure Flight, you're up first."

Coda flew wide circles around the entrance, keeping an eye on Azure Flight's approach and their forces outside the hive. The enemy force was nearing the hive's entrance, and Emerald Flight had already launched a volley of missiles. Judging by the size of the enemy force, Emerald Flight wouldn't be able to hold out for long. But they didn't need to. They just needed to hold the enemy off long enough for them to find the Overlord.

Azure Flight entered the tunnel. Having seen how the turrets were displayed, their computers locked onto their targets quicker, and they were able to release three waves of missiles before the plasma struck.

Coda studied the readout on his HUD. The tunnel's defenses were much more imposing than any they'd run into before. The Overlord seemed more concerned with his own people attempting to overthrow him than with an outside force assaulting the planet. That made Coda wonder how much autonomy the individual Baranyk had when the Overlord wasn't controlling them. In some way, he actually empathized with them.

The tunnel's defenses appeared nearly insurmountable. They'd lost multiple flights just breaking into the tunnels, and this presented a much bigger challenge. And they didn't have the reserves they'd had before.

*We can't use the same strategy as before.*

Blue plasma fire poured from the tunnel like water from a faucet, incinerating everything in its path. Phantom was about to order the next flight in when Coda opened a direct channel.

"Phantom, it's Coda. You're on a private channel. We don't have the numbers to assault the tunnel the same way as before. We've already exhausted nearly half our forces."

"If you've got another suggestion, I'm all ears."

"Some of our Hornets are still equipped with Welcome Parties, right?"

"Yes."

"Two of those should do it."

Coda could almost hear the drone CAG thinking. They'd had to be very careful using the Welcome Parties when entering the hive since a mistimed blast would have collapsed the tunnel system and made it impossible to enter, but here, the debris would fall downward, leaving nothing but a hole above.

"All right," Phantom said over the wide channel, "change of plans. Bombers, form up. Two per run. Target opposite sides of the tunnel, launch, and retreat. The rest of you, give the tunnel a wide berth. It's coming down."

Two drones per flight had been equipped with the Welcome Parties. They were bulky and had enough mass that it reduced maximum speed and made performing even basic maneuvers trickier. They shifted into their own formation while the rest of the squadron created some distance between them and the tunnel.

Two bombers broke away from the formation and made for the mouth of the tunnel. From Coda's vantage, they looked like little more than specks of dust being sucked into a long tube. As soon as they disappeared, Coda pulled up their live feed on his HUD. The plasma turrets were already charging, their exteriors beginning to glow.

"Bombs away," one of the pilots said. Their Hornets bucked as the heavy missiles detached and zipped for the sides of the tunnel. Before the missiles had gone far, the two drones flipped nose to tail and burned hard, racing for the exit.

The first spit of plasma fire appeared as the missiles struck.

A terrible but intensely gratifying explosion rocked the chamber. Rock and debris fell from the ceiling, and for a brief second, Coda thought the entire chamber ceiling was about to collapse. A massive shock wave exploded from the tunnel, and half its length broke away. It tumbled toward the surface of the chamber. Rock, fire, and smoke trailed behind and crashed against the floor, sending up plumes of dust and debris.

"Next wave!" Phantom bellowed.

Two more bombers disappeared into the dust. The next explosion was even more devastating than the first. The already-damaged tunnel exploded outward, sending boulder-sized chunks careening into the colony, destroying homes and community buildings.

When the dust finally settled, the scope of their efforts became apparent. The tunnel had completely fallen away from the chamber's ceiling, leaving a terrible maw where the entrance had been.

Coda pumped his fist excitedly. They'd done it and without losing any more fighters.

"Phantom, this is Waddle," a voice said over the radio. Waddle was Emerald Flight's flight leader. "We did what we could, but the enemy is inbound. I repeat, the enemy is inbound."

Glancing at the battle map on his HUD, Coda saw the enemy fighters had broken through Emerald Flight's resistance and entered the hive. They weren't more than five minutes away.

"Collapse the tunnel," Coda said.

"What?" Phantom said.

"Collapse the tunnel," Coda repeated. "There's probably another way in, but it'll slow them down."

"And eliminate any chance we have of getting our drones out of here," Phantom said.

"This was always a one-way mission."

"If we're wrong..." Phantom said. "Or if he's not there... We won't get another chance."

"We're not going to get another chance anyway," Coda said.

Phantom's resigned sigh was clearly audible through his flight helmet. "You're right. Do it. Bombers, collapse the tunnel. The rest of you, form up. It's time we saw what's waiting for us above."

Coda moved into formation as the bombers broke away. Their work was done in moments, the Welcome Parties making quick work of the tunnel entrance. As Phantom had said, that isolated the Hornets in the chamber and would at least make retreat much more difficult, but that was the farthest thing from their minds. Not this close.

"What is that?"

It took Coda a moment to figure out what the pilot was talking about. He'd thought it was just the aftermath of the tunnel collapsing, but no, this was different. It sounded like distant thunder, and it was coming from...

Deep cracks formed in the ceiling as dust and debris fell downward.

"Fall back!" Coda bellowed.

Too late.

The ceiling around the entrance to the Overlord's chamber shattered, then the entire thing was coming down. Shards of rock tumbled, crashing on drones and habitats alike. Coda did his best to dodge the falling debris, but it was more luck than skill that saw him through it. He didn't know how long rock rained down, but when it was over, only a handful of Hornets remained.

Breathing heavily, he surveyed the scene. It was tough to make out through the thick dust, but it appeared much of the colony had been destroyed. Above him was the remains of an empty chamber. He had no idea what it had looked like before its floor had fallen away, but hovering at its center was a single Baranyk fighter. Flat black in color, its lines were sharper than others, and silver stripes decorated its sides. He'd seen that coloring before. Seen those stripes.

It seemed the Overlord had a fighter of his own.

Coda punched his engines and angled his stick to engage.

It didn't respond.

For a brief moment, Coda thought that he was under the Overlord's control again. Or that his fighter had been hit with a signal that had rendered it inoperable. But then he remembered the lag time. Two seconds in a fighter was an eternity. And, it proved, more than enough for the Overlord.

The enemy fighter rocketed forward, plasma fire erupting from its front turrets, eliminating two drones Coda hadn't even seen. Then it was banking hard, moving in pursuit of another.

Finally, Coda's fighter was moving, racing toward the spot the Overlord *had been*. Coda was already trying to turn, but the Overlord's flight pattern was too random, he had no way of keeping him in his sights. Every time he turned, he'd spot the Overlord, but just as quickly as he came into his sights, the enemy was gone again.

One by one, the Overlord systematically destroyed what was left of the Hornet squadron. Somehow, he saved Coda for last. It was almost as if he knew Coda was behind its controls. By then Coda had all but given up. He'd throttled back enough that his drone was doing little more than hovering. The Overlord came on his six.

He didn't fire.

Coda spun, and several lethargic moments later, his ship rotated at his command. Coda squeezed the trigger, opening his cannons, all the while knowing it was a useless endeavor. It took two seconds for the signal to arrive in the drone operation bay. His fighter was destroyed before he ever knew it.

His terminal went black.

They'd found the hive. Discovered the Overlord. And failed.

# 57

*Bridge, SAS Abraham Lincoln*
*Jovian System, Sol System*

THE WORLD SNAPPED BACK INTO FOCUS AS THE *ABRAHAM LINCOLN* completed its jump. Admiral Orlovsky sat in his admiral's chair on the bridge, fingers digging into the armrests. He expected chaos, a system under siege, humanity fighting for its very existence. Instead, he found stillness.

The red, orange, and white bands of Jupiter shone brightly, its moons little more than shadows against its backdrop. Earth may have been the ancestral home of humanity, but Jupiter, with its habited moons and stations, could support greater numbers and had become its economic hub more than a century past. And it appeared as it would have any other day since.

The night sides of Europa and Ganymede shone with orange artificial light, and Jupiter Station, the largest station in the Sol System, blinked steadily. Space traffic would be too small to make out at their distance, but Orlovsky could almost see the hundreds of ships commuting between the moons, harvesters braving the planet's storms to mine important gasses, and others using any of the dozen JumpGates to move to more distant locations.

A terrible worry gripped his heart like a fist. Where were the Baranyk? Had he guessed wrong?

"Report," Orlovsky said. The vanguard, fifteen of the fleet's most powerful ships, had arrived first and would have already taken readings from across the entire system.

"The *New Dubai* is reporting no enemy activity," his tactical officer, Lieutenant Erikson, said.

Orlovsky sat back in his chair, rubbing his chin in nervous habit. Had the fleet simply beaten the enemy here? Even if the enemy had improved their jump capabilities, Orlovsky doubted they would have been able to jump straight to the Sol System the same way the fleet had. The JumpGates may have been limited with how many ships they could send per jump, but they were still capable of sending ships farther than any individual jump drive. Arriving first wasn't out of the question.

He squashed the wriggling doubt threatening to take root in the back of his mind. He'd rolled the dice, believing he knew the enemy's next move. He couldn't second-guess that now. One of the worst traits a leader could have was indecisiveness. If he started second-guessing his decisions, the crew would follow his lead and second-guess *him* as a result. Until he had reason to believe he was wrong, it was best to move forward as planned.

"It appears we've arrived before the enemy," Orlovsky said. "Have all civilian and nonessential personnel evacuate to Earth and Mars, and have the fleet take position. We're moving forward with attack plan Delta-Four."

"Aye, sir," Lieutenant Erikson said.

The battle plan would divide the fleet into several smaller forces. Even with the system's defenses, they didn't have the strength to take the enemy head-on. Their best hope was to divide their number and force the enemy into as many separate battles as possible. Jupiter and its four Galilean moons naturally lent itself to that strategy.

With his orders being relayed and the fleet in motion, there was nothing left to do but wait. Wait and pray.

It took a little more than an hour for the rest of the fleet to arrive and an equal amount of time for them to move into position. The evacuation was slower, though there was nothing that could be done about that. No matter how well coordinated their efforts, moving several billion people took time.

Every minute felt like an hour, every hour a day. Orlovsky refused to let doubt nag at him but couldn't keep his hands from becoming clammy or the sweat from dripping down his back. It had often been said that the time leading up to a battle was more troubling than the battle itself, and it couldn't have been truer in that moment.

That was why, after several hours and a short sleep shift, it was almost a relief when Lieutenant Erikson bellowed, "Contact!"

Something akin to relief flooded through Orlovsky. He'd been right. And even better, they'd beaten the enemy to the location and moved their forces into position. More often than not, he who controlled the terrain won the battle. That idiom had been tested recently, but it was better than the alternative.

That relief, however, was quickly replaced with tempered nerves as more of the Baranyk fleet arrived. They assembled on the outskirts of the Jovian System, well beyond the Galilean moons, nearly eleven million miles from the planet itself.

Location is nearly impossible to predict in space. The distances are so vast they're nearly incomprehensible, but based on prior battles, Orlovsky had guessed about as well as any man could. The enemy had assembled on the outskirts of the system, biding their time until their full force had arrived, then took a slow and methodical approach into the system. He hadn't known if that was some sort of technical limitation, but so far, the Baranyk had employed the strategy like clockwork—and today was no different.

The biggest gamble had been assembling the Sol Fleet in the Jovian System and not at Earth. Destroying the hub of humanity would devastate their war efforts in a way that would effectively end the war. Destroying their home planet, on the other hand, would be more of an emotional blow.

Fortunately, the Jovian System offered more defensive measures. With ninety-two different moons with orbits ranging from 128,000 kilometers from the planet all the way to 24 million kilometers, there were ample places to hide strike forces.

Leda, Himalia, Lysithea, and Elara were all moons a little more than

11 million kilometers from the planet, and while they were too small to build any sort of infrastructure on, they were more than large enough to hide multiple ships. Better yet, they were located *behind* the gathering enemy.

"Lieutenant Erikson," Admiral Orlovsky said. "Send in the strike forces. Let's hit them before they have a chance to get their hands up."

"With pleasure, sir."

The final battle for humanity was underway.

---

Buster's drone was dead. No lights. No guns. No power. Around him, two full squadrons, nearly fifty fighters in all, were dead as well. Little more than space debris flying at a predetermined course.

It was exactly as he wanted it.

Moments before, the *Olympia* and *Monaco* had crept around opposite ends of Himalia, just enough to launch their drone squadrons. After a quick burn, the squadrons shut down all systems except life support and raced toward the assembling fleet. There were already more than one hundred enemy vessels and more arriving every minute. Buster's squadrons had one job and one job only: to thin the ranks and wreak havoc.

Buster watched the countdown in the corner of his HUD. His ship wasn't measuring speed or angle of approach, and he was still too far away for visual. The attack vector and time to contact had all been measured long before he'd ever launched. There was little to do now except trust their calculations. They were about to find out just how accurate those calculations had been.

3…

2…

1…

Buster flipped the power switch on his terminal, and the drone came alive. Speed, distance, vector, and battle readings flooded his HUD.

"All fighters report in," Buster said.

One by one his pilots acknowledged they were online.

*Good.*

It had been a risk to enter the battle in a powered-down mode. The

Hornets were reliable but, like all things, prone to error from time to time and not designed to operate like a light switch. It seemed they had been able to avoid any issues, however. A good omen for the battle to come, perhaps?

"Prepare to break formation in ten seconds," Buster said. "You know your targets. Let's do ourselves proud."

Like the timed burn and the following dark flight mode, the opening sequence of the attack had been preplanned. The two squadrons were to break into their subflights, creating eight separate strike forces of six fighters a piece, and because their primary mission was to destroy as many capital ships as possible, they were equipped with a full complement of CapKillers. What they'd lack in maneuverability, they made up for with sheer destructive power.

The enemy fleet was coming into visual range now, their blue drive signatures growing in size so that they now burned brighter than the stars surrounding them. Since they were coming in from behind the enemy line, that's what they'd target first. Even if they didn't destroy the enemy capital ships, they'd incapacitate them and remove them from the upcoming battle. As CAG, his subflight took the heart of the formation.

Red targeting brackets surrounded the centermost ship. He was locked on. Buster took one final steadying breath.

"Break!"

The Hornet squadrons broke with practiced precision, shattering from a revised delta formation into their individual strike formations. Only seconds after that, pilots bellowed that missiles were away.

"Azure-1, Fox-Two!"

"Bronze-4, Fox-Two!"

"Emerald-Six, Fox-Two!"

Buster's display lit up with yellow indicators as the infrared-guided CapKillers streaked toward their targets. They hadn't hit yet before a new wave was launched, these targeting more of the ship's center mass. By the time the fighters were cresting the aftmost part of the ship, they were missiles away again. Three CapKillers per ship to ensure they inflicted maximum carnage while also spreading the love to as many enemy ships as possible.

The three missiles hit in quick succession. Explosions lit the black, burning hot and orange. Yellow-and-black-streaked carapace-like material shattered outward as various gasses and fluids billowed into space.

"Splash one!"

Eight separate runs, eight separate ships, eight examples of perfection.

They didn't have time to celebrate. The enemy fleet had jumped in with a few kilometers' space between them, but at the Hornets' speed that meant they were on the next enemy vessel in moments. The next three fighters in the formation had already locked onto the second targets. A fresh succession of pilot communication rang over the comm.

"Crimson-Four, Fox-Two!"

"Emerald-Three, Fox-Two!"

A fresh set of yellow indicators raced toward their enemy counterparts, followed by two more in quick succession. Just like the first wave, these struck without fail. The attack run had been a thing of beauty—precise, coordinated, and deadly. Somewhere behind Buster's fighter, one of the enemy vessels went critical.

The explosion was white hot, and in its wake the ship shattered into two main chunks that veered toward other ships in the line. They might as well have been moving in slow motion, but even then, the other enemy vessels couldn't move their behemoths fast enough. The pieces of the destroyed ship crashed into two others, creating a chain reaction of destruction.

It was a goddamn work of art. A Picasso of devastation.

And they weren't done. Each drone in their squadrons had been armed with two of the CapKillers—any more than that and they wouldn't have been able to maneuver at all—and so far each fighter had only launched one. Since they were launching them one subflight at a time, that meant they had two more runs left, and the Baranyk ships were already launching fighters.

"Enemy fighters inbound," Buster said. "Stay on target and provide cover fire for the CapKillers. Let's bring this mission home."

Buster's next target was a massive carrier that was one of the ships launching fighters. The enemy ships spewed from its hull like escaping oxygen before coalescing into a stream of fighters several kilometers long. Buster's targeting brackets went solid. He had tone.

"Azure-One, Fox-Two!" Buster shouted.

Just behind him in the Hornet formation two more pilots bellowed their missile launches. They tore into the enemy capital ship with the full might of the Sol Fleet. Fire cascaded down its bow.

*Another capital ship down.*

By then the enemy fighters were on them. Plasma fire streaked past his Hornet, and the one in the dash-two position exploded into a sea of shrapnel. Thankfully, it didn't destroy any of the other fighters in the formation. Even better, it had been one of the Hornets that had exhausted its CapKillers.

"Bollywood," Buster said, keeping the line to his entire flight open but talking specifically to Azure-Six. The other pilot, of Indian descent, had earned his call sign because he looked like an actor from the Bollywood era of Indian cinema. "We're spent. No more CapKillers. Let's see if we can draw some of these fighters off the rest and give them time to finish the mission."

"Sounds good, sir."

"On my mark, cut thirty-degrees positive-Z," Buster said. "That should give the rest of you two, maybe three seconds. Make them count."

Affirmatives from the rest of the flight came in.

"And... Break!"

Buster pulled back on his joystick, bringing his fighter above the orientation line. Bollywood moved into the dash-two position off his starboard wing. Behind them, the front of the enemy formation cut away in pursuit. They were on Buster and Bollywood in moments, but the maneuver had accomplished what it needed to accomplish, giving the fighters still armed with CapKillers critical moments to use them.

Voices bellowed across the comm as the last of the CapKillers were released. Buster watched with half an eye as he and Bollywood spun their Hornets to engage the incoming wave of enemy fighters. They may not have any missiles left, but they still had cannons. The front of his Hornet erupted as he squeezed the trigger.

Unlike the missiles, cannon fire didn't register on his HUD. Like tiny fireflies, they sparked into the black before being lost forever. Several enemy fighters exploded, organic carapace and fluids caking those around them. At their speeds, the enemy fighters were unable to take evasive maneuvers, and several more were destroyed from the shrapnel.

In the end, there were too many of them, and Buster and Bollywood were overrun. Shortly after that, the rest of Azure Flight was as well. In their wake they had destroyed six enemy capital ships, not counting the rest of the squadron.

*Maybe that'll help even the odds.*

They'd soon find out, because four ships and a full complement of fighters were inbound to Himalia. The mission had been a success, but Buster couldn't help but think they were little more than a sliver in the enemy's foot.

More capital ships poured in, already replacing the ships he and his pilots had destroyed. He couldn't help but shake the feeling that it hadn't been enough.

*No matter what we do, it's never enough.*

# 58

*Bridge, SAS Redemption*
*Distant Orbit, Baranyk Homeworld*

"Commander Garcia is reporting that decks thirteen, seventeen, and thirty-five have been cleared of Baranyk activity," Lieutenant Poiu said.

"Good," Captain Coleman said absently. "Keep me apprised of their progress on the remaining decks."

"Yes, sir."

The boarding party had been an unexpected wrinkle in their battle plans but, in the end, had proved to be little more than a distraction. That was largely because of the ship's depressurization alerts and rapid communication from the crew. Had they been even a minute or two slower, the enemy would have gained unfettered access to the drone operation center.

*Little good it did us.*

He'd just watched as the Hornet squadrons had found the Overlord's location and blown its entrance like a battering ram against an ancient castle. That was before the Overlord had collapsed the chamber's ceiling, destroying the bulk of their fighters in the process. What remained, he had single handedly destroyed in a fighter of his own. Where he was now, Coleman had no idea.

Would he have left? Coleman expected not. There was no reason to anymore. There were no more human fighters in the area, and the tunnels offered maximum protection. Couple that with the enemy fighters that had returned to help repel the Hornets, and Coleman himself wouldn't have withdrawn.

No... The enemy leader was still there. Problem was, Coleman was out of Hornets.

*But you still have the Forgotten.*

"Moscow," Coleman said, opening a direct line to his CAG. "What's your status?"

"Locked and loaded, sir," Moscow said.

Moscow's confident bravado eliminated any underlying reservations Coleman had. His pilots had a purpose, they knew that purpose, and as a former pilot, he knew it himself. They were there to perform the impossible. To fly harder and faster, to push the limits more than anyone else in the fleet. When you were in the cockpit, there was no time for doubt or second-guessing. There was only time for action.

And it was time for action.

"Assemble your pilots and meet me in the ready room in five minutes," Coleman said.

"Aye, sir."

Coleman closed the line and immediately opened a new one. Time for action indeed.

---

CODA SAT IN HIS DRONE OPERATION BAY, STARING AT THE BLACK SCREEN OF his VR helmet in disbelief. He'd found the Overlord. He'd damn near stared him in the face. And the bastard had slipped through his fingertips like the eel he was.

"Fuck!" Coda screamed. He pounded his fist against the terminal and jumped to his feet, ripping his flight helmet off. "Damn it! We were so close!"

If the terminal's chair hadn't been bolted to the floor, he would have flung it across the room. Instead, he looked to the vaulted ceiling of the operation center and closed his eyes. It was almost too much to bear. He'd been given a second chance, entrusted with a critical mission, and he'd failed. When Coleman, the fleet, and his *father* had needed him most, he'd failed.

Disappointment of a kind he'd never felt before burned through his veins. He felt empty, drained, dead. He couldn't decide if he wanted to find a dark hole to hide in or burn the entire ship down.

Instead, he did... nothing.

He didn't know how long he stood there like that. Eventually, it was a friendly voice that brought him out of his apathy.

"Coda?"

Coda opened his eyes. The voice came from the earpiece they'd implanted after he'd been named CAG.

*Damn, those days feel like a lifetime ago.*

"Sir," he said mechanically.

The voice on the other end was his friend and mentor, Captain Coleman. "I have one question for you," he said. "Did you use the training simulations of the Baranyk tunnels I provided?"

"Sir?"

"I'm asking, Coda, if you and the Forgotten flew the same training scenarios as the Hornet squadrons."

An awkward silence.

"We did, sir." Coda had no idea where this line of questioning was headed. "Why?"

"Tell me," Captain Coleman continued, ignoring Coda's question. "Who was faster? The Forgotten or the Hornets?"

"The Forgotten, sir," Coda said. "It wasn't even close."

"And among the Forgotten, who was the fastest?"

Any other time, and the question would have brought a smile to Coda's face. In this moment, however, all it did was remind Coda of everything he couldn't do. Everything he'd lost and couldn't be. How he'd failed in the one task he'd been given.

"I was, sir."

"That's what I thought," Captain Coleman said. "I need you in the Nighthawk ready room. You have a briefing in two minutes."

"Sir?"

"You heard me, Commander."

"I don't understand, sir."

"Then I suggest you get your ass to the ready room so I can explain."

Two minutes later and slightly out of breath, Coda was seated in the stadium seating in the Nighthawk ready room. Moscow sat to his right, Squawks to his left, with Nails beside him. Others milled about behind them. The soft leather of the seat embraced him like a mother's hug. The faint smell of sweat and hydraulic fluid was his cologne. This was where he was meant to be. What he was born to do.

The door to the ready room hissed open, and Captain Coleman strode in. "Be seated," he said before anyone could call "attention on deck" and strode directly for the podium.

"Less than ten minutes ago, our drone fighters identified the Overlord's location." Coleman toggled his terminal and brought up the image of the chamber under the mountain. The vertical tunnel that the Hornets had destroyed was still intact in the image and was marked by a large red circle. "The entrance to his chamber was located here. It was heavily guarded with dozens of plasma turrets. Our forces were able to neutralize the defenses and blow a hole into the chamber above."

Coleman clicked his terminal again, and the image changed to show the aftermath of their assault. The tunnel had collapsed to the ground, leaving a jagged maw in the chamber's ceiling.

"However," Captain Coleman continued, "before our forces could proceed, the Overlord triggered a defense protocol that collapsed the chamber's ceiling, destroying the majority of our forces. The rest were destroyed by this..."

Another click, and the Overlord's fighter filled the screen.

"He has his own starfighter?" Moscow asked.

"Yes."

The word echoed through the ready room and was followed by quiet chatter. Coda didn't say anything. He just stared at the image. He didn't need to—it had been taken directly from his fighter and would be forever burned into his memory.

"This is your target," Captain Coleman said. "We do not have any intelligence on it beyond what you see here. But expect it to be bigger, faster, more maneuverable, and more powerful than anything you've faced before."

"When are we going in, sir?" Moscow asked.

"The *Redemption*'s computers are plotting the intrasystem jump now," Captain Coleman said. "We'll jump into high orbit and launch fighters. The enemy force that engaged us in orbit have since returned to the hive, so our expectation is that you'll have a clear path to the hive. After that, expect enemy resistance. You may also encounter fleeing dropships returning with surviving marines. But make no mistake, this," he pointed at the screen, "is your *only* objective. Am I clear?"

A chorus of "Yes, sirs" reverberated through the room.

"There's one final wrinkle," Captain Coleman said. "The enemy fighters were inbound on the Hornets' location, so they collapsed the tunnel leading to the chamber. We know based on scans that there are additional entrances to the chamber, but you'll need to find them on your own. Any questions?"

Silence was the only response until Squawks decided to chime in.

"So all we have to do is make an incredibly difficult intrasystem jump, get to the surface unscathed, and navigate a complex tunnel system without a map without getting blown to bits by the hundred or so fighters patrolling the hive?"

The quip elicited a bout of nervous laughter.

"Don't forget the Overlord," Nails added.

"Of course," Squawks said. "Let me try again. Intrasystem jump. Complex tunnel system. Don't get blown up. And then fight the bigger, badder Baranyk leader in his bigger, faster starfighter with the fate of humanity hanging in the balance."

"There you go," Nails said. "That's better."

"Well," Squawks said, blowing his cheeks out. "Good thing you've got us. We've *forgotten* how to say no."

That actually brought a small grin to Captain Coleman's face. "I know how you feel, Squawks. Do us proud."

"Always, sir."

"All right," Captain Coleman said, returning to business. "If there are no other questions, lock and load."

Coda stood with the rest of his squadmates but hung back as they filtered through the doors to the hangar bay beyond. He sought out Captain Coleman.

"Why, sir?" Coda asked. "Why me? Why now?"

"Because you're the best, Coda," Captain Coleman said as if it were truly as simple as that. "And you have the most to lose. That means you'll fight the hardest. And right now, we need that."

"Thank you, sir." Coda gave his captain the finest salute he could muster.

"Good luck out there, Commander."

Coda strode through the doors, back straight, chin high. There were a thousand logical fallacies with Captain Coleman's line of thinking, but when it boiled down to it, Captain Coleman believed in him.

And that helped Coda believe in himself.

# 59

*Cockpit, Nighthawk*
*High Orbit, Baranyk Homeworld*

The moment Coda was thrown back in his seat and felt the welcome return of real G's, he understood he had been wrong about everything. He'd thought returning to the cockpit of his Hornet was a reunion of sorts, that the Nighthawk ready room had been home, but in both situations, he'd been wrong.

This… This was home. This was him.

Every nook of his fighter was his, a relationship forged through thousands of hours in its cockpit. From the shape of the gel seat to the way his fingers had smudged the controls, wearing paint in unique shapes and angles specific to only him. The g-forces were old friends. The zero-g an ex-lover. Rocketing through the launch tube and into the black, blood rushing from his body into his extremities, he grew lightheaded as if he were suffering from the brain fog after a first kiss.

He and the rest of the Forgotten immediately formed up into six flights of four fighters apiece, all in finger-four formations. Coda had gotten his wings back, but he hadn't been placed back in command. That was fine with him as long as he was in the cockpit. Flying at his wing and wingman for the mission was Rocket, someone who had sadly earn his call sign based on the bright-red color of his hair and the way his pale skin blushed furiously whenever he grew embarrassed or strained. They were in Moscow's flight, angling for the planet. Coda had never flown with Rocket before, but this was a different kind of mission, and the unique bond wingmen had would be less important.

*If we find the Overlord, he's mine.*

Cutting through the upper layer of the planet's atmosphere, his fighter bucked and kicked. The temperature in the cockpit rose as the fighter's heatshield glowed red and orange from the friction. Sweat beaded on his head and slid down his back. Even that brought a smile to his face.

Once they were through the atmosphere, they approached the hive entrance at full burn, angled up its peak, shot above the entrance, and performed an inverted dive into the tunnel.

Even with their nose- and wing-mounted lamps, visibility was limited inside the tunnel, and they relied heavily on computer-aided sight. If anyone had expected that would result in slower speeds, they were sorely mistaken. The Nighthawks ripped past rock formations, stalagmites, and stalactites fast enough that they were barely recognizable. They darted around bends and flipped into the first chamber.

Once inside, they quickly assessed the various chambers branching off from it, and Moscow ordered each flight to proceed into one on their own. In essence, they were racing through a maze at breakneck speeds, hoping someone would make it to the end.

The particular branch of tunnel Coda, Rocket, Moscow, and Dumper had ventured into was one of the few that had largely been unexplored. Moscow ordered them to reduce throttle by twenty-five percent, which allowed their onboard computers to scan ahead and plot an optimized flight path that avoided obstacles. They had just enough time for the computer to scan, analyze, visualize, display, and give the pilots the precious half-second to adjust.

Tunnel after tunnel, chamber after chamber they ventured, each one taking them farther away from the hive's center. Moscow saw it too, and when none of the branching tunnels from the latest chamber seemed promising to get them back on course, they doubled back to find one that did.

It was tedious work without radio chatter. They couldn't risk any distractions. Even the main comm was quiet as every fighter in the squadron struggled with the dangerous speeds.

The minutes ticked by, each more agonizing than the last, and Coda began to sweat in earnest. Not from heat or physical exertion but the immense focus the flight required.

They'd seen thousands of Baranyk as they'd ripped through various tunnels and chambers, but none were fighters. Nothing that posed a threat. Beyond the exterior defenses, it seemed the Baranyk had little in the way to repel invaders. That shouldn't have surprised him. They were basically flying through alien cities and towns, racing down streets and highways, around farms and lumberyards.

"Shit!" someone screamed.

Coda jumped, tweaking his joystick to the right and narrowly missing a protruding rock formation. His HUD didn't show any enemy signatures, and the confines were too close to risk a look at the battle map, but it was clearly not his flight under attack.

"Contact! Contact! Contact!" the pilot said in rapid succession.

"Report!" Moscow bellowed. "Where are you?"

"Aaaarrrgghhh!" the pilot screamed before the line went dead.

"Report!" Moscow said, but nobody else from the flight reported in. "Shit."

It wasn't until they entered another chamber, this one some sort of storage yard, that Coda called up his battle map. They were getting more central in the hive but were several levels below where they needed to be. He'd thought about the hive all wrong. The hive wasn't just a maze but a three-dimensional labyrinth. And they were trying to navigate it at a full sprint.

The other flight had been more successful in finding an alternate entrance to the Overlord's chamber, which indicated that the enemy forces were staying close to the Baranyk leader. That was good. They wouldn't run into the monsters roaming the labyrinth's corridors—at least not until they drew closer to the prize.

"Stay focused," Moscow said. "It could be us next."

Moscow led them into a tunnel that led back toward the surface. Based on the computer estimates, they were under the mountain range, which meant they were getting closer. They followed it into another chamber then another tunnel that continued to lead upward.

*This is it. This is the yellow brick road that's going to take us to Oz.*

As they shot through the tunnel into another chamber, Coda's HUD immediately flashed red, and emergency claxons rang.

"Contact!" Moscow bellowed. "Evasive maneuvers!"

In the dash-three position, Coda and Rocket shot starboard, Moscow and Dumper to port. Plasma fire ripped through the space where the formation had just been, close enough that Coda could feel the heat through the reinforced glass of his cockpit canopy.

The chamber was much larger than the tunnel, giving him the room and freedom to check his battle map. They'd come upon a full flight of Baranyk fighters, twelve in all, and forced to take evasive maneuvers they were already at a disadvantage.

Coda shot toward the chamber wall, eliminating one of the angles the enemy had at their disposal, and raced around the chamber's edge as the Baranyk formation split into two.

"We've got six fighters coming around on our tail," Rocket said. "Moving into firing position."

Coda grunted an acknowledgment. If they were in the black, he would rotate his fighter one hundred eighty degrees and attempt to pick one or two of them off. Here in the chamber with the planet's gravity, that wasn't possible.

"How high do you think that ceiling is?" Coda asked.

"No idea," Rocket said. "One hundred meters, max?"

That wasn't too far from his guess. "Tall enough. On my mark, dive negative-Z, forty degrees toward the chamber floor, then sharp, positive-Z eighty degrees. When they're in vertical pursuit, drop chaff. We'll let gravity do its work."

"That's—" but the rest of Rocket's remark was cut off as plasma fire peppered their flight path, narrowly missing both fighters.

"Now!" Coda bellowed.

He shoved the stick forward, diving toward the chamber's surface. Despite his obvious reservations, Rocket did the same, and as they were about to bottom out, they ripped their joysticks back, shooting toward the ceiling of the cavern.

The maneuver put intense pressure on Coda's lower back, and his stomach did somersaults in his chest. The Baranyk fighters mimicked the maneuver, but with more fighters and a wider formation, one clipped a rock protrusion and broke apart, leaving a yellow smear against the gray rock.

*One down.*

As soon as the enemy fighters performed the second part of the maneuver, going vertical, Coda shouted, "Chaff!"

Fist-sized hunks of metal shot out of the backs of both Nighthawks directly into the incoming fighters. Even at these reduced speeds, the chaff tore jagged chunks from the Baranyk fighters, sending them careening into each other and the nearby chamber walls.

"Four down," Coda said as the red indicators blinked out on his HUD. "Two left. Cutting to port, sixty degrees on three. Once we're clear of this wall, break into a Helix maneuver."

"Roger."

"Mark!"

Coda threw his joystick to the left, veering away from the wall toward the center of the chamber. Rocket, despite never having flown with Coda before, was right on his wing. He then shot away hard to starboard as if peeling away. Coda moved in the opposite direction simultaneously, putting significant space between the two of them.

As Coda hoped, the remaining Baranyk fighters moved into individual pursuit, one on each of them. As soon as he was far enough, he eased his joystick in the opposite direction, turning his fighter starboard just as Rocket moved his to port. The maneuver brought the two fighters veering toward each other at a rough forty-five-degree angle. Most importantly, it meant they had a clean firing angle on each of the enemies in pursuit.

"Gold-3," Coda said. "Fox-Four!"

He squeezed the trigger just as Rocket shouted his intent to fire.

Coda's Nighthawk kicked as the missile released and rocketed away. A separate missile from Rocket's fighter zipped toward him. It was an unnerving sight, even if Coda knew he wasn't the missile's intended target.

The chamber flashed with orange fire as Coda's missile exploded into the Baranyk fighter behind Rocket. A split second later, Coda's

Nighthawk lurched as a second explosion erupted behind him, Rocket's missile finding its target.

Coda yelled victoriously.

"Splash six!" Rocket added.

The celebration was short-lived, however, as Coda reassessed the battle map. Moscow and Dumper weren't having the same luck against their pursuers. They'd clipped two of them off, but the four remaining enemies sprayed plasma fire across their bow.

"Moscow, I'm sending you a beacon now," Coda said. "Trident maneuver. Acknowledge."

"Received," Moscow said. "Thanks, Coda."

"Just get there."

The beacon appeared on Coda's and Rocket's battle maps. Since Moscow and Dumper were on the opposite side of the chamber, it meant the four Nighthawks were now flying toward each other.

"Trident maneuver," Coda said again, this time for Rocket. "Two-second stagger."

"Understood."

As with the Helix maneuver, both fighters veered from their current flight path, Coda once again to port and Rocket to starboard. Together, they made the outer prongs of the so-called trident, with the middle prong created by Moscow and Dumper in the middle.

Once he was wide enough, Coda cut hard back to starboard, racing toward the beacon. Nobody was there yet. They weren't supposed to be. He raced to the spot they *would* be.

As Moscow and Dumper came into view, Coda's targeting computer locked on to the lead fighter in pursuit. Since he was coming in at an angle, he had a clear view of the fighter's broadside.

"Gold-3, Fox-Four!" He squeezed the trigger.

The missile took the lead fighter, but its destruction didn't cause any other deaths.

"Gold-4, Fox-Four!" Rocket bellowed a moment later. His missile had a similar effect, taking out another Baranyk fighter.

Coda continued his trajectory, ripping through the space the enemy fighters had just been, now behind Moscow and Dumper's flight path. He turned hard to starboard, preparing for another attack run when a bright flash flared in the edge of his vision.

"No!" Moscow screamed. "Dumper! Dumper, do you copy?"

But the remains of Dumper's fighter fell to the chamber's floor.

"Dumper! Goddamn it!"

The enemy opened fire again. Moscow's erratic flight path was the only thing that prevented him from becoming slag as well.

"Moscow," Coda said. "Moscow, listen to me. I'm almost in position. Cut thirty degrees to port on my mark. Do you hear me? Moscow?"

"Yeah."

"Good," Coda said. "Mark!"

Moscow ripped hard to his left, giving Coda another clean angle. He made this one count. The missile took off the right half of the enemy fighter, sending it crashing into the last remaining fighter. Both went down, breaking apart against the chamber floor.

The silence that followed was heartbreaking. Coda knew that pain. He'd felt it on too many occasions. The sense of loss was palpable, but the suddenness of it all was the most difficult to process. One moment, you were whole. The next, a piece of your soul had been ripped away.

"Moscow," Coda said.

"He was my friend," Moscow said.

Coda was struck by how many layers there could be to such a simple statement. "I know. And he would have wanted us to complete the mission. We have to get out of here before more fighters arrive."

"I know," Moscow said, but his fighter didn't alter course.

Coda took the moment to scan the battle map. It seemed they had come up in a chamber parallel to the one they were trying to get to. If there was only a tunnel that went—

"There!"

Coda spotted the tunnel mouth on the adjacent wall. Unless it veered off at a crazy angle, it should lead directly to the central chamber.

"Moscow, we're so close. Let's finish this. Sending you coordinates now." He sent another beacon. A blue indicator appeared on Coda's HUD as it would Moscow's and Rocket's, with arrows pointing in the proper direction. Rocket formed up on Coda's wing.

Moscow sighed deeply. "Let's finish this."

His fighter banked hard, moving with purpose for the tunnel entrance, and soon he shot past Coda and Rocket, taking the lead. Coda and Rocket fell into formation behind him.

As Coda expected, the tunnel led directly into the central chamber. It felt larger than Coda had expected, seeing it in the flesh, and was easily twice the size of any they'd entered before. At its center was what remained of the massive tunnel that had extended downward from the ceiling like an arm holding the rest of the Baranyk down. It now lay shattered against the city below.

A deep, unnerving presence washed over Coda like a thick stench. It felt wrong and seemed to penetrate his every pore.

"He's here," Coda said. "I can feel him."

As if the Overlord had heard him or maybe felt him too, a squadron of enemy fighters poured from the maw in the tunnel's ceiling and made directly for their three fighters. And at their head was a fighter bigger and more menacing than the rest.

It was the Overlord.

# 60

*Cockpit, Nighthawk*
*Hive, Baranyk Homeworld*

CODA IMMEDIATELY FIRED TWO MISSILES. THEY SHOT TOWARD THE Overlord with blistering speed, but before they closed the distance to the enemy, a mass of ships behind the Overlord's fighter zipped past their leader, sacrificing themselves by jumping into the missiles' path. The rest flooded toward the three Nighthawks.

"Evasive maneuvers!" Moscow said, darting to port while Coda and Rocket moved starboard.

They weren't going to last long. The Overlord had close to thirty ships to their three, and because of their previous engagement, all three were already running low on missiles. They still had cannons, but that wouldn't be enough to handle these kinds of numbers.

"All forces," Moscow said over the comm. "We've found the Overlord. I repeat, we've found the Overlord. Uploading a data package now that provides the route we took to get here. We are outnumbered and need immediate assistance."

"Acknowledged and received, Moscow," Squawks said. "We're on our way."

It was good to hear Squawks's voice, good to know he hadn't been part of the flight that had previously been shot down, but any good feelings that brought were quickly replaced when the enemy opened fire. It was like trying to dodge hail in a hailstorm. Unrelenting plasma fire sprayed across his fighter from bow to stern, narrowly missing wings and fuselage.

The enemy forces had divided into two flights when the Nighthawks had split. According to his computer, that left thirteen fighters on each of their tails. The only chance they had was to divide those further and start to pick off a few. That and hope Squawks could arrive in time to provide assistance.

"Rocket, break away," Coda said. "There's no use in remaining as a fighter pair."

"Agreed." Without another word, Rocket darted away.

As Coda had hoped, nearly half the enemy fighters on his tail broke away in pursuit.

Coda let out a long breath. It was time to strap in. The only reason he hadn't been shot down yet was because the fighters behind him weren't as tight on his six as they could have been. Nor did they have the guided missiles of the Nighthawks.

He ducked and dived, dodged and weaved, falling into a steady rhythm. Blue fire shot across his bow, narrowly missing him on a dozen different occasions. It was only a matter of time before his luck ran out.

His body moving automatically on nothing more than thousands of hours of training, Coda assessed the situation. He'd lost sight of the Overlord, but that feeling of dread and oppression hadn't relented. He was still present. He wouldn't have given up his front-row seat to Coda's destruction. If Coda could just hold out long enough, he would get his chance.

Rocket had darted toward the deck and was weaving in and out of the various city structures. If he'd thought that would slow the enemy's fire, he was dearly mistaken. They fired at him with reckless abandon, taking no caution and not caring when their plasma fire shattered homes and buildings. The Overlord's disregard for Baranyk life was appalling.

It also gave him an idea. "Rocket, I'm adjusting thirty-five degrees to port. If you climb positive-Z, that should give you a clear shot at the fighters on my tail."

"Do it," Rocket said.

Coda banked his fighter, adjusting to his left. It moved him closer to the middle of the chamber, flying toward the large tunnel that had broken from the ceiling and crashed below. Rocket was coming around it now, having used the debris for cover, then shot upward.

Rocket performed the maneuver perfectly and knifed directly into the enemy fighters on Coda's six. A missile hit the fighter dead center in the middle of the mass, but not before plasma fire that had missed Rocket's ship struck another Baranyk fighter. The formation shattered as enemy fighters swerved to miss the friendly fire coming in their direction, and two more crashed into each other in the chaos. Four fighters on Coda's tail had been eliminated, and Rocket had expended only a single missile.

"Great work!" Coda bellowed. "Moscow, cut six degrees to starboard, fourteen degrees positive-Z, and I'll pay it forward."

Moscow grunted a response, clearly too under duress to say more, but did as instructed. His course brought him racing past Coda, relatively perpendicular to Coda's own trajectory. Coda targeted the lead fighter and squeezed the trigger, sending a missile on its way. He immediately thumbed the firing switch to cannons and shot off two more quick bursts.

His attack wasn't as devastating as Rocket's, but he eliminated two Baranyk fighters in the process. It gave them time to breathe. Not much, but some.

With his sliver of freedom, Moscow cut harder to starboard, jetting toward the center of the chamber. It caused him and Coda to fly past each other. Moscow opened fire again, and it wasn't until then that Coda realized the enemy had been forming back on his tail.

"Thanks, Moscow," Coda said.

Their CAG still didn't answer. He shot toward Rocket, who had made it to the chamber ceiling, near the black maw that was the entrance to the Overlord's chamber, but was looping back around and diving toward the surface. The route put them close to a collision course.

"Break left!" Moscow bellowed as their two fighters screamed toward each other.

Rocket swerved hard, grunting under the strain. His ship banked to port. As soon as it was out of firing range, Moscow laid on his cannons.

Plasma fire mixed with his cannon fire, peppering the flight path of the Baranyk fighters pursuing Rocket. In a single instant, half the fighters on Rocket's tail were eliminated, nearly half from friendly fire. The Overlord was getting a hard lesson in the power of teamwork.

They weren't out of the woods yet, though. Even if they had decimated the enemy forces, almost half still remained, and they were regrouping. The Overlord himself rose slowly out of the city's wreckage. His black ship was all sharp edges, striped and menacing. The remaining fighters swarmed around him, shielding him and making it abundantly clear who was in charge.

Coda and Rocket looped around the chamber's edge then reassembled with Moscow in a simple parade formation. Unlike in the black, where the two forces could have floated in space, neither moving, almost standing like two gunslingers on a dirt road in the old west, they flew in a steady circular pattern. They were like two opposing weather patterns circling each other, a hurricane of destruction on the horizon.

Coda's fingers tapped the joystick in anticipation, waiting for the standoff to end. He knew where this would lead. The two formations would dart toward each other and open fire, then any remaining fighters would bank hard to make another run, hoping they were faster at getting into position and get a cleaner shot. With their numbers disadvantage, Coda thought he knew how that would end.

He was about to say something when he caught a glimmer of movement out of the corner of his eye. Almost simultaneously, four new green icons appeared on his battle map.

"Hello, boys," Squawks said over the comm. "I heard you were having a party. Thanks for the invite!"

His flight, flying in a finger-four pattern, increased thrust and shot sharply at the mass of enemy fighters. Their timing couldn't have been more perfect, allowing them to close the relatively short distance toward the enemy's flank. Four missiles raced ahead, exploding in the center of the Baranyk mass.

"Now!" Moscow screamed.

Their three ships raced forward, unleashing three of their own missiles. For the first time Coda could remember, the Baranyk seemed panicked. Their mass exploded outward, enemy ships flying in every direction. In response, the two Nighthawk formations broke into fighter pairs, moving to engage.

Coda only had one target in mind.

The Overlord, perhaps sensing a potential defeat for the first time since engaging, raced toward the dark maw in the ceiling.

"The Overlord is trying to escape!" Coda yelled. "I'm in pursuit!"

"Not alone, you're not." Moscow's and Rocket's fighters formed up on his wing. Together, the three of them entered the maw.

# 61

*Cockpit, Nighthawk*
*Hive, Baranyk Homeworld*

THE OVERLORD'S CHAMBER HAD BEEN DESTROYED WHEN HE'D COLLAPSED its floor on the chamber below. That meant the black maw had existed *above* even the Overlord's chamber.

Speeding into it, Coda had to immediately reduce throttle. On the other side wasn't another chamber or even a tunnel like the ones they had flown through before. This was narrow and uncut and looked like a natural formation, not the engineered style of the rest of the hive.

*An emergency exit?* Coda wondered.

Within the narrow confines of the tunnel, the Nighthawks fell into a basic trail formation, the three fighters flying directly behind one another, fifty meters between them. Having entered the tunnel first, Coda was in the lead of the formation, with Moscow behind and Rocket bringing up the rear.

Coda switched his HUD's view from his normal vision back to the computer-aided sight they'd used in the other tunnels. It gave him a green flight path to follow to avoid the boulders, stalagmites, and stalactites that rose from the floor, dropped from the ceiling, and protruded from the walls.

"What's your status, Coda?" Moscow asked. "You have visual on the enemy?"

"Negative," Coda said.

The tunnel was too narrow, with too many obstacles, twists, and turns to see much beyond what was directly in front of them. He doubted Moscow even had a visual on the rear of his Nighthawk most of the time.

When Coda had been a child, his father had enjoyed watching weekend sprint races on the stream. Twenty racers would climb into what almost resembled starfighters and would race through incredible terrains across the galaxy—canyons, across rocky, windswept deserts, frozen tundra, and more. The speed was incredible, the tension high, the wrecks as exhilarating as they were catastrophic.

Those racers had never flown through anything like this. The tunnel was barely wide enough to fit his Nighthawk, its walls little more than a few meters from the tips of his wings. The ceiling was so low, he thought he could almost reach out and touch it—and that wasn't the worst of it.

Without warning the tunnel would squeeze together, making an opening that was nothing more than a vertical slit in the rock. Coda had to flip his fighter ninety degrees so that his wings were vertical to squeeze through then immediately flip it back horizontal on the other side to maintain maximum maneuverability.

Another time he came head-on to a rock wall, where the tunnel seemed to end even though the flight path showed a one-hundred-eighty-degree horizontal spin, followed by an inverted dive. Coda performed the maneuver perfectly, but it left him lightheaded with black stars creeping in from the edges of his vision.

Behind him, Moscow cursed, and Rocket screamed, but both made it through the sudden obstacle.

Righting his fighter, Coda came into a hollowed chamber. Like the tunnel, it felt like a natural cave formation, and at its far end was another opening. He made for it, wondering how much more of the tunnel there was. There hadn't been any junctions or intersections, and they had to be nearing its end.

Coda was two hundred meters into the tunnel, Rocket just entering its confines, when he screamed over the radio.

"Contact!" Rocket yelled. "Shit! He's on my six."

"Come again?" Coda said.

"He's on my six!"

Coda risked a quick look at his battle map and saw a single red indicator directly behind Rocket's fighter. *How is that possible?* There was only one possible answer. He must have found a spot to hide in the chamber then moved into pursuit the moment the Nighthawks had entered into the new tunnel.

"He's opening fire!"

From Coda's vantage at the tip of the formation, he couldn't see the blue plasma fire, but he heard the panic in Rocket's voice.

"There's no room! I can't—"

The line went dead.

"Rocket!" Coda bellowed.

No answer.

"Rocket!"

Still nothing.

"He's gone, Coda," Moscow said. There was something in his voice that said he was next. Without Rocket behind him and without room to take evasive action, there was nothing Moscow could do.

*No*, Coda thought, grinding his teeth. *No. Not again.*

"Increasing thrust twenty percent," Coda said.

"Increasing... Coda, that's insane."

Coda's flight suit tightened around his limbs as the recommended flight path had him yank back on the stick, climbing again. They were moving in a rough vertical path toward what would be the top of the mountain range. It was their only hope. If they couldn't beat the Overlord in the tunnel, then they would have to best him outside it, and Coda was confident the tunnel had an exit somewhere. They just had to find it.

"What does Captain Coleman say all the time?" Coda asked, his voice strained from the weight of the G's.

"Speed is life," Moscow said.

"Speed is life," Coda repeated.

If Coda had thought the previous speed was pushing his limits, then this was truly on the edge. His fighter moved at nearly the same speed the computer could take the readings from its sensors and calculate a flight path. Coda had less than half a second to get the reading and perform the flight action.

His flight helmet was wet with sweat, his heart beating a steady staccato. He had no time to think. No time to question. Just read and react. Read and react.

"He's gaining on me!" Moscow said.

*How is that possible?* The Overlord's fighter was larger than the Nighthawk. If it was a tight fit for them, it had to be absolutely suffocating for him.

"He's opening fire!"

"Increase thrust five percent!"

"Coda!"

"Do it!"

"Aaaaghhh!"

"Moscow!"

"He missed!" Moscow screamed.

Coda could see it in his mind's eye. They had just come to a switchback that had them cut hard to starboard then almost immediately back to port. The natural formation must have shielded Moscow from the fire —but it wouldn't for long.

"Increase thrust five percent," Coda repeated. "Create some distance."

"Roger."

Coda made his own adjustment. The hum of his thrusters increased, the vibration in his seat intensifying. The boosted speed left him with barely three-tenths of a second to read and react. He widened his eyes, maximizing blood flow, refusing to even blink.

Eyes burning, Coda moved his fighter, pitching, swaying, looping, and climbing. They were only climbing now. No more horizontal movement. No more chambers.

The tunnel grew tighter. Narrower. Something registered on his HUD. Bright. Small. Growing larger. It seared his eyes like a fire poker to the pupil.

Then white fire washed over his ship. Coda screamed, slamming his eyes closed from the pain, knowing that the reaction meant his death. He waited for a screech. A violent twisting. Anything that would mark his end. It never came.

Coda opened his eyes to slits. The white fire had changed to gray clouds. He opened his eyes wider, taking in the full view of the Baranyk sky. His HUD had darkened, compensating for the harsh light of the surface, allowing his eyes to adjust.

They'd done it. They were out of the tunnel.

Coda cut thrust, allowing the planet's gravity to slow him, then flipped back around and fell toward the rocky mountain range. He had just completed his maneuver when Moscow's Nighthawk flew out of the hole in the mountainside.

Coda tightened his hand around the stick, fingering the firing stud. As soon as Moscow's fighter was out of the line of fire, he squeezed. Cannon fire erupted from the nose of his fighter, peppering the tunnel's entrance just as the Overlord's fighter emerged. It bucked under Coda's fire, and chunks of carapace ripped free.

Overspray slammed into the mountain, sending dust and rock exploding into the air and collapsing the tunnel. For a brief moment, Coda thought he had done it, that he'd brought the tunnel down on the Overlord, but then the Overlord shot out of the dust like a dark comet.

He raced skyward. With Coda still in his dive, the two ships barreled toward each other. Blue plasma fire blasted toward Coda, forcing him to corkscrew. He didn't have time to switch to missiles and get a lock. He squeezed the trigger, firing three bursts of cannon fire. Most missed, but some of the third struck, blasting off more chunks of the Overlord's fighter. His ship rocked but continued its climb, shooting past Coda. Whatever that ship was made out of, it was a stronger material than the normal Baranyk fighters.

Coda pulled back on his joystick, leveling out his dive, then banked hard to port, expecting the Overlord to be in his own dive, pursuing Coda's Nighthawk. Except he wasn't. He was still climbing. Coda pulled back again and plotted an intercept course. He maximized his burn. The dive and time it had taken to level out his fighter had given the Overlord a significant lead. He disappeared into the clouds.

"Moscow, I'm in pursuit, but I lost visual. Copy."

"Copy," Moscow said. "I'm moving into a better attack vector."

Coda had lost visual on him too. He was somewhere in the gray clouds above the surface.

Coda could hear the strain on Moscow's voice. He had to be banking hard.

Distant cannon fire echoed across the horizon. Moscow had opened fire. "Damn it!"

"What?" Coda asked.

"He slipped past."

"He's going to orbit," Coda said. "We can't let him get there."

Coda didn't understand the physics of it, but something about gravity wells made interstellar jumps impossible. That was why every jump the *Redemption* had performed had been done no lower than a high orbit and why the more powerful JumpGates were located deeper in-system, away from any planetary bodies.

The Overlord was fleeing, doing everything he could to escape the attack and jump to another system.

"*Redemption* actual, this is Moscow. We've flushed the Overlord from his hole, but he's fleeing to orbit. We need all available units. I repeat—we need all available units."

"Copy," Lieutenant Poiu said over the comm. "We've got a bead on your position and will attempt to box him in, but, Moscow, there are no other fighters. I repeat, there are no available units."

The implication of Lieutenant Poiu's words was clear.

"It's up to us," Coda whispered, barely loud enough for his own ears to hear. If they lost the Overlord, they might never get another chance.

"Roger," Moscow said. "Coda?"

"Yeah?"

"That ship's too strong for cannon fire. We'll need to hit him with missiles, but I'm too far for lock. The *Redemption*'s computer can help, but I'm not confident he'll get close enough to them either."

"So, what's your plan?"

"Have you ever been bird hunting before?"

It was such a strange question at a strange time that Coda didn't know how to respond. "Uh... No?"

"Well, the concept is simple enough. The *Redemption* is moving into position, but all that's going to do is make the Overlord alter course. It might give me enough time to get into a firing position, but if not, I'm going to flush him toward you."

Coda's recovery from the dive had moved him several kilometers away from the mountain range. He was in pursuit but at an angle, unlike Moscow, who was more closely on the Overlord's six.

"I'm sending you coordinates now," Moscow said. "If it works, if I'm able to flush him... do you remember our last battle at the Academy?"

"Of course."

In the final battle between their two squadrons, Coda had employed a tactic known as the Coleman Diamond, named after their eventual captain. It leveraged a formation that included a lot of fighter movement to mask a single fighter going dark. That fighter was the knife in the night, the one that could change the entire battle by cutting the head from the snake.

The tactic had worked. In that battle, Coda's fighters, which had powered down as the rest moved into formation, moved silently toward Moscow's capital ship, only powering up at the last second when Moscow couldn't do anything about it. They'd destroyed his capital ship and become the Ace Squadron of their graduating class.

"Good," Moscow said. "We're only going to get one shot at this. Once you're clear of the planet, power down to critical systems only. I'll flush him your way, giving you a clear shot. Make it count."

"Copy," Coda said.

Moscow's coordinates came in a moment later, and Coda altered course to move into position. By now, he was nearly fifteen kilometers from the surface and above the cloud cover. He still didn't have visual on Moscow or the Overlord, but he watched the readings on his HUD. Because the *Redemption* had jumped in nearly directly over the hive, it had been close to an intercept position already. The Overlord didn't know it yet, but he was flying into a trap.

Two minutes ticked by, and the light haze of atmosphere burned away, leaving nothing more than the black of space and glimmer of stars beyond. The pull of the planet's gravity lessened as the familiar feeling of weightlessness returned.

Spotting the *Redemption*, the Overlord suddenly altered course. It was nearly a fifty-fifty chance. If the Overlord moved hard to port, then he would slip away. Hard to starboard, and he would move toward Coda.

Moscow must have foreseen this decision and had slightly adjusted his course so that he was off the portside of the Overlord's ship. In doing so, if the Overlord moved in that direction, Moscow would have a cleaner attack angle.

Coda could almost see the calculations in the Overlord's brain and knew what direction he would head. Coda powered down his Nighthawk, keeping nothing but his targeting, weapon, and life support systems active.

Captain Coleman must have seen the same thing, because when the *Redemption* opened fire, it shot over the portside bow of the Overlord's ship. At that distance, they had no hope of hitting the fighter, but he wasn't about to run into a stream of antiaircraft fire either.

The Overlord angled hard to starboard, avoiding the fire, and moved directly toward Coda's position. Even if the Overlord somehow got close enough to get a visual, there was no way he would ever see Coda's powered-down fighter. The Nighthawk's matte-black exterior made it all but invisible in the black, and its surface was resistant to radar, lidar, and other forms of detection.

Surprisingly, Moscow's Nighthawk was faster and more maneuverable than the Overlord's. Every time the Baranyk fighter moved to climb farther, Moscow moved into a better attack position. It prevented the Overlord from gaining too much altitude and forced him to move in a more horizontal direction. The Overlord would eventually get clear of the planet, but he would have to take the long way to get there.

Coda stayed off the radio. He wasn't risking anything giving away his position. Seconds ticked by, and the Overlord grew closer. Coda was the assassin in the night, the sniper in the bell tower, Moscow's hunter waiting for his prey.

Targeting indicators appeared on Coda's HUD as the Overlord came into range.

For years, Coda had dreamed about restoring honor to his family's name. He'd been the squadron leader of the Ace Squadron at the Terran Flight Academy. He'd become CAG of the Forgotten, the first and last line of defense for the Sol Fleet while their Hornets had been inoperable. He'd even found his father, a person the entire world thought dead, and learned the truth behind his actions.

Since that day, Coda had thought about little else than destroying the

Overlord. Even more since his father had been captured in the Baranyk network. When the targeting indicators grew bold and the steady sound of tone filled his cockpit, Coda couldn't help but think it was all too easy. But it really wasn't, was it?

He'd given up everything for this moment. He'd left his mother behind. Lost friends and mourned comrades. Seen more death and destruction than any human being should ever witness. He'd been scarred internally and out. Physically, mentally, and emotionally destroyed. He would never be the same, likely incapable of living what most would deem a normal life.

But through it all, he had grown more human. Driven by incessant dedication and prone to rage, Coda had learned to forgive. Not only his father but even his former adversary, Moscow. Nothing, he realized, could have been more profound, more poetic, in a sense, than Moscow driving the Overlord toward him.

Teamwork.

Comradery.

Love.

Forgiveness.

That was what separated them from the Overlord. What made them human. And in the end, it was that humanity that made them victorious.

Coda squeezed the firing stud. With his fighter's engines and navigational thrusters powered down, his fighter bucked, swaying in the zero-g. He squeezed the firing stud a second time, releasing a second missile.

As if seeing the trap spring, the Overlord attempted to dart away. Too late. The first missile struck. It exploded, sending large chunks of carapace into the black. Still, the Overlord continued, though clearly weakened.

Coda thought he heard a distant scream in the back of his mind. Maybe it was his connection to the Baranyk network. Maybe it was just his imagination. It could have even been his own triumphant hollering.

The second missile struck. The Overlord's ship exploded. Vaporized.

He waited for something. He didn't know what. Maybe some sort of galactic boom. A shock wave across the universe. An exclamation point to their efforts. It seemed odd that the entire war could end with a single act, something little more than a pair of flashes in the night, all but invisible from anything more than a few kilometers.

Coda sat in silence, his body trembling with adrenaline, relief, and immense satisfaction. It wasn't until he powered his ship back on that he heard the cheers. They shook him out of his introspection.

Moscow's voice was the first voice he could make out on the radio. "You did it!" he screamed.

"No," Coda said over the din. "We did it. *We* did it."

# 62

*Bridge, SAS Abraham Lincoln*
*Jovian System, Sol System*

The Baranyk fought with a ferocity Admiral Orlovsky had never seen. Unlike the slow, methodical march through the human systems, now that they were in the Sol System, the heart of humanity, the enemy attacked like an angry bear.

In the aftermath of the *Olympia* and *Monaco*'s attack on the rear of the still-forming enemy fleet, the Overlord had moved fast. The response was so swift and devastating, the two human capital ships had to jump to a fallback position and rejoin the bulk of the fleet. Even then, more than half of their Hornet drones had been wiped out, and each ship took severe damage.

Dozens of ships attacked each of the Galilean moons. The outposts on Io and Calisto had been destroyed in minutes, the ships hiding on their dark side eliminated nearly as quickly. Stations on Ganymede, more populous and defensive, had lasted little longer. Europa, the main habitat in the Jovian System, had fared the best, but that said little.

The system burned. Millions, perhaps more, were dead. Remnants of ships floated through space, some pulled to the surface of Jupiter's moons, where they produced new craters. Others were drawn to the planet itself, lost forever in Jupiter's massive storms. The space surrounding the system was equal parts graveyard and scrapyard. A place where all things, human and machine, went to die.

"Sir!" Lieutenant Erikson said. "A contingent of the enemy fleet has broken off, sir."

"Where are they headed?" Admiral Orlovsky asked.

"Toward the inner system," Lieutenant Erikson said.

That meant only one thing. Earth. The bastards weren't happy just eliminating their ability to wage war. They had to destroy the humans' ancestral home too.

Admiral Orlovsky studied the battle map. It was the most complex battle he had ever seen. More ships, more fighters, more planets, moons, and stations, each with their own individual defenses. It hadn't been enough. The fleet was in shambles, fighting two dozen different skirmishes and losing all of them.

He didn't have the ships to spare. He'd long since ordered in their reserves. They'd already lost. The weary side of him just wanted to be done, to finally be free of the pressure and anguish, to die so that he could find peace.

A small piece of him believed that Coleman was still out there. That they still had a chance. If his old friend was successful, what kind of world would he return to? Would there be *anything* to return to at all? That tiny ray of hope, above all else, kept him going.

"How many ships broke away?" Admiral Orlovsky asked.

"It was a small contingent, sir," Lieutenant Erikson said. "Six ships in total."

It was amazing how quick the new reality had set in. Two weeks ago, six ships would have been a massive attack force. In the new reality, it was barely worth mentioning.

"Have the remaining Io and Calisto forces jump to the inner system," Admiral Orlovsky said.

"There's only four ships remaining, sir," Lieutenant Erikson said. "The *Barcelona*, *Columbia*, *Endeavor*, and *Williamsport*."

"They'll have to be enough," Orlovsky said.

"They have all reported considerable damage."

"Look around, Lieutenant. Any ship that's still around has sustained considerable damage."

"Understood, sir. Sending the..."

"What is it, Lieutenant?" Orlovsky pressed, more than half expecting another quip from his tactical officer.

"It's the enemy, sir. They've stopped firing."

Orlovsky was on his feet in moments. "They've *what?*"

"They've stopped firing, sir," Lieutenant Erikson said. "All of them at once. I've never seen anything like it, sir."

Orlovsky strode toward the battle map and gripped the padded railing. He squeezed it, feeling the rubbery surface squish between his fingers.

The battle map didn't display anything smaller than a ship-to-ship missile. It was still teeming with those, but each of them were friendlies streaking toward the enemy capital ships. Most of the enemy vessels were in orbit around the Jovian moons and had been assaulting the surface. Those were now strangely quiet. Even the enemy fighters had stopped.

Well, not *stopped*, rather stopped maneuvering. They flew in the same trajectory as they had before... whatever it was had happened. It was almost as if someone had hit the pause button on the enemy's side of the battle.

The same couldn't be said about the Sol Fleet. They used the small reprieve to inflict as much damage as possible. Rejuvenated drone fighters swarmed into enemy formations, attacking enemy ships without hesitation, shattering their assault as if they were nothing more than toys on a table and the Hornets were a sweeping hand. Capital ships launched volleys of rail-gun strikes. Nighthawk squadrons looped in, delivering CapKillers, laying waste to strategic targets.

"What's the status of the enemy contingent?" Orlovsky asked.

"They're still moving, sir."

"They should have jumped by now," Orlovsky said. Something was most definitely off. The small trickle of hope grew to a steady stream. Had Coleman done it? Had he destroyed the Overlord?

"What should I tell the fleet, sir?"

"Tell them to fire at w—"

"They're moving again, sir!"

The battle map came alive with new activity. The directionless ships were now maneuvering again. Except they weren't moving to attack. They were *retreating*.

*If the Overlord is dead, shouldn't the rest of them be lifeless?* Fleet Intelligence had called them drones after all.

*That's not what Chadwick believed*, Orlovsky reminded himself. He'd said that the Baranyk were slaves. Forced to do their master's bidding. If that master was dead, it stood to reason that they would make their own decisions.

Several of the red indicators disappeared off the battle map.

"They're jumping, sir!"

"Where?" Orlovsky knew it was a stupid question. Science fiction movies and books always talked about jump signatures, but there was no such thing in the real world. Once a ship jumped, there was no way to determine its destination.

"Looks like the edge of the system, sir."

"Zoom out," Orlovsky said, surprised.

The battle map zoomed out. The disappearing ships were indeed moving toward the edge of the system. Not toward Earth. Toward Saturn. Farther from the home of humanity. Within moments, every ship in the Baranyk fleet had disappeared, reassembling on the outskirts of Saturn.

*Except... No.* Not every ship was accounted for. Only about half of the enemy ships had regrouped with the rest.

"Have the fleet pull in," Orlovsky said. "Regroup. Keep an eye on the enemy. If they so much as twitch, I want to know about it. Send our Io and Calisto forces to Earth and another to Mars. Try and locate the missing ships."

"Sir?" Lieutenant Erikson said. "Where are you going?"

"I need answers," Orlovsky said. And there was only one place he was going to get those.

Sick bay was busier than Orlovsky had ever seen it. Pilots, ship personnel, even engineers filled every bed, corner, and available floor space. Medical personnel moved between them with harried expressions, blood covering their scrubs.

Orlovsky didn't even try to find the doc. He went straight to O'Neil.

The prevailing theory was that Joseph O'Neil had somehow been captured by the Overlord during his time in the Baranyk network and was being held against his will. If the Overlord was gone, then maybe O'Neil was free. If he was free, maybe he had answers.

The door to O'Neil's makeshift room opened, and Orlovsky's hope was immediately dashed. The man lay unconscious on the gurney, his features sallow and emaciated. He looked more like a corpse than most of the injured in the medical ward.

Orlovsky grabbed O'Neil's arm and gave it a soft shake. Maybe the man just needed a little extra coaxing to come out of it. A physical stimuli. He didn't respond, so Orlovsky shook him again. Still nothing.

"O'Neil," Orlovsky said. He even snapped his fingers in front of the man's face. Nothing worked. "O'Neil."

The door to the small room opened. Dr. Sullivan stepped in then froze when her eyes found the admiral's. "Sir, what are you doing in here?"

"Looking for answers." His eyes fell on O'Neil once more.

"Did you find any?" she asked.

"No. No, I didn't."

# 63

*Hangar, SAS Redemption*
*High Orbit, Baranyk Homeworld*

A SEA OF PEOPLE WAITED FOR CODA AND MOSCOW WHEN THEY RETURNED to the hangar bay. Coda couldn't hear them through the Nighthawk's canopy, but they were jumping up and down, clapping, and pumping fists into the air. There were hugs and tears between members from every function, from engineering to the marines.

When he popped his canopy, a sonic boom of cheering crashed over him. He'd never heard anything like it. He slid the canopy into its fully open position, stood, and removed his flight helmet. He didn't know how it was possible, but the ovation grew louder. He raised his flight helmet in the air and pumped his fist in reply, letting out a triumphant yell. The crowd roared in response.

Across the hangar, Moscow dealt with a similar mob. He and Coda made eye contact then climbed out of their fighters and down the ladders that had been rolled beside their cockpits. Coda was mobbed the moment both his boots hit the deck. People slapped him on the back, offering congratulations, and a few even cried as they voiced their thanks.

Coda nodded to each, smiled at most, gave high-fives and hugs, and said thank you in return. It was a moment he could only have dreamed about—a moment he *had* dreamed about ever since entering the Academy.

Coda and Moscow found each other in the middle of the throng and crashed into each other, pounding each other on the back with triumphant ferocity.

"We did it!" Moscow screamed. "Holy shit, we fucking did it!"

Coda was laughing now, a permanent smile tattooed on his face. The moment hadn't felt quite right without his friend. With their arms around each other's shoulders, they held up their flight helmets again. The mass of people screamed their gratitude, one step away from pure pandemonium. Coda and Moscow spun, taking it all in.

Another sound entered the fray, and Coda turned to see a squadron of Nighthawks entering the hangar. The crowd parted, giving them a place to land. Those closest to the landing zones swarmed around the new pilots. Coda looked from fighter to fighter, searching for his friends.

Squawks wasn't difficult to find. He had his flight helmet off in seconds and drank in the attention. He held a hand to his ear as if he couldn't hear the crowd, willing them to get louder. Then he pumped his hands in the air, encouraging them even more, all the while beaming from ear to ear.

Nails was more circumspect. She sat in her cockpit, head down. Coda wondered what was going through her mind. Had she lost someone? Was the moment too big to comprehend? Coda didn't know, and it wasn't the right time to find out.

The crowd parted as Squawks made his way through it toward Coda. When he finally saw Coda, Squawks bounded into a sprint and crashed into him as hard as he could. It took everything Coda had to stay on his feet.

"You crazy sonuvabitch, you did it!" Squawks bellowed, then he turned and gave Moscow a vicious shove. "You're bad, man. You're bad!"

Coda and Moscow could only laugh. Sometimes there wasn't anything else to say, and Squawks usually made up for it.

"Just remember," Squawks continued, "as you're drowning in women and going on all of the talk shows, just remember who saved your ass down there."

Coda's smile was so big it hurt. "I will."

After all, they had done it together. Not just Coda, Moscow, and Squawks, but Rocket, Dumper, and the rest of the Forgotten. Phantom and the rest of their drone pilots. Sergeant Haniger, Corporal Abernathy, and their marines. Commander Payton and his engineers. Doctor Poiu and Doctor Rydell. Not to mention Captain Coleman and the ship's executive crew.

*Speaking of the captain, where is he?*

Coda's eyes went back to Nails's starfighter. Captain Coleman had his daughter in a tight hug. Her face was buried in his shoulder, and he held her as if she were a child again. With everything happening around him, the energy, the raucous crowd, the screams, the celebrating, and congratulations, it was that small, quiet moment that hit him the hardest.

That was what they had fought for.

It was also a reminder that his mission wasn't complete. The Overlord was gone, but the Baranyk were still out there. *What does that mean for my father?*

Coda pulled away from Moscow and Squawks and began threading his way through the crowd.

"Where are you going?" Moscow called after him.

"There's one more thing I have to do," Coda said, and then he disappeared into the Nighthawk locker room. Nobody followed him. They were too caught up in the celebration.

Coda stripped out of his flight suit, and after donning the standard-issue slacks and tank top, he left the locker room behind.

He returned to his bunk in the pilot barracks. If anyone found him, they would think he was sleeping and wouldn't disturb him. Since losing his private quarters, that was the best he could hope for.

Lying down, he placed his hands on his chest and closed his eyes. After the celebration in the hangar, it was difficult to slow his heart rate and steady his breathing, but once he had, connecting to the network proved as simple as it always had. In moments, Coda left the familiar sights, sounds, and smells of the *Redemption* behind and floated in a place that was simultaneously nothing and everything.

Coda noticed the difference immediately. The wrongness that had permeated the Baranyk network like an oil slick over water was gone, and in its wake was a distant sense of relief. As he floated through the network, the pinpricks of light that so often resembled stars pulled away from him.

Were they afraid of him? Fearful that he would assume the Overlord's place and subjugate them? Or were they simply doing everything they could not to provoke him? To show they weren't like their ruler?

Coda tried to give off a sense of assurance that he wasn't there for violence. That seemed to help. At least the lights didn't pull away as quickly. A thought came to him, and he projected an image of his father. It was painful to recollect, but he thought of the last time he'd seen him, when they'd sat in the abandoned baseball stadium and been attacked by the Overlord and his minions.

Coda didn't hide his anguish. He did the opposite, letting it radiate from him like a signal from a radio. He knew the others could feel it, because he'd felt it too. His father had done the same to him when they'd first met in the network. Even the Overlord had radiated his feelings of cruelty and oppression.

He was about to give up and continue the search himself when a single light broke away from the rest. It floated toward Coda, almost unsure, like an anxious dog slowly approaching with its head low, tail between its legs. As it drew closer, Coda had the impression of a Baranyk warrior. This one had been in the hive and had watched with its own eyes as the Overlord collapsed its chamber and destroyed their city. It had lost other Baranyk dear to it.

Their grief was a shared experience that bridged the gap between species in a way that normal language never could.

*It's over*, Coda attempted to say. He projected an image of the Overlord's ship exploding. *He's gone.*

The Baranyk warrior recoiled.

*No,* Coda thought. *I'm* sorry.

Showing the destruction of their leader clearly wasn't the right decision. He tried channeling a different image, one of the human survivors helping clear the rubble from the fallen city, then their fleet leaving the system behind.

*We can help each other.*

That appeared to quell some of the Baranyk's fears. The feeling of uncertainty solidified into resolve, then the light was racing away. At first,

Coda thought he had scared it away for good, but it paused then raced farther away, only to pause again.

*It's waiting for me to follow.*

Coda chased after it, and when he did, the light didn't stop. The Baranyk led Coda through the network, past millions of other consciousnesses until eventually they found one that wasn't like the rest.

His father had told him that it was possible to tell a human consciousness from a Baranyk's, and he'd been right. It was difficult to put into words, but the moment Coda saw the light, he knew it belonged to his father.

Coda raced toward it, and as he neared, the image of the network disappeared, replaced instead by a cave. It was not unlike the hive's chambers, only smaller. There were no light sources, but it was well lit. The rocky walls and stone floor were a yellow-brown shade. There were no entrances or exits, and at its center was a single slab of stone where his father rested.

Joseph O'Neil was almost unrecognizable. He was emaciated and pale except where the dried blood had stained his skin. His lips were crimson and chapped, eyes sunken and hollow, hair thin and brittle. His clothes had been ripped away, leaving a pale body crisscrossed with cuts, littered with bruises, and two punctures where the Baranyk warrior's forelimbs had pierced him.

Coda went to him in a rush and took his hand. "Dad? Dad, it's me. Can you hear me?"

His father didn't respond, but he was breathing, and Coda could feel a faint pulse. There was obviously no air in the Baranyk network, but if his mind was projecting critical life functions, that was a good sign, wasn't it?

"Dad, it's Callan. I'm here. I found you. Can you hear me?"

His father didn't move.

Coda looked around, helpless. His father was connected to a network that didn't require wires, cables, or plug-ins of any kind. Coda didn't know how to force him to disconnect. The empty chamber didn't offer any clues, and try as he might, Coda couldn't think of anything. So he went back to the only thing he knew to do.

"Come back, Dad." He patted him on the cheek. "Come on, Dad. It's me. I'm going to get you out of here, but I need some help. Come on."

What if he disconnected while holding his father's hand? Could he lead him out of the chamber? Coda started to try, but as the chamber grew fuzzy, he lost his connection with his father. Panicking, he scrambled back, clawing at the network as if he had fallen into a hole and was trying to scramble back to the surface. Whatever he did worked, because he was back in the chamber.

Firmly back in the network, he rested his hands on the slab and slumped his head. "What am I going to do with you?"

A scraping noise brought his head up. Across the chamber from him was the same Baranyk that had led him to his father. Years of fear boiled to the surface, and Coda stepped back hesitantly. He held his hands in front of him as if trying to ward it off, and he looked around the chamber for anything he could use as a weapon.

The beast's triangular head watched him, cocking from side to side as if measuring him. Its steps were slow, almost tentative, as it made its way across the chamber toward his father.

"Stay away from him," Coda said.

But the alien didn't listen. It crawled to the center slab where Coda's father lay and stood over him, eyes taking in his frail body. When it looked up, it met Coda's eyes again. If the Baranyk had wanted to hurt his father, it could have. And if it'd wanted to hurt Coda, there had been opportunities.

"Can you help him?" Coda asked.

The Baranyk warrior made a strange sound in reply.

"Please."

The Baranyk made the sound again. This time, Coda realized it was coming from the alien's antennae, but he didn't know what it meant.

"Please," Coda said again. "I need him. *We* need him. Only he can tell the others the war is over. If there's anything you can do, please do it."

The Baranyk warrior dipped its head, something Coda took as a submissive gesture. Then it rose sharply on its hind legs, its razor-sharp forelimbs flaring outward.

"No!" Coda screamed. He'd seen those limbs drive straight through his father's chest.

An ear-piercing shriek rang through the chamber, so loud Coda had to cover his ears. Still, the sound seemed to pierce his brain. The pain was unbearable, as if a creature were trying to burrow its way out of his head. His scream echoed the Baranyk's, creating a terrible harmony.

Coda crashed into the wall, his legs weak, unable to take any more. He didn't know how long it lasted, but when it finally stopped, his vision was blurry. He gasped and tried wiping away tears. Tiny lights sparkled at the edges of his vision. It took several moments for him to get his breath back. When he did, he found his father still on the stone slab, without any new wounds. The warrior hadn't attacked him. *Then what did he do?*

Suddenly, his father moved. It was a small thing, almost imperceptible, but it was there.

Coda was at his side in an instant. "Dad? Dad, can you hear me?"

His father moved again, his arm moving sluggishly toward his head, legs stretching slowly.

"Dad, it's me. I'm right here. Go slow."

One by one, each of his father's limbs moved until eventually, his eyes opened. He looked at Coda, recognition slowly appearing. "Callan?" His voice was raspy and little more than a whisper, barely making it past his lips, but Coda heard it.

"Yeah," Coda said. "I'm here."

A sliver of a smile.

Coda's eyes must have drifted to the Baranyk warrior waiting on the other side of the stone slab, because his father's head turned. When he saw their former enemy for the first time, his body visibly tensed, eyes going wide with fear.

"It's okay," Coda said. "He's here to help."

"Help?"

"Yes," Coda said. "I couldn't get you to wake up."

"There was a noise," his father said slowly, his head turning sluggishly back to Coda.

"Yeah."

"Pain."

"That too," Coda said. "Listen, Dad, I need you to hear this. We did it. We killed the Overlord. It's done. I don't know what's happening at home, but they need to know. Can you do that? Can you tell them?"

"Done."

"Yeah," Coda said. "It's done. It's over. It's all over. We just have to get you home."

"Home."

Coda nodded. "Yeah, Dad. Home. Are you ready to go home?"

His father slowly reached up, his hand cupping Coda's face. His skin was dry and scratchy, but it felt better than anything Coda had ever felt in his life. He placed his hand over his fathers and leaned into it.

"Not without you," his father said.

A dam of emotion broke inside, and tears welled in Coda's eyes. "I'll be there soon, Dad."

His father made a sound somewhere between a groan and acknowledgment. "Promise?"

"I promise."

"Okay."

He cast another uneasy look toward the Baranyk. Coda did as well.

"I made a promise to you too," Coda said. "And I have every intention of seeing it through."

The cold black eyes of the Baranyk just stared at him, its antennae buzzing slightly. For some reason, he had the distinct impression that the alien had understood him.

# 64

*SAS Redemption,*
*High Orbit, SAS Redemption*

THE *REDEMPTION* AND ITS CREW REMAINED IN THE BARANYK SYSTEM FOR four days. Captain Coleman initially resisted Coda's pleas to assist with the cleanup, but in the end, Coda had won out. He'd even flown the first dropship and led the first cleanup crews. Unsurprisingly, Squawks and Moscow had joined him for that. They were a squadron, after all, and whatever one of their brothers did, they did as well.

Eventually, hundreds of the ship's crew joined in, working side by side with their former enemy. It was difficult, labor-intensive work, and Coda worried the peace would shatter at any point. He had to remind himself that this wasn't the standard postwar effort so often leveraged by the victors. These people—and the longer Coda spent among them, the more he believed they *were* people—or at least individuals—had fought a terrible war among themselves before they'd ever discovered the humans.

There was no communication between the two races. No peace talks or conversations about war retribution. Simply hard labor to clean up a city destroyed by war.

When the humans left, the Baranyk lined up on the edge of their city and rose onto their hind legs, their forearms stretched to the sky, and wailed in that high-pitched squeal of theirs. Coda could only guess at the meaning, but he waved from the ramp of the dropship as it took flight and left the city, entering the tunnel that would take it to the surface.

Coda didn't know what would happen with the Baranyk after they returned to human space. That was a topic for politicians and military leaders. He was just a pilot. Give him a mission, and he would see it through. Though he hoped this was the beginning of a long peace between their races. There was a lot they could learn from each other, and just like the Baranyk, humanity needed time to rebuild.

The return flight took over four thousand individual jumps and nearly three months. Coda kept himself busy with his shipboard responsibilities. The *Redemption* had suffered significant damage during the attack and took months to repair. Their Nighthawk and drone squadrons needed to be rebuilt and repaired, and until the war was officially declared over, they were still on high alert. That meant CAP schedules needed to be created and flown and trainings completed, including the ones out-of-touch politicians mandated. Even in the deepest depths of enemy territory, the bureaucracy knew no bounds.

In the evenings, the pilots assembled in the small storage locker off the hangar and told stories about friends and old comrades. The nights were filled with good friends and laughter. It was the first time in Coda's life that he could just *be*, and they were some of the best days of his life.

They talked of their past and even more of their future. With the battles over, the most popular topic was what they would do when they got home. Having gotten a taste of high speed in confined spaces, Squawks had his sights set on the high-stakes starfighter races. It was the closest thing he would be able to find to the adrenaline rush of flying his Nighthawk and riding that knife's edge between life and death. "The women don't hurt either," he would add with a mischievous grin.

Moscow's Russian pride was too strong. He intended to stay with the Sol Fleet, likely moving into a leadership role to prepare for the next war. Coda had told them that the galaxy was teeming with life. If humanity had gone to war with the first alien species it had ever come across, then it was a damn good bet there would eventually be a war against another.

Nails, on the other hand, couldn't wait to get out. She'd joined the Forgotten to get closer to her father, specifically to understand what her father had seen in the Nighthawks all these years. What she'd found hadn't impressed her. Sure, she enjoyed the camaraderie, and the speed was addictive, but contrary to what many believed, she could find those things elsewhere. Coda wasn't so sure, but he never voiced his opinion.

For himself, he didn't have an answer, and it became something of a running joke. Coda was good at telling others what to do but struggled to set a path for himself. He needed orders. When the nights came to a close and Coda lay alone in his bunk, he wondered if it was because he'd lived so long with a singular goal that he'd never thought about what would come after it. Or maybe as a fighter pilot, he'd never truly expected to survive long enough to see the end of the war.

Captain Coleman had long since taught them that death was their comrade, always lurking, always present on every mission they ever flew. Whatever it was, whatever he decided, he had time to figure it out.

When he wasn't drinking with his squadmates, he communicated with this father through the Baranyk network. It had taken weeks before Joseph O'Neil was well enough to leave the medical ward, but he had fulfilled his promise. Admiral Orlovsky and the rest of the Sol Fleet knew of the Forgotten's success, that the Overlord was dead, and that the Baranyk were no longer a threat. The enemy had long since left the Sol System, likely headed back to their own home world to rebuild, like humanity.

Of his personal life, Joseph said little, only that he was healthy and had been released from the hospital and pardoned from his crimes. It was a quiet affair, one apparently without any hoopla or celebration. His record had been expunged, and he was allowed to retire. No press conference or formal writ of apology. The Sol Fleet moved forward as if the incident hadn't occurred. As if his father hadn't been vilified for decades. It was for the best, Coda told himself. His father was done with the fleet, and now he could live in peace.

When they finally returned to human space, they took the first available JumpGate back to the Sol System. Somehow, word had traveled ahead of them, and an honor guard of ships waited to escort them home, Admiral Orlovsky's *Abraham Lincoln* at its head.

The admiral shuttled to the *Redemption*, where he personally thanked and congratulated the men and women of the ship, promising a great award ceremony accompanied by the world's leaders and streamed live for all its citizens once they'd had a chance to recover. In the meantime, they had his eternal gratitude.

For Coda, Captain Coleman, and others, the admiral brought other tidings. They spent days reviewing their briefings, reviewing the battle, and answering a thousand questions from the fleet's top brass. During this, Coda realized an important detail he hadn't noticed before.

In the aftermath of the Overlord's death, the Baranyk civilization had fractured. Fleet Intelligence's best guess was that the forces assaulting the Sol System had divided into two distinct and separate groups. The first had jumped away entirely to parts unknown. It was widely believed that they'd returned to their home system, but there was no actual evidence to support that theory.

The second group had lingered for a time on the edges of human space, watching and observing. They'd made no aggressive moves, but their continued presence kept the fleet on high alert. They had since fallen back, and recent probes showed they were rebuilding their defensive line on the edges of their own system.

Admiral Orlovsky and the top brass didn't take it as an act of war, but they weren't as convinced the war was over, either.

"When a power void is created," Admiral Orlovsky reminded them, "someone always aims to take control. It's a universal truth, proven since the dawn of time, and it appears the Baranyk are no different."

Coda wondered about the truth of the statement. There were different kinds of power. Different kinds of leaders. It didn't mean that whoever took the mantle of the Baranyk's next leader would be like the Overlord. Maybe they would value peace. He could only hope, just as he could only hope that his efforts on their home world wouldn't go unnoticed. From what he'd seen, the Baranyk were capable of incredible things, not just great technologies but also art and architecture. Surely, they believed in protecting those things as much as humanity did.

The *Redemption* docked on Luna, the hub for all of Earth's space travel, and Coda prepared for a flight to Earth. He had nothing to pack and slung a single duffel over his shoulder. There was a muted set of goodbyes in the barracks. The previous night, they had all gotten well and truly drunk, and the tears had flowed as freely as the alcohol. Captain Coleman had even joined them.

All that was left was the final goodbyes shared between friends and comrades. They promised to see each other again. They were forever brothers and sisters, forever Forgotten. If anyone needed anything, they were only a short message away.

Coda was the last to leave. He stood in the empty barracks, taking mental pictures of it, wondering if he would ever be back. He still didn't know what he was going to do next. With a final deep breath, he left it behind and boarded a shuttle to Luna.

As the doors opened, he shuffled out, watching as loved ones rushed forward, barreling into each other. There were fierce hugs, kisses, and enough tears to fill an ocean. He smiled as husbands and wives embraced. As fathers hugged children who, in some cases, had never even seen them in person.

He didn't have a wife or children to hug, but he did spot a familiar face. He stood tall and proud, his shoulders firm, and healthy. Gone were the sunken features and his emaciated form. He didn't know how much of that had been a projection in the Baranyk network, but here, his father looked as he had in Coda's imagination. The very definition of a hero.

Coda smiled and fought back the lump in his throat, what little good it did him. When he embraced his father, the tears fell freely.

"God, it's good to see you," his father said.

"You too," Coda said. "I didn't expect to see you here."

"Glad I could surprise you."

Coda pulled away and wiped his eyes. "It was a good surprise."

"I didn't come alone."

Coda followed his father's gaze. Standing to the side of the terminal was a small woman. The years hadn't been kind to her. She was shorter than he remembered—and frailer, as if she'd spent the time in a constant state of worry and regret. She smiled and waved at him awkwardly, clearly equal parts happy and concerned.

"Go say hi to your mom," his father said. "She's missed you."

His father didn't have to say it twice. Coda dropped his duffel and bounded to her.

"Callan," she said as he took her in his arms. "I'm so sorry." He felt her warm tears on his shoulder.

Coda couldn't talk. Couldn't breathe. There are few things in life a person needs more than a mother's hug. With his arms holding her tight, and his father smiling and watching on, Callan "Coda" O'Neil finally released the burden he'd been carrying since his father had disappeared. With his family together, he was finally whole.

If you enjoyed The Forgotten Fleet, please consider leaving a review on Amazon. Aside from purchasing a book or recommending it to other readers, leaving a review is the single most helpful thing you can do for an author and I'd be incredibly grateful.

# ABOUT THE AUTHOR

Craig Andrews graduated from Portland State University with a Bachelors of Arts in English. Growing up on a healthy diet of fantasy and science fiction, some of his favorite memories include being traumatized by the TV shows Unsolved Mysteries and The X-Files. He currently lives in a small town outside of Portland, Oregon with his wife and two boys.

Craig Andrews Mailing List

craigandrewsauthor@yahoo.com

www.ingramcontent.com/pod-product-compliance
Ingram Content Group UK Ltd.
Pitfield, Milton Keynes, MK11 3LW, UK
UKHW010840061025
8245UKWH00038B/558

9 798992 883718